PASSING GLORY

PASSING GLORY

REAY TANNAHILL

CROWN PUBLISHERS, INC.
New York

T 1571 P

Published by Crown Publishers, Inc., 201 E. 50th Street, New York, New York 10022. Originally published in Great Britain by Century Hutchinson Ltd. in 1989.

CROWN is a trademark of Crown Publishers, Inc.

Manufactured in the United States of America

Library of Congress Cataloging-in-Publication Data

Tannahill, Reay.
    Passing glory / by Reay Tannahill.
        p.   cm.
    I.   Title.
    PR6070.A543P3   1989   89-10020
    823'.914—dc20   CIP
    ISBN 0-517-57329-6

10 9 8 7 6 5 4 3 2 1

First American Edition

Contents

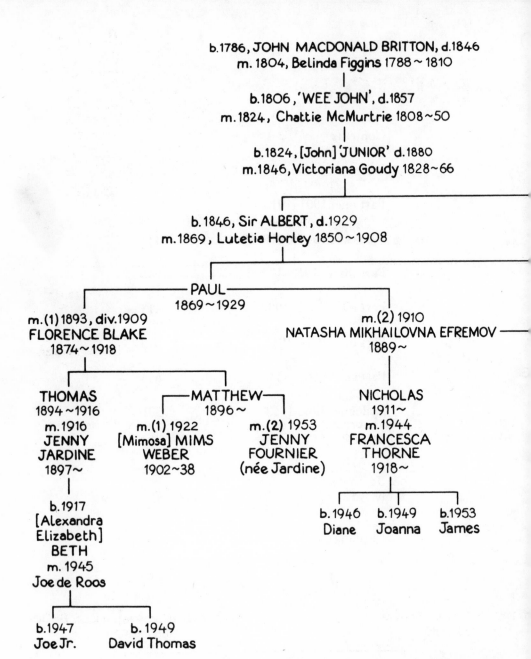

b.1786, JOHN MACDONALD BRITTON, d.1846
m. 1804, Belinda Figgins 1788~1810

b.1806, 'WEE JOHN', d.1857
m.1824, Chattie McMurtrie 1808~50

b.1824, [John] 'JUNIOR' d.1880
m.1846, Victoriana Goudy 1828~66

b.1846, Sir ALBERT, d.1929
m.1869, Lutetia Horley 1850~1908

PAUL
1869~1929

m.(1) 1893, div.1909
FLORENCE BLAKE
1874~1918

m.(2) 1910
NATASHA MIKHAILOVNA EFREMOV
1889~

THOMAS
1894~1916
m.1916
JENNY
JARDINE
1897~

MATTHEW
1896~

m.(1) 1922
[Mimosa] MIMS
WEBER
1902~38

m.(2) 1953
JENNY
FOURNIER
(née Jardine)

NICHOLAS
1911~
m.1944
FRANCESCA
THORNE
1918~

b.1917
[Alexandra
Elizabeth]
BETH
m. 1945
Joe de Roos

b.1946
Diane

b.1949
Joanna

b.1953
James

b.1947
Joe Jr.

b. 1949
David Thomas

JARDINES

BRITTONS

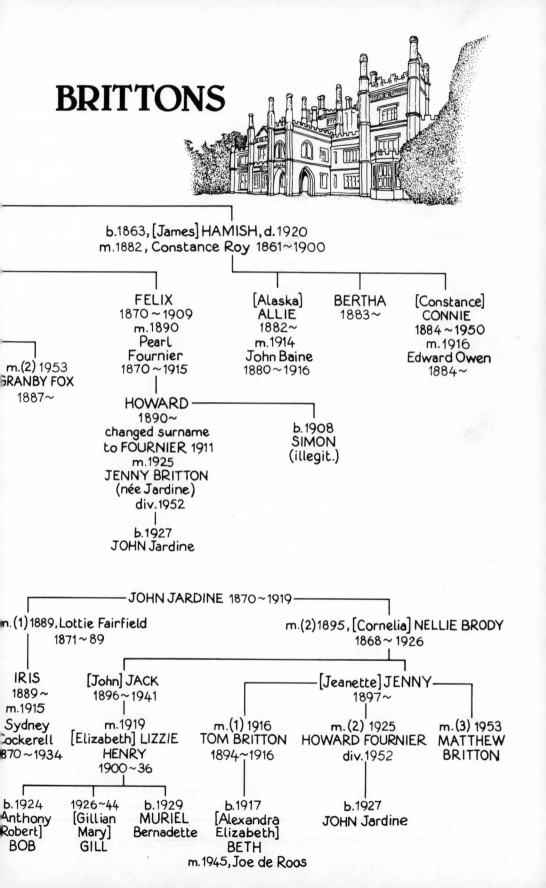

b.1863, [James] HAMISH, d.1920
m.1882, Constance Roy 1861~1900

FELIX
1870 ~ 1909
m.1890
Pearl
Fournier
1870 ~ 1915

[Alaska]
ALLIE
1882~
m.1914
John Baine
1880 ~ 1916

BERTHA
1883~

[Constance]
CONNIE
1884 ~ 1950
m.1916
Edward Owen
1884~

m.(2) 1953
GRANBY FOX
1887~

HOWARD
1890~
changed surname
to FOURNIER 1911
m.1925
JENNY BRITTON
(née Jardine)
div.1952

b.1908
SIMON
(illegit.)

b.1927
JOHN Jardine

JOHN JARDINE 1870 ~ 1919

m.(1) 1889, Lottie Fairfield
1871~89

m.(2)1895, [Cornelia] NELLIE BRODY
1868 ~ 1926

IRIS
1889~
m.1915
Sydney
Cockerell
1870 ~ 1934

[John] JACK
1896~1941

[Jeanette] JENNY
1897~

m.1919
[Elizabeth] LIZZIE
HENRY
1900~36

m.(1) 1916
TOM BRITTON
1894~1916

m.(2) 1925
HOWARD FOURNIER
div.1952

m.(3) 1953
MATTHEW
BRITTON

b.1924
[Anthony
Robert]
BOB

1926~44
[Gillian
Mary]
GILL

b.1929
MURIEL
Bernadette

b.1917
[Alexandra
Elizabeth]
BETH
m.1945, Joe de Roos

b.1927
JOHN Jardine

Prologue
December 1918

Prologue

1

IT WAS late on a Friday afternoon in December 1918. Friday the thirteenth. Naturally.

Matthew Britton – intrepid aviator, popular poet, reluctant darling of the British press – rounded a bend much too fast, stampeded a herd of cows, and took a nose-dive into the ditch.

And then had to sit and listen while the cowherd, a chit of a girl in a disreputable old army greatcoat and pudding-basin hat, gave him a piece of her mind.

It wasn't the way conquering heroes were supposed to return from the wars.

2

'. . . more sense than to come tearing round corners on narrow country roads in a motorcar that size. You must have been doing thirty-five miles an hour at least! What if there had been something coming in the other direction? It's bad enough as it is. I was taking those cows home for the evening milking and they'll be all over the place by now . . .'

Except for the girl's voice, everything was amazingly quiet. December in Dorset was a month of lowering grey skies and dripping black trees, of ochre-yellow mud underfoot and decaying vegetation in the dells. A month, according to Matthew's grandfather, when any civilised man would rather be somewhere else.

One of the dripping black trees dripped down the back of his neck, while the Hispano-Suiza settled a little, its bonnet burrowing contentedly into the decaying vegetation and the bramble canes weaving themselves through the spokes of its wheels. Matthew wiped a splash of ochre-yellow mud from his goggles. The girl's voice flowed on,

'. . . and it'll take hours to round them all up. We're very short-handed just now. I've only got two boys from the village to help me.

3

Are you all right?'

He turned the goggles on her, and said politely, 'Thank you, yes.'

He wondered who she was. In the gathering dusk, he could see that she was fair-haired, wide-eyed, about nineteen or twenty years old, and pink with annoyance. Her face didn't mean anything to him, but there was something elusively familiar about the voice and manner. Bossy little madam! He said, 'How do I get a tractor to haul me out of here?'

'You'd be better with the plough horses and they're down at Sardingley. You'll have to wait.'

He didn't mind waiting. He had no urgent desire to find out whether the broken leg, cracked ribs, fractured collarbone and bullet-riddled shoulder he had acquired a few weeks ago were sufficiently healed to permit him to disentangle himself from this damned motor without suffering a relapse.

'Aren't you getting out?' she asked.

No question about it. He'd met her before, and he hadn't liked her much then, either.

'Who the devil *are* you?'

She was at a disadvantage. It wasn't easy to match a pair of flying goggles, glare for glare, but she did her best. 'I don't see what it has to do with you, but I am Mrs Britton. Who are *you*?'

It took no very intricate process of reasoning for him to arrive at the conclusion that this must be his brother Tom's widow, Jeanette, although he wouldn't have thought she was Tom's kind of girl at all. And it still left him in the dark about where – or whether – he had encountered her before.

Abandoning the problem for the time being, he said sardonically, 'I, my dear Mrs Britton, am – er – Mr Britton.'

'You're not!'

'All right, I'm not.'

She digested this for a moment. 'You must be Matthew.'

'Who else?'

'Well, you might have been Howard.'

Cousin Howard, tall and calm and fatly smiling. Revolted, Matthew said, 'Certainly not. Anyway, he hasn't been a Britton for years. Changed his name by deed poll when he took a spite against the family.' She was looking mystified, and he couldn't resist getting some of his own back. 'You're not very well up in the family history, are you?'

'No, I'm not, but I can *perfectly* sympathise with him! Are you

4

going to get out of that motor, or are we going to stay here all day carrying on this ridiculous conversation?'

'My dear Jeanette . . .'

'Jenny,' she said automatically.

A dozen years vanished as if they had never been.

My name's Jenny. Do you want a sweetie?

'Oh, my God!' he said disgustedly. 'Not Jenny Jardine?'

All he had known about his brother's marriage was that Tom had made an ass of himself by marrying out of his class and in suspicious haste; that his wife's name was Jeanette, and that she had worked at the Britton shipyard on the Clyde. It hadn't occurred to Matt to wonder whether he himself might know her, but now it seemed that he did – not as a marriageable young woman but as an officious, pigtailed little brat in a white pinafore and black boots.

'Well, there's no need to be rude about it!'

'Puffers,' he said, remembering. 'Toffee lumps.'

And the first of the many days in his life when he had come near to death.

She corrected him, as he might have guessed she would. 'Not toffee lumps; Cheugh Jeans. Didn't you know it was me?'

'No.'

A cow peered inquisitively over her shoulder and she said, pleased, 'Oh, Daisy! What a clever girl you are. Have you brought the others back with you?'

And that was too much, Matt decided. He was damned if he was going to go on sitting in a half-wrecked car in a ditch, providing a raree-show for a herd of bloody cows.

The dusk turned suddenly to dark as he began to remove his goggles and flying helmet, shrugged out of his heavy leather coat, ran his fingers through his hair and then, the decorations on his chest clanking like the High Priest's breastplate, set about extricating himself from the motor. It wasn't as bad as he had expected. Not quite.

Helpfully, Jenny Jardine produced a torch, asking with interest, 'Why are you wearing all your medals?'

'Not from choice, I assure you. They gave me a ceremonial send-off from the hospital, with the whole of Fleet Street in attendance. That's why I'm all dressed up in my flying kit. It is also . . .' He stopped, because it suddenly became necessary to grit his teeth. 'It is also why I was driving so fast. I know of no other means of escaping the press, short of stealing a plane. Which I nearly did, except that I couldn't be sure someone hadn't ploughed up the south lawn.'

'No,' she said. 'It's still there. It would make quite a good landing field, I should think. But I'm surprised the press were still chasing you after a hundred miles. They must be awfully persevering. Are you sure I can't help?'

'I can manage.'

He was breathless when he reached the road, and very pale in the light of her torch, but she didn't make the mistake of offering him her arm. So he leaned carelessly against the Hispano-Suiza's spare wheel and said, 'I don't suppose any of your cows are broken to bridle?'

She was able to see him properly at last, the adult incarnation of the boy she remembered, without pleasure, from her childhood. Dark, waving hair; long, firm mouth with a cynical lift at the corners; eyes that, despite their bleak exhaustion, were of a most beautiful deep, dark blue; an austerely handsome face that would, some day, have the same arrogant distinction as his father's. He looked thirty, but Jenny knew that he couldn't be more than twenty-two. He was eighteen months younger than Tom had been.

He had changed beyond recognition. But she recognised him, just the same.

He said tartly, 'When you've finished . . .' and she realised that she was shining the torch full in his face.

'Sorry,' She lowered the beam.

It was extraordinary. The eyes, the nonchalance, the refusal to admit to a pain she could read in every lean, wilfully relaxed line of his body – she and Matthew Britton had met much more recently than all those years ago on the Clyde. She remembered the first day of the battle of the Somme and the infuriating, muddy, blood-soaked, nameless young captain with the raging fever who had staggered out of an ambulance to faint in her arms. She had wept a little for him afterwards, and hoped he wouldn't die.

It seemed better, on the whole, not to say anything about it, or not now. He obviously didn't remember; nor would she have expected him to.

Prosaically, she remarked, 'You don't look to me as if you're fit to ride a tortoise, let alone a cow. Will you be all right here for half an hour while I cycle up to the house and send someone down to collect you?'

'What an admirable notion. Will you take the cows with you, or shall I send them?'

6

3

THE Lanchester, driven by the butler, arrived within fifteen minutes, followed by two shire horses and four conscientious objectors doing duty as farm labourers. Soon afterwards, a sinister jangling noise resolved itself into two small boys laden with the chains for the plough harness, and two others with instructions to take the cows back to the byre for the milking.

Supervising the salvage operation, Matt felt almost benevolent towards the younger Mrs Britton; she was efficient, if nothing else.

Towards the elder Mrs Britton, who was twenty-nine years old, Russian, gorgeous, and his stepmother, he did not feel benevolent at all. In fact, he had the strongest possible desire to wring her neck. It was one of several reasons why he had discharged himself from hospital a week before time.

As the Lanchester crunched up the drive in the gloom, he saw that the great country house known as Provost Charters had been illuminated from end to end, like an oceangoing liner, to welcome home the family's son and heir. He saw, too, that there was a reception committee gathered under the porte-cochère. His father and grandfather were there, with Jenny Jardine and a couple of children whom he took to be his seven-year-old half-brother and two-year-old niece. But he scarcely noticed them at first, because at centre stage front – as always – was Natasha.

Her hair was like butter under the lights and her Arctic blue eyes like stars. Beneath a diaphanous wrap bordered with white fox, she was wearing a spectacular gown of richly coloured gauzes and satins that he had seen once before, at Sarajevo in 1914. By Paquin, he remembered, after a design by Bakst. And since it was a garment ludicrously inappropriate for five o'clock of a December afternoon in Dorset, he knew with amused exasperation that she must have rushed upstairs to change the minute she knew he was back.

She was impossible, infuriating, exhilarating, enigmatic, and a darling. He adored her; had adored her ever since the day in 1910 when his father had brought her home as his second wife. She had been just twenty-one years old, and Matt fourteen, and she had changed his life; laughed with him and cried with him, encouraged his aspirations, forgiven his sins, sympathised with him in his dilemmas, charmed all his troubles away. She hadn't a single flaw that he could perceive.

It didn't in the least diminish his desire to wring her neck.

He smiled dutifully at his father and grandfather – the one tall, handsome and supercilious, the other white-haired, robustly built, with a gaze deceptively blank and owl-like – then grinned at the children, young Nick almost bouncing with excitement and little Beth angelically fair and innocent. Amused, he saw that Jenny Jardine, looking much the better for having shed the greatcoat and pudding-basin hat, was watching him as warily as if she expected him to keel over and die of his confrontation with the cows. She would be quite a pretty girl, he thought, in any company other than Natasha's.

Then, at last, beaming affably, he bent to receive his stepmother's passionate, scented, and protracted embrace and to hear her murmur huskily, 'My darling, *darling* Matthew. We thought we had lost you.'

When he straightened up again, feeling a trifle heated, Jenny Jardine's eyebrows had almost disappeared into her honey-coloured hair, and his grandfather's eyes held an unmistakable glint of malice. The smile on his father's lips had given way to a look that took Matt back headlong through the years, to a time when it seemed as if weary distaste was the only expression Paul Britton's face ever wore. Though not for the same reasons as now.

If you can keep your head when all about you are losing theirs and blaming it on you . . . During the last four years, Matt had discovered that there were no flies on Mr Rudyard Kipling.

So, keeping his head in the approved fashion, he said lazily into the silence, 'Shall we go indoors?'

4

HE had come to Provost Charters partly because he needed to convalesce and partly to have things out with Tasha, but mainly because he wished to make clear to everyone that, for him, no homecoming would ever be permanent; that he was not open to emotional blackmail; that 'the son of the house' was not a rôle he proposed to play.

He was going to become what *he* wanted to be.

Not until much later did he recognise the irony of making such a declaration to four of the five people who, between them, had been largely responsible for shaping what he already was.

Part One

1901–1914

One

1

LONDON, one of the liveliest, noisiest cities in the world, was so
crowded and yet so quiet on that chill, dank February morning in
1901 that it was making everyone nervous.

If the first Mrs Paul Britton – whose nerves were a force to be
reckoned with even at the best of times – had known what Queen
Victoria's funeral held in store, she would undoubtedly have stayed
in bed. But she had no gift of prophecy and would, in any case, have
refused to believe that, merely by reproving her sons' nanny, she
was sparking off a train of events that would disrupt the lives and
fortunes of the entire Britton family for fifty years to come.

It all began trivially enough, as they trooped down the pillared
and porticoed front steps of 8 Upper Hyde Park Gardens and
waited to cross the Bayswater Road into the Park. Indeed, Paul
Britton felt no more than a twinge of all-too-familiar exasperation
when his wife moaned suddenly and laid a compelling, kid-gloved
hand on his arm. Following the line of her gaze, he saw, as he would
have expected, that there was nothing worth making a fuss about,
so he said merely, 'Yes. Quite so.'

Then, with the praiseworthy object of directing her attention
elsewhere, he glanced up at the yellow-grey blanket of cloud that
lay, thick and oppressive, over the chimneys and treetops, and
remarked, 'Do you know, I believe that, despite appearances, the
rain may hold off.'

But Florence ignored him. In the light, languid, carrying voice
whose pitch she never troubled to vary (except, occasionally, in
church), she exclaimed, 'The *vulgarity* of it! What do you suppose
can have possessed the woman? If we were not late already, I should
send them back. Perhaps I still should. Paul, is there time?'

'I think not.'

'Are you sure? Because, really . . . *Brown* shoes!'

To her husband, sons, uncle and cousins, it seemed as if the whole
of the Bayswater Road must be able to hear her. Four-year-old
Matthew, trotting along with the schoolroom party a few yards
ahead, gulped worriedly. Beside him, he could feel Nanny Flott
swelling like a balloon getting ready to burst. It was a pity, because

she had been quite good-tempered earlier on. So good-tempered that Matthew and his brother Tom, who had been told only that they were being taken to see the Queen's funeral procession, had decided that a funeral procession – whatever exactly it was – must be some kind of rather jolly treat.

Matthew peered down at his neat brown shoes with the short, buttoned gaiters. He thought they looked rather nice with the brown tunic and matching knee-long knickers, but he always seemed to be wrong about everything. Gentlemen only wore *black* shoes in town. When he grew up he was going to have red shoes, or green ones. Or blue ones to match his legs. He wished little boys weren't expected to be hardy. His knees were freezing.

Without turning her head, Nanny said, 'The boys always wear brown shoes with their Buster Brown suits, ma'am.'

'Oh, yes!' sighed her mistress. 'I am well aware of it. I would have spoken to you about it long before now, except that I make it a rule not to interfere with your management of the schoolroom. But on a day of national mourning such as today, I would have hoped for some sign if not of taste, at least of respect.'

Matthew opened his mouth. When they were getting dressed that morning, Nanny had sewn black bands round his and Tom's sleeves and tied black silk scarves under their stiff Eton collars, finishing them with a pussycat bow at the front. Tom had eased his finger round his neck, grumbling that the scarf made the collar beastly uncomfortable, but Nanny, instead of giving him a box on the ears as she would have done on any ordinary day, had only said that no little boy in her charge would ever be criticised for failing to show respect for the dead.

Matthew wondered whether, if he told his mama the bit about respect, she might forgive Nanny and put her back into a good temper. On the other hand, it would mean breaking the iron rule that children should be seen and not heard, which would probably cancel everything out again. Nanny was always going on about well-brought-up little boys not speaking until they were spoken to, and it wasn't just a Nanny-rule because, only yesterday, their father had said the same thing.

He had been explaining to them that God had sent for the Queen to come and join Him in heaven – Her Majesty Alexandrina Victoria, sovereign of Great Britain and Ireland, of Australia, Canada, India, New Zealand, a good deal of Africa and the Far East, some very pretty islands in the Caribbean, and a rather small bit of South America. Which, if you added it up, papa had said, meant

12

that she had ruled over six hundred million people and a third of the surface of the globe.

It struck Matthew that it must have kept her awfully busy, and he had said so.

His father had stared at him in the way that made his nose look a mile long. 'You are impertinent, Matthew. I take it you know what "impertinent" means?'

'Yes, papa.' It was one of Nanny's favourite words.

'Nor do I recall giving you permission to speak without first being spoken to. I should not need to remind you that little boys should be seen and not heard. I will have to have a word with Nanny about this deplorable assertiveness of yours. At four, you are quite old enough to have learned propriety.'

Matthew sighed to himself. He had no idea what 'deplorable assertiveness' meant, but it was sure to be something disapproving. Nobody ever patted him on the head and told him he was a good boy. The trouble was that, although he knew the rules and tried very hard to stick to them, when he got excited about something he usually forgot.

He closed his mouth again. Perhaps it would be safer not to explain to mama about the respect thing.

Nanny said grimly, her eyes fixed straight ahead, 'I apologise, ma'am. I will know better in future.'

Matthew sneaked a glance at her. When he had seen men cooking chestnuts or potatoes on open braziers in the street, he had noticed how the heat shimmered round the coals. Nanny was shimmering, just like that, only it wasn't heat. It was temper.

Oh, *bother*!

2

QUEEN VICTORIA had died at Osborne House, her home on the Isle of Wight, so the journey to her final resting-place at Windsor had needed a good deal of intricate organisation involving the royal yacht 'Alberta', several special trains, and a ceremonial procession through London that had been planned to give as many of her subjects as possible the chance to pay their last respects to the short, stout, unamused old lady who had occupied the throne since before most of them were born.

Although the procession was not due to pass through Hyde Park for two hours yet, the place was as full of people as it could hold.

'Dear me,' said Paul Britton to his Uncle Hamish, who had come down from Scotland for the occasion. 'It looks as if physical force may be required. I hope your elbows are in their usual excellent trim?'

Hamish, one of those sturdy, middle-sized men whose air of steamroller competence disguised rather than revealed the acuteness of his mind, gave a snort of laughter. There was certainly no likelihood of them getting where they were going without a fair bit of pushing and shoving. The East Carriage Road was already banked ten or twelve deep behind the pipeclayed crossbelts of the soldiers and sailors lining the route, while milling around in the hinterland were not hundreds but thousands of latecomers trying to find a vantage point. The leafless branches of the plane trees seemed to be accommodating every chimney boy and crossing sweeper in London, and all of them sucking oranges.

Despite the crowds, the quietness was uncanny. There were none of the ordinary street sounds. No clatter of horses or rumbling of carriages, no rattling of cabs or cracking of whips. No barrel organs, no men with tin whistles, no flower sellers, no cat's-meat men. No cries of 'Chairs to mend', or 'Knives to grind'; no voices calling, 'Muffins and crumpets', or 'Fish all alive!'

Instead, the air vibrated with subdued movement – the rustling of coats and skirts, the squelching of galoshes in the mud, the occasional scrape of a hard shoe on the gravelled paths, the sniffling of numberless cold noses, the slither of cloth on cloth as arms were raised to grasp or point or direct. Consultations were carried out wordlessly, by means of raised eyebrows, shaken heads, and so much silent mouthing that Hamish felt as if he'd been inspanned into some vast Workers' Educational Association class on 'Lip-reading for the Millions'.

As he and Paul began forcing a path through the crowds, Paul sighed dispassionately. 'Well, well. I suppose one must expect to rub shoulders with the great unwashed on a day like today.'

It was the kind of remark that always riled Hamish. Fine for Paul, with his privileged background, his elegance, looks and brains, to patronise ordinary folk, when the brutal truth was that he didn't know much about anything beyond country houses and Oxford colleges and the intimate, secretive world of career diplomacy – in which, Hamish grudgingly admitted, he'd gone a long way considering he was still only thirty-one. Hamish himself, who was half

14

a dozen years older than his nephew and managed the shipyard on which the whole family's fortunes depended, reckoned that *he* knew better than to judge folk by whether they'd had a bath or not!

Paul's low voice resumed, 'After all, it is a day that marks not only the passing of the Queen, but the end of an era.'

Battling through the crowd alongside, Hamish just managed to stop himself from saying, 'And high time, too'. His nephew was about the hundredth person this week who'd told him it was the end of an era, and maybe it was true. But Hamish, a man of few illusions, didn't believe eras ended as tidily as that. He wouldn't have bothered to come at all if his daughters hadn't pestered him into it. All the way from Glasgow just to watch a coffin go by. It beat him why women got so much pleasure out of funerals but, being a kindly man, he hoped they weren't going to be disappointed.

A good many folk, he knew, were predicting that the procession wasn't going to come up to scratch. Everyone had always assumed that, when Victoria died, there would be the funeral to end all funerals. Black horses, with black plumes and trappings, drawing a black hearse containing a black-palled coffin. A mile-long cortège of servants and pensioners, the men with crape round their hats and the women dabbing their eyes with black lace handkerchiefs. Foreign monarchs and distinguished guests shrouded in black greatcoats. Mourning bands on every sleeve, naval and military. Gold braid decently dimmed. And all to the strains of 'the Dead March in Saul'.

It should have been like that, but it wasn't going to be, because Victoria, imperious, incorrigible and inconvenient to the last, had said in her Will that, when she went to join her dearest Albert in a better world, there were to be no undertakers, no mournful music, and no black trappings of any sort or kind.

She was going to join Albert in a white gown, her white wedding veil and her white widow's cap. And she was going to travel in a white-draped coffin on an open gun-carriage drawn by eight cream-coloured horses with purple streamers plaited through their manes. The houses along the processional route were to be hung in purple with white bows, and visiting dignitaries were to wear their normal ceremonial dress.

Which meant Austrians in bright red breeches, Germans in pale blue and crimson, Japanese in mauve and yellow, Russians in grey hung about with jewels and gold chains, and the Staff in scarlet ablaze with orders.

It was not at all what Her Majesty's subjects had expected. Nor, indeed, quite what some of those closer to her had bargained for. One result of her ban on undertakers had been that Kaiser Willie – who happened to be over on a visit at the time – had found himself landed with the job of laying out the body. It was generally reported that he had done so without demur, being very attached to his grandmother, but not everyone had been so philosophical. There had been a mutinous muttering of bandsmen when the parts were handed out for the Balmoralised, but still barbarous Scotch coronachs that, relieved by Chopin and Beethoven, were to be played during the march. There had also been something approaching communal apoplexy among furnishing store managers when they discovered they had been far too clever about whisking White Sale goods out of the windows and having them all dyed black.

Chuckling, Hamish glanced back to make sure that the family party was still intact. The boys' nanny appeared to be improving the shining hour by putting her two dark-haired, blue-eyed charges through a murmured catechism from *The Child's Guide to Knowledge*.

'Thomas. Tell me who introduced the fashion of wearing black silk stockings into England?'

'Queen Henrietta. Her consort King Charles I seldom wore any other.' Six-year-old Tom managed to sound virtuous even in a whisper, and his younger brother glared at him.

'Matthew. God has made Great Britain the most powerful of all nations. Why should we therefore govern our Empire with mercy and justice?'

'Er . . . Because if we do so, He will continue to bless and prosper us.'

Hamish chuckled again and allowed his eyes to travel on to where his own three girls were following with Paul's wife, Florence. To his partisan eye, it seemed that, at eighteen, seventeen and sixteen, they were nice-looking lassies, very suitably attired for the weather and the occasion in beige, half-caped Anderson waterproofs ('as worn by the Royal Princesses'), with neat black bonnets and gloves.

He suspected that, if he hadn't put his foot down, they would have been got up, like Florence, in the highest of funereal style. The size and shape of Florence's hat reminded him of nothing so much as a plateful of dead ravens, while her mourning dress under the sealskin cloak was so covered with dangling jet beads that she might have been mistaken for a mobile chandelier.

He was just reflecting, with unchivalrous satisfaction, that she was likely to lose a good few of her beads in the crush, when she raised

16

her voice. 'Paul! Paul! How much further? This mud . . . These vulgar people . . . Are we nearly there?'

Several of the vulgar people turned to look at her, but Paul did no more than raise an airy hand in acknowledgement. Hamish was interested to see a trace of malice on the handsome, autocratic face.

And then, a few moments later, they reached the Apsley House corner and Paul, with a courtesy that lost nothing from being re-inforced by muscles developed on the hunting field, directed a hand, arm and shoulder into a small gap in the rear row of spec-tators, and said, 'Excuse me. Excuse me. Thank you. Excuse me, please!'

You had to give him credit, Hamish thought. Fox the butler – together with the groom, the undergroom, the stable boy, the boot boy, one of the footmen and three of the maids – had been despatched at five o'clock that morning to reserve positions at the front of the processional route until the family arrived.

In no time at all, the changeover had been accomplished and Paul was saying to his departing butler, 'Thank you, Fox. That will be all.'

It wasn't all as far as Hamish was concerned. 'Where are the servants going to watch from? They'll have a job finding someplace at this late stage.'

'Hamish, Hamish! This democratic Scotchness of yours!' Paul smiled. 'I don't know, but since Fox has a large family of his own, I would be prepared to wager that his children have been fulfilling the same task for their father as he has been fulfilling for us.'

He glanced along the row. 'Now. Are we all in a position to see the procession, when it comes?'

3

THEY waited and they waited. Matthew did his best not to fidget. It wasn't too bad at first, because one of the soldiers in front of him was trying to hide the fact that he had hiccups. His face was bright red and different bits of him kept jerking one after the other – shoulders, elbows, rifle, medals, busby and even, once, his knee. Matthew found it hard not to giggle; he wondered whether Tom was watching, too, but didn't dare lean round Nanny to find out.

Nanny was in a terrible temper. 'I don't want to hear a sound out of either of you,' she had said in the voice they knew only too well. Not a sound meant not a sound.

After a while, Matthew lost interest in the soldier. You would have thought the army would teach you simple things like putting a key down the back of your neck.

Carefully, he sneaked a glance at the people round about. They were all very respectable, most of the men in top hats and black overcoats with big astrakhan fur collars, and the ladies in velvet and fur and jet. None of the ladies was half as pretty or nicely dressed as Matthew's mother.

He wriggled. He was beginning to feel uncomfortable. He wished he knew what everyone was waiting for.

Peeping through the space between the hiccuping soldier and the one next to him, he caught the eye of a boy on the other side of the road, peeping back. The boy stuck his tongue out.

Matthew stared at him in a very superior way. Some boys didn't have a nanny to teach them manners.

Weren't they lucky.

He shifted his feet. Nanny took no notice. If she'd been in a better mood he might have risked whispering to her about what was worrying him, but he didn't dare. He shifted his feet again.

He wished the 'funeral' would happen and give him something else to think about. Sometimes, when he woke up crying from a nasty dream, Nanny would snap, 'What's the matter, you bad boy?'

And he would say, 'I don't like what I'm thinking about.'

And Nanny would say, 'Well, turn over on your other side and think about something else.'

It did work, sometimes, but it wasn't much help here and now. He clasped his hands in front of him and wriggled his fingers inside his coat. Please let something happen soon, he thought.

4

THE procession came at last, the sweetish, melancholy strains of Chopin drifting ahead of it under the lowering sky. Among the throngs at Hyde Park Corner there rose a single reverberant murmur, like the rush of water over a distant weir, before all movement ceased and even the susurration of breath in a hundred thousand throats was stilled.

Slow-stepping, rigid, unexpectedly soft-footed, the Scots Guards, the Irish Guards, the Naval, Colonial, and Indian Army detachments began to emerge into Piccadilly from the top of St James's, out of the thin fog that always settled on the streets of London in winter, on days when there was no bustle to dispel it.

By Hamish's reckoning, it took twenty minutes for the vanguard to slow-march along Green Park until it reached the Apsley Gate and began to wheel into Hyde Park and the East Carriage Road; and even then the main part of the procession was still far off and the tail not yet in sight. Twenty relentlessly paced-out minutes that numbed the brain. Even Hamish, who was not given to flights of fancy, began to feel as if the whole of London, the whole of life, had been suspended.

His eyes, sliding like everyone else's over the ranks of Hussars and the flying-wedge of officials beyond, settled with a kind of mute satisfaction on the gun-carriage with its disconcertingly small burden. And as he traced the lines of the white-palled coffin with the Royal Standard over it and the crown, the orb and the insignia of the Garter on top, he became conscious of an emotion that wasn't sorrow, or even regret, but something he couldn't quite put a name to. If it hadn't been overstating things, he might have identified it as a sense of the littleness of humanity in the immensity of history.

Here she came at last, the old widow-woman who had ascended the throne as an eighteen-year-old girl just two years after his own great-grandfather had founded the Britton shipyard. Sixty-three years ago. Sixty-three years that had seen the triumph of steam-ships and railways, the introduction of gas lighting and electricity, of photography and typewriting machines, the invention of the telephone and this new-fangled thing called a motor car.

Sixty-three years of winning wars, large and small; of acquiring subjects brown, black and yellow and trying to make coloured Englishmen of them.

And none of it would have happened if she hadn't had the whole-hearted support of the growing body of people who thought of themselves as the upper middle class, people like the Brittons, who had made money through hard work and hard bargaining, and then polished their manners to match their brass until no one could have told that their blood wasn't blue, but plain, common red.

19

But what did it all mean in the great design? Hadn't the wheel been of as much significance in history as the railway, the arrow as revolutionary as the Gatling gun? Not for the first time, Hamish wondered how long the upper middle class would survive, now that there were Labour members in parliament and trade unionists in the factories and shipyards. How long, come to that, would the grandeur of the British Empire last, now that men of good intentions were telling the once-benighted heathen all about the virtues of freedom and democracy?

Abruptly, Hamish brought his eyes back into focus. Around him, for as far as he could see, every man's hand had risen to his hat – but the sound of thousands of heads being bared, all in the same second, amounted to no more than the whisper of a leaf falling. Even the music had passed and died away into the distance.

He shivered. He wasn't sorry he had come, after all, but he wished it was over. Top-hat in hand, he glanced briefly along the row at the rest of the family. Paul's expression was one of polite indifference, and although Hamish couldn't see Florence's face under her veil, the wisp of black lace she was holding was as pristine as if it had just come from the laundress. But the girls were sobbing satisfyingly into their handkerchiefs, and Nanny Flott, oblivious of young Matthew tugging at her sleeve, was staring at the approaching gun-carriage as avidly as if this were the high point of her life. Well, maybe it was.

In another minute or so, the four pairs of fine cream geldings would be drawing level, one of each pair with a postilion astride, one led, but the faint clop of hooves only made the silence more profound. Nothing moved except the horses and the coffin behind. Nothing breathed. The diamonds in the crown caught some refraction of light from the orb and glittered balefully.

There she went, Victoria Regina, ruler of the greatest empire the world had ever known. And all her glory come to dust.

5

IT WAS at this ill-judged moment that Matthew Britton – four years old, ignored, and absolutely desperate – at last succeeded in attracting the attention not only of his nanny but of his papa, his mama, his uncle, his cousins, and a thousand or two scandalised strangers including the new king, Edward VII.

The acoustics in the Park that day would have satisfied Henry Irving himself, and Matthew's piercing treble carried beautifully as, into the hushed and reverent air, '*Wee-wee!*' he shrieked, almost dancing with the urgency of it. '*Wee-wee!* Wee-wee! Nanny, Nanny, I'm *bursting*! Nanny, *please*! I must have a wee-wee! *Now*!'

Two

1

ON THE CLYDE, four hundred miles to the north of London, Queen Victoria's funeral seemed like a terrible waste of a Saturday.

It wasn't that Clydesiders lacked respect for the old lady, and it most certainly wasn't that they did not enjoy a good funeral. There were few things they relished more. But, since the Scottish Sunday was a day of unrelieved tedium and gloom, Saturday afternoon and evening were the only time in the week when the working man had any real liberty, and he had a rooted objection to people telling him what he should do with it.

All very well for the government in London to declare official mourning and shut everything down. In London they had a procession to watch. But there was no procession in Glasgow or its neighbouring borough of Paisley and – much, much worse – no football, either.

'It's like a week wi' twa Sabbaths', grumbled John Jardine, surveying with disfavour the plateful of cold fried bacon and potatoes his wife had dished up for his dinner. Nellie wasn't much of a cook at the best of times, and today she wasn't even trying. Ostentatiously, he reached for the mustard.

Four-year-old Jack and three-year-old Jenny eyed him doubtfully. Although they were still a bit hazy about the days of the week, they knew enough to be deeply bothered by having their father at home on a Saturday morning. Especially when 'home' had suddenly stopped being the friendly tenement flat they had lived in all their short lives and become a cold, empty house. There didn't seem to be any neighbours in it at all.

Their mother had brought them to it last night in the carrier's cart, when it was dark and raining, and the first thing the carrier had unloaded had been the big chest of drawers. Their mam had pulled out two of the drawers, already lined with blankets, and put the children to bed in them.

'There you are,' she had said. 'Lovely wee cots for you. Just you go straight off to sleep, because I don't want to hear a cheep out of you. I'm busy.'

22

Obediently silent, they had watched while the carrier unloaded other bits of furniture, boxes, trunks and more boxes, until at last, in the chaos of their small world, they had fallen into a restless doze.

But this morning they had been a little comforted to wake to the sight of familiar chairs and tables and plates and mugs, and a fire struggling to burn in the kitchen range.

'It's our new house,' their mam said. 'Our lovely new house. Sit up properly, Jenny, and eat your porridge or I'll smack you. We're going to live here, instead of at the shipyard. There's a nice wee garden for you to play in. You'll like it.'

They were too young to understand that their mother, a connoisseur of what was 'done' and 'not done', was saying what it was correct for mothers to say under such circumstances. But they were not too young to understand that, if she told them they would like the new house, they would like the new house and no nonsense.

2

THE only thing that mattered to Nellie Jardine was that she herself liked it. Worshipped it. Having her own 'proper' house was something she hadn't even begun to dream about until a year or two ago.

Until her marriage five years before, Nellie Brody had lived all the twenty-seven years of her life with her parents and eight brothers and sisters in a tenement in Govan, in Glasgow; eleven people in two rooms, with no bathroom and a single toilet on the stairs that they shared with the shifting population of the neighbouring flats.

Nellie, the eldest daughter, couldn't remember a time when she hadn't been an unpaid drudge; it was desperation that had led her to try and better herself. Starting at fourteen, she had worked her way up from general skivvy in a Corporation primary school to the post of nursemaid-teacher at the Douglas Road Private School, where the staff were so underpaid that no one with proper qualifications was prepared to work there. Nellie did well. She'd had enough experience with her own brothers and sisters to have no trouble at all in disciplining the 'difficult' wee ones whose parents had been persuaded by the school's advertising to fork out good money for them to be educated there.

'No little Child whose Thoughts may stray, Will fail to learn The Douglas Way'. It didn't sound like an 1890s Dotheboys Hall.

Time passed and Nellie's accent refined itself until the glottal stop of Govan vanished as if it had never been and Kelvinside would have claimed her for its own. She even managed to buy the cloth to make herself some decent clothes by sneaking an occasional few pennies from her wage packet before she handed it over to her father, an unemployed and increasingly unemployable dock labourer to whom every missing threepenny bit meant a dram of whisky the less. It earned her a good many drunken clouts about the ears, but she didn't care.

She had been wearing a smart, new white blouse with a high collar that hid the bruise on her jaw when John Jardine had come to the school to see whether it might be a suitable place to send his orphaned six-year-old daughter Iris, who was being very slow to learn.

On her wedding day, Nellie's mother and sisters had told her how lucky she was to have caught a steady widower like John Jardine for a husband, a shipyard foreman only a couple of years older than she was, with a regular wage, a flat with a real bathroom in a good tenement, and nothing on the debit side except wee Iris. A fine-looking man, too, with his long, silky moustaches, his curly brimmed bowler, and the gold watch chain with the amateur football medal dangling from it.

Nellie knew it and was grateful. During the first months of the marriage her temper was so much improved that she did no more than smile thinly when her sister Effie told her, with the brutal candour characteristic of all the Brodys within the bosom of the family, that she was hardly recognisable as the bossy, spiteful Nellie they knew.

'She didny even hit me, honest she didny,' Effie reported wonderingly when she got home, but Mattie, the third and sharpest-witted of the five girls, shook her head and opined that it wouldn't last.

She was right. After a while, Nellie developed new ambitions. What she wanted was not a rented flat in a tenement where everyone knew everyone else's business and the neighbours were all cut from the same ungenteel cloth, but a house. A house with a garden and neighbours whose work didn't involve dirtying their hands. A house of which she could say grandly, 'It's our own, of course.'

John Jardine wouldn't hear of it at first. He liked where he was, and he liked the neighbours, and if Nellie didn't enjoy having the shipyard at the back door that was just too bad. She'd made her bed, etc etc.

Eight years earlier, Brittons' had had the notion of building decent tenements on the edge of the yard for their most valued employees, the foremen. They'd spared no expense, or not very much. The eighteen flats all had gas lighting and running water, and were uniformly built to a plan of parlour, bedroom, living-room-kitchen and scullery; each flat had its own bathroom, with a proper toilet and a bath big enough to double as a fitting-out basin for the *Campania*. Mr Hamish Britton was proud of his neat little row of three-storey tenements, and in John Jardine's opinion he had every right to be.

The place suited John Jardine in all kinds of ways. It was handy for work during the week, and handier still on Saturdays, because it meant he had time for a snooze after his dinner – Nellie's inevitable broth, brown stew, and jam roll and custard – before it was time to say, 'Well, I'm away to the match, Nellie', and take himself off to cheer on St Mirren. Nellie complained that he was football mad, and more than once he'd heard her tell people, with an unconvincing laugh, that the first word the babies had ever uttered (after 'mam' and 'da') had been 'fitball'.

But he had no regrets about marrying her. All women nagged their men, and he didn't have to listen. Nellie kept the place clean, and she was a competent mother, and prepared to put up with his demands in bed without making a fuss about it; she'd known the theory of that, but not the practice, when he's married her. No reasonable man could ask for more.

Because of John Jardine's stubbornness, it took Nellie two ex-tremely repetitive years to get her way. The wee ones were picking up a very slack turn of speech. They needed more space; wee Jack shouldn't be sharing the bedroom with the girls. They needed a garden; Nellie didn't like her children risking their necks in the shipyard.

It was true enough that all the foremen's children looked on the yard as their own private playground. Even the management turned a blind eye, on the principle that what couldn't be cured must be endured. Granted, some of them occasionally fell in the water or got treed halfway up a gantry, but they were retrieved with unfailing good nature by any fitter or riveter who happened to be around, and very soon learned to draw their own dividing line between safety and danger. In John Jardine's opinion, the yard was as good a place as any for them to learn sense.

But there was a limit to any man's endurance, and in the end he gave in and handed over the hundred pounds that represented most of his life's savings in exchange for a little stone villa in a lace-curtained terrace about a mile from the yard.

Nellie was in the seventh heaven. Now, at last, she could feel that something was really hers. Now, at last, she would be able to give full rein to her passion for appearances – for gentility, respectability, cleanliness and tidiness. And godliness, of course.

Her smile, always firm-lipped, had stretched until her cheeks were as round as apples, and her weak hazel eyes had worn a dazed look as she paced out No.2 Rashilea Terrace for the first time, planning where to put things.

There was a lovely parlour downstairs at the front where the walnut suite could go, with its full complement of ornaments and embroidered mats and crochet-edged antimacassars. She would invite some of her new neighbours in to partake of afternoon tea. She'd get out the French-polished cake stand and the lace doileys, and give the EPNS an extra polish, and wear the satin-striped purple gown with the buttons down the front and the cream lace collar.

At the back of the house there was a good-sized kitchen with a cooking range and a fine big recess. Like most married couples, Nellie and John Jardine slept in a bed built into the curtained-off kitchen recess, the warmest spot in the house – the only warm spot in the house – while the children led a spartan existence in the unheated bedrooms. Rashilea Terrace had three bedrooms, one large and two small, opening off the little hall upstairs. On the half-landing, built over the scullery extension, there was a bathroom with a rooflight.

It was all exactly what Nellie had wanted, and the only hurdle that remained was the removal. She knew her husband would expect to set out some morning from the tenement and come home in the evening to the new villa, all neat and tidy and welcoming; like all men, he regarded flitting as woman's work. But Nellie saw no reason why she should do everything herself and it occurred to her that, if she arranged the removal for the Friday evening before Queen Victoria's funeral, John would have neither work nor football as an excuse for not helping her the next day.

He wasn't going to be pleased. Nellie smiled. It always gave her satisfaction to come off best.

3

JACK and Jenny went on sitting, wide-eyed, watching their da work his way through the cold bacon and potatoes and mustard. They could tell he was riled with their mam.

She whisked the plate away from under his nose, saying, 'Are you done? There you are, Iris; you can take that to the scullery.' His teacup vanished, too, just as he was reaching out his hand.

Busily wielding the brush and crumb-tray, Nellie said, 'We'd better get on if we're going to finish upstairs before it's time to light the gas. Iris can unpack the linen after she's washed the dishes.'

Eleven-year-old Iris was looking almost as grumpy as their da.

And then it was the wee ones' turn. 'I don't want you two under my feet. You'd better go out and play. Iris will button your coats and boots up for you. But don't go far.'

Hand in hand, they walked out into the back garden. There was a heavy, wet white mist hanging over the fields beyond the gate, and whatever their mam said they didn't think they were going to like it here.

They didn't hear their father's sudden chuckle. 'Poor wee mites! They look like the orphans o' the storm. Will they be all right?' Or their mother's impatient, 'Of course they'll be all right. Come on, now. Let's get on.'

There were no leaves on the bushes, and only the dank dead stalks of old flowers sticking up from the sodden earth. Jack and Jenny walked right round the garden, slowly. It wasn't very interesting. They walked round it again, skiffling their feet disconsolately. It didn't take long. Jenny said, 'Wish we had our ball. Iris couldny find it.'

'Bet she didny really try,' said Jack.

'No.'

'Will we play tig?'

'Awright.'

Playing tig was fine in the shipyard, where there were all sorts of things to run round and you could get behind a pile of plate mouldings or baulks of timber or even coal, so that whoever was chasing you could see you but couldn't touch you. Even though Jack could run faster than Jenny, she was better at staying out of reach and it sometimes took Jack ages to catch her and shout, 'Tig! You're het!'

But it was no fun in the garden. Jack caught Jenny the minute she started running, and she couldn't catch him at all.

They gave up.

They began to get cold, and Jack's nose was running, but they didn't dare go back in before their mother called them.

'Wish we had your peever. Or your skipping rope,' Jack said.

'Aye.'

It gave them an idea. There was a hook in the house wall with the ragged remnants of a washing line attached to it. They began rummaging round the flowerbeds and among the dead leaves in search of the rest of the line. But it wasn't there. All they did was get dirty.

Jack said, 'There's some trees along the field there.'

'Mam didny say we had to stay in the garden,' Jenny agreed.

So they didn't.

Small though they were, they were both quite good at climbing the scaffolding round the ships' berths. Jack had once climbed up a whole six feet and their da had come and lifted him down and said he was proud of him. When they reached the trees, they discovered that the trunks of the nearest ones were too thick for them to climb, but there was one further along that looked about the right size, and had branches quite low down. Jack beat Jenny to it and took possession.

'It's *my* tree. There isny room for the baith o' us. Find your own tree. I dare you.'

So Jenny stuck her cold pink nose in the air and ran off.

4

'HUV ye found one? I canny see.' Jack's voice sounded funny.

'Aye, I'm here,' Jenny squeaked, and her voice sounded funny, too. She couldn't see him, just like he couldn't see her, because the mist had suddenly spread right down to the ground.

'Are you awright?'

She didn't answer, because she wasn't all right but didn't want to admit it. She had skipped straight up her tree, expecting it to be like the wooden scaffolding she was used to, rough, safe and solid. Instead, the trunk was smooth and slippery, and the little tree was bending and swaying as if it was trying to shake her off. She didn't

28

know how far she was from the ground, because she couldn't see it. It must be a long way. Her hands were beginning to slip, and she'd lost the knobbly bit her foot had been resting on.

In all their limited experience, neither of the children had ever encountered total emptiness, silence, or loneliness. Even in the fog, there had always been lights in the yard, and a warm red glow from the foundry, and plenty of shouting and banging and clattering, and people to rescue you when you got into trouble. This white mist with the darkness behind it, this smothering quietness, this blanked-out isolation were new and unutterably frightening.

The tree shuddered again as Jenny moved, and she let out a wail. 'I'm stuck, Jack. I canny get down. Jack, I'm feart.'

It felt better when his voice came back to her. 'Och, you silly wee thing. How did ye get stuck? Where are you?'

'I'm here.'

'Dinny be daft. Where's here?'

'*Here!*'

She heard him slithering down his tree, and an 'Ow!' as he landed. Then everything was quiet again except for some scufflings and rustlings, as if he was moving about.

His voice, sounding cottonwoolly, said, 'Say something so's I can find you.'

'I'm going to fall off!' she squealed. 'Where are you? Can you make out where I am? Oh, Jackie!'

'Haud on.' He was sounding frightened, too. 'I'm feart of the baith o' us getting lost!'

Stoutly, she said, 'Hansel and Gretel,' then she slipped a little and the tree shook wildly. 'Oooh!'

Even at four, Jack had his head screwed on. 'I dinny ken where you are, but I ken where *I* am. I'll away and get somebody,' he announced.

'Don't tell mam!'

'I'll get Iris.'

Then there was nothing but wet white mist and silence. 'Jack?' she gulped, and then more loudly, 'Jack?' But he'd gone.

She couldn't see, and there was nothing to hear. Her knees began to shake and her arms were aching. She sniffed, and it was nearer a sob. Then, because of the dampness, the sob became a cough, and the cough became a sneeze, and the tree gave a last violent jerk and she couldn't hold on any longer.

Limbs thrashing wildly, she fell into the soft white blanket that wasn't soft at all.

5

IT WAS more than an hour before Jack and Iris found her, because she had fallen into a deep ditch which, added to the mist, muffled their shouts almost completely. It was an hour Jenny was never to forget in the whole of her life, an eternity of misery and loneliness and hurt in a steep, hard, prickly box with a wet, white, dark-shadowed emptiness above and around her that was far, far more terrifying than the worst nightmare she could ever have imagined.

Iris scolded her, of course, once she found that Jenny could stand with a bit of help, and even walk. 'Whit a fuss aboot nothing! And it's jist a toty wee tree, too. You must have fallen squinty-ways. And you're filthy. Your mam'll skelp your breeks.'

But she was good just the same. She made sure their parents were upstairs before she sneaked the wee ones into the scullery and wiped their faces, and combed out Jenny's wet, mouse-fair hair, and took off their coats and brushed them down.

The greenish-yellow light and steady hiss of the gas mantles in the kitchen, the ashy-red crackling glow of the fire, were the most comforting things in the world. But Jenny couldn't stop shaking and her arm was aching like a great big throbbing bruise, so that when her mam came down the stairs her face began to crumple and the tears welled up.

'Tssst!' said her mam crossly, walking straight past her towards the scullery. 'Iris, fill the kettle! And Jenny, whatever it is that's the matter, stop that at once. If you want to cry, you know where to go.'

It was a rule in the Jardine house that, if you wanted to cry, you went to the bathroom. Nellie Jardine said, just let a child think it could get its own way by crying, and there was no end to it. Even when they were babies in their prams, she'd never picked them up when they cried. They'd been the quietest and best-behaved babies in the neighbourhood, which just went to show.

It was a very cold bathroom, but it was a long time before Jenny mastered her tears enough to go back downstairs again.

Jackie was on the floor playing with his building bricks, and Iris was setting the table for tea.

Jenny's mam looked round from where she was pouring boiling water into the teapot. 'That's better. Now, what were you girning about?'

'I'm sorry, mam. I fell, mam. It's my arm. It hurts.'

When Nellie Jardine discovered that the child's wrist was broken, she did at least have the grace to take her into her arms.

But for Jenny there wasn't any comfort in it.

Three

1

ON A warm June evening in Dorset, five years after Queen
Victoria's funeral, Matthew Britton broke all the rules again –
though this time deliberately and much less publicly – by sneaking
out of the house when he was supposed to be asleep, and making for
the water garden. It wasn't that he passionately wanted to watch
the goldfish popping up through the lilies for their bedtime snack;
more that he didn't see why he shouldn't, if he felt like it. He was
very tired of rules, rules, rules.

He almost pranced along the path that ran beside the cutting
garden, where the flowers for the house were grown and the still,
soft air was overpowering with the scents of clove pinks and lavender and nicotiana, cottagey things that old Comstock the gardener
insisted on growing in the hope that some of their vigour might
rub off on them wunnerful-fine danged lilies, delphin-eye-ums
and roses young mis'ess did allus be want'n for to fill up her
danged vaases and bowls. Comstock made no bones about having
been happier in the days before Mr Paul and Mis'ess Florence had
come to share Provost Charters with Sir Albert and her La'ship, but
since the head gardener was the human equivalent of an ancient
monument everyone just had to sigh and put up with him.

If either Mr Paul or Mis'ess Florence had been at home, Matt
wouldn't have dared to kick over the traces, but his father was busy
being diplomatic in Rome, and his mother, who suffered from a
well-publicised delicacy of constitution, was, as so often, staying at
the London house within reach of her favourite doctors.

Matthew, therefore, had no qualms about proceeding blithely
on his way along the crazy-paved paths and through the gaps in
the sheared yew hedges that made a formal framework for the
ten smaller gardens into which Provost Charters' main garden was
divided, reflecting as he went on how jolly it was to have the whole
world to himself under the clear-as-clear, lemon-pale sky. No, not
quite lemon; more like lemon pith, which didn't sound nearly as
poetic. But he was trying very hard these days to be accurate with

words. Lemon pith to the west and the faintest turquoise above, with one or two stars beginning to show.

At nine years old – coming up ten – Matthew liked being alone, which was just as well. It was something he had been forced to learn after his Great Disgrace five years before.

There had been the most terrible dust-up about the episode at Queen Victoria's funeral. According to his father, Matthew had offended against *all* the canons of propriety; had displayed a complete lack of decency, respect, self-control, discipline and shame; had been, in fact, not simply tiresome or naughty, but bad with a capital B.

And he had been punished accordingly. Fifty strokes of the cane and a week on bread and water had been only the start. After that, his father had told Nanny coldly, 'My son is to speak to no one until he can prove he has mended his ways, however long that may take. And no one is to speak to *him*, except you, and only when it is unavoidable. After tonight, neither his mother nor I wish even to see him again until he has learned to control himself and behave like a decent, respectable member of society.'

It had been awful, and since it was difficult to persuade people you were being good when you weren't allowed to point out how good you were being, it had taken two whole years before the torture-by-silence had been relaxed. Even now, he hadn't been entirely forgiven; in fact, he had found that the only way to avoid offending against propriety, the only way to stop people complaining that he had said or done something he shouldn't, was to do and say as little as possible.

Only in public, though. In private, he'd been lucky enough to stumble on the most splendid way of letting off steam without any-one knowing; rather like kicking the furniture, but not so painful.

It had happened on a day when Nanny had never stopped going on at him. She hadn't been speaking to him directly, of course; instead, she had talked and talked and talked, and complained and nagged and snapped – but always looking in Tom's direction and never referring to either of them by name. It was 'he' this, and 'he' that, and 'he' the next thing, until Tom's face had turned red and started to pucker up, and he had screeched. There was no other word for it, he had *screeched*. Matthew was grateful. If Tom hadn't screeched, he would have. As it was, it was Tom who was given a shaking that rattled his teeth and sent to bed without any supper. Nanny, haling him off by the ear, said loudly that 'he' could practise his letters for the next hour.

33

Left alone in the schoolroom with pencil and slate, Matthew had sat raging inside. Nanny was horrible! Viciously, he had stabbed at the slate and then begun scrawling on it.

The slate was narrow, the slate pencil clumsy, and the words short. Accidentally at first, and then by intent, he managed to make everything come out in rhyme.

> I hate Nanny Flott,
> Shes a blot,
> Shes a blot,
> And I wont care a jot,
> If she gose to pot.

He had been so please with this effusion that he had felt a hundred times better almost at once, and since then, with his poetry as an outlet, he had found it possible to be quite cheerful and irreverent inside, while appearing on the outside to be the boring little prig everyone wanted him to be.

2

THERE was a creak in a tree above his head, and he was startled for a moment. One of the barn owls? But it wasn't. With an almost inaudible rustle, something long and shapely floated down to catch in one of the lower branches, something green and gleaming, its iridescent eye lustrous even in the pale light of the afterglow. A peacock's tail feather. Matthew stretched up his hand.

It was one of the sad things about summer, when the cock began shedding his plumage. No more dazzling displays; no more sweepings of his train; no more unfurlings of the huge rainbow fan of feathers. Or not until next spring.

Because his eyes were on the feather in his hand and his nostrils still full of the scent of pinks, Matthew neither saw his grandfather nor smelled the smoke of his cigar until it was too late.

There was an ornate wrought-iron bench on the paving that surrounded the pool, and Sir Albert's tall, heavily built figure was lounging on it, knees crossed. He was wearing his quilted velvet smoking jacket and a smoking cap to match, pillbox-shaped and trimmed with braid. The cigar was in one hand and a large crystal tumbler in the other.

Weakly, Matthew said, 'Good evening, grandfather.'

Sir Albert stared at him unblinkingly, and then, miraculously, the wide white arrow-shaped moustaches lifted at the corners and he said, 'Ah ha! Welcome. Didn't think you had it in you.'

He had a rusty, dark brown voice. Matthew's father's voice was a dressy mid-blue, and his mother's a thin pinky-lilac like Michaelmas daisies.

'Care to join me?' Sir Albert went on, waving a hand spaciously.

Dutifully, Matthew sat down.

'You're too well-behaved, you know. 'Tisn't good for you.'

Matthew blinked, but since a reply was clearly expected, said politely, 'It isn't good for me when I'm *not* well-behaved.'

His grandfather gave a breathy sound that might have been a laugh, and raised his glass. 'Well, I suppose there's that. But no need to go to extremes. Yes, sir, no, sir, three bags full, sir. It's getting damn' boring having a little plaster saint around the house.'

'Mama doesn't think I'm a saint.'

His mother was the only person whose distaste for him was really worrying. To the best of Matthew's understanding, mothers were supposed to love their sons, but his didn't even like him. She didn't like Tom much, either, but at least he hadn't disgraced himself with a capital D.

The funny thing was that, at the time of the Great Disgrace, his mother had been less upset by his lack of self-control than by what he had failed to be self-controlled about. She was so disgusted, she had said, that it made her feel ill just to look at him. And things hadn't improved much, even after five years.

A few months ago, in desperation, he had confided the whole story to his tutor, Mr Morland, finishing up, 'And after all, everyone has to go to the bathroom some time! Even ladies. Why is it so awful?'

Mr Morland was a thin, stooping, immensely polite man who always wore a shabby tailcoat on which the chalk powder lay like snow, and a black wideawake hat over his dust-coloured hair. From his pocket drooped a large red handkerchief, which he used for everything from mopping his forehead to cleaning his spectacles, wiping ink from his hands, and flicking invisible specks off his chair seat.

35

In answer to Matt's question, he had removed his hat, rumpled his hair, put his hat on again, and used his stick to take a swipe at the hedgerow.

At the end of this performance he had said, a lot less fluently than usual, 'Ladies, well . . . Yes, they do feel strongly about it, you see. They've all been so gently reared. All those dainty little lace handkerchiefs and things . . . cleanliness and godliness . . . purity of mind and body. So – er – bodily functions, well, even though they're necessary, the ladies think of them as dirty and nasty. Messy. Not always – um – precisely rose-scented, either. Understandable, really. And someone like your lady mother, with her refined sensibilities – well, someone like she can be made to feel quite ill even by the mention of anything unclean. Probably can't help it. Probably gets the shudders every time she thinks about it.' Mr Morland had a rush of inspiration. 'With some people it's spiders. With some people it's snakes. With your lady mother it's – er – bodily functions.'

Just his luck, Matthew had thought at the end of this rambling discourse. Why couldn't he have had a mother who didn't like snakes? There hadn't been any of those at Queen Victoria's funeral.

'I see,' he had said doubtfully. Ladies were awfully difficult to understand. Perhaps his sensibilities weren't refined enough.

In a voice half smothered by Havana, Sir Albert muttered something that sounded uncommonly like, 'Fool woman.' Then there was a slurping sound as he refreshed himself. 'Enjoy being goody-goody, do you?'

Matthew wished his grandfather wasn't such a single-minded old gentleman, but at least he seemed prepared to talk. Matt wondered whether the brandy might have something to do with it. Its apple-y, throat-catching smell was something he had learned to associate with unusual chattiness in his elders. Even his mother. He'd noticed, because most times his mother didn't say anything, so when she *did* speak to him he always attended extra carefully on the off chance she might say something nice.

'Used to be a jolly little brat once,' grumbled Sir Albert. 'Not any more. Too much discipline, that's your trouble.'

'Mama says I need it. I have to be brought up the same way as papa was brought up, the way countless generations of Brittons have been brought up. The way all proper gentlemen are brought up. She says physical chastisement is a way of helping one to remember what's right and what's wrong.'

The shallow, expressionless eyes swivelled towards him. 'Says that, does she? Well, don't blame me just because you get walloped

36

like your pa did. Your pa's upbringing was your grandmother's concern.'

'But you beat him when his moral wellbeing required it. Mama *told* me.'

'Well, of course,' snorted his grandfather. 'I beat him whenever your grandmother said I should. Never argue with Lutetia.' He nodded sagely. 'Lutetia always knows what's what.'

Matthew didn't doubt it. His grandmother was the most intimidating woman imaginable, loud-voiced and full of vitality. Tall and well-built, she took big strides like a man, and her dresses were made from strong, serviceable materials in serviceable colours. Since she was almost always on her way either to or from the stables, she often had a whip in her hand, and you could tell where she had passed because she left a trail of muddy footprints and hairpins behind her. Talking to her was a bit like standing on the edge of the Blackmoor Vale being buffeted by the wind.

Sir Albert, however, staring at the goldfish pond, abandoned her ladyship without a quiver. 'Said all that, did she? Your mama. That bit about countless generations of Brittons? The bit about gentlemen?'

'Yes.'

'Mmmm. She's right about one thing, y'know. Fine thing to be a gentleman. Look at me. I like it. I'm a happy man. Mind you,' he went on solemnly, 'wouldn't have been a gentleman if I hadn't worked hard at it. Lessons in elocution. Lessons in deportment. And then Lutetia.'

The sky was dark now, but it was a muted darkness, as if the moon was just over the horizon; blue velvet pinpricked with diamonds. In spite of the hedges, there was a sense of space all round, an impression of the wide, well-tended acres that had always been of more importance to the owners of Provost Charters than the house that stood on them.

Matthew was mystified. *He* hadn't had lessons in elocution. He hadn't had lessons in deportment, either, unless being told to stand up straight counted as deportment. And he couldn't quite see what being a gentleman had to do with Grandmother Lutetia. He said, 'I don't think I understand.'

'What don't you understand?'

'Everything. I mean, anything.'

His grandfather shifted. 'Well, come on then. Never find out about things if you don't ask.'

Golly! No one had ever said that to him before. They usually said speech was silver but silence was golden. His mind darted around. There were so many things he wanted to ask! While he sorted them all out, he made do with, 'Why did you take elocution lessons?'

Sir Albert tossed his cigar butt into the pond. It landed on a lily leaf and lay there glowing. He watched it for a moment. 'Stands to reason, doesn't it? Who ever heard of a gentleman with a Glasgow accent and Glasgow manners?'

Putting his glass down on the paving, he rose and stretched his limbs, one by one, with the slow carefulness of a cat, treating himself at the same time to an enormous yawn.

Matthew, perched on the edge of the bench with the peacock feather in his hand and his mouth slightly open, said, 'Aren't there any gentlemen in Glasgow?'

'Well, of course there are. But not *English* gentlemen.'

Then, fists on comfortably upholstered hips, the old man peered down at him, and when he spoke, it was in the communing-with-himself style that increasingly led his wife to fear, at the pitch of her voice, that he was entering his dotage.

'Well, well, I see! Countless generations, eh? Brat thinks the family came over with William the Conqueror, like as not. No one's told him.'

Bending suddenly, he picked up not only his glass but, from behind the bench, a half-full decanter which he held out to Matthew to carry.

'Seez a haud o' that 'steed o' sittin' there like a fart in a trance,' he admonished his stupefied grandson. 'We'll take a wee dauner an' find sumplace comfier to park wurselves.'

3

OUTSIDE the western boundary wall of the house, the land sloped down in a series of gentle folds before taking a dive into the Blackmoor Vale, smooth and featureless under the night sky as a bolt of black bombazine. Sir Albert settled himself on the turf with a sigh of satisfaction. 'That's better. Getting curlicues on my backside from that damn' bench.'

Matthew, resigning the decanter to him, surveyed the turf closely for a patch free from stinging things. It was all very well for grandfather to plump himself down without looking, but Matthew was wearing no more than a much-laundered and somewhat shrunken flannelette nightshirt and he had never forgotten the time when, much less scantily clad than now, he had sat down inadvertently and hard in a patch of nettles. It had ruined his faith in Nanny and her proverbs. 'Tender-handed stroke a nettle, and it stings you for your pains; grasp it like a man of mettle, and it soft as silk remains.' You couldn't grasp a nettle much more mettlesomely than by sitting on it, but he hadn't been able to sit on anything else for days.

Click, click. Click, click, click. Click, click, click, click.

Muttering, Sir Albert put the Automatic Magic Pocket Lamp back in his pocket and produced his little silver case of wax vestas.

'Now!' he said, drawing carefully on his newly lit cigar. 'You can forget all this came-over-with-the-Conqueror stuff. We didn't.'

'But Howard says . . .'

'Howard?' His grandfather looked for a moment as if he were having trouble placing Howard. 'Oh, your Uncle Felix's boy. Well, that's on his mother's side. Your Aunt Pearl. We don't count her. No, it's good old Jockie we're interested in. That's the chap who got things going. Your great-great-great-grandfather.'

Matthew, conjuring up a mental picture of the family tree in the big Bible in the drawingroom, took a moment to identify 'good old Jockie' as the one at the top. John Macdonald Britton. Matthew had always thought of him as large, imposing and bearded like the pard, a kind of scaled-down replica of Abraham or Moses. It was really quite shocking to have him scaled all the way down to 'good old Jockie'!

And as if that wasn't bad enough, it turned out that good old Jockie wasn't even a proper Britton.

'He was born a Macdonald in 1786, in Morar. On the mainland across from Skye, y'know? My brother – your Great-uncle Hamish – bought a house there a few years back, sentimental idiot, though when he has time to stay in it beats me.'

Matthew found his voice. 'He's going next summer,' he volunteered. 'He's invited Tom and me to go, too, on a visit.'

'Oh, he has, has he? Take a mackintosh with you. And don't interrupt me. Now, when Jockie was twelve he ran away and joined the navy – wanted to see the world, or some such rubbish – and served all the way through the Napoleonic wars as a ship's carpenter. Then he went back to Morar.'

'It was his son, Wee John – my grandpapa – who told me how the family got its name. Seems that almost everybody in Morar was a Macdonald or a Macdonell, and half of them called Ewen or John or Jockie; they're all versions of the same name. So they had to be known by nicknames. Jockie's father rowed the ferryboat, so he was "Ewen Ferryman". That sort of thing.

'Now, it seems Jockie had a terrible habit of boasting about his last ship, a frigate called the *Britton*. It'd been French originally, name of *Le Breton* – "the man from Brittany" – and when it was captured and transferred to the British Navy, the clerks at the Admiralty translated the name into English. That's why the two "t"s. Anyway, according to Jockie, the *Britton* won the war single-handed. One dashing exploit after another. Never talked about anything else. So the Morar folk started calling him Jockie Britton. He knew they were making fun of him, but he couldn't very well complain. Even stuck to it afterwards, when he went to Glasgow to work. Jockie Macdonalds were ten a penny there, too.'

Sir Albert paused to refresh himself and Matthew shook his head. To talk about John Macdonald Britton as a ten-a-penny Macdonald called Jockie! It was almost blasphemous. Like calling the Holy Ghost 'Spookie'.

It was worrying, too. Jockie didn't sound like a very high-class kind of ancestor, certainly not the kind Matthew's mother had been going on about. He frowned, wondering if she knew all this.

To his grandfather, however, he said encouragingly, 'Yes? And?'

4

'WELL, in Glasgow, Jockie found work building fishing boats and whalers, and he soon knew all there was to know about wooden-hulled sailing vessels. But he was ambitious, d'ye see, and after the navy he'd had enough of doing what he was told. He was soon convinced that steam was the thing of the future, so he spent all his spare time studying hull design.'

Sir Albert's voice stopped as if someone had snipped it off, and he peered at his grandson. 'Don't know *anything*, young feller-me-lad, do you? I can tell from your face. Wondering what hulls have to do with steam power. Pay attention, then. Point is, sailing ships need cod's-head bows and mackerel tails to compensate for the forrard stress of the masts and sails, whereas with steam, where the power source is inside the body of the vessel, it makes for better sailing if the hull's symmetrical about the midships. *Now* d'ye see?'

'Yes, grandfather.' It was amazing. Matthew had never heard his grandfather talk about anything but farming or politics. It hadn't occurred to him that the old man might have hidden depths.

Sir Albert's cigar had gone out. This time he didn't even bother with the Magic Pocket Lamp.

'Hmmph. Well, I won't waste breath on things you're not going to understand. But what happened was that Jockie went to a yard called Woods' at Port Glasgow and concentrated on hull design, while Wee John was apprenticed to David Napier who'd just started making marine engines. Before that they'd mostly used land engines with a few special refinements. Clever chap, Napier. Him we had to thank for surface condensation, and the steeple engine, and . . .'

Matthew said, 'Grandfather . . .'

'Eh? Oh. Well, never mind that. The end was that in 1835 Jockie and Wee John started their own yard. Found a site near Paisley where the river Cart joins the Clyde. They were just changing from wooden to iron hulls when I was born in 1846, and I can tell you, I knew more about rivets and castings and pumps and compound engines by the time I was your age than you know about multiplication tables and Caesar's Gallic wars.'

The old man had been sounding quite nostalgic, and then, all of a sudden, he made Matthew jump a foot in the air by exploding, 'God save us! I thought I was doomed to live with them for the rest of my life! Dust and glare and hot-metal smells and enough noise to split your skull. I was so grateful when Hamish came into the world that I sat down and cried. I was seventeen at the time.'

He took a huge gulp of brandy. 'I was never very strong, of course. Suffered from ill health all my life. Still do. Well, you know that. That's why I'm always having to go to Baden-Baden to take the waters'.

Matthew nodded sympathetically. He wasn't acquainted with any other elderly invalids, so he didn't know whether they all looked as healthy as his grandfather.

'Anyway, it was clear from when he was an infant that Hamish had a natural turn for the business. So I removed myself. Always fancied the life of an English country gentleman. Took those elocution lessons you were asking about. And deportment lessons. Then I set out to look for the right property and the right wife.'

41

He sighed. 'Never looked back after I found Lutetia. Old county family, you see? Made sure the local gentry accepted us. Took care we never did anything vulgar or *nouveau riche*. It was all of five years before she let me add those turrets to the house, and put in a bit of stained glass.' He contemplated his cigar tip moodily. It was obvious there were some things that rankled. 'And those marble pillars in the hall. Not real marble, just *trompe l'oeil*; painted plaster. The real stuff's *nouveau riche*, d'ye see? Means you've a lot of money and that means you're not proper old landed gentry. Queer thing, ain't it?'

Matt assented whole-heartedly, but he was still bothered by all these countless generations of noble ancestors his mother had talked about. A notion occurred to him.

Tentatively, he said, 'You don't think perhaps *Jockie's* great-great-great-grandfather came over with William the Conqueror?'

Sir Albert snorted happily. 'Not a chance, m'boy. Not a chance. Came over with one of Darwin's apes, more like! No, you'll just have to make the best of the pedigree you've got and keep quiet about it. Mind you, can't see anything wrong with being *nouveau riche* myself – well, I wouldn't, would I? – but there's no denying that the more of a gentleman you appear to be, the more people respect you. One of the laws of Nature. Your Great-uncle Hamish says it won't last, but he's always had funny ideas.'

'Yes, grandfather. No, grandfather. But please, you haven't told me how you got sirred.'

'Think that's what makes me a "proper" gentleman, do you, having a title? Well, I got it for what they called "services to industry", meaning the shipyard. What it really meant was services to the Tory party. I was free with my money when they needed it. Mind you, it cost me more than it should have done. I'd have been content with a knighthood myself, but your grandmother was determined on a baronetcy. Wanted a title that could be passed on. Speaking for myself, I don't see why my sons and grandsons shouldn't earn their own titles. Haven't got much family feeling, I suppose, when you really get down to it.

'But there it is. I got what I wanted. I'm a happy man. And if you can say as much when you're in your sixtieth year, young Matthew, you can count yourself lucky.'

5

SIR Albert, if pushed, would have claimed that he had told young
Matthew the family history because the boy was entitled to know.
But it would have been truer to say that the brandy, which had
induced in him one of his rare fits of garrulity, had also tempted
him to the indulgence of putting a spoke in his daughter-in-law's
wheel. For the languid and snobbish beauty who was young
Matthew's mother, he had no time at all; he couldn't understand
why Paul had married her. Not that Felix's wife was any better –
worse, if anything! – but at least Sir Albert didn't have to share
a house with her.

His grandson's reaction to the revelation that his mother had
been telling him something less than the truth didn't impinge on Sir
Albert's thought processes at all. Indeed, if he even noticed the boy's
abstraction over the next few days, he put it down to the imminence
of his father's return from Rome.

But Matthew was deeply disturbed by the new light his grandfather had shed on the aftermath of the Great Disgrace, and there
wasn't anyone he could talk it over with, not even Tom, who was
away at prep school.

In the last year or two, having reached the age of being able to
think about things, Matthew had decided that when he grew up he
wasn't going to submit to the stupid conventional values according
to which he had been judged, and condemned, on the day of Queen
Victoria's funeral. And he was going to be a lot more tolerant of
other people's sins than anyone had been of his.

Those decisions weren't affected by his grandfather's revelation.
But this ancestry business! He wondered, at first, whether he'd got
it all wrong, what his mother had said to him, but he knew he hadn't.
There had been too much about the honour of the family, and
how he had let the side down and betrayed his breeding. Brittons
didn't do this, that or the other – and certainly not what he had
done. His mother hadn't known how it was *possible* for him to
have behaved so. And for little Matthew John Britton to have
become known to *every*one as 'the boy who disgraced himself at
Queen Victoria's funeral' had set generation upon generation of
blue-blooded Britton ancestors revolving in their graves.

43

But now it turned out that there were only three generations to do any revolving, and that the Brittons didn't have an ounce of breeding to betray, nor an ounce of honour to be upheld.

All of which meant, on a personal level, that Matthew had suffered the thrashing of his life, two years of isolation, and another three of continual nagging as a punishment for not behaving like the perfect little gentleman he wasn't.

The long and distinguished lineage of the Brittons was a fraud. Grandfather Albert's nobility was a fraud. The marble pillars were a fraud. And as for a mother who not only didn't like you and didn't love you – but lied to you . . .

Frowning heavily, Matthew began to wonder whether there was anyone or anything in the whole wide world a boy could rely on.

Four

1

PAUL Britton had every justification for feeling pleased with himself when, a few days later, he arrived back at Provost Charters on leave. After six years at the embassies in Paris and Rome, he had just been given a posting to St Petersburg and was as excited as a boy.

It wasn't likely to be a rest cure. The Bloody Sunday massacre of January 1905 had been followed by a series of revolutionary outrages, a mutiny on the battleship *Potemkin,* and a general strike; a thousand people had died in the streets of Moscow as recently as Christmas. But order had been restored and so, according to report, had all the splendour and barbarism that made Russia one of the most exciting countries in the world.

Snow and shimmering golden domes, court intrigues and Byzantine mosaics, trackless wastes, moujiks, ikons . . . Paul's brain told him it wasn't like that, but his imagination insisted that it was.

In future, visits home were going to be few and far between. That didn't worry Paul, and he knew it would not worry Florence. Their thirteen years of marriage had been impossible almost from the start.

He had been twenty-four when they were married, and she nineteen, and he had been enchanted by her pretty-kitty ways. But those had vanished on the other side of the altar. It had been years before he realised that it was the challenge and the winning that gave her pleasure; in the prize itself, she had no interest at all. The only times, since, that he had seen her transformed into the enticing creature she had been when he courted her, had been when they were at a party or a ball and she had decided to teach some other man's wife a lesson.

He was, however, concerned about the effect of his absence on the boys. Not so much Tom, who was a normal, healthy, straightforward lad, but Matthew. Once or twice Paul had found himself wondering whether he might have been too harsh with Matthew over the episode at Victoria's funeral, because there had been a spark in the child once that seemed to have gone, a spark that had made him more engaging than his elder brother. Paul

45

caught himself up on that. It was wrong for a father to indulge in favouritism. What troubled him now was that the boy had become almost too well-behaved, as if all the spirit had been drained out of him. Paul hoped it was only a stage.

Dorset was looking very lush, very English, very fertile, as Sir Albert's chauffeur drove him away from the little market town in the north of the county where, almost fifty years earlier, the Salisbury and Yeovil Railway Company had obligingly decided to put a station.

Paul had a pleasant sense of coming home. He had never contemplated farming Provost Charters' five hundred acres himself, but one couldn't grow up in the country without developing an interest in the land and its use. Now, he found himself assessing everything that was going on. Observing the men with slashers and billhooks hacking away at the undergrowth in the lee of the hedges, and the others with dock lifters prying dandelions up by the roots, he reflected that it was useless labour in this heavy clay; the roots always broke off and sent up half a dozen new shoots to replace the one that had gone. A mile further on, he noticed that Will Beton, who farmed the land adjacent to Sir Albert's, had set some women hoeing between the rows in his fields of peas. The women looked up inquisitively when they heard the De Dion pass, and Paul watched half a dozen pea plants keel over as the hoes strayed from their path. Beton wouldn't be pleased about that.

Bearing left, the De Dion trundled down into the dip at Sardingley Bottom, and then chugged and jerked its way up the other side. Really, Paul thought, horses were much quieter than motors, and just as fast. The speed limit for motorcars was twenty miles an hour, but he wondered how many roads there were in the county where one would dare travel at more than ten.

And here was Provost Charters at last, the cow parsley making its annual takeover bid on the banks outside the eight-foot high garden walls and the big, wrought-iron lodge gates standing open. The De Dion backfired vigorously three times and then put-put-putted up the drive as if it owned the place.

Paul, born at Provost Charters, had been the merest child when Sir Albert had embarked on the improvements that brought the original, modest Georgian house into line with mid-Victorian taste. He had no memory at all of what the place had been like before his father tacked on the vast public rooms, the conservatory, the servants' block, the battlements, the turrets, and the porte-cochère;

46

before he garnished the interior with a marble staircase, moulded plaster ceilings, carved wainscotting, and gilding everywhere.

If it had been anyone else's house, Paul would have shuddered fastidiously at its Victorian excesses, but because Provost Charters was his home he literally failed to see them. What met his gaze was not a vast, pretentious pile but an evocation of his childhood; not the vulgar whole but the quality, even the charm of its separate elements – the soft, golden sandstone, the richly modelled detail. His eyes came to rest with pleasure on the beautifully maintained gardens, the mature creepers, the windows of the bedroom that had always been his, the sun striking into the library where he had spent so many happy hours, and seeing them he was content. Provost Charters wasn't a specimen of architecture, not something on which one exercised one's critical faculties. It was home.

He was surprised to see that there was no one waiting to greet him under the porte-cochère. In fact, there wasn't a soul in sight.

'Thank you, Janson,' he said, stepping down from the closed passenger compartment into the warm June breeze. Windless days were rare on the edge of the Blackmoor Vale, and the smells of farming always at war with the scent of roses.

'How do you like the new motor?' He had to raise his voice to make himself heard above the engine.

The young man's round, high-coloured face lit up. 'Fine, surr. Fine. 'Ur new traansmission makes a difference you woo'n't believe.'

And that was certainly true; engineering was a closed book to Paul.

'We'm having a mite o' trouble with 'ur brakes – them leather linings burns out faast on the roads round 'ere – but otherways she'm a beauty.'

It was always a mistake to ask questions of an enthusiast. Paul said, 'Excellent,' and turned towards the steps, but Janson's voice followed him.

'Will you be wanting the motor again, Mr Paul, surr? I 'as to drain 'ur radiator, you see, if she'm not going out again today.'

'No, I shan't want it – her – again, thank you.'

47

2

FIVE minutes later, he was wondering whether he should have been quite so positive about it.

A slightly flustered Fox had the door open by the time he mounted the steps, but Paul, his mouth open to enquire where everyone was, closed it again almost at once. From the sound of things, there was a small riot going on in the morningroom.

Welcome home, he thought.

He handed his trilby, stick and gloves to Fox and shrugged himself out of his ulster. One of the white marble statues in the hall eyed him emptily and he eyed it back as, from the general clamour, he singled out Nanny Flott's voice, his mother's, his wife's, and what sounded like one of the boys saying, 'Yes, but . . .' over and over again. Paul's lips tightened.

'That will do, thank you,' he said, as Fox made to precede him towards the morning room, and the butler ducked his head and departed, murmuring something about seeing to Mr Paul's luggage.

It was several moments before anyone noticed Paul standing in the doorway, surveying a room that seemed uncomfortably full of people. Forming, as it did, part of Sir Albert's Gothic improvements, it had a high, ornately plastered ceiling, wainscotted walls, and tall, narrow, leaded windows embellished with emaciated stained-glass representations of St George and the Dragon with attendant knights. There were enough chairs, *chaises-longues* and occasional tables to fill Mr Selfridge's new department store.

Florence, her voice high-pitched and unusually loud, was standing in the centre of the room with one hand on her bosom and the other clutching a crumpled sheet of notepaper, while before her, as Paul had surmised, stood an indignant Matthew, at least an inch taller than he had been the previous summer and considerably more vocal. Nanny had him by the arm in an iron grip, while his grandmother, Lutetia, in riding dress as usual, stood with her back to the empty fireplace. A white-faced maid was doing her best to make herself invisible, and the two men present – Sir Albert and the tutor-fellow – had removed themselves as far as possible from the scene of battle and were deeply engrossed in a discussion of one of the Eastlake oil paintings that disgraced the walls.

At last, with something of a slam, Paul closed the door and said with icy politeness, 'Good morning.' There was immediate silence, and seven heads turned as one. 'I was under the impression that you were expecting me, but it appears I was wrong. Perhaps someone will be good enough to enlighten me as to what is going on?'

His wife and son both opened their mouths, but as it had clearly occurred to neither of them that pleasure would be an appropriate response to the return of their lord and master, Paul waved Matthew to silence and looked at Florence enquiringly. For a moment, she stared back at him. Then she moaned, 'Your son . . . Your abominable, disgusting son . . .' and burst into tears.

Lutetia said bracingly, 'Really, Florence!' and Matthew made a sudden movement as Paul leaned forward and took from his wife's grasp the paper that appeared to be the source of the trouble.

Without looking at it, he said, 'Must I ask again? What is this all about?'

'Tidying up the schoolroom,' replied his mother succinctly. 'The maid found the paper in the toybox, and since she can't read and thought it might be something important, some kind of list, she brought it to her mistress. That was half an hour ago, and there's been no stopping Florence since.'

Paul looked down. He didn't know what he expected. Wondering what a ten-year-old boy could possibly have got up to, to warrant such a furore, he had a brief and unpleasant mental picture of the *ragazzi* of Rome, but dismissed it at once. Nothing of that sort was likely in the wilds of the Dorset countryside.

And it wasn't anything like that. His initial reaction, as he read what was written in his son's juvenile hand, was exasperation that Matthew should still not have mastered the use of the apostrophe. Afterwards, he was aware only of a desire to laugh.

> My mamas a pretty lady
> And I loved her very much
> Because she always smelled so nice
> And was so soft to touch.
> But I do'nt like her any more
> Not cos she says I'm bad,
> And that she ca'nt forgive me
> For making her feel sad,
> But cos I think it is'nt fair
> That when I ask her why

She tell's me things that *are'nt true.*
Its *wrong* to tell a lie!

Scrawled at the end was a kind of codicil. *Why is she allowed to tell lies when I'm not?*

Paul read the thing again. On second reading, it wasn't so funny.

Matthew, returning his father's gaze, said defensively, 'It's *my* poetry. Other people aren't supposed to read it.'

'I will speak to you later.'

Florence's hysterical sobs were grating on his nerves. First, the journey from Rome, then three hours on the train from London, then that damned De Dion; and now Florence.

'My dear, I think you should ring for your maid. When you are calmer, we can have a talk.'

Welcome home.

3

PAUL tapped on the door of his wife's dressing room.

There was a moment's silence and then a rustling sound and the click of a drawer before her voice, unfamiliarly hoarse, said, 'Come in.'

He had given her an hour's grace and her attack of hysteria seemed to have subsided. She was sitting before her frilled and flounced dressing table wearing a frilled and flounced crêpe-de-chine robe in her favourite shade of mauve pink, with her long, dark hair unpinned and her frock tossed carelessly over a chair. Scattered on the floor were petticoat, corset, stockings, shoes, and half a dozen sodden handkerchiefs. They had fallen in such a way that the whale-boned corset looked unpleasantly like a headless corpse.

She didn't speak, but from the little enamelled box in her hand took a violet-scented lozenge and slipped it into her mouth, watching him through eyelids still red and puffy despite the fresh layer of *Poudre d'Amour*. He had told her when he brought the stuff back from Paris that, if it were applied delicately, it wouldn't show, but the message appeared to have escaped her.

After a moment, she turned back to the dressing table and began rummaging among the chaos of combs and bonnet brushes, ring trees and glove powderers, buttonhooks and hatpin stands. He could see in the mirror that she was sucking hard on the lozenge and felt no surprise when what she turned out to be looking for was her scent bottle. The inevitable Oriza 'Parma Violet'.

'Don't trouble on my account,' he said. 'It would need more than violets.'

Two or three years ago, she had tried to explain away the smell of brandy that hung about her by claiming that Mrs Beeton recommended brandy and cold cream applied to the scalp on alternate nights as an excellent hair tonic. He had drawn her to him until there was only an inch between his lips and hers, and that had been the last time she had tried that excuse.

The frown lines showed up like claw marks on her high, smooth forehead. 'I had to calm my nerves.'

'Yes.'

Standing directly behind her, he surveyed them both impersonally in the glass. Even with her eyes swollen, Florence's beauty still had that cool, brittle precision that he had once mistaken for intelligence. He himself had changed into riding dress, and the buff waistcoat and breeches, the black stock, coat and boots, suited him well. They made a handsome couple.

As she began winding up her hair again, he said, 'It will not do, Florence.'

'What will not do?'

'The brandy. Your lack of interest in anyone but yourself. Your attitude to Matthew.'

Having selected three or four hairpins from their cut-glass box and placed them between her lips, she removed one and began anchoring the first coil of hair in place. It was one way of avoiding answering.

He said, 'I can wait.'

He waited until she had used up the pins and then, as she stretched out for more, placed his hand firmly over the box and removed it. She swung round, then, the colour spreading over her face, and he said, 'I would like an explanation, if you please.'

'An explanation? I see. The great man is back, and it is time for the annual accounting. You enjoy catching me out in something you disapprove of, do you not?' She laughed waspishly. 'Whereas I have no idea of what I might catch *you* out at, if ever I were to come to Rome!'

51

'It is rather late to think of that now.'

Her chin jerked up. 'And what am I supposed to deduce from that?'

'Nothing dramatic, I assure you. Merely that, if you had chosen to come abroad with me at the beginning of our married life instead of pleading the delicacy of your constitution – of which I cannot say I have ever seen any particular signs – we might now be happier than we are.'

She closed her eyes and drew in a breath, then with sudden, blind violence sent her hairbrush hurtling into the fragile disorder on the top of the dressing table. The china ring tree snapped and sent a shower of golden hoops spinning over the edge, and the glove-powderer, as it toppled, loosed a puff of scented talc into the air.

Jumping to her feet, she began to stalk about the room, stumbling a little in her feathered, high-heeled slippers.

'Oh, God! Oh, *God*! In thirteen years of marriage, I have borne two living children. They were both very difficult births, especially Matthew's – but you would know nothing about that. I have also suffered two stillbirths. And three miscarriages. But my loving husband has never seen any particular signs of the delicacy of my constitution! Oh, no!

'Oh, no! You have never seen any signs of my being ill, because you come home for a few weeks, share my bed whether I want you to or not, and then disappear for six months or a year, leaving me alone to suffer the consequences.' She gave a hysterical gasp. 'Or not quite alone! I do have the support of your mother, who treats me like a mare in foal. Not one of the more valuable mares, of course!'

He detested scenes and was quite unaccustomed to them, even from Florence. She knew as well as he did that it was axiomatic in married life that, whatever the emotions beating within a wife's bosom, they should remain there. For her to make any kind of scene before her husband, especially about something as sordid as childbirth, was quite unacceptable. And since Paul had never seen any reason to dissent from the commonly held view that the head of the household was someone set apart, someone whose word should be law and whose will unquestioned, when he began to lose his temper it was less over what his wife was saying than with the fact that she was saying it at all.

Icily, he said, 'Control yourself. And pray and do not take that tone with me.'

It stopped her only for long enough to allow him to add, 'I was not aware that you felt so strongly on the subject . . .' and then she was off again.

'Not aware? How should you be? When have you ever listened to what I say? When have you ever talked to me about anything beyond the weather, or which play we should see in London, or how crusty old Comstock is becoming these days?'

He made a sound of impatience. 'You exaggerate. In any case, I cannot imagine that you would wish me to bore you with talk of politics or finance or foreign affairs.'

'Dear me, no. No conversation about anything important. Politics or finance or child-bearing or – or – bed.'

'*Florence!*'

She fell silent, staring out of the window at the wide, peaceful, uneventful countryside. She knew it had never occurred to him to try to see things from her point of view. Husbands didn't. They married because they needed a superior housekeeper, a hostess, and someone to go through the disgusting ritual necessary to give them sons. Someone who made concession after concession and received nothing in return but financial security and the dubious honour of being 'a married lady'. Someone whose manners and looks were all that mattered; who wasn't expected to have feelings.

It seemed extraordinary to her now, how much she had wanted to marry Paul Britton. She had thought married life would be very little different from courtship – until her wedding night, when she discovered what she was expected to do in bed. Her mother, with six daughters to get off her hands, had told Florence nothing calculated to frighten her.

After that first night, Florence had tried to discourage her husband by every politely deceitful means she could think of, but it hadn't saved her. Nor, later, had it occurred to him that her increasingly obvious dislike of conjugal relations, her lack of affection for her sons, might have something to do with the history of her confinements. She knew he thought her a prude and would not have taken the suggestion seriously even if she had dared to put it into words.

He knew nothing, of course, of the obstetrical details – which were far too indelicate for any wife to discuss with her husband – but she had always written, afterwards, to tell him how ill she had been, hoping it might make him stop and think. It hadn't. Very likely he had thought, with distaste, that she was looking for sympathy. And gradually, as the years went by, she had

53

found depression and lethargy beginning to eat into her like a cancer, until she was ready to grasp at any kind of relief. Lacking friends and happiness, the only stimulants were pettishness, and spite, and brandy.

Her husband said, 'That is quite enough, Florence! Have you *no* delicacy of mind?'

It was not the kind of discussion he cared to prolong, so he continued, 'But we will let that pass for the moment. What I cannot allow to pass is your lack of control with Matthew this morning.

'From what he tells me, I gather that, some time ago, you led him to believe that the Brittons had a long and honourable pedigree. I cannot imagine why you should have done so, when he was bound to find out that it was untrue?'

She said dully, 'It was a misunderstanding. I wished him to feel utterly ashamed of himself. As he deserved.'

'I see. Not very intelligent, since he has now discovered the truth of the matter. However, although perhaps he was at fault with that very juvenile poem of his, the basic fault this morning was yours.'

He paused, measuring his words, and because he detested everything that had been said between them in the last ten minutes, they were harsher than they might have been. 'Your display of "nerves" was wholly unforgivable, and I can only say how disgusted I was to find *my* wife behaving with the lack of decorum one would more readily expect from some Billingsgate fishwife.'

He had no warning at all except for her harsh gasp of 'Fishwife!' before she threw herself at him like a wildcat – teeth bared, arms flailing, hands clawing; the long slender nails reaching out furiously to rip and slash and tear at his eyes and face – and the sheer unexpectedness of it held him frozen for a moment. Her nails were already raking at his cheek before he succeeded in catching her wrists, and gripping them, and holding them one-handed while he brought the flat of his other hand across her face in a blow that rocked her whole body.

He had never hit a woman in his life, and would not have imagined himself capable of it.

Releasing her abruptly, he almost flung her away, and she fell clumsily on the bed, the mauve robe open over her lacy, revealing slip. But Paul Britton was not one of those men in whom anger bred arousal. This pretty, spoilt, hysterical and utterly self-centred woman was his wife, the mother of his sons – and he had no feeling at all for her except revulsion.

He stared at her, and went on staring, a weary distaste on his face. This was his wife, and would go on being so. However they felt, they would have to suffer each other for another thirty years or more. There was no way out, no possibility of divorce, not only because divorce would damage his career but because there were no grounds that he knew of. It was scarcely possible to imagine Florence being unfaithful to him; Florence, who cringed even at the thought of intercourse and lay immobile, with her eyes closed, waiting for it to be over. Nor could she divorce him. He had been unfaithful to her often enough, but although a man could divorce his wife for adultery, adultery was not a sufficient ground for a wife to divorce her husband; the law required him to be more of a sinner than that. It didn't occur to Paul that by striking Florence he had laid himself open to an additional charge of cruelty.

He said, 'Shall I have some lunch sent up to you on a tray?'

She shook her head, numbly, and he turned on his heel and left her.

4

MATTHEW was feeling exceedingly pleased with himself. No thrashing beyond an automatic box on the ear from Nanny. An unexpected afternoon off from lessons. The sun shining. And, best of all, his father had said, 'We must see if we can persuade your mama to forgive you.'

He made a bee-line for the stables, saddled up a surprised pony, and said, 'Let's go! Down into the Vale for muscle, and up again for wind. There's a good girl.' Grandmother Lutetia had strong views about the right kind of exercise for fat little ponies.

It was just after four when, full of fresh air and merriment and half-thought-out poems, Matthew returned Lady Jane to her stable, brushed her down, and made off for the front of the house in search of a piece of minor poetic detail to do with Virginia creeper. Having got as far as 'the greenness of the leaves unfurled, against the summer wall', he had to have a look at a live specimen to see whether it should be 'unfurled' or 'unfurling'. He liked 'unfurling' better.

To his surprise, Janson had the De Dion coupé parked on the gravel.

'Hallo,' Matthew yelled over the noise of the engine.

'A'noon, Maaster Matthew.' Janson smiled and went on polishing the brass.

Who could be going out in the motor at this time of day? It was very unusual. Matthew said, 'My father going somewhere, is he?'

'Beg paardon?'

Matthew repeated the question in a smothered shout. He didn't want anyone to hear him and tick him off for being inquisitive.

Then Janson glanced up towards the steps.

Matthew's mother was standing there in her mauve travelling dress with the pink braid on it, and a mauve hat with a veil and a lot of feathers. She was carrying her dressing case and the little plush bag with the muff warmer inside, while her maid, also coated and hatted, was almost invisible under a load of travelling rugs, bonnet boxes, and the tea basket.

Matthew took his cap off dutifully and then, his mouth slightly open, looked back at the motor and saw that the big Combinati trunk and a couple of valises were strapped on the back.

There was no expression at all on his mother's face – or none that he could see under the veil – as she picked up her skirts and descended the steps slowly and carefully. After the scene that morning, Matthew didn't know whether he dared say, 'Good afternoon, mama.'

She walked straight past him without looking, in a trail of violet perfume, and Janson helped her into the motor, closed the door firmly, then got up in the driving compartment and began fiddling with the brake.

Matthew took a deep breath and stepped forward. 'Good afternoon, mama,' he said, and there was a question in it.

Then, and only then, did Florence Britton put her veil up and survey her bewildered younger son. There was an apathy, a deadness in her face, a dullness in her violet eyes, that someone older than Matthew might have read more accurately than he was able to. To him, all they conveyed was rejection. That, after all, was what he was accustomed to.

After a moment or two, she let the window down a little and spoke through the gap. 'Good afternoon, Matthew,' she said, her voice throaty. 'Although I am afraid . . .' She hesitated. 'I am afraid that it is also goodbye. I am going away and I do not think I shall be coming back. I hope that some day you will learn to be a good boy and a credit to the family.'

Matthew stared at her blankly. He had heard what she said, but the message didn't seem to be reaching his brain. She didn't mean those words. She *couldn't* mean them. This wasn't the way world-shattering events happened – was it? Mothers, even if they didn't like their sons much, didn't just drive out of their lives for ever with no more than a goodbye and an instruction to be good.

It wasn't really happening.

Then his mother pulled up the window, and leaned forward to tap on the partition, and Janson pushed the brake stick, and the De Dion began to move. There was the usual salvo of reports from the exhaust and the familiar, crunching put-put-put as the motor crossed the gravel.

Matthew just stood where he was, as it moved away towards the bend in the drive, his legs paralysed and his mind in turmoil. He knew he had to do *some*thing! What would a good boy do in the circumstances? He felt a panicky certainty that she wouldn't come back if he behaved like a *bad* boy. But the only thing he could think of to do was go rushing after the De Dion shouting, 'Mama! Mama! Come back, please come back!' and since good boys never shouted or made a fuss he couldn't do that.

By the time he had reached this despairing and useless conclusion, the Combinati trunk was disappearing from view and the last puff of exhaust fumes dispersing on the breeze.

He heard himself saying in a small, childish, desolate voice, 'Don't go, mama.'

5

AND then he thought – what was he moaning about?

If she was going away for ever, it meant she could never be nasty to him again. She could never tell him lies again. He didn't have to worry any more about whether he could trust her or not.

So he stopped moaning, and planted his fists on his hips, and yelled after her at the top of his voice, 'All right, *go*! And good riddance. You're just a fraud like everybody else. Fraud, fraud, fraud! I don't *care* if you never come back!'

Then he threw his cap down on the gravel and gave it such a kick that it went soaring right into the middle of the largest and spikiest shrub in the garden and was never seen again.

He was absolutely furious with himself when he discovered that he was crying.

Five

1

IT was a nice day.

Jenny Jardine, her teeth cemented into one of the outsize toffee lumps known as Cheugh Jeans (two for a farthing and you could make them last for hours), reconsidered the word 'nice' as, using her feet for brakes, she skidded Iris's old bicycle to a halt beside the gap in the shipyard fence. *Was* it a nice day?

With six whole weeks of school holidays ahead, with the sky blue and the sun shining, it was more than a nice day. Cheerfully, Jenny dinged her bell in time with the riveters' hammers. Clang! Clang! Ting-a-ling. Clang! Clang! Ting-a-ling. It was more than a nice day. It was a *lovely* day.

Jenny was careful about things like that. Her mother said exaggerating was a kind of lying, and lying wasn't allowed at No.2 Rashilea Terrace.

Jack had wasted ages trying to teach Jenny how to lie, but he said her face always gave her away. In the end, she'd asked, 'Why do I have to? Why can I not just say what's true?'

'Suffering duck!' Swear-words weren't allowed at No.2 Rashilea Terrace, either. 'How did I get you for a sister? You canny "just say what's true" because I'll no' have you clyping on me, that's why!'

'I'm *not* a clype.'

'Are you not! It just needs mam to say, "Where's our Jack?" and you *tell* her. And if that's no' clyping, I dinny ken what is!'

'Well, I won't if you don't want me to,' she said obligingly.

'Huh! Fat lot o' good that'll be. One look at your face and she'll know I'm doing something I'm no' supposed to.'

'Why don't you behave, then?'

It seemed to her a perfectly sensible thing to ask, but Jack, sounding just like the stopper coming out of a fizzy-lemonade bottle, yelped, 'In the name of the wee man! Of all the daft questions!'

At nine-and-a-half, Jenny could scarcely have foreseen that her life was going to be full of people reacting very much as Jack did to her infuriating reasonableness. As it was, she merely assumed, as usual, that there was something she had misunderstood, or didn't know, and that everything would become clear to her some day. She hoped it would be soon. It would be nice to see things the way everyone else did.

She said, 'Sorry, Jackie. I'll try not to let on.'

But now it was she who was doing something she wasn't supposed to. According to Jack.

Jack said that Mr Britton had rounded the boys up at the shipyard last night and told them he couldn't afford to have the place turned into a school playground for the next six weeks. 'I know you laddies always manage to slip in, in spite of not being supposed to,' he'd said, 'but there's getting too many of you and I'm afraid there's no two ways about it. Boat daft you may be, but you'll have to find somewhere else to go and play.'

Jenny was suspicious. She couldn't see why Mr Britton, who was always nice in a brisk kind of way, should suddenly want to stop them playing in the yard when he'd always turned a blind eye before. If her dad had told her, she would have believed it, but she had the feeling that Jack had made the whole thing up just to stop her getting in his hair while he was up to something he shouldn't be. Their mum only needed to tell Jack not to do something and he went straight off and did it. Jenny could understand why, but it seemed to her awfully silly to go asking for trouble.

Anyway, she thought, even if what Jack had told her was true, Mr Britton had only said 'laddies'. Girls didn't count. And she was dying to see how they were getting on with the wee puffer they were building in the new berth. She was every bit as boat daft as any of the boys.

Jenny's passion for ships had vaguely religious undertones, though not of a kind any minister of the kirk would have recognised. As she saw it, some ships had a life after death and some didn't – 'death', in her highly individual view, meaning the moment when a vessel's outfitting was complete and it steamed out of the Britton yard for ever. It had a life beyond only if she *wanted* to see it again, or thought it likely that she might.

According to these exacting standards, horrid, dangerous things like Admiralty gunboats died the minute they rounded the Watter Neb where the river Cart joined the river Clyde. Passenger liners did too, because although Jenny admired them she couldn't imagine ever being rich enough to sail in one.

Not so the steam coasters called puffers, in Jenny's view the real wee pets among the immortals. She didn't know why she liked them so much. Maybe it was because they were the right size for someone who wasn't very big herself; sixty-six feet long at most. Or maybe it was because they were so nice and sensible, carrying a mast with a gaff trysail forrard just in case something went wrong with the engine. In a stiff breeze it helped to save coal, too. Jenny knew all about coal consumption at sea. You didn't grow up in and around a Clyde yard without learning that kind of thing pretty early in life.

But the real truth was that the puffers had personality. They reminded Jenny a bit of Jack, because no matter how clean they were, they never looked it. And sometimes when Jack got cross, she was able to imagine great columns of dirty black smoke and five-foot tongues of flame issuing from the top of his head, where he had a tuft of hair that stood up just like a puffer's smokestack.

She giggled to herself, and then sighed. If only the future would hurry up and come. *Some* day she'd go on a puffer as it jinked its way north among the green and purple islands of the Hebrides, delivering the oil that kept the lamps of Ardnamurchan burning, and the tea that quenched the drouth of the crofters of Barra. *Some* day . . .

In the meantime, she badly wanted to know how Ship No.363 – which was how the newest puffer was listed in the yard books – was getting on.

Peering through the gap in the fence to make sure there was no one in sight, she manoeuvred the bicycle in. The children never entered the yard by the main gate because if anyone saw you they shouted at you to go away, and no one shouted louder or longer than the gatekeeper, Old Girny Grosset, the sourest man on the Clyde. But once you were in, nobody bothered very much. Which was what made the by no means accidental gap in the woodyard fence so convenient, hidden as it was behind the timber stores.

With a struggle, Jenny shifted the Cheugh Jean from one side of her mouth to the other and debated whether to head for the berths or the fitting-out basin. The hull of Ship No.363 had been very nearly ready for launch last week, so she plumped for the fitting-out basin.

61

2

IT TOOK her almost ten minutes to wend her way through the woodyard, past the neat stacks of pallets, the mountains of scaffolding, the squared-up piles of struts – six-by-six, four-by-four and two-by-two – the planks for the gangways and working platforms, the great baulks of timber for shoring up the hulls. As daughter of the foreman carpenter, Jenny knew what everything was for without even thinking about it.

With a cheery wave at Billy Bulmer, her dad's best journeyman – who shook his head at her reprovingly – she nipped through the space between the pattern store and the spar shed and emerged on the north wharf of the fitting-out basin to find that she'd guessed right. Because there she was, the dear wee puffer, shaped like one of Jenny's mother's Turkish slippers. The quarter-deck was nearly finished.

No one was working on her. Everyone was too busy with the other ship tied up beyond – the 5,000-ton passenger-cargo vessel (No.354) otherwise known as the s.s. *Fleuron*. Her superstructure was complete, her funnel banded with the white, blue and grey of the Asterisk Line, and she was in the delicate process of being masted. This was something that even daughters of foreman carpenters didn't see every day, and it was quite exciting to watch the great big new hammerhead crane on the wharf, with 'Britton' written in huge letters along it, manoeuvring the foremast towards the ship and the point on the deck where it was to be stepped.

Then, suddenly, it stopped being exciting and became too exciting.

It wouldn't have been so bad if there had been a screeching noise or something. But there wasn't any special sound at all as the steel hawser slipped on the pulley and the huge spike of the mast dropped like a stone for a full twenty feet before the man in the cab managed to stop it. There was a terrible jerk, and the mast began swinging back and forward like some enormous pendulum. Jenny nearly choked on the sweetly melting toffee that followed her own indrawn breath down her throat. Then, almost at once, there was an outburst of shouting from the deck that was audible even above the din of the yard, followed by another terrible jerk, as the mast dropped again. And stopped again.

It was only then, moving forward so as to see better, that Jenny realised that some of the shouting was directed at a boy standing on the wharf — a total stranger, about Jack's age, very posh and upper-class in his oatmeal-coloured tweed jacket and knickerbockers, with a matching cap on his head and a square, bright brown box hung round his neck. What was he *doing*, just standing there!

He was leaning forward a little, as if he was trying to make out what the men on the ship were saying, and it dawned on Jenny that he probably couldn't even see the crane because of the shed between it and him. But he was right underneath the mast. If it slipped just once more . . .

Two of the men were leaping down the *Fleuron*'s gangplank, but Jenny was nearer.

She ran faster than she'd ever run before. It was less than a hundred yards but by the time she reached the boy, she was out of breath. And her teeth were stuck together. She tried to say something but all that came out was a kind of honking sound. So she took hold of a couple of handfuls of his jacket, and tugged.

At first he just stared at her with an air of well-bred mystification, but then, more as if he was afraid she was going to tear his jacket than anything else, allowed himself to be dragged slowly away from the danger zone towards where the peaceable wee puffer swayed sedately at her moorings.

Still gasping and gulping, Jenny pointed upwards, and the boy's eyes followed hers just as the mast dropped another half-dozen feet.

The boy's mouth opened silently and closed again. After a while, he said, 'Oh,' and after another while, 'That could have given me a bit of a headache, couldn't it?'

Unfamiliar with the English habit of understatement, Jenny didn't believe her ears. With a violent effort, she yanked her teeth free from the Cheugh Jean and squeaked, 'It could have killed you.' He smiled a bit disbelievingly, and then started fiddling with the fastening of the brown box hanging round his neck. After a minute, he opened it and took out a black box.

'I didn't see the crane,' he said. 'I suppose I was standing too close to that shed. And one doesn't expect to have great big dangerous things dangling above one's head. I don't, anyway. I really think I ought to have a reminder of it.'

He braced the black box against his tummy, peered into a little glass window in the top, and then tilted the box up a bit. 'With all the din, I couldn't hear what the men were shouting. Shipyards are very noisy, aren't they? Anyway, thank you very much for saving my life.'

And about time, too!

He still didn't look at her. With his eyes on the box, he pushed down a metal lever on the side of it. Then he twisted a thing like a butterfly nut on the top, looked into the window again, and moved the lever up. Despite the general clamour, Jenny heard the tiny click quite clearly.

Sounding, although she didn't know it, very like her mother, Jenny said tartly, 'You shouldn't be having to thank me. You shouldn't have been standing there. Asking for trouble. Don't you know *anything*? And what's that box thing, anyway?'

Matthew didn't have the pleasure of Mrs Jardine's acquaintance, but the bossy little girl in the blue cotton dress, white pinafore and black boots reminded him of Nanny Flott, to whom he had waved a relieved farewell just a year ago.

He said, 'I know lots of things. It's just that I've never been in a shipyard before. How would *you* get on if you found yourself in the country for the first time?'

She didn't even have to think. 'Not very well, but at least I'd have the sense to be extra-specially careful, just because.'

The boy began to put the black box back into the brown box. '*One* of the things I know is how to take photographs,' he said in a nose-in-the-air voice. 'You don't even know what a camera looks like.'

'I do *so*!' Jenny exclaimed, stung. 'I've had my photy took with my mum and dad and Iris and Jackie in a proper studio with a *proper* camera. If that thing's a camera, I don't think much of it. I bet it takes rotten pictures!'

She was beginning to wish she hadn't gone to all that trouble to save the boy's life. She didn't like him at all. He had a plummy voice and a starchy smile, and he was stuck up.

On the other hand, she had had good manners dinned into her ever since she could remember, and there was no doubt about it – she had just been rude. She ought to apologise. Her mum said people should never do or say things they might find themselves *having* to apologise for. The fact that he had been rude first was no excuse.

Suitably ashamed of herself, she muttered, 'I'm sorry.' Then, from the pocket of her starched white pinny she took the creased and slightly sticky screw of paper containing her only remaining Cheugh Jean and held it out to him. 'My name's Jenny. Do you want a sweetie?'

64

He hesitated. But although he had no conception of the heights of self-sacrifice her offer represented, he could recognise an olive branch when he saw one. 'Thank you very much. My name's Matthew Britton.'

She didn't look impressed. She just stood there hanging onto the sweetie-poke like grim death while Matthew fought to detach the toffee lump from it. A little distractedly, he said, 'I'm Mr Hamish Britton's . . .'

It came free at last with a ripping sound, and he said 'great-nephew' and popped the Cheugh Jean straight in his mouth, paper shreds and all.

Some time later – the *Fleuron* having been safely masted and the crane operator made to wish he'd never been born – a very good-looking boy of about thirteen, with dark wavy hair and the blue-est of blue eyes, came strolling down from the head of the fitting-out basin to where Jenny was explaining to Matthew how puffers had got their name.

'Early models . . . non-condensing engines . . . exhaust led up the funnel . . . puffing noises . . .'

Matthew was listening with speechless incomprehension, reflecting on the folly of asking a polite question of someone who didn't know the difference between a polite question and an invitation to bore the questioner silly.

The newcomer grinned at them in a friendly way, especially at Jenny, whose hazel eyes were enormous. 'Hullo,' he said. 'I'm Tom Britton. How do you do?' He had awfully good manners.

Jenny went on staring, and Tom, accepting her interest as no more than his due, turned to his brother and said, 'Thought we'd lost you, Matt. Cousin Connie says it'll soon be time for lunch. Up at the offices. Are you coming?'

Manfully, Matthew tried to answer, but the Cheugh Jean had him in thrall and all he could manage was something that sounded like 'Glup!'

3

'LETTING the side down', said Sir Albert firmly, planting his large, well-manicured hands flat on the table before him. It was his only sign of emotion.

'Rubbish,' said Hamish, equally firmly.

'You can't retire. You're only forty-four.'

'Yes, I can. You retired at twenty-one.'

'That was different.'

'No, it wasn't.' Hamish stopped, and tipped his spectacles forward on his nose. 'But maybe it was, though! I don't remember you doing a fourteen-hour day at the yard, six days a week, fifty-one weeks a year!'

The others sitting round the boardroom table were so accustomed to their chairman and managing director bickering that they scarcely even noticed. Hamish's secretary and eldest daughter, Allie, recorded the exchange with a single, dispassionate shorthand symbol and hoped Connie hadn't brought that witless new maid to serve the lunch. Also, that she'd remembered that James McMurtrie had joined the Temperance movement and would want tea with his steak-and-kidney pudding instead of wine.

James, a cousin of sorts, had inherited a ten per cent holding in Brittons', but attended board meetings primarily as representative of the Eastern Empire Steam Navigation Company, which his grandfather had founded in the 1850s. Brittons' had accepted shares in Eastern Empire in part-payment for its first ships and it had been a good investment; whenever Eastern Empire needed a new ferry or one of the specialised craft that plied the estuaries of India and Burma, Brittons' was the automatic choice to build it. But James wasn't the man his grandfather had been. Or even his father, in whom the old man's engineering and mercantile genius had already been diluted.

Allie knew that her own father was fed up with James. At breakfast that very morning he'd said, 'The fellow's got about as much gumption as a big, long drink of water, and about as much notion of what makes folk tick. With all these amalgamations going on, he'll find Eastern Empire taken over before he knows what's what. Royal Mail's got its eye on him already.'

And now here was Paul – drat the man! – cutting in to suggest, with ill-concealed boredom and only faintly concealed malice, that if Hamish was determined on retiring, perhaps James might take over the post of managing director.

Hamish leaned back in his chair, tucked his thumbs into the armholes of his waistcoat, and surveyed the ceiling, conscientiously giving credit where credit was due. Paul had a fine mind; good seconds in Classical Mods and Literae Humaniores at Oxford; unusually swift promotion in the diplomatic service; likely to go a good deal further since he was still only in his thirties. It was a pity there were times when he didn't seem to have as much common sense as you could balance on a threepenny bit.

Aloud, Hamish said, 'James has enough on his plate as it is. He'll not want to give up Eastern Empire . . .'

James's thin mouth opened beneath the under-nourished moustache, but Hamish was carefully not looking.

'. . . and there's no way he can manage both.' The chair legs thumped to the floor again, and Hamish leaned his forearms on the richly waxed walnut of the big, rectangular table and gazed round at his fellow directors.

'It's a full-time job, and it's going to get fuller. We're in a grand position now we've expanded the site. We've built sixty-five ships in all, these last ten years, and we've got the new berths, the new plating shop and the new light engineering shop. We've nearly completed preparations for the change-over to turbines, and . . .'

'Can't imagine why we're going over to turbines,' Sir Albert said testily. 'We should be listening to this Herr What's-his-name. Diesel. Damn' clever thermodynamics. High compression ratios – that's where the future lies. Not in your rubbishing turbines.'

There was a moment's thunderstruck silence, which Hamish broke at last. 'And what do *you* know about it?' he asked witheringly.

'I know high compression ratios mean high thermal efficiency. Oh-h-h, yes, I still read *The Engineer*, m'boy. I keep up with the times.' The owlish gaze had a glint in it.

Hamish sniffed. 'Pity you don't honour us with your well-informed presence more often, then. If you ever bothered to read the Minutes of the Board Meetings, you'd know we agreed to change over to turbines more than two years ago.'

'Children, children,' murmured Paul.

'Aye, well.' Hamish wasn't sure that Albert wasn't right, though nothing on earth would have induced him to admit it. Diesels might very well be the engines of tomorrow; but this was today and all the Clyde yards were putting their money on turbines. Abandoning Sir Albert and Herr Diesel, he glared at the portrait of John Bell Britton the Second, in all the high Victorian glory of whiskers and frockcoat, and said, 'Anyway, the point is, I've had enough. I want a rest. I bought my house in Morar the summer they finished the Mallaig railway. That was six years ago and I've only had time to get there twice.

'Now, I've got things all nicely settled here. The order book's comfortably full and everythings's ticking over fine. I expect there'll be a slump over the next year or two – we're about due for one –

but we've enough capital reserves to get us through. I can't see that there'll be any serious problems as long as we don't do anything daft, and as long as the naval orders keep coming. So it's as good a time as any for me to go and someone else to take over.'

Elegantly, Paul Britton flexed his shoulder muscles; the only thing to be said for the boardroom chairs was that they did keep you awake. 'That sounds sensible enough,' he drawled. 'But in case you were about to ask, I have to say that the answer is no, not I.'

'I should think not,' exclaimed his father with unflattering promptitude. His gaze swivelled round the table. 'Now, let's take this thing systematically. Number one, Hamish is going, and he doesn't care whether he lets the side down or not.'

Hamish snorted.

'Number two, my own health isn't up to it, as you all know.' His stare dared anyone to contest it. No one did.

'Number three, Paul doesn't know a keel from a hull, and anyway he'd rather get back to St Petersburg.'

Paul smiled.

'Number four, James is too busy . . .'

James opened his mouth.

But Sir Albert's gaze had passed on. 'Which only leaves Felix.'

All eyes turned towards Felix, whose pale, fine skin gradually lost what colour it had.

Felix, a year younger than Paul, bore little resemblance to his brother in looks and none at all in temperament. Though he was of above average height and build – fair of flesh, even – there was a fragility about him that was surprising in the son of such a stalwart pair as Lutetia and Albert. Once or twice, Paul had caught himself wondering whether their mother had played Sir Albert false, but it seemed unlikely; she had always been more interested in breeding horses than humans. Unfortunately, she was also prone to order both species around in the same uncompromising manner, and while Paul hadn't minded, or even paid much attention, Felix had always been a born candidate for bullying.

It was unlucky for Felix that, where his mother had left off, his wife had taken over, even if in a very different style. Pearl, fourth daughter of an impecunious but genealogically impeccable Gloucestershire landowner, was the purest of early Victorians born quarter of a century after her time, a woman whose sweetly domineering saintliness concealed a will of iron. Or so it seemed to Paul who, however lukewarm his affection for his brother, very much disapproved of the emotional pressure Pearl brought to bear on him, draining him when he most needed his strength, soothing him when he needed to be stimulated, and encouraging him to refer all his decisions to God; rather as if God was a more reputable kind of Delphic Oracle. They had married young, and during the sixteen years since then Paul had watched his brother lose what little self-confidence he had and fade into a man whose nerviness was little short of distressing. The only time he behaved like a normal, rational human being was when he was immersed in his law books, because only then did Pearl, who laboured under the delusion that the law was a branch of Christian justice, leave him to his own perfectly capable devices.

Briefly, Paul wondered why he and Felix should both have been so unlucky in their wives.

Felix exclaimed, 'Oh, I say, father, have a heart! I mean – I'm a lawyer, not an engineer. I wouldn't be competent ... No, I really couldn't. No, I don't think . . .'

But Felix knew already that he was going to have the job foisted on him, like it or not, because it suited everybody else that it should be so.

Hamish, equally aware of it, surged into action, allowing his guilty vision of the beauty and peace of Morar to blind him to his nephew's manifold deficiencies. Returning his spectacles to their proper place on his nose, he said with a nice blend of briskness and reassurance, 'The yard doesn't need an engineer, Felix. We've dozens of those. We need a businessman. Now, you've a good head, and as long as you know in general terms how a ship's put together, there's experts enough on the strength to keep you straight on the technical side. And you can call on me for advice any time you need it.'

'Yes. Thank you,' Felix said distractedly. 'But no, I couldn't. I mean, we'd have to move up here, to the Clyde, and I don't think Pearl would like that, especially with Howard just having been apprenticed to the best accountancy firm in the City. She won't want to leave the boy in London on his own. I'm sure she wouldn't like it, though I could ask her, I suppose . . .'

Sir Albert's patience, a frail thing, fell apart. 'What d'ye mean "ask her"? Don't ask her, *tell* her!'

Paul wished Felix had the guts to reply, 'The way you *tell* mother?'

'Damn it all, m'boy!' Sir Albert went on. 'You know as well as we do that if you don't take the job we'll have to get someone in from outside, and I won't have that. This had always been a family firm, and as long as I'm chairman it'll stay that way.'

Felix took a deep, quavering breath and said, 'Yes . . .'

Sir Albert didn't gave him time to get to the 'but'.

'Right, then! That's settled.' He slapped his hands down on the table with reverberating finality. 'Now, what else is there on the agenda? Item 8: Any other business. There isn't any. Item 9: Date of next meeting. Allie can settle that. Good! That's it. I declare this meeting closed. I want my lunch.'

4

ALLIE, neat as a pin in crisp white blouse and grey flannel skirt, raised a capable hand to ruffle Matthew's hair. 'And what have you been up to this fine morning?'

Matthew, just about to help himself to what the grown-ups had left of the smoked salmon, wasn't accustomed to having his hair ruffled, and certainly not by a cousin he scarcely knew. He could only just remember Allie, Bertha and Connie – A, B, and C, as Uncle Hamish had helpfully pointed out – from their visit to London at the time of his Great Disgrace six years before. But he'd taken a strong liking to Allie in these last two days, and that was something that had never happened to him before. She was the nicest, cheerfullest lady he'd ever met, which was funny, because she was quite old. Tom said she must be twenty-five at least.

Smothering his instinctive protest, he smiled back at her, though it wasn't a very spectacular smile. He'd lost what little he'd had of optimism about people after his mother's departure last year. She hadn't come back to Provost Charters once since she left, and his father, in an unguarded moment, had said it would be most improper if she did.

Improper? Like terriers, Matthew and Tom had worried at the word for days on end. What could possibly be improper about their mama coming back to see them? Tom, who had learned a lot during his first year at prep school – a good deal of which he imparted to Matthew behind locked doors at dead of night – was convinced she had found Another Man, that she had abandoned the respectability of hearth and home for the superior delights of Living in Sin. The only alternative, he said, was that she had been kidnapped for the White Slave trade. Either way, she couldn't possibly come back to her family. Because there was no question about it. She must have been doing you-know-what. Matthew didn't know what, and he had the feeling that Tom didn't either, or he would have told him.

Allie said, 'Did you have a look round the yard?' and Matthew nodded. He hoped she wasn't going to ask them what they thought of it.

They'd had a very interesting conversation the evening before in Uncle Hamish's house at Castlehead, a house quite different from Provost Charters in that it was smaller – it only had ten bedrooms, including the servants' – and very plain indeed. It looked, in fact, as if it had been built by someone exceedingly strong-minded to last for ever and ever, amen, and woe betide it if it didn't. But in spite of its stern grey solidity it was much more comfortable inside than Provost Charters; even the chairs were nice and squashy and covered with a bright, pink-patterned white cloth. Allie said she had chosen the covers, and persuaded Uncle Hamish to have all the panelling painted white to cheer everything up. Matthew had come to the conclusion that Allie was jolly good at cheering things up.

'Just wait till you see the ships in the harbour!' she'd said. 'They're a real allsorts mixture. Atlantic passenger steamers, and funny fat cargo boats that look like floating hatboxes, and big bright-funnelled South American traders bristling with derricks. Then there are steamers from the China seas, with their names written on the bows in strange, exotic scripts and pig-tailed Chinamen for crews.

'Sailing ships, too! Did you know they can still clip hours – sometimes days – off the Australian record? And then there are four-masted Frenchies from New Caledonia, and carriers from Rangoon or Harbour Grace, and Chile and the Persian Gulf. And ore tramps from Bilbao, and Italian fruit boats, Channel packets, and Highland steamers. I can't tell you how thrilling it all is!'

Matthew and Tom had looked forward to seeing it very much, but what they hadn't realised was that Allie had been talking about the main harbour of the Clyde, which wasn't by any means the same as the shipyard. The yard, they discovered, was a couple of miles downstream from the harbour and dead across the oily bronze waters from another shipyard, the one known as Clyde bank, which belonged to one of Britton's major competitors, John Brown. They'd felt seriously let down by the absence of four-masted Frenchies and ships from the China seas.

Tom, trying to change the subject, said, 'Matt found a girl friend. She gave him a toffee lump. He knows all about those puffer things now, because she told him.'

71

If Matthew hadn't had a plate in his hand and Allie's arm half round him, he would have kicked his brother where it hurt most. Tom was always trying to take him down a peg.

Allie looked at Tom quizzically, as if she was wondering whether he wanted his hair rumpled too. Then she held Matthew away from her at arms' length and looked at him and said, laughing, 'A girl friend? My goodness. But if you've been hearing all about puffers, I don't need to ask who it was. Jenny Jardine. She's a little monkey, that one, but I sometimes think it's a pity girls can't be engineers. She'll just have to make do with being a secretary like me, and walking out with a *man* who's an engineer.'

It took Matthew's mind right off his troubles, and from the look on Tom's face, he was pretty intrigued, too. Twenty-five years old – and walking out?

Matthew said, 'Oh, really? Is it someone at Brittons'?'

'Not now. He's doing what most marine engineers on the Clyde do after they've finished their apprenticeship and before they settle down. He's a Chief Engineer with the Mount Line. Sails all round the world.' One hand went to the opal and pearl drop in her ear. 'See? He brought me these, all the way from Australia.'

'They're very pretty,' Matthew said dutifully. 'What's he called?'

'John. John Baine.'

'Is he nice?'

'Of course.' The boys' attempt to hide their astonishment struck Allie as very English and rather amusing. She supposed they must think of her as being as old as their mother and nowhere near as pretty. Allie was ready enough to admit that, being built on lines more functional than elegant, she wasn't any great beauty compared with Florence, but she had well-set, grey-blue eyes and the high-boned Britton nose, and John Baine thought she was a handsome woman. Which was all that mattered.

'Eat up,' she said, 'and I'll take you on a proper tour of the yard this afternoon. We might just have time to go up to the harbour afterwards. You'll have to see everything today, because the train for Morar leaves at the crack of dawn tomorrow.'

There seemed to be no way out. Matthew glanced down at the smoked salmon and discovered he'd lost his appetite. He didn't know if he could stand any more noise. 'Is Morar a quiet place?' he asked, all wide-eyed innocence.

But Allie wasn't fooled. She laughed. 'You'll see! After a week of only the seabirds' song, you may find yourself yearning to be right back here at the yard with Jenny Jardine and her puffers.'

Six

1

THE golden dome of St Isaac's shone like an alternative sun over the winter roofs of St Petersburg, and the gleaming spire of the Fortress Church pierced the flurrying snow like some gilded Excalibur borne aloft over a landscape 'clothed in white samite, mystic, wonderful'.

Paul Britton smiled briefly at this odd and inappropriate fancy. Why *did* the Russians gild their cupolas and turrets? An Oriental love of magnificence, perhaps? After two years, he had come to the conclusion that Russians were far more Oriental than European; fatalistic, lacking in initiative, venal, unpunctual. Awaiting the arrival of a minor official who should have been in his office an hour ago, he was reminded of the drollery credited to one of his predecessors at the embassy, a certain Lord Frederic Hamilton. A nation, Lord Frederic had said, that could render Your Excellency as *Vashe Vysokoprevoskhoditelstvo* clearly had no sense at all of the value of time.

Morosely, Paul stared out of the double windows at the Troitsky Square and the frozen river Neva, at a world almost unpeopled and a sky filled only with snow. Such light as there had been was dying, though it was no more than two in the afternoon. Here, on the Gulf of Finland, the winter day lasted a mere four hours and the sun – when it shone – shone so low in the sky that its rays never reached the streets. An occasional sledge swept north or south along the lamplit, tree-lined artificial avenue that crossed the ice of the Neva, but the lamps were dim and the fir trees had no roots. A few moujiks in sheepskins and red shirts plodded their way towards one of the wooden taverns that appeared on the Neva in December and vanished with the April thaw. And that was all. Emptiness.

This was how he had first seen St Petersburg, and his disappointment had been acute. The dazzling city of his dreams turned out to be nothing more than a gigantic stage set; a huge huddle of grandiose monuments built on a quagmire; of state buildings vulgarly painted and leprous with flaking plaster; of private houses smelling of drains and cabbage soup and leather; of wanly lit theatres and even more wanly lit shops; of uneven pavements, and slovenly soldiers; of a damp and penetrating cold outdoors, and, indoors, suffocation from the steam heat and hermetically sealed windows.

And then summer had come and he had wondered how he could ever have found it dreary, for in summer the Neva ran sparkling and swift, and the sun shone on tender new greenery, and a faint opal haze lay over everything, lending a classical purity to the architecture and transforming the crude reds and blues of the façades into Venetian rose and cobalt. By then he had begun to learn Russian; by then, too, he had Russian friends.

Now he was in his third winter, and he had been home only once. The work had been unremitting, some of it bureaucratic, some of it local and political, some concerned with matters of international moment. Paul had lost count of how many times he had spent half the night in the Chancery while the cypher clerks coded and decoded urgent telegrams. Last year there had been the Triple Entente between Britain, Russia and France – an alliance fertile with misunderstanding, especially in the matter of the clause guaranteeing British support for Russia in the area of the Dardanelles. No one, on either side, had any real idea of what it meant, or was even intended to mean. And this year, Austria-Hungary had annexed Bosnia and Herzegovina, and Mother Russia, in her role of 'Protector of the Slavs', had first of all made a great fuss and then been forced to back down. Which was just as well, because the Russian army was in no state to fight a European war.

There was no doubt in Paul's mind that there was going to be a new crisis before long, precipitated by German intervention in Turkish affairs. He hoped that it wouldn't blow up out of all proportion, because he was entitled to some home leave and was beginning to think he would be wise to take it.

Where *was* the pompous little man from the Governing Senate? From – shades of Lord Frederic! – the *Pravitelstvuyushchiy Senat*. Withdrawing his gaze from the darkening outdoors, Paul swung back to his desk and took out the Christmas letters he had just received from his sons.

2

HE couldn't remember the kind of epistles he had penned to his own parents, but Tom's was much what one would have expected from a fourteen-year-old at the end of his first term at public school.

Casual references to long trousers and Eton jackets and top hats. Vain glorious asides about a possible tryout for the second rugger fifteen. Heavy hints that a new airgun would be appreciated. A bit about midnight feasts of sparrows roasted over the embers of the dormitory fire.

Paul frowned. One didn't send one's son to public school to be mollycoddled with fires in the dormitory.

After that, there was Baden-Powell's new Scouting movement – tents, campfires, tracking, woodcraft, just the kind of things that had always appealed to the boy. Silence on the question of academic achievement, which was just as it should be.

Tom, thought his father, was bidding fair to turn into a normal, manly, sensible chap. But Matthew, now twelve-and-a-half and in his last year at prep school, hadn't a word to say about rugby, roast sparrows or Scouts.

'I was awfully sorry you couldn't come with us to Morar that time you were home. It was smashing. We went again this summer. Wasnt it decent of Great-uncle Hamish to invite us? Allie was there too. Its' amazingly quiet. Tom goes shooting and is learning to fish, but I like it better just looking at the sky. There are the most eckstrordinary clouds, and they look diffrent every five minutes. I think it would be very exiting to be up in the sky, much more exiting than shooting at birds and catching boring old fish. I think I like Morar better than Provost Charters but Tom doesnt.

'Uncle Hamish drives around in a very pekuliar old motorcar. Its' called an Arrol-Johnston dog-cart, and you cant see any machinery so it looks as if someones left the horses off by mistake. Uncle Hamish says its' well desined for these bad Highland roads. I think motors are interesting.

'We went to the shipyard again on our way to Morar and Mr Jardine – thats the foreman carpenter – showed me how to use his

75

laith and said I had a real talent for it. It would be nice to make things with my hands I think.'

Matthew's father wondered, sorrowfully, how he had managed to sire a son with no interest in gentlemanly pursuits, no grasp of punctuation or spelling, and a professed love for rude mechanicals.

And it looked as if, with the aid of Hamish's middle daughter, Bertha, he was in danger of acquiring some other odd ideas.

Eighteen months before, Grandmother Lutetia had broken her neck – 'taking that bitch of a mare of hers over the water jump,' had written her grieving husband. 'Damned disobliging of her.'

It had placed Paul in a quandary, because it meant there was no one to exercise even his mother's arbitrary supervision over the boys during their school holidays.

There had been no question, of course, of Florence returning. Paul and she, in the presence of their solicitors, had met before he left England to find that absence had made neither of their hearts grow fonder. She was living with her parents in Cambridge, and it appeared that she was being squired around by a middle-aged academic with more milk-and-water in his veins than blood. They would suit very well, Paul had thought with unaccustomed savagery.

And then it had occurred to him to invite Bertha – buxom, homely, and reassuring – to preside over Provost Charters and act as substitute mother. It looked, now, as if this had not been the happiest of inspirations.

'Bertha took me to a new kind of exhibition last spring. It was called the Ideal Home Exhibition and it was ever so interesting. Did you know there are machines that can wash clothes all by themselves or almost all by themselves? They make a terrible noise, though. And then in June there was a great big meeting in Hyde Park we went to, though not Tom because he was still at school. There were thousands of people there, and lots of policemen to make sure everybody behaved. It was all about ladies wanting things gentlemen wont let them have. The ladies are called sufferajets (I dont know if thats spelt right). Anyway, it was very thrilling and Bertha stood there and cheered and I cheered too . . .'

Paul groaned.

'I am sure Cousin Bertha would wish to be remembered to you, and Great-uncle Hamish too. Very confidenshully, I dont think Uncle Hamish is really enjoying being retired. He talks an awful lot about the yard and what Uncle Felix is doing wrong, and though Crannoch Lodge is full of stags heads and pictures of Highland cattle and other exiting things, he says it can be awfully boring

76

and dreich (thats the right spelling, I asked him) compared with his nice comfy house at Castlehead and, anyway, he likes spotted lorrels better than heather. And when the puffer lands on the beach to deliver the flour and tea and fewel for the Arrol-Johnston, the men have an awful time getting away again because Uncle Hamish wont stop talking.'

It was clear to Paul that something was going to have to be done, and he could think of only one thing to do. Although the solution depended on a number of factors, not least the profitability of the shipyard, it might, he thought, with an excitement to which he had been a stranger for a very long time – it might be viable.

3

IT wasn't a decision to be taken lightly, and during the next few weeks Paul studied it from every angle. Not until one midnight in March did he realise that he was deluding himself; that the decision had been made in the very moment when the idea first entered his head.

With other members of the diplomatic corps he was attending Easter Mass in St Isaac's. Simple curiosity had taken him in his first year; the poignancy and majesty of the occasion had drawn him back.

For the half-hour before midnight, the great church, packed to its doors, stood in incense-laden darkness while black-robed priests chanted the Russian Office for the Dead and re-enacted the search for the body of Christ. And then, as the first stroke of midnight pealed out, the Metropolitan of St Petersburg cried, 'Christ is risen!' and the guns of the fortress boomed out the salute.

Tens of thousands of unlit candles, their wicks touched with kerosene and linked by a single thread of gun-cotton, had been strung round the cathedral in such a way as to outline every feature of it – every arch, pillar, cornice, doorway – and at the very moment when the Resurrection was proclaimed, an acolyte touched a match to the cotton. Small, blue and magical, the spark raced along the invisible thread, and the candles – one by one – leapt into immediate life, so that in a matter of seconds a girdle of light had been thrown round the cathedral, blazing on a barbaric splendour of jewels, ikons and mosaics, on gold, silver and bronze, porphyry and jasper, malachite and lapis lazuli. And then the great doors were thrown open and the clergy appeared with their long, flowing white beards, gemmed crowns, and vestments of cloth of gold, while the choir burst into the Russian Easter Anthem, and every member of the huge congregation lit another, separate taper. The explosive transformation from darkness to dazzling light, from funeral dirge to paean of glory, was unimaginably thrilling.

But although Paul, standing with his fellow diplomats in their allotted place behind the railings of the ikonostas, felt the same thrill in this year of 1909 as he had done in 1908 and 1907, it was superseded almost at once by a sensation of breathlessness. As the tapers were lit among the congregation, his eyes, independent of his will, flew to the throng, searching. Ludicrous, he knew, when there were so many thousands present.

But then his gaze was inexorably drawn towards a point on the northern side of the building, where one of the lamps cast a rose-red glow over peasants in sheepskin standing shoulder to shoulder with nobility in sables.

And she was there. She was there, vivid eyes lowered and bright hair dimmed by a heavy black veil. The answer to all his needs. The fount of the passion in his heart. His obsession.

4

WHEN Paul had arrived in St Petersburg, he had carried a letter of introduction to one of the city's most distinguished residents, the Princess Betsy Bulgarin. He had been fortunate to find favour in the old lady's eyes, and invitations to her Sunday 'At Homes' had followed.

'No one dull,' she had said. 'I hold a *salon* in the old French style. About thirty guests. Conversation and supper. You and Monsieur Garamond will be the only Europeans but, naturally, as civilised people we all speak French and English.'

No one expected foreign diplomats to learn more Russian than was needed to instruct a waiter or a cab driver, but Paul had felt bound by courtesy as well as convenience to apply his mind seriously to it; it had pleased him to find that his old talent for languages had not deserted him. And it had proved worthwhile in every way, because when his Russian acquaintances discovered that he was genuinely interested, they had opened their homes to him – a privilege rarely accorded to foreigners.

Tonight, he had been invited to the Princess's for the traditional after-Mass supper that broke the rigorous forty-day Lenten Fast of the Eastern Church.

'*Khristos voskres.* Christ is risen!' his hostess greeted him. She was tiny, but wonderfully stately, clad as always in plain black dress and lace cap.

'He is verily risen,' Paul responded.

'We are happy to greet you, Pavel Albertovich. As you see, many of my guests have already arrived and supper has begun. Will you join them?'

As he entered the great first-floor reception room, he found himself marvelling, as always, at the Englishness of so many of the great St Petersburg houses. Or Scotchness. After the Napoleonic invasion in 1812, patriotism had forbidden the Russian nobility to employ French architects, and one result had been an influx of men trained by the Adam brothers. The Russians called their version of the Adam style *empire russe,* but the first time Paul had crossed the threshold of the splendid residence belonging to Count Orloff-Davidoff he had been completely taken aback, wondering for a moment whether he had somehow been transported back to London and Lansdowne House. The resemblance was uncanny.

The Princess's reception suite was vast and elegantly panelled in white and gold, lit with crystal chandeliers, and with golden damask drapes over the windows. But although the shelves and display cabinets were crammed with the most exquisite china, bronzes and *objets d'art,* the walls – as in so many St Petersburg houses – held not a single painting worth looking at. It was a mystery that Paul hoped someone would offer to explain to him some day. It was not the sort of question one could ask straight out.

The atmosphere was like a Turkish bath. Murmuring, 'Christ is risen!' or 'He is verily risen!' to left and right as he passed, Paul made his way through the crowd to the buffet table. Once he had reached it, he had no intention of straying, though not for reasons of gluttony. Russians, brought up to the *zakuski* table from childhood, might be able to stand around juggling plates and glasses with the most perfect aplomb, but it was a knack which Paul had not yet mastered. He felt an ill-timed twinge of amusement at the thought of what Florence would have made of it all.

Unlike his hosts, Paul had not been forbidden meat, butter, eggs and cheese for the last forty days, but even so the buffet looked delightful, laden with all the traditional foods that would appear on twenty million Russian tables tonight, tables rich and poor, high and low. Cold ham; brightly decorated hard-boiled eggs marked with the letters XB to signify 'Christ is risen'; *kulich,* a kind of brioche covered with white icing; and *paskha,* a confection of curd cheese, cream, butter, fruit and nuts, imprinted with the Orthodox cross and, once more, XB.

To the servant, Paul said, 'Vodka'.

At almost the same instant a voice spoke behind him – a warm, mischievous, feminine voice. *'Khristos voskres,* Pavel Albertovich!'

By some miracle, his hand remained steady and he was able to receive the glass from the servant without dropping it. Carefully, he placed it on the white damask cloth, and turned.

'He is verily risen.' He had to take a breath before he could go on. 'It is, as always, a joy to see you, Natasha Mikhailovna. What a fortunate chance that we should both be overcome by hunger at the same moment!'

'Chance?' The luminous ice-blue eyes widened in mock indignation. 'It is no chance. I wish to speak to you, and practise my English, and evair eebodee knows one finds you always near to the *zakuski* table!' An enchanting smile robbed the words of any possible offence.

Automatically, he said, 'Everybody.'

'Ev-ree-bodd-ee?'

Natasha Mikhailovna Eᶠemov was the most alluring young woman in St Petersburg, not because she was a beauty in the accepted sense, but because she wasn't. Or not if one ignored her figure, which wasn't easy to do, since it was a small and perfectly proportioned hour glass, gowned tonight in a décolleté sapphire-blue satin that displayed her soft and shapely shoulders to perfection. But in other ways, in looks and, Paul suspected, in character, she was a study in contradictions.

In the months since he had known her, she had always worn her silky yellow hair piled up and puffed out into the cottage-loaf style so fashionable in Europe, but beneath it her cheekbones were unmistakably Slav, her mouth wide and full-lipped, and her jaw verging on the square. Yet the bold cast of her features was the last thing one noticed. When they met, Paul's invariable first impression was of delicacy, of the fine creaminess of her complexion, the soft glow in her cheeks, and the way she held her lips very slightly apart so that she had a look of childlike innocence that wasn't altogether belied by the intensity of light in the clear northern eyes.

She was nineteen years old, and he, more than twice her age, was besotted.

Gathering himself together, he said, 'May I serve you something?'

'*Grand dieu, non!* I have eaten long ago, thank you. You are so late. I saw you in the cathedral, by the ikonostas, looking very distinguished – evening dress becomes you well! – and I thought, "The poor Pavel Albertovich! It will take him a long, *long* time to escape through all those people!"'

He smiled, ridiculously flattered. 'Whereas you were intelligently positioned near one of the doors.'

'But of course. So! Now, you must eat. I shall leave you and we will talk later.'

'No, please. Tell me – why did you wish to speak to me?'

She smiled at him with the vitality that she knew to be her greatest charm, and shrugged her shoulders so that there was a shimmer at her throat from the sapphires and diamonds studding the little blue enamel Fabergé egg she wore as a pendant. She thought Paul Britton an attractive man, and wonderfully cosmopolitan. He had breeding, and appeared to have no wife, and she was fairly sure that he had money. He was also, unless she was mistaken – which, with men, she rarely was – very much aware of her. His tour of duty in Russia could not last much longer, and she was very bored with St Petersburg.

She said artlessly, 'I think perhaps you will not like it, but . . . You have travelled so much. You are a man of the world, yes? Then, is it true that in Paris the ladies are giving up their . . .'

She paused, no longer artless but provocative, and he knew that she was right and he wasn't going to like it. Praying that no one within earshot was fluent in English, he half-frowned and half-smiled and said, 'Giving up their what?'

Her hands described two outrageously explicit curves, and she murmured, 'Their corsets!' Then her mirth bubbled over. He had no doubt at all that she was teasing him simply for the pleasure of seeing the expression on his face, but there was no malice in the richly infectious chuckle. Half a dozen faces turned, smiling, in their direction.

She said, 'Please, Pavel Albertovich? You must tell me! How may I be in the *avant-garde* of fashion if I do not know these things?'

Her gaze was so limpid in contrast with the brazen impropriety of her question, that for a moment Paul could only stammer. 'My dear Natasha Mikhailovna, I . . . I . . . I have no idea!'

She chuckled again. 'Pooh! I do not believe you. Confess, you only pretend that you do not know, because I shock you.' Her voice became coaxing. '*Please!* Please tell me! You *must* know!'

She was utterly disarming. He found himself laughing back at her as he might have laughed when he, too, was nineteen years old and free from care. 'Very well! I deny that I am an expert, but I believe you may be right. If you are to be *avant garde,* you must look not only soft and flexible, but – er – limp. Though that does not appear to me to be the style of thing that would suit you at all!'

But before Natasha, about to bubble over again, was able to reply – with, he suspected, something even more hair-raising – her aunt materialised beside them.

'*Khristos voskres,* Pavel Albertovich,' said the countess reprovingly, and then, without waiting for his response, 'Natasha, this public merriment is quite unseemly. You should know better. What will Pavel Albertovich think of you?'

But that was something Pavel Albertovich had no intention of divulging. Not yet. First he had to go back to Scotland to arrange things.

His self-discipline slotting neatly back into place, he said courteously, 'I think, Zena Fedorovna, that Natasha Mikhailovna charms all who know her.'

5

'A YOUNG lady?' Hamish said.

It had been a long way from the British Embassy in St Petersburg to Crannoch Lodge, Morar, Scotland, and Paul was in no very sweet temper when he arrived. But Hamish had seen no reason to trail down to Glasgow when he was enjoying life fine in Morar. If there was something Paul wanted to talk about, there'd always be a welcome for him at Crannoch Lodge and the fresh air would do him good. Why didn't he bring the boys?

'A young lady?' Hamish repeated. And then, his tone changing, 'A *Russian* young lady?'

He exhaled a large cloud of Havana smoke.

Paul said drily, 'She speaks English,' and then, after a pause, 'Not perfectly, but she is highly intelligent and will soon learn.'

It was his turn to blow out a cloud of smoke.

'One, two, three,' said Hamish, and both men spun on their heels and began to march back whence they had come, along the length of the glass-roofed terrace that fronted the house.

Crannoch Lodge had been erected in the 1880s by a Lancashire industrialist with more money than sense, and though he hadn't gone as far as battlements and turrets and minstrels' galleries, he hadn't been able to resist some highly carved and exceedingly dark panelling, several deer-forests'-worth of stags' heads, the occasional tartan carpet, a few polar bearskin rugs, and any number of bibelots on the lines of goat's horn inkwells, bronze eagles, and address books nicely got up in snakeskin.

Hamish admitted that it was a bit like living in the Natural History Museum, but he'd bought it lock, stock and barrel and hadn't bothered to change much. Or not in the main part of the house. Allie had appropriated the old drawing room and done it up as her own parlour in white paint and chintz, and very nice it looked too.

The terrace had been one of the industrialist's brighter ideas. Provided the rain wasn't actually coming in horizontally from the sea (which wasn't unheard of), it enabled the occupants of the house to indulge in a gentle constitutional in the open air even when it was wet. As, in Paul's experience, it was, four days out of five.

Hamish puffed out another huge cloud of smoke, directing it carefully at an approaching swarm of midges. They hesitated briefly, and before they could reform and regroup Paul added his contribution and they fled in disarray.

'It's interesting, you know,' Hamish said. 'I'm told they really like cows better than humans. Fairly puts you in your place to think that even those wee bloodsuckers consider you a poor second-best to the beasts of the field.'

'Then I suggest you put a cordon sanitaire of Highland cattle round the house,' Paul said astringently. 'Otherwise, by the time I leave here I won't want to see another cigar for as long as I live. I'd rather be bitten.'

'They're unco' early this year,' Hamish said absently. 'It's been a mild winter. What age did you say she was?'

'I didn't.'

Oh, well, Hamish reflected philosophically. If Paul didn't want to say, he didn't want to say.

After a moment, Paul went on, 'She is young enough to be a friend to the boys as well as a mother, and she has great warmth and vitality.'

Hamish regarded him with a sapient eye. 'Oh?'

But Paul's rather ascetic face gave nothing away. He had aged very little in the last few years, except for a touch of grey at the temples. Hamish, no Lothario himself, had a momentarily envious vision of exotic young women strewing themselves, by the dozen, round his nephew's elegant feet. Maybe a second marriage wouldn't be such a bad idea after all.

'I'm flattered you should be telling me all this,' he said hypo-critically.

'I'm sure you are. Hamish, do we have to keep on marching up and down this damned, midge-ridden terrace, or can we go indoors and consort with some less active *ferae naturae?*'

Out of sheer contrariness, Hamish took him into Allie's parlour, where there wasn't a stag's head or a stuffed eagle in sight. Then he poured brandy into a pair of balloon glasses and said, 'Aye, well. So what *do* you want to talk about?'

'This. I cannot marry Natasha unless I divorce Florence, or she divorces me. And if either happens, my career in the diplomatic service will be in jeopardy. The service dislikes scandal.'

Hamish said, 'Oh, aye?'

'Now, I might simply be posted to some minor, distant consulate for a year or two. But I *might* be asked to resign, and I must make provision. Even now, most of my income comes from the shipyard, since the Foreign Office isn't notably generous to its employees. But I should be in quite serious difficulties if I lost my diplomatic salary *and* found my income from the yard diminishing. Especially with the recent Budget. Income tax at one shilling and two pence in the pound, supertax on incomes over five thousand pounds, death duties at ten per cent. . . What on earth possessed Asquith to appoint this fellow Lloyd George to the Exchequer?'

Hamish shrugged. 'Horse-trading,' he said. 'It's what politics is all about.' Outside, there was one of the skies that always sent young Matthew into raptures, a study in contrasts – robin's egg blue, roiling charcoal, and a great bank of cloud like a polar landscape brilliantly underlit by the sun. And beneath it all, a sea like a millpond, smoke-blue and molten silver. He said, 'So, now we're getting to it.'

'Now,' Paul agreed, 'we are getting to it. I spent two nights at Provost Charters on my way here, and father confirmed what I already suspected. Felix is making a godforsaken hash of things at the yard.'

Hamish sniffed. 'Aye, well. You could put it like that. I'd better tell you, I suppose.'

84

What emerged was a sorry tale of attempts to undercut competitors, poor estimating and bad contracts, special retooling that failed to pay for itself, lack of departmental control, general management incompetence. All compounded by Felix's refusal, in the slump, to take on Admiralty contracts because his wife didn't approve of ungodly weapons of war.

'And that's it,' Hamish concluded. 'Two years ago, when I retired, I left the yard with reserves of a wee bit under a million pounds. Now there's a net deficit of a quarter of a million.'

Paul had always had plenty of self-control, and the habit of a lifetime held even when he saw everything he desired in danger of slipping out of his grasp. Even so, the tension in him was almost palpable when he said, 'I see. In fact, Felix *has* made a godforsaken hash of things, just as I suspected. Then you'll forgive me if I ask, why has nobody stopped him?'

Abruptly, Hamish put his brandy balloon down on the table. It was cut crystal with a heavy base, otherwise it would have shattered.

'Because you were away. Because your father's too idle. Because James McMurtrie's a fool. And because Felix won't listen to me. There's nothing unusual in that. Not many managing directors like having their predecessors telling them what's what.'

Paul opened his mouth, and closed it again. Felix might not be prepared to listen to Hamish, but the board would have done. Why hadn't he said something? How many board meetings had he missed? Didn't he want to raise a fuss because, if Felix was sacked, he himself would have to go back to the yard instead of staying here, lotus-eating, in Morar. If you could call it lotus-eating to sit in this barren, beautiful, lonely landscape with nothing to do all day but twiddle your thumbs.

Paul wasn't a diplomat for nothing. He said only, 'Well, I'm here now, and I can stay for a month, not more. We have to decide how to salvage the situation, if it can still be salvaged. And there doesn't seem to be much doubt about the first move. Felix must go.'

Without expression, Hamish said, 'He's your brother.'

But Paul looked at him as if he were talking Pushtu. 'Yes? Does that have some significance that escapes me?'

6

IT TOOK Paul three days to convince Hamish that the only solution was for him to go back to the yard, 'just for a year or two. Just to sort things out.'

Then they left for Glasgow to set up an urgent board meeting.

Only after five telephone calls and a great deal of cranking and shouting did Paul succeed in persuading his father to rush up to Glasgow at a few days' notice. Sir Albert couldn't see the point of it, and Paul's attempts to be at once noncommittal and persuasive were frustrated by recurring bursts of static on the line.

In the end, the old man bellowed, 'All right! All right! Can't stand this damned instrument! Specially with Millie Brown sitting there in the Post Office eavesdropping on every word I say!' There was a sharp, eloquent click, and Sir Albert snorted. 'Damned nosey parker. Wish I'd stayed in Baden. I'll come up on Wednesday. Will that do you? And tell Hamish to get some decent claret in. The last lot was terrible.'

James McMurtrie wasn't much easier. Next Thursday? No, he had meetings all day. He supposed he might be able to fit one more in, just – though it would still be extremely inconvenient – if it could be arranged for six in the evening, or preferably half-past. He couldn't see why Paul wanted to call an extraordinary board meeting, anyway.

And Felix was most difficult of all. It had been Paul's intention simply to ask for a board meeting, and leave it at that. But Hamish had threatened to go straight back to Morar if Paul didn't give his brother due warning that they intended to ask for his resignation.

The trouble was that Pearl was present, already gracious and silver-haired at thirty-nine, her heavy-lidded, deep-set eyes glowing with Christian charity, her mouth set in a sweet perpetual smile, and enough strands of pearl choker round her throat to make Paul think of one of those giraffe-necked African princesses. For two solid hours, Pearl never stopped talking and Felix never started. Spruce as ever on the outside, he seemed to his brother to have become hollow within.

What with the tea and sandwiches and dainty little cakes, Felix's blank-eyed weariness and Pearl's inexhaustible flow of pious clichés and prying personal questions, Paul wasn't entirely sure, when he left, that Felix had understood his rather oblique references to management reorganisation. Looking back a few days later, he realised that he should have ignored the rule about never discussing business before the ladies, and come straight out with what was afoot.

But by then the damage had been done.

7

MATTHEW, arriving at the Castlehead house after a blissful week in Morar on his own – Tom having elected to leave when his father did and go straight back to school – discovered that everyone was down at the yard for some meeting. So, since he didn't want to kick his heels around the house for hours, he thought he might as well go down and given them all a surprise.

It was beginning to get dark when he arrived, but a stout, smiling, motherly lady in Allie's office told him the meeting was still going on.

'Oh, well,' he said. 'I'll just go and have a walk round. Do you think you could be very kind and make *quite sure* they know I'm here, if the meeting finishes before I come back? I wouldn't like them to go home without me.'

She promised she would make quite sure.

There was still a lot of activity going on down by the river bank. Though most of the berths were dark, the two right at the end on the left were brightly lit by flares. The riveters were having a fine old time. The noise was terrible.

They must be working overtime to get a couple of ships ready for launch, Matthew decided, and felt rather pleased with himself that he'd reached such a conclusion without even having to think about it. It made him feel very knowledgeable. He'd just go down and have a quick look. Though the road was dimly lit, the offices were bright, so he would be able to find his way back easily enough, provided he didn't go right along to where the men were working. He didn't think his ears could stand it, anyway.

Pattern shop on the left. Mould loft on the right. He congratulated himself. And that was the boiler shop over there. Or was it?

He stopped in the middle of the road, trying to remember, and got the fright of his life when, about six inches behind him, he heard the urgent ting-a-ling of a bicycle bell.

He jumped the wrong way.

It took several moments before he and the cyclist succeeded in disentangling themselves, picking themselves up, and counting their bruises. Then they peered at each other through the gloom.

Recognition was mutual.

His hand still clasped to a grazed knee, Matthew thought bitterly that he might have known. He said, 'Oh, it's you.'

The girl of the toffee lumps, rubbing her elbow vigorously, said, 'Yes, it's me. Why aren't you over at the side under the lights, where people can see you, instead of standing around looking glaikit right in the middle of the road?'

Matthew didn't know what 'glaikit' meant, but it didn't sound very polite. It was as if the last two years had never been. He found himself glancing upwards in case there was a crane overhead, but the sky reflected enough light from the flares to let him see that there wasn't.

It made him feel pretty silly, so he said snappishly, 'I don't think much of your beastly bicycle lamp, if you can't see a fellow until you nearly run him down!'

They glared at each other.

Matthew saw a gawky eleven-year-old with an oval face in which the only determinate features were a pair of large, widely set eyes which he vaguely remembered as being hazel; long mousy-fair hair tied back with a ribbon; a dark cloth coat, and a dark tammy with a pompom on top; white socks and dark, laced-up boots.

Jenny saw a boy a year or two older than she was, and several inches taller. He was wearing short trousers and a school blazer with wide light-and-dark stripes, and a stiff collar with a narrow tie. His hair was slightly wavy and dark, but his face was visible only as an assortment of strong shadows, all of them firm-looking and a bit crosspatchy. She had no difficulty in remembering that his older brother had been a whole lot nicer.

She said, 'What are you doing here, anyway?'

'Waiting for my father and my uncle. They're at a meeting. What are *you* doing here?'

'Waiting for my dad. He's the foreman carpenter. He's working late, and he said I wasn't to go home until he could come with me.' With a certain pride, since the children of the yard were normally considered perfectly capable of looking after themselves, she added, 'He doesn't think it's right for his daughter to be out on the roads by herself after dark.'

'I should say not.' Matthew suddenly made the connection. 'Are you Mr Jardine's daughter?'

'Yes.'

'Oh.' It gave him a new perspective. Mr Jardine had been the nice man who'd said he had a real facility with lathe and spokeshave and why didn't he try his hand at carpentry.

Matthew looked at the girl more civilly. 'I was just going down to see what they were doing in the berths.'

Jenny had no idea why he had suddenly become polite, but she never held things against people. So she picked up her bicycle, settled her tam more firmly on her head, and brushed the worst of the dust off her coat. Then, on a kindly impulse, she brushed Matthew down, too. She couldn't reach his shoulders very well, because he was so much taller than she was.

'I'll come with you,' she said.

They walked in silence for a few moments, Jenny wheeling her bicycle.

'Is your brother here?' she asked.

'No, he's gone back to school.'

'I've got a brother, too. He's called Jack. He's two years older than me.'

'Oh. So's mine.'

'Two years older? Is he?'

'Yes.'

'Have you any other brothers or sisters?'

'No.'

'I've got a half-sister. She's called Iris.'

'Oh.'

Jenny decided the boy wasn't just glaikit. He was fushionless. He wasn't even trying to make any contribution to the conversation. She gave up. Anyway, she couldn't think of anything else to say.

They reached the walkway that ran along between the iron-workers' shed and the berths.

Jenny took a deep breath. 'The river isn't very wide here, that's why all the berths lie at such an angle to it.'

He had no idea what she was talking about.

She persevered. 'When the ships are launched, they slide out stern first – that means backwards – into the water. Then they just swing round a bit to get parallel to the banks, you see? If the berths were at right angles, the stern would go crashing into the opposite shore.'

'Oh.'

'Afterwards, they go round to the fitting-out basin to be fitted out.'

'What with?'

'Mmm? Oh, everything,' she said vaguely. 'Well, everything that gets added on after the hull's finished. The superstructure and cabins and things, and the boilers sometimes; it depends. You remember the fitting-out basin, don't you?'

He did.

Each of the berths, secretive, sinister and dark, seemed to have the skeleton of a ship in it. The one directly ahead consisted of no more than some scaffolding with a few girders inside, but Matthew thought he'd better not ask the girl about it in case she told him.

Jenny said, 'That one over there on the right's beginning to look like a proper ship. If you want to go over, I'll show you. The frame's made of a whole lot of standing-up U shapes fixed together, with the deck beams across the top. Oh, fiddle!' She stopped and shook one foot vigorously. 'I've got a chuckie in my boot. I'll have to take it off.'

'What's a chuckie?' Even before the words were out, he was regretting them.

'A wee stone.' But she didn't start giving him a lecture on geology. Instead, she propped her bicycle against the shed and began balancing on one foot while she unlaced the boot from the other.

Matthew picked his way over to the berth she'd pointed out, his eyes on the obstacles underfoot. Not until he was well inside the hull did he stop and look round. It was enormous. There was a dark spaciousness that made it feel like a big, empty cathedral, and the din coming from the other end of the row of berths emphasised the silence in a way that didn't have anything to do do with noise or lack of it. It was eerie.

Jenny's voice followed him. 'Watch where you're going in case you trip. Can you see? Just a minute and I'll come and explain it to you.'

Oh, jiminy! The puffer all over again. Automatically, Matthew looked upwards.

It wasn't a crane this time.

At first, his eyes couldn't make sense of it.

Then, with a brutal suddenness, his insides rose into his throat and all the breath rushed out of his lungs. He doubled over as if some huge, invisible fist had punched him in the stomach. Even while his disbelieving brain was still interpreting what he had seen, his physical being was gasping and retching, making horrible tearing sounds as his lungs tried to drag the breath back into them. There was a chill all through him so that every separate nerve and muscle seemed to be shivering and hurting. He swallowed hard, and again, and again. Then, steadying himself against the hull with one hand, he managed somehow to find his way out of the ghastly place onto the walkway, where he was urgently and comprehensively sick.

Jenny dropped her boot and limped over to him. In a small, uncertain voice, she said, 'What's wrong? What is it? What's wrong?'

He couldn't answer at first, and she didn't connect his sickness with the ship. She said, 'What's wrong? Did you eat something that didn't agree with you?'

If she hadn't been there, he would probably have gone on kneeling and shivering and gagging for ages before he was able to brace himself. But, somewhere in the recesses of his mind, he could hear Nanny Flott saying, 'Pull yourself together. You are making an exhibition of yourself. Gentlemen *never* make exhibitions of themselves. Pull yourself together.'

He hauled himself upright. His legs were shaking and his voice didn't sound like his at all, but it wasn't too unsteady when he said, 'You mustn't look. But . . .

'There's a man in there. Hanging. With a rope round his neck.'

8

THE board meeting had been very unpleasant, so that even Allie hadn't given more than a moment's thought to whether or not young Matthew had arrived safely from Morar.

It was clear from the start that Felix recognised this wasn't a run-of-the-mill board meeting and that he was going to have some explaining to do, but it was also clear that his imagination hadn't progressed any further. He believed, without a shadow of doubt, that he had done as well as anyone could have done in the circumstances.

It seemed at first as if James McMurtrie was on his side.

'As far as the retooling is concerned,' James said, his mouth prim under the thin moustache, 'it has always been my opinion that you must spend money in order to make money. Research and retooling pay dividends in the end. Build a better mousetrap and the world will come flocking to your door.'

'Not,' rejoined Sir Albert smartly, 'if there aren't any mice within a hundred miles.'

But James ignored this sally. 'In any case, all the yards are suffering from the recession. It is hardly to be expected that Brittons' should be exempt.'

'Oh?' enquired Sir Albert, with exaggerated interest. 'Perhaps you'd like to tell us how many other yards have lost more than a million over the last two years?'

Ill-advisedly, Felix intervened. 'Beardmore's.'

His father's stare was unblinking. 'Just so. And I was hearing today that Vickers, as major shareholders, are so dissatisfied they're wanting to sack Beardmore himself.'

Felix said, 'Yes. The usual story. I sometimes wonder whether managing directors have any other role than to act as scapegoats. However, that is hardly the point at issue.'

He sounded dog-tired, and Paul reflected that forcing him to resign was going to do him a kindness.

'The board is perfectly well aware,' Felix went on, 'of the difficulties I have had to contend with. I have explained them before and I will explain them again, if you wish.'

'Spare us,' said Sir Albert.

Allie wished her uncle wouldn't overdo it. It was typical of him that, having ignored the whole problem for so long, he was now behaving as if Felix had deliberately reduced the shipyard to a shambles so that he, Sir Albert, would find himself landed with the job of setting it all to rights again. The trouble was that, although Allie and Paul and Allie's father and Sir Albert himself knew perfectly well that Sir Albert was an idle, cynical old rascal, Felix took every word he said to heart. Allie had been working closely with Felix for the last two years, and she was sorry for him and worried about him. She didn't know how much more his nerves would stand.

He had recently taken to wearing pince-nez. Now he removed them and rubbed a trembling thumb and forefinger over the bridge of his nose. 'Very well. But capital investment is what we need. What we must have. It seems to me that the members of the board might be prepared to offer individual guarantees . . .'

'Are you being facetious?' demanded his father, with his customary sublime disregard for the laws of probability. 'Good money after bad? Not a hope, m'boy. Not a hope!'

After a moment, Felix replaced his pince-nez. They made him look very lawyerly and deceptively uninvolved. 'I'm sorry you feel like that. One alternative, which you might prefer, would be to raise a debenture mortgage to cover our losses until the situation improves. It would, however, be restrictive, and I believe we might do better to consider a share issue . . .'

'We – might – not! This is a private limited company, and a private limited company it will remain, as long as I have any say in the matter.' It was obvious to everyone except James McMurtrie and Felix that Sir Albert was having the time of his life.

Hamish, watching Felix from under half-closed lids, found himself wishing he had never retired in the first place; it wasn't decent that someone like Felix, spiritless but by no means stupid, should have been pitchforked into a job he was quite incapable of handling. The boy was a bundle of nerves, and living up to the high expectations and elevated standards of that dratted saintly wife of his wasn't helping.

Felix said, without expression, 'Then I have nothing else to suggest.'

'But I have.' It seemed to Paul that things had gone far enough, and he was regretting that he hadn't given his brother a blunter warning. 'It seems, Felix, that the cut-throat world of heavy industry is not your natural habitat, and that you might be happier if you returned to the law. We would perfectly understand if you felt that everyone's interests would be better served if you were to offer the board your resignation.'

The silence was punctuated only by the whisper of Allie's shorthand pencil. Felix was so still that he might have stopped breathing.

After a moment, there was a faint shuffling as, with unnatural care, he began aligning the papers before him into a neat pile. Then he cleared his throat. 'Am I to understand that you have found someone' – he cleared his throat again – 'someone more suitable than I, to take over?'

Calmly, Paul said, 'Hamish is prepared to return as caretaker.'

There was another silence. Hamish had never seen any particular resemblance between Felix and his father, but when at last the younger man looked up, there was something of Sir Albert's blankness in his eyes. 'As caretaker?' he said. 'So even a caretaker

93

is preferable to me. You cannot trust me to stay on until you find someone permanent?'

It wasn't really a question, and even if it had been no one would have cared to answer it.

Allie glanced meaningly at her father, and he raised his voice for the first time.

'Don't upset yourself, laddie,' he said peaceably. 'You're not cut out for the job; we should have seen that. It's not your fault. We all had our own reasons for pushing you into it. And it's been a hard two years for someone with no experience. Now me, I've worked on the Clyde for upwards of a quarter of a century, and that means I know ways of sorting out problems that no one fresh to the job could even guess at.'

'Thank you,' Felix said. 'But don't try to be kind. It's insulting. The truth is that you all think I've failed, and you're not prepared to give me a second chance.'

'We can't afford to!' said Sir Albert, tactless to the end. 'We're not made of money, you know. Another year like the last, and we'll all be bankrupt.'

It was then that Felix's control broke. Suddenly, all the blood rushed to his face and away from it again, leaving his fine-grained skin a dirty grey-white. He was shaking with barely repressed hysteria.

'Oh, don't think I don't understand! I'm the scapegoat. Or, no – perhaps not! Because I imagine none of you would concede that the board has any sins requiring to be carried away. So I must be the second goat, the sacrifice to the Lord. Yes, that's it. I know my *Leviticus*, you see!'

Allie, worried and embarrassed for him, glanced round the table and saw that all the men were simply sitting, eyes lowered, faces expressionless, wishing he'd get it over with.

Felix swallowed. 'And I know something else, too. All that's been said here this evening has been carefully rehearsed beforehand. You, Paul – you probably arranged who was to say what, so that you could ease me out with the minimum of fuss. That would be like you. You like things *civilised*, don't you! You'd like me to agree that I've been at fault, and say I'll resign and no hard feelings.'

He was on his feet now, his shaking fingertips resting on the table before him. His neat dark suit was impeccable, his neat white collar pristine, his neat brown hair unruffled in the uncompromising, greenish light of the gas lamps. It was only his eyes that were dishevelled.

'Well, I won't. I *will not* resign. I have slaved to the point of exhaustion, day after day, sometimes well into the night, contending with problems that no one – not even Uncle Hamish – could have settled successfully. *None* of the yard's troubles can be laid at my door.

'The truth is that not one of you knows what work and worry really mean. You're inhuman. I cannot imagine why I should ever have thought you might feel even a modest gratitude towards me for ruining my health and happiness in a task you were all too blindly selfish to take on yourselves. All that concerns you are your dividend cheques and the knowledge that your capital is safe.'

He took a deep, wavering breath. 'Look at you now! Sitting there feeling mildly embarrassed, mildly contemptuous. Wishing I would finish and be gone.'

If he had thought anyone was going to have the grace to deny it, he was mistaken.

When he looked round the table for the last time, his mouth was trembling. 'Well, I will go. But *I will not resign.*'

No one tried to stop him. No one even looked up until he had left the boardroom, closing the door behind him with quiet, fumbling haste.

'Oh, dear,' Paul sighed after a moment. 'How very distressing. One has always so disliked scenes. Never mind, he will see sense in the long run.' There was a general atmosphere in the boardroom of everyone beginning to relax again, as he went on, 'In the meantime, what we have to do is get down to retrieving the situation. Hamish, I imagine you should be able to persuade the bank not to call in the overdraft? They know you well enough, and trust you.'

Hamish opened his mouth, but Sir Albert was ahead of him. 'I'd be obliged,' he barked, 'if you'd remember *I'm* in the chair. Right? Right! Very well, then, where do we go from here?'

It was almost an hour later and the meeting was approaching its conclusion when there was a hasty knock and the door burst open, setting the gaslight trembling and the cigar-laden air swirling.

It was Matthew.

Paul said coldly, 'Really, Matthew! How dare you! Go and wait for us outside . . .'

Then he saw the boy's pallor and distress, and said, half rising, 'What is it? What is the matter?'

Matthew gulped. 'Down in one of the berths. . .' He was breathless, and looked as if he had run all the way.

95

'Papa, he's – he's hanging from the deck beams. I think he's dead.'

It was as if the next words didn't bear saying, but he managed to get them out in the end.

'It's Uncle Felix.'

9

'I AM the resurrection and the life, saith the Lord . . .'

The rain was coming down in torrents as they carried Felix's coffin from the black-plumed hearse into the church that stood on the side of the hill.

'Lord, thou hast been our refuge: from one generation to another. Before the mountains were brought forth, or ever the earth and the world were made . . .'

The church in the village of Provost was Norman, with a square tower and simple, ancient ornamentation; small enough for it to have been unnecessary to hire professional mourners. Indeed, it was more than adequately filled by Brittons and Fourniers, acquaintances from the county, servants, representatives from Felix's old law office, even two of the foremen from the shipyard.

'Now is Christ risen from the dead, and become the first-fruits of them that slept. For since by man came death, by man came also the resurrection of the dead . . .'

The funeral invitations had said, discreetly, that full mourning would be observed, and the church was a nightmare in ebony. Pearl, wearing a huge black hat swathed with acres of black veiling, would have been recognisable only by guess if she had not been leaning on the arm of her nineteen-year-old son, Howard.

Matthew, eyeing his cousin unobtrusively, reflected that no one could ever fail to recognise the Horrible Howard. Tall, calm, and commandingly built, he always looked a bit like Zeus taking a stroll down from Olympus to make sure all those vulgar chaps on earth were toeing the line. It was quite extraordinary, Matthew had thought sometimes, how limited was the range of expressions that showed on Howard's long, rectangular, slightly fleshy face. Bland No.1 and Bland No.2, and that was pretty well the lot.

It was still pouring when they emerged into the churchyard, a place whose headstones told their own story of a once bustling village that had of late years been almost emptied of its people. The dripping trees framed a view down onto the wetlands, clothed now in the thin, patchy, violent green of spring.

'Man that is born of a woman hath but a short time to live, and is full of misery . . .'

The ground was so waterlogged that the fronds of evergreen lining the grave were afloat in a greasy, khaki-coloured lake. And when the handsome oak coffin was let down, its patina of beeswax shedding water like some monster from the deep, there was a surge of mud that caused one or two of the mourners to hop back from the edge with more haste than was seemly. There was a squelching, sucking noise as the coffin settled into its final resting place.

'Forasmuch as it hath pleased Almighty God of His great mercy to take unto Himself the soul of our dear brother here departed, we therefore commit his body to the ground; earth to earth, ashes to ashes, dust to dust . . .'

It was Howard who was to cast the token handfuls of earth upon the coffin. True to form, he didn't look specially upset, but Matthew thought he really must be, inside. Everyone knew that he and his mother were very close, so he must be sad about his father's death even if only for her sake. Wondering, suddenly, how he himself would feel if his father had died under such circumstances, Matthew decided he'd be jolly cross with whoever had made him upset enough to want to kill himself.

Then he forgot about it because, if foresight counted for anything, Howard would go far. No soiled gloves for him. From beneath his overcoat he produced a small silver goblet which Matthew last remembered seeing in Grandmother Lutetia's display cabinet. Using it as a trowel, he scooped up a few glutinous yellow lumps of mud and allowed them to plop – one, two, three – onto his father's coffin. Then he opened his hand and allowed the goblet, too, to drop.

Matthew dug Tom surreptitiously in the ribs, and Tom nodded, equally surreptitiously. Grandmother Lutetia's goblet should rightly have been his some day, and Howard hadn't even *asked*. It was pretty rotten of him, considering how possessive he'd always been about his own things. One Christmas a few years ago, he'd fetched Matthew a hefty clout over the ear just for borrowing his pen without permission.

'I heard a voice from heaven, saying unto me, Write, From henceforth blessed are the dead which die in the Lord . . .'

Uncle Felix hadn't died in the Lord, if that meant what Matthew thought it meant, but everyone seemed to be giving him the benefit of the doubt. The official story was that he had been inspecting some work the men had been doing on the ship's deck beams and, slipping, had become entangled with the rope that had hanged him.

'Lord, have mercy upon us.'

There was a responding murmur of, 'Christ, have mercy upon us.'

'Lord, have mercy upon us . . .'

The forest of black umbrellas dipped in unison. 'Our Father, which art in Heaven . . .'

The minute the 'Amen' was out, there was a general atmosphere of fidget, as if everybody was dying to get in out of the rain. Matthew felt quite sorry for them all, because they probably didn't know that Aunt Pearl didn't approve of funeral baked meats and all they were going to get was a glass of brown sherry and a slice of Madeira cake. Oh, well, at least it was over.

But it wasn't, quite.

Because the widow raised her head and into the impatient silence said, very genteelly but with the ear-rasping clarity of an inferior boy soprano, 'For I have heard a voice as of a woman in travail, that bewaileth herself, that spreadeth her hands saying, woe is me now! for my soul is wearied – *because of murderers.*'

All movement ceased, and there wasn't a sound except for the heavy, relentless patter of raindrops.

Matthew's eyes slid sideways. It sounded like a bit of Bible, but everyone else was looking just as blank as he felt; except the vicar, who was frowning slightly, as if he didn't like unauthorised additions to his burial service.

It was difficult to make out who Aunt Pearl was looking at across the grave – Paul, Uncle Hamish, Grandfather Albert, or all three of them.

And then her voice rose again. 'Whosoever doeth not righteousness, is not of God, neither he that loveth not his brother. He that loveth not his brother abideth in death. Whosoever hateth his brother is – *a murderer.*'

Well, at least that was one question answered.

Paul Britton's lips tightened and it was clear that he was wondering how to put a stop to the thing, but Aunt Pearl didn't look stoppable. Howard might have done something, but Howard was just standing there at her side, a foot taller than she, motionless and quite expressionless.

Silence or no silence, you could tell that everybody was thinking furiously. The county gossips were going to have a fine time with *this*.

Aunt Pearl threw back her veil and her heavy-lidded eyes were like deep, gleaming pools in the pallor of her face. She opened her mouth again. What *was* she going to say next?

No one found out – except that it was something to do with Cain and Abel – because she had scarcely begun before Uncle Hamish stopped her. There was something infinitely reassuring in the way he raised both black-gloved hands to the brim of his top hat to settle it more comfortably on his head before walking unhurriedly round the grave to where she stood.

'And He said, the voice of thy brother's blood . . .'

Uncle Hamish's hand came to rest, firmly but uncompromisingly, on Aunt Pearl's free arm and his voice over-rode hers, magically draining away all the tension.

'Aye, well,' he said prosaically. 'It's natural for you to be upset at such a time, but it won't do to get things out of proportion, you know. What you need is a nice glass of sherry, my dear. That'll set you right.' He nodded to the vicar. 'You'll join us up at Provost Charters, will you, vicar? Aye, fine.'

Pearl's audience, as suddenly as it had fallen still, came to life again and began to move away. Paul Britton, smiling faintly, strolled off with a military-looking gentleman from Minton Magna, and Matthew, shamelessly eavesdropping, overheard him murmur, 'Poor woman. My brother and I had a minor disagreement an hour or two before his accident, and she has convinced herself that his distress of mind made him careless. Ah, well. But tell me. Your dairy herd must be thriving in such an early season? I do not remember ever seeing the grass so lush at this time of year.'

It sounded jolly convincing, Matthew thought.

'Come on,' Tom's voice said in his ear. 'Let's take the short cut back and see if we can grab some cake. Honestly, isn't Aunt Pearl awful? Fancy making an exhibition of herself like that!'

'Yes! And Howard just *stood* there!' They squeezed through the gap in the hedge. 'Never mind. Race you back! It's all over now!'

But despite his own carefree words, Matthew wasn't entirely convinced that they had, indeed, heard the end of it all.

Seven

1

PAUL Britton brought his new wife home to England just before Christmas the following year, and Tom and Matthew met them off the boat train at Victoria.

They had been waiting at the barrier for almost fifteen minutes before they were granted the privilege of seeing the happy couple stroll towards them, followed by a mountain of cabin trunks and surrounded by a vast entourage of valets and maids and stewards and attendants, all of them bowing and scraping like mad.

'My God,' Tom muttered. 'Father must have greased every palm on the train.'

But Matthew scarcely heard him. All he could think of was that their new stepmama was ab-so-lute-ly gor-r-r-geous.

She was carrying an enormous white fox muff and wearing a coat that would have turned any woman green with envy, an amazingly beautiful thing made of some dark, supple, velvety fur with a wide collar and deep hem of snowy ermine. Her hat was even more amazing, approximately the size and shape of an umbrella, with what looked like a fully-grown swan nesting on top.

And as if all that wasn't enough, the face that looked out from under this outrageous confection was the most exotic either of the boys had ever seen, with slanting cheekbones, a wide curving mouth, and eyes that sparkled even from twenty yards away.

Their father bent his head and said something to her, pointing to where the boys were standing, and she smiled at them dazzlingly.

Very gently, Matthew let out his breath. 'Oh, whoopee!' he thought. 'Oh, definitely whoopee!'

Beside him, Tom groaned, 'Will you look at that hat! God, isn't she *awful*?'

Tom had made up his mind in advance that he wasn't going to like her. He said it was disgusting that someone as old as their father should be getting married again, especially to someone like the Countess Natasha, who wasn't only foreign but young enough to be his daughter. Or so Bertha had told Cook, who had told the second parlourmaid, who had told the new chauffeur, who had told Tom.

100

'I'll be so embarrassed I won't know where to look! Can't you just imagine what kind of female she is? And a blonde, on top of everything. Russians are supposed to be dark-haired, so hers must be dyed.'

Matthew, who had only recently discovered why suicide blondes were called suicide blondes, said doubtfully, 'Dyed by her own hand? No, surely not. Not if she's a countess. She'll have a hairdresser to do it for her. Anyway, what does it matter! I think it's exciting having a real, live countess for a stepmother.'

'Oh, *will* you grow up! I can tell you, when you've been at Eton a bit longer and learned something about the world, you'll find that practically all foreigners have some tuppenny-ha'penny title that doesn't mean a thing in a civilised country. And I'll tell you something else. All blondes are whores. Or if they aren't, they'd like to be!'

Tom's prejudices had naturally encouraged Matthew in the hope that their new stepmama would turn out to be a Good Thing, but he hadn't anticipated just how Good a Thing she was going to be. She looked not only absolutely gorgeous, but full of beans, and *fun*!

Without regret, he jettisoned his serious, well-bred expression and beamed back at her for all he was worth.

Thus, unwittingly, he franked himself straight into Natasha's good graces, because until that moment she had been contemplating the figures of her two stepsons with deep disfavour.

She had not been pleased to discover that Paul had a family. If they had been very small children, she thought, they might have been manageable, but two boys only a few years younger than she was herself? She had even gone so far as to warn Paul – with the mischievous smile that deluded him into thinking she wasn't entirely serious – that she believed herself to have very little maternal instinct. But all he had done was smile back, and lower his body onto hers, and move inside her in the way that melted her whole being; and afterwards, had led her for a second time, and then a third, along that ineffably exciting path that culminated in the ecstasy that was, she sometimes thought, what she had been born for.

The starched, mechanical smiles which were all the boys at first vouchsafed her had filled her with an irritable presentiment of boredom. Her own smile should have been enough to charm them without there being any need for her to exert herself further. She disliked having to *work* at charming people; it was boring, and if there was one thing that Natasha abominated, it was being bored. Most people succumbed to her in the end, of course, but she had occasionally come across some who didn't, people who believed that everyone should be as grey and conventional as they were themselves. With them, she had no patience.

But, just as she was resigning herself to making an effort with her stepsons, the face of the younger one lightened and broke into the most blinding, enthusiastic, heart-warming grin. It made him look astonishingly like Paul at his best; handsomer, if anything, because there was none of the reserve that made Paul appear cold.

What a nice boy! Natasha felt a rush of warmth and a strong inclination to hug him.

Instead, virtuously, she held out her arms to both of them.

Tom was too tall to get in under the hat, which made everyone laugh except him. But Matthew, who had been fretting for months because he wasn't growing as fast as he would have liked, just managed it, and found himself being not only hugged but kissed.

It was lovely. She smelled delicious, and her eyes laughed at him as she exclaimed, '*Magnifique*! Why did not Paul tell me I was to have a beautiful dark Adonis for a son?'

Matthew had never been called an Adonis before, and certainly not beautiful, but after his first instinctive revulsion he found he didn't mind. After all, she was foreign and foreigners were funny.

Tom, however, was disgusted – and it showed.

2

MATTHEW had never enjoyed himself so much as he did that Christmas, but Tom had a very hard time of it.

Natasha was everything that, conventional to the marrow of his sixteen-year-old bones, Tom disapproved of. Even her laughing insistence that they all eat rice pudding on Christmas Eve, as they did in Russia, set him off muttering about heathen customs. It was unfortunate that his muttering wasn't quite *sotto voce* enough; unfortunate, too, that since Natasha's English accent wasn't reliable, he made the mistake of assuming that her understanding was also inferior.

The result was that to Tom's unutterable horror and Matthew's delight, they were treated there and then to their very first display of their new stepmother's temperament.

Her colour flaring above the sapphire-blue dress and collar of pearls, the second Mrs Britton rose to her feet, picked up one of the best Baccarat crystal glasses, and tossed it, with the greatest verve and impeccable aim, straight into the marble fireplace.

Then, with scarcely a pause, she turned and said, 'In Russia it is considered unlucky if one breaks nothing at a festive meal. Also, I feel better for having done it. If I had controlled myself, I would have – I would have – Paul, *j'aurais jeté un froid?*'

'Cast a wet blanket over everything,' her husband said helpfully.

'Thank you. I would have cast a wet blanket over everything for the rest of the evening, which would have been very uncomfortable for all of us.'

Enraptured by this superb disregard for the conventions that had been the bane of his young life, Matthew thought it a jolly sensible attitude to take, even while he waited breathlessly for his father to launch into a lecture on propriety. But he didn't. Astoundingly, he laughed, and took his wife's hand in his, and placed a kiss on her palm.

Then he put the lid on Tom's day by ticking him off for bad manners.

Not even the spiffing presents their stepmother had brought were enough to reconcile Tom to her, though they were presents that showed she knew *just* what a boy wanted. There was a watch for each of them, one of the new kind that you strapped round your wrist. Some jolly boxes, brightly lacquered with what she said were traditional Russian designs. One of the new, self-filling fountain pens. And a real silk shirt each, the very latest thing, with buttons all the way down the front so that you didn't need to pull it over your head.

Tom's thank-yous were formal in the extreme, but Matthew was so thrilled that he risked giving her an enormous hug. She didn't mind at all; she even seemed to like it.

He said, 'We've never *ever* had presents like this before. Nanny used to spend all year knitting horrible brown pullovers for us. And Aunt Pearl used to give us books about missionaries in darkest Africa. And Uncle Stephen brought us the kind of jigsaws that gave you brain fever.'

She chuckled, a nice warm chuckle. 'And what did you give them in return? Did you give your mama a pretty scarf, like this one you have given me?'

Matthew gulped. This was carrying disregard for convention a bit far. He glanced around, but although Tom looked as if the taxidermist had got at him, their father's face was perfectly noncommittal and Sir Albert's after-dinner gaze as blank as it always was. Matthew couldn't understand it. It was his impression that stepmothers were supposed to behave as if real mothers didn't exist.

But no one came to his rescue, and, floundering, he found that the only present he could remember was a vile blue-and-yellow kettle holder he'd done in cross-stitch when he was about six. 'Polly, put the kettle on', it had said.

'But I thought that was silly, because mama's name wasn't Polly. So I picked it out when Nanny wasn't looking, and sewed in "Florrie" instead. There wasn't space for Florence, you see. And mama nearly had a fit, because she said it sounded as if she was a servant. Nanny gave me a good walloping, but looking back I think it was quite funny, don't you?'

Natasha put an arm round him and squeezed his shoulders. 'I think it was sad, when you had gone to so much trouble! And if you wish to sew a kettle holder for me you shall do so, and if there is no space for "Natasha" you may put "Tasha", for that is what I wish you should call me. For two such big boys to call me "stepmama" would make me feel very old, which I would not like at all.'

It took a moment for Matthew to overcome the suspicion that it would be disloyal to their real mother to enter into such an intimate relationship so readily. He wasn't even sure he should have told the kettle-holder story at all, because it had made Natasha think badly of her. Then he thought, what difference could it possibly make? 'All right!' he said cheerfully. 'Thank you very much – er – Tasha!'

But Tom, who was always a bit out of his depth with people who weren't in the rule book, didn't say anything and from then on expended a great deal of effort in avoiding calling their new stepmother anything at all.

3

AT occasional weekends and during the school holidays over the next few months, Natasha watched with possessive satisfaction as Matthew began to blossom. Paul, who had told her how subdued the boy had been before, attributed the improvement entirely to her influence, and was amused when she accepted the tribute as no more than her due.

'And why not?' she said. 'False modesty is excessively dull. Quite bourgeois, in fact!'

Although no one but she was aware of it, she would have taken a good deal less interest in Matthew if there had been something else to divert her mind. But Natasha, like Nature, abhorred a vacuum, and always reacted to the uneventful patches in her life either by becoming impossible to live with or doing what she could to make something – anything – happen. It was one of the many things Paul did not yet know about her, and she had hoped that he might not find out for quite some time, because she was fond of him and did not wish him to be worried.

But she had not expected to find herself in a state of boredom so soon, and certainly not because she had become *enceinte* with the child Paul so much wished to father. About the child she was philosophical. Although, privately, she had taken all the recommended precautions, no precautions were wholly reliable, and she and Paul had put them through a testing that had been quite as rigorous as it was pleasurable.

It was just that it had happened too quickly. She was aware of an unfamiliar sensation of unease; unease at being twenty-one years old, and pregnant for the first time, in a foreign country whose ways she did not wholly understand, with people who understood her scarcely at all. That was why she had given in to Paul's insistence that she spend the months of waiting in the tranquillity of the Dorset countryside.

She detested it. To Natasha, the country was somewhere one went to for a few days or perhaps – reluctantly – weeks, before returning with relief and gratitude to town. Green fields and fresh air? Pooh! Country air was not, after all, so very fresh when one considered the silaging and the muck-spreading and the cowsheds. While as for country society – men with complexions like underdone roast beef and women with faces like horses – was it for this, she demanded tempestuously of Paul after one particularly leaden dinner party, that she had left her beautiful, beloved St Petersburg? He had been very sympathetic, very understanding, very quick to say that a good night's rest would make her feel more like herself.

'I do not wish a good night's *rest!*' she had exclaimed, and harmony was instantly restored.

By some miracle, she had succeeded, and continued to succeed in guarding her tongue on the subject of Provost Charters. Paul, describing life in England to her, had spoken of the English country house as something that embodied everything of graciousness, tradition, dignity and beauty, and she, who had always been passionate about beauty, had looked forward very much to presiding over just such a house. A a result, Provost Charters had come as a serious shock, its Victorian vulgarity offending her in every tiny detail. It seemed to her very strange that Paul, sophisticated and knowledgeable as he was, was uncritically blind to its deficiencies. To him, it was the family home, and there was nothing more to be said.

The delicate hints Natasha had dropped about new furnishings had met with a flat negative from Sir Albert – who was happy enough to flirt, in an elephantine way, with his new daughter-in-law but had no intention of allowing her to cut up his comfort – and a light dismissiveness from Paul which had annoyed her very much. It was the first time he had ever refused her anything.

He did not know it yet, but after she was delivered of the child she intended to persuade him to dispose of the London house, which was his, not Sir Albert's, and almost as dreadful as Provost Charters. It was clear that Paul's first wife had had not one ounce of taste. Natasha had felt quite ill at the sight of so much dark brown paint and varnish, so much clutter. Not a surface that wasn't covered with vases, bronzes or knick-knacks, and one could scarcely tell what colour the walls were for the prints, engravings and majolica plates that covered them. What Natasha wanted was one of the fashionable new mansion flats, on which she could exercise her own taste to the full. She had no intention of spending any more time than was absolutely necessary buried alive in this unspeakably dreary English countryside.

In the meantime, deprived of redesigning either of her homes, she devoted herself to redesigning her younger stepson.

4

'STYLE,' she said, 'is more important than book-learning. To be a beautiful dark Adonis is good. To be a beautiful, *stylish* dark Adonis is much, much better.'

Her eyes were dancing, and Matthew grinned back at her, in no danger of taking her seriously.

'Go on, then,' he said. 'Teach me how!'

What Natasha could not understand was why such an engaging boy should have to be taught at all. It appeared to her as if, until now, his emotions had been crumpled up into a ball, like a half-finished sketch on a sheet of paper that needed to be uncreased again, and smoothed out, and given shading and perspective.

Paul had been evasive when she asked him, although she knew some of it had to do with his reluctance to talk about his first wife. 'As a small child,' he said, 'Matthew was seriously naughty. It upset his mother very much, and there were problems. She could feel no warmth towards him. That was all.'

'How *very* mysterious!' Natasha had exclaimed, but he would say no more and she was too proud to coax.

It was exasperating that he would not talk about Florence, because Tasha was quite naturally curious about the woman, and would have expected Paul to have enough perception to recognise that, the more reticent he was, the more curious she was likely to become.

Not that she was jealous of her predecessor. They were not in competition, and even if they had been it would not have occurred to Natasha to doubt that she would win. She always did. But she *was* inquisitive. Knowledge of any kind was worth having; one never knew when it might come in useful as a weapon in some unanticipated war.

Now, she eyed her stepson, faintly chiding. 'Style,' she said austerely, 'is not something that can be *taught*. It is an instinct developed by observing others who are possessed of it.'

'Like you?'

'Like me,' she agreed. 'And you must understand that it is not only a matter of clothes. It is a matter of having an air. It is a matter of attitude. It is not possible to be at the same time stylish and – and *collet-monté* – what is the English? – prim and proper.'

She pointed imperiously. 'There!' and Matthew, already burdened with an enormous basketful of mushrooms, bent down to add some more.

He looked at them doubtfully. 'Are you sure these aren't poisonous?'

'Of course! I am a Russian.'

'Does that mean you know all about mushrooms? Or all about poison?'

'You are a wicked boy! All Russians go mushroom-hunting in the summer. It is a tradition. We know everything about them.'

Matthew sniffed the damp, dark smells of wet moss, sodden earth and rotting leaves, and chuckled. 'I believe you. But you know, it's not awfully stylish scrabbling about for mushrooms under hedges in a drizzle!'

'On the contrary! Knowledge of fine food is always stylish. Did your mama never take you mushroom-picking?'

Matthew's laugh cracked in the middle and emerged as a neatly bisected hoot of mirth. 'That would have been the day! No. Not like mama at all.'

'What *was* like mama?'

'What? Oh, I don't know . . . She . . . No.' He coloured, and broke off. 'I can't tell you.'

It was too much for Natasha. She almost shrieked, '*Voyons*! Was she pretty, fashionable, unusual, conventional? I know nothing of her. Was she kind to you? Did she scold you? Did she ignore you? I do not understand why there should be all this mystery!'

In the end, he took so long to stumble through the tale of his relationship with his mother that Natasha, easily bored, would have lost interest completely if she had not been tantalised by the suspicion that he was leaving out something vital. There was nothing in what he said to explain what had caused the silly woman to take such a damaging dislike to him.

Sorrowfully, she said, 'Matthew' – which always emerged from her lips as Mathieu – 'I thought we were such good friends. Can you not tell me what *really* happened?'

She was wearing a voluminous, hooded cloak that hid her swollen figure, and instead of looking absolutely gorgeous she looked young, and reproachful, and deceptively soulful. Matthew felt a tremendous rush of affection for her and realised, in a moment of revelation, just how much she had changed his life. He felt he would do almost anything to repay the warmth she lavished on him.

Even to the extent of telling her about the Great Disgrace.

By the time he was halfway through, her shoulders were shaking and there were tears of laughter in her eyes. He was a little offended, and at the end surveyed her doubtfully. 'Is it funny? Is it really funny?'

'My poor, poor Matthew,' she gasped. '*Eh, la belle affaire*! Was that the "serious naughtiness" of which your papa told me? What a very ridiculous thing to cause so much trouble! And to worry you so much that, even now, you can scarcely bear to talk about it. *Of course* it is funny. And it is a very excellent example of what I have been saying. To take it seriously – that is conventional. When you learn to laugh at it, that will be style!'

He couldn't learn to laugh at it straight away. But he might be able to soon, he thought, now that the most wonderful person in the whole wide world had put it in perspective for him.

Feeling two inches taller, he grinned and said, 'What shall we do with these idiotic mushrooms?'

PART TWO

1914–1918

One

1

PARIS, Vienna, Zagreb, and now Brod. Ah, Brod!

'Oh, I say! Would you cwedit it? It's weally quite scandalous!'

Charlie Thompson always had trouble with his 'r's when he was upset. Now, a look of outrage on his thin, anxious face, he struck a match and peered more closely at the greasy, dog-eared notice high on the wall of the compartment. 'Do you know what this says?'

Matthew, crouched in the aisle trying to cram two large leather suitcases into a space designed for one emaciated string bag, muttered a few well-chosen words about railroads in general and Balkan railroads in particular, and levered himself to his feet. In the process, he knelt on something sharp and cracked his funny bone on the corner of the bench. Hell!

'No, Charlie,' he replied politely. 'I don't know what it says.'

If he'd had even the most superficial acquaintance with the Serbian Croatian tongue, he would have been travelling on his own instead of having to listen to Charlie Thompson asking idiotic questions. But although he had pointed out to his father that at eighteen (just), with a year at Oxford and two visits to the Riviera behind him, he neither needed nor wanted a guide, philosopher and friend, his father had been adamant. Matthew would travel out to Bosnia with the new attaché, who spoke the language, and he would on all occasions defer to that gentleman's judgement, since he was five years Matthew's senior.

It had ruined everything, because Matthew had a lively spirit of adventure and a passionate sense of romance, whereas Charlie Thompson had none at all. Possessed, instead, of an abounding, ill-directed vigour, he had rushed Matthew round all the right museums, along all the grandest of Grand Avenues. He had decreed that they should eat not in restaurants but in hotels, where the tablecloths were clean and they didn't put garlic in everything. He had vetoed all exploration of the night life of Paris and Vienna on the ground of having to be up early next morning. He had never stopped criticising slovenly foreign habits. He didn't approve of talking to strangers. He had ensured that he and Matthew were first in to breakfast every morning; first in to dinner every evening.

They hadn't missed a single train. Twice, they could easily have caught the one before the one they were aiming at.

Charlie Thompson, in fact, was the most perfect specimen of English insularity Matthew had ever come across, and Matthew couldn't imagine what he thought he was doing in the diplomatic service. And in the Balkans, too.

Oh, well, only a few more hours now, and they would have reached the end of their journey. Sarajevo the Golden. Matthew hoped it was going to be worth it.

Charlie shook out the match. 'Never thought I'd find myself having to twanslate this kind of thing. What it says, woughly speaking, is: "Any passenger who finds live parasites in the carriage, please to inform the guard."'

Matthew couldn't help laughing. 'It's a trick!' he said cheerfully. 'They're trying to discourage us from swatting beastly bugs on their nice clean upholstery.'

Charlie had no sense of the ridiculous. '*Clean* upholstery! You can't have looked. I'll light another match . . .'

Matthew said, 'Charlie, why did you choose to learn Serbian Croatian? Why not something more civilised, like French or German?'

Charlie stared morosely at a small boy in a large fez, who recoiled slightly and snuggled in closer to the bundle of black veiling that was presumably his mother.

'I did,' he said. 'But everybody speaks Fwench and German. I thought that, with a new cwisis in the Balkans every other year, I'd have more chance of a posting.'

It made sense, within limits. Matthew sat down on the bench, forcing the cassocked priest already in possession to move over, which he did with un-Christian lack of goodwill. 'But why do you want a posting at all? I mean, you really are terribly English. I don't think you even like being abroad.'

Charlie shook open a fresh handkerchief, spread it out on the opposite bench, and sat on it. 'I don't. But I'm a third son.'

'Oh?'

'Third sons of the Thompsons are supposed to go to India. First sons stay at home, second sons go into the army, third sons join the Indian Civil Service.'

'And fourth sons?'

'Go into the Church. Though the family usually stops at thwee. Anyway, I thought family twadition be blowed. I don't want to be a District Officer in some outpost of empire. Think how dashed uncomfortable it would be to find oneself on the North-west Fwontier or some place like that. Makes even the Balkans look attwactive by comparison. How's your head?'

'Mmm? Oh, fine.' They had changed trains at midnight, when everything was pitch dark outside and only marginally less dark within. Twice, Matthew had hit his head on the roof as they battled their way along the carriage looking for seats; it was a narrow-gauge railway and the rolling-stock was proportioned to match. But the locals were obviously used to it. There was a Turk, as tall as Matthew, who had fought his way from platform to seat without even denting his fez. On the other hand, if their language was anything to go by, the six Austrian soldiers had dented almost everything.

Matthew glanced round, trying to pierce the gloom. The passengers were a varied lot – Turks and Austrians; a Catholic priest; an Orthodox priest further down the carriage; two men in the traditional peasant dress of lace-edged shirts, embroidered waistcoats, and wide trousers tucked into short socks; another two who looked as if they might belong to Sarajevo's colony of Spanish Jews.

Matthew's father had told him little about Bosnia except that it was 'politically sensitive, but otherwise varied and interesting', which hardly amounted to a rave review. But he did know that, six years earlier, Austria had annexed the country from the Turks, much to the annoyance of Serbia, which had been hoping to beat the Austrians to it. The Bosnians themselves, it seemed, weren't much bothered, or so it said in *Bosnia and Herzegovina: Some Wayside Wanderings,* the book that had furnished Matt with most of his information about the place. He had become quite attached to its authoress, though he felt that the fact of her being married to someone called Otto Holbach cast a certain doubt on her impartiality in the matter of the 'great things' the Austrians were doing for Bosnia. Encouraging industry. Putting up European-style hotels. Splashing out on fancy new public buildings. And so on.

Maybe they'd clean up the trains next.

Charlie leaned forward. 'Did you hear that?'

'Hear what?'

'The soldiers. The Archduke Fwanz Ferdinand – you know, the heir to the Austrian thwone? – he's coming to inspect the army in Bosnia next week. Manoeuvres and things. That's why these chaps are on their way to Sarajevo.'

'Are they, indeed!' Bloody Austrians, Matt thought. And bloody Germans, too, come to that. Ever since he had reached the age of awareness, their arrogance and aggressiveness had seemed to be hanging over Europe like a thunderstorm waiting to break. 'Well, if you ask me, both the Austrians and Germans are getting too big for their boots. Someone's going to have to teach them a lesson one of these days.'

Charlie began to look even more harassed. 'Ye-e-es. I suppose so. Do you weally think there's going to be a war?' He had very few positive opinions of his own – except about nightlife, and garlic, and catching trains.

'Oh, all the chaps at Oxford are sure of it! Unless you diplomats can prevent it, of course.'

'Yes, well, there's no need to wub it in. I know I'm the lowest form of diplomatic life.'

Charlie being injured was worse than Charlie being insular. Matt said soothingly, 'Come on! I wasn't getting at you. Just being cynical about the Service in general. That's the trouble with having a father who's been in it most of his life.' He raised a quizzical eyebrow. 'You don't look as if you fancy taking up arms for King and Country. Are you wishing you'd chosen the North-west Frontier after all?'

Then, watching Charlie grope his way towards an honest answer, he was engulfed by a wave of boredom. If he wasn't careful, he'd have Charlie baring his soul all the way from here to Sarajevo, though at least it wasn't likely to be the kind of soul so many young men had bared to him over the last year or two. Rugby toughs, most of them, though there had been one thin, ascetic, studious young man with a premature bald spot who'd been a surprise. Matthew hadn't bared his own soul in return. He'd just said no, very firmly, and moved the photograph of Rachel to a more prominent position on top of the bookcase.

Damn. He didn't want to think about Rachel. If only human relationships weren't so complicated. He didn't want to be involved with people. What he wanted was – what? Beauty. Significance. The lyrical spirit.

No harm in hoping.

He said bracingly, 'Never mind. Even if there is a war it won't last long. Just long enough to clear the air. Shall we try and get some sleep?'

There wasn't much likelihood of sleeping on the hard wooden pews, whose upholstery was as thin as it was filthy, but it was better than talking.

Matthew placed his hat, with care, on the roof rack. It was a rather splendid hat with a wide brim that made him look like an artist – a

Royal Academician, at the very least. He had bought it because he knew Natasha would admire it. As he tucked his rolled-up Norfolk jacket behind his head and redistributed his legs among the mound of baggage, he found himself smiling and wondering what arrangements his father had made for Tasha and the baby when they had come out last year. Probably hired a special train. A clean one, with cushions and pillows and the air sprayed with rosewater.

Dear Tash, who would be twenty-five next week. It was more like having a sister than a stepmother. There was a very special present for her in his inside jacket pocket, a little scent bottle of translucent white jade that he had bought in the Fabergé shop in Bond Street. He didn't know whether she wanted to be reminded of Imperial Russia, but she adored Fabergé.

They hadn't seen each other for ages. Baby Nick would be a toddler by now. It would be fun to see father again, too. Tasha had mellowed him almost beyond recognition.

Roll on, Sarajevo! Matthew smiled, and drifted off into a doze.

2

THE station was dingy and disreputable. Tasha, exquisite in cream and sugar-pink, looked as out of place as a Botticelli down a coalmine, and all the passengers, including Charlie, gaped at her. But she had eyes only for Matthew. She wasn't smiling, and for a moment he thought something dreadful must have happened.

Jumping down from the carriage, he said, 'I'm probably covered with smuts from the engine and I smell like an old-clothes shop. Tash, darling! How are you?'

She didn't hold out her arms to him. Instead, after a moment, she bent and placed a kiss on the back of his hands the way Bosnian women did (or so it said in his book). Then, at last, she laughed, and her eyes began to sparkle, and she allowed him to hug her, and positively glowed at him when he exclaimed, 'You look marvellous. Worth every mile, every furlong, every yard, every foot of the journey!'

They stood arm in arm for almost ten minutes, watching Charlie and the servants sort things out with the porter, a swarthy fellow in fez, cummerbund, and baggy breeches whom Matthew would have taken for a brigand if it hadn't been for the enormous brass numberplate that proclaimed his official status. And eventually, after some money had changed hands, the servants were permitted to carry the baggage away and toss Charlie's into the one-horse buggy that was to take him to his hotel, and strap Matt's onto the back of the motorcar destined for the place called Ilidze, where Paul and Tasha had taken up residence.

Tasha began chattering as soon as the motor was on the road. 'I hope it is not too hot for you, though by midday it will be, I assure you. Now, we do not have our own house, you understand . . . Oh, look there! That great fortified place on your right is the barracks. Yes. Well, you know I dislike houses. So boring to have to look after them. So your father found this hotel . . .'

Matthew couldn't imagine what was the matter with her. She sounded like some twittering debutante.

'Ah, this is better. Now you will see the interesting Sarajevo, much less depressing than that flat, dusty, crumbling part near the station. And the river is dramatic, the Miljacka.'

The motorcar was an open one, so she kept her parasol up, placing Matthew's eyesight at risk every time she moved, which she did continually, pointing in one direction or another, making gestures of emphasis, smoothing her gloves or straightening her hat.

'And those are the official buildings and government offices along the bank. Austrian, of course. Yes, even the one with the Mauresque arches. That is the Town Hall . . .'

She reminded Matt of Charlie in Vienna. Laughing, he interrupted, 'For heaven's sake, Tash, there'll be time enough for guided tours later on. What I want to know about is you and father and the baby. Are you enjoying yourselves? Are you well? And where's this Ilidze place, this hotel we're going to?'

Abruptly, her lips snapped closed, and Matt felt a tension in the air before she settled back into the corner of her seat and began toying with the wrist-loop of her parasol.

'We are all quite well,' she told him carelessly. 'You will see for yourself. Your father is busy, of course, because the – what is the word? – the repercussions of the Balkan War last summer have not died down. Turkey and Bulgaria are resentful. And Serbia is uneasy. And Albania is in anarchy. It is all very – er – engrossing, I am told. But you will hear about that from your father.'

Paul Britton had been little more than a year in idleness after his divorce and remarriage, because early in 1912 the diplomatic service had discovered an urgent need for an experienced man in the Balkans. Russia, as always, was trying to manipulate the Balkan states and Paul's experience in St Petersburg made him such an obvious choice for the posting that his marital misdemeanours were smartly brushed under the carpet. He had refused to have Tasha with him at first, but she and the baby had joined him in May 1913 at a time of temporary, if illusory peace.

Matthew was surprised at what Tasha said. He had thought everything was fine now, with no one fighting anyone, or showing signs of wanting to. The London newspapers scarcely even bothered to mention the Balkans these days. It was all Ireland, Ireland, Ireland, and the danger of civil war there.

'And the baby?' Tasha went on. 'Oh, he will astonish you. He is quite a big little boy now. He runs about and talks and plays all day. His energy must be seen to be believed.'

Matthew waited for her to tell him how she herself passed the time, and whether it amused her to be a diplomat's wife in this hot, pungent melting-pot of Eastern and Western cultures, but he waited in vain.

'Yes,' she went on, 'and Ilidze. It is Sarajevo's pleasure resort. There were Roman baths there once – in the days of Diocletian, one supposes – and it is still possible to bathe today. The hotel where we live is in a park, very well cared for, and there are trees and balconies and servants, and one eats in the garden. We are excellently looked after, and it is all much more convenient than having our own house. We may even borrow the servants when we wish, for picnics and such things. And one is not isolated. Your father is very much occupied, but in the hotel there are always people to talk to, and parties.' She shrugged. 'You know. Things going on. You will like it.'

He could feel the smile of amused understanding spreading across his face and, impulsively, stretched out an arm to give her shoulders a sympathetic squeeze. 'Poor Tash. You're bored. Is that it?'

For a moment, she didn't react, but then she gave an uncontrollable shudder that startled him and exclaimed petulantly, '"Is that it?" Is *what* it? I have no idea what you mean.' The colour was burning in her cheeks.

Even so, he couldn't believe she was going to throw a tantrum at *him*, so he grinned at her in the way she always responded to, and said, 'Steady on, Tash! It's me, your dark Adonis, the budding poet. Remember? And if you don't stop poking me in the eye with that damned parasol, I shall write a verse about you.'

There was no answering smile, so without pausing he went on, 'Let me see. A limerick, I should think.

There was a young lady of Bosnia,
With a parasol pink as a – as a rosnia,
She waved it about,
When the sun it came out,
Which for her was divine –
Although for the young-gentleman-sitting-next-to-her, it wasnia.'

Considering that it was extempore, it wasn't bad at all.

For a moment, everything seemed to hang in the balance, and then the intractable look disappeared and she dissolved into a chuckle and, furling up the offending parasol, announced, 'You are very clever to make me laugh when I do not wish to. It seems that Oxford agrees with you.' She surveyed him appraisingly. 'Yes, and it is lovely to have you here, even if you *are* all smelly and covered with smuts from the engine. And your hat is most dashing. *Is* there such a thing as a rosnia?'

'Of course! It's a cross between a rose and a – an attack of insomnia. How long before we get Ilidze? As you so indelicately remind me, I need a bath. Not to mention a decent breakfast.'

3

THE next few days were immensely pleasurable. It was hot, so hot that the buildings seemed to waver in the midday sun. But in the morning it was a delight even for Matthew, who wasn't one of Nature's early risers, to go out into the hotel gardens before the dew was off the grass and wander along the avenues of acacia trees, breathing in the fragrance of flowers and looking out on the pastoral timelessness of the scene beyond, where shepherds tended their flocks and the thin sound of their flutes pierced the air like horns of elfland faintly blowing.

Tasha never appeared until well into the morning, so Matthew breakfasted with his father in silence, and went in to Sarajevo with him, to wander alone for an hour or two, sometimes in the modern European city with its fine shops and electric trams, but more often on the other side of the river amid the minarets and orchards and terraces of the Turkish quarter, and the cheerful cacophony of the markets.

The smells were amazing – a whole delirious dispensary of them. Sunbaked dust and spices. Leather. Coffee. Sewers, or lack of them. Mutton and warm bread. Hot metal. Dill, garlic, cheese. People and patchouli. His guidebook had let him down badly. Mrs Holbach had been too busy with churches and mosques to spare more than a paragraph for the Carsija. Shame on her.

One morning, yielding to *force majeure*, he took his infant half-brother with him. Nick was not quite three, abominably forward for his age, and adept at getting what he wanted by the simple expedient of being a pest if he didn't. Fortunately, as pests went he was a most engaging one, with golden-brown hair, bright blue eyes, and a grin in which mischief and yearning were combined in proportions guaranteed to melt even the hardest heart.

It melted a good many hearts in the market, where so many pedlars and stallholders pressed Turkish Delight and halva, almonds and raisins and lollipops upon him that Matthew began to feel seriously embarrassed. It was only on the way home that he discovered why Nick had been so set on going to the market with Matthew and Matthew alone. 'No one else,' the child confided happily, 'lets me k'cept things from all those nice people.'

Matt couldn't help laughing. Young Nicholas Mikhail Britton, it seemed, had learned at a very early age to know a sucker when he saw one. It occurred to Matt to wonder whether it was a trait he had inherited from his mother.

4

A FEW days later, Tasha insisted that Matthew must see the famous waterfalls at Jajce, which meant setting out at dawn.

'It is sixty miles as the crow flies, but we are not crows. Also, the road was designed by a gentleman whose previous employment was in a corkscrew factory.'

Matthew laughed, and she laughed back. 'Ah, ha! I see you are like Paul, who does not believe there are such things as corkscrew factories. But wait until we have travelled the road before you commit yourself.'

It was, indeed, quite a road, but Tash had assured him that

Jajce was one of the most picturesque small towns in the world, and Matt readily believed her when they came in sight of it, its romantic little hilltop castle standing proud above the tented roofs and minarets that draped the slopes, the whole ringed with silvery, cascading waters and framed like a jewel amid dark green velvet heights.

Tash showed it off to him as if she had been personally responsible for its creation, but it soon became too hot for walking and they made for the river, where there was a platform, Tash said, from which one could see the river Pliva hurl itself into a ravine a hundred feet below.

'We will not go there now, however,' she said. 'It is spectacular but it is loud, and the noise will make us feel hotter than we already are. We will leave the falls until after lunch.'

Matthew, who was healthily hungry, had no fault to find with this programme. The servants had set out their picnic on a patch of grass overhung by trees and bathed in the cool, fresh airiness of the falls, a spot where by some minor miracle of Nature – the configuration of the rocks, perhaps – the noise level was no more intrusive than the whisper of distant traffic.

There were raw cured ham and figs; then cold chicken and a crisp salad; then a flaky, honeyed pastry. The white wine, after an hour wedged in the rushing water, was perfectly chilled. And there was excellent coffee, something of a rarity in Bosnia.

Afterwards, the servants cleared away and were given permission to wander where they chose, but to be back in one hour precisely.

Matthew stretched himself out luxuriously on the grass, his head pillowed on his jacket. 'What a sybaritic life the diplomatic service leads,' he said. 'Almost, I am envious.'

'You would like to be a diplomat?' He coulds tell from her voice that she was smiling.

'No.'

'Why not? Because it would not give you time to be a poet?' The smile was still there.

It was very endearing, this conviction of hers that some day he would be a poet, a real one. He knew better. Poetry was only a game to him, even if it happened to be a game that Mr Rupert Brooke and his friends had recently made fashionable in the universities. Matt, with the facility he had learned in childhood, had tossed off a few celebrations of love and laments over its loss – feeble, sentimental stuff – which had been much admired by his fellow-undergraduates though not by his tutor. Matthew had been pleasantly surprised, since it was the first time he had descried in that gentleman the faintest sign of taste or judgement.

'Don't laugh. It's not fair,' he murmured drowsily, keeping up the charade. 'I couldn't be a poet *and* a diplomat. Though I could be a poet and a carpenter, I suppose.'

'Do you still do that? Working with wood the way that man at the shipyard taught you?'

'Jardine. Yes, sometimes. There's a lot of satisfaction in being good with one's hands. The only trouble is, I can never think what to make.'

She chuckled. 'I have the same problem, *exactly*, with embroidery and *petit point!* So. Not a poet and diplomat. Not a poet and carpenter. A poet and something else?'

'What else?'

The truth was that Matt felt restless and rootless, impatient with Oxford even after so short a time. It wasn't something he ever said, because it sounded arrogant, but the place was too young for him. The isolation of his childhood had forced him into an early maturity, and then Tash had shown him how to apply the veneers of adulthood. As a result, when he had gone up to university, he had felt a decade older than the supercilious youths of the Claret Club, the sporting hearties, the wits of the Union, the earnest Fabians. The casual self-assurance this had given him had led to his being accepted by his elders, almost at once, as the only Freshman worthy of notice. Which was flattering. He quite enjoyed being sought after, even if he didn't place much value on it.

But now he had this sense of impatience, this anxiety to get to grips with the future even though he lacked any clear vision of what the future might be. There was something out there beyond the mists on the horizon, something exciting, something romantic, something that would exercise him in mind and body and spirit. But what?

There had been a family suggestion a couple of years before that, since he had once declared an interest in machines he might take over the shipyard from Uncle Hamish some day, but Natasha had thrown a truly spectacular tantrum and the idea had been dropped like a red-hot coal. Matthew had been grateful. His own feelings about the yard were not simply ambivalent but actively anti. Noise and cranes and suicides. Bossy little girls with toffee lumps. Puffers. In the end, it had been Tom who was sent straight from Eton to the Clyde, to learn the business. And Tom had resented it bitterly, holding Matt personally responsible.

Sensing Tasha move slightly, Matt said again, '*What* else? The trouble is that I just don't know what I want to do.'

'Why not be a poet all the time?'

'Because even poets must eat,' he said. 'I wonder if Aristophanes feasted on raw ham and fresh figs?'

'Juvenal did. And on wild asparagus. And "lordly eggs, warm in their wisps of hay".' Tasha was astonishingly well educated in her own undisciplined way.

'No,' he said, and stretched again, sensuously. It was splendid here in the lightly shaded sun and the freshness of the falls. He felt like a pampered cat. 'No, it won't do. If I'm to be a poet and live in a garret, I shall have to reconcile myself to what's to be found in the shops. And put in a lot more practice with my chafing dish.'

'Your what?'

Smiling, he turned his head. 'You don't believe me? Twelve shillings and sixpence in Harrods. And a cookery book to match. I can produce as good a supper in my rooms as you would get in Hall.'

She was watching him with the fixity that usually meant her mind was on something else, so he said provocatively, 'When you come home, I will give you Polly Lobster, and some walnuts and green peas, and perhaps Lady Effingham's Eggs as a savoury.'

'Who in the world is Lady Effingham?'

'I've no idea. I know her only by her eggs. But I can assure you that they have been admired by any number of people.'

'You mean you entertain in your rooms?'

'Of course.'

'Who?'

'Oh, people.'

'Young ladies?'

He couldn't help laughing. She was paying attention now, all right. Why were women always so fascinated by thoughts of romance? 'Certainly not. I have far too much regard for their reputations.'

It wasn't quite true, but he didn't want to talk about Rachel. They had fallen into love, and out of it, so quickly. His vanity had been sadly piqued when, just as he was preparing to break it to her, with infinite tact and sensitivity, that his feelings had undergone a change, she had forestalled him. 'You are a darling,' she had said, with the frank modernity that was her greatest charm, 'and very easy to love. But I have decided that my studies must come first.' Then, blowing a daring smoke ring, she had added, 'But we must always be friends.'

124

Fortunately, Pamela had come along soon after – Pamela of the white frock and blue ribbon sash, who was not only willing but anxious to be made love to in the starlit, early summer dark of the walled garden, where the lingering warmth of the sun filled the air with strong, sweet, separate scents of herbs, and blackcurrant bushes, and the first strawberries of the season. It had been a charming little affaire, but unfulfilling.

'Do you have a young lady?'

'Dozens! They queue up at my door. I am the envy of the college.'

'Do you go to bed with them?'

'*Tasha!*' He was honestly shocked. Though he loved the way she said what she thought, there were times when she did go it a bit!

She made a derisive little sound in her throat that, in a man, would have been a grunt, but didn't pursue the subject. Instead, switching to a deeply serious tone, she said, 'It was so very *strange* the other day, when you came off the train. You had become not just a young man, but a man. So suddenly. You had changed so much.' She paused, and when she resumed her voice sounded quite distressed. 'I was afraid you were not my Matthew any more.'

'Changed? That was only because you've never seen me in my artistic hat before!'

He wasn't conscious of having changed at all, except a little on the outside, but during the last few days he had found Tash's manner oddly disturbing – brittle and artificial. Could this be what was wrong, he wondered, why the old ease and freedom seemed to have gone and he found himself having to tread warily with the only person from whom he had never kept back even the smallest part of himself? Well, if that was all it was, it could be remedied easily enough.

'I haven't changed,' he said stoutly. 'I did change – *you* changed me – when father brought you home to England. But since then, not at all.' He grinned. 'I can honestly assure you that I still am, and will eternally remain, your ladyship's most obedient – humble – and devoted – servant.'

Sitting up, he swung round, intending to conclude his little speech with a mock flourish of hand to heart, but even as he turned he found she was leaning towards him, her gaze luminous and her own hand stretched out.

'My beautiful Adonis,' she said, and laid the tips of her fingers on his lips.

He froze.

If the atmosphere hadn't been so highly charged, it would have been funny, but, as it was, the gesture and the ridiculous words – echoes from the easy, extravagant affection of the past – were horribly embarrassing. He found himself repressing an urgent instinct to look round in case someone was watching.

Damn and double damn.

She was so fluent in English nowadays that it was easy to forget that she didn't always recognise the faintly ironic undertones that certain words and phrases had acquired over the years; phrases like 'obedient, humble and devoted'. It wouldn't have mattered if she weren't so demonstrative, but how could he convey, without hurting, that the caresses that had been unexceptionable when he was a schoolboy might, nowadays, very easily be misinterpreted by people who didn't know any better?

He moved his head a little, instinctively, and perhaps in the movement there was a hint of what had been in his mind, because she at once withdrew her hand.

And then, of course, he felt guilty.

At a loss what to say or do, he rose after a moment and picked up his jacket and asked with a slightly forced smile, 'Shall we look at the falls now? I imagine we ought to be starting back soon.'

She had already begun to gather up her purse and parasol, and he couldn't see her face. But as he swung the jacket over his shoulder he remembered the package in the inside pocket. Her birthday present. He had been carrying it around with him for safety; one never knew, with hotels. He had intended to give it to her tonight, at her birthday dinner, but it occurred to him that now might be a better time.

She opened the package as she always opened packages, with a bright excitement, and gasped when she saw what was inside.

The last time he had given her a present, she had offered him her cheek and he had planted a smacking, youthful kiss on it. But this time she merely said, her voice melodious, 'Oh, how beautiful! What a thoughtful boy you are.'

It made him feel about fourteen again, and a bit of an idiot. What *was* the matter with him, that he should be letting his imagination run away with him?

5

IT HAD been a tiring day, but no one would have guessed it when they sat down to dinner on that late June evening in the garden at Ilidze. The air was soft and scented, and there were nightingales singing.

Every head turned as Natasha appeared, wearing a gown that was like nothing Matthew had ever seen before, except in the theatre. A wondrous thing of rich colours and gauze and satin, its multiple layers anarchic, and yet not so anarchic as to conceal the soft and shapely figure beneath. Her hair was dressed close to her head, throwing the exotic cheekbones into relief and emphasising the faint slant of the ice-blue eyes which, tonight, were brilliant. There was more colour than usual in her cheeks.

'In the theatre?' she repeated, fair brows lifting, as Matthew held the chair for her. 'But of course. The *Ballets russes* and *Schéhérazade*. The dress is Paquin but the design is Bakst. Thank you.'

She smiled blindingly at the heavy-jowled gentleman at the next table, who scrambled to his feet, clutching at his napkin, bowing and very nearly scraping. The gentleman's wife, an unusually fine specimen of Gretchen-at-the-spinning-wheel, didn't look nearly so enthusiastic.

Paul had succeeded, for once, in getting away from the office at a respectable hour, but the strain of the last two years was beginning to tell. Although the increasing grey in his hair merely added to his distinction, the line of his cheeks had become hollow rather than lean and the long nose that had always seemed to his sons to have been specially designed for looking down, was longer and thinner than ever.

Nothing, however, had impaired the supercilious courtesy with which he treated everyone in the world except Tasha; for her there was an unfailing softening of the eyes that spoke of tenderness and tolerance, as if she were an uncritically adored though sometimes wayward child.

When they were all seated, Paul moved aside the glass goblet with the candle in it and said, 'I am pleased to hear that you have both had an enjoyable day but, Matthew, I must repeat my regrets at having to desert you for so much of the time. We seem scarcely to

127

have had the opportunity to talk. However, the pace should slacken when Franz Ferdinand's visit is over. You may think the comings and goings of our Hapsburg friend have nothing to do with me, but I am afraid they have. You cannot imagine how anxious London is to know which troops he is reviewing, and where and when and why, and what weaponry is being brought out that we did not know about before.'

He held out a hand for the menu. 'Yes. I can recommend the stuffed aubergine and the pilaff, or the spiced kebabs. Not the roast veal. And there is some champagne on ice for us.' Reaching out, he took Tasha's hand in his. 'For tomorrow's birthday girl.'

Matthew had to swallow a grin. Anyone less like a sweet little English 'birthday girl' than Tash in her bird-of-paradise gown would have been hard to imagine.

'Though what', his father went on, 'Dom Pérignon would have had to say to champagne with stuffed aubergines, I can't imagine.'

Tasha laughed intimately into his eyes. 'He would have considered it sacrilege, of course. So I will have the champagne, and you may have the aubergines.'

They talked about the road to Jajce, and the picnic, and the waterfall, and when those topics had been exhausted Paul said, 'Matthew, have you heard from Tom? I don't think I have had more than two letters from him in the last two years.'

'You're honoured! I've had none, though I've seen him in London a couple of times. The moment Uncle Hamish lets him off the leash, he comes dashing up to town for debutante balls and school reunions. I gather that Glasgow is a kind of Arabia Deserta where social life is concerned.'

Softly, from somewhere down at the end of the garden, there came the voice of a *sevdalinka* singer, melancholy and intriguing, the note-scale as mysterious as the words and the spirit behind them.

'I have no interest in his social life,' Paul Britton said, leaning back to allow the waiter to remove his plate. 'How is he shaping up at the yard?'

'All right, I think, now he's resigned to it. It was a bit hard on him at first that no one had time to teach him. I mean, Uncle Hamish was already run off his feet because of the rearmament programme, and then, of course, the *Titanic* went down and every ship that *could* be adapted to take extra watertight compartments *had* to be adapted. It seems to have been just one crisis after another. But I've the impression he's got a grip on things now.'

128

Tasha, taking no part in this conversation, had been sitting, patently bored, glancing round the other tables, up at the sky, outwards into the haunted dark. Now, her patience exhausted, she turned back to her husband and stepson and announced, with bell-like clarity, 'Thomas is a stuffed shirt!'

It was undoubtedly the champagne talking.

At neighbouring tables, several heads turned and Matt reflected that, if this had been England, everyone would have been looking busily the other way.

Paul said, half smiling, 'Natasha darling, please!'

Tasha bridled. 'We have had enough of Thomas. He is boring. The shipyard is boring. Sarajevo is boring. Even my husband is boring, because he is so much occupied with his work that when he comes home he is too tired to make love to me.'

Matthew, aware of a craven desire to get up and run, began with great concentration to peel a pear.

They needed Uncle Hamish, he thought. That gentleman, having at first had his doubts about Tasha, had been an early convert to her charm, if not an uncritical one. In fact, he had made it his mission in life to ensure that she didn't forget she was living in democratic Britain, not at the Court of the Czars, and in pursuit of this praiseworthy object habitually addressed her as 'hen', which was proletarian Glasgow's version of 'dear' or 'luv'. It didn't discompose Tash in the least. Indeed, it usually made her chuckle. But there was no denying that she came nearer to being a model of propriety in Uncle Hamish's company than in anyone else's.

To Matthew's relief, after a pregnant moment his father said no more than, 'Quite so, my dear. But things will be better soon.'

'Soon, soon, soon! It is almost my birthday, and I wish to be not-bored *now*. Does that oaf with the moustaches bring his so-called wife to Sarajevo with him?'

This time, Paul did twitch slightly. 'Natasha! Not here, please.'

Tasha ignored him. 'The Duchess of Hohenburg,' she explained to Matthew. 'She was the Countess Sophie Chotek, and too base-born to be a suitable match for the next Emperor of Austria. So it was a morganatic marriage and she is never treated as royal. She cannot even sit beside him on public occasions. Paul, you have not answered me. Does she accompany him?'

'Yes. They arrive on the 28th. It seems he regards the visit as a special treat for her, since he is coming in his military, not his imperial rôle, and it is therefore permissible for her to appear with him in public.'

129

'A treat? To inspect the army? *Mon dieu!* But there must be a party, a reception, yes?'

'I – er – yes.'

Champagne or no champagne, Natasha was perfectly capable of recognising when her husband was looking shifty.

'Good,' she said with exaggerated precision, toying with a silver cheese knife. 'Where and at what time?'

'At the Town Hall. My dear, have you finished? Shall we go indoors?'

'I wish to stay here. When is this reception? They are very late with their invitations. The 28th is the day after tomorrow. But never mind. I look forward to it. I wish to see whether she dresses as badly as everyone says.'

'Well . . .'

Her blue eyes opened fully on his. 'Well, *what?*'

And then the cat was out of the bag. In view of the less than amicable relations between Russia and Austria–Hungary, Mr Paul Britton had been invited but his Russian wife had not.

There was a moment's heavy silence before Tasha's colour rose and she gave vent to a sound not unlike the rustle of distant thunder.

Matt thought, 'Oh, God!'

With stupefying suddenness, she sent the cheese knife somersaulting through the air to bury itself in a tub of geraniums, while with her other arm, almost simultaneously, she made an impassioned gesture that swept the table half-clear of its contents. Then, even as Paul hurriedly pushed back his chair to escape the fusillade of flat champagne and coffee grounds, she sprang to her feet, picked up the large and expensive-looking glass fruit bowl, and dashed it to the paving. There was an extremely gratifying crash, and the fruit rolled all over the place.

Natasha, with satisfaction, surveyed the havoc she had wrought and then sat down again, while a waiter, with admirable presence of mind, brought them some more coffee and the heavy-jowled gentleman at the next table retrieved two peaches and a small bunch of grapes from under his chair and, with a courteous clicking of heels, presented them to Paul, who received them with aplomb.

After a while, Matthew said helpfully, 'Tash, darling, I think you may have some splashes on your frock.'

It was not well received. 'Nothing,' Tash replied grandly, 'is more bourgeois than worrying about one's clothes.'

130

But her expression, as she sipped her coffee, was hard to decipher and there were no self-exonerating references to old Russian festive customs. Matthew wondered whether the trouble, now, went too deep.

In the end, Paul took a deep breath and said, 'My dearest, I know you are disappointed, but . . . I wish you would not.'

And then, with characteristic suddenness, Tasha was Tasha again, exotic and exhilarating, her charm almost incandescent. It was as if the night had suddenly lit up. She raised her husband's hand mischievously to her lips. 'Then I will be good. Has it – has it tired you?'

'No.'

Matthew wouldn't have believed that a single monosyllable could convey so much. Staring down into his cup, he wondered when it would be safe to raise his eyes again.

When he did, they met Tasha's full on, and he discovered that the melting smile was for him, too.

It was all very disturbing.

6

RUSSIAN she might be, but Mrs Paul Britton had no intention of being deprived of the pleasure of criticising Sophie Chotek's clothes, so it was arranged that Matthew should escort her into Sarajevo in time to watch the arrival of the imperial party at the Town Hall and that they would then stroll along to the Hotel Europa for coffee. The motorcar would pick them up at the river bridge and bring them back to Ilidze in time for lunch.

But it didn't work out like that.

The day started well. As if to make up for her moodiness of the past week, Tasha was in her most enchanting humour even before he told her how marvellous she looked. Which she did, in a soft silk dress whose long, narrow, ice-blue tunic top was sashed over an ankle-length white skirt with a hem scalloped in matching blue. The sash ended in a fall of blue silk roses, and there was a posy of them on the front of her hat, which in other respects was exactly like a beehive.

'But a most elegant beehive,' he assured her as he handed her into the open car, and she sparkled at him all over again.

There were no excited throngs in Sarajevo, no banners waving as there would have been in London on the occasion of a royal visit, no soldiers in the streets and only about a hundred police – though that, admittedly, was the entire local force. The crowds were, in fact, there, but they had an air about them as if it was all pure chance, as if they might deign to stroll over and take a look when something began to happen, but in the meantime had better things to do. It was, after all, the great Serbian festival of *Vidovdan*, which was more important than a mere Austrian archduke.

'Peasants!' exclaimed Tasha with a bright contempt, as they took up their position opposite the Town Hall. 'They have no sense of occasion. Royalty is royalty after all, even if that oaf with the moustaches is not someone one would choose to know socially.' She consulted her white enamelled fob watch. 'They should be here soon, surely? I thought Austrians were never late.'

'You're thinking of Germans.'

'Am I?'

'Something's happening, though.'

Far away in the distance, in the direction of the station, the crowds seemed to be converging at the roadside, as if the procession was coming into sight. Sarajevo was a place always filled with noise, but Matthew would have expected to hear cheering if there had been any, and there wasn't. If it was indeed the archducal cavalcade approaching, it seemed that Franz Ferdinand wasn't being hailed with the rejoicing usually accorded to conquering heroes.

Tash, her arm in his, said, 'Is that the first of the motors? I think I see the sun glinting on metal.'

Matthew did, too.

And then there was an echoing bang, and the crowd opened and closed again, and the glint of sun on metal vanished.

'Oh-oh,' Matthew said. 'A burst tyre.'

Nothing happened for another ten minutes, although there seemed to be a certain amount of activity going on. The vehicle might have swerved after the burst, of course, and one or two bystanders could have been injured. If what they'd heard *had* been a tyre bursting.

Natasha sighed. 'Why are they taking so long? I am tired of standing here. The sun is becoming unpleasantly hot.'

And then the crowd in the distance opened up and the motors appeared. Because of the angle of vision, Matt didn't realise at first just how fast they were travelling, but as they drew near it became very obvious. And the sharpness with which the chauffeur of the third vehicle braked in front of the Town Hall steps suggested a nervous disposition.

But Franz Ferdinand and the Countess Sophie were seated stiffly in the back of the open vehicle, and when they prepared to descend it was with no perceptible signs of haste.

Tash was right about one thing. The Archduke didn't look like a man one would choose to sit next to at dinner. When he removed his ceremonial helmet prior to handing his wife down, an *en brosse* haircut was revealed that made his head look as square and solid as a block of wood, while the pale eyes, with their prominent lower lids, were so lacking in expression that they might have belonged to a dead fish. But expression there most certainly was around the mouth, clearly visible despite the huge, handlebar moustaches. And it looked like fury.

'*Ahhh!*' Tash sighed in accents of bliss. 'What a truly dreadful hat! How can she bear to be seen in such a thing? Those feathers, so *démodé*! And look at her figure. My dear, she's still wearing *corsets*!'

Matthew smiled absently, watching the couple stalk up the front steps and disappear between the lines of welcoming dignitaries, most of them wearing fez and cummerbund. He found himself wondering what had happened back there. Nothing serious, presumably.

Turning to Natasha, he said, 'Well, that's over. You've seen the Duchess of Hohenberg. Was she dowdy enough for you? Let's go and have our coffee. Shall we have Turkish, or that dirty dishwater they call European?'

They had been seated in the padded, panelled, curlicued and entirely un-Bosnian lounge of the Europa for no more than ten minutes when Charlie Thompson materialised in the doorway.

'Hullo,' Matthew said, and added without thinking, 'Coffee?'

'No, really, Matthew! I don't know how you can dwink that Turkish stuff. It's wevolting! Anyway, I haven't time. Have you heard what happened?' He sounded as if he had run all the way from the Town Hall.

Tasha, who had been too absorbed by Sophie Chotek's corsets to think about anything else, said, 'What do you mean, "what happened"?'

'The bomb.'

'The *what?*'

Matt said, 'So that's what it was! Come on, Charlie. Tell.'

'I'm twying to! Someone threw a bomb at Fwanz Ferdinand's motor. A gwenade, I suppose. But it bounced off the side and

133

exploded in front of the one with the aides-de-camp in it. One of them was injured quite badly, a Colonel – I can't remember his name – oh, yes I can – Colonel Merizzi.

'Anyway, you have to hand it to FF. He stopped his own motor and went back to see what had happened. Then he ordered Colonel Whatsit to be taken to the Bawwacks Hospital while everything else pwoceeded as if nothing had happened.'

'Yes, I see!' said Matt. 'Well, that explains why the chauffeur was driving so badly.'

Tash stared at him indignantly. 'Was he? I did not see that! You did not say anything to me!'

'Didn't want to upset you.' Though, now he thought about it, Tash was much more likely to be upset by lack of excitement than by excitement. 'So what's the situation, Charlie? What happens now? Did they catch the fellow?'

'We can't find out. The police gwabbed a few bystanders, but how do you prove a man *had* a gwenade if no one saw him throw it?'

'That's true enough. What about the reception?'

'Well, FF and the Duchess are still at the Town Hall, as planned, and everyone seems to think they'll go to the Bawwacks Hospital afterwards to see Colonel Whatsit, and then dwive stwaight out of town to the manoeuvres. The reason I'm here is your father wants you to take Mrs Bwitton back to Ilidze immediately. You never know, if it turns out to be a genuine tewwowist conspiracy, they might twy again.'

Matt, suppressing a reprehensible desire to hang around just in case they did, said, 'Dear me, yes. What a thrilling prospect. The only thing is – what's the time? – yes – it's another thirty-five minutes before the driver's due to meet us.'

Charlie, who had been perched on the very edge of a chair, hopped to his feet. 'That should be all right. The woyal party isn't expected to leave for about an hour, so you should be well out of the way by then. I'd better get back now. Your servant, Mrs Bwitton. Bye, Matthew.'

Natasha said, 'But I do not wish . . .'

Charlie, however, was already disappearing through the tall twin doors with their sandblasted glass panels and flaking brown varnish. Tasha stared after him, incensed. 'What a breathless young man! It was most impolite of him not to wait to hear what I was trying to say.'

Matt grinned. 'Diplomatic deafness, it's called. Anyway, I suppose we ought to go down to the bridge fairly soon, in case your driver happens to turn up early.'

'But I do not *wish* to return to Ilidze. That young man could have taken a message back to Paul that we intended to stay and see the fun.'

'What a shocking thing to say!'

She stared at him forbiddingly. 'Do *you* not wish to stay? No! I do not believe you can be such a – what is the word? – a milksop!'

But though he couldn't help laughing, he said, 'I can think of other words, and no, I won't be coaxed. If anything happened to you, my father would kill me. If I didn't kill myself first.'

'Would you do that?'

A year ago, it wouldn't have occurred to him to doubt that she was teasing. As it was, he had to take a deep breath before he said lightly, 'My dearest and most darling Tash, the ground would be positively strewn with corpses if even a hair of your head was harmed. So be a good girl, and don't argue.'

She rose to her feet with immense dignity. 'You will oblige me, Matthew, by remembering that I am your stepmother and that I expect to be addressed with suitable respect.'

Then she held out her hand and added austerely 'You may button my glove, serf.'

That was more like it. At least he knew where he was, now. Bending, he began to struggle with the tiny buttons, saying obsequiously, 'Yes, stepmama. Of course, stepmama. As you wish, stepmama. But the word you want is "varlet".'

7

THAT was how they happened to witness the event that was to change the history of the world.

Because Francis Ferdinand, Archduke of Austria, nephew of the Emperor Francis Joseph and heir to the thrones of Austria and Hungary, was in no mood to be gracious to the Burgomaster and Council of a town that harboured terrorists. So he listened stonily to the Burgomaster's stammered address of welcome, replied angrily, and left with his wife at his side. They had been in the Town Hall for not much more than half an hour.

When Matthew and Tash reached the Appel quay their own motor hadn't arrived, but there was a small and rather aimless-looking crowd hanging around and before long Matthew found himself caught up in conversation with a man anxious to practise his English.

'What's everyone waiting for?' Matthew asked. 'The royal party isn't coming this way, is it? I thought it was taking the other direction.'

The man shrugged. 'Who can tell? Rumour say this. Rumour say that. One knows not until one sees, or not sees, for himself.'

Matthew frowned and wished the Ilidze car would get a move on. It was all very well for Tash to stand there hoping something exciting would happen, but he felt responsible. However, there must be at least another ten or fifteen minutes before he needed to begin worrying in earnest.

And then Tash said, 'Oh, look!' and there was the blasted cavalcade, tearing along at forty miles an hour.

Without warning, the crowd began to converge at the roadside.

'Oh! How exasperating!' Tash exclaimed. 'If they all stand close together like that, I will not be able to see! We must move forward.'

Firmly, Matt put his arm round her waist. 'Stay where you are! They're going too fast for you to see anything anyway.' She didn't struggle but stood obediently motionless as he scanned the crowd.

No more bombs, he thought. Please. Surely no one would try anything against a convoy moving at that speed.

Then the air was rent by an ear-splitting squeal that almost made his heart stop beating.

It turned out to be only the imperial motor braking. It stopped, and reversed a few yards, and stopped again.

Tasha said happily, 'How very obliging! I can see perfectly now. *Mon dieu*, Matthew, her corsets! Perhaps she may after all be forgiven them, though not the frock. She looks as if she is *enceinte*.'

'As if she's what?'

'Oh, you Englishmen! Such ignorance. As if she is expecting a child!'

The chauffeur, it seemed, had missed the turn on to the bridge, and was now having trouble with his gears. He was taking an eternity to find first again.

Indeed, he was still struggling with the lever when an innocuous-looking bystander clad in a European topcoat over a dark suit stepped forward from the crowd, mounted the running board, drew a pistol from his coat pocket, and fired.

Once. Twice.

In the frozen waste of time that followed, a brilliant scarlet stain began to spread over the side of the Duchess's much-maligned frock, and purple drops appeared and multiplied on the Arch-duke's fine blue braided tunic.

Afterwards, Matthew recognised that only a few moments must have elapsed before everyone stopped staring and began to react. He himself, starting forward instinctively to help lay hands on the culprit, was halted by Tash's voice behind him crying, 'Oh, the poor thing!' Reminded that his first duty was to her, he hesitated, and turned, only to find that she had vanished.

Then everything dissolved into chaos. In a matter of seconds, the crowd that had been numbered in scores swelled to hundreds as people from other parts of the route came running to see what had happened. And many of the bystanders who had been present from the start were trying to fight their way out, to turn their backs on what had happened, to blind their eyes to the bloody scene and their ears to the bubbling moan that must be the sound of poor Sophie Chotek dying. Franz Ferdinand's *en brosse* head was already as motionless as the block of wood it resembled and his fish-cold eyes were blank and staring.

But his blood still dripped.

There was some kind of scrimmage going on over to the left, and then a furious outbreak of shouting and pushing. The new voices were the voices of authority, and the thwacking sound that of police scabbards being used to clear a path. Another motor appeared and decanted a general or two, and there were women in black veils keening and men in waistcoats and cummerbunds crying out to Allah, and all the time Matthew was using shoulders and elbows and knees to try and bore his way through to wherever Tasha might be.

He found her at last as the police dragged the assassin away to the police station, followed by most of the crowd; a young man of Matthew's own age, shielding his head against the blows. By then, much too late, there was a tight wall of soldiers round the motor that was now a hearse, and Tasha was standing nearby with no hat, the pins coming out of her hair, and blood on her hands.

She stared at him dizzily, and he thought she was going to faint. But instead she talked, and talked, and talked, and when he found her hat at last, the trodden-on white beehive with the ice-blue roses, she tossed it into the river without a second glance.

The police refused to allow the Ilidze car to approach the bridge, but the driver had enough sense to come and find them. Matthew sent him to the hotel for some brandy. He thought Tasha might be the better for it, and he knew he would. And then they drove out of Sarajevo.

Sarajevo the Golden.

Tasha said, 'I held her hand, and spoke German to her a little, because I only know it a little. But I thought it might be a comfort to her to feel there was someone who spoke her language. To feel that she wasn't dying quite alone in a foreign land. The poor thing, the poor thing! She was wearing a gold chain round her neck with holy relics to protect her against misfortune!'

Matthew held her all the way back to Ilidze while she sobbed as if her heart would break.

8

A LITTLE over three weeks later, on 23 July, Austria–Hungary, convinced that Serbia had been behind the assassination, sent her an ultimatum couched in impossible terms. That same evening, Paul Britton told Matthew that he was to escort Natasha and Nick back to England at once.

'And I mean at once. You will start tomorrow. I have told young Thompson to make the arrangements. He will go with you.'

'But . . .'

'Credit me with some knowledge of what I am talking about. Serbia will make concessions, but this time they will be useless. We have all been burying our heads in the sand for too long. All the great powers have convinced themselves that because last year and the year before they managed to stop the trouble in the Balkans from spreading to Europe, they will be able to do it again. This time I believe they are wrong.

'Austria–Hungary will declare war on Serbia. Russia will mobilise in Serbia's defence. Germany will send an ultimatum, which Russia will refuse. Germany will declare war. And since France is Russia's ally, France will be drawn in.

'We won't be able to stay out. And I can tell you – if, this time, the world *is* going to fall apart, it will fall apart in weeks. Not months, not years. If you set out tomorrow, you will probably get back to England before Armageddon. But only just. I should have sent you sooner.'

'What will you do?'

'I must stay here until I am ordered home. I shouldn't think it will be long. What will *you* do?'

138

'Have I a choice?' Matthew said. 'I'll fight, of course. "The cause being just and the quarrel honourable." *Henry V*, Act IV, Scene something-or-other.'

Paul Britton, studying his son, recognised that the boy was half looking forward to it. Not only that. He also recognised that – tall, handsome, charming and assured though he might be – Matthew *was* still only a boy. Eighteen, and quite untried.

After a moment, he said in a tone devoid of expression, 'Yes. I suppose you must. But for all our sakes, try to emulate the Abbé Sièyes. You remember? When someone asked him what he had done during the French Revolution, he replied, "I survived". Look after yourself.'

Then, for the first time in his life, Paul Britton embraced his son.

Two

1

JENNY Jardine, busy ladling fried potatoes onto the plates, nearly dropped the pan when Jackie yelped right in her ear, 'Lloyd George! I'm fair sick of Lloyd George!'

She said. 'I wish you wouldn't do that. I didn't hear you come in. What's the matter now?'

He was brandishing a newspaper. 'Did ye see this? Did ye see it? What yon wee nyaff said to the shipbuilding employers the other day? "We are fighting Germany, Austria, and Drink, and the greatest of these is Drink." Did ye ever hear the like? He says the men in the yards are producing less than they did in peacetime because they're getting higher wages and drinking more and staying off work because they're stotious . . .'

'Did he really say stotious?'

'No, of course he didn't. He's whit they call an or*a*ytor. Wouldny recognise a decent, honest word if it came up and poked him in the pinny. "Inebriated", he said. And he says he knows of one publican in Scotland who fills a hundred bottles of whisky every Saturday night for his shipyard customers to take home and drink on Sunday when the pubs are closed. And why not, jist tell me that! But *he* says it canny be allowed. *He* says he'll have to increase the tax on drink. *He* says he'll have to pass a law stopping the pubs from staying open in the afternoons . . .'

'Will you get out of my way, Jackie!'

Jackie didn't budge. 'Aye, weel, it's anither conspiracy against the workers, that's whit it is, and . . .

'There's your tea, and will you stop standing there like a stookie. Sit down and eat it before it gets cold.'

Iris, who had just come in, wearily pushed him down into his seat at table and then subsided herself, moaning, 'My feet are killing me. You don't need any help, Jenny, do you?'

'No, it's all right. Bad day?'

'I seem to have done nothing but run up and down steps. I'll either have to get a new job or some new shoes. Customers, honestly! "You could get me wan o' they tins of biscuits from the top shelf, Miss Jardine . . . Och, they've got coconut on them; he

140

doesny like coconut ... Whit aboot that kind ower at the end there? No, further, you'll huv tae move the steps ... Aye, yon wans ... Och, no, there's nae chocolate wans in them ... Mebbe I'll just take four o' they fly cemeteries on the coonter." It's enough to drive you demented.'

Jack, momentarily diverted, glanced round the table at the scones and cakes Jenny had baked that afternoon. 'Hey, why huv *we* no' got any fly cemeteries? I could just go a fly cemetery.'

Jenny said, 'Because we haven't. And I wish you wouldn't call them that. It puts me right off. They're raisin slices.'

'Hah! Where's mum and dad?'

'Mum's letting out her dress for tonight and dad's gone down the road to get the results edition. Jackie, will you eat your tea before it gets cold!'

'Why huv we got fried potatoes wi' our mince? We always have mash.'

'I thought it would be a change.'

Iris couldn't help giggling as Jenny turned bright pink with annoyance; a pretty, fair girl with big eyes and an air of shyness that made you wonder if she was a throwback. Jardines weren't usually backward in coming forward.

Iris herself, at twenty-four, was nothing out of the ordinary either in looks or brains. She'd decided the best she could hope for in life was to marry Mr Cockerell, who owned the corner dairy where she worked. He was a middle-aged bachelor and a bit set in his ways, but he'd said this very day that he didn't know what he'd do without her. When they'd been busy at the stocktaking in January, he'd even told her she could call him Sydney, though not in front of the customers, of course.

Knowing that everyone else in the house was going to be out this evening, she'd very daringly suggested he might like to drop in for a cup of tea if he happened to be passing, and he'd said well yes, he might. He hadn't even blinked at the thought of just 'happening' to be passing a house situated at the farthest end of a half-mile cul-de-sac. Iris hoped the leerie wouldn't skip Rashilea Terrace when he came round to light the street lamps, as he sometimes did when he wanted to get home to his supper. She hoped, too, that Jackie wouldn't eat all the shortbread Jenny had made. Sydney was partial to a nice bit of shortbread.

Every time Iris thought about herself and Sydney, which she did quite often, she had a vision of the two of them twenty years on, a stone or two heavier in their clean white overalls but still behind

141

the same marble-topped counter, wielding the same butter patters, shovelling sugar into the same blue paper bags, and formally addressing each other as 'Mr Cockerell' and 'Mrs Cockerell'. It was a satisfying picture, and the sooner they got started the better.

Iris yearned for a nice, comfy home of her own, with no Nellie Jardine bossing her about, and no Jack blethering on about workers' rights. Where he got his notions from, she didn't know. He was quite unlike their dad, who never got worked up about things.

However, sore feet notwithstanding, she was contented enough with life this Saturday evening not to want to spoil Jack's fun. She said chattily, 'So what's the latest conspiracy against the workers, then?'

Jack told her at length, while Jenny fixed her attention on her plate and tried to close her ears. She had very mixed feelings about Jackie. Some of the time she looked up to him as her big brother, but at other times she could cheerfully have strangled him. This was one of the other times.

Iris said, 'I read about that. Lord Kitchener says the army in Flanders isn't getting the munitions it needs because of poor time-keeping and drunkenness in the factories.'

Jack snorted. 'It's lies, lies, that's whit it is. Anyway, whit does Kitchener know aboot anything? He's jist making excuses because the army's made sich a cock-up of things!'

There was an ear-splitting, 'Jack!' from the doorway, and everybody jumped.

'Language!' said Nellie Jardine. Considering how often she told them that cleanliness was a state of mind, she was remarkably quick to recognise a dirty word when she heard one.

Jenny brought her parents' plates over from the range where they had been keeping warm, and her mother eyed hers disapprovingly and said, 'Fried potatoes? We always have mash with mince.'

2

JACK reached for a scone. 'It's aye the same. Blame the workers! I dinny believe the army *is* short of shells. Shove over the jam, Iris.'

Jenny said, 'Oooh, what about that battle at Neuve Chapelle last month! It said in the paper the soldiers hadn't even enough shells to spare for a preliminary bombardment!'

It was the wrong example to choose – the only time in almost nine months of war when the British army had actually succeeded in breaking through the German lines – and Jack took her up on it like a shot. 'Aye, weel! That's why they won, because they didny give the Huns any warning; maybe they should try it again.'

'That's not the point, and you know it isn't. The point is, all those poor men are suffering and *dying* in the trenches just because they haven't got enough munitions. And,' Jenny concluded belligerently, 'they're getting paid a shilling a day while you go on strike for an extra *tuppence* an *hour*. I think it's scandalous.'

Unaccustomed to having his views so hotly contested in the bosom of his family – which was more inclined to change the subject – Jack said, 'Aye, weel, but *they*'re getting free bed and board.'

Even his mother put down her knife and fork to stare at him, while his father abandoned his attempt to concentrate on the finer points of the Rangers v. Celtic match.

John Jardine hadn't changed in all the years his family could remember. He looked the same. He weighed the same. His moustaches were still long and silky and sandy-grey. He still went out to work in his black serge suit, the waistcoat with the braided lapels, the gold chain with the hunter watch on the end, the stiff collar and black tie and high-crowned, curly brimmed bowler hat. He still never sat around in his shirt sleeves. He still never spoke unless it was necessary.

Now, he looked at his son and said bluntly, 'If you're that keen on free bed and board, why d'ye no' take a dauner along to the recruiting office? They'd be blithe to see you. You'd maybe get a prize for being the one-and-a-quarter-millionth volunteer, and a nice cushy billet in the trenches at Ypres. And then *we* wouldny have to go on listening to your blethers.'

'It's no' blethers. In the opinion of the Central Withdrawal of Labour Committee . . .'

John Jardine rustled his newspaper impatiently. 'Och, away and boil yer head, laddie. The opinion of the Central Withdrawal of Labour Committee cuts about as much ice with me as a kennel full of wally dugs. It fair scunners me to think how many years it's taken to build up a decent union organisation on the Clyde, just to huv it a' put to waste by a bunch of glaikit buggers that call themselves shop stewards.'

His wife opened her mouth.

143

'Hold your tongue, wumman! And you needny look so black-affronted, either. If my language offends your genteel sensibilities, you can take them off into the scullery.'

With awful dignity, Nellie Jardine rose to her feet, gathered up the dirty plates, jerked her head meaningly at the girls and disappeared. But the girls stayed where they were. It was the longest speech they'd ever heard their father make.

'Now, jist you listen to me, laddie,' he went on in a tone rarely used and never disobeyed. 'You and your ten bloody thousand Clyde engineers out on unofficial strike instead o' building ships to beat the Germans – you've brought nothing but shame and disgrace on the whole union movement. And I'll tell you whit else you've done. You've left responsible union leaders withoot a leg to stand on when the government makes up its mind to outlaw strikes for the duration, as it's bound to do. They'll huv tae give in.'

Jack opened his mouth but his father, having said his say, had retired behind a barricade of pink newsprint and even Jack had more sense than to waste his breath arguing.

Nellie Jardine's face appeared round the scullery door. 'Jenny, you've got the dishes to do before you get dressed for the dance. And Iris, you didn't make a very good job of dusting the front room before you went out this morning; you'd better take the duster round again, and see you do the chair rails this time. Jack, get the coal in, and we'll need a pail of dross to bank up the fire when we're out this evening.'

Iris said, 'I'm going to be in.'

'Oh, so you are. Well, remember. There's no need for a roaring blaze just for you.'

Iris wouldn't have put it past her to count how many lumps there were in the scuttle.

3

'WE'LL have to do something to celebrate. See you off in style,' Uncle Hamish had said, and Tom had thought he'd meant dinner at the Club and perhaps a visit to the theatre.

He had been horrified when Allie broke it to him that his twenty-first birthday and simultaneous departure for the navy were to be marked by a dance attended by all the yard's most valued employees

– accompanied by wives where applicable – plus the office staff. Which, said Allie cheerfully, was the only way of ensuring there were enough young ladies to go round. Did he have a young lady of his own he wanted to bring?

He didn't, not in Scotland, and she knew he didn't.

'Good,' she said even more cheerfully. 'That means you can partner the girls from the tracing office. It'll do wonders for morale. They all go into a swoon every time you pass by.'

'But ...' Even after three years at the yard, he knew the tracers only as an anonymous roomful of sensible shirtwaists and celluloid cuffs. 'Allie, I won't know what to say. I'm all right with girls of my own class – I mean, debutantes and old pals' sisters and so on – but *tracers*!'

'Well, don't say anything, then. Just smile sweetly and gaze down into their eyes. Remember, you'll be the boss some day, and in the meantime you're the handsomest young man they've ever set eyes on. So make a note. Saturday the twenty-fourth of April, 7.30 until 11.30. You might even wear your uniform and give us all a thrill.'

What a way to celebrate his coming of age, he'd thought, and failed to cheer himself with the reflection that it wouldn't have been much better at Provost Charters, with his father in Athens and no one in residence except Grandfather Albert, Natasha, and that spoilt little brat Nick.

But at least he could have nipped up to London and had a night on the town with some old pals, or taken Marjorie or Dolly to dinner and had a good, satisfying cuddle afterwards. It was a terrible strain on a chap, living in Scotland where the manners and morals of one's own class were so different from what they were in England; where one didn't even know what the other classes' morals and manners were; and where the brothels were good for nothing except a dose of clap.

He'd always been uncomfortable in Scotland, even when he and Matt, as boys, had gone up to stay with Uncle Hamish in Morar. Not that he'd shown it, of course. He'd enjoyed impressing the chaps at school with descriptions of his uncle's Highland shooting lodge; making them laugh with tales of how the grouse and blackcock, in the weeks before the Glorious Twelfth, strolled across the lawn with that knowing air of theirs, as if they were saying, 'Yah, boo! You can't shoot me. It's out of season.' Making a joke of the way the Highlanders treated 'English young chentlemen' as if they were beings from another planet.

145

As far as Tom was concerned, it was the Scots who were beings from another planet. They behaved as if everyone was equal, which was manifestly silly. He remembered one of the chaps at school – a bit of a bounder – who was always going on about something he called 'class distinctions', and wondered if that was why he had such a problem with the Scots. But he didn't think it was. It was more a matter of knowing where you were with people. Tom liked to know where he was.

The evening of the dance was cold, but at least it wasn't raining. Tom, impeccable in the smart new uniform that had arrived that morning from his tailor, stood inside the main door with Uncle Hamish and watched people arriving, his heart descending steadily towards his boots. In spite of all Allie had done with bunting and flags and flowers, a chill mist seemed to hang over everything. The gas lamps were harsh, the portraits gloomy and forbidding, the office doors unmistakably office doors. Even the guests looked depressing, the men so stiff that they might have been starched into their clothes, and the women in dresses that had evidently spent most of their long lives in mothballs. A faint smell of camphor began to permeate the atmosphere.

Uncle Hamish, as if he knew what Tom was thinking, said breezily, 'Don't you worry, they'll unwind after a few drams and an eightsome reel or two. And Connie's got a lovely buffet laid out upstairs, with a great big birthday cake. Your uniform's a good fit.'

'Thank you.' Tom tried to look as if it meant no more to him than any other new suit, but he couldn't resist shooting his cuffs just for the pleasure of admiring the single gold stripes on the sleeves. There was no doubt about it. Uniform did something for a chap. It was jolly decent of Uncle Hamish to let him go off to the navy when he was needed at the yard.

Determinedly virtuous, he spent the first half hour of his coming of age party listening to an appallingly well-informed discussion about war production between Uncle Hamish and his friend and competitor, the redoubtable William Beardmore. A German spy would have had the time of his life. At one stage, Tom thought Beardmore was going to blow a gasket about Kitchener's recruiting drive.

'Whit's the use of raising a million volunteers in the first six months of the war – jist you tell me that! – when half o' them would have been better here at home making arms for the other half to fight wi'? It's a fine thing when the gunners on the field of battle run out of shot and shell halfway through the forenoon. And maist o' that wasted, forbye! The men's that ill trained they couldny hit a barn door at ten paces. It's a shambles, the whole jing-bang, jist like everything else aboot this bloody ill-organised war. S'help ma bob, I could tell you . . .'

To Tom's modified relief, it was at this moment that a reproachful Allie materialised at his side. She didn't wait for a gap in the conversation; you could die of old age waiting for Willie Beardmore to let you get a word in edgeways. 'I'm ashamed of you all,' she interrupted. 'I'm sure Mr Beardmore didn't come here to talk shop . . .' Mr Beardmore, who, as she well knew, had come for precisely that, glowered at her, but she went on unblushingly, 'Come and let me introduce you to a lady who's dying to meet you. And Tom, I hope you know the steps of the "Flowers of Edinburgh", because Miss MacIntyre needs a partner . . .'

4

BY HALFWAY through the evening Tom was feeling pretty worn and was grateful when he found himself face to face with a shy, quiet, fair girl who didn't look as if she was about to do what most of his other partners had done, and put him through a stiff *viva voce* on his life history.

She didn't. She danced very correctly, and looked rather self-conscious, and scarcely said a word. So much so that he began to feel uncomfortable after a while and volunteered, 'I'm sorry, but I didn't catch your name when Miss Britton introduced us.'

'It's Jeanette Jardine, but I'm called Jenny. My dad's the foreman carpenter.'

'Oh, yes. How do you do, then, Miss Jardine?'

Jenny smiled nicely, if a little distractedly. She had the feeling that one of her stocking suspenders was slipping.

'How do you do,' she repeated. 'We've met before, actually.'

'Yes, of course,' he said.

It forced him to look at her more carefully. Fair, delicate complexion. Ordinary sort of nose. High cheekbones. Soft mouth, with a rather nice, kissable Cupid's bow. Big hazel eyes that were a surprise when she looked up and gave you the full benefit of them. Honey-coloured hair with wisps escaping from the coil at the back. Good figure, as far as it was possible to tell under the long, straight, tunic dress, whose dusky pink colour couldn't be said to flatter her. Neither tall nor small. She wouldn't have caused a head to turn in London, but she was a definite improvement on most of the girls here.

He still couldn't remember having seen her before.

Expertly, he steered her round a traffic jam caused by Uncle Hamish and William Beardmore who, to their partners' ill-concealed annoyance, were standing swaying in the middle of the floor with their discussion still going at full throttle.

'. . . availability of lyddite and TNT,' said Uncle Hamish.

Beardmore wattled like a turkeycock. 'Dinny talk to me aboot explosives . . .'

Tom said hopefully, 'The tracing office?' There wasn't anywhere else it could have been.

The girl said, 'Actually, I do work in the tracing office, but it wasn't there. It was a long time ago, when you and your brother were at the yard with your father. I was explaining all about puffers to your brother, and you came down to the fitting-out basin to find him.' She gave the tiniest of giggles. 'I thought you were terribly dashing and grown-up and good-looking.'

Then she blushed. In terms of the law according to Nellie Jardine, making personal remarks, even complimentary ones, was Not Done.

But Mr Tom didn't seem to mind at all. He smiled down at her warmly. 'I remember now. My brother said it was very interesting, what you told him about the puffers.'

'Did he?'

'Oh, yes. Honestly,' he lied.

'I met your brother another time, too. The night Mr Felix . . .' She stopped. It was hardly the kind of thing to talk about at a dance and, anyway, the memory of that night still gave her the shivers when she thought about it. 'How *is* Mr Matthew?'

'Matt? Oh, fine, I imagine. He's in the army. Dashed right off and joined up the week war broke out.'

'Did he? How funny.'

Jenny thought of the hundreds of men in cloth caps and bowlers and straw hats who had crowded round the recruiting office in the centre of Paisley when war broke out. And the posters saying, 'Your country needs YOU', with the picture of Lord Kitchener and his finger pointing right out of the poster so that it looked as if it really did mean *you*. And the processions through the streets, led by a few soldiers in uniform, with the bagpipes playing and hundreds

148

more men in ordinary clothes marching along behind, singing and cheering, on their way to take the king's shilling.

Jenny just couldn't imagine Mr Matthew Britton mobbing the recruiting office or singing in the streets. Maybe if you were a member of the ruling classes there was some special place for you to go and enlist, where you didn't have to queue.

Tom Britton said, 'Funny?'

'No, well . . . He didn't look to me like the kind of boy who would do that sort of thing.'

'Why not?'

'I don't know, really. I just didn't think he was awfully exciting.' Then, recognising what a singularly tactless thing it was to have said, she rushed on, 'Oh, dear, I didn't mean *that*! I meant – I meant, *excited*. I meant, not the kind of person who would get excited enough to do that sort of thing.'

Worriedly, she stared up at him and hoped she hadn't put her foot in it unforgivably – because Tom Britton, for eight whole years, had been the hero of her dreams, her untarnished and untarnishable ideal of young love.

She could still remember her first sight of him, the dark-haired, blue-eyed youth from another world who had strolled down to the fitting-out basin as if he owned the place. She hadn't known then that, one day, he would; or some of it, at least. He'd been tall for his age and she'd thought he had a tremendous air about him, looking so assured, so much at ease with his hands thrust carelessly in his pockets. Quite unlike his sulky brother, despite their physical resemblance. And even though his grin had been the grin of almost-a-grown-up dealing with children, she hadn't resented it at all. She had wished she could be grown-up, too.

And now he was even handsomer. His black hair had a wave in front, and his brows were very straight over the dark blue eyes. She didn't remember his nose being crooked; perhaps he'd had an argument with a cricket ball. But that, and the hint of a cleft chin, made his good looks quite unusual; in fact, she thought him heart-stoppingly wonderful.

She could have cried with relief to find that he was still smiling at her. More warmly than ever, in fact.

She didn't know, and couldn't have guessed, that Tom, who had been irritated by his brother for the first fourteen years of his life and envious of him for the last four, had conveniently forgotten how long it was since Jenny had met him, and was thinking how refreshing it was to come across a girl who wasn't bowled over by

149

young Matt's charm. She was really rather a nice little thing. He was beginning to feel as if they were quite old friends.

He said gaily, 'Oh, he can get excited, all right. I suppose he's a bit of a romantic, really, and I can tell you, it gives him some pretty funny notions. He even used to write *poetry* when he was a child, and I'm not sure he still doesn't.'

'Poetry? Oh.' This came out on such a descending note that Tom could have hugged her. Then she brightened a little. 'Like Mr Brooke?'

'Like who?' The valeta was coming to an end, and Tom hoped to God the next dance wasn't going to be another of those heathen reels. The place was feeling pretty overheated by now – except when someone opened the main door and let in a freezing blast – and Uncle Hamish had been right about everyone unwinding on champagne and birthday cake and sandwiches and whisky. He kept a proprietorial hand on Jenny's arm.

'Mr Rupert Brooke,' she said. 'The soldier poet. Some of his poems were in the papers a few months ago. I know two of them off by heart. They're terribly touching. Sad, but sort of – uplifting. "If I should die, think only this of me, That there's some corner of a foreign field, That is forever England." You know? Everyone was talking about them.'

'Oh yes, I remember now. No, I don't think Matt aspires to the heights of publication. Anyway, he's probably too busy for poetry these days!'

The orchestra came back to life.

'Good,' Tom said. 'It's a waltz.' He bowed gallantly. 'May I have the pleasure, Miss Jardine? And I must say, whichever corner of a foreign field my young brother happens to be in, he can't possibly be enjoying himself as much as I am!'

5

JUST after dawn the following morning, a bleeding, filthy, coldly sweating Lieutenant Matthew Britton was lying plastered against the side of a sandbank on a crimsoning beach at Gallipoli, his heart filled with the horror of death and mutilation, his head bursting with the smells of blood and smoke, his mind stupefied by the noise around him – the chatter of Maxims, the crack of field guns, the rolling boom of the naval broadsides; the flat, intimate thud of bullets biting into flesh; the screams and the moans; the no less terrible counterpoint of grown men whimpering for their mothers or their God.

All eternity seemed to have passed since the murmuring moment at sea when twenty thousand men, quiet and careful, had clambered down from their transports into the strings of open boats, to be towed inshore by a crazy assortment of coasters and trawlers and paddle steamers before taking to the oars for the landing. There had even been a converted collier whose captain took her in so close that the two thousand men on board could walk down the gangways slung along her sides, step into an anchored lighter, and cross over it as if it were a bridge straight on to dry land.

It must have looked good on paper.

But on paper there had been no Turkish regiment and no field battery ensconced on the ridge commanding the beach, raking the foreshore and the bay, volleying death at the men jammed in the open boats, sending bullets rattling like hailstones along the sides of the collier so that the soldiers on the gangways fell singly and separately, one after the other, like targets at a coconut shy. The name of the collier was the *River Clyde,* and the moment Matthew had seen it he had gone cold in his stomach and felt a presentiment of death.

There was no shelter at all on the wide, exposed beach, except behind the shallow sandbanks that followed the line of the water. They were only about four feet high, and several hundred un-crossable yards short of the first of the rocky gullies that climbed to the ridge of the plateau. Among the men clinging like khaki limpets to the seaward side of the banks were the remnants of the first group who had made the dash from the collier, about twenty in all. There had been two hundred of them to start with. The rest were strewn in the water, on the reef, along the beach, keeping company with the dead and wounded from the open boats.

Men were still coming ashore.

Matthew felt a sudden flurry behind him, and a corporal of the 29th, white of face, his uniform spattered with blood that didn't seem to be his, dived into the bank at his side just as a shell dropped half a dozen yards away, sending up a surge of shrapnel and wet sand and filthy sludge from the crater it made in the beach.

The newcomer spat the dirt out of his mouth and said un-excitedly, 'Cor-bleeding-Christ! Wot a welcome! Just like my old woman when I've been aht at the pub. Move over, mate!' And then he saw the pips on Matthew's shoulders and achieved a parody of a salute. 'Sorry, sir! It's like wot the preacher says, my eyes was blinded by the glory to come. Thought I *was* gone to glory back there.'

When Matthew, clinging to what he had been taught, said idiotically, 'Name and rank?' he could see the man wondering whether he was going to be put on a charge for insolence to an officer.

'Bonny, sir. William Bonny, Corporal.'

'Very good.'

He couldn't say, 'Thank you', although he could think it. He needed Corporal Bonny more than he had ever needed anyone in his life before; not because the man was all in one piece, but because he appeared to be capable of hanging onto his sanity even in the midst of raving bedlam. A rock. Not to cling to, but to give one a sense of solid ground under one's feet.

It was like some small, sudden miracle. Although Matthew's head was still swimming, though he was still feeling sick and his eardrums were bursting, although the horrors around him had not diminished, they seemed to be less oppressive than they had been a moment ago.

His mind even began to work again. When he looked at his watch, he discovered that it was only ten minutes since he had stepped out onto the gangway of the *River Clyde*; that although it had felt like an eternity, he couldn't have been lying for more than about five minutes with his nerves raw and his mind blank, holding the sodden field dressing from his kit against the wound in his thigh and wondering when someone was going to get them out of here.

A glance along the sandbank told him there were no other officers in sight, only privates and a couple of NCOs. A moment before, it wouldn't have meant anything. Now it did; it meant that, however little he relished the prospect, the 'someone' who was going to have to get them out of here was Lieutenant Matthew Britton, because there wasn't anyone else.

It made no difference that he was only eighteen coming up nineteen, spoilt, inadequately trained, and petrified. In the army's view, a year at Oxford had qualified him for a commission and endowed him with the right and the duty to tell other people what to do, even when their lives depended on it. Right from the start, he had thought it a queer way of looking at things. Queerer than ever, now.

6

THE realisation that it was up to him had a bracing effect.

'Got your breath back, corporal? You're going to have to help me get these men away from here and up towards the gullies.'

'Yessir.'

The Turks were riddling the beach with machine-gun fire just a couple of feet away from them, as if determined to get at the men crouched in the shelter of the bank, but the corporal didn't bat an eyelid even when a stray bullet cut through the lip of the bank and he had to shake sand out of his ear.

He had a solid, muscular face, with a down-turned mouth, eyes that verged on the boot-button, and short eyebrows sprouting like wings from the deep clefts above his nose. Matthew took him to be somewhere in his late twenties, and one of those men who prided himself on remaining phlegmatic whatever the circumstances. He was amazingly reassuring.

Matt said, 'You can see there's no cover on the beach except for the sandbanks, so we have to move away in order to leave them clear for the men coming ashore with the next wave.' And that sounded terse and decisive enough! 'Some of our fellows seem to have reached the gullies already. I don't know whether they landed before the shooting started, or whether they found a route from here. Anyway, let's see if we can follow them.'

Corporal Bonny said, 'Yessir. Wot about your leg, sir? Is it bad?'

'I don't think so. Messy, that's all.' Three cheers for the stiff upper lip. 'I doubt if I can walk but, all things considered, who wants to walk?'

Corporal Bonny made an indecipherable sound in his throat. 'You're right there, sir. Want to keep our heads down and proceed by means of alternating oscillations of belly and arse, like wot it says in the book.'

Matthew was astonished to hear himself laugh aloud.

About fifty yards to the right of where they lay, the bank curved inland in a way that struck a chord in his memory. If this had been Morar, he would have guessed at a freshwater rivulet descending from the hills and cutting itself a bed in the sand; and he would have expected the bed to form a kind of ravine, with the banks arching over into a bluff. If it was the same on Cape Hellas, the bluff could provide cover for the men to work their way inland to shelter. Even a little cover was better than none.

'Corporal,' he said . . .

Oscillating belly and arse as to the manner born, Corporal Bonny began making his way towards the bend, sometimes on the beach, more often slithering over the men lying against the bank. At one stage, Matthew thought he had been hit, but the burly figure emerged safely from the flurry of sand, and Bonny shook himself like a wet dog and proceeded stolidly on his way. It seemed a very long time before he reached the bend, vanished round it, and then reappeared to signal that Matt's guess had been right.

The problem, now, was to get the men moving. Waving and shouting and passing messages wouldn't do. Half of the men probably wouldn't move at all, and the others were only too likely to jump to their feet and make a run for it, which would be suicidal.

So, with a good deal of pain and difficulty, Matthew began dragging himself along the line. The first three men looked as if they wouldn't have a brain amongst them even at the best of times, but when Matt shouted to them what to do, they did it. When they had manoeuvred past him, he turned to the next man, whose pale face was puddled with blood from a scalp wound; he moved, too, and the next, and the next, and the next. After that, the men weren't lying singly but piled on top of each other, in layers.

It made things more difficult, because they had to disentangle themselves without straying into the Turkish field of fire while, all the time, the beach around was erupting with bullets and shrapnel and great gouts of sand from the shellbursts.

Even so, the operation wasn't going too badly until he reached a surly looking bastard with a patch of sandbank all to himself. He was older than most, and a dozen years older than Matthew.

Matt shouted at him, explaining what he was to do, but the fellow didn't move. He just stared.

Then, 'Move fucking inland?' he yelled back, as a machine-gun stitched a line of holes along the beach eighteen inches from Matthew's foot. 'On *your* fucking say-so? Stuff you, you little cunt-sucker! First fucking chance I get, I'm going fucking well out, not in.' And he jerked his thumb towards the sea and the ships of His Majesty's Navy, reeling in the recoil from a broadside.

Matthew was interested to find himself capable, even now, of disliking the man's foul-mouthed monotony, but if it had been a matter of insolence alone, even of disobeying an order, he would have let it pass, and to hell with Army Regulations. Today had disabused him of any idea that he was superior to his fellow men. He was just as plain bloody terrified as any of them.

But if this man disobeyed his order, others might, too. He could feel them all watching, and waiting. And if that happened, the men who landed from the next wave of boats would find no shelter, and there would be more carnage, more blood to be added to the oceans already spilled. And he, Matthew Britton, would be responsible.

It was not going to happen. He would have no man's death laid at his door, unless he willed it.

He drew his revolver and, sick with desperation inside, said steadily, 'You may take your choice. Do as I say, or I will shoot you here and now for mutiny in the face of the enemy.'

He thought for a moment that the man was going to call his bluff. He didn't even know, himself, whether it was a bluff, and never would. For several seconds they stared into each other's eyes. Once, the man even began to turn his head away, a contemptuous half-smile twisting his mouth. But Matthew put every last ounce of determination into his expression, clenching his jaw and setting his nostrils flaring, striving his uttermost to look like the fanatic disciplinarian he wasn't. Not for a moment did he allow the hand holding the revolver to tremble or deviate.

It worked, in the end. The man went. Snarling, and wilfully clumsy; but he went. Matthew had no sensation of triumph; no sensation at all except of a heart pounding like a steam piston.

Scarcely aware of the revolver still in his hand, of his gritted teeth and savage eyes, he turned to the next man and found that it wasn't a man, but a thin, pallid boy of about seventeen, shaking like an aspen, his face awash with tears. Matthew spoke to him, shouted at him, but, deaf with the deafness of panic, he didn't understand.

Matthew had always been told that the only cure for hysteria was to shock the victim back to his senses. So he raise his free hand and hit the boy hard, first on one cheek, then the other.

For a single, brief moment, the flow of the boy's tears ceased. Then he flung himself out of Matthew's reach, and lurched to his feet, and ran towards the sea. And before he had gone a dozen paces, was cut in half by a burst from a Maxim gun.

Three

1

HMS Indefatigable
Somewhere at sea
25 May 1915

Dear Miss Jardine,

How very kind of you to write to me with all the news of what is going on at home. You are quite right that we do not see newspapers very often at sea. They do, of course, come at the same time as letters, but by then they are too old to be interesting. Yes, the Zeppelin raids on the coast of England were very shocking, and the sinking of the *Lusitania* was a terrible thing, with all those innocent civilians drowned, but it is just what you would expect of Germans. That is why we are fighting them. We keep a sharp eye open for submarines here, I can tell you!

It was very interesting to learn that, even in Paisley, ladies like your aunts are beginning to drive electric tramcars and work in factories, though I cannot think it is right. The sooner the war is over and we can return to a civilised existence, the better.

It is very kind of you to offer to knit me some socks. Luckily, we do not seem to get our feet wet very often, but when winter comes I am sure I will find myself wearing several pairs all at once, to keep warm. I take a size nine.

I am sorry my own letter is so short, but I am kept very busy. I hope you will write again.

Yours sincerely,
T.B. Britton, Sub-Ltnt.

Miss Jenny Jardine to Sub-Lieutenant Thomas Britton

2 Rashilea Terrace
Paisley, Renfrewshire
30.6.1915

Dear Mr Tom,

Here are your socks at last. I am afraid I am not a very quick knitter, as you will already have gathered. What a pity it is not possible just to run socks up on the sewing machine! I hope they fit alright. If they are too big you can always wear them over some smaller ones.

I think of you very often and hope you are alright. Though I know it is quite exciting being at sea, it must be lonely as well as dangerous. I mean, I am sure you have made many friends on the ship, but it is not the same as being with your family and people you have known for a long time. Do you miss the shipyard, or does it seem very dull and ordinary to you now? I hope not.

Yours sincerely,
Jeanette Jardine

Lieutenant Matthew Britton to Sir Albert Britton et al

On the field of battle
July something, 1915

Dear Grandfather and Natasha (plus the brat!),

You've no idea how pleased everyone here is to get letters from home. If only the hostilities were as well organised as the postal services!

Anyway, it was good to have your news.

So Tasha wants to know what trench warfare is like, does she? Well, what happens is that somewhere around dawn you shoot off a few shells at the opposition – just to let them know you're coming – and then leap over the parapet of your own trench and run as fast as you can towards the enemy, whose nationality I cannot reveal without annoying the chap whose

157

job it is to censor this letter, but who have woken up and are standing in *their* trench taking potshots at you. The great advantage of their trenches being so near yours is that you don't have far to run.

With luck, you frighten them out of their trenches, which you take over with congratulations all round, wishing you had remembered to bring something to eat with you. After about half an hour, some other chaps from your side very decently come and take over so that you can go back to your own trenches for breakfast (where you discover that some thieving rotter has eaten your bully beef). After another half an hour, the chaps who relieved you come running back complaining that the beastly enemy has just pinched his trenches back again. So you say sympathetically, 'Oh, bad luck, old fellows!' and do the same thing all over again the next day.

And that, dear Tasha, is what trench warfare is like!

Now, what else? Oh, yes! Your little gifts to ease my life in the trenches are a constant delight. It's quite amazing to think that somebody, somewhere, should have been clever enough to foresee that the fighting soldier might one day find himself in need of a bullet-proof barometer! However, I hope you won't think me ungrateful, my most darling Tash, if I say that mad and misbegotten 'trench requisites', though fun, aren't a first priority out here. If you want to make me laugh, just send me Asquith's latest speech about 'our brave fellows' striking 'another deadly blow' at the enemy.

What I really need and want are large and continuing supplies of Oxo and Lemco. I know you think they are ruining my palate, but they're not half as ruinous as the water here without them. And by the way, Tash, are you *quite* sure the only place that stocks Oxo is Harrods? Have you tried the village shop?

Is father still in Athens? I'm glad to hear that Nick is growing so fast. Please keep writing. It means a lot.

All my love,
Matthew

P.S. Have you heard from Tom? He really must be the world's worst correspondent!

158

Sub-Lieutenant Thomas Britton to Miss Jenny Jardine

HMS Indefatigable
30 July 1915

Dear Miss Jardine,

Thank you very much for the socks, and I am sorry I have taken so long to write. They fit very well and are knitted beautifully.

In spite of all the discomforts, I am really enjoying being at sea. The air is a lot cleaner and fresher than it is on the Clyde, so I am feeling very healthy, although a little tired and short of exercise. One cannot go for a good long stride on shipboard, and of course I miss the shooting and fishing, too. But one has to make sacrifices.

Again, thank you very much for writing. Letters are always welcome, and with my father and brother being away and my stepmother much occupied with household matters, I don't hear very often from them. Of course, I do hear regularly from my cousin, Miss Allie Britton, and am always getting cards from old school pals.

I hope you will not think I am being presumptuous if I sign myself

Yours sincerely
Tom
(T.B. Britton, Sub-Ltnt.)

Miss Jenny Jardine to Sub-Lieutenant Thomas Britton

2 Rashilea Terrace
Paisley
Renfrewshire
18.8.1915

Dear Tom,

I am very pleased that you feel we know each other well enough by now for you to ask me to think of you as 'Tom' instead of 'Mr Tom' or even 'Sub-Lieutenant Britton', which is a bit of a mouthful besides taking up rather a lot of space! I do hope you will call me 'Jenny'.

I am feeling very proud of myself at the moment, because Miss Allie has just promoted me to be her assistant instead of working in the tracing office. She says I am so knowledgeable about the yard that I will be very helpful to her. I should not be boasting about it, I know, but I am so pleased that I can not resist telling you!

I have just begun to learn shorthand and typing, and she thinks I should learn to drive a motorcar, too, because you never know when it might come in useful. It is all very exciting.

We are tremendously busy at the moment, like all the yards. Since this time last year we have completed two light cruisers, five destroyers, six barges, two submarines and six torpedo-boat destroyers. (Oh, dear, do you think someone will censor that bit?) It is quite a lot, you must admit, though Beardmore's, Fairfield, and John Brown's are a little ahead of us. However, they are bigger than we are.

Mr Hamish says he does not know what will happen after the war, because with all the British yards working on warships, foreign yards are bound to try and steal our markets for merchant ships – among non-belligerents, I mean. However, there is nothing to be done about it, is there?

Miss Allie asked me to send you her regards, and says she will write soon. I must stop now, but I will write again soon, too.

Yours sincerely,
Jenny

Mrs Paul Britton to Captain Matthew Britton

Provost Charters
Dorset
September 10 1915

Matthew, my darling boy,

I cannot think where the time goes to in the English countryside, but you will understand that I do not write to you more often because there is nothing at all to say! Only what a neighbour tells me is called 'a chronicle of small beer'. The meaning of this I do not understand, since I know nothing of beer.

If one may speak of a chronicle of small consecrated wine, however, I must tell you that your Aunt Pearl has died. Her son

Howard telephoned to ask me to inform Paul, and I enquired (as one does) of what did she die? Of a broken heart, he said.

You will, no doubt, be enchanted to know that she forgave Paul before she died – *but for what*, I ask? Why do I know nothing of what is evidently some great drama in the history of the family?

Well, you were perfectly right about the village shop. I have bought you six dozen packets of Oxo, ten bars of Lifebuoy soap, some peppermints, cigarettes, pipe tobacco, matches and a few other minor items. One of the maids will pack them all up for you.

I am most hurt that you do not wish to have any more special trench requisites. Last week I saw some protective goggles made entirely of leather, with slits for you to see through, but since you are so ungrateful I did not buy them.

Your father hopes to be home soon, instead of chasing spies in Athens. Nick continues to grow. Sir Albert is well, though he complains often about the war, which prevents him from taking the waters at Baden. We suffer no food shortages, or anything unpleasant like that. Your brother has sent me one of those postcards where you cross out what does not apply. You know:

$$
\text{I am} \left\{ \begin{array}{l} \text{A 1} \\ \text{In the pink} \\ \text{Rather sick} \end{array} \right.
$$

It seems he is A1.

Why have you not sent me any of your poetry since you have been away? So sad that young Mr Brooke should have died. His work was quite inspiring. You must be inspiring, too, my Matthew, then you also will become fashionable.

With fondest love from us all,
Tasha

2

MATT couldn't very well write and tell her that plagiarising a bit of Gilbert and Sullivan was the most inspiring and fashionable thing he'd done during all the long months of fighting back and forth over the same few hundred yards of useless foreshore.

161

Dead bodies had been piling up all over the place, because there was no time to bury them and nowhere to put them, anyway. Even the trench walls were full to bulging point. There was one particular hand that kept poking out, a hand that seasoned campaigners had fallen into the habit of shaking as they struggled along the trench, declaiming in the fruity tones of some juvenile lead in a West End comedy, 'How do you do, my deah chap! How *are* you?'

After a while, the joke had begun to wear thin, and it had occurred to Matt to paraphrase a bit of *The Mikado*.

> Here's a how-de-do!
> Though we buried you,
> When your time had come to perish,
> Still your mem'ry we do cherish,
> Shake a hand, pray do!
> Here's a how-de-do!

Its success had been so instantaneous that, within days, it was adopted as a regimental ditty and unofficial marching song.

It might not be up to Mr Brooke's standards, but Matt had the feeling it was a song the singers would never forget. Those of them who survived.

3

HE HAD tried writing real poems, 'proper' poems, too, but had torn most of them up. Iambic pentameters and Petrarchan rhyme schemes were too ludicrously inappropriate in the context of this weird, bitter, intensely personal war, where you spent your days and nights separated by no more than fifty yards from thousands of enemies whose sole purpose was to kill you.

It had astonished Matt how quickly everyone, including himself, had become accustomed to living in hell on earth, hardened to the shelling, heat, dysentery, lack of exercise, lack of food; to the endless, raging thirst and nothing to drink but a daily tot of rum and water that tasted as if a corpse had been soaking in it; to being permanently filthy, with whiskers an inch long and feet that weren't out of their boots for a week at a time.

In some ways, the monotony was the worst thing. Day after day it was the same. Attack, counter-attack, counter-counter-attack, losing men all the time, never winning much ground or giving much away. Short of retiring into the sea, there was practically nothing to give away, anyway. And afterwards, the field telephone would ring insistently, and there would be some fat, clean, pedantic clerk on the other end wanting to know precisely how many rounds of ammunition each man had fired and then, as an afterthought, the size of the butcher's bill.

Even so, Matt found he never quite got used to going out twice daily in the expectation of being killed or wounded. It was a curious sensation; like having some Great Nanny in the Sky tell you to swallow your medicine like a good boy and it turning out not to be as nasty as you'd expected. Even though you knew that, next time, it probably would be.

Must be. Because wherever Matthew went, whatever he did, he did in the certainty that, very soon, the bullet with his name on it would find its homing. Justice would be served. It had been *his* impatience, *his* lack of perception, that had led to a panic-stricken boy being cut to ribbons during the landings on V Beach, and it seemed to him that there was no other way in which his guilt could be purged.

The fatalism that possessed him didn't, of course, silence his imagination, but it did help him to keep the fear tamped down somewhere among the convolutions of his guts where it didn't interfere with his thinking. And because he had fast reactions and a good brain, he was lucky, and went on being lucky. Behind his back, his men started calling him The Blessed Brit.

He didn't escape entirely, of course. He was blown through the air more than once, knocked out several times, and seemed to be forever shaking bullets out of his clothes. But it was always superficial, a matter of a little blood and a few bandages, and he succeeded in being extremely nonchalant about it all. In fact, he succeeded in being extremely nonchalant about everything. There was no reason, he had decided, why Corporal Bonny should have a monopoly on consistency.

4

THEY had landed on Sunday, the twenty-fifth of April 1915, their object to take Constantinople and divert Turkey's attention from Russia. In November, they were still exactly where they'd been when they started; still clinging to a couple of nail-pairings of the Gallipoli shore; still sharing the beaches with the dead, because there was nowhere else for either of them to go.

Lord Kitchener came out in person, then, and decided it was all a waste of effort. It was, the War Cabinet admitted, a pity about the quarter of a million British, Australian, New Zealand and Gurkha troops who had been killed or maimed in the meantime. But war was war.

The evacuation took place in December and January, without a single casualty. Matt had the feeling there was a moral there somewhere, if only he could think what it was.

Seven weeks later, his division exchanged the trenches of Cape Helles for the trenches of the Somme. They thought it was an improvement, at first.

Four

1

SUB-LIEUTENANT Thomas Britton was looking unbelievably hand-some in his naval uniform, with his eyes bluer than ever in the deeply tanned face and new little lines at his temples which crinkled when he smiled.

Jenny had been holding her breath for the whole of the four days since he had walked into Allie's office and announced that he was home on a week's leave before he had to rejoin his ship at Rosyth. Her heart hadn't stopped pounding, her palms were clammy, and she veered from moment to moment between extremes of agitation and bliss. She couldn't sleep, either, but that was all right because she didn't want to. Drowsing and dreaming were so much nicer. She wasn't herself at all.

Last night, he had taken her to the picture-house in Glasgow to see *The Birth of a Nation*, which had been very exciting, though not as exciting as sitting next to him in the darkness and letting him hold her hand. She had called to her mother that she was going to spend the evening at Iris's and scurried out of the front door before mum, who didn't even know that Tom was home, had time to say a word.

And tonight, Allie had allowed her to leave the office promptly, because it was a lovely evening and in late May you could get in a full round of golf before dark.

'Tom says he doesn't get much exercise on the ship.'

Allie had raised a quizzical eyebrow. 'Jenny, I know it's a bit late in the day, but be careful. I wouldn't like to see you hurt.'

Privately, Allie knew that Jenny was going to be hurt, whatever happened. Right now, the girl thought the sun shone out of Tom's eyes, but when the glory dimmed she was going to discover that Tom was really a very ordinary young man after all.

Or was she herself just being envious, Allie wondered, because she had never felt that kind of thrill? She and John Baine had walked out for five years and been engaged for another five before they'd finally been wed, just after war broke out. She was thirty-three years old now. Old enough to be a grandmother. And if the war didn't end soon and give her her husband back, she'd never even be a mother. But at least she'd known the man she was marrying, known that they loved each other enough in their own down-to-earth way to live together, not just tolerantly but happily, for the rest of their lives.

She smiled and said, 'And having done my duty by giving you a friendly warning, you can have tomorrow morning off, if you want. Tom's only got another couple of days and I'm tired of him prowling round the house like a bear with a sore head!'

'Oh, *thank you!*' Jenny, who had been brought up to regard self-control as the cardinal virtue, had to restrain herself from throwing the rules to the winds and hugging Allie for all she was worth.

2

AND now she couldn't believe it. They were on the fourteenth tee when Tom, as if struck by some great revelation, exclaimed, 'Gretna Green!'

She was halfway through her swing at the time, so it wasn't altogether surprising that she should have sliced the ball. In silence, their eyes followed its erratic flight through the air; in silence, they watched it landing on the edge of the fairway; in silence, they saw it trundle into the rough.

After a dazed moment, Jenny said, in a polite small voice, 'I beg your pardon?'

'Let's run away to Gretna Green and get married!'

Just then, the four players who were coming round after them arrived on the thirteenth green.

Tom teed up his own ball, addressed it, raised his club, and hit it any old how.

'Oh, dear,' Jenny said. 'Right into the bunker. You'll need your niblick.'

Tom glared at her. 'Damn the niblick! Did you hear what I said?'

'Yes,' Jenny said weakly.

They shouldered their golfbags and started walking.

'Yes, you heard? Or yes, you'll marry me?'

She opened her mouth, 'Yes, I . . . Do you think you should wave those people through? We oughtn't to hold them up while we're finding our balls.'

Teeth gritted, Tom turned and waved to the following party, who waved back, much obliged. Then he drew Jenny to the edge of the fairway.

'*Yes, you what?*'

If it had been one of his London girl friends he would have felt like throttling her for being coy. But his London girl friends were in the past, now, and this was Jenny, who probably didn't even know what being coy meant. Tom felt exasperated and warm and protective, all at the same time. Marjorie and Dolly hadn't even written to him at sea, but Jenny had, and though he had smiled at first, a bit condescendingly – because her early letters had been very stilted indeed – he had come to depend on them and, in a funny kind of way, on her. She had been the only person who *had* written to him with any regularity this last year, and she always made it sound as if *he* mattered. He'd had a few letters from Allie, brisk and brief and friendly; two self-centred notes from Natasha, which he could easily have done without; an occasional jokey card from one or other of his old school pals; and one communication from his father, now back at Provost Charters, which had been so redolent of paternal surprise over his eldest son taking so long to place his services at the disposal of King and Country that Tom had ripped it up and tossed it overboard.

Civilians just didn't seem to have any conception of what war was like. Except Jenny. She even seemed to know how a chap felt.

During these last four days Tom hadn't been able to stop thinking about her or do anything but wait impatiently until the hour came when he could see her again, share her lunchtime sandwiches at the office, walk part of the way home with her after work. He was ashamed now of having taken her to the picture-house last night; somewhere in the back of his mind he'd had the idea of finding out how far he could go with her, and then his conscience had reared its head and all he'd done was hold her hand. This morning he had waylaid her halfway down Rashilea Terrace and escorted her to the yard, because he had to be sure that their tiny intimacy of the previous evening hadn't, in retrospect, upset or embarrassed her. He recognised that he was wearing his heart on his sleeve, but he didn't care, because she was shy, and nice, and pretty, and adorably sane and sensible in this otherwise mad world.

And he had just realised that he loved her.

Anyone who knew him would have seen proof of it in the fact that he was behaving and thinking completely out of character. Certainly, if there was any warning voice at the back of his mind, he didn't hear it. 'A carpenter's daughter? An ordinary little typist! And what about that vulgar mother of hers? And the sister who's married to a grocer, and the trade unionist brother? No breeding. No money. What will your father think? What will your friends think?'

In a way, it was the golf course that clinched matters. After five years of living on the Clyde and aboard ship, Tom had become so accustomed to Scots accents that he no longer even noticed that his darling had one. He forgot, too, that golf in Scotland wasn't, as in England, a game only for the upper classes. And he didn't know enough about clothes to recognise that Jenny's trim brown-and-white-striped golfing outfit had been homemade from cotton at ninepence-three-farthings a yard.

What he did know was that there was something about her that didn't have anything to do with looks or class – a sweetness, openness, innocence and honesty, and a subdued but very real sense of fun. It seemed to him that he could take Jenny anywhere, and be proud of her, and if anyone had suggested otherwise he would have blacked the fellow's eye without a moment's hesitation.

He loved Jenny and, after a year of war, he knew that he needed her. He needed someone to be his; someone to come home to; someone to whom *he* mattered more than anyone else in the world. Other people had stable, civilised families to support and sustain them, but the Brittons had never been like that. Even Uncle Hamish and Allie, kind though they were, expected him to stand on his own feet. Which was asking a bit much of a chap. People weren't born to be solitary.

Jenny, her eyes like stars, said fervently, 'Yes, I . . . *Oh, Tom!*' just as he told her in a loud, authoritative tone, 'I think it went in just about here, didn't it? Let me help you look.' A second or two later, he was nodding a 'Yes, indeed! Fine evening!' to the four gentlemen as they strode past.

Obediently, Jenny bent her head and surveyed the rough, heathery stubble underfoot. The notion of marrying someone who, for years, had appeared to her very much in the light of a demi-god, was so dazzling that she couldn't quite convince herself that he meant it. Ever since she had begun to dream dreams of romance, Tom had always played the leading rôle. In those dreams he had kissed and embraced her, and then gone down on one knee to her. Not to ask her to marry him, but to explain why he couldn't. Their worlds lay too far apart. And Jenny – a practical and reasonable girl even in her dreams –

had understood, and thought their grand renunciation rather sad and very beautiful.

But this was reality. *Real* reality. And he must have meant it because he had come out with it so impetuously, as if he couldn't help himself. It was wonderful, marvellous, stupendous, glorious. She had never been so happy in her life. There was nothing in the world she wanted more than to be married to Tom. She didn't believe it.

3

WHEN the other players were out of earshot, she looked up at him and said, blushing, 'Yes, please, Tom. I would like to marry you. Do you really want me to?'

He couldn't hug her in the middle of the golf course. So he turned bright red, and pointed, and said, 'There's your ball. What'll you use? The brassie? *Oh, Jenny, will you?* Let's go tonight. I'll borrow Uncle Hamish's car. He won't mind.'

She breathed, 'Oh, yes!' and then she thought, 'Oh, no.'

She couldn't possibly run away to be married in a cheap cotton golfing dress and a woolly tam. She wanted to wear her new tailored costume with the flared skirt that came a daring three inches above her ankles, and the pale blue blouse, and the meringue-shaped hat, and the new flowered petticoat with the broderie anglaise frills on it, and clean *every*thing.

And even as she hesitated, something else occurred to her, and she felt duty-bound to point out that there was really no need for them to incur the expense of going all the way to Gretna Green.

It was only the English who needed to elope to Gretna, which was handily placed a few yards over the Scottish border, because in Scotland, unlike England, you could get married at sixteen without parental consent and without even a church or a minister. All the happy couple had to do, provided that one of them had been resident in Scotland for three weeks, was declare before two witnesses that they wished to marry. And that was it. They were married.

And the law was the same all over Scotland, so there was no real need for Tom and Jenny to run away at all.

Tom was a trifle dashed. Though it hadn't occurred to him before, one of the undoubted charms of running away was that they wouldn't have Jenny's mother to contend with. Repellent visions of rings, engagements, bottom drawers, displays of presents and white weddings flashed across his mind. It was enough to put you off the whole idea of marriage, especially when you were obsessed by a desire to hug Jenny, and kiss her, and make love to her *right now*, not six months or a year in the future.

Jenny, horrified by his expression, went on very hurriedly indeed, 'I didn't mean let's *not* run away. I just meant perhaps we didn't have to run away so far!'

His brow lightened. 'Of course! We could go somewhere much nicer. What a smashing idea!' And then, 'We could go to St Andrews or North Berwick and play golf there.'

She was too busy being relieved to realise that he was making a joke; he didn't make jokes very often. 'Oh, yes! And either of them would be much nearer Rosyth for you, too, when you have to go back.'

She really was a darling!

4

SHE had to let Jackie into the secret, because he walked in just when she was getting her suitcase down from the attic above his bedroom.

'Shhh!' she said.

'Whit are you wanting that for?'

She told him.

'In the name of the wee man! You'll be the talk of the steamie!'

'I don't care.'

Jack, momentarily bereft of words, stared at her – at his docile wee sister who never offended anyone, never even argued with anyone. Except him, sometimes. 'Whit's come over you? D'ye no' want to live? Mum'll kill you.'

'I know. But it's my wedding and if I want to run away I'll run away. Getting married's something private between Tom and me, and mum would just spoil it.'

'Well, that's true enough. But jings, she'll go off her tot!' He began to chuckle. 'Let me be here when she finds out!'

Jenny said obligingly, 'Do you mean that? Because I was wondering how to leave her a note so that she wouldn't get it too soon. You can give it to her tomorrow night, if you like.'

170

'Oh, thank *you*! Don't you play the innocent with me, my girl. D'ye think my head buttons up the back?'

She giggled. 'No, but will you? Honestly, I can't think of any other way of doing it. Unless you'd just like to break it to her for me?'

'Ye're a cheeky bizzim and ye'll go the Bad Fire if ye're not careful!' But he wasn't altogether joking when he went on, 'Though I tell you, it's only the fact that it's going to rile our mum that reconciles me to you marrying one of the bosses. It's asking for trouble marrying out of your class, and dinny come crying to me when you find out.' A hideous thought struck him. 'My God, he's no' a Catholic as well, is he? That would fairly put the lid on it.'

'No, he isn't. He'd have said if he was. And no, I won't! Honestly, you and your class-this, and class-that! People are just people and there are nice ones and nasty ones. And Tom's a *nice* one!'

'He can afford to be!' But Jack's face relaxed. Even if she'd got her values all wrong, she was still his wee sister. 'Away and do your packing, and I'll sneak the case out for you in the morning.'

She smiled at him gratefully and then began, rather abstractedly, to brush the faint film of dust off the suitcase with her bare hand. Dust wasn't allowed at Rashilea Terrace, even in the attic.

After a moment, her eyes resting noncommittally on her brother's Reserved Occupation badge, she said, 'Jackie, I can't ask mum, and I haven't time to go and see Iris, so there's only you. Do you know . . . I mean, do you have any idea . . . I mean, what do people do when they're married?'

He looked at her for a moment, uncomprehending, and then light dawned and he sat down with a twang on the bed and began to go through the motions of tearing his hair.

'Are you telling me you don't know?'

'No. I mean, yes. I mean, yes I don't know.'

He wanted to be sure he had it quite clear. 'Ye mean our mum hasny told ye anything?'

'No. All I remember is her saying to Iris last year that men enjoyed it and women just had to put up with it.'

'Aye, she *would* say that. And Iris hasny told you anything either?'

'No.'

'Surely some of the lassies at school must have blethered about it? In the playground or someplace. I know a good few of them that could give lessons.'

'*Jackie*! Well, if they did, I didn't hear them, or I didn't understand.'

He shook his head in disbelief. 'I'm jiggered! Ye wouldny think it was possible! And ye never thought to ask?'

'No. Well, it's not really the kind of thing you *can* ask, is it?' She was beginning to get annoyed. 'Anyway, I've always just assumed mum would tell me when I needed to know.'

It was easier being an unofficial strike leader any day. Some of Jack's mates on the Clyde Workers' Committee were in jail right now, and he wished he was with them. He groaned. 'All right. How far has your precious Tom gone?'

'Only up to the house at Castlehead,' she said, surprised, and then, observing that her brother was breathing heavily through his nose, put two and two together and added, 'He's kissed me. Is that what you mean?'

'No, that's no' whit I mean! Has he put his hand inside your blouse, or between your legs?'

'*Jackie!*' she went scarlet. 'Of course he hasn't!' It was modesty speaking, not awareness.

'Jeez-oh!' Stiff-necked and pig-headed though he was, Jack had a kind heart. He knew that he was probably going to make it all sound dirty because he couldn't think of any words that would make the mechanics of the thing fit in with women's fushionless notions of love. But he had to try. It wasn't fair to Jenny to let her land up in the marriage bed without a notion what to expect.

He said, 'Aye, well. See now, pet. It's one of they things that doesny sound awfu' nice when you explain it, but I'll try.' There was a long, long pause while he meditated. 'Aye. Well, here goes. It's like this, see. Fellows and girls. They're different – oh, suffering duck! – they're different shapes down here.' He indicated a point vaguely south of his middle, and hurried on before she could give the matter too much thought. 'Well, ye know *that*! Anyway, the – the bits jist sort o' fit into each other. And when ye both move about, it feels great.'

It wasn't the most inspired explanation of all time, and she looked at him as if she was hoping he didn't mean what she thought he meant.

Suddenly, he had a brainwave. 'It's like a cylinder and piston, when ye think aboot it. A steam pump. Basic engineering, that's all. You're the cylinder and he's the piston.'

She opened her mouth, but that was as far as Jack felt himself competent to go; he shook his head firmly. 'No, enough's enough. So long as ye've got the general notion, ye'll be fine. Tom'll be careful wi' you. Jist don't get a red face about it, or ye'll spoil your fun.'

She was still looking doubtful and, suddenly, it all became too much for him. His voice sliding up into something perilously close to a wail, he assured her, 'It's quite respectable, ye know. It is, honest! Everybody does it!' and then subsided into a wheezing, uncontrollable paroxysm of mirth.

Jenny, throwing a worried glance at the door, poked him vigorously in his black serge ribs. 'Jackie, will you shush! She'll hear you! And you wouldn't wheeze like that if you didn't smoke so much!'

But her brother's mirth was extremely catching, and after a moment she too began to giggle until the pair of them were rolling about on the fat feather quilt, gasping and hiccuping and hugging themselves to ease their aching ribs, while from over the headboard the steel engraving of John Knox glowered balefully down upon them.

Jenny only just had the presence of mind to kick the suitcase under the bed when Nellie Jardine came clumping up the stairs, demanding to know what all the noise was about and why Jenny wasn't in the scullery ironing the things that she, Nellie, had been slaving away all day washing, down at the steamie.

5

IT WAS bucketing the next morning, so Jenny had to pack her good costume. Her mother wouldn't have let her out of the house until she'd discovered why she was wearing it in such weather. Nor could she either wear or pack the hat that looked like a meringue, so she had to make do with her dark blue flannel costume and the navy felt hat with the feather. But none of it mattered.

Jackie left her standing with her umbrella up and her suitcase in her hand not far from the main road, at a spot where there weren't any houses, or nosey neighbours peering out from behind the lace curtains and castor oil plants. The speculative builders who'd put up Rashilea Terrace had started work not at the main-road end but at the far end, with the intention of working back from there. Unfortunately, they'd run out of money halfway, so there was a field-bordered stretch between the houses and the main road which had

173

its uses, especially for courting couples. Not that there were many of those in the terrace.

Jenny didn't have to wait long. After about five minutes, Tom drove up in Mr Hamish's 15.9 Arrol-Johnston Grand Tourer, silver-grey and satiny and stately with its cape hood up and the rain flowing smoothly off the flares of the bonnet and radiator.

She climbed in, and Tom kissed her and took a nine-point turn to get the motor facing in the right direction again. Then he told her that he had decided they ought to go straight to the Town Hall because it had occurred to him that it might be sensible to declare themselves man and wife in a place where somebody could give them documents to prove it.

Jenny thought it was very clever of him, and said so, then found herself chattering nervously all the way into town while he concentrated on his driving.

'Poor Jackie, the greens will be too wet for his bowling match this afternoon ... Don't the Fountain Gardens look nice? ... Did you know that the Town Hall is said to have risen in silence, like Solomon's Temple?'

Tom, negotiating the corner of Love Street, steered well clear of the electric tram lines and said, 'No. How did they manage that?'

'The masons dressed the stone off site and then carried it there and put it all together, just like a big jigsaw.'

'Very ingenious. Oh, good, we're here.'

Jenny knew one of the clerks, so they didn't have to prove residence, and there were so many hasty marriages these days that the man didn't even raise an eyebrow, but just told them to clasp hands and declare themselves married.

Then it struck Tom that Jenny needed a wedding ring, and ought to have an engagement ring, too, so they went and bought a plain, wide gold band, and a dainty little half-hoop of graduated diamonds in a chased setting. Tom's eye lighted on a solitaire that he thought was just the thing, but Jenny said shyly, 'It's lovely, but it's awfully big. I'd really rather have something I can wear all the time – if you don't mind?'

He gave in, laughing, and threw a possessive arm round her shoulders. 'All right, something you can wear even when you're washing the dishes! But when the war's over and you never have to wash the dishes, I'll buy you the biggest and most beautiful solitaire I can find.'

Jenny laughed back. As if she'd dream of putting even her dear

174

little baby diamonds in hot water and soda! 'All right, but I'll always love this one best.'

She kept the rings on and her gloves off when they left the shop, and sneaked a glance at them as she climbed into the motor to wait while Her Husband cranked the starting handle. Suddenly, she felt quite dizzy.

He got in beside her. 'Well! That's done! St Andrews, here we come. And with the weather like this, thank goodness for four-wheel brakes.'

6

JENNY had never been in a hotel in her life. She had only been away from home once, when the Jardines had gone to a boarding house at Brodick.

Her father said holidays were an invention of the Devil. You didny work, so you didny get paid, *but* your wife thought you could jist conjure up money out of thin air, to feather the nest of some old wifie at the seaside whose notion of 'full board' was kippers for breakfast and sausages for tea. No, thank you, said John Jardine; once was enough. And since Nellie had no more idea than any other wife how much her husband earned, her arguments didn't carry conviction.

Jenny couldn't imagine what her dad would say about a place like this. It must be awfully dear. And what was he going to say when he found out about her and Tom? She hoped he wouldn't be upset. Jackie had probably handed over her letter by now.

The hotel was huge and overpowering, a bit like the Town Hall smartened up with thick carpets and chandeliers and chairs covered in uncut moquette. The reception clerk was even snootier than the head sales assistant at Cochran's the Drapers, and addressed them as 'Sir and Moddom' as if he didn't believe a word of it.

The fact that Jenny was often shy with people who mattered to her didn't mean she was prepared to be condescended to by people who didn't. So, while Tom arranged things with the clerk, she stood and surveyed the reception lounge as if she wasn't really very impressed, and when she was sure the clerk was watching, allowed her eyes to rest disdainfully on the divot of mud some golfer had tracked in on the carpet. It gave her great satisfaction, as she and

Tom departed in the wake of a porter, to hear the man summon a minion and hiss at him, 'Dustpan and brush!'

And then they were in their big, comfortable room, and the porter had gone, and the door was closed, and she had nothing except the chintz curtains and electric light and the fine view of the links and the sea to divert her mind from the fact that she was married to her adored Tom and would just have to put up with whatever lay ahead, because he would enjoy it even if she didn't. It was an awfully big bed. Did it happen now? she wondered.

She raised her face obediently to be kissed, and it was a different kiss from the one he had given her last night. He was shivering a bit, too, and she thought the cold wind must have got into him. Then, just as she was running out of breath, he withdrew his lips and said, 'We ought to go down to dinner. Did you bring a pretty frock?'

'Yes.' Her sewing was much better now that Allie had said she could use her nice new treadle machine, and Allie helped with the fitting. Allie had very good taste.

'I'll find an empty bathroom and change there. Don't be too long! I'm ravenous, aren't you?'

Connie Britton had made some very nice sandwiches for Tom's lunch – with cold ham in them and butter on both slices of bread – but only enough for Tom. He had decided that, until the knot was tied, discretion was the better part of valour, so hadn't told the family what he was up to. Like Jenny, he'd left a note.

'Yes. I'll be quick.' Then Jenny stood on tiptoe and, for the first time, kissed Tom instead of waiting to be kissed.

He threw his arms round her waist, lifted her off her feet and swung her round in an excited circle. 'Whoopee! We're married. Jenny, I love you, I love you, I love you. Let's eat our dinner *quickly*!'

7

THERE was one thing about her wedding day that changed Jenny in a way that Tom, who scarcely knew his bride, didn't recognise and Jenny herself was only vaguely aware of at the time. It wasn't being in love, or getting married, or even the consummation that still lay ahead. It was the giving of that kiss.

Long afterwards, looking back, she could see how barren her childhood had been. No warmth, no embraces; no glow of maternal love. Nothing but self-discipline and self-containment. Until her dying day she would remember the time when, aged five, she had clutched at her dad's sleeve to attract his attention so that she could confide something to him, and her mother had said, 'Don't paw your father. He doesn't like it.'

The words hadn't chilled her at the time because she was too young to have any standards other than those of Nellie Jardine, and there was, too, a core in her of – what? obedience? fatalism? – that was to stay with her all through her growing up. Where people and relationships were concerned, she didn't question, she simply accepted, taking the world as it came, unaware of missing anything and certainly not unhappy. It meant that she had even been able to fall in love with Tom, and accept that he loved her, without it seriously impinging on her inner state of suspended animation, her feeling of being no more than a character in some interesting and occasionally amusing puppet show.

But when she reached up, voluntarily, to kiss him, when she made that one small gesture of independence, she put an end to eighteen years of mere existence and embarked on real life, with all that it entailed.

8

SHE WAS fizzing with happiness and excitement as they went down-stairs for dinner. Tom had told her she'd be the prettiest girl in the place, and she had said he would be the handsomest man, and they'd both laughed and uttered blushing disclaimers. And then they entered the hotel restaurant and discovered that every table seemed to be occupied by gentlemen with broken veins and ladies who looked as if their corsets were killing them, and not one of them a day under fifty.

Jenny nearly disgraced herself by giggling, especially when they passed one of the tables and its occupant growled in a port-pickled, terribly-terribly English voice, 'Pretty little thing, what!' Tom didn't help by nudging her to make sure she'd heard.

She was awed but, because Tom was there beside her, not in the least alarmed. She had never seen anything like the restaurant before – the white damask, the silver and crystal, the bright lights, the dozens of hurrying waiters. She had never seen a menu before, either, but her spirits faltered only for a moment because Tom said, 'Would you like me to order for both of us?'

What she ate she never really knew. There was a fish she hadn't heard of, and chicken à la something else she hadn't heard of, and a chocolate pudding with a French name, but it was all delicious, as much for its unfamiliarity as its taste. They didn't have fish very often at Rashilea Terrace, because Nellie Jardine was always suspicious of its freshness, while chicken was a Christmas treat in place of everyday rabbit, and pudding meant either jam roll or apple tart. The wine – which Jenny thought of and drank as if it were still lemonade – was heavenly, cool and refreshing to offset the rich sauces. And though it was strange not to find bread, jam, scones and cakes on the table, she supposed that after three courses people didn't really need them.

Tom said, 'You don't want coffee, do you?'

'Don't I?' She had never tasted coffee and it seemed a pity not to.

'No.' He shook his head at the waiter, and then looked at her and said huskily, 'Let's go up.'

9

THEY almost floated upstairs, and were scarcely inside the room before Tom had his arms round Jenny's waist, and was kissing her just under the ear and holding her to him very tightly indeed. Sensing – and, in her innocence, misinterpreting – the tension in him, Jenny thought she ought to show him there was no need to be nervous, so she waved both arms gracefully in the air, like wings, and in lilting tones declaimed, 'Soft eyes look'd love to eyes which shpake again, And all went merry ash a marriage bell'.

Tom raised his lips a quarter of an inch and said, 'Mmmm?'

'Byron. It'sh the bit about . . .'

He had no interest in Byron, so he placed his mouth firmly on hers and at the same time, very decisively, began to unbutton her frock. She would have liked to warn him that the inside ties always got themselves into knots, but she couldn't free her lips without struggling, and that wouldn't have been very polite. Anyway, he seemed to be managing quite well, because her frock soon dropped

178

to the floor, and he buried his face in the hollow of her shoulder, and put his hands on her waist, and they stood like that for quite a long time. Jenny thought how nice it was. She felt warm and comfortable and a little weak about the knees.

He stepped back after a while, still holding her, and his blue eyes, unusually brilliant, looked into hers as he said, 'Do you know what happens?'

She would have smiled except that she found she was smiling already. 'I think sho.'

'I'll be careful with you. I'll be gentle. I promise.'

'I *know* you will. *Of coursh* I know.' Waving an airy arm, she stepped out of the circle of her frock and reeled slightly. 'Oooh! Why is the world going round?'

He caught her, laughing, and exclaimed romantically, 'Love is why!'

'Is it? O-o-o-h, *yes*. It'sh love that makes the world go round. How silly of me.'

She thought it would be nice to stroke his cheek, so she did, and found herself swept into another embrace which left her breathless and vaguely mystified by the hard bump on his body just above where his legs joined. Then she forgot it as the embrace ended and he twirled her dizzily round so that he could take the pins out of her hair.

'One, two, three, four, five . . .,' he counted, tossing the pins over his shoulder as he did so. She didn't like to mention that they were going to have to pick them all up again, because she didn't have any spare ones. They looked untidey, too.

Reminded, she slipped away from him as he removed the tenth and last pin from the descending, honey-coloured coil and bent to pick up her frock. The world went round again, but strong-mindedly she ignored it and, shaking the frock out carefully, steered a slightly erratic course towards the wardrobe. Her bride-groom watched with his mouth slightly open as she struggled to turn the key. It didn't seem to want to be turned.

'What in God's name are you doing?'

She was surprised. 'I have to hang it up. It'sh very bad for clothes to leave them lying around. They get all creashed.'

'*Drop it!*'

'But . . . Oh, all right,' she said obediently, and compromised by laying it over a chair.

'*Come here!*'

She came.

179

He couldn't help laughing as she stood before him, wide-eyed and expectant and slightly and delightfully tipsy. So he gave her another hug and a quick kiss before he set to work and unbuttoned her waist petticoat. And after that he gave her another kiss and slid one hand down into the soft, warm silky space between her breasts, only to remove it because it had such an unsettling effect on him. Instead, he took her wrists and lifted her arms so that he could draw the camisole over her head.

It was made of some clingy stuff that attached itself to his sleeve and distracted him for just long enough to allow her to bend down and pick up a couple of hairpins from the floor.

It was too much. 'Will you stop it!' he yelled. 'How can I be gentle and nice with you if you won't let me do it my way!'

'Oh, Tom,' she said remorsefully. 'I'm sorry.'

'Would you just stand there!'

'All right.'

The neat, practical beige knickers had to come off, and Jenny got her foot tangled in the elastic and Tom's hands began shaking. Then the suspenders had to be undone, and the small pink corselet unhooked. By that time, all that was left was underslip and stockings, and Tom was almost crying as he took his wife in his arms and held her, pressing her body tightly against his. He scarcely knew what to do about the hot, molten throbbing in his loins, so violent was it, and when she stirred slightly in his arms he cried out desperately, 'No! No, don't move! *Don't move!*'

She didn't. She stood perfectly still, because that was what he wanted, but she said in a small, worried voice, 'Are you all right?'

He nodded, and succeeded in smiling, and after a few moments regained some measure of control, although he had no idea how long it would last. He didn't know how gentle he could be with this raging urgency inside him, but he was terrified of frightening her or hurting her any more than he could help.

He had intended to sit her on the edge of the bed and roll down her stockings, slowly and erotically, but he didn't dare. He had already seen what nice legs she had. So he said hoarsely, 'My darling, take your slip and stockings off and get into bed. I won't be a moment.' Then he turned away and began to tear off his own clothes, strewing them around him, cursing the buttons, unfastening the braces so hurriedly that they sprang up and slapped him and made his eyes water.

When he turned again, naked and covering himself with his hands in case she should be frightened by the size and stiffness of him, all he could see of his bride was two bare legs and a pair of neat, firm, rounded and appallingly desirable pink buttocks disappearing under the bed.

He gave a strangled moan of, 'What are you *doing?*'

Then he lunged across the room and hauled her out, and threw her on the bed and himself on top of her. And even as she squeaked, 'But my engagement ring fell off', his fingers were concluding their feverish exploration and he was sliding as smoothly inside her as if they had been made for each other. A brief gratitude washed through him even as he placed one urgent hand behind her head and the other beneath her, raising her hips and holding her while he drew back and thrust forward, once, powerfully, encountering resistance and hearing Jenny's cry of pain and shock, and then feeling the blessed yielding.

Sighing, shaking, he buried himself fully within her and dropped his lips on hers and murmured thickly, 'It won't hurt any more, my darling. Oh, my darling! Trust me.'

And because she was Jenny, she did.

That first time, the climax overtook him before he had managed more than two strokes and Jenny lay, and waited, and when his gasping was over, asked interestedly, 'Wash that it?' although what she really meant was, 'Ish that all?' She didn't know how she felt, other than sore.

But later, he was able to give more care to her, to ease her along so that she learned there was pleasure in it for both of them, even if she didn't quite understand why it excited Tom so much more than it did her. The first few times reminded her irresistibly of Jack's cylinder and piston, but after that it became more like a kind of rather nice massage and she thought she could see why, as Jackie had said, everybody did it.

And perhaps the abruptness of her initiation had been no bad thing. As she sensibly reflected, there had been no time at all for nerves or embarrassment.

10

THEY should have had only one night away, but Tom became alarmingly decisive and telephoned Allie and told her they were married and that his wife wouldn't be in to work on Monday because they were staying on in St Andrews. Jenny, he said, would come with him to Rosyth, where he had to rejoin HMS *Indefatigable* on Monday afternoon, and would then drive back to Paisley alone.

Yes, Admiral Beatty would be missing him, ha, ha! No, he had brought all his kit with him, so there was nothing to be sent on. Yes, the motorcar was running well and the weather on the east coast was fine and clear, just as you would expect at the end of May. Their room at the hotel had a splendid view of the golf links and the sea but, no, he didn't think they'd be playing. They – er – hadn't brought their clubs. And yes, Jenny and he were wonderfully happy and many thanks for Allie's congratulations.

Jenny was very brave when they parted; braver than Tom, if the truth were told. But she drove back to Paisley slowly and carefully, not even seeing the scenery that had been unsee-able because of the rain on Saturday, and sniffling most of the way to control the tears Jardines weren't supposed to shed. Though now that she wasn't a Jardine any more, but a Britton, she supposed she could cry when she felt like it.

The last place she wanted to go was home.

She and Tom, wrapped up in the present, had scarcely talked about the future. He had suggested, without much conviction, that she might like to go and live with his father and stepmother at Provost Charters, but she had recoiled from the idea; she couldn't possibly go there without Tom. So he had said she ought to look for a temporary home for them in Paisley or Glasgow, and that did seem to be a possibility, once he arranged some money for her.

But in the meantime, there was mum to be faced.

She went to Castlehead first, to return the Arrol-Johnston and make her peace with Allie and Mr Hamish, but there was no need. Allie greeted her severely with, 'Well, you're a fine one!' and then laughed and threw an arm round her shoulders and said, 'Come on in. Connie's produced a celebration supper, and there's a bed made up for you if you want to spend the night. You're one of the family, now.'

It was almost as if Allie could read her mind, because she said the next morning, 'Unless you want to stay here with us – and you're welcome to – I'd suggest you go home and settle things with your mother as soon as you've finished breakfast. And if you need an excuse to get away, you can say I want you in the office by ten.'

Jenny was in the office by half-past nine. There had been no delighted welcome home from her mother, but she had expected none. 'What will people think? That you couldn't wait to do the thing decently, that you *had* to get married!' And Nellie's horror of scandal was only too obviously reinforced by a sour resentment over being cheated out of her role as Mother of the Bride and deprived of the opportunity to boast of her daughter's splendid conquest and her rich and influential new relations. Including a Sir.

Jenny had been prepared, and was able to face it with a semblance of calm and her head high. But she was shuddering inside, and when Nellie Jardine turned maudlin – 'Could you not have told *even your own mother?*' – she began to feel genuinely queasy and said, 'I have to get to the office. If you want to talk about it, you'll have to wait till tonight.'

Tuesday evening, Wednesday morning, Wednesday evening, Thursday morning. It seemed as if her mother would never let it go. Jenny went to bed at night exhausted, and it took hours before she was able to wipe the unpleasantness from her mind and fall asleep, smiling, with her memories of Tom.

But then, at teatime on Thursday, her father paused in the middle of plastering rhubarb-and-ginger jam on his scone and said in the tone that halted even Nellie in her tracks, 'Will ye stop girning, wumman! Folk would think all ye wanted was to ruin the lassie's happiness. Well, Tom Britton may no' be the man I'd have picked for her, but she isny a bairn and she isny a fool. If my wee lassie's happy, that's all that matters. So jist hold your wheesht. What's done is done, and I dinny want to hear anither word aboot it.'

Nellie Jardine folded her lips and retired into the sulks. It was a great improvement. So much so that Jenny woke next morning thinking how silly she had been to let her mother get her down; it had almost made her forget how happy she was.

Defiantly, she put on her best gingham shirtwaist and the white pudding-basin hat, and set out for the office on her bicycle. It was the second day of June and there was a slight, balmy breeze from the south-east that had spring-cleaned away the smoke of the shipyards and factories and left the sky blue and almost clear. Jenny waved blithely across the road at old Mrs Cowan, and wondered if the sun was shining at Rosyth, too. Raising her left hand to her lips, she dropped a little kiss on her rings, and then began to warble, *Keep the Home Fires Burning.*

But the words were far too melancholy, and she soon changed to *Rule, Britannia! Britannia rule the waves! Brit-t-ons never, never, never shall be slaves!* It wasn't easy to sing an extra 't' into 'Britons' but she managed it somehow.

The relief was enormous. Now she could start thinking about the future instead of wasting energy protecting herself against her mother. And today, at the office, she might even manage to get some of the torpedo-boat destroyer estimates done for the Admiralty, if Allie didn't have too many letters for her to type.

Allie hadn't arrived at the office, which was unusual. She was always there on the dot. Oh, well. . . Jenny took the cover off her typewriter and began on the estimates.

It was almost midday when Allie appeared, when she walked through the door, and took off her hat. When she nudged her hair into place in front of the little mirror in the corner, and then stood for a moment with her back turned. When she didn't respond to Jenny's mock-censorious greeting, but went to her desk, and sat down, and folded her hands before her and looked at them.

When she raised her eyes again and said, in a voice that wasn't hers, 'Jenny. . .'

11

'JENNY, I'm afraid I've got bad news for you.'

It didn't occur to Jenny that it had anything to do with Tom. She had kissed him goodbye on Monday and today was only Friday. So she said, mildly worried rather than frightened, 'Yes?'

'There's been a big naval battle on the Jutland Bank. The whole of the Grand Fleet . . .'

Allie stopped as if she couldn't go on, and Jenny knew then that it was the end. The end of everything before it had even begun. She knew it while her skin prickled and the small of her back went cold, and she thought, no. Please, no. No. No. No.

She knew it even while she fixed her eyes on Allie, willing her to say that this had nothing to do with Tom.

Throatily, Allie went on, 'Jenny, the *Indefatigable* was sunk.'

Into the long silence, Jenny said, 'Survivors?' Her voice sounded far away and very thin.

But Allie just sat there opposite her, white as a sheet, the knuckles of the hands clasped in front of her looking like bare bone. Her cheeks were hollow and there were tears in her eyes.

'A few. But not Tom.'

'They'd take to the boats. He'll be in one they haven't picked up yet.'

Allie met her gaze. 'A shell hit the magazine and the ship rolled over and went straight down. They didn't have time to take to the boats.'

Jenny leaned shaking elbows on her typewriter and pressed her fingertips hard against her forehead. Her chin was shaking, too, but she stopped that by clamping her lips between her teeth. She wasn't going to cry because it was wrong to cry in public and, anyway, it would upset Allie more than she was upset already.

She felt a hand on her shoulder. 'It would be quick, Jenny. And drowning is the friendliest death. Remember that.' Allie's grip tightened a little. 'Now – I don't know what you want to do, but I've sent to the carpenters' shop for your dad.'

'Thank you.' There was a little cut glass jug of bluebells on Allie's desk. Jenny hadn't noticed before what an intense blue they were. 'When did it happen?'

'Wednesday. Admiral Jellicoe had news on Tuesday that the German High Seas Fleet was up to something, so the Grand Fleet went out to meet them. Beatty's battle-cruisers from Rosyth, and Jellicoe with the destroyers and cruisers from Cromarty and Scapa Flow. Then there was the battle.'

'Who won?' She ought to care, but she didn't.

'Nobody. Nobody won. But we lost fourteen ships and there were six thousand men killed.'

Jenny looked up at that. '*Six thousand*! Oh, Allie, how dreadful!'

'Yes,' Allie said. 'And all in four or five hours. Think how much better they could have done if they'd taken more time to it.'

Her tears looked as if they were about to spill over.

It was only then Jenny remembered that John Baine, Allie's husband, had been with the fleet at Scapa Flow. Falteringly, she said, 'Allie, what about John?'

The other woman stirred slightly.

'John? Oh, he's gone, too. The *Warrior* took such a battering that she sank halfway home. I don't even know whether my man was drowned or blown to bits.'

12

'JENNY, my poor lamb,' John Jardine said, and held out his arms.

Despite his aloofness from life at Rashilea Terrace, which had become more pronounced over the years, Jenny had always loved him and knew that he was fond of her. So she rose to her feet, and went to him, and stood in the circle of his arms with her face buried in his shoulder.

He looked at Allie. 'And John Baine, too, I hear. A fine man. A sad loss.'

Allie's head was slightly bent and she was running the tips of two fingers over her eyes to smooth away the moisture in them. 'Thank you. And another seventeen men who used to work here at the yard. Willie Maxwell, Jim Kennedy, Geordie Allen . . .'

'Never! Och, that's terrible. There's no doubt? There's been nothing in the papers.'

'No, there wouldn't be, not yet. My father was talking on the telephone to one of our suppliers at Burntisland last night, and he'd seen the ships limping back to Rosyth. You can't keep that sort of thing quiet. So my father telephoned someone he deals with at the dockyard. They knew the worst by then, but we didn't have confirmation until this morning. I've spent most of these last hours breaking the news to the men's wives. And I've spoken to the minister. He'll do what he can for them.'

John Jardine shook his head and the long, silky moustaches brushed his daughter's cheek. 'You'd no need to do all that. You, wi' your own loss to bear.'

Allie sighed. 'They're our folk. I couldn't leave them to the clatter of the knocker and the boy with the telegram.'

Jenny had a faint perception of what Allie must have been through. Her voice half-muffled in her father's shoulder, she said, 'Where do you find the strength?'

'You can find the strength for most things, if you have to.' It wasn't a boast, or a rebuke, or an assurance; just a flat statement.

Then her tone changed, as if that was a subject on which there was no more to be said. 'Now, John Jardine, what are we going to do about Jenny? You can tell me to mind my own business if you want, but I think she'd be better staying with me for a few days, rather than go home.'

John Jardine, feeling his daughter move slightly in his arms, interpreted the movement correctly. Already, in his mind, he could hear Nellie going on, and on, and on. A judgement. A judgement on Jenny for running away with a man. That, interspersed with displays of unconvincing sympathy. Nellie wasn't a bad woman, or even an unkind one. It was just that some time, somehow, her own human values had got submerged under the dead weight of the values she aspired to. She didn't recognise real feelings any more, not even her own. There was an American fellow who drew comic strips called 'Keeping up with the Joneses' and it was Nellie to a T.

'Would you no' rather be on your own?' he asked.

Allie shook her head. 'I wouldn't be suggesting it if I didn't think it might help both of us.' Which wasn't altogether true, but it would have been on her conscience for the rest of her life if she'd let Jenny go back to that mother of hers. For a moment, she felt a healthy flush of annoyance with John Jardine for marrying such a woman, which was ludicrous, since the child was Nellie's daughter as much as his. Heredity was a queer thing.

'Jenny?'

'Yes, dad, please. I'd like to stay with Allie, if you don't mind.'

He found it sad – though he had no feeling of responsibility for it – that home should seem such an unwelcoming place to her, but he said, 'Fine. Tell me whit you need, and I'll get Iris to pack it for you and take it up to Castlehead.'

Allie nodded approvingly.

It crossed Jenny's mind that her mum would probably never speak to her again. But it didn't matter. Nothing would ever matter again.

She didn't even have a picture of Tom to remember him by.

187

Five

1

AT ground level lay the marshy lagoons of the Somme, set in a valley pocked and cratered like some landscape of the moon but streaked with green in spite of everything. In June, nothing in the world could stop the grass from growing.

Above was the wide, wide arch of the sky, blue and torrid, where larks in the morning sang in counterpoint to the whine of shells, and the wind sighed as it combed and teased the gun-smoke gently across the firmament, from horizon to far horizon.

The sky was yellow now, and in the west lay the glowing embers of the day. Another day gone, another day survived. Somewhere in the British trenches, someone was playing *Pack up your troubles in your old kit-bag* very slowly on a mouth organ; it was a meagre, mournful sound.

Underground, twenty steps down from the gas-blanket door that shut the dugout off from the main trench, Captain Matthew Britton was sitting on a box at a rough table with maps and notes and brigade reports scattered before him and an indelible pencil behind his ear. He wasn't alone, but in war no man ever was, except in the privacy of his mind or his death.

Over in one corner, Lieutenant Keith Whalley had his lanky length stretched out on the wire-netting and sandbag contraption that passed for a bunk, his crooked, whimsical face bent over a letter from home. Sergeant Bonny and the cocky new transport officer, Sam Simmons, were similarly engrossed, sitting like badly matched bookends back to back against the wooden prop supporting the roof, while Second Lieutenant Conyers Middleton, clever, opinionated and deplorably untidy, had one hip hitched on the corner of Matthew's table.

The atmosphere was a suffocating compound of dampness and chloride of lime, of mud, sackcloth, cooking grease, sweaty flesh, and unwashed clothes. The only light came from a couple of candles that conjured up baleful, moving shadows out of the stinking dark. Everyone was suffering from sore feet and trench mouth and indigestion.

Con Middleton, scanning what was known officially as the Corps

Intelligence Summary but unofficially as *Comic Cuts*, suddenly said, 'Hark at this. They're going to put up a memorial to Kitchener when the war's over. It never ceases to amaze me, the effect dying has on the reputation of public figures. Kitchener hasn't had a sou's worth of influence this last six months, but just because he manages to get himself drowned, he's everyone's hero again.'

No one paid any attention except Matthew, who said, 'Middleton, if you insist on sitting on my desk, for God's sake sit still.'

A fat grey rat emerged from behind a pile of sandbags and squealed like a baby trying to attract attention. Absently, Sergeant Bonny picked up the throwing-at-rats boot and threw it. The rat sat down and licked its paws and then retired, sneering.

There was a crump ten feet above them. Fritz passing the time of day, or a British shell dropping short. Matthew upended his tin mug and shook out some crumbs of chalk that had fallen from the ceiling.

All life seemed to be suspended here on the Somme in June 1916, because the really serious fighting was going on a hundred miles to the south-east, in the Verdun salient, where the French, even after seventeen weeks of bloody battle, were still standing fast against the Germans. Pétain had said, 'They shall not pass', and it was no secret that, to date, two hundred thousand of his men had died to make that promise good. But there were rumours that, very soon, there was going to be a Big Push elsewhere, and the likeliest 'elsewhere' was right here.

Matthew tipped the last of the whisky into his mug.

'Well, I never!' said Sergeant Bonny. 'My mum says there's twenty-seven buds on 'er rose bush. Wot abaht that? Wonderful wot you can do on that 'orrible old London clay!'

Knowing it was expected of him, Keith Whalley murmured, 'Yair. But you want to see what you c'n grow in Sydney, mate.' He didn't even bother to raise his eyes.

Matthew scarcely heard them.

His father had written, 'One can only conclude that the so-called Battle of Jutland was a grossly mismanaged affair from start to finish. I have been unable to discover any details of your brother's death; I am told that less than a dozen survivors were picked up out of the *Indefatigable*'s total complement of 1031 men and officers, and that none of them can provide any information on the matter. We are all, of course, deeply distressed.'

Poor old dad, Matthew thought, having to admit to emotion. Will he be 'deeply distressed' when I go, too?

'It will surprise you, no doubt, as it surprised me, to hear that Tom chose to marry two days before he rejoined his ship, without deigning to inform anyone. Fortunately, there seems to have been no question of compulsion. Most ill-judged, however, and of course it leaves his affairs in some disorder. One must feel sympathy for his widow, Jeanette . . .'

Matthew took another gulp of whisky and, remembering Tom's taste in girls, reflected that Jeanette would get over it fast enough. What had those dashing debutantes of his been called?

'. . . who is very young – only eighteen – and an employee of the yard.'

And that was a different kettle of fish.

'Whatever my personal feelings about Tom's choice of bride, family duty compels me to insist that she come here to Provost Charters to live. As I am sure you will agree, it would be most unsuitable for your brother's widow to continue typing letters, or whatever it is she does, in the family business. Fortunately, Hamish says she is perfectly presentable.'

Matthew almost felt sorry for the girl.

'I imagine you will wish to send her your condolences. You may address them to her at Provost Charters, as I have suggested she come here as soon as can be arranged. In the meantime, I hope you are reasonably well and not at the Front somewhere. Natasha and Nicholas send you their love. I remain, Your affectionate father, Paul Britton.'

Matthew said, 'Bonny! Get out another bottle. And smartish!'

He was feeling slightly light-headed already, but it didn't matter because it was Keith Whalley's turn to go out with the wiring party tonight.

Reminded, he removed the pencil from behind his ear and made a note to indent, yet again, for new wirecutters. The ones they were using were as blunt as butterknives.

2

TOM. Dead. *Thy brother Death came and cried, wouldst thou me?*

Alas, poor Tom. Clean, decent, upright. A pleasant, kind-hearted, conventional chap, with ordinary good looks, ordinary charm, ordinary intelligence, and an ordinary assortment of human virtues and vices.

The army would have suited him better than the navy. Matthew had watched young subalterns just like Tom go out to die in hundreds, and knew that in the wider scheme of things they had done so in tens of thousands, most of them sprigs of the nobility and gentry. *Debrett's Peerage* had had to postpone publication because it couldn't keep up with the casualty lists.

He sighed to himself. Strange the things one remembered; small things. Such as how much of his own eighth year he had spent pussyfooting round the withy plantations with a pigeon's feather in his hair and a cardboard tomahawk in his hand, just because Tom had been obsessed by Kingston's *Adventures in the Far West*. Matt, whose tastes ran more to the 'Lays of Ancient Rome', would rather have been playing Brave Horatio, Captain of the Gate.

He had no idea how other brothers got on. He and Tom had never been close, but although they had irritated each other, they had enjoyed a kind of companionship and an occasional closeness. Until, he supposed, Tasha had arrived and driven a wedge between them. It hadn't been her fault.

He was going to have to write to Jeanette, as he had learned to write to so many grieving widows. 'Dear Mrs So-and-So, As your late husband's commanding officer, I write to offer you my deepest sympathy and that of all his comrades in the Company. Your husband's bravery, selflessness and devotion to duty were as outstanding as his cheerfulness in the face of adversity . . .'

Where the hell was that bottle? 'Bonny! Get a move on, damn you.'

'Yessir.' The sergeant's voice floated out from behind the pile of sandbags that protected the Company's rum ration and the officers' small private store of delicacies from prying eyes and thieving fingers. 'And wot abaht the Gentleman's Relish, sir? Shall I get it out for tonight? It's the last pot.'

'I suppose so.'

There was a mouse burrowing in the sugar basin, head down, rump in the air, gorging itself. Matthew eyed it morosely.

Dear Mrs Britton, As your late husband's brother, I write to offer you my deepest sympathy and that of all his comrades in the Company of life. Your husband's bravery, selflessness, and devotion to duty . . .

Bonny's hand plucked the mouse out of the bowl. 'Will you have your meal now, sir?'

'Go to hell.'

'Yessir. Tea or Oxo, sir?'

How could he write to the girl? What could he say? 'Bonny, why are you doing the mess orderly's work?'

'Stow's down at the dressing station, having his foot seen to, sir.'

'Oh, very well. Thank you.'

Dear God, it was Tom who had gone now, like all the others. His brother Tom. His brother Death.

3

HE spent the watches of the night inspecting the sentries, worrying about the wiring party, and making a brief and foolhardy foray out into no-man's-land to see how they were getting on.

And then, as the darkness thinned, he stood for a while in one of the trenches and stared out over the bleached sandbags at the white seams marking the Boche positions on the facing hill, and the ghostly, leafless, limbless trees; at the pale and derelict road wavering its way into nowhere; at the craters filled with stagnant water and the tangles of wire and the drunken posts that held them up.

The dawn chorus began at last, and it was stand-to, with tots of rum all round as the white sky flushed pink, and the rats scuttled along the parapets, and the dandelions opened along the rims of the communicating trenches and the poppies reared their blood-red heads out of the morning mist.

4

ON THE twentieth of June, ten days before the date everyone was betting on for the Big Push, Matthew's brigade commander gave him permission to go up with a pilot of the Royal Flying Corps to have a look at the division's gun positions from the air.

A number of staff officers had been trying to persuade the Brigadier for weeks past that, with Boche reconnaissance planes so active, camouflage was necessary, but it had taken a direct hit on one of the batteries and a couple of near misses to convince him that Fritz hadn't just struck it lucky and that these new-fangled flying machines might not be the irrelevant toys he had always thought them. Dangerous toys, so he sent his youngest and most expendable captain.

Matthew was more than willing, not only because it made a change from the trenches, but because he had begun to develop an interest in aeroplanes in the Dardanelles, mainly thanks to Bonny, a mechanic in civilian life.

The pair of them had been down at the small sheltered area of V Beach euphemistically known as the Rest Camp, Bonny with his face blackened by a blow-back from one of the howitzers and his left arm tied up, Matt recovering from an attack of malaria that was troubling him less than the fact that he seemed to be itching everywhere, from the whiskers on his chin, via a thousand or two insect bites, to enough half-healed minor injuries to stock the entire out-patients' department of a London teaching hospital.

They had been sitting staring out to sea, yearning for a swim, when Bonny exclaimed, 'Cripes! An 'ydroaeroplane ship! With a couple of seaplanes aboard. Short 184s, by the looks of them. Little beauties. Wot I wouldn't give to be up in one o' them!'

It was the first time Matt had ever seen Bonny display emotion, and he was sufficiently intrigued to follow it up, even though, to start with, the corporal's unholy dedication to his subject reminded Matt forcibly of the girl at the shipyard and her beastly puffers. But perhaps because the circumstances were so very different, or because he had always found more beauty in the sky than in the sea, he found himself beginning to take note of what the boys of the Royal Naval Air Service and the Royal Flying Corps were up to.

Now, the opportunity of actually going up in a plane was far too good to miss. Scrounging a lift in a staff car, a stately 25 horse-power Vauxhall D, he arrived just after first light at the straggle of huts, tents and aeroplane sheds that comprised the aerodrome of Bertangles. He was clad, as instructed, in his warmest clothes and two pairs of gloves, and the pilot handed him a leather flying helmet and goggles, saying, 'Cold up there, and you don't want an eyeful of oil from the engine. Let's go, before Fritz starts cluttering up the skies.'

It was tricky squeezing into the observer's place through the forest of wires and the struts that held the upper and lower wings in position; and although Matt had known – in theory – that the body was just linen stretched over a slatted wooden framework, he found it disconcerting to see the neat, blanket-stitched seams running along the sides. What a frail thing it was, to venture into the heavens! It was the first time he had ever been in, or even near an aeroplane and he found himself reflecting, with amusement, on the gap between theoretical knowledge and physical actuality. In no way did the machine resemble the winged motorcar of his imagination. He wasn't even sitting behind the driver.

He twisted round. 'What kind of aeroplane is it?'

'Aeroplane?' There was surprise in the young man's voice. 'This isn't an aeroplane. It's the decision-making half of a suicide pact. The only reason we're still here is that she's trying to keep me guessing whether the prop or the joystick'll go first.' He was studying the dashboard controls as he spoke. 'BE.2a and government-designed, if you really want to know. Slow, and uncommonly hard to manoeuvre. The tail falls off if you try to be too clever. Clyde built.'

'Help!' said Matthew, only half-humorously. 'Let me out of here!'

The pilot laughed. He was about the same age as Matthew, and his name was Ben. 'Belt yourself in. We'll do a few stunts later and hope the boss isn't looking. Can't resist 'em on a lovely morning like this.' He tied his chin straps. 'Right, we're ready to go.'

'Great.'

'Don't be too sure. You'll sing a different tune if we meet one of the Fokkers. They've machine-guns mounted and, as you may have noticed, we haven't, though one of our chaps damn' near shot himself down the other day in a Bristol Scout. Loosed off with a Hotchkiss, and the synchronising gear wasn't working, so he sawed his propeller in half. Got your revolver?'

'Are you joking?'

'No. You won't hit anything, but it'll make you feel better. Nothing more frustrating than sitting in an unarmed plane being potted at by someone with a Spandau. Always carry a rifle myself.'

Then the engine caught, and that was an end of conversation, although they hung about for five minutes before Ben yelled, 'Chocks away!' and the mechanics stood clear, and they started to zigzag over the bumpy turf. Matt was wondering if they were ever going to get airborne when the plane lurched off the ground onto the smooth highway of the air.

The weather was perfect and visibility excellent, because most of the smoke from the big guns had dispersed during the night. Matthew could scarcely believe it. It was wonderful, glorious, incredible. After the trenches, the air was like champagne. He hadn't breathed anything so pure since he was last in Morar. What wouldn't he give to be over Morar now! Over that dark and silver sea, the pure white sands, the seal islets, the amethyst hills. It must be a magical sight from the air. Strange that he hadn't thought of Morar since the war began.

The plane, whatever Ben said about it, seemed to be climbing quite fast, and the sheds soon dwindled into children's playthings while the valley itself spread out before them like a great rippling, falling sheet of green cut-velvet with, traversing it, the wide and ragged ribbon of the Somme.

It was amazing how many patches of trees were still standing, how many fields under cultivation; how many tranquil clusters of toy houses and farmyard animals there were only a few miles to the west, where the shelling hadn't reached. And the large cluster to the south, the one they were leaving behind as they banked into a turn, must be Amiens.

Something poked him in the back and he turned to discover it was the business end of Ben's rifle. The pilot grinned at him, and then mimed that he should hang onto his hat. So he did, and Ben began practising stunts, looping the loop, doing nosedives and any number of other tricks Matthew didn't know the names of. There were times when Matt wasn't sure where his stomach had got to, but the plane's tail didn't fall off.

He found himself laughing aloud, his blood singing. He had no doubt at all that air was the most marvellous, stupendous, invigorating element, and was scarcely aware of a noise level that, on the ground, would have had him cursing and stopping his ears. All grief, all worry, all weariness had left him. Sincerely and deeply, he pitied the poor mortals down there below, who had no idea of what real living was. There was no question at all that flying was what he had been born for.

It annoyed him to have to concentrate on the reconnaissance he was here for. There was a considerable amount of activity on the roads behind both sides of the Front, long lines of troops moving up, supply columns, Pioneers engaged on road mending, and on the British side what looked like the better part of a cavalry division.

There were tents going up, too, big camouflage-daubed ones; the new Main Dressing Station for Z-Day – Zero Day, the day of the Big Push. And as for the 29th's artillery emplacements, what with the newly turned earth, the gouged-out tracts and the shadows they cast, the Brigadier might as well have hung out signs saying, 'Here be dragons'.

Like a child at the end of a long-awaited treat, Matthew didn't want to go home. But they were back at Bertangles after being in the air for less than an hour. As they landed with a series of bouncing bumps and much waggling of wings, Matthew concentrated his mind on the problem of organising an immediate transfer to the Royal Flying Corps. The trouble was that, although it was high-level policy to encourage transfers, the 29th Division strictly forbade them to men on active service in France.

Because of his preoccupation, it took him a moment to notice that Ben had burst into song and another moment to catch the words.

> Oh, the bold aviator was dying,
> And as 'neath the wreck-age he lay, he lay,
> To the sobbing me-chanics about him
> These last parting words he did say:
>
> Take the cylinders out of my kidneys,
> The connecting rod out of my brain, my brain,
> From the small of my back get the crankshaft,
> And assemble the en-gyne again.

The message didn't escape Matthew, but he was accustomed to the gallows humour of the trenches and all he did was laugh. War was death, and this, surely, was the way to go.

Ben, who had been impressed at first by his passenger's lean, dark, intelligence, his tired blue eyes and air of authority, was interested to discover that he was no more than a fellow fool, after all.

5

THE day of the Big Push broke in a mist that promised brightness to come, and C Company's officers breakfasted in the dugout at six, unwashed and unshaven, while the air shook and the earth juddered under the last stages of the preliminary bombardment.

Matthew felt stiff and cold, depressed and thick-headed, and his mind persisted in sliding away from the here and now, up into the sky, and the sunlight. To the blessed peace of Morar, with its salt-white sands and silver seas. To Provost Charters, on a scented midsummer noon. Even to Sarajevo, with its pale hot buildings and pale hot dust.

Zero hour was 7.30a.m. and the bombardment ended on time, but the officers in the dugout, who were to go over with the second wave, stayed out of the way as they had been ordered to do, while above them the first wave of a hundred thousand infantry, most of them untried volunteers laden with half their bodyweight in weapons, gas masks, emergency rations – even carrier pigeons – clambered out of the trenches, lined up, and set out on their slow plod towards the enemy.

Z-Day. Zero-Day. The last day.

For how many?

After a while, Matt said, 'I shall go above, and see what's happening. Let me know the minute any orders come through.'

'Yes, sir.' It was Con Middleton. 'Where'll you be?'

'Hyde Park Corner.' He wasn't trying to be funny. All the trenches had names, easier to remember than official numbers.

Hung like a Christmas tree with field glasses, water bottle, gas mask, revolver and map case, he emerged blinking into the light and made his way along to the viewpoint, studying the waiting second-wave men as he went. They seemed to be talkative enough, which was a good sign. The trouble started when fear gripped your diaphragm so tightly that you couldn't speak.

It was unlikely that, today, any sniper would have time to spare for long shots, so Matthew sat on the edge of the parapet where the men could see him and think that, if the captain wasn't worried, they needn't be.

The landscape swam before his eyes. His head, his muscles, his very bones felt as if they were on fire, and his limbs seemed to be made of lead. But he succeeded in training his glasses on the opposite hillside.

He thought, at first, that some quirk of the bombardment had tossed sandbags, hundreds and hundreds of them, onto the barbed wire, and murmured to himself, 'That's handy. Makes it easier for the men to cross.'

And then he saw that they weren't sandbags.

The sun was shining brilliantly now, flashing on the fixed bayonets of the tail-end of the first wave, on the men still trudging across the pock-marked wilderness towards the heavy artillery and the spitefully chattering machine-guns and the barbed wire that was almost invisible behind the piled and strewn bodies of those who had gone before them.

There were runners dashing back and forth with messages, and spotter aircraft skimming the attack lines, their purpose to radio progress reports back to HQ. Matthew couldn't focus on them, but he knew they were there.

What were they saying? Objective attained; objective not attained. Boche resisting fiercely. Some 580 Royal Fusiliers out of the original 700 draped bleeding or dead over the wires. Inniskillings have caught up with artillery forward barrage, and lost two-thirds of their number. Twenty-two officers of 2nd Middlesex regiment lost out of twenty-six, and 601 men out of 700.

By the end of this day there will be 19,000 dead and 38,000 wounded, the heaviest losses of any single day in the entire history of the British army.

But no one knew any of that, yet.

In the meantime, the valley of the Somme dissolved before Matthew's aching eyes into a mirage of smoke drifting pink and grey and black; of machine-guns spewing out sparks like some mad Brock's benefit; of shrapnel bursting in small, blue-white puffs, and canister in black and shells in huge brown gouts.

At Hyde Park Corner, birds fluttered above the trenches, cheeping nervously, and the breeze ruffled the coltsfoot, and the poppies sprang scarlet against the bleached sandbags and chalky soil.

Con Middleton was at his elbow. Time for the second wave to move.

Matthew raised a clumsy whistle to his lips, waved a leaden arm, and said thickly, 'Right! Are we ready? Let's be off.' It was only as they stepped out into no-man's-land that he realised what was wrong with him.

He was just clear-headed enough to wonder, with an unsoldierly giggle, whether the malaria or the guns would get him first.

Six

1

'JERUSALEM, Jerooooosalem, lift up your heart and sing, Ho-san-na, i-in the high-yest, Hosann-ah-ha to the king.'

Struggling towards consciousness, Matthew decided he must be at a funeral. He must have died, and they'd forgotten to tell him. He couldn't think of any other reason for someone to be singing psalms over him.

But if you were dead with a couple of bullets in you – he remembered that – you wouldn't be aware of a temperature rampaging around somewhere up in the stratosphere. Nor would you have this irritable feeling that the psalm-singer hadn't got it quite right.

Next time he came to, he wished the psalm singer would shut up. The time after that, he managed to work out that the source of all these damned hosannas was the ambulance driver, bundled up in army greatcoat and tin hat and rejoicing, no doubt, to be going home from a Somme-ful of corpses to his nice, cosy Casualty Clearing Station with its wards full of soon-to-be corpses and the mass graves already dug and waiting in the field nearby.

It was one of the jollier psalms, but the fellow was singing it in a light, mournful voice, half under his breath, as if his mind wasn't on it. He sounded very young.

Then the ambulance, a converted Paris taxicab with shelves for the stretchers sticking out at the back, bounced into and out of a nasty pot-hole and just before the vibrations reached Matthew and sent him plunging back into darkness, he saw the driver make a grab at his tin hat, which had been dislodged by the jolt.

Fair hair, and a hand with a tiny sparkle of diamonds on it. A *woman* driver? It couldn't be.

The road was choked with troops and ammunition wagons and staff cars, with detachments of cavalry, strings of gun horses and mule limbers. It took two hours for the ambulance convoy, struggling against the tide, to reach the Casualty Clearing Station and find it full to overflowing. There was no longer any space even on the floors, so that new cases had to sit if they could, or lie on their stretchers in the open. Some had fearful wounds, but it gave them

199

no priority. The surgeons were already working without respite on wounds no less fearful.

Matt's driver couldn't at first find anyone to come and lift the stretchers down from the ambulance. But she seemed to be a strong-minded and stubborn young woman, and through the advancing and receding mists of pain and fever Matt heard her laying down the law to someone.

'This ambulance is *not moving* until it's been unloaded. That means it'll go on cluttering up the courtyard, stopping the other ambulances getting in. It means it can't go back up to the Front to collect more wounded. And *that* means there won't be space at the Advanced Dressing Station for the new wounded being brought in from the battlefield. Now just you find somebody to give me a hand *right now*! It could all have been done twice over in the time you've stood there arguing!'

Matt wouldn't have been surprised to hear her add, 'And I don't care if you *are* a general.'

But he thought he detected a trace of desperation under the common-sensical Scots voice and governessy manner.

He lay and meditated. One bullet had torn a path diagonally across his chest, deflected jaggedly from rib to rib, and the other had gone through his left shoulder, missing spine and jugular by a fraction of an inch. Or so the doctor at the Dressing Station had said, adding in a harassed way that he couldn't judge how much of Matthew's raging fever was due to the bullets and how much to the malaria.

There was nothing wrong with his legs except their weight and the chill in them, and his stretcher was on the bottom tier.

'Lady in distress,' he told himself hazily. 'Officer and gentleman. Do the decent thing. Up the workers.'

One of the other patients looked at him and groaned as he began to struggle crabwise out of his stretcher, but the remaining four lay silent. Twice he almost passed out before he found himself perched, at last, on the tailboard of the ambulance. He couldn't see the dressing on his shoulder but the sling was a brilliant scarlet. Oh, well. The ground looked a very long way away. Not a yard under eighteen inches.

'*What* are you doing there?' said the bossy Scots voice.

Ask a silly question . . .

'Waiting for a bus,' he said. And then, because his enunciation had been slurred, which might give a wrong impression, he raised his head and stared at her austerely through the mud and blood. She wasn't any too clean herself.

She peered at him. 'Are you *drunk*?'

'Certainly not. Or only on the waters of the Pierian spring.' That didn't come out very clearly, either. Kindly, he added, 'The spring of the Muses,' just in case she hadn't heard of it.

'Don't be idiotic. And how do you expect the men to lift you down from that position? Have you no sense? Do you want to kill yourself?'

If she was going to be like that about it . . .

'O Death, where is thy sting-a-ling-a-ling, O Grave, thy victoree?' He fixed his eyes on the ground and manoeuvred himself swiftly and competently off the tailboard. 'The bells of Hell go ting-a-ling-a-ling, For you, but not for me.'

But although the manoeuvre was, indeed, swift, it turned out to be less than competent, because his knees buckled under him and the exhaustion, pain and fever surged up in a great engulfing wave. Not for the next forty-eight hours was he to know anything of the world at all.

2

FOR Jenny, the days after Tom's death had been a nightmare of condolences and mourning clothes and visits from the minister, but there had been a cruelly fleeting quality about everyone's sympathy, as if people thought that being married and widowed in four days made the whole thing unreal. Made the grief less. No one said, 'You'll soon get over it', but she knew everyone was thinking it.

No one said, either, that Tom had been an outsider, but during the church service she had thought her heart would break from the conviction that she alone was thinking of him.

As the melancholy words and measured notes of the burial hymn echoed through the plain grey building, Jenny knew that it was John Baine and the other seventeen men from the yard who came first in everybody's thoughts; in the thoughts of Allie, and Mr Hamish, and her own father, and all the rest of the congregation standing there in the simple wooden pews, dressed in their best rusty black, with hymnbooks in their black-gloved hands. Even the minister somehow conveyed that each of the eighteen Presbyterians who had died mattered more to God than the one Episcopalian.

Now the labourer's task is o'er
Now the battle-day is past;
Now upon the farther shore
Lands the voyager at last.

Oh, Tom, Tom! My lonely voyager.

3

AFTER that, things had got worse, not better. Jenny had begun to feel like a bone being fought over by two dogs.

Or, said Allie – too bleak of heart to trouble about minding her tongue – two bitches.

Their mourning had been twelve days old and it was a fine, sunny June evening when, at Allie's suggestion, they had left the office early to walk over the Gleniffer Braes and breathe some air that wasn't shipyard air, and be reminded by the sight of plants growing and the sound of birds singing that, in some ways at least, life did go on.

So they had climbed the hill, two women wearing their darkest clothes and black armbands, and found that it was true. The grass sprang green over the ruins of Stanely castle, the briars swayed frail and pink on their tall, thorny stems, and the rough turf of the hillside was bright with dandelions as regular and golden as pats of salty butter. The great sheet of water that was Paisley's reservoir lay calm and cool and serene in the evening light. An idle mavis was singing from amid the fresh green of the birches and an infant blackbird trailed around on its father's heels, tsee-tsee-tsee-ing for its supper.

Blind to it all, Jenny said, 'Allie, I don't know what to do.'

She had assumed that, after a while, she would go back to Rashilea Terrace and the cold haven of the familiar, and take up her life again as if her brief marriage had never been.

It was what her mother expected of her, a mother overflowing with sympathy, because that was what mothers did. Jenny shouldn't be staying with the Brittons. 'My bereaved wee girl should be at home with her mother, where she belongs.' She had even come up to Castlehead to say so, sitting in the drawingroom with her

202

coat and hat still on and her handbag on her lap, sipping tea from a real bone china cup. Black coat, black gloves, black shoes, black handbag. Black cotton stockings wrinkled round the ankles. Black hat with bits of jet on it and a small fan of black lace standing up at the back.

But then had come the request – the command – from Provost Charters that Jenny should go to live there and take up 'her rightful place' as the widow of the family's eldest son. The family whom Tom had made sound very upper-class, very traditional, very frightening. There had been telephone calls and letters from Tom's father and a call, too, from his stepmother Natasha, warm and sympathetic and foreign. Cynically, Allie had wondered what had come over her.

Now, Allie said, 'I can't advise you. I know your mother, and I know Natasha, and there's no possible way of choosing between them. You don't exist, you don't matter. All that matters to them is how you fuel their view of themselves.'

The light evening breeze began to ruffle the grass. Allie, her eyes unfocussed and her fingers cupped round the little spray of roses tucked between the top two buttons of her jacket – roses of so deep a red that they were almost black – hesitated for a moment. In business, you never mentioned politics or religion; on a personal level you never talked about money. The contents of your wage packet or bank account – if you had one – were as private as . . . well, as the contents of your wage packet or bank account. But this was a special case.

'Jenny, have you thought about money?'

'How do you mean?'

'There might be a third possibility. Tom didn't just live on his salary, you know. There was a legacy from his grandmother, and Paul put five per cent of the yard's shares in his name when he was born, so there's dividends as well. There might be enough to give you some kind of independence. The only thing is, I don't see how he could have had the chance to make a Will, or change one, between the time you got married and . . .'

Her voice trailed off. She sounded exhausted, and Jenny saw her clearly for the first time in twelve long days. Kind, considerate, self-contained Allie. Jenny felt a rush of tenderness for her, and was ashamed of having been so dependent, so demanding, although she hadn't intended to be. She exclaimed, 'Oh, Allie! Don't worry about *me*. I'll manage, really I will. But you look so worn. You take everyone's burdens on your shoulders. Isn't there anything

I can do to help?'

To help? Allie was so tired that it was as much as she could do to string half a dozen words together. Looking at Jenny, anxious and concerned and faintly pink about the eyes, she thought, she doesn't recognise it, but she's lucky. A brief, bright happiness with someone she scarcely knew, a dream she can cherish, a bliss uncontaminated by the realities of everyday life.

A bliss unenriched by friendship and companionship. Allie knew one of the hardest things she herself was going to have to do was stop saving up all the small, amusing things to tell John next time he came home. She was going to miss him. All of him. Half of herself.

One of the black-red rosebuds disintegrated into a flutter of petals.

With something of her old asperity, she said, 'Just don't tell me that time is a a great healer! If one more person says that to me, I won't hold myself responsible. Now. If Tom *didn't* make a Will, the law says that you as his widow are entitled to the first £500 of his estate. Over that, you have to share half and half with his father.

'What worries me is that if Tom *did* make a Will before he knew you, and didn't have time to change it, you may not be entitled to anything at all except by courtesy of Paul Britton.'

'I don't want money. It wouldn't be right.'

'Don't be silly! You can't do anything without it.'

The sun was almost down and the sky a lovely pale turquoise fading in the west to a rich, peachy gold. Suddenly, desperation flooded through Jenny so violently that her whole body began to shudder. She couldn't – she *couldn't* – go to Rashilea Terrace or Provost Charters. There had to be some other answer. She had to get away, right away. Now.

Allie understood, and in the end it was Allie who supplied the answer. 'You know Bertha works with the Scottish Women's Hospital in France? Suffragettes. All women, from the doctors down.'

'I don't think I could be a nurse!'

'No. But you could drive an ambulance.'

4

AND so Jenny had fled from everyone who had a claim on her.

.Just before she left, she received a note of condolence from Tom's brother, the brother he hadn't liked very much and whom she herself remembered without pleasure. Though it wasn't a note, not really.

> Better the kindly deep, the name unsung,
> Than some grand, polished monument of stone
> Or wooden cross, anonymous among
> All those in France's soil so thickly sown.
> No graven words, no scrawled 'Here sleeps the brave',
> Only a sense that some of what was he
> Informs each dark and silver-shining wave
> In the vast, changing splendour of the sea.

It seemed to Jenny a very peculiar way to express sympathy. What did it matter if Tom had a headstone or not? What mattered was that he was *dead*.

5

SINCE drivers were urgently needed, Jenny found herself in France little more than a fortnight after taking the decision. It had been a terrible rush, and she had been feeling tired and sick by the time she arrived at Amiens, even though the journey, the unfamiliar sights and smells and food, had helped to take her mind off things. It had been strange to find that people even *looked* as if they ought to speak a foreign language. For the first time, she was grateful that she had been taught French so thoroughly at school and that, like most Scots, she seemed to have the knack of it.

She had expected to have a day or two to recover; perhaps some training in mechanics so that she could make temporary repairs to her vehicle if anything went wrong.

But there hadn't been time.

Jerusalem, Jerooooosalem . . .

There was a faint mist, with the moonlight shining behind it so that the trees and posts by the roadside loomed up as dark, menacing, unidentifiable shapes. Jenny shivered. Mist had always frightened her, from as far back as she could remember. Iris said it probably had something to do with her adventure the day they'd moved in to Rashilea Terrace, but Jenny had been too young to have any recollection of it. All she knew was that she hated the whiteness and the silence and the feeling of being shut in.

She wished she hadn't gone dashing ahead without waiting for the convoy. What if she got lost again, for the second time in one day? That was how she had landed up at the Front this afternoon, at the Advanced Dressing Station instead of the Casualty Clearing Station behind the lines. She was so new that she hadn't even recognised the signs that should have told her she was getting far too close to the battle.

She hoped to goodness this was the right way to Amiens.

Double-declutching, she misjudged the revs, and the gear went in with a grinding shriek that tore the night apart and made her feel as if her teeth were being ripped from their sockets. The Renault might look like an Arrol-Johnston, but it didn't behave like one. One of her new load of patients moved restlessly in the back, but all six had been stuffed with morphia for the journey to Base Hospital, so it was probably all right.

Never in her life had she been so afraid or so upset. Or so angry. She had thought she could imagine something of what war must be like, but she had been wrong. And it was all so *unnecessary*. The whole dreadful business could probably have been settled before it began, with the application of a little common sense and goodwill. But instead there was this stupid, futile notion that there was something fine about fighting, something glorious.

One could have felt a decent scorn if it had only been the statesmen, safe in their beds in England. But it wasn't. Because this very day she had seen men who wouldn't give in to the horror of their wounds because giving in would have been contrary to their fine, noble, stupid, suicidal idea of heroism. Like that idiotic, muddy, blood-stained young captain, with his stiff upper lip, and his Oxford accent, and the airy nonchalance that he was going to cling to, even if it killed him. Which it probably would.

It was four weeks and three days since Tom had been drowned.

Jenny gave a little snuffle of misery. The exasperating young captain had had blue eyes just like Tom's.

She hadn't any patience with him, but she hoped he wouldn't die.

Then she had to stop the ambulance, and get out and find a bush she could disappear behind in order to be drearily, retchingly sick.

6

SHE put it down to strain and weariness and revulsion, as she was to put down all the other discomforts and irregularities that afflicted her body over the next few weeks – weeks of unremitting tension and increasingly familiar horror. Dressing pails full of amputated arms and legs; the sweet smell of sepsis and decay, resting like a miasma over the hospital and the ambulances, impregnating everybody's clothes, hair and skin; the raw, ghastly, gurgling sound of chest casualties fighting for breath; men with blind eyes; the clutch of hands reaching out for help when help there was none; the foreknowledge that everything one touched would be sticky with blood and tissue and mud and vomit.

It was the middle of August when Jenny at last realised that she was pregnant. It seemed, at first, too much to bear.

Seven

1

PAUL Britton, standing on the platform at the station watching the passengers descend from the London train, had formed no mental picture of his widowed daughter-in-law but assumed that, since Tom had married her, she must be reasonably pretty. Hamish had told him on the telephone that she was 'a nice, sensible lassie and perfectly presentable', which was more than, at first, Paul had dared to hope. It seemed unlikely that there would be more than one pretty, presentable, pregnant young woman travelling alone on the morning train, and Paul anticipated no difficulty in recognising her.

But he was wrong. He was beginning to wonder whether she had missed the connection, when a rather prim Scots voice said at his elbow, 'Excuse me, are you Mr Britton?'

The girl who was standing there reminded him of nothing so much as a bedraggled sparrow. Wisps of fair-ish hair were coming adrift from under her plain brown felt hat, a pull-on of the style favoured by English nannies, and her pregnancy was scarcely noticeable under the ankle-length khaki greatcoat, its skirts creased, splashed and muddy, which she wore over a serviceable two-piece suit in an indeterminate green and brown tweed. There were heavy rings round her eyes and her nose was sharp with fatigue.

For a disoriented moment, Paul tried to remember whether his farm manager was expecting another Land Girl this week.

Then the sparrow spoke again. 'I'm Jeanette. I must look awfully disreputable. I'm sorry. But I've been travelling since the night before last. The Blighty ship was packed and the train from Dover was late. They have to go awfully slowly in the blackout, don't they? We didn't get in until early this morning and there was an air raid on, so I spent the night in Waterloo station. The train here was packed, too. I couldn't get a seat.'

The words came out in such an unemotional monotone that there seemed very little for Paul to say other than, 'Oh?' Conventional expressions of sympathy were not, in any case, very much in his style and he was already wondering, with dismay, how Natasha was going to react to this sadly commonplace young woman. Although he didn't really have to wonder. He knew.

So he did no more than smile briefly and say, 'Yes, it is often like that, I fear. How do you do? Is that your suitcase?'

Bracingly, Jenny reminded herself that she hadn't expected any great show of warmth, anyway.

He said, 'The motor is in the forecourt. Perhaps you will allow me to lead the way?'

He turned, making no move to pick up her suitcase, so she picked it up herself and followed him, a dismal anger beginning to well up inside her. But when she caught up with him, he was saying to his chauffeur, 'A small brown suitcase. You will find it on the platform, by the pillar.'

There was a faint frown on his brow when he turned and saw her carrying it, as if she had criticised his manners or his breeding or one of the other things the upper classes set such store by. Oh, drat!

Why had she come? Why had she come?

She didn't at first recognise the make of car, a tourer with a short, wide box-like bonnet and a flat, clean-cut radiator grille, but even before she identified the badge she saw that the headlamps were electric, which meant it was probably a Lanchester. Not that she cared. It was just that being observant about motor vehicles had become second nature to her over these last months.

At least she didn't have to carry on a strained conversation with her father-in-law all the way back to Provost Charters, because he sat in front with the chauffeur and she and her battered cardboard suitcase had the back to themselves. The October sky was grey and sullen, the little town no more than one long, uninteresting street, and the countryside flat and featureless. Jenny was so tired and discouraged that she absorbed no more than a vague impression of it all.

And then they came to Provost Charters. Tom had told Jenny that it wasn't a specially grand house, and she'd taken the statement at face value, forgetting that his idea of grandeur wasn't necessarily the same as hers. She'd expected something like Castlehead. But what she saw, as they crunched up the drive, was an edifice that appeared to her horrified gaze to be not much smaller and scarcely less impressive than the City Chambers in Glasgow, complete with battlements and parapets, leaded windows replete with stained glass, a massive pillared portico, and something at the back that looked like a church tower.

The chauffeur took the motor right in under the porte-cochère, but it wasn't until Sir Paul and Jenny had both descended that

Natasha appeared to welcome them and Jenny suffered her second serious shock of the day.

Was this – *could* this be? – her stepmother-in-law?

'Fair, flashy, and self-centred', Tom had said, and Allie hadn't been much kinder. But what Jenny saw was an exquisitely groomed, strikingly exotic young woman only a few years older than she was, with hair of a rich and ravishing gold, brilliant blue eyes, and a perfectly proportioned figure clad in the simplest, most beautifully cut slate-grey gown, with a six-inch-wide darker grey belt resting on her admirable hips. There were enormous pearl studs in her ears and her dark grey shoes had heels not a fraction under three inches high.

Jenny had no way of knowing that Natasha, reflecting that Tom's poor little widow had probably been cut off from news of the latest fashions for some months, had self-sacrificingly dressed her hair without elaboration and selected one of the oldest and plainest gowns in her extensive wardrobe for the occasion. Paul had said he wished her to be kind to the girl, and she desired to show that she grudged nothing – or not very much – in such a cause.

On a waft of some impossibly expensive fragrance, she stretched out both hands to Jenny and said with a blinding smile, 'Welcome to your new home. Come inside. You must be tired after your journey.' She rolled her 'r's deliciously, but no one could possibly have mistaken her for a Scot.

'Thank you.' Jenny had never felt dirtier, dowdier, or plainer. 'How do you do?'

She would have been happy to take advantage of Natasha's invitation to enter, except that her stepmother-in-law, having delivered it, remained where she was, staring. Staring, with her perfect lips very slightly open over equally perfect teeth, as if her greeting had been carefully rehearsed for the daughter-in-law of her imagination and she was having difficulty in adjusting to the reality.

Jenny's hackles were already beginning to rise when the unmistakable figure of Sir Albert appeared. Although Jenny hadn't been sure about Paul Britton, whom she remembered from the night of his brother's death seven years before only as a tall, aristocratic, low-voiced silhouette, Sir Albert had been at the yard for board meetings several times since then, and his was a face that wasn't easy to forget.

At once bluff and impersonal, the old man barked, 'Tom's girl, is it? Well, come in, then. Get out of the way, woman.'

Natasha, thus unceremoniously addressed, threw an amused sideways glance at him and obediently stepped back.

'Come in,' Sir Albert said again. 'Looking a bit peaky, aren't you?'

For what seemed like the hundredth time, Jenny said, 'Thank you. How do you do?'

Then she went in.

The contrast with the hospital billet in which she had spent the last few months was so ridiculous that, if her sense of humour hadn't been somewhat in abeyance since Tom died, she would certainly have giggled.

> I dreamt that I dwelt in marble halls,
> With vassals and serfs at my side . . .

Marble halls was right. There were gleaming, mottled pillars all over the place, with huge, gilded plaster seashells between them and soapy white statues and busts perched on columns and brackets. The floor was intricately patterned with cables and dragons in tasteful shades of turquoise and peach, and the ceiling painted in rectangular panels of the same colours with heavy, golden mouldings surrounding them. Straight ahead, the ceiling disappeared completely to accommodate the well of a noble staircase whose twin flights curved upwards to meet where the ceiling would otherwise have been; enfolded in their embrace was a larger-than-life sculptural group that appeared to represent Venus with attendant nymphs. *Just* like the City Chambers in Glasgow.

A vassal relieved Jenny of her trenchcoat, and passed it on to a serf.

Rebuking her puritan conscience – which was showing signs of having an apoplexy – Jenny took a deep breath, gave a twitch to her draggled skirts, and stalked across the tesserae in her mother-in-law's elegant wake.

2

BY THE end of a week, Natasha was showing perceptibly more signs of wear and tear than her stepdaughter-in-law.

Or so it appeared to Paul, entering his wife's bedroom late the following Thursday evening to discover her seated before the mirror in a flame-coloured peignoir, with the diamonds still in her ears, looking like some beautiful, distraught bird of paradise.

Without preliminary – rather, in fact, as if she was reaching the climax of a tirade whose only previous audience had been herself – she exclaimed, 'I have been so *good*! I have been an *angel*! But it is too much. She is gauche, and ill-bred, and – and – *impossible*. I will not have her here. It is not *reasonable* that you should expect me to share our home with her. She must go!'

Although the tragedy in his wife's aquamarine gaze would have done justice to *The Duchess of Malfi*, Paul didn't make the mistake of underestimating it. The variations in Natasha's moods had become more marked during the six years of their marriage, and he had found it necessary to learn when her resort to high drama arose out of something that mattered and when it did not. This time, it mattered.

He had been expecting an outburst for days, but until tonight she had, indeed, been behaving amazingly well in the face of considerable provocation. Unwitting provocation, which made it worse.

The essential difficulty was that Natasha saw society as irrevocably divided between 'us' and 'them'; between the upper classes to which she had always belonged, and the others, barbarians all and worthy only to be despised. The division, in her view, was absolute. It was as impossible for a member of the lower classes to become one of the upper classes as for a non-Hindu to become a caste Hindu. The structure of society simply didn't allow for it.

It was an unsurprising legacy of her Russian past but in a country with as many gradations of class as Britain, it limited her attitude towards people rather severely.

Paul himself, while accepting the basic class premise, was naturally – in view of his own ancestry – more flexible, but he would not have denied that, every day for seven whole days, Tom's widow had done something to demonstrate that she was to be numbered among the barbarians. It was abundantly obvious that she didn't know the rules, didn't belong, and perhaps never would.

The first evening, it had been the Zeppelin. Sir Albert, raising a forkful of roast beef to his lips, had asked absently about her journey and she had replied at rather too much length, as if she thought they really wanted to know. Then, after five unnecessarily detailed minutes, she had come to the enormous, glowing red Chinese lantern she had seen in the sky over London just before the train drew in – a Zeppelin, internally aflame.

Paul had said, 'Indeed? I suppose that must have been only the third or fourth destroyed since the bombing raids began. Tom's brother Matthew – you won't know, of course, that he transferred from the army to the Royal Flying Corps a few weeks ago – tells me it is remarkably difficult for our fighter pilots to pierce the hydrogen cells. It is apparently necessary for them to concentrate all their machine-gun fire on a single area of the hull.'

'Yes,' she said. 'I know. But what surprised me was how long it took for the flames to burn through the skin. When they did, it looked just like a fire-flower hanging in the sky. It was so beautiful that you forgot there were twenty men frying to death inside.'

She clearly hadn't been able to understand why an inimical silence should have fallen in the panelled dining room with the white damasked table, the flowers, the silver and the crystal. Even the faint rustle of activity from the serving room next door had been stilled.

Paul would have shrugged it off, but after a moment Natasha, at her most charming, had suggested to the girl that, while such reflections might not be out of place in the surroundings of some field hospital, they were not acceptable at a civilised dinner table. The girl had coloured right up to her ears and said scarcely another word all evening.

The next day's contretemps Paul knew of only from Natasha, who had engaged to show the girl round the house. The music room and the conservatory, the drawing room and the library, the morning room, the billiard room, the smoking room. Within half an hour, Natasha said, she had been ready to scream with vexation and ennui over the girl's ignorance of everything to do with art, architecture and decoration and her patent lack of enthusiasm for the house and all it contained. The Gothic arches, the tapestried furnishings, the portraits, the plants, the armorial stained glass, the statues, the sporting paintings, the Turkish couches, the lunettes – none of them had moved her to more than a polite, 'Yes', or 'I see', or 'Oh, really?' And when they went upstairs it had soon become clear that, under her breath, she was keeping count, as if she couldn't conceive why a family of four should need thirty bedrooms and three bathrooms. Especially three bathrooms with Ionic pilasters, Siena marble walls, and carpets on the floor.

Leading her daughter-in-law downstairs again, Natasha had remarked, 'The nursery floor is above, but you do not wish to visit that – it is very much what you would expect it to be – and the servants' wing is just a servants' wing.'

And then, Natasha reported, *exactly* as one might have expected, the girl had exclaimed, 'Oh, I'm looking forward to seeing that, especially the kitchen.'

'The *kitchen*?'

'I wondered whether you had one of the new gas cooking ranges?'

For Natasha it had been too much, really too much. 'I have no idea!' she had said, and had then explained, kindly but firmly, the rules of protocol governing a gentleman's residence. 'The servants' domain is the responsibility of the butler and housekeeper, not of the mistress of the house. You may not inspect it. It would be intrusive and exceedingly – ah – ill-bred to do so.'

The next day had been Sunday, and Jeanette had said she couldn't *possibly* attend a Church of England service; she was a Presbyterian. When Natasha, smiling and helpful, had pointed out that she herself was of the Russian Orthodox faith but *she* attended, the girl had just looked at her, and had relented only after Paul's reminder that the Church of England was Tom's church.

And still things hadn't improved. At dead of night on Monday, Marriot the butler, armed with a poker, had discovered that the suspicious noises emanating from the service room were caused by the younger Mrs Britton rummaging through the cupboards in search of something to eat – just as if she had not had an ample four-course dinner a few hours earlier. Marriot had taken it upon himself to explain to her that, if she required anything *at any time*, she should ring for one of the servants.

Then, on Tuesday, when Natasha was telling her about Matthew's convalescence, and his poetry, and his transfer to the Royal Flying Corps, she had let it be seen that she had no interest in Matthew at all, which had annoyed Natasha quite seriously. And on Wednesday, Natasha had caught her scolding little Nicholas for jumping up and down on one of the tapestried sofas in the music room, wearing muddy outdoor shoes, and had told her rather sharply that it was quite *bourgeois* to concern oneself with material possessions and that she absolutely forbade Jeanette to try and teach Nicholas otherwise.

All in all, it had been quite miraculous that Natasha had succeeded in controlling her temper for so long, although Paul knew that her tantrums rarely sprang from anger alone. The trouble more often was boredom, while criticism, real or implied, was another infallible spark.

Ruefully aware that his wife's self-control couldn't last, Paul had nevertheless been as startled as Jeanette when, this evening, the explosion had come. For a moment he had been unable even to identify the cause.

Now, he smiled slightly, and Natasha mistook the reason for it. Two enormous tears welled from her eyes. 'But she called me . . . She called me . . .' Her voice broke.

Taking her into his arms, he looked down at her and said, 'I was smiling at something else. I was smiling because the mere sight of you still gives me so much pleasure, and will do until I die.'

She gave a little sniff. '*Vraiment?*'

'*Vraiment*. But no matter what she called you, my darling, we cannot sent her away. It is Tom's child she is carrying, and that child cannot possibly be born and raised in some artisan's cottage on the Clyde. It must grow up here at Provost Charters. It will, after all, be a Britton, and this *is* the family home.'

'Pooh! Family home!'

He ignored it, because although she was temporarily at odds with the world he believed that, deep down, she was coming to love Provost Charters as much as he did. 'I mean it,' he said, carefully sweeping aside the heavy fall of her hair and placing his lips no less carefully on the warm, silky nape of her neck. 'And if she is to stay, it seems to me there is one thing that must be done, and you who must do it.'

3

'THE four Cs,' Natasha said. 'Cut, colour, clarity and carat weight. These are what determine the *value* of a diamond. The two elements which give it beauty – its brilliance and its fire – come from the way it transmits light. Jeanette, are you attending?'

'Yes', said Jenny, whose attention was, in fact, wholly concentrated on preventing her stomach from rumbling. She didn't know whether it was an effect of pregnancy, but it had been going on for weeks.

Natasha detached a sapphire and diamond brooch from among the miscellany of scarves, shawls, and other floating draperies with which she adorned her person during the winter months. Accustomed to the steam-heated indoors of St Petersburg, she had not yet learned English fortitude in the matter of winter temperatures. However large the fires – and at Provost Charters they were large – she much disliked being baked on one side, frozen on the other, and attacked from all directions by icy, whistling draughts.

215

She handed the brooch to her daughter-in-law. It was a pretty, extravagant piece of nonsense, shaped like an eye, with delicate rays of diamonds fanning from the corners in to the large, round sapphire at the centre. Even Jenny, who knew next to nothing about jewels, could see that the workmanship was exquisite. Not that wild horses would have forced her to admit it.

'Those diamonds, of course,' Natasha said, 'are the merest chips, ten carats perhaps, but you see what effect a true artist can achieve with stones of little value. The artist, of course, is Fabergé. What do you know of Fabergé?'

'Who?'

Natasha drew in a breath of purest exasperation. The greatest jeweller who ever lived, and this dreary girl knew not even his name!

Paul had said, 'You must teach her how to behave in the kind of social circles in which she will be moving in future. And how to dress, and appreciate the elegancies of life. Because, clearly, someone must teach her. I cannot imagine what possessed Hamish to describe her as "presentable"! No doubt some of her deficiencies may be put down to her war work and the fact of her being – er – *enceinte* – while that rather wooden manner may be attributable to nervousness, but . . .'

Natasha, fired by memories of Mr Shaw's *Pygmalion*, had been intrigued by the thought of transmitting her own pleasure in matters of beauty and style to someone who knew nothing. Indeed, she had been very nearly reconciled to Paul's suggestion even before his hands moved from her waist and began to travel slowly and erotically downwards; before, delicately, they parted the graceful, silken folds of her peignoir; before, sinking to his knees, he murmured, 'But however well the girl learns her lessons, she will never come within a million miles of her beautiful, and very, *very* desirable teacher.'

It had not, at first, occurred to her that the little *bourgeoise* would feel anything other than gratitude for the effort that she, Natasha, proposed expending on her. The need, after all, was so obvious. But now she was beginning to wonder.

'Very well. Peter Carl Fabergé is a native of St Petersburg, though of French Huguenot origin. He is an old man now, but he employs many hundreds all of whom are committed to his own standards of craftsmanship, which are unsurpassed. You see from that brooch that he has a charming sense of caprice. He has, too, an unerring appreciation of how to combine colours and materials. *Jeanette!*'

'I'm listening.'

216

'His enamels also are enchanting, for you must understand he makes not only jewels but *objets de luxe* and *objets de vitrine* – trinkets, delicate little fantasies of great beauty, sometimes useful, sometimes not.'

'Fantasies?'

Much encouraged by the fact that Jeanette had at last said something other than 'Oh?' Natasha smiled at her. 'My aunt in Petersburg has a little spray of cornflowers, made of gold, enamelled in translucent blue and set with brilliant-cut and rose diamonds. It stands in its own small rock crystal vase and is quite, quite lovely.'

'It sounds as if it must have been awfully dear.'

Natasha snatched her brooch back. 'We are speaking not of cost. We are speaking of taste. Anyone, even vulgar people, may have beautiful things if they have a sufficiency of money, but it does not mean that they have taste. Real taste is for oneself, not for others, and it shows in the small perfections of life.'

'I don't understand.'

'*Mon dieu!* It shows in the – in the white jade scent bottle or lipsalve case that no one but the owner and her maid ever see; in the enamelled handle of a parasol or riding crop that is most often hidden in one's hand; in the nephrite ashtray or agate bell push that are *au fond* objects of the merest utility. Can you not understand that, if one must see a bell push every day, it is better that it should be beautiful rather than ugly?'

'I suppose so. But you have to be able to afford it, first.'

Tasha could have screamed. 'Of course. But what I am saying to you is that, first, one must have sufficient taste to *wish* to afford it!'

She rose to her feet. 'I am going to change. And I must tell you that tomorrow we have guests from St Petersburg who will stay with us for three days. Our talk will be all of Russia and of no interest to you, so I think you might prefer to dine in your room while they are here. Yes?'

There was a moment's pause, then, 'Yes. If you'd rather I did.'

4

THERE were other guests during the course of the next few weeks, and there was always some good reason why Jenny should not join

217

them for dinner. But early in December, miracle of miracles, Bertha wrote to say that she was due for leave and thought she might manage a night at Provost Charters on the way home if she could wangle a passage to Portland. There weren't many Blighty ships heading that way, but there was always a chance.

Bertha had been Jenny's sheet anchor throughout the months in France, practical, kindly and placid, someone who never allowed things to get out of proportion. Jenny waited for her with a longing that amounted almost to craving. This, she thought, must be what it was like to be a drunkard in the hour before opening time. She would never have dreamed it possible to feel so homesick – not for Scotland, not for home, but for a friendly face and someone she could actually talk to. She couldn't bear it if Bertha didn't come.

But Bertha did come, ten days before Christmas, and Jenny felt quite faint at the sight of that stolid, homely figure with the matter-of-fact voice, gruff smile, and unbecoming clothes. As Bertha herself said, she was no oil painting and she'd better things to do than dress up as if she was. It was a dreadful struggle for Jenny not to throw her arms round Bertha and weep all over her and almost as much of a struggle to disguise the anxious need to feel that Bertha was *her* guest, had come only to see how *she* was getting on.

But she had forgotten that Bertha had lived at Provost Charters for three years, looking after the boys, and that she knew Paul quite well and Sir Albert very well indeed. Though not Natasha. Tactfully, Bertha had left Provost Charters the day before Paul brought his second wife home, and had met her only once since then, and briefly.

Desperate to talk, Jenny became more and more frustrated as the hours before dinner passed, and then dinner itself, with Bertha asking knowledgeable questions about the farm, and hearing all the county gossip. It was clear that she and her Uncle Albert got on like a house on fire.

Afterwards, when the ladies left the gentlemen to their port, Bertha disappeared upstairs for a moment and returned to the music room with her knitting. 'Got to get on with this,' she said, settling down on the sofa and looking very much at home. 'It's a scarf for dad's Christmas.'

Jenny took a deep breath. 'I'll get mine, too. Baby bootees!'

Ever since she had arrived, she had spent all her spare moments working away grimly in her bedroom; there were so many things the baby would need. Now, fired by Bertha's example, she couldn't think why she hadn't brought her knitting downstairs before. What did it matter that it didn't measure up to the Fabergé!

When she reappeared, it was to find Bertha's needles flashing busily and Natasha – seated as usual in the velvet armchair to the left of the huge, carved, pulpit-shaped fireplace – idly flicking over the pages of a magazine. In the hours since Bertha had arrived, she had alternated between silence and a brittle, butterfly charm.

Bertha said, 'The men have gone off to the billiard room to knock some balls about – and there's no need to look so scandalised, young Jenny! I'm a member of the family, after all, and it gives you and me a chance to catch up.'

Since Bertha didn't even glance in Natasha's direction, Jenny strong-mindedly didn't either, but plumped herself down on the chesterfield and said, 'Oh, yes, please. Tell me *all* about *every*thing that's been happening.'

From then on, the only sounds in the music room were the clicking of needles and the clacking of tongues.

'D'you remember the corporal in ward 11, the leg wound? Well, he . . .'

'And what about Sister Freebairn? She must have . . .'

'They ran out of sterile dressings just when . . .'

'But if the Renault broke down, I don't see how . . .'

Neither of them noticed when, after about half an hour, Natasha threw down her magazine and went over to the piano to search through the pile of sheet music on its top. And even when she began playing, their only reaction was gratitude that it should be something reasonably melodious and not too noisy.

Jenny said, 'And what about Beaumont-Hamel? There must have been . . .'

'Well, according to Driver Ruddiman . . .'

The Tchaikovsky came to an end, to be succeeded by something that sounded to Jenny, who had no musical education, like a random, tuneless, clashing of exceedingly loud chords. With a heaven-help-us smile at Bertha, she raised her voice and said, 'It seems as if these new Commer First Aid lorries . . .'

But Natasha, catching the glance and interpreting it correctly, brought her recital to an abrupt conclusion with a violent discord that had nothing to do with Stravinsky and everything to do with plain old-fashioned bad temper. Jenny and Bertha looked up in surprise.

Natasha's face was coldly unexcited when she spoke, but her words ate into the echoes like acid into glass.

'You observe,' she said, gesturing, 'these magnificent arches? The walls stencilled in gold? The chandeliers? The Turkish carpets? The upholstered chairs and chesterfields? The conservatory with its tropical plants?'

Jenny and Bertha raised mystified eyebrows.

'You would imagine, from all these, that this is a gentleman's residence, would you not? And yet you sit there chatter-chatter-chattering about vulgar, boring people and things – you sit there *knitting*! – as if it were the hovel of some Russian peasant! Well, I will not have it, do you hear me? *I – will – not – have – it!*'

Bertha, unimpressed, went on with her knitting, reflecting that Natasha was the kind of silly female who gave the idea of votes for women a bad name.

But the effect on Jenny was cataclysmic, because Natasha had been offensive not only to her, but to *her* guest.

After a second's frozen silence, she tossed the plebeian needles, wool and baby bootees down on the carpet and levered herself to her feet. Then, fists on hips, she met her stepmother-in-law's intolerant gaze across the Steinway, and launched into some of the things she had been dying to say for every single day and every single hour of the last seven unspeakably miserable, relentlessly self-controlled weeks.

'Oh, won't you!' she grated, her customarily soft voice sounding as if it were being dredged up, resisting, from somewhere deep in her diaphragm. 'Oh, *won't you!* How *dare* you talk to people like that! What *you* enjoy is always good taste, isn't it? But what *other* people enjoy is ill-bred and boring! Well, I – am – fed – up – with you and your stupid rules and your stupid opinions. And I – have – had – enough – of your beastly, horrible condescension and snobbery. You think you're better than everybody else just because your rotten ancestors made such a good job of grinding the faces of the poor. Well, you're not! You've no *right* to look down on other people.

'You've no *right* to look down on Bertha and me just because we come from the Clyde. Because we've always *worked* for a living! You've no idea what that means! And there's something else you've no idea of.' Her voice suddenly became unstable. 'You've no idea what it's like to find yourself a widow when you've only been married four days, and then discover you've a baby coming!'

Although Natasha's brows had risen at first, after a moment a flickering, equivocal smile had settled round her mouth. She sat where she was and made no attempt to interrupt.

But Bertha did. Laying a hand on Jenny's arm, she said, 'Jenny, don't. It's not worth upsetting yourself.'

'Yes, it is! It's been boiling up for weeks. You don't know what it's been like, Bertha! Silly rules about what you can say and can't say at table. Being told you're vulgar just because you wonder what kind of cooker there is in the kitchen. Being sneered at because the baby makes you hungry at the wrong hours. Having your education improved with lectures on stupid bits of jewellery that probably cost enough to keep a whole family for a year. Being accused of being *bourgeois* when you try to stop a spoilt little brat from ruining the furniture . . .'

She was becoming more overwrought with every word she uttered, so that what she said was coming out in gasps and jerks. Bertha, conscious of a strong desire to slap the satisfied smile off Natasha's face, said again, 'Jenny, don't.'

Jenny clutched at her arm. 'No, but you don't *know* how awful it's been. She hasn't said *one kind word* to me since I arrived. All she's done is let me see that she thinks I'm plain, and common, and dowdy, and ignorant, and – and . . .'

Natasha, at last, rose to her feet and said superciliously, 'And quite impossible. My dear Jeanette, if you insist on making such a vulgar exhibition of yourself, I should prefer that you do not advertise the fact to the entire household, including the servants. Lower your voice, please.'

It was deliberate provocation, but Jenny failed to recognise it as such. Nor, all her attention on Natasha, was she aware that Paul Britton and his father had been standing in the doorway for several minutes, Sir Albert, post-prandially cheerful, giving vent to chortles of *sotto voce* mirth.

Her voice soaring half an octave, Jenny shrieked, 'Did you hear that? She says it's vulgar for *me* to raise my voice. When you should have heard *her* just a week after I arrived! I came in here, and she was standing in front of the fire, and one of those scarves of hers was floating almost in the flames, and I wanted to warn her. I had to call her *some*thing, and I'm just as much Mrs Britton as she is, and "Natasha" wouldn't have been very polite when I scarcely knew her, so I called out, "Mother! Be careful!"'

She didn't see the spasm of laughter that crossed Bertha's face as she rushed on. 'You've never heard such a screech as she let out. I don't know why. I mean, she *is* older than me and she *is* my stepmother-in-law, but she said I was being insulting and offensive. She even threw a vase at me, but she missed and it broke against the wall and all the flowers fell out. And if *that* isn't vulgar and ill-bred, I don't know what is. And she never even thanked me for warning her when she might have been badly burned!'

Then, all at once, Jenny ran out of steam. 'Not that I'd have expected her to,' she wailed. 'She doesn't want me here. And I don't want to *be* here. I only came to Provost Charters because I knew my darling Tom would have wanted his baby to be born here, and I wish I hadn't. But I'm here now, and I'm *not* going to be trodden on. I'm *not* going to be driven away. I'm staying, whether she likes it or not. Do you hear me? I'm staying! *I'm staying!*'

And on this militantly miserable note, fled the room.

5

BERTHA bent down and, picking up the forgotten knitting, began to smooth out the little white bootees.

Then she looked at her uncle and said, 'You're a real old scally-wag, aren't you?'

'Me?' Sir Albert's snowy moustaches, which in their arrow-headed descent from lip to jaw gave him such an air of lugubrious respectability, twitched offendedly.

'Yes, you. You've been enjoying yourself fine, these last weeks, haven't you?'

'She's not *my* wife!'

No one had any doubt who he was talking about.

Dispassionately, Bertha replied, 'No, but someone ought to keep her in order, and you can't expect Paul to do it. I've never seen a man so besotted.'

Natasha took a deep breath and opened her mouth, but it was clear even to her that anything she said was unlikely to be attended to, so she closed it again. Paul was standing with his hand resting on the mantelpiece and his eyes on the fire. Sir Albert was getting out a cigar. Bertha went back to knitting the scarf for her dad.

Without looking up, Paul said, 'My dear, I think perhaps we may have been a little insensitive where Jeanette is concerned. She is clearly very upset and . . .'

'*Upset!* What right has *she* to be upset? Did you hear how she spoke to me? That *that* should be all the thanks I receive for the trouble I have taken! When I think . . .'

222

'Yes,' her husband interrupted. 'Yes. But perhaps a little more tact would have been advisable. A little tact and understanding.'

The soothing, almost subservient note Natasha was accustomed to hearing in his voice when he spoke to her was absent, and that infuriated her even more than Jenny's outburst had done.

Her own voice sizzled. 'Tact? As well be tactful with a – with a crocodile! Why should I trouble to be tactful with a girl who is interested only in adding up the cost of my jewels and counting the bedrooms. Who has neither sensitivity nor finesse, and whose every look is a criticism! How *dare* she criticise! No, no, *no*. I have said before, and I say again, I will not have her here! She must go!'

No one moved. No one spoke.

Then Sir Albert gave voice to a resounding 'Harrumph!' He didn't like being forced to make decisions; on the other hand, once he had accepted the necessity, he always entered wholeheartedly into the spirit of the thing. Blowing out a vast, suffocating cloud of Havana, he announced with gusto, 'You're forgetting. This is my house. And if you, young woman, force Tom's girl to leave . . .'

With satisfaction, Bertha began casting off. Heartless old scoundrel that he was, he was going to do the right thing for once.

'. . . if you force Tom's girl to leave, then you can go too.'

'Father!' Paul exclaimed, but was ignored. Sir Albert was much too busy daring Natasha to defy him.

Thought she could twist her father-in-law round her little finger, did she? Well, she thought wrong, seductive little witch that she was. Not even Lutetia had ever got the better of Sir Albert except when he couldn't be bothered to stop her.

His daughter-in-law's ice-blue eyes glittered back at him, but she spoke only one word.

'*De-lighted!*' she said.

It took Bertha a good half-hour to persuade everyone to see sense, but she managed it in the end, even though Natasha, grandly conceding that Jeanette's behaviour might – just might – be put down to the emotional disorders of pregnancy, concluded, 'But I will never forgive her, you understand. Never!'

As Bertha retired upstairs to see what could be done about calling young Jenny to order, it was with a gleam of amusement in her eye. It seemed to her that Uncle Albert was actively looking forward to sharing the house with two women who loathed each other.

6

JENNY, deeply disturbed by the fact that she should have been capable of such an outburst, was no less amazed by the effect it had on her. The violent paroxysm of tears to which she had given way as soon as she reached the privacy of her room, the furious pummelling of her mattress and the vicious satisfaction of kicking a fallen pillow all over the place, didn't just restore her to normal, but gave her a sense of faintly bellicose wellbeing that was without precedent in the whole of her experience.

Afterwards, she collapsed onto a pouffe and sat surveying the rather antiquated but sinfully luxurious bedroom, with the four-poster bed, the enormous wardrobes, the easy chairs, the sewing table and the new cabbage-rose curtains that must have cost at least fifteen shillings a yard. Weeks ago, she had calculated that there were eighteen yards in them, which meant that it would have taken every penny of her wages at the shipyard for nine whole weeks to pay for them. She had been very much shocked.

But that had been then. This was now. Glaring at the largest, cabbagiest rose, she said, 'Impossible, am I? Well, we'll see about that!'

By the time Bertha came upstairs, Jenny was peacefully asleep, looking no more than faintly tear-stained.

But next morning, before the chauffeur drove her to the station, Bertha took time to give her some very sound advice and one result was that, a few days later – days during which everyone behaved as if nothing at all had happened – Jenny set out for the county town to spend money. Her darling Tom, despite Allie's forebodings, had found time to see a lawyer and make a Will in his wife's favour before the *Indefatigable* sailed, so she had an income of her own even though, until now, her Calvinist conscience had forbidden her to spend any more of it than she absolutely had to; it seemed vaguely improper to spend money one hadn't earned. And in these last months, too, it had seemed right to save it for the baby.

But her view of the matter had changed, and now she was going out to buy confidence. She began at the hairdresser's where, nervous but resolute, she had her hair ruthlessly chopped off and shaped into the practical and rather dashing short bob that the dancer, Irene Castle, had recently made fashionable. As the coiffeur told her, '*Very* suitable for hair as fine as yours, madam, and quite a transformation, if I may say so.'

Afterwards, daringly, she had lunch not in a tearoom but at an hotel, and then bought two new costumes, one in fire-engine red and the other in cream. Both had flared skirts ending above the ankle and wrapover jacket tops, the red one with a stand-up collar and the cream with quilted lapels, and both could easily be adjusted to accommodate her thickening waist. They might not be in the very height of the mode, but no one could possibly have called them dowdy. And to conclude the most extravagant day of her life, she bought a hat to go with the red costume, a hat with a shallow crown and a wide brim that balanced the whole thing beautifully.

As, full of guilty delight, she stood admiring the effect in the mirror, the baby didn't just move inside her, but actually kicked, so that she gave a gasp, and then a rather startled laugh. Was it saying, 'You look nice'? She realised that this was the very first time she had thought of the baby as a *person*. It was the strangest feeling.

7

AT SIGHT of the red costume, Paul Britton blinked, Sir Albert beamed, and Natasha said, 'Very – ah – striking'. But Jenny wasn't downcast. She hadn't bought it for them, except as an indicator that, if she was going to be made over, she was going to be made over in her own way.

She and Natasha became inordinately polite to each other, Jenny addressing her stepmother-in-law as 'er – Natasha', and Natasha abandoning 'Jeanette' for its less formal diminutive. Jenny gave up her extreme self-restraint and said what she thought, though striving always – if not with invariable success – for courtesy, while it seemed as if Natasha was seriously endeavouring to expunge the words 'ill-bred', 'vulgar' and '*bourgeois*' from her vocabulary.

At Christmas, Jenny gave Natasha a beautifully illustrated book about jewellery, and Natasha presented Jenny with a simple little string of rather nice pearls. They both expressed their thanks charmingly and even gave each other a peck on the cheek.

Then, at Hogmanay, Jenny – encouraged by Sir Albert – insisted they all stay up to see the New Year in with a dram of whisky and some of the shortbread and black bun that, with the willing connivance of Mrs Redick, the cook, Jenny had secretly baked in the lovely new gas range in the kitchen. Natasha didn't utter a word of criticism. Indeed, she commended the shortbread and said how amusing it was to indulge in folk customs different from one's own.

Later in the month, she took Jenny up to the nursery floor so that they could discuss what needed to be done. Nick and his nanny, who was to be the new baby's nanny, too, accompanied them, and Nick told his mama and his half-sister-in-law, very decidedly, how everything ought to be arranged to suit the baby's convenience. Jenny said what a clever little boy he was, and Natasha smiled benignly upon her.

No one could have guessed how deeply they detested each other.

8

THE beginnings of Jenny's war with Natasha, her obsession with proving that a carpenter's daughter from the Clyde was every bit as good as some decadent Russian countess, had the useful secondary effect of taking her mind off her pregnancy.

Jenny knew as little about this as she had known about sex before Jack told her. But Jack couldn't help her this time, and Iris was useless because her brain seemed to dry up when she had to put things on paper, and you couldn't talk about intimate things on the telephone, with the operator probably listening in. All Iris did, therefore, on the strength of one baby of her own and another on the way, was assure Jenny that, whatever was – or wasn't – worrying her, it was probably perfectly normal. Jenny wished she could believe it, thinking it must be a lot easier when you had a husband to comfort you and five of his sisters to advise you; not to mention mum just round the corner.

Even so, when Nellie Jardine telephoned Provost Charters to suggest she might come and stay when the baby was due, 'so as to be near my own wee girl during the most important days of her life', Jenny went cold all over. She was amazed, afterwards, at the number of cogent arguments she managed to think up during the time limit imposed by Nellie's consciousness of the telephone bill. Badly though Jenny wanted someone to talk to, her mum wasn't a person you did 'talk to'.

Before she left France, she had summoned up the courage to ask Matron if it was normal when you were expecting a baby to be sick and have indigestion, day in and day out, and Matron had said,

226

'Sakes alive! Yes, of course it is! Now will you get those stretcher cases off to Base Hospital and start worrying about something useful for a change.'

Then, when she had been buying Natasha's Christmas present, she'd steeled herself to ask in the bookshop if there was something to explain how babies were born, and the assistant had said with distaste, 'I have no idea, madam. We would never stock books about *that* kind of thing.'

Even the doctor wouldn't tell her more than that everything was coming along famously, adding – in almost so many words – that if the blue-blooded multitudes of his other patients were content with his assurances, it wasn't up to a mere Mrs Britton to question them. The doctor, in fact, reminded Jenny forcibly of her mother five years earlier when her periods had begun. All her mum had said was, 'It's just one of those things that happen because you're a girl, and you have to put up with it.' When a puzzled Jenny had asked, 'But what makes it happen?' the reply had been, 'Never you mind. Now go and get on with your homework.'

It seemed quite wrong to Jenny that no one would tell her what was going on inside her own body, more wrong than ever when her back began to ache so much that she felt as if giant hands were try-ing to tear her in half; when the first pains, cramping and terrifying, came and went for days before the midwife pronounced them as 'proper contractions'; when the *real* pains began. When, breathing in shallow jerks, shivering uncontrollably, hovering sometimes on the very verge of consciousness, she remained true to her upbring-ing and didn't – wouldn't – scream or weep, even when she was convinced she was dying. Instead, she repeated Tom's name over and over, as if it were a talisman.

The pain and the anguish went on for-ever, and still the baby wasn't born. What was happening? *She didn't know what was hap-pening.*

And then the midwife said, 'Good, you can help now. Gather your muscles together and push when I tell you.' And it was better to suffer and do something than to suffer and do nothing. So she pushed, and pushed, and the wringing, relentless torment inside her seemed to take on a direction, a purpose, and through the haze she realized that the end must be near.

Then, with startling suddenness, the figure of the midwife began to dissolve before her eyes into a struggling, ghostly vision of her baby – her baby and Tom's – a miniature, sentient human being fighting to be born; a small, fragile, infinitely delicate thing as

227

breakable as glass. She knew that the baby must be suffering as she herself was suffering. She thought of its tiny bones, its insubstantial lungs, its faltering heart being crushed and twisted and mangled by what was going on inside her.

She cried aloud then, because she couldn't believe the baby could possibly emerge alive from such a brutal passage into the outside world.

But then the midwife said, 'Stop!' and she stopped. And there was a gliding sensation, and a blessed moment of nothingness. And then, almost at once, a little mewling sound, and a hiccup, and a cry that became louder and steadier and more insistent.

Someone put a bundle in her arms. Her daughter. Her daughter, and Tom's. And as she hugged the baby to her, at last Jenny gave in to tears, tears that began in a helpless gasping of pain and thankfulness, and grew into a torrent that, by some loving miracle, washed away all but the memory of nine long months of loneliness and hurt.

Eight

1

'GENTLEMEN always make the best pilots,' Matt's instructor had said encouragingly, welcoming him – as one gentleman to another – to the RFC training field on Salisbury Plain in the autumn of 1916. 'Look at Guynemer and this new chap Richthofen. Can't fault 'em. Good hands for a horse, d'ye see? It's in the blood.'

It hadn't stopped them getting shot down and killed.

Now, on a mid-September evening in 1918, cruising along above the shadowed, secretive clouds, Matt found himself thinking that he'd prefer to put his money on nasty, low cunning any day. The last two years' crop of fighter aces hadn't a drop of blue blood among them – Billy Bishop, Canadian roughneck; Eddie Rickenbacker, race-car driver from Ohio; René Fonck, abrasive successor to Georges Guynemer; Hermann Goering, who had inherited Richthofen's flying circus. Not to mention the late Major Mick Mannock VC; the late Captain Albert Ball VC; and the late Major James McCudden VC.

Reminded that he had no pressing desire to become the late Major Matthew Britton VC – or even just DSO and Bar, MC and Bar, DFC and *Croix de Guerre*, which was all he'd managed to collect so far – Matt squeezed his aching eyes tight shut and opened them again, then shifted his feet on the rudder pedals and eased the joystick forward so that the nose of the plane dipped to give him a clear view of the horizon, which was blessedly empty.

Often, you could get more reliable information from a single-plane foray behind Boche lines at the tag end of the day – when all sensible fliers had gone home to supper – than from orthodox patrols in full light, when your attention was apt to be distracted by ground fire and swarms of angry Fokkers. There was only one snag, apart from finding your way back to base in the gathering dark, which was that you couldn't photograph what you saw, and the generals were reluctant to believe anything unless they had pictures to prove it. Matt thought they were wrong there; a good eye was more reliable than a bad picture any time.

Tonight, he hadn't even brought a PBO along, because a Poor Bloody Observer meant a two-seater plane, and two-seaters were

229

bigger and noisier and more obtrusive than his beloved SE.5a scout. But it was a nervy business without one. Even now, with the Hindenberg Line broken, the Boche in full retreat, and the *Jagdstaffeln* short of both pilots and planes, you couldn't be sure of having the skies safely to yourself.

Now, with only one pair of eyes, Matt did what he regularly did in a seemingly empty sky and took the plane round in a fast, tight circle before returning to his heading. Even if he survived the war, he thought, even if he went on flying until the ripest of ripe old ages, he would always find himself expecting danger from above and behind.

It was time to turn back into the headwind that blew eternally from the west, across northern France and into Belgium, making the journey home almost twice as slow as the journey out – though at least you knew where you were going. Matthew had been let down times without number by faulty compasses. Now, he preferred to trust to the wind and the stars.

God, he was tired. The trouble with being one of the select band known to an admiring press and public as 'lone hunters' was that you had to do everything yourself. Smothering a yawn, he eased the stick forward for another look at the horizon.

2

DEAD on cue, the clouds ahead of him tore apart, and it was a trio of fighters, and they were painted half red and half blue with big black crosses on their wings, and they weren't outdated Albatroses or dozey old Rumplers but Fokker D.VIIs, which could outclimb and outmanoeuvre anything else in the sky.

It said in the books that the qualities essential to the lone hunter were coolness, self-control, good gunnery and exceptional eyesight.

Matthew, sweat breaking out on his forehead and his goggles steaming up, called upon his Maker in terms of which the padre would not have approved, gave the joystick a shove that nearly sent it through the instrument panel and did his best to force the right rudder pedal through the floor.

In his opinion, it was absolutely the wrong time, place and odds for a dogfight, for trying to look a dozen ways at once, for being deafened by the hammer of guns and blinded by the streams of tracer, for being unhappily reminded that you didn't have enough hands or eyes to manoeuvre the plane while at the same time aiming and firing the Lewis gun mounted on top of the wing and the Vickers on the fuselage.

For being grimly aware, as you fired and missed, and fired and missed, that you only had five hundred rounds of ammunition per gun and that those five hundred rounds would be gone in a mere fifty seconds. If you lived so long.

There was only one place to go and that was down. The Fokkers might be great at climbing, but the SE.5a knew how to dive.

He thought, to begin with, that he was going to get away with it, because he knew the Fokkers would have to bank out of their climb, and turn, and dive, and they wouldn't risk diving blind, all three of them, into the cloud. But he hadn't allowed for the recklessness of men who, after four long years of fighting, knew their country to be on the verge of final defeat.

He was no more than three hundred feet below the cloud cover when, throwing a glance over his shoulder, he saw that they were there, and even as he turned forward again the plane gave an appalling kick and a shuddering jerk and then began thrashing about. The stick went light and useless in his hands.

With despair griping at his guts, he recognised that it had happened at last, and it was farewell Matthew Britton. The elevator control cables had been shot away, and he wasn't in charge any more.

The force of gravity was taking over. With the nose almost vertical, the whole plane began to shudder and vibrate. The big Wolseley Viper engine roared like half a hundred lions and he could see the wing fabric fluttering and distorting. The speed was building up, and he was heading straight for the ground, and he knew what was going to happen when he got there.

Be damned to that. There must be something he could do!

Briefly, he wondered what the Fokkers were up to, but there was no possibility of turning to find out.

He was down to about a thousand feet now, and he had to think of something. Something that didn't involve the bloody elevator controls! There was nothing that didn't involve the bloody elevator controls!

And then an idea flashed into his head.

Gently, gently, he began to wind back on the tailplane adjustment. All his instincts screamed *Hurry it up, hurry it up!* but he resisted them because it was a hideously imprecise control and it was the only chance he had.

231

Would it work? Dear God, would it work?

Nothing happened.

Come on, he willed it. Come *on*!

Slowly, sluggishly, the nose began to lift. And his heart with it.

He was still going to crash, but if he could get the nose up sufficiently it might be a survivable crash.

He was concentrating so hard that he didn't even hear the renewed burst of fire from the Fokkers. But he felt it; felt a violent blow to his left shoulder and then, unbelievingly, heard the engine stop dead. Crankshaft gone.

It was bloody annoying, especially since the field below looked just about big enough, assuming he got the plane down in one piece, for it to bounce around to its heart's content until it finally got bored and stopped. It was time someone invented brakes for aeroplanes. Parachutes wouldn't be a bad idea, either.

But he was going to have to land, like it or not, at quite the wrong speed, from quite the wrong height, and at quite the wrong angle. One-handed, too, which didn't help.

Seconds later, the wheels hit the ground and collapsed, and the fuselage did a nice job of ploughing up the field, and the tail went up and the nose went down and the fuel began to pour out. And a familiar refrain drifted into Matt's head.

> And when at the Court of Enquiry
> They ask for the reason I died, I died,
> Please say I forgot twice iota
> Was the minimum angle of glide . . .

The Fokkers hung around until they heard a whoosh and a roar and saw the flames leap to the sky. Then they levelled out and headed for home.

3

IT WAS Paul, as Matthew's next of kin, who received the official notification that his son was missing. He told no one for a week, a week during which he pulled every string he could think of in the attempt to find out just what 'missing' meant. Someone told him brutally that, if Major Britton was a fighter pilot, what it meant was 'dead'.

Matthew had failed to return from a lone evening patrol fifteen miles behind the enemy lines. That was all anyone was able to tell him. Until recently, if the Boche had killed or captured someone as notorious as Major Britton, they would have contrived to let his squadron know. It was one of the unexpected courtesies of war, and the Allies did the same in return; less than six months earlier, they had given Richthofen a formal funeral. But now, after the failure of Ludendorff's offensive, the Allies were striking hard, again and again, and the Germans were pretty well walking back. It was no longer a situation in which the courtesies were observed.

All anyone could do was recommend Paul to hope and pray that, if the plane had crashed, his son might have been thrown clear.

Returning home exhausted and discouraged from London, Paul broke the news to Jenny first, not only because she was the least involved but because over the last eighteen months, to his own surprise, he had become coolly fond of her and had come to trust her good sense.

He said, 'You must help me with Natasha. She has always been very close to Matthew, perhaps because she did so much for him when he was a boy. He had been rather – repressed until she came. I know you and she do not see eye to eye on many things, but if you could make a special effort to be gentle with her, and tolerant . . . Not to be upset, not to be sharp, if she should be difficult. It would help me, too.'

'Of course.'

He was looking very drawn as, unexpectedly, he took her hand and patted it, and said inconsequently, 'Both my sons . . .'

She reminded him gently, 'But you still have Nick.'

4

SHE didn't mourn Tom any more. She looked back on their brief marriage as something infinitely sweet and distantly sad; complete in itself. Life changed, people changed, and she had known Tom so briefly that he seemed to her, now, almost as unreal as he had been during the years of her adolescence, when she had worshipped an image of him in her dreams. She sometimes thought that she could as easily have pointed to any of the family portraits on the walls of Provost Charters and said, 'I was married to him.' The baby had given her a reason for looking forward, not back. If she still, occasionally, found herself shedding a sentimental tear over the past, it wasn't for herself or her lost love, but for Tom as Tom, the young man who had been robbed of life, and living, and changing, and becoming whatever he might have been.

His daughter wasn't like him at all, or not to look at. She was fair and dainty and hazel-eyed, and had the most engaging way of looking at you as if she weren't sure whether you were being serious or not. Her name was Alexandra Elizabeth, because the Czar had abdicated a few days after she was born and the names Nicholas and Alexandra had been on everyone's lips – especially Natasha's. It was a pretty name and Jenny had had no other preferences, but she found herself calling the baby Beth, because Alexandra seemed such a grown-up name for a baby.

Jenny could never have foreseen that so many of the world-shaking events of 1917 and 1918 would become linked inextricably in her memory with the stages of her adored daughter's infancy; and yet she found herself laughing, even during the blackest days, at the baby's genius for doing the right thing at the right time.

At a month old, she gave her first real smile; it happened on the very day America entered the war on the side of the Allies. And when the first American troops paraded through London – clean, vigorous, well-fed and full of a self-assurance that the weary nations of Europe no longer possessed – Beth produced something that looked very much like a clap of her tiny hands. A week or two later, Allied morale reached rock bottom and she turned fractious with her first tooth.

After that, it was time to embark on the long adventure of learning to walk. It took her three months, during which Jenny estimated that she had covered about five miles – in time and distance an almost exact match for the Allied advance through the Belgian mud to Passchendaele.

When the October revolution broke out in Russia, Beth was at the stage of playing pat-a-cake with Nick; by the time President Wilson outlined his Fourteen Points for peace she had progressed to playing ball.

By June 1918 it had reached the stage where Jenny wasn't even surprised that, with the Germans less than sixty miles from Paris, the baby should catch measles from Nick and be dreadfully, miserably ill. A trifle hysterically, she wished the Allies would mount a successful counterattack. Any more disasters on the Western Front,

234

and this ridiculous child of hers would probably die of the epidemic influenza that was killing people off in their thousands.

With a superstitious shudder, she thrust the idea from her mind, recognising that – with the enthusiastic cooperation of everyone else at Provost Charters – she was in grave danger of protecting the child too much, of suffocating her with love.

Sir Albert, in particular, was besotted, sitting with the baby in his arms for an hour at a time, making chuckling noises and encouraging her to tug his moustaches, while six-year-old Nick, who had constituted himself her guardian, hovered close by, anxiously adjuring his grandfather to be careful. Paul, who had seen very little of any of his sons during their babyhood, softened instantly at the sight of his granddaughter, and even Natasha, unable to discern any trace of vulgar ancestry in the delicate little face and form, fell victim to her confiding charm.

Jenny had laughed until her ribs ached when, very early on, Nanny had taken it upon herself to warn young Mrs Tom against referring to Mrs Paul as 'Granny' in that lady's hearing. 'For one cannot deny, madam, that Madam is inclined to be sensitive.'

'I wouldn't deny it for a moment,' Jenny gasped. 'And thank you for mentioning it to me, Nanny. I'll be very careful!'

5

TO GIVE honour where honour was reluctantly due, Natasha had been behaving very well ever since she had decided that it was incumbent upon her to make some personal contribution to the war effort.

What that contribution was to be had been the subject of a debate so protracted that Jenny had seriously blotted her copybook by suggesting that Natasha was being unnecessarily finicky.

'Think of all the occupations open to women these days! Railway porters, chimney sweeps, cobblers, ration-book clerks, margarine packers, people who make bandages and crutches . . . Surely, amongst all those, there must be one to suit your talents?'

Natasha had not been amused, though Sir Albert had.

What she had done in the end was array herself in her most exquisite apparel and sally forth to give pianoforte recitals to the officers at a nearby convalescent home. She was an enormous success. No one could have doubted that the very sight of her did wonders for their morale and even their health, and if any of them felt that her playing was a high price to pay for being permitted to feast their eyes on the most exotic young woman they had ever seen, none of them was so ungentlemanly as to say so.

Her contribution to the war effort did not, however, end there, or not after she discovered that some of the grandest ladies in the country had begun inviting a few of the better class of officer to complete their convalescence with a visit to Such-and-such Castle or So-and-so Hall. Just for a few days, no more, but it served as gracious acknowledgement of the officers' heroism, alleviated their hostesses' boredom with all-the-year-round country life, and encouraged the servants to keep the bedrooms aired.

Nothing could have been more precisely calculated to appeal to Natasha, and neither Paul nor Sir Albert had any objections. The result was that from mid-1917 on, there were always half a dozen pleasant young men mooning around the house, very much on their best behaviour and all of them, to some degree or other, in love with their hostess. Especially Major Granby Fox, who was somewhat older than the rest and so smitten by Natasha that he could hardly find a word to say, but simply sat and gazed at her with doggy-brown eyes. Since he had left, not a week had passed without chocolates or flowers arriving on the doorstep; it turned out that he had placed a standing order with Harrods before returning to the Front.

Fortunately, Paul chose to find it amusing. Or so it seemed to Jenny, who didn't yet know that Natasha was difficult to live with only when she was bored; and she had been very bored, during the first years of the war, because of Paul's insistence that she remain in the safety of the countryside. Paul's amusement, in fact, disguised a profound relief.

Jenny had never seen Natasha in top gear before, and it was an education. Even she was forced to admit that Natasha was an admirable hostess. Few other women, she suspected, could have presided at all successfully over house parties at which stiff-upper-lipped young British officers were required to mix with the rather excitable White Russian refugees who passed through Provost Charters in a steady stream in 1918.

They were refugees whose emotions reached fever pitch when the news came that the Czar and his entire family had been massacred. Then it was that Natasha insisted on having the children brought down from the nursery to be introduced. Jenny thought it not only morbid but unhealthy the way the various princesses and

236

countesses, misty-eyed and broken-voiced, insisted on clutching little Nicholas and Alexandra to their jewelled bosoms; none of Natasha's friends, it seemed, were among the unfortunates who had fled their estates with only the clothes they stood up in. But there wasn't much Jenny could do to stop it without provoking a crisis, which would have been a pity when Natasha was in such a consistently good humour.

In such a good humour, in fact, that – acknowledging the exigencies of the times – she had them all eating shepherd's pie once a week, and even refrained from telling Jenny more than once a day that she would be grateful if she would bath more often.

6

THE sad truth was that, however many baths she took, Jenny smelled strongly of the cowshed.

As soon as she had recovered from the baby's birth, she had begun to fidget over having nothing to occupy her. There was no question of volunteering to do something useful around the house, and Paul politely declined her offer of secretarial help in the farm office. It would be unsuitable, he said, and in any case they had a woman who had been with them for years.

After a few weeks had passed, weeks of inexpert flower arranging and exercising Sir Albert's Labradors on long, tedious walks round the estate, Jenny was desperate, so desperate that, in the end, she found herself taking over the management of the small dairy herd belonging to the home farm – a task that could scarcely have been more ill-suited to a girl who, brought up in an industrial town, was terrified of cows.

To Paul and Sir Albert, and indeed the government of the country, the great need was for wheat, and that was the end to which all their energies were directed. Paul scarcely even noticed when the cowman went off to the trenches and six Land Girls in succession put in for compassionate leave after a week of having to get up at the crack of dawn to do the milking. But Jenny, suddenly and heatedly maternal, had no opinion of wheat as baby food, and pointed out to her father-in-law with a frequency which he found exceedingly tiresome that every mother in the country was desperate for milk, eggs, butter and cheese for her children.

Paul said, 'The government is bound to introduce rationing soon. It will make things easier, and at least it will guarantee fair distribution.'

'Yes, but "soon" isn't "now". And they'll still need milk to distribute!'

'Possibly. But I fear there is nothing we can do about it. Now, if you will excuse me, I have a great deal of paper work to get through.'

Breathing heavily, Jenny had gone off and asked one of the farm labourers' wives to teach her how to milk a cow. Then she had marched heroically down to the cowsheds and set about convincing two dozen suspicious shorthorns that she was in charge and didn't propose to stand any nonsense from them. Five o'clock in the morning wasn't her favourite time of day and it wasn't easy.

But by the autumn of 1918 she had become quite attached to them, and fretted over their health and wellbeing almost as much as she did over her daughter's. They were her little herd and she was proud of them.

Though not Maybelle, who had a beady eye and a spiteful temper.

7

HER mind was on Maybelle when, with a much-needed cup of tea in her hand, she walked reeking in to the morning room on the day after Paul had broken the news to the family about Matt, and found Natasha there.

The previous evening had been one she would have preferred to forget. Natasha hadn't given way to an orgy of grief. Instead, her warm, lovely complexion had turned a pasty white and her eyes had become dull as she sat silent and shivering uncontrollably within the protective circle of her husband's arm. She didn't seem to be aware of him, or of anyone.

After five minutes that had seemed like hours, she had said desolately, 'Not Matthew. No.'

Jenny had thought it very silly of Paul to break the news to the whole family at once. It didn't ease the blow; all it did was encourage them to feed on each other's sorrow. She wondered, briefly, whether a similar scene had been enacted when Tom had been killed, but knew that it hadn't. Tom had never been beloved in the way his younger brother was.

She said, 'Missing doesn't mean the end, you know,' but Natasha ignored her. She knew herself that it had been a facile thing to say, even though Paul backed her up and Nick, with all the earnest trustfulness of childhood, said, 'God wouldn't *let* Matt be killed. He's probably just hurt himself and can't get back. He's probably hiding somewhere.'

But Natasha said emptily, 'I saw an aeroplane crash, once.'

And that, last night, had been all.

This morning it was different. Natasha, who never allowed herself to be seen when she was less than impeccable, was sitting at a table in her blue velvet dressing robe, her hair tumbling down her back and tears pouring down her cheeks, rummaging through an untidy heap of papers. Usually, her elegance gave her an ageless quality, but now, although she clearly hadn't slept at all, she looked very much younger than her twenty-nine years.

'Matthew's poems,' she sniffled in response to Jenny's startled enquiry. 'Here's one.' She put a paper to one side. 'Oh, and here's another.'

Jenny hesitated and then, since she didn't seem to have much alternative and was, in any case, mildly curious, put her cup down and said, 'May I see?'

The poems, most of which were clean copies, were written in a crisp, distinctive hand that seemed to Jenny to be nine parts controlled and one part impatient. It wasn't the kind of copybook one was taught in school.

> Strange now to think how first we welcomed war,
> Like longed-for thunder in the sultry air . . .

Tidily, Jenny put the poem face down on a corner of the table.

> I have no right to fear the giving,
> Who have known comfort, and good times, and tenderness . . .

The next one reminded her of Shakespeare on a bad day.

> If life for death be some divine exchange,
> And all the soul's great splendours may be bought . . .

The one after that had overtones of Shelley.

Say not, 'He was'. He is a presence still,
A presence at the dawn, at dusk, and in the night . . .

As it joined the others on the pile, she wondered whether Matthew had no voice of his own.

It seemed probable. To her, he was a study in contradictions. She remembered him as a rather monosyllabic, standoffish youth and knew that Tom, under the veneer of brotherly amiability, hadn't cared for him much, either. But to everyone else at Provost Charters, Matthew was the golden boy of the family, handsome, brave, and clever, everything that the young, upper-class English male was supposed to be. Jenny wrinkled her nose. Even if the face he presented to the world had changed, she could still imagine condescension written all over it.

And then she remembered that he was probably dead, and felt ashamed of herself.

She had plodded through several more poems before she came to one so different that she wondered whether it had been written by someone else. And yet the handwriting was the same, or almost the same; a little younger and more ragged.

It wasn't a very good poem, scarcely a poem at all, but there was an honesty about it that was raw and shocking. Here were no carefully rounded phrases or uplifting thoughts; instead, it was a description of the first night in the Dardanelles, when the men who had survived the landings – 'Clerks, tailors, farm boys, factory hands, Whose only former sight of death, Was grandad in his coffin' – had raked over the beaches sorting out the wounded from the dead. Many of the dead had lain appallingly injured half the day, helplessly awaiting the new wounds that would kill them.

The M.O. says that you can often tell
What happened, from the blood.
'This bullet here put out his eye, d'you see?
Then shrapnel to the jaw and through his liver.
That sticky darkness where his balls should be,
That's the machine-gun. Splits you like a cleaver . . .'

The whole poem ran to almost three pages and ended on a simply-phrased note of compassion, almost of fatalism, that was alien to everything Jenny thought she knew about her brother-in-law.

Lonely the suffering. Lonely the death.
Rest now, in peace, my friend.
We'll take the disc from round your neck,
And bury you, and notify your folk,
And write, 'The End'.

'How old was he when he wrote this?'

'Which? Eighteen, I suppose. Oh, God! Where *are* the ones he gave me when he was convalescing after the Somme. They were so splendid.'

It seemed a strange word to use. 'Did he always . . .'

Jenny could have bitten her tongue off but, fortunately, Natasha hadn't heard her.

After a moment, she tried again. 'Does he always show you his poems?' She had wondered, sometimes, whether Natasha's vaunted closeness to her 'darling boy' might be no more than a reflection of her own need to be first in everyone's eyes, but if he had been in the habit of showing her what he had written, there must have been more to it than that. Writing had always seemed to Jenny to be a baring of the soul.

'Of course.' Natasha raised her head, and her hands were suddenly still. 'I remember when he was in hospital. He was so pleased with himself, because he wanted to transfer to the Flying Corps and there was some stupid rule that said he could not do so when he was in France. So he was *happy* to be wounded and sent back to England.

'I asked him why he had not written any poems for so long. I had just read some by a young man called Sassoon and I did not like them at all. They were bitter and ugly. And Matthew said, "But that is what war is like."'

Her swimming, ice-blue eyes were staring blankly ahead as if she were seeing Matthew again, and talking to him in the officers' convalescent ward of a London hospital on a dusty summer's day. Jenny could imagine it all easily enough – grey-green walls, thirty or forty beds, perhaps some stained cut-glass vases with flowers in them; a few officers loafing about in dressing-gowns; others in bed, smoking and reading the newspapers; a gramophone churning out *At the Fox-Trot Ball* or *Everybody's Doing It*.

A million miles from the trenches.

'The ignorance of everyone at home here disgusted him. What he called the self-seeking, and the way everyone so effusively praised "our brave boys", without stopping to imagine what the trenches

241

were really like. People who sent parcels of food and books and, by doing so, thought their duty was done.'

She stopped suddenly, and then said, as if it had occurred to her for the first time, 'People like me.'

The tears overflowed, but she brushed them away and went on, 'And then he said, "Look in that drawer, and you will see the poems I have been writing. You can take them home with you."

'So I did. But they were just as harsh as Mr Sassoon's and I told him so when he came here to finish his convalescence. I said they were not at all what I expected from my darling boy.

'He laughed at me, and took them away and brought them back, saying, "There you are. Is that more the kind of thing you wanted?" And he had made them rhyme properly, and although they were still sad, they were not depressing because, at the the end, he added a little twist of – of dark humour. There was one – I will find it in a moment – about a very well-bred officer who was mortally wounded, but did not mind dying – "For, really, dear fellow! The noise! And the people!" One knows *exactly* how he felt!

'I told Matthew that he was very clever, and these were precisely the kind of poems *everyone* wanted to read. Not romantic and uplifting, like Mr Brooke's, which none of us can believe in any more, but not crude, like these new young men. And he laughed again, and said, "Keep them, if you like them." And – and – and then he went back to the war.'

She produced one of her husband's handkerchiefs from her pocket, and blew her nose, and said, 'So I am going to have all his poems printed and put in a book – a beautiful book – and I shall send it to all kinds of important people, and it will be his memorial.'

Jenny, at first taken aback and then shocked, exclaimed, 'But should you? They're so personal. Natasha, you *can't*!'

It was the wrong thing to say, even if it did restore Natasha briefly to herself. Her fair brows lifted. 'It is not for you to tell me what I can or cannot do.'

8

AND that was how Matthew, limping filthily and comprehensively bandaged out of a half-ruined cellar near Tournai on the last day of October, found himself a hero.

'Bang on the nail,' crowed one of the war correspondents accompanying the advancing British force. 'Couldn't have timed it better, old son! The posthumously published poetry of a fighter ace is one thing. But when the bloody corpse comes back to life on publication day, that's a story!'

PART THREE

1918–1929

One

1

ON Friday the thirteenth of December 1918, Jenny stood under the porte-cochère of Provost Charters watching Matthew Britton's return to his ancestral home and thinking, 'Well, really!'

The extravagance of Natasha's welcoming embrace didn't surprise her; Natasha was the most self-indulgent woman imaginable, emotionally as in every other way. But Jenny found it more than a little confusing to see the brittle and guarded young man who, an hour earlier, had stampeded her cows and crashed his motorcar, displaying such uninhibited – not to say uncalled-for – enthusiasm. He didn't seem to have any more sense of propriety than his stepmother!

Unobtrusively, Jenny glanced round. She herself, impartially prejudiced, would have apportioned the blame for the disturbing little scene equally between Natasha and Matthew, but she knew that Paul was constitutionally incapable of blaming Natasha for anything. He, poor man, was looking quite hurt, while Sir Albert had the gleam in his eye that usually meant he was wondering whether it might be worth stirring things up a bit more.

It seemed to Jenny that diversionary tactics were required, so she gave Nick and Beth a little push, murmuring, 'Say hello to Matthew!'

Nick needed no encouragement. Before anyone could stop him, he had leapt up to fling both arms round Matthew's neck and then, with seven-year-old abandon, hauled himself up to sit astride his brother's hips, legs locked round his waist.

Before their eyes, all the colour drained out of Matthew's face and his mouth tightened until the muscles of his jaw and neck stood out like cords. Jenny thought he was going to faint, which wouldn't have surprised her.

After his aeroplane crash three months before, he had spent six half-starved weeks in a Belgian cellar without medical attention or painkillers, his broken bones and bullet wounds roughly tended by an elderly farm labourer; then there had been the spell in hospital, being taken apart and put together again; and today he had topped things off by putting the Hispano-Suiza in a

247

ditch. There probably wasn't a bone in his body that wasn't giving him agony.

Since no one else showed any signs of doing anything, Jenny stepped forward and detached a protesting Nick from his perch, setting him down on terra firma and saying calmly, 'What a detestable boy you are. Where are your manners? You're supposed to be introducing Beth to her new uncle.'

'Oh, I forgot! So I am.'

As the child reached out to take Beth's hand and lead her forward, Matthew's eyes met Jenny's for the briefest of moments and she saw in them a rueful thanks. It made her feel more charitable towards him, even though it annoyed her unreasonably that he wouldn't admit to feeling as if he were at death's door.

With care, Matthew dropped to his heels so that his face was almost on a level with Beth's, and smiled at her, and said, 'Hello! Are you going to be my best girl?'

He had an unusually attractive smile when it wasn't complicated by past strains and present tensions, and it was only a matter of seconds before Beth's wide-eyed and doubtful stare vanished and she lit up inside and placed her free hand confidingly in his. 'Yes, please,' she breathed.

And so, when they went indoors soon after, Matt re-entered his ancestral home after his years away not with his father's arm benevolently round his shoulders or his stepmother's lovingly round his waist, but with an ecstatic child hanging onto each hand as if they would never let go.

Jenny, meeting Natasha's baleful glance, smiled at her brilliantly.

2

DURING the days that followed, civilised behaviour was in the ascendant and no one did or said anything that might upset anybody else. Even so, Jenny couldn't help noticing that Natasha was working very hard at being sweet and loving to everyone – except Jenny, of course – while Sir Albert was unusually chirpy and Paul at home for a much larger part of the day than usual.

As for Matthew, Jenny didn't know what to make of him. The boy of the shipyard, the airy young captain of the Somme, Tom's over-indulged brother, Natasha's 'dark Adonis' – he was none of these.

Not even by mixing them could she produce any approximation to the lean and faintly caustic reality. The lavishness of his response to Natasha's welcoming embrace, she soon decided, must have been some kind of aberration. Perhaps he'd had a temperature.

More irritated than intrigued, she couldn't think why she was letting it bother her, except that she was interested in people and usually rather good at reading them.

Not knowing who he was, of course, made him difficult to talk to. In fact, she wasn't sure there was anyone *there* to talk to, because it seemed to her that the man inside Matthew Britton was almost completely detached from the one who had come home to his family, the one who behaved as if he were perfectly fit in mind and body, his convalescence no more than a convenient fiction that enabled him to spend Christmas in a comfortable house in the country instead of some cold, draughty RAF station.

None of his family seemed to notice that there was anything wrong with him, and Jenny readily admitted that he kept the charade up very well. Indeed, when Nanny Baylis descended on him the day after his arrival with a predatory gleam in her eye that spoke as clearly as words of hot gruel, and rugs over knees, and weeks of gentle invalidism, he leapt successfully to his feet and said, 'I think I'll take a gun out. It'll make a change to shoot at something that can't shoot back.'

Jenny, sighing over the folly of men in general and this man in particular, said, 'May I recommend the rabbits? Unless you don't care for green vegetables, of course.'

'Cabbage thieves, are they?'

'Incorrigible. If you'd like to wait a moment, I'll get a coat. Your father had a grand reorganisation in the gunroom a few weeks ago, and I'd better come and show you where everything is.'

The fleeting surprise on his face annoyed her. Even if he did have other things on his mind, he had no right to make her feel like an ignorant outsider.

She said abruptly, 'Why the surprise? I'm perfectly capable of telling a gun from a broomstick.'

It was a cold, dank, windless day, the kind of day that got into your bones; beyond the stables, the rooks were wheeling and chattering among the leafless birches, but all else was silence. As Jenny and Matt walked along the path behind the servants' wing, she said, 'There are scarves and gloves in the gunroom, if you need them.'

'Thank you. But I'm inured to cold. You can catch frostbite above the clouds in an open plane. And please don't misunderstand me. It's just that my mind isn't adjusted to thinking of you in terms of Provost Charters rather than the shipyard; of sporting rifles rather than puffers and Cheugh Jeans.'

'I've every right to be here, you know!' She was aware of sounding defensive, and exasperated by it, but his indifferent courtesy demoralised her more than Natasha's open contempt had ever done. 'I'm just as much a part of the family as – as anyone else.'

'Tash, you mean? I suppose so.' He didn't look at her, and he didn't sound convinced.

But even as she exclaimed, 'Yes, of course I am,' she knew it wasn't true and that his scepticism was perfectly fair, even if he didn't have to be so offhand about it. Incurably honest, she changed the words almost before they were out of her mouth. 'No, I'm not.'

Then he did turn his head, and looked at her appraisingly. 'Did you really expect to fit in here? I was listening to you and Tash last night with something akin to awe. A thin layer of honey over unplumbed depths of vinegar. Both of you. Why *did* you come? You must have known it would be a case of different worlds.'

She sighed. 'It seemed the obvious thing to do. Tom would have wanted his child to be born at Provost Charters.'

Matthew said nothing, and she went on drearily, 'Though I don't know, any more. Until the war was over, there seemed no purpose in planning ahead, but now ...' She couldn't very well confess to what was really worrying her – that she might become like Natasha, living a pointless existence with nothing to do but spend money or stir things up to relieve her boredom. 'I can't stay here doing nothing.'

He shrugged. 'Well, don't. Why should you?' He clearly couldn't understand why she was making such heavy weather of it.

'Because if I don't stay here doing nothing, I have to go somewhere else and do *some*thing,' she said. 'Have you any suggestions? Women have had a good many opportunities during the war, but we'll all find ourselves right back at the kitchen sink again when the men come home from the trenches!'

He half-laughed. 'You can hardly expect me to see anything wrong in that. Anyway, there's no law that says *you* have to do what other women do. From what I remember of you, I should have thought you were perfectly capable of saying to hell with convention.'

She unlocked the gunroom door. 'Easier said than done.'

'Why? Convention's no more than a formula for mediocrity. It's like the rules of a gentleman's club, designed to ensure that other people don't offend you. Or excite you.'

'Here's the key to the gun cabinet,' she said, rattling the bunch with unnecessary vigour, 'and this one's for the ammunition drawers. The cleaning materials are in that cupboard under the window. And it's all very well for you to sneer at convention. You're rich. You can afford to.'

His crack of laughter stopped her halfway to the door. 'Rich? My dear good girl, what makes you think that? You don't know much about money, do you? My grandfather's rich. My father's moderately rich. But I can assure you that, except possibly on paper, I am *very* far from being rich.'

'Yes, well everything's comparative, isn't it?' she said, and then turned her head sharply to see her small daughter tiptoeing in through the door. 'Beth! What are you doing here without a coat? Where's Nanny? Have you slipped out without her knowing?'

But Beth scampered past her, making straight for Matthew with an expression that was half mischief and half anxiety on her face, holding out both hands to him as if he were the one person she had been waiting for all her short life. As if, Jenny thought with a sudden, sick feeling, her unknown father had come home from the war.

Matt, grinning, swept the child up into his arms, saying, 'Oh, dear! What cold hands! Here, tuck them inside my jacket and warm them up.'

Jenny couldn't speak for a moment, but then, observing her daughter's look of blissful idiocy, she sighed and said, 'Honestly! Children! I'm sorry, Matthew. You'll probably have her following round at your heels like a puppy until she gets used to your being here. Now, Beth, you're not to be a nuisance! Do you hear me?'

But Matt, chuckling down at the child, said, 'Nonsense! I don't think I've ever been followed around by such a pretty girl before. I don't mind in the least.'

3

HE was to revise his opinion before many days had passed.

On the Wednesday evening, emerging from the civilian bliss of a pre-dinner bath, he tucked a towel round his waist and went over to the mirror to shave.

It was an effort. Everything seemed to be an effort at the moment, because with the sudden relaxing of nerves that, for the last four years, had been as tightly coiled as watch springs, he had been overcome by an almost paralysing sense of lethargy. Every commonplace remark, every smile, cost him an incalculable effort, even if he was being quite successful in not letting it show; at least, none of his self-centred family had noticed, though he wasn't so sure about Jenny Jardine. Of all the unlikely girls for Tom to marry! He must make an effort to behave as if she *was* one of the family now.

He was using his left hand to stretch the skin taut from temple to jaw while, with the right, he drew the cutthroat razor carefully over his cheek, when he felt the towel round his waist un-tuck itself and begin to slide gently towards the floor.

Swearing under his breath, he lowered a hand to retrieve it.

What his hand connected with, however, was not the towel but something much less yielding – a head of soft, fair hair with a pretty little two-year-old girl underneath.

It wasn't even as if he'd needed confirmation that his nerves weren't up to much, he thought as, letting out a squawk like a Victorian virgin, he dropped the razor, clapped his hands over the more intimate parts of his anatomy, and did a faster about-turn than he would have thought humanly possible, considering that he was almost completely hemmed in by washbasin and child.

'Close your eyes!' he commanded, scanning the bathroom for another towel. The child was standing bang in the middle of the one he had been using, and it dawned on him that it must have been she who had loosened the damned thing by tugging on it to attract his attention.

'Why?'

'Never mind. Just do it.'

'Will I get a nice surprise when I open them again?'

'Yes. No. I mean . . . Close your eyes!'

After that, things deteriorated rapidly, because there didn't appear to be another towel, and every time Matt, his legs crossed like an end-of-the-pier comedian trying to prevent his trousers from falling down, picked Beth up from the towel and planted her on the floor with her back to him, she bounced round again, giggling merrily and conveying that she regarded it all as a lovely game.

And when at last he had a grip on the towel and was hurriedly shaking it out preparatory to rewrapping himself, a puzzled little frown suddenly came over her face and she stretched out an investigative hand towards him.

He leapt back so precipitately that he dropped the towel again and very nearly toppled over into the bath.

Reflecting, a trifle hysterically, that he would have been feeling distinctly hot under the collar if he'd been wearing one, he said with a despairing clutch at authority, 'You shouldn't be here, sweetheart. Nanny's probably looking all over the place for you! Why don't you run along and I'll come and see you later when you're tucked up in bed!'

But Beth was as single-minded as any other child when there was something she didn't understand. Taking another step forward and pointing, she lisped, 'What's 'at, Uncle Matt?'

He blushed. God help him, he *blushed*, even as he groaned to himself at the thought of all the things well-brought-up girls weren't supposed to know about until their wedding night.

His sister-in-law wasn't going to be at all pleased.

4

HALF an hour later, emerging from his room clean and decent and impeccably clad in full uniform – the only formal wear he possessed that still fitted him – he caught sight of Jenny descending the stairs from the nursery floor.

She didn't look as if she knew anything to his discredit, or nothing more than usual, so he hesitated for a moment before he said, 'Jenny, can we have a word? Er – about Beth.'

'Oh, dear!' she said, as he joined her and they turned towards the main staircase. 'Is she being a pest?'

He chuckled, running one long finger along the line of his jaw almost as if he expected to find traces of soap still there. 'It's not so much that. The thing is, since no one but grandfather and I use the blue bathroom, I don't usually bother to lock the door, and this evening Beth came pattering in, looking for me, when I was – er – a trifle underdressed. I just thought I ought to mention it, in case you discovered that she was rather more – er – knowledgeable about – er – some things than you would like. I wouldn't want anyone else to get the blame.'

Raising his eyes from the treads, on which he had been concentrating with unnatural care, he saw without surprise that Jenny was tight-lipped with mortification; in a moment, she was going to give him a thorough ticking off. Trying to avert it, he went on lightly, 'Don't be too severe with me for leaving the door unlocked. I've already been punished enough. I almost had a seizure when the child pointed at me and enquired, "What's that?"'

But he had only made matters worse. Jenny flushed scarlet, and opened her mouth to speak.

Unfortunately, neither of them had noticed that Natasha was right behind them on the stairs.

She had been deliberately silent, because she strongly disapproved of her darling Matthew having private conversations with Jenny and wished to discover what it was that was absorbing the pair of them. Indeed, she might have gone on eavesdropping right to the end if Jenny's suddenly heightened colour had not presented her with a perfect opportunity for pointing out to Matthew just what a boring, provincial little prude the girl was.

With a soft trill of laughter that caused the guilty pair to start like frightened rabbits, she exclaimed, 'My dear Jenny! How ridiculous you are, blushing like a nun over something perfectly commonplace when you have borne a child and must know *something* about men! Admit it! I have had to warn you before about this mealy mouthed hypocrisy of yours!' The roguish smile that accompanied her words was intended to reassure Matthew that she was not being unkind – but Jenny knew better.

Descending the three steps that separated them, Natasha linked her arm in Matthew's and gave it a playful squeeze. 'And Matthew, my darling boy, you must not encourage her. So boringly *bourgeois*.'

Jenny, furious with herself – and Matthew – for giving Natasha such an opening, glared at her while she tried to think of some suitably cutting reply, but before she could find one Matthew himself came to her aid.

In other circumstances, he might have viewed Tasha's rudeness as no more than an extreme case of Tasha being Tasha and, although he would probably have tried to gloss over it, would still have been in sympathy with her on general principles. Primness and propriety bored him every bit as much as they did her.

But on this occasion, he thought she was being much too rough with Jenny. And besides, she was in his black books.

'My dear Tasha, you are leaping to the most vulgar conclusions,' he said acidly, ignoring the fact that Jenny – and he himself – had leapt to precisely the same conclusions. 'As it happens, I still have a raw, nasty-looking, stitched-up scar running over my hip bone to my abdomen. That was what interested Beth, as you would have discovered if you had not heard only a part of the conversation. It occurred to me that Jenny might think it undesirable, as I do, that a child of Beth's tender years should be exposed to the ugly effects of physical injury.'

And that, he reflected with satisfaction, ought to repay the debt he owed Jenny for saving him from Nick's over-enthusiastic attentions the previous Friday.

For a moment, Natasha's ice-blue eyes and Jenny's hazel ones rested bemusedly on his expressionless face, and then dropped to meet across his uniformed chest.

Natasha said suspiciously, 'Then why was Jenny blushing?'

If Matt could do it, Jenny could. Loftily, she said, 'Simple annoyance over the fact that your darling boy seems to have forgotten that the free and easy manner of life to which he has been accustomed during these last four years of war is not acceptable in a civilised household.'

Matt, who had never had the misfortune of being condescended to by his stepmother, looked mildly taken aback, but Jenny was pleased to see that, for once, she had succeeded in rendering Natasha speechless.

5

MATT hadn't intended to talk about his plans, or the other thing that concerned him, until he was feeling more like himself. He wouldn't have chosen, either, to lay his cards on the table before the season of goodwill was over; he didn't want to end it prematurely.

But the conversation on Christmas Eve took a turn that gave him no alternative, and the result was to be one of the most disruptive evenings in the whole history of Provost Charters.

They were all, save Jenny, sitting lethargically before the fire in the drawing room, digesting an excellent dinner, while Jenny was up a ladder putting the finishing touches to the Christmas tree. This irritated Natasha, who disliked people being busy around her when she was idle, but his brother's widow, Matt noted, ignored her. With dry amusement, he reflected that there couldn't be many carpenters' daughters from the Clyde with the stamina and strength of mind to hold their own against an English stately home *and* Natasha.

'An improvement on Christmas Eve last year,' his father remarked idly.

'Oh, I don't know. At least at Cambrai we didn't have to swallow Russian rice pudding.'

Natasha chuckled. '*Mon dieu!* Do you remember my first Christmas here? And Tom, with his "heathen foreign customs"!'

Matthew flicked a glance at Jenny who, with a small frown of preoccupation, was moving a candle a couple of inches to starboard and showed no signs of having heard.

'And our first experience of your destructive habits,' he remarked. 'I'm amazed we have any decent glasses left. Your aim was always excellent. I can't tell you how many times I gave thanks that the Hun archies didn't have Russian training.'

Sir Albert exhaled a large cloud of Havana. 'Shoot at you, did they?'

'Y-e-e-e-s.'

'Never liked Germans.'

'No?'

'No. Baden-Baden's full of them. Clicking their heels. Bowing. All that beer and *wurst*. The Stephanie's a damn' good hotel, mind you, but I've always preferred Menton myself. Good thing the war's over. I can start taking the waters again. You should try them yourself, young Matthew.'

Ignoring the old man with the ease of long practice, Paul said, 'You will certainly need a holiday. I imagine you must have had enough action and excitement to last you a lifetime. It is a pity that Hamish is determined to retire so soon. He has fixed on the day the Peace Treaty is signed, whenever that may be. In about six months, I suppose. And since you ought to have at least three months overlap with him, I am afraid it will not allow you as long a break as you would like.'

Matt sat for a moment with his teeth clenched on his pipe stem and his hands beginning, very slightly, to shake. He had expected to hear urgings to go back to Oxford, to take time to think before he made up his mind what he was going to do. He had even anticipated mention of the shipyard. But he hadn't foreseen this arbitrary disposal of his future. It hadn't occurred to him that he wouldn't be asked.

Carefully, he said, 'You're not seriously suggesting I should take over the shipyard?'

'Naturally.' His father was faintly surprised. 'Though if Tom had been alive, of course, the question would not have arisen.'

'Tom didn't want to take over the yard.'

Paul sighed, a man who, knowing his word to be law, found any discussion of his decisions the merest waste of time. 'He recognised that it was inevitable.'

'Uncle Felix didn't want to take over the yard, either.'

The atmosphere was suddenly still.

Matthew said, 'But he, too, did what he was told.' And since he was sufficiently angry to feel the need to draw blood, went on, 'You, on the other hand, never do anything you don't want to do. Doesn't it embarrass you?'

'*Matthew!*'

'You're still under fifty, father. Why don't *you* take over the yard?'

6

SOMNOLENTLY, Sir Albert muttered, 'He doesn't know a keel from a hull.'

Father and son stared into each other's eyes. The resemblance between them was very marked.

Abruptly, Paul flicked his cigar into the fire. 'I will overlook your impertinence, Matthew. I will merely remind you – much though it grieves me to have to do so – of your duty to the family.'

'To hell with the family.'

No one believed him at first.

His father said coldly, 'It seems I must also remind you that you are not in some RAF Mess but in your stepmother's drawing room, where such language is not acceptable. You . . .'

But Natasha, rising suddenly and gracefully to her feet, crossed the room and placed a protective arm round her stepson's shoulders. Her voice vibrating and her accent very strong, she exclaimed, 'No, Paul! You cannot *possibly* expect my darling boy to bury himself in a dirty, dreary shipyard. I will not permit it!'

Jenny, who had been busily pretending to herself that she wasn't involved, couldn't repress a twitch of annoyance. How dared That Woman call the shipyard dreary! It was also very silly of her to try to intervene between father and son, especially in a way that could only exacerbate Paul's temper.

Paul ignored his wife. 'No, Matthew. You go too far. You are my son, and you will do as you are bid.'

How many times during his childhood, Matt thought suddenly, had his father spoken to him in just those terms? Old habits died hard. His marriage to Natasha had mellowed him for a while, but it hadn't lasted.

Rising, as much to free himself from Natasha's arm as to knock out his pipe on the hearth, Matt said, 'Don't be a fool, father. You can't get away with that kind of thing nowadays. Queen Victoria's been dead for almost eighteen years. We went to her funeral, remember?'

And afterwards, Paul Britton had surveyed his son as if he were something regrettable that had crawled out from under a stone, and told him that his behaviour had been indicative of some terrible flaw of character which had to be corrected before it was too late. Matt still found it difficult to laugh at the memory of his Great Disgrace. The cause had been ludicrous, but the sequels bitter, and the lessons he had learned had not been the ones his father had intended to teach. To distrust the people who should have been closest to him; to hate convention and injustice.

Through all the years since, Matt had tried to love his father, because he still believed he ought to. But he couldn't.

He said, 'No. Let me make one thing quite clear. I hate the shipyard, and have always hated it. For that reason alone, I would refuse to take on the job. But there's another reason. The era of the ship may not be over, but it's passing. The future is in the air, and since nothing in the world will make me give up flying, I intend to make it my future, too.'

'You will do no such thing.'

Matthew's temper snapped. 'Bloody hell! Will you understand that I am not four years old any more? Don't talk to me about what I will and won't do. I will do exactly what I please, and that is *final!*'

There was an inimical silence and everyone's head turned in irritable surprise when Jenny decided to break it. She thought it extremely short-sighted of Paul Britton to take that arrogant tone with his son, and found that she had a sneaking sympathy with Matt; she, too, knew what it was to be dictated to. Anyway, the temperature needed lowering.

Calmly, she said, 'A future in flying? Surely aeroplanes can't compete with ships? They can only carry one or two people.'

The warning note didn't escape Matt, and since he had no desire to find himself irrevocably at odds with his father, he took a breath and replied, 'Some day they'll carry dozens, and when that time comes I'd like to set up a passenger airline. In the meantime, there are plenty of other things to do. I can afford to buy a couple of war surplus planes, probably a Bristol F.2b two-seater for general work, and a Sopwith Camel single-seater for racing.'

'Racing?'

'It has its purpose. If planes are to be improved, they have to be tested in the air. Racing's just an extension of that, with the additional attraction of prize money. It's not only a matter of speed. It's fuel economy, too, and checking the effect of different elements of design. If the internal combustion engine could be coupled with the perfect airfoil, it would make the most astonishing difference to performance, and. . . Well, you can't be expected to understand about that.'

'Thank you,' Jenny said, 'but I'm not one hundred per cent ignorant. I do know something about marine engines, old-fashioned though they may be, and there's really nothing new in the concept behind test flying. There have been things called sea trials for centuries.'

Matt had forgotten how much she'd known about engineering even when she was a child, but before he could apologise, she said, 'Never mind. What else do you propose to do?'

He could sense Natasha seething over the fact that Jenny was monopolising his attention, and it tempted him to answer at more length than he would otherwise have done. 'Enter for the *Daily Mail* prize first of all. Before the war, they offered £10,000 for the first plane to cross the Atlantic. No one's won it yet, but it's a safe bet that, in the spring, everyone will be after it. It would give me capital.

'And then, since the war has wrecked most of the Europe's railway network, I'll start ferrying business passengers around. London to Paris is only two-and-a-half hours in a plane compared with the better part of a day by train, ship and train. Perhaps I can get a contract for carrying mail by air; the Americans have been doing it recently and it seems to be working not too badly.'

His father had risen and gone to stand before a simpering portrait of Mrs John Bell Britton the second. Now, his back to the room, he said sarcastically, 'You do not propose, then, just to go straight out and kill yourself doing exhibition flying, like that man Beaney?'

'Beachey. Not from choice. But I'll go barnstorming if I must. And I'll take people joyriding, and I'll loop the loop for as long as

259

anyone will pay to watch. Make no mistake about it. I know what I want to do, and I intend to do it.'

Paul turned and looked at him consideringly. 'It appears to me that you are drunk on danger, but however that may be, you can scarcely expect me to condone your desire to commit suicide.'

'No?' Matthew removed his empty pipe from between his teeth. 'I don't remember you taking that line when I volunteered for the army in 1914.'

'That was different.'

There was a rumbling snore from Sir Albert.

'Was it? Perhaps. But at least, in future, I'll be risking suicide on my own terms, and on the basis of my own judgement, not that of some fool general who thinks of the casualty list as "the butcher's bill".'

His father's eyes were impervious. 'No doubt. It is not a subject I have any interest in discussing. Indeed, if you are not prepared to do your duty by your family, I have little interest in discussing any other plans you may have.'

Matthew considered pointing out that, after four years of doing his duty for King and Country, he was entitled to think of himself for a change. But he left the words unspoken. His father's face was closed. Realising for the first time that Paul Britton understood no better than Sir Albert what the war had meant to those who fought in it, he felt a sudden, regretful contempt.

And then his father slammed the door on all emotions but one. 'Perhaps I should add,' he said, 'that when you find yourself in the Bankruptcy Court, you will be wasting your time if you come to me for help.'

It wasn't the clever, controlled diplomat speaking. It was a self-centred, disappointed, spiteful man.

Matthew ground out, 'I won't. Don't worry, I won't!' And as his father walked out of the room, added bitterly, 'Not if you were the last man on earth.'

7

AS the door closed on the echoes of this deeply felt cliché, Natasha said consolingly, 'My poor, darling boy, never mind. For even if your horrid planes send you bankrupt, you will be able to make millions and *millions* with your poetry!'

One of the Christmas tree baubles, victim to Jenny's suppressed hiccup of hysteria, dropped to the carpet and rolled to a halt halfway between Natasha and Matthew. She stared after it for a moment, and then decided she hadn't the courage to go and pick it up.

'Ah, yes,' Matthew said savagely. 'My poetry. That is something else we have to talk about.'

The slim and elegant volume of his poems – bound in sapphire blue leather embossed in silver with a winged helm and oak leaves – was something that no one had done more than mention in passing since his return home. Paul and Sir Albert had no great opinion of poets as a breed, and Matt knew that Tash had been waiting until she could catch him alone before she raised the subject. He had been very successful in avoiding being caught alone.

Now, she made the mistake of thinking that his tone of voice was left over from the exchange with his father, and smiled blindingly. 'Was it not clever of me? You want to know how it all – came – about . . .'

As her voice trailed off, Jenny said politely, though not very loudly, 'Would you like me to leave?' Neither of them heard her.

'How dared you!' Matt said, and it was so obviously a preface rather than a question that even Natasha had enough sense to remain silent.

'How *dared* you take those idle, shallow scribblings and present them to the world as poetry? As *my* poetry! Soulless nonsense, cheap versifying that I should have torn up, would have torn up, if it hadn't seemed to matter so much to you. I left them for your amusement, because you were the one who was so anxious for me to work at them, and I owed you so much that I would have done anything to please you. And what happens? You publish the things, and because I died and was resurrected the whole damned world has gone mad about them. Have you any conception of how nauseating it is to be known as "Our dashing young English Poet-Hero"?'

She opened her mouth.

'No, don't interrupt. I have hated fraud for almost as long as I can remember. The fraud of "the family", the fraud of convention, the fraud of this house, the fraud of my mother's love. And now you have made me party to becoming a fraud myself! I don't think I can ever forgive you for that.'

Natasha went quite white and her face was so full of distress that Jenny almost felt sorry for her. Almost.

'But we thought you were dead,' she said pitifully. 'I wanted you tc have an epitaph, and your poetry . . . It mattered so much to you. You told me it did. Why do you now say it does not?'

'Oh, *God*, Tash! It mattered to me when I was six years old, when I had no other outlet for my feelings. After that, all it ever was was a means of amusing myself. I found it satisfying to play with words; a kind of one-man chess. And in the trenches, it took one's mind off things when the library parcel hadn't arrived. Everyone was doing it; it was practically a cottage industry. But it was no more than intellectual exercise for most of us – and quite untruthful, because what we were doing was prettying up an intolerable reality with rhymes and rhythms. It was escapism on a par with *The Prisoner of Zenda* or *The Thirty-Nine Steps*. Adventure without pain or heartache.'

Jenny spoke up, and this time her voice was clear and deliberate. 'The poem you sent me when Tom died. Was that untruthful? No pain or heartache?'

Characteristically, Natasha was diverted. 'Which poem? When Tom died? Why do I not know about this? Why did you not give it to me for the book?'

But Jenny was staring at Matt, clear hazel eyes meeting arrested dark blue.

'It was honest,' he said after a moment, 'but an evasion nevertheless. There's no reason why you should understand, but I was in a frame of mind where, if I hadn't been able to fall back on rhyme and rhythm, I don't think I could have written at all.'

'That,' she said reflectively, 'is the second time you've told me there's no reason why I should understand.'

Her voice was surprisingly soft and pleasant when she wasn't bossing people about.

Natasha wished the stupid girl would go away and stop demanding Matthew's attention. It was insufferable. It was also outrageous that Matthew, her darling boy, should dare to criticise *her*, Natasha, when her only thought had been of him.

The colour flared in her cheeks, and her diamond earrings glittered balefully as she tossed her head. 'I do not care what you say. The world has accepted you as a real poet. No one has said a single unkind thing about your poems. You are only being unpleasant to me because I did what I did without your knowledge.'

Matt turned back to her. 'No one has said an unkind thing about Matthew Britton, "poet", because no one wished to say an unkind thing about Matthew Britton, "hero". *Can you not see the distinction?*'

'Do not shout at me! I will not have you shout at me!'

'I will shout at you if I bloody well want to shout at you!'

Sir Albert slept peacefully on, and Jenny discovered that the star she was tying to the tree was lopsided.

'No, you will not! And it is most unjust when you owe all your fame to me!'

'*I do not want fame.* Not that kind.'

Natasha's voice rose to something perilously near a shriek. 'Not want fame? How can you speak to me so? How can you be so ungrateful? When I think of all I have done for you! How much I have loved you! How I cared for you and encouraged you when you were an unhappy boy! The weeks and months of time I lavished on you, making you what you are!'

'A fraud, my dear Tash,' he said. 'I was your hobby. That was all.'

Then, as his father had done, he stalked out of the room.

Natasha cried, 'No! Oh, no!' and stood for a moment with her breath coming fast and her perfect lips very slightly open over those irritatingly perfect teeth. Her eyes were wide and shocked. Then, even as the door to the conservatory closed behind Matt, she picked up her ice-blue satin skirts and, with another scarcely audible, 'No!' ran after him.

Some little time later, Jenny descended from her ladder and walked over to the window, saying, as she passed Sir Albert's chair, 'The fun's over. You can come out now.'

Sir Albert opened an innocent eye. 'Everybody gone to bed, have they?'

She could see the Vale only as an ocean of darkness, no less dark and mysterious for the tiny pricking of lamps that marked its habitations. The sky was pitch black, so black that she wouldn't have known it had begun to snow if it hadn't been for the light spilling from the window. She shivered in revulsion. She would have given anything for brightness, and people, and human warmth.

Sir Albert stretched. 'I'm off, too, then. G'night, girl.'

'Goodnight. Sleep well.'

After he had gone, she economically turned down all the lamps except those round the tree, and went back to work.

8

SHE had learned to derive a certain pleasure from the English Christmas. It was a festival no one bothered about much in Scotland, though there were presents, of course, and stockings for the children, and roast chicken for tea. But although the children might shout their requests up the chimney to Santa on the eve of Christmas, all the adults went to work as usual on the day itself, and there were no trees and no decorations other than paper chains. It was New Year that mattered to the Scots.

Jenny had discovered that trimming the tree was a very soothing occupation, placing the baubles and tinsel and stars to their best advantage and deciding which of the smaller presents the branches would bear. She was in no hurry. Although she could think of at least one good and tactful reason for abandoning her task and going to bed, she couldn't leave the tree unfinished, and if she didn't go at once it didn't much matter when she went.

There was a strong scent of pine needles, and candle wax, and wrapping paper. The dying logs crackled in the fireplace and the house shifted and creaked, as old houses always did. The lamps hissed gently and a wandering draught rustled the curtains. From the conservatory came a barely perceptible quiver of sound, so faint that it might have been the plants murmuring in their sleep.

The conservatory was glazed all round, from its semicircular garden front to the series of windowed doors that connected it with the drawing room, the music room, and the hall. It had been the architect's praise worthy intention to provide as many green vistas indoors as he could contrive, and he had contrived very well. But the privacy offered by the lush, twining greenery to the occupants of the conservatory was sadly illusory. It was really quite easy to see in from outside.

Conscientiously, Jenny kept her eyes averted.

Half an hour had passed and she was almost finished when the door opened and Matthew emerged into the drawing room, his face unreadable but his eyes chill and bleak as the North Sea in winter.

Jenny recognised, without surprise, that he had forgotten she was there, and the slight frown that crossed his brow told her he was seeing her as an intruder. It hurt.

Neat and controlled in her simple, finely pleated green silk frock, she looked down at him from her ladder and said, 'I live here. Remember?'

And then, before he could speak, she added primly, 'And no, don't start on me. I'm strictly a non-combatant.'

His eyes in the subdued light weren't blue or, indeed, any colour. They were just dark – and fathomless. She couldn't read them at all as she stared down into them. He was shaking slightly, in a way that was unexpectedly, shockingly familiar, though at first she couldn't think why. And then she remembered her wedding night with Tom and her brows came together in puzzlement.

His lips tightened. But, before she could say anything more he gave her goodnight – with something of a snap – and strode swiftly from the room.

It was all very mysterious. She would dearly have loved to know what had been going on in the conservatory since her single and quite accidental glimpse through the door. Sheer vulgar curiosity. She should be ashamed of herself. With a flourish, she placed the fairy on top of the Christmas tree.

With a flourish, it fell off.

9

SHE was still glaring at it when she remembered something she was perfectly sure Matthew had forgotten. Skipping down the steps, she ran after him.

'Matthew! Matthew!' she whispered. 'Father Christmas!'

He was already halfway up the stairs, but he stopped as suddenly as if he had been turned to stone.

'That is *all* I need,' he said. 'Oh, *hell!*'

She had never heard anyone put so much intensity of feeling into one word before, and she had to gulp before she said, 'I'm sorry. I'd do it myself, but I'm absolutely sure the children will manage to keep one eye open even in their sleep. And it's Beth's first real Christmas. She was too young last year.'

'Yes, all right. There's no need to make a song and dance about it. Just give me a moment or two. Where's the outfit?'

'I'll get it.'

It was laid out in one of the box rooms, and Jenny found

herself sniffling a little as she picked it up, all scarlet and white and furry and *cosy*. It should have been Tom playing Santa for his daughter at her first real Christmas, slipping into her room with the sack on his back and the brightly coloured stocking in his hand. Smiling down at his daughter in her pretty, flower-sprigged cot and wondering whether she was really asleep, or only pretending. Dutifully swallowing the mince pie and glass of milk left on the hearth, and then slipping out again, leaving an aura of love and happiness behind. But Beth, poor pet, didn't have a daddy to do all the things daddies did.

So it had to be Uncle Matthew. Jenny lurked behind the door, watching, as Matthew went first to Nick's room to leave his stocking. Nick gave a great sigh, and turned over, but it seemed he was genuinely asleep, which was a relief. The previous Christmas, he had leapt out of bed, shrieking with excitement, just as Sir Albert was sinking his dentures into the mince pie, causing Sir Albert to flee incontinent and subsequently to swear off the whole enterprise for ever.

Tonight, it was Beth who was awake. Her eyes were wide open and questioning, but she didn't move. Matt, whatever his state of mind, carried it off beautifully, holding a finger to his lips, and pretending to search in his bag for the stocking, and then seeing the mince pie and milk and pretending to be surprised and delighted. He swallowed them with every evidence of enjoyment, his eyes resting on the child in the cot, so that Jenny, watching through the slit between the hinges of the door, felt quite benevolent towards him. Then he went over to Beth, and stroked her hair, and murmured, 'Good night, little one. I have to be off, now. I've lots of other presents to deliver, and the reindeer don't like to be kept waiting, you know. Be a good girl and go to sleep, and tomorrow you can have a wonderful Christmas.'

There were tears in Jenny's eyes, even as she said briskly, 'You're awfully good at it. Thank you.'

She couldn't see much of his face under the moustaches and beard, but he smiled at her in the cynical way that made her nervous. 'A pleasure, ma'am. Though if there are to be any more Christmas Eves like this one, I shall insist on a stiff slug of whisky in the milk next time.'

10

NEXT DAY, everyone behaved terribly, terribly well. You could have cut the atmosphere with a knife.

On festive occasions, it was Sir Albert's custom to revert to the French tradition of table service, which had been universal in his youth but had long since gone out of fashion. His excuse was that it gave the table servants time off, but Jenny suspected him of baser motives. Such as being able to carve himself the most luscious slices off the turkey, and help himself to the crispest roast potatoes and the curliest bacon rolls.

This Christmas, however, Matt had been deputed to carve and, as he did so, Nick enquired brightly, 'Did you have turkey when *you* were young, Matt?'

Matt, feeling every one of his twenty-two years, said with a lopsided smile, 'Yes, just like this. All golden brown and crackling. I can't tell you how we looked forward to it! We weren't spoilt all the year round the way you little monsters are today.'

'I'll have that leg,' said Sir Albert, 'and a couple of slices off the bosom.'

Matt grinned. 'Anyone else want bosom? Jenny, shall I chop some up for Beth?'

'It's all right, thank you. I'll do it.'

'We're *not* spoilt,' said Nick belligerently.

'Yes, you are. You haven't even glanced at the sideboard since you came in, whereas Tom and I used to sneak down and feel quite dizzy just looking at it. Lovely shiny candied fruits in lacepaper-lined boxes, and a basket of pineapples and grapes and bananas. Bananas were something new, then. And there were Carlsbad plums – you won't have had those because of the war – and pre-served ginger, and nuts and raisins and things. Oh, and there was something else new. Fry's Chocolate Creams. They were a great treat!'

'Chocolate creams a *treat?*'

'Pass the salt, brat. You'd have thought they were a treat, too, if all you ever had for breakfast was porridge and cocoa. And mutton broth for lunch.'

In Jenny's experience, Natasha ought to have exclaimed, 'My

poor darling boy!' but she didn't. She didn't even glance up from her plate.

It was Paul who said, rather distantly, 'You exaggerate.'

'I don't. I suppose you never really knew what went on in the nursery. Yes, grandfather?' Matt passed the bread sauce, as requested, and went on, 'But you did know that Christmas dinner was the only meal of the year we were allowed to share with you. Mulligatawnay soup, cod's head and shoulders in oyster sauce . . .'

'*Cod's head!*' It was Nick again.

'. . . then turkey and stuffing and sausages and forcemeat balls. Then a great big muscular Christmas pudding – not these puny little pies – wreathed in blue flames, with a sprig of holly in the top and a handful of silver threepenny bits mixed in with the currants. I remember it took us most of the afternoon to eat our way through it all, and Nanny always dosed us with Gregory's Mixture before we went to bed. But it was worth it. The only decent meal we had the whole year.'

'You exaggerate,' his father said again.

'The hell I do. We were brought up in the same good old tradition as you were. Or so we were always led to believe.'

'Possibly, but I do not recall being deprived of nourishment.'

'Rubbish!' said Sir Albert, spearing a sausage. 'You were, you know. Always thought it was cruelty to dumb animals, myself, but Lutetia made the rules and she said English gentlemen never over-fed their sons in case they couldn't find a horse to take their weight when they grew up. Damn' good sausages, these. Martinmas pig, are they?'

Jenny said very little throughout the meal, but listened, and wondered, and observed how wifely Natasha was being. Not once did she call Matthew her 'darling boy', and when Matthew, Sir Albert and Jenny took the children out of doors afterwards to build a snowman, she didn't even watch them from the window.

It made Jenny feel extravagantly cheerful. For more than two years now, she had been yearning for someone to put Natasha in her place, and it seemed clear that, in the conservatory the previous evening, Matthew must have done just that.

11

THE shipyard didn't crop up again for another two days and, this time, the contenders were reconciled to being sensible about it, even if the bitterness remained.

Paul was at his desk in the library when Matt, his mind on air versus rail mileages, entered in search of an atlas. He was crouching down to scan the oversize shelves when his father said, 'It seems we have no option but to turn to Howard.'

For a moment, Matthew thought he had misheard. Howard? Whose father had committed suicide at the shipyard, whose mother had blamed Paul for it, who had himself felt so much distaste for the family that he had changed his name from Britton to his mother's maiden name of Fournier.

He glanced up and asked, surprised, 'Are you in touch with him?'

'I have an address. He is in the army, Paymaster-General's department, or something of the sort.'

'Oh, yes, I'd forgotten he was an accountant.' Nobly, Matt didn't make any remarks about nice, cushy desk jobs. He found the atlas and rose to his feet. 'But surely . . .'

'If you are thinking of that old business, I am sure he has forgotten it by now. It was his mother who made an issue of it at the time, but he wrote two or three years ago to say that she had "forgiven" me before she died. Obliging of her! That ridiculous scene at the funeral was mere foolish emotionalism, the outburst of a silly, unhealthily devout woman under the stress of bereavement.'

It was one way of putting it, Matt supposed.

'In any case, it was all ten years ago now. Past history. I will ask Howard to come and see me.'

12

HOWARD arrived garlanded in gold braid, shoulder pips, Sam Browne belts and swagger sticks.

Matt, comfortable in shirt and pullover and a pair of ancient tweed trousers, extended a leisurely hand. 'Dressing down for the country, Howard?'

His cousin smiled. 'I haven't your excuse for being in civvies. The only damage one sustains in a desk job affects a part of one's anatomy that one hesitates to mention in the presence of someone convalescing from – ah – more heroic injuries.'

Matt laughed. 'Oh, don't think I haven't had a bullet in the arse before now, and very disabling it was. Good journey down? You're earlier than we expected.' Carefully, he didn't glance at the staff car and official chauffeur.

'Yes, the roads were clear after the thaw. We left early and made good time. I have to get back tonight.'

'What a pity,' Matt said, without troubling to sound as if he meant it. 'Well, I suppose we'd better go in and get started.'

'How delightful. I am consumed with curiosity to know why I have been summoned.' Anyone looking less consumed with curiosity would have been difficult to imagine.

Matt had no very enthusiastic memories of Howard. Tall and calm, six years older than Matt and four year older than Tom, he had always been much too lofty to play with them when they were boys and, in their dislike of him, they had been for once united. Tom had said that, although Howard wasn't fat, he had a fat smile that he, Tom, would some day wipe off Howard's face. It hadn't come to that, because Howard had vanished from their life after his father's funeral.

Nowadays, he and Matt were much of a height. But where Matt was lean and easy-moving, Howard had an air of the parade ground about him that matched his uniform better than his occupation. He looked stalwart, well-fed, well-groomed, and perhaps a little too well-pleased with himself. And, at twenty-eight, he still had his fat smile. Some day, Matt thought, he was going to look like a benevolent basset hound.

If it had been left to Matt, he would have put a straightforward business proposition to Howard in the library and then, the matter settled one way or the other, would have taken him in to lunch with the family. But his father, still the diplomat, was incorrigibly averse to doing things in a straightforward fashion.

'Business last,' he had said, 'in case relations should become strained during the course of it. Nor would one wish even a satisfactory discussion to carry over into lunch. I have no idea whether Howard is civilised enough to know the rules. Young people are so slovenly these days.'

Matt caught Jenny's unwary eye and detected an unfamiliar and entirely human glint of amusement in it. It made a pleasant change. Since he'd arrived home, she'd run the gamut of being brisk, polite, annoyed, colourless and defensive. It was a relief to discover there was a chink in her armour. If his father hadn't been watching, he would have winked at her.

Howard behaved beautifully at lunch, giving no hint of any impatience he might feel; conveying, indeed, that he had come to Provost Charters solely to renew his acquaintance with a branch of the family with whom he had regrettably lost touch. He had a pleasant enough manner, somewhat formal, even slightly ponderous, but he seemed able to hold his own on most subjects, and Matt could see that his father and grandfather were favourably impressed. Natasha he handled with a repulsively olde-worlde courtesy that caused her to sparkle as she hadn't sparkled for a week.

Howard didn't flicker an eyelash when, over coffee in the drawing room, Paul raised the subject of the yard, the family's dependence on it, and the importance of finding someone trustworthy to manage it. Someone, he revealed after a good deal of delicate beating around the bush, like Howard.

For a scarcely perceptible moment, Howard went still, but then, smiling fatly, said, 'My dear Uncle Paul! I am not *altogether* sure that your suggestion is in the best of taste.' Then before anyone had time to be embarrassed he went on, 'However, I shall say no more on that head. Tell me something about the place nowadays. Having inherited my father's ten per cent holding, I know of course that it has been doing well.'

'Doing well?' erupted Sir Albert. 'I should say so! Three million pounds profit, 1914 to 1918, and that's in spite of that villain Lloyd George's excess profits tax.'

'You are referring to gross profit, of course,' Howard murmured. 'So we have to deduct depreciation, management commissions and dividends, which takes us down to about half. And you must have put – what, a million? – to reserve. Even so, it seems adequate.'

'Adequate? What d'ye mean, "adequate"?' Sir Albert barked and then, deciding he couldn't be bothered, settled back in his chair and resigned from the proceedings.

'So?' Paul asked.

It was Jenny who waited most intently for the answer. She had nothing against Major Britton – Major *Fournier* – who seemed pleasant enough and would undoubtedly be competent at anything he turned his mind to, but he wasn't the right person to handle the workers in a Clyde shipyard. If there was one particular breed of Englishman the Glasgow working man couldn't stomach, it was the officer and gentleman. One look at Major Fournier and every man Jack of them would walk out on strike.

There was something else, too. Shipbuilding wasn't about money and balance sheets and maximum efficiency. It was about people and craftsmanship and flexibility and – love. All those would suffer if profit was the only criterion, which meant that quality would suffer, too, and so would business. It would be a vicious circle. Anyone who knew about shipbuilding knew that, but outsiders didn't seem to understand.

Jenny's instinct also told her that Major Fournier wouldn't dream of letting the yard tender for anything less profitable than big, smart passenger liners and the like. Her darling puffers wouldn't interest him at all.

Suddenly, she was overcome by a wave of homesickness for the yard, for the noise and the bustle, the people, the excitement, the sense of something happening. She'd rather have ships than cows any day; would joyfully exchange the soft English dusk for the garish light of the working flares; longed for the vulgar clamour of the seagulls on the Clyde instead of the unearthly dawn screech of the Provost Charters peacocks in spring.

For the first time she honestly admitted to herself how much she hated the English countryside. She detested the hunt and the hounds and the pink coats, the smells of cut grass and muck spreading, the winter dampness and the chill, cutting winds. The flatness and the silence. She hated the deep dark holly wood that never showed a berry and always made her think of something nasty out of the Brothers Grimm. She loathed the bats that, in the summer dusk, swooped and wheeled and chittered wherever flying insects congregated. She loathed the insects themselves, come to that. And there were spiders at Provost Charters, huge and malevolent, as big as mice, that were the most repulsive things she had ever seen.

Silly though it might be, the calm, green, well-tended acres of the English countryside gave her claustrophobia. They, and Provost Charters. Matthew Britton's return had let in a welcome breath of fresh air, but that was something that wouldn't outlast his visit.

She dragged her attention back to the discussion. Say no, she willed Major Fournier. Say no.

'So?' Major Fournier repeated, gazing at his uncle in majestic enquiry. 'Ah, I see. No, no, Uncle Paul. I have not the remotest desire to inherit Great-uncle Hamish's mantle. I am an accountant and I intend to remain one. So I fear that, unless you fancy the job yourself, you must be resigned to employing a managing director who is not one of the immediate family. Someone, perhaps, from one of the other yards who knows everything about the technical side. It would, of course, be necessary to keep a close family eye on him, and there I might be able to help. Indeed, I think I may say I would be prepared to commit myself to serving as a non-executive director, if you were to invite me to join the board . . .'

'What?' Paul said. 'Oh. Er, yes. Yes, of course.'

Sir Albert, awakened by a surreptitious kick from Jenny, rumbled, 'Eh? What? Oh, yes. Yes, definitely.'

And that was that.

From Jenny's point of view, Major Fournier had said all the right things. Unaware of Natasha's speculative eyes on her, she allowed herself to smile a little warily at Matthew, who must, she thought, be feeling as relieved as she was.

13

JENNY felt rather pleased with life that evening as she changed into her favourite green silk dress, which she had bought because it was simple, elegant and restrained. Privately, she considered Natasha's dinner gowns more than a little vulgar; over the last two years, every new one had been more startlingly seductive than the last. Tom had been absolutely right in describing Natasha as 'fair, flashy and self-centred', and Jenny had found herself worrying about it once or twice, for Paul's sake.

Dabbing a trace of powder on her nose and pinching her cheeks to give them colour, she wondered why he, who had been quite unperturbed by his wife's adoring young officers, should disapprove so strongly of her relationship with her stepson. He was a clever man, however besotted, and Jenny would have expected him to evaluate it, as she herself had done once the shock of that first embrace had worn off, as no more than a slightly risqué game in which Matthew responded with amused artificiality to Natasha's flirtatiousness. Irrelevantly, Jenny found herself thinking that Matt had, after all, improved a good deal since he was a boy; she had been feeling quite kindly disposed to him since Christmas Eve.

273

Reflecting that Paul clearly couldn't be jealous of his own son, she thought there must be something else behind it. Indeed, she wondered whether he had perhaps always disapproved of Matthew. The more she saw them together, the stronger grew her feeling that Paul's love for his son had more of duty in it than warmth. It was as if his entire stock of human emotion was reserved for Natasha. And that was a strange alliance, when you considered it.

But Jenny had no intention of considering it, not this evening. She didn't know why she was feeling so happy. Partly, perhaps, because the talk of the shipyard had made her feel bright and knowledgeable for a change. It was more usual for her to spend her time trying to disguise the difficulty she was having in following conversations full of allusions that had meaning for everyone except her. Having a shared class background, she had discovered, was like having a shared private language. Once or twice she had even found herself remembering, wryly, how dismissive she had been of Jack's warning that it was asking for trouble, marrying out of her class.

Never mind, she was learning. Not because she wanted to be absorbed into the class to which she belonged only by marriage, but because the knowledge would be useful when, at last, she became herself.

After a last look in the mirror, she turned out the lights, and opened the door preparatory to going down to dinner.

There were two linked shadows at the end of the corridor, and she heard Natasha's voice murmur, 'Matthew, my love! Kiss me!' and Matthew's low response. 'Not here, Tash. Don't be a fool.'

14

WITHOUT knowing how it had happened, she found herself back in her room, leaning against the closed door, shuddering with revulsion.

It wasn't possible that she could have been so wrong!

What had happened in the conservatory on Christmas Eve must, it seemed, have been *quite* different from what she had thought.

She had never been more shocked. It was awful. It was indecent. It was immoral.

She was going to have to send a message downstairs saying that she wasn't feeling well and didn't want any dinner, because she knew she was incapable of looking Natasha and Matthew in the eye and pretending that she didn't know.

It took her half an hour to calm down enough to wonder why she was reacting so violently; half an hour to recognise that it wasn't moral outrage that possessed her.

It was jealousy.

15

'LIKE a fox getting in the henhouse!' exclaimed Mrs Redick, the cook, two weeks later. 'I've never seen a place empty so fast. Can I tempt you to a piece of Victoria sponge, Mr Marriot?'

The butler stretched out a hand, saying sentimentally, 'Just like the old days. Very peaceful it used to be before the war, with Mr Paul away in the diplomatic, and Sir Albert taking the waters at one of his spas, and the boys at school. Before your time, of course. I remember when I first came here – in 1912, it was – I thought it an ideal situation for someone like myself, with leanings toward the contemplative life.'

Mrs Redick, who disliked being idle and considered Mr Marriot a lazy good-for-nothing, all manner and no substance, sipped her tea thoughtfully.

Young Mrs Tom had been the first to go, which had been a surprise. Quite a shock, in fact. There hadn't been any family quarrel – the servants would have known – but Mr Paul had cut up stiff when he heard that she wanted to go back to the Clyde and live with her parents and work at the shipyard. He'd said it wasn't proper, and – if he had but known it – the servants agreed with him. But young Mrs Tom, pleasant though she was, had a very stubborn streak, and off she'd gone, with the baby and not even a nursemaid, within a week of making her mind up.

Mrs Paul had waved her goodbye, saying that she did hope dear Jenny would find her work not too taxing and that she would be *wonderfully successful* in her new life.

No more than three days later, the Major had finished repairing that dangerous motor of his, and said it was time he was off, too, to see about buying his aeroplanes. Mrs Redick had shaken her head and remarked, 'It is my belief, Mr Marriot, that if the good Lord had intended us to fly, He would have given us wings,' and Mr Marriot had agreed.

The Major had also said he must find somewhere to live. Mrs Paul had been very upset when he'd told her he didn't want a room in the London flat Mr Paul had just taken in the mansion block near the Albert Hall. It would be more convenient to have a place of his own.

His father hadn't said a word. The whole staff knew, of course, that he disapproved so strongly of his son's flying plans that they were barely on speaking terms.

And then, forty-eight hours after the Major's departure, Mrs Paul had declared that she really must do something about arranging for the London flat to be redecorated and furnished. Furthermore, she wished to begin living again, and going to galleries and theatres. It was quite shocking that she hadn't seen *Chu Chin Chow,* although it had been running for more than two years.

The result was that she and Mr Paul had disappeared in a great flurry, leaving Sir Albert with the house to himself. And since he was bored at Provost Charters on his own and Europe still wasn't settled enough for him to take the waters at Menton or that Baden-Baden place he was always talking about, he had gone traipsing off to spend the rest of the winter at Bournemouth.

All of which had left young Master Nicholas and his nanny in sole possession.

It wasn't what Mrs Redick was used to. She went on sipping her tea and wondering whether, now that the war which had tied the family to Provost Charters was over, it was always going to be like this. All coming and going. Not what *she'd* call a proper family home.

Perhaps it was time to look for a new situation.

Two

1

'WELL, well! Aren't you a pet!' Allie said, smiling down at Beth. 'Come on in, Jenny. Is it nice to be home?'

Firmly repressing a desire to burst into tears, Jenny said, 'Lovely. How's everybody? I see Castlehead hasn't changed.'

Neither, she supposed, had No.2 Rashilea Terrace. In her memory, it had been a spotlessly clean little stone villa redolent of dusters and wax polish; a place full of good walnut furniture and dark oil paintings of stormy seas; of prints of John Knox and 'The Gleaners'; and incomplete sets of Scott and Dickens bound in artificial leather. But now she knew that it must always have been poky and over-furnished and badly lit; the kitchen must always have smelled of unaired bed, and the entire house of tripe and onions; there must always have been rust marks in the bath and cracked putty round the windows.

It wasn't Rashilea Terrace that had changed. It was Jenny, and she was embarrassed and ashamed. She hadn't realised how much the moneyed comfort of Provost Charters had distanced her from her old life, how it had contaminated her. Even her accent had almost gone and her hair and clothes were such as had never before been seen in an artisan's cottage on the Clyde. She didn't know which world she belonged to.

But Beth knew. Rashilea Terrace wasn't what she was used to and she didn't like it at all, however much she was crooned over by the stout, heavily corseted woman she had been instructed to call 'Granny'. One look had been enough to tell her that 'Granny' belonged to the servant classes.

Beth missed her nanny, and she missed Nick, her playmate and protector. She had made a terrible fuss about being taken away from her adored Uncle Matt. And to Jenny's exasperation, she also missed 'Tashy', who was pretty, and cuddled her, and smelled lovely, and made her laugh.

Now, inspecting Allie's pleasant drawing room, Beth smiled shyly and said, 'Nice.'

Jenny raised her eyebrows in mock despair. It was the first thing the child had approved of since they'd got back. 'Sit down

277

and be a good girl,' she said. 'Your Aunt Allie and I have a lot to talk about.'

One thing at least promised to work out well. Jenny was to take over from Allie at the shipyard. Allie had made up her mind that when her father retired, she too would leave. John Baine's death, she said, had fated her to live the rest of her life alone and, that being so, she might as well get some enjoyment out of it. So she proposed opening a dress shop. A good one.

Jenny said, 'What fun! Are you going to adopt a French accent and call it "Madame Allie"?'

'Well, I can't call it "Madame Alaska" or the only trade I'd get would be Eskimos.'

'*Alaska*? I always thought you were an Alison!'

'Certainly not. I had the misfortune to be born on the day Elder's launched my namesake, which displaced 7500 tons and was the first ship to cross the Atlantic in less than a week. Brittons' had made the boilers, and my father got a bit carried away.'

Jenny gave a hiccup of mirth. 'Oh, Allie, you've no idea what a joy it is to be able to laugh again, without having to stop and think first.'

'What? Nothing funny at Provost Charters?'

'Funny-peculiar, yes. Funny-comical, no. But you're going to stay on at the yard long enough to teach me all I need to know? Frankly, I'm terrified.'

Allie smiled. 'Don't worry. If you come back fairly soon, we'll have four or five months, and unless you've forgotten everything you ever knew, that should be plenty. It'll be a load off my mind having you back. I was dreading having to break in an outsider, because the new managing director – whoever he turns out to be – is going to need a company secretary who really knows what's what.'

'Oh, how I wish Natasha could hear you say that! You can't imagine how condescending she was about it all! I promise you, I'm going to be the best company secretary there's ever been – present company secretaries excepted, of course – if only to teach dear Natasha that a girl from the Clyde is *not* to be looked down on by a *damned* Russian countess.'

Well, well, Allie thought. The words were humorous but the feeling underlying them most certainly was not. Knowing from Bertha that Jenny and Natasha had not hit it off in the early days, Allie – who had as much ordinary human curiosity in her make-up as anyone else – hoped Jenny wasn't going to leave her to put

278

two and two together about what had happened since. Her letters hadn't been exactly revealing.

For no particular reason, or none that she was aware of, she said, 'What did you think of Matt, by the way?'

But Jenny's attention was momentarily distracted. 'Beth, pet, will you sit still!' she exclaimed. And then, 'Matthew? He seemed perfectly pleasant. Now, will it do if I start the week after next?'

2

FOUR months later, which also happened to be three years to the day since his brother had died at sea, Matthew Britton was looking for a nice, cosy trough where he could ditch his plane between the mountainous wave crests of a stormy mid-Atlantic, and thinking as he did so, 'See you soon, Tom!'

All that effort for nothing. Whoever won the *Daily Mail* great Atlantic air race, it wasn't going to be Matthew Britton and Bill Bonny.

The shortest route, 1880 miles, was between Ireland and New-foundland, and most of the competitors had decided to start from Newfoundland, where they could rely on a tailwind to keep down fuel consumption. It wasn't a matter of penny-pinching, but a matter of weight. Matt's Bristol, despite all Bill Bonny's tinkering with the Rolls-Royce Falcon engine, couldn't be relied on to do more than seven miles to the gallon, and an Imperial gallon weighed 7.2 pounds. Matt had worked out that he'd need well over a ton of the stuff to be on the safe side – which meant that the fuel was going to weigh more than the plane. Like everyone else, he'd spent a lot of time worrying about whether he was even going to get off the ground.

There was no nonsense about an official start to a race such as this. You set off when you felt like it, which meant when you'd finished putting together again the machine that had had to be taken apart for the sea journey out. And when the weather was right, of course.

Harry Hawker and Mac Grieve, in their Sopwith, had been first away on the eighteenth of May. They'd managed to get off the ground all right, but had finished up in the sea; it had been a week before anyone knew they'd been picked up by a tramp steamer. Freddie Raynham and Fax Morgan had gone next in

279

their Martinsyde, but they hadn't gone far; only a few yards beyond the end of the so-called runway. Fax Morgan had lost an eye in the crash.

Twelve days later, it had been the turn of Matt Britton and Bill Bonny. Matt hadn't even noticed the date; all he'd thought was that the weather was less unfavourable than usual. To Bill, he'd said, 'If we don't go now, we never will.'

Lumbering along through the mud, trying to take off in something that was less a plane than a giant fuel tank with wings, Matt wondered briefly whether there was any history of insanity in his family. Because he was almost out of space, and there was a stone dyke just ahead, and if the plane didn't lift within the next dozen yards there was going to be an almighty quantity of highly inflammable fuel looking for employment.

The nose lifted; sluggishly, but it lifted. They were airborne.

Matt took a deep and slightly uneven breath, had a mental picture of Jenny Jardine looking disapproving, and then another and very different picture of Natasha. She was saying something.

'Shut up, Tash,' he muttered, but her voice went on echoing in his head.

'When we believed you had crashed, there was nothing in the world I could think of for days but of your plane going up in flames, and of you injured, and trapped, and burning, and screaming, and dying in the most terrible agony.

'It was then I knew how much I loved you.'

And because he had been thrown clear in the crash and hadn't been burned, and because in the conservatory that evening there had been other more urgent and important matters at issue, he had ignored the first part of what she was saying and exclaimed, 'Don't be a fool, Tash. You're married to my *father*.'

Ever since, he had been trying without much success to forget the whole episode. He was going to have to try harder. For one thing, he couldn't afford to be distracted by images of flame every time he had a sticky take-off or landing.

3

THEY crossed the Newfoundland coast at twelve hundred feet under patchy cloud. Matt knew that Bonny, sitting in the navigator's cockpit back-to-back with him, would be radio-ing the ground, 'All well after take-off'.

And then a hand came round his shoulder with a note saying, 'Prop sheared off the generator. Radio dead.'

Great. Who needed it, anyway? Turning his head so that his voice was carried on the wind, he yelled, 'Start navigating.'

You could get very lost in 1880 miles of sky. Bonny had a standard naval sextant for shooting the sun and the stars, and even with sun or stars blotted out, he could still navigate by dead reckoning as long as he was able to see the sea. Crosswinds could easily carry you fifty miles off course in an hour and play hell with your dead reckoning, but there was a nifty little gadget called a drift bearing plate that enabled you, when sun and stars weren't visible, to read drift and speed from the waves below and make compensations in the dead reckoning. The trouble started when the waves weren't visible, either.

The engine throbbed steadily as they flew on. After a while, Bonny passed Matt a mug of coffee from the Thermos, and after another while, a sandwich. Darkness was approaching. The last weeks had been a time of such acute strain that Matt was filled with euphoria over the fact of being in the air again at all, however dangerous the venture, whatever troubles lay ahead.

But by the time four hours had passed, and then five, and six, he was beginning to be affected by the monotony of flying over the ocean, even though he was kept wakeful by having to make constant corrections to stop the plane from skittering around. It was as if his mind and eyes had lapsed into a state where they need something to fidget about. He found himself taking a dislike to the shape of the fuselage; square as the old Boxkite. It needed streamlining. There were some splashes of heavy mud, churned up during take-off, sticking to one of the wings. He would have brushed them off, but he couldn't reach and they began to annoy him, so that his eyes kept returning to them independently of his will, like a tongue exploring an aching tooth.

Deliberately, he tried to fix his mind on the future, all the things that would have to be done when he got back to London. So much depended on whether the Bristol stayed in the air as far as Ireland; if it did, the future was in the bag. The prize money had risen to £13,000 now, because two other sponsors had turned up to add to the *Daily Mail*'s original £10,000.

Matt and Bill Bonny, in partnership, were going to sink all except five hundred each into the commercial flying venture.

Bonny had no other capital and Matt's, such as it was, was already committed. He'd even had to sell the Hispano-Suiza to get them over to Newfoundland. Smiling wryly, he remembered Jenny Jardine saying, 'You're rich!' But all he had was a five per cent holding in the shipyard, which gave him a small income; he wasn't entitled to sell it.

Even the tiny flat he'd found for himself in London was going to be a drain on his resources. But he had to have it. He couldn't, under any circumstances, share the family flat near the Albert Hall.

He couldn't risk being alone with Natasha ever again.

4

SHE WAS the only person he had ever loved. She had been an anchor to him, another self, a living warmth permeating his heart and senses.

He had thought there was nothing sexual in it. Even when, once or twice in the past, she had made him vaguely uneasy, she had been quick to disarm him into believing that she was just being Natasha – teasing, exhilarating, melodramatic – not a stepmother, but a sister or cousin with a wicked sense of mischief. And because he had wanted to believe, he had believed.

But last Christmas Eve he had discovered how very naive he had been.

This time, there had been no possibility of error. Her arms had been round him, and she had held him as if she would never let him go. Her eyes shining like aquamarines in the dim, steamy warmth of the conservatory, she had cried, 'Matthew! My darling, darling Matthew. Forgive me for what I did with your poems. It was only because I love you so very much!'

She had been insanely alluring in a high-waisted, ankle-length, ice-blue satin gown draped with georgette that revealed rather than concealed the brevity of the bodice and the clinging lines of the skirt. Her hair had been pinned up at the back, with the heavy, waving curls framing her face confined by a satin bandeau that circled her forehead, its colour an exact match for her eyes. The curls threw her slanting cheekbones into strong relief, and her lips were parted and breathless.

War had taught him control over his physical desires, but his body had been starved for months and now it stirred with appalling and unheralded violence.

She was so close to him that she would have had to be very innocent not to know how she was affecting him, and she gave a gasp of relief and triumph. Then her hips were swaying against his, and she was clinging to him so that there was no millimetre of space between them along the whole length of their bodies. If the difference in their height had not been so great, her lips would have been on his, too, and there would have been no possibility of going back, ever.

He had remembered, with a faint sense of delirium, how on the afternoon of his arrival he had kissed her sardonically, intensely, insincerely, just to teach her a lesson. Disaster, even then, had been close.

He remembered, too, his father's face.

Because of that, he was able to make a supreme effort of will and ignore the raging fire inside him, to grasp her arms and tear them from round his neck, to push her away from him and hold her, his wrists like iron, at a sensible distance.

'*What are you thinking of?*'

But this was Natasha, and she was too deeply physical, her craving too strong for her not to fight back in the only way she knew. 'I love you!'

'Don't be a fool. You're married to my *father*!'

'What has that to do with anything? I cannot help what I feel for you, what I have always felt for you since that day at Sarajevo, when I first saw you as a man, though you were still so very young. When you are away from me, I can forget you, but when I see you – when I feel you – near to me, I love you so much I cannot bear it!'

'Love me so much? Or want me so much?'

'*What is the difference?* I – love – you.'

Her voice was rising and she began to struggle in his grip.

He could feel the sweat breaking out on his forehead, not only from simple physical desire but because it occurred to him that his father, with whom he had just quarrelled, might not have gone upstairs after all, but only to the music room. From which it was not difficult to see into the conservatory.

It mattered not at all that he felt little warmth for his father. Some betrayals went beyond the limits of tolerance.

'*Will you be quiet!*'

Immediately, she stopped struggling, but her eyes remained

fixed on his, luminous as they had been throughout, and she said huskily, 'There is one way you can silence me. Kiss me. Kiss me not as a friend, but as a lover.'

He had to put a stop to it, whatever it cost. 'Kiss you as a lover? Or as a bitch in heat!'

The faintest of smiles flitted across her face. 'Words. What do words matter? All that matters is that you cannot ignore me. You *do* want me, as much as I want you! Oh, my darling, my darling Matthew – please! Let us be happy!'

Never in his life had he been aware of such intense sexual magnetism. Her eyes, lips, face and body smiled at him, enticed him, draining him of all sensations but one . . .

5

THERE was a tap on his shoulder, and Bonny passed him a note. It said, 'Need to see the stars.'

They climbed through the cloud cover into moonlight at just above six thousand feet. It was freezingly, achingly cold. But after Bonny had fiddled with the sextant and discovered that they were almost halfway to Ireland and dead on course, the cold didn't seem to matter so much. And the plane, having used up a third of her load of fuel, was beginning to handle better.

Matt dropped down a thousand feet and skimmed the top of the clouds. The moon was hazy and misshapen, the cloud shapes weird and distorted, the light eerie, the sense of space infinite. The engine droned on and on, endlessly, as they flew towards the dawn.

But the calm ended with the dawn, because dead ahead, stretching from left to right as far as Matt could see, an enormous bank of cloud reared up, sheer and solid as a cliff, too tall to be surmounted, too wide to be circumnavigated. It was either fly into it and hope to find the way through, or turn and go back. Matt flew into it.

It was a nightmare of air pockets and gusts and gales, of turbulence that tossed the plane upwards and pushed it sideways; dropped it like a stone; threw it around like some invisible giant bouncing a rubber ball; smothered it in freezing mist; bombarded it with hailstones. There was no longer any horizon to cling to or judge by, and soon Matt found that he didn't know whether they were flying straight, or at an angle, or upside down. The plane began playing tricks of its own and the bubble in the lateral level indicator, the spirit level that should have told him whether or not his wings were straight, disappeared like mercury off the top of a thermometer in a heat wave.

He didn't know where he was or what he was doing. He didn't notice, until his blindness almost killed them, that the needle of the air speed indicator wasn't moving, so that, with no frame of reference, he was flying slower and slower until, without realising it, he was on the brink of stalling.

And then the plane shuddered violently, and the engine wasn't turning over fast enough to keep them airborne, and he knew from his breathing and his stomach as well as from the whirling compass and the swinging altimeter needle that they were spinning down and down uncontrollably through the dark, and he couldn't make corrections because he still had no frame of reference, and they were down to two thousand feet, and fifteen hundred, and a thousand, and five hundred. They were spinning out of control, and still they were inside the cloud and still there was no horizon to tell him what to do.

And then at last they hurtled into the open and the raging sea was only two hundred feet below them and the plane was almost upside down so that the sea was like the sky and the sky like the sea. But it was enough. In spite of everything, his reactions were still fast, and he whipped the plane out of its spin, and levelled it out and gave it throttle.

And the propeller bit into the air, and they were flying again.

Just like that.

He had been piloting the plane for twelve consecutive hours and hadn't slept for eighteen hours before that. His shoulders were aching, his face burning, his eyes smarting and his back a screaming torture. But they were still alive and aloft and, with luck, on course.

It was only as, gently, he tried to take the Bristol up to a safer height, that he discovered the crisis wasn't over, because the mad descent had done something to the wings, probably cracked the rear struts, so that he wasn't getting lift. Was it that, or was it ice? Even those stupid divots of mud weren't helping. After four long years of surviving everything the Boche could throw at them, were he and Bill going to be defeated by a mere patch of cloud?

The plane was battering along no more than forty feet above the waves, taking a tossing from surface gusts and rain squalls that were putting a shocking stress on the fabric. Matt opened the throttle and prayed.

But no one was listening.

He didn't dare take a hand off the controls, so that Bonny practically fell out of the plane stretching to hold the sodden note-pad in front of Matt's goggles. The raindrops were streaming down them like sticks of barley sugar, which made the message difficult to read, and he didn't want to read it anyway, because what it said was, 'Second fuel tank ruptured.'

That was when he began looking for a nice, cosy trough among the waves to land in.

He managed to turn and mouth, 'That's it, then!' at Bill Bonny, and to point downwards. And Bill, expressionless as always, nodded and brandished his Very Pistol. At least they ought to be near the shipping lanes by now.

Matt began blowing into the tube that inflated his special waist-coat. There would be only two planes in the race now, Kerr's Handley Page, and Alcock and Brown in the Vickers Vimy. Matt found that he didn't really care very much which of them won. He was thinking that Tash would be pleased he'd drowned, rather than burned to death.

6

'YES, I know, dad,' Jenny said patiently. 'But I'm only a glorified bookkeeper. And female. And twenty-one years old. You don't think the board's going to listen to me?'

In less than three weeks now, Allie was leaving the yard and Jenny would be on her own. She was petrified with fear every time she thought about it, because going back to the yard had not been a return to heaven after all. It hadn't occurred to her that she would be popular with no one – a girl who'd married one of the bosses and come back, smart and anglicised, to step into a nice, comfortable job she hadn't earned.

And she herself hadn't improved matters, because she'd been determined to show Paul and Sir Albert and, above all, Natasha, that she was thoroughly capable. So she'd gone round not only the office but the works, placing a critical finger on every evidence of sloven-liness that could possibly be regarded as her business, and some that couldn't.

To begin with, Allie had left her to it, on the principle that you were more likely to correct errors within yourself when you discovered them for yourself, but in the end she'd sat Jenny down one evening in the house at Castlehead, shoved a glass of sherry in her hand, and said, 'Now, see here . . .'

Jenny had been grateful, and now she was trying to stop being Mrs Britton and get back to being the Jenny Jardine everyone had known since she was a toddler no older than Beth.

'Amatchurrs!' said her father. 'And they've gey bad memories, forbye. There was maybe a boom in shipbuilding during the war, but we're at peace now, and if that doesny mean slump, my name's no' John Jardine.'

He had aged a great deal during Jenny's years away, in his features and in the way he moved. His drooping white moustaches were yellowed with nicotine, and he wheezed a bit, and his cheeks were a mass of broken veins, but it was the heavy pouches under his eyes that Jenny noticed most; those and the invincible pessimism that now possessed him. In both mind and body, he was a tired man.

'Is it true they're wanting to convert the South Yard to take nothing but broad-beamed vessels?'

'Yes.'

'Frittering money away. They'd be better keeping it in an auld sock under the bed to pay the men when the slump comes. Whit did Mr Hamish huv tae say aboot it?'

'Nothing. Well, it was his last board meeting and he said he didn't want to poke his nose into decisions that were the rightful province of the new management.'

'Whit aboot the others? They're ignorant, Guid kens, but they're no' fools.'

Jenny, a bouquet of knives and forks in one hand and the best EPNS condiment set in the other, sighed. 'Dad, I have to get this table set. Why don't you move over to the fireplace? And if you want to know, Sir Albert and Mr Paul said the same as Mr Hamish. James McMurtrie's going to be running the yard from now on and Mr Fournier's promised to keep a stern accountant's eye on him. Howard Fournier – Mr Felix's son, remember? He'll be up and down from London quite a bit.'

Gloomily, John Jardine shook his head. 'Let's hope he's a better man than his faither.'

Just then, Jenny caught a glimpse of her brother holding the gate open for the mysterious 'someone' he'd said he'd be bringing home to tea, and told herself, as she hurried to lay out the last of the

287

knives, 'It isn't possible. I didn't see what I thought I saw.' Jack never brought anyone home except on the Sabbath, and then it was always a fellow engineer starched up in his Sunday best and intimidated into monosyllables by the thought of tea in Mrs Jardine's front room. But today – to Nellie Jardine's annoyance – it was Monday. And it wasn't a fellow engineer.

Jenny looked out again just to make sure and said, 'Dad! It's a young lady. Jack's brought *a young lady* home to tea!'

7

AND that was only the beginning. Because the young lady was part Irish, and a Roman Catholic, and she came from a slum in the Cowcaddens of Glasgow, and Jack said they were going to be married.

Nellie Jardine looked as if she were about to go off in a dead faint, and even Jenny, who had learned in the last three years to be tolerant of religious differences, was horrified.

But Jack was her brother and she did her duty by him. 'How exciting! When's the wedding? Though I must say, Miss Henry, I think it's very brave of you to take on this brother of mine. He's a terrible handful.'

Jack gave her a quick glance of gratitude, an expression that didn't sit comfortably on his harassed face.

His betrothed was dark-haired and pale, with a poor complexion, and her clothes were cheap and tawdry. But though her accent was thick, her voice was gentle and her smile shy to the point of timidity. She wasn't pretty, but Jenny could see that, for Jack, her patent helplessness might have the charm of novelty.

'Och, I'm no' brave,' the girl said. 'I couldny look for a kinder man. Will ye no' call me Lizzie?'

'Of course, Lizzie. And I'm Jenny.'

Not brave! Jenny felt her brain reeling. Miss Lizzie Henry didn't look very bright, but she couldn't be so stupid as not to know what she was letting herself in for. Whatever it might be like in other parts of the country, in Glasgow any couple contemplating a 'mixed marriage' found themselves under the bitterest attack from all sides and then, if they persisted, shunned by family, friends, even by neighbours. Jenny wasn't sure what Catholics thought of Presbyterians, but she did know that the average Presbyterian's view

288

of 'Papists' deserved to go in the dictionary as an example of bigotry carried to its rampant extreme.

The plates of cold ham and salad that were Nellie Jardine's unfailing solution to the hospitality problem were already on the table. As they began eating, Jenny asked, 'Have you broken the news to your parents yet, Lizzie?'

'Aye.'

It would have been better left there, but John Jardine raised his voice for the first time, and his tone wasn't friendly. 'They'll no' be well pleased. And whit's the priest got to say aboot it?'

Jack snapped, 'Look, dad! Lizzie and I are gettin' married whether you like it or not, and if you're thinking we *huv* to get married, you're wrong. Forbye, whit the priest's got to say is *my* business. I'll deal wi' him.'

And then Jenny thought, so that was what it was really all about! It was about Jack being Jack, born rebellious, born pig-headed, born cranky; born to resist authority, whatever shape it took. He'd even gone to prison twice, once in 1917 for leading an unofficial strike – that was when Nellie Jardine had refused to let him live at home any more – and once, earlier this year, for inciting a riot at the demonstration in George Square over the Forty Hours Strike. And now he was taking on the might of the Catholic Church. Taking it on – however fond of Lizzie he might be – mainly because the might of the Catholic Church in Glasgow was mighty indeed.

Into the uneasy silence, she said, 'Lizzie, can I pass you the scones? They're good. I know. I made them.'

It drew a small, nervous smile from Lizzie, but everyone else went on looking as if they were suffering from a surfeit of pickled beetroot. In a minute, someone was going to say something unforgivable, and Jenny knew who. She was thankful she'd taken Beth down to Iris's to play with her cousins.

When Nellie Jardine spoke, her voice was as mean and her face as tight as the knot of hair on top of her head.

'Jack Jardine,' she said, 'The day you wed is the last day you cross the threshold of this house.'

Jack didn't even bother to raise his eyes from his plate. 'Is that a threat or a promise? Talk aboot founding a League o' Nations to keep the peace! Fat chance, when a Protestant canny even marry a Catholic withoot gey near starting a war. But don't fash yersel; we'll no' be making any more inroads into your cold ham and salad after today.' He paused, and then added in a conversational tone, 'Lizzie's a fine cook.'

It was deliberate provocation but his mother ignored it.

Nellie Jardine had intended to make her point and then retire into a dignified silence, but curiosity won the day. 'Are you turning?'

'Don't be daft,' replied her undutiful son. 'Can you see me as a Papist? The priests'll no get their hands on *me*. If Lizzie believes all that mumbo-jumbo, that's her lookout. I'm staying in the kirk.'

'And what about the bairns, if you're blessed with any?'

'We'll see aboot that when it happens.'

Puzzled, Jenny glanced at Lizzie who, lips shaking, was trying to swallow a mouthful of scone. They all knew perfectly well that, unless Lizzie swore that her children would be brought up in the Catholic faith, no priest would ever bless her marriage. Could Lizzie be so blindly in love with Jack that she was prepared to risk her immortal soul for him? Trying to discount the sisterly prejudice that made this hard to believe, Jenny still sensed that Lizzie *must* have promised – hoping, no doubt, that if she prayed often enough and fervently enough, Jack would come round in the end. If so, she didn't know Jack at all.

Jenny felt desperately sorry for the girl. Though she herself had no idea what it meant to be blindly, passionately devoted to God and the Church, she did know what it meant to be blindly in love.

8

SHE also knew what it meant to be in love clear-sightedly, painfully, and self-critically.

At half-past two the next morning, she sat at the open window of her bedroom gazing up at the clouds and the stars and thinking about it. The one man in the world who mattered to her, the man who, four weeks ago, would have drowned if a passing ship hadn't picked him up, was off again, incorrigibly, on the first east-west crossing of the Atlantic. Not in a small plane this time, and not as the pilot. This time he was going as a crew member aboard the R34 airship. Jenny had seen it being built at Beardmore's earlier in the year, and had been interested, but no more. She hadn't known, then, how much its 643-foot length, its two million cubic feet of gas, its five Sunbeam aero engines would come to matter to her.

It had been due to take off from East Fortune as soon after midnight as the weather permitted (if it permitted), and then to head across Scotland towards the northern tip of Ireland. Jenny didn't know whether there was any likelihood of her seeing it, but to have gone sensibly to bed when it might be passing overhead would have been impossible.

She knew how foolish it was to sit there yearning, but it was all she had. All she could ever have.

She had been completely stunned, that evening at Provost Charters, to discover that, against all the odds, she was in love with Matthew Britton, and not only stunned but mystified. During the previous eighteen months, several of Natasha's young officers had attempted an assault, not on her virtue – they were too gentlemanly for that – but on her lips, and she had felt no desire other than to smile and pat them on the head and murmur, 'Down, boy!'

But with Matthew, who hadn't even touched her and scarcely seemed to notice she was there half the time, everything was different. She supposed there must be some chemistry at work, a chemistry that had nothing to do with his resemblance to Tom which, except for the dark waving hair and the intense blue of his eyes, was slight. Matthew was far deeper and more complex than Tom had been, or could ever have been.

Part of the mystery was that, even while loving him, Jenny was frightened of him. Frightened of his careless assurance, and his dismissiveness; of the curling, cynical grin that kept everyone at a distance; worst of all, of the brilliance of his smile when he was honestly amused, a smile so infectious that you found yourself joining in even when, stupidly, you didn't know what was amusing him. It was seldom anything obvious.

But none of it mattered. It didn't even occur to Jenny to wonder whether she liked him; liking had nothing at all to do with being fascinated, infatuated – lost. She tried to imagine him taking her in his arms and kissing her, and it needed only a moment's dreaming for the dream to become urgent and physical. When all the muscles in the lower part of her body sprang, of their own volition, to melting, quivering life, Jenny discovered a new dimension to love, thrilling and beautiful and terrible.

After a while she had been overcome by the most wonderful sense of exhilaration and challenge. She had sat before her mirror, eyes shining, her breath coming fast and her heart full of ambition. She had been in love before, blindly, with Tom, and it had been exciting and it had been sweet. But she was no longer an ignorant, romantic schoolgirl; she was twenty-one years old and past the

291

stage of submitting peaceably to the dictates of other people, and events, and destiny.

Natasha *shouldn't* have him; not Natasha, of all people. She, Jenny, was going to take Matthew away from her. She didn't know how, but she would. She *could*. She would fight with every ounce of will she possessed.

On reflection, she was annoyed that Matthew had allowed himself to become entangled with Natasha, though not unduly troubled. Men were men. She even allowed herself to think of Natasha with pity as well as jealousy and scorn – because however much Natasha wanted Matthew, she could never have him except, perhaps, for a few brief and illicit moments. If Natasha had been Scots or English, the possibility of a liaison wouldn't even have occurred to Jenny; respectable women didn't do that kind of thing. But Natasha was a foreigner and everyone knew that foreigners were loose in their ways. Even so, nothing could ever come of it, because even if something were to happen to Paul, both the law and the Bible absolutely forbade a man to marry his father's wife. Or widow. It was a most satisfactory thought!

For an hour, a week, a month, a lifetime, Jenny had sat feeling ridiculously happy, her whole being concentrated not on the battle but the victory. Smiling, she had fallen asleep at last in the divine certainty that Natasha couldn't win. Which meant that she herself couldn't lose.

And then, at three o'clock in the morning, she had wakened – wakened with the name of King Henry VIII repeating itself, ridiculously, over and over in her mind. At first, she couldn't think why. And then she remembered her history lessons at school, and how England had left the Church of Rome because the Pope had permitted Henry to marry his dead brother's wife. Which was against the laws of church and state. All the universities of Europe had been consulted, and had confirmed it.

As Jenny buried her face in the pillow and wept her heart out, all the misery she had felt over Tom's death came back to her, the sense of everything being over before it had even begun. But, then, she had had something to remember. This time she had nothing at all, and never would have.

9

HER immediate and overmastering desire had been to run away, a desire no less desperate than it had been when she fled to France two-and-a-half years before. Then, she hadn't even tried to persuade herself that she was being mature and sensible. This time she did.

It had been urgent for her to put the greatest possible distance between herself and Matthew Britton, and she had done so, but the pain and longing had grown no less over the months. She was perpetually being reminded of him. She couldn't avoid reading about his career in the newspapers, while Nick wrote to her regularly from Provost Charters and she saw Paul at board meetings. It meant she knew all the unimportant things about him, such as how the loss of the Bristol had affected his plans, and that he and Mr Bonny might stay in America for a while before they made up their minds what to do with the unexpected £5,000 consolation prize they had received for not-quite-crossing the Atlantic. About his personal life she knew nothing at all.

She didn't want to.

She tried not to allow her thoughts to stray to him, except when, as tonight, she was anxious and exhausted. Her mother had a genius for upsetting her even at the best of times, and this evening hadn't been the best of times, or not after Jack had made his announcement.

Shivering, Jenny tried to concentrate on the fact that, like Allie, she was going to have to live the rest of her life alone, and that it was becoming imperative to live it somewhere other than Rashilea Terrace. She needed a flat, a little house – she didn't know which – but a place where she could make a home for Beth and feel that she was in control of things.

She was furious with herself, every time she thought about it, for running away from Provost Charters straight to Rashilea Terrace. She hadn't been thinking clearly, and it had seemed the natural place to go. Until she had walked through the front door.

When the sky began to pale into the early dawn of the northern summer and still she had not seen the gondola lights, she knew that the R34 with Matthew Britton on board must have passed beyond her arc of vision. It hardly seemed worth going to bed, so she stayed where she was until Beth woke, as she always did when the light began to penetrate the washed-out damask of the curtains, and came pattering through crying, 'Mummy! Mummy! Want to play A, B, C!'

10

WHEN she went downstairs, her mother told her sourly, 'Your father says he's not getting up. He's got a headache. All very well for some of us! You'd better tell Mr McMurtrie he's caught a bad cold.'

It wasn't a cold. Later in the day Nellie had to get the doctor in, in spite of the expense, because her husband's temperature had risen alarmingly, and he complained of pains in his eyes and ears and was so dizzy he couldn't sit up.

He died at four the next morning, one of the last victims of the influenza pandemic that had killed thousands in the summer of 1918 and the spring of 1919, and his last words were to Jenny as she sat by the bedside, under the strictest instructions from the doctor not to touch him, not even to hold his hand, and watched him go downhill so quickly that was quite unreal.

'Look after your mother, lassie,' he gasped. 'There's a wee bit insurance, but I dinny ken how she'll manage. And she'll need you ... needs someone to nag at ... she's no' bad woman, she's just ...'

She never discovered what else he had wanted to say, because his voice tailed off and he never spoke again.

11

'I KNOW fine where he caught it,' Nellie Jardine wept. 'Rubbing shoulders with all those folk at the football!'

Miraculously, he hadn't passed it on to anyone else in the family. 'I suppose because he was such an undemonstrative man,' Jenny said sadly to Allie. She couldn't bring herself to tell Allie that even the hollows in the six-foot bed that, for twenty-five years, John

Jardine had shared with his wife, told their own tale of a life lived at arm's length.

Allie looked round from the rails of coats and costumes and frocks that had taken over one of the spare bedrooms at Castlehead, stock for the splendid new shop she was opening in September. 'What age was he?'

'Forty-nine.'

'Aye, well. He wouldn't have had much longer anyway, Jenny. Not many working men last beyond their early fifties.'

'I know, but it was a shock.' Jenny shook her head at the black blouse and skirt Allie was holding up. 'No, I ought to have a frock.'

'I've only autumn things. But I'll telephone a few people and see what I can find. With your legs and figure, you'll suit the new tubular line and you might as well have something decent you can wear later.'

'Yes.'

She didn't sound as if she cared very much and Allie knew it wasn't just her father's death that was troubling her, but the consequences. 'Your mother?'

'She's in a terrible state. She's discovered all his virtues now he's gone. What else would you expect?'

Allie could imagine it. 'Come downstairs and let's have a cup of tea.'

In the end, Jenny burst out, 'Allie, could I have a cigarette, do you think? And I have to talk to you, or I'll probably go mad. I don't know what to do. Before this happened, I was all wound up to find somewhere of my own to live, and now – well, I don't see that I can!'

'Somewhere of your own? Is Rashilea Terrace so awful?' If the self-controlled Jenny was reduced to smoking, it must be.

'There you are, you see! That's what everyone will think. Yes, of course it's awful and I hate every minute of it. But what matters is the effect it's having on Beth. I thought she'd still be young enough to adjust quite readily, but I was wrong. Poor baby, torn away from her lovely comfortable home and dumped in dreary, unwelcoming Rashilea Terrace! She's losing all that sweet, confiding charm of hers. She's beginning to girn and misbehave and throw tantrums.'

Nervously, she stubbed out the cigarette and went to stare out of the window at the glossy black-green of the holly trees that screened the road from sight. The grass was dappled with strong shadows and the gold splashes on the spotted laurels were so bright they might have been flowers.

After a moment she went on, 'The only reason I haven't moved before now is because – well – you know I don't love my mother, but I do have a sense of duty. What the neighbours think matters so much to her, and if I leave everyone will say what they always say – there's something wrong. I'm immoral, or my mother's intolerable. Or both. That's what's held me back these last months. I couldn't bring myself to be so cruel to her.'

Allie shook her head. 'You should have gone when you could.'

'I know. I can't now. And I don't know if I can – ever.'

If only Jack had chosen to marry some decent Presbyterian lassie, Allie thought, everything might have worked out. But not Jack. Oh, no.

She said, 'After things have settled down, you could come and live here, if you wanted to. We're your family, too, so you'd have an excuse.'

Jenny turned, and although her back was to the light and Allie couldn't see her very well, there was a sparkle around her eyes. She sniffed vigorously. 'Oh, Allie, you're so good! But you don't want a baby in the house and, anyway, it would probably upset my mother even more. *What* am I going to do?'

Prosaically, Allie said, 'For the time being, find a good strong-minded nursemaid for Beth! The poor mite deserves *some*one's undivided attention.'

'Of course, *yes*! I hadn't thought of that. Dad wouldn't let me employ one when we came home because he said he wasn't going to have anyone other than himself paying for a servant in his house, and he couldn't afford one and we didn't need one. I suppose it would help, and it would fairly raise mother's stock with the neighbours, but . . .'

Allie shook her head. 'But for the next few months, young Jenny, you haven't much choice. You are well and truly stuck at Rashilea Terrace.'

'Yes,' Jenny said, and then, with a watery smile, 'Oh, Allie, why is life so *awful*?'

12

'KEEP your bloody feet still, can't you?' Matt yelled, paying urgent attention to the controls.

Keith Whalley, precariously balanced on the upper wing of the JN-4D, managed to make a rude gesture at him without even checking in the punch he was swinging at Bill Bonny's jaw.

Matt hoped it looked more realistic from the ground than it did from up here. Fortunately, they had lighted on one of the few small towns in Iowa that wasn't yet blasé about planes and aerobatics. You could nearly always tell. If you flew low over a place and everyone rushed out to look, it was worth giving a display; but if only a few heads turned, it was better to head straight on for the next spot on the map, with hope in your heart and fuel calculations in your head.

The plane rocked again as Bill Bonny staggered slightly, and Matt guessed that Keith had probably misjudged things, not for the first time, and landed the punch instead of pulling it. It wouldn't be surprising. After three years of barnstorming, they were all getting bored and stale. What they needed was some new tricks that, added to the $5-a-head rides, would bring in the last few hundred pounds they needed to reach the target they had set themselves before going back to Europe or, in Keith's case, the Antipodes.

Bonny, justifiably irritated, enveloped his opponent in a bear hug, and the OX-5 engine, entering into the spirit of the thing, spat half-a-pint of oil in Matt's face.

Enough was enough. Wiping his goggles, he gesticulated to his partners and then waved up the support plane. After that, it was a matter of Bonny sliding into the front cockpit of the Curtiss while Keith Whalley swung his muscular length down by way of the struts until he was hanging from the landing gear, three or four feet above the support plane, on to whose wings he dropped. It wasn't the easiest of manoeuvres. On one occasion, he had slid off right into the pilot's lap, an unrehearsed thrill for all concerned; so much so that the pilot, landing with six feet of Australian still tangled up in the controls, had lost his nerve and sold his plane to Matt there and then for $700.

13

THE crowd had pretty well evaporated by the time they landed, but the three small boys who had been looking after the box office on the promise of a free flip were still there with the takings, a less than princely $22.23. The pilot of the support plane, a free-lance, accepted his $10 and departed, while Keith and Bill Bonny made off across the fields in search of a gasoline station and a soda fountain.

Matt would have gone with them except that there were some cows drifting around and he had learned not to trust cows. Their habit of grazing with their tails to the wind made them a handy substitute for a windsock, but they had an unhallowed passion for the nitrate dope used to stiffen a plane's wings and, left to themselves for half an hour, could lick enough of the stuff off to leave the fabric sagging like a dowager without her corsets.

He grinned to himself, thinking that was something Jenny Jardine probably didn't know about cows. Or perhaps she did. Anyway, he'd never dare tell her about it or, sure as fate, she'd tick him off for wasting his time stooging around the States, enjoying himself, when he should have been doing something useful.

She'd be right, of course; she usually was. Because he *had* been wasting time.

It had started off as deliberate lotus-eating. The first days in New York, when the crew of the R34 had been fêted in typically enthusiastic American style, had been enormous fun, so much fun that when, after a party one evening, Matt had found himself in Central Park, dancing smoochily in the warm moonlight with a pretty girl, he had realised that he had been in danger of forgetting what fun was. The war had been over for almost nine months, but only that night had he felt the weight of it lift from his shoulders, only then had he admitted to himself that he was unutterably tired of being responsible and disciplined and *serious*. He had lost four irreclaimable years of his youth, years during which, under happier circumstances, he might have enjoyed himself and sown his wild oats and come to terms with the adult world.

He decided he had a lot of catching up to do. Even so, if it hadn't been for a fluke, he would probably have controlled his new-found levity and pursued, without quibbling, the course that he and Bill Bonny had mapped out for themselves. It had been their intention to study, over a period of perhaps six months, how the American aviation industry was developing and then go home and put the experience to profitable use. But instead, one day on Broadway, they had caught sight of a familiar figure standing staring up at the Woolworth Building; a tall, rangy, bare-headed young man who could never have been mistaken for an American.

'Keith Whalley!' Matt had exclaimed.

And Keith Whalley it was, the sun-streaked blond hair and sky-blue eyes, the large nose with the break halfway down, the loosely bracketed mouth and the head poised casually on a neck that resembled a small tree trunk – all were quite unchanged since he had been one of Matt's lieutenants on the Somme. Although he had transferred to the air force during the last months of the war, he had been posted to a squadron south of Matt's and they had lost touch.

Now it appeared that, after four years of living with Poms, he was making his unhurried way home to the land of sun and space and sheep, mulling over the possibilities for an out-of-work flier. It had occurred to him that the Yanks, who had wide open spaces of their own, might have an idea or two he hadn't thought of.

Nothing could have been more natural than that they should pool ideas and resources, and it had seemed a pity not to see as much of America as possible; one never knew when there would be another chance. So, instead of driving around in $300-worth of secondhand Model T, they had invested $4,000 in a secondhand Curtiss JN-D4, and begun working their way round the country, freezing in Boston, roasting in Atlanta, stewing in Los Angeles, shivering in San Francisco.

It hadn't taken them long to discover that the greatest danger inherent in an aerobatics career was starving to death. Especially when Prohibition came in and there were no more saloons with free lunch counters where you could eat your fill for the price of your drink.

But they'd survived. During their three years they had counted the brides at Niagara Falls, and the pigs in the stockyards of Chicago. They had seen Bill Tilden winning the National Singles Championship, Man O' War running the greatest race in history at Aqueduct, and Jack Dempsey delivering the knockout to the 'invincible' Carpentier. They had been revolted by *Abie's Irish Rose*, enthralled by *Shuffle Along*, excited by Joe Oliver and Louis Armstrong's cornet duets, and bored stiff by Paul Whiteman.

They had been offended by Secretary of Commerce Hoover's declared intention to take over primacy in world trade from the British Empire, and considered it pretty cheeky of him to talk about America having a mission to reform the Old World.

They knew all about Republicans and Democrats, the Ku Klux Klan, and Sacco and Vanzetti. They'd seen Buster Keaton, Mary Pickford, and Douglas Fairbanks, and read *Main Street* and Mencken and Edna St Vincent Millay.

The only things they hadn't done had been to learn to play Mah-Jongg and participate in a dancing marathon; Keith would

299

have liked to, if he hadn't needed his feet for mid-air combat.

In short, they reckoned, they had learned all about America except how to get into a speakeasy in a town where they didn't know anyone to vouch for them. Which meant almost every town. There were times when they would have given anything for a pint of beer.

14

IT WAS two hours before Matt's partners reappeared, Bill rolling a fifty-gallon drum of gasoline before him, and Keith with his pockets stuffed with Coca-Cola bottles, a bag of food on one arm, and a girl on the other.

She was the most dazzling girl Matt had ever seen, with a heart-shaped face, luminous green eyes, shining red-gold hair, and the prettiest mouth set in a mischievous and quite enchanting pout. The only thing he could possibly cavil at as, admiringly, he watched her approach, was that she didn't walk very gracefully.

Keith, exuberant as always, shouted. 'Hey, mate! We found a sheila. Ain't she a beaut? Her name's Wattle.'

'*Wattle?*'

The girl tossed her head, and laughed. 'He's kidding,' she said. 'Of course it isn't Wattle. He says that's what I'd be called in Australia. My name's Mimosa. Mimosa Weber. My friends call me Mims.'

Matt began to feel more cheerful. 'Hello,' he said. 'How did a girl like you allow herself to be picked up by an oaf like him?'

She tossed her head again, and he wondered if she knew how teasing a movement it was, setting the lovely hair aflame – she'd been sensible enough not to have it bobbed – and showing off the pertness of her nose and the pure line of her jaw.

'He didn't pick me up,' she said. 'It was me. I mean I picked him up.'

Keith, standing behind her, was wearing a wide grin, while Bill Bonny, refusing to be involved, began filtering the gasoline through a chamois into the tank.

'Easy to do,' Matt said encouragingly.

She surveyed him a trifle warily, clutching her coat tightly around her, and then took a deep breath. 'You're the boss?'

300

He couldn't place her accent. He didn't think it was Iowa; he wasn't even sure it was American. 'Yes. Are you English?'

'Sort of. I was born in England, but my stepfather's American. Anyway, that doesn't matter. I've a proposition.'

It wasn't, presumably, the kind of proposition that instantly sprang to mind. 'Whalley, why don't you offer the lady a Coke?'

Keith shook his head, grinning more broadly than ever.

The girl said in a rush, 'I've got my pilot's licence, and I've done some wing-walking, and I'm tired of working as a clerk, and you've got two two-seater planes and only three of you. And I can see from the way you fly that you're good. Will you take me on?'

Matt opened his mouth and closed it again. When he opened it for a second time it was with the firmest intention of saying no.

She could see it, and before he had time to speak said breathlessly, 'I can pay!'

Then, without waiting for a response, she threw open her coat and, with a teasing smile, began to raise the skirt of her frock an inch at a time.

Matt had never in his life seen anything so improbably seductive. He knew that his face must be a study.

And then he got the point, because firmly strapped to each leg, just above the knee, was a king-size hot water bag.

'Bourbon,' Mims said, her piquant little face brimming with laughter. 'I hope you like it. I'm afraid I couldn't get Scotch.'

Three

1

JAMES McMurtrie's moustache looked as ill-nourished as it had ever done, and the abstemious years as an adherent of the Temperance movement had reduced his body to match until Jenny thought she had never seen such a stringy man. Or such a gloomy one. He looked like the personification of one of the deep depressions the weather reports were always talking about.

Jenny held no brief for strong drink, but she had come to the conclusion that people who crusaded against things that ordinary people enjoyed usually did so because it allowed them to feel tall and strong and righteous. Which nearly always meant arrogant and bigoted and not to be trusted when it came to recognising and tolerating ordinary human frailties and needs. After three years of working closely with James, she thought he fitted the pattern very well.

It wouldn't have been so bad if he himself had been remarkable for brains or competence, but he was incorrigibly mediocre. Jenny, sitting in on meetings with potential customers, had more than once found herself analysing – with a trace of malice – the faint air of puzzlement on their faces.

What they were thinking, she knew, was, 'This man is a member of the Western Club. And the Conservative Club in Bothwell Street. He's a Mason. He's a pillar of the kirk and a member of the Glasgow town council. So he can't be – can he? – as commonplace as we think he is. He must have hidden depths.'

Jenny could have told them that he didn't. He just had large ambitions and believed that what mattered wasn't what you knew but who you knew. Reluctantly, Jenny had come to see that, whatever she had once thought of Howard Fournier, he would have made a much more convincing managing director than James.

302

2

NOW, Adam's apple bobbing, James was presenting his formal report to the board.

For once, everyone had turned up, even Sir Albert, seventy-five years old and still in rude health despite his piteous pleas to the contrary. Jenny was rather touched when he greeted her with a smacking kiss on the cheek and the demand that she bring Beth to see him before he went back south to civilisation. Allie, on whom he had billeted himself, was very patient with him considering how revoltingly proud he was of having outlived Hamish who, though sixteen years younger, had died a year after retiring from the yard. 'From boredom,' Allie had said succinctly. 'Poor love. I'm going to miss him.' Jenny missed him, too, not only because he had been kind to her but because there had been so many times recently when she would have welcomed his advice.

James droned on, and on, and on, until Paul interrupted him, his voice cool and supercilious as ever. 'Forgive me, James, but are we to understand that the profits for 1922 are likely to be *less* than 1921? I find that hard to accept.'

The year 1921 had been a dreadful one, and Jenny knew, from her own dividends, what a nasty dent it must have made in everyone else's income.

James, who was good at dissimulating only when he had been geared up to it in advance, found himself in a quandary. 'Early days, early days!' he muttered, running a forefinger along his moustache. It was clear that he didn't want to make things look too black in case he got the blame; on the other hand, no one would believe him if he tried to make them look rosy.

Jenny glanced at Howard, wondering whether he knew what James was going to propose as a solution to the crisis, but Howard's face was as blandly unreadable as always. He would have made a fortune as a poker player.

James went on, 'On the basis of the first two quarters, however, it looks as if the figure may be in the region of – ah – £85,000.'

The previous year's profit had been £150,000.

There was a stunned silence, then, 'That's the ba' up on the slates,' said Sir Albert gloomily.

Jenny swallowed a giggle. It was the only real sign Sir Albert gave of advancing age, this tendency to revert to the idiom of his youth when he couldn't remember the English for what he wanted to say – which in the present case was something like, 'That's torn it!'

With a sniff that appeared to involve every muscle in his face, the old man reverted to standard English. 'What am I supposed to live on, eh?' And then, as an afterthought, 'And everybody else, too, come to that.'

Paul said, 'James, I think some explanation would be in order.'

James signed ostentatiously. 'You know most of it already. What do you want me to explain? I mean, it all goes back to 1919. Wage rates had soared during the war, but though we all knew they were going to be hard to sustain, every yard in the country anticipated a world shortfall in shipping as a result of wartime losses. So we all went ahead with capital investment despite it. We knew that the market for *merchant* shipping would be more competitive than pre-war, but we thought we could bank on naval orders because, although the Admiralty were taking their time about it, there seemed no doubt they would still have to replace the lost tonnage at some stage.

'You will all recall that, as recently as last year, the board agreed to Howard's suggestion that, since there is so much engineering work in destroyers, we should apply for a guaranteed loan under the Trade Facilities Act to modernise the engine shop. And then came the Washington Conference! A disaster that no one could have foreseen.'

And one, reflected Jenny, watching the sober faces around the table, that would be inscribed for ever in the hearts of every shipbuilder in the country. Because the Washington Conference of 1921–22 had concluded a naval convention by which Britain, America and Japan agreed not to build any capital ships for a period of ten years. It had meant that all contracts for the new battlecruisers, the 'super-Hoods', the big profit-makers, had been cancelled, and that even run-of-the-mill naval orders were no longer to be a cushion against the harsh realities of postwar shipbuilding.

Paul repeated thoughtfully, 'A disaster no one could have foreseen? I wonder. Hamish would probably have anticipated something of the sort, wily old bird that he was. He was a pessimist from experience, whereas we are all optimists despite experience. Looking back, I think he would have put his foot down on raising that unfortunate loan on the basis of mere speculation.'

Everyone looked at Howard, but he just went on sitting there, looking politely interested and saying nothing. It had been his idea, but scarcely his fault, Jenny thought. He was an accountant, not a shipbuilder, and accountants, she had learned, were great believers in making use of other people's money to finance things, as if the interest repayments were a mere bagatelle in comparison with the paper benefits of improved capital valuation. Uncle Hamish, on the other hand, had been a firm believer in earning the money first and spending it afterwards, and only on what you really needed. Jenny thought that was a much safer way to do things, but whenever she asked Howard what was the point of having a high capital valuation on something you weren't going to – indeed, couldn't – sell, he reeled off an alarmingly fluent answer couched, of course, in the accountancy jargon she didn't pretend to understand.

Paul shrugged. 'Ah, well. Water under the bridge. Go on, James.'

'Well, the situation in these last months has been that we have heavy interest repayments going out and very little cash coming in. As I reported earlier, Asterisk and two of the smaller lines have instructed us to suspend work on ships they have in the berths, because their sector of the market is in trouble, too. We extracted compensation from them, of course, but it has still left men and machinery idle.'

Jenny liked that 'of course'. There hadn't been any compensation clause in the contracts James had signed, and it had been she who had gone out on her own initiative and done some very hard bargaining.

James went on, 'Oh, and I should add that I hope the board will approve the decision I made last month to tender for two cable ships at a price that will show no profit at all. It will, however, allow us to pay the wages of a nucleus of our best and longest-serving men.'

That had been Jenny's idea, too. James would have laid the men off without a qualm. 'They have their dole money nowadays, at the taxpayers' expense. I see no reason why we should pay out twice.'

For once, Jenny hadn't allowed herself to be diverted by James's peculiar reasoning processes. 'Fifteen shillings a week!' she'd exclaimed. 'Plus five shillings for a wife and a shilling for each child! No, really, James. It's *our people* we're talking about.' She had sounded just like Allie, and perhaps that was why James had given in.

There was a tap on the door and Jenny's secretary, Madge, appeared with the tea tray. As she unobtrusively distributed cups and napkins and cucumber sandwiches – with a special side order of bloater paste for Sir Albert – Howard plucked an invisible thread from the cuff of his impeccable sleeve and said in measured

305

tones, 'It appears, then, that the Britton yard's continued liquidity depends on an upturn in the market.'

Sir Albert turned puce, not without justification. 'We're no' that dunderheided that we canny work that oot for wurselves,' he snapped. Then, his owlish glance transferring itself from Howard to an afflicted Jenny and back again, he continued genteeley, 'And as chairman of the board, I may add that if that is the most constructive contribution Howard feels able to make to this discussion, I don't know what he's doing on the board at all. It wusny *me* that invited him.'

Wearily, Paul said, 'Father!'

Howard looked completely unabashed.

'I have a suggestion to make,' James announced, folding his hands on the table before him and treating everyone to his authoritative look. 'It seems to me that if we are not to go staggering from crisis to crisis, what we need is a substantial injection of capital. I believe we would be wise to consider a share issue . . .'

With a crash, Sir Albert put his cup down on the table, missing the saucer completely. 'I don't believe this,' he said. 'Did you hear that, Paul? Did you hear that, Felix?'

It was Howard who broke the ensuing silence. 'Not Felix,' he said. For the first time since she had known him, Jenny detected a flicker of something that might have been anger in his eyes.

The old man's face showed the confusion in his mind as he floundered back through the years remembering the last time someone had suggested going to the stockmarket. It had been April or May, he thought, and it must have been after dark because the gaslights had been burning and the air full of cigar smoke. A long time ago. And someone had killed himself outside in the night, and the conscience he hadn't known he possessed had never been quite comfortable again.

'Felix,' he mumbled. And then he was back in the present, as suddenly as he had left it, and saying with his familiar belligerence, 'I won't hear of it. We'd find ourselves taken over in no time. The Lithgows are sinking every penny they've got into buying up competing yards. And look at Fairfield, now that Hatry's got them in his clutches. You, too, James. Edged out of your own Eastern Empire Company. No, I won't have it.'

Paul said, 'Well, I don't know, father, but if I were a prospective customer and saw all these empty berths of ours, and the equipment rusting away, I'm not sure I wouldn't take my order elsewhere. James may have a point. What is your view, Howard?'

Howard had a face that spoke reliability and judgement in every line of it, so that, even though his mouth curved upwards at the corners, cradling the long upper lip in a way that suggested smugness lurking in ambush, one felt as if he were entitled to be smug. He would never utter an opinion that had not been carefully considered.

'I find myself,' he said weightily, 'inclining towards the chairman's view. For an outsider to acquire a controlling interest in Brittons' when the family, in the past, has gone to so much trouble to prevent that happening would be most regrettable. There are, of course, steps that might be taken to prevent it, but we need not, I think, spend time on them at the moment.

'The sad truth is that, just as rust and empty berths are the first thing the customer sees, so also are they the first thing the investor sees. It would be necessary for the yard to refurbish itself very considerably *and* to have a full order book before we could contemplate, with equanimity, any excursion into the stockmarket.'

Jenny, who yielded to no one in her admiration of Howard's syntax, wasn't always so impressed by his reasoning although, feeling ignorant and insignificant as she did, she rarely questioned it aloud. On this occasion, however, she said rather apologetically, 'But there are signs of an upturn, you know, especially in new liner tonnage. Wouldn't that make it a good time to look for investors? We could easily prove the yard's potential, and it would take comparatively little capital for it to "refurbish itself" and return to full efficiency. I should have thought investors might find it quite tempting to be offered entry on the ground floor.'

As always when she spoke at board meetings, there was a momentary pause as if everyone was having to come to terms with the fact that Tom's widow not only had a voice but was entitled to use it. What they would never come to terms with, Jenny knew resignedly, was the fact that she was at least as well informed about shipbuilding as they were. Better, because she didn't just regard it as a source of income. She loved it.

Howard smiled at her, with the superior masculine smile she was coming to know so well and which, despite her awe of him, always induced in her a desire to pick something up and hit him over the head with it. 'My dear Jenny,' he said, 'there are unfortunately very few investors with such acute intelligence as yours. Most, I fear, are also – with justification – nervous of the Red Clyde tag. No, we would have to be very sure indeed that your "upturn" was real before we could risk such a venture.

It would do incalculable harm if the bottom were to fall out of the market just when we were in the middle of seeking a quotation.'

Since Howard was the only one intimately acquainted with the workings of the stockmarket, what Howard said was law. It was a pity, Jenny thought despairingly as the meeting broke up without reaching any useful decision, that the non-executive directors seemed content for Brittons' to go on staggering from crisis to crisis until something happened to improve the situation. If it ever did.

Gathering up her papers, she left the men to their sherry and gossip.

3

SHE was on the telephone about half an hour later when there was a knock on the door of her office.

'Come in!' she called and, when she saw it was Howard, smiled and signed that she wouldn't be long and waved her hand towards a chair.

But Howard preferred to stand, glancing out of the window towards the berths and then turning to survey Tom Britton's widow, who was being fluent and decisive over something to do with turbine parts. It interested him, because at board meetings she was usually retiring to the point of invisibility.

Not that he would have expected anything else, of course. It would be most unbecoming for a girl of twenty-four – or whatever she was – to put herself forward among a gathering of men who were superior to her not only by experience but by the very fact of being men.

It was Howard's impression, however, that young Mrs Britton had both technical competence and a quick intelligence. Certainly, she had learned a good deal since the early postwar days when, with tiresome frequency – and usually at the precise moment when he was sitting down to dinner – she had telephoned to ask what to do when she was unable to get the books to balance. He had made it a point of principle to help, with the result that, in the three years since then, she had increasingly turned to him for information and advice.

She was a good-looking young woman, well turned out, with a reserve in her manner that was not unattractive. That she was a trifle in awe of him was only natural.

She replaced the receiver at last, looking at him enquiringly, and he said, 'I merely wondered whether you needed me to sign anything or glance through some figures. What about the estimates for that trawler? We must take care not to cut them too near the bone.'

'How kind of you! No, I think everything's under control – though there's a mysterious form here from Whitehall. Perhaps you might know something about it?'

Howard glanced at it. It was simple enough if you knew how the Civil Service mind worked. After he had explained it to her, he said, 'I am returning to London on the overnight train. I wondered whether you might care to have dinner with me beforehand?'

It wasn't a suggestion made on impulse – Howard never did anything on impulse – though he made it sound so. He could see that she was taken aback and a little hesitant, as was perfectly proper.

'I'm not sure whether I can,' she said. 'And I'd have to go home first.'

'Of course. We will dine at the Central Hotel in Glasgow, so you will wish to change.'

She gave a slightly shame-faced giggle. 'It's not only that. It's more that I have to drag Beth away from the wireless!'

His eyebrows rose. 'The wireless! But she's only – what? – five?'

'Yes, but age knows no frontiers where tickling at the cat's whisker is concerned! And if she's not doing that, she'll be bouncing round the garden on her pogo sticks. When she *should* be learning her sums. Take my advice, Howard. Never be a mother.'

He laughed. 'I won't. What I would suggest is that I come with you – I have a hired motor – and wait while you change and call your daughter to order.'

Jenny couldn't think what to do, and stared at him blankly for a moment. It would be a rare treat for her to have an evening out in the great big civilised world that lay beyond the narrow-minded confines of Rashilea Terrace; the world she had learned about at Provost Charters and had tried to convince herself she wasn't missing. And even though Howard made her nervous by being so large and lordly and clever, he was perfectly pleasant. The only thing was, she didn't in the least want to introduce him either to Rashilea Terrace or her mother.

But then she committed herself almost without thinking. 'Oh, no. You don't want to sit around waiting for me. I can quite easily meet you at the Central.'

He wouldn't hear of it, and she had to invent the excuse of letters to sign and another urgent call to make in order to get him out of the office so that she could telephone her mother and warn her.

When they arrived at Rashilea Terrace just after six, there was a fire struggling to burn in the front room and Nellie was splendidly attired in her best purple matelassé frock. Her colour was high, and her surprise at seeing them unconvincing and a touch breathless, but the graciousness of her 'Good evening, Major Fournier,' would have reduced any lesser man than Howard to a jelly.

Howard, however, merely inclined his head and shook her hand with the benign blankness of a politician at a Women's Guild luncheon, and Jenny wondered what he was thinking and then decided she didn't want to know.

Fortunately, Beth came dancing in just then and Howard looked at her with genuine interest, and Jenny was able to say, 'Beth, why don't you show – er – Uncle Howard how the cat's whisker works, while I run upstairs and change?'

She changed at Olympic speed, and was still fastening the belt of the leaf-green frock under her fashionable new cape as she ran downstairs again to find Beth sitting, hands in lap, watching Howard with owlish curiosity while Nellie, with a glass of sweet sherry in her hand – the only alcoholic liquor she was prepared to admit into her house – told him, 'Of course, Mr Hamish Britton himself said to me that the death of my late husband, Mr Jardine, was a terrible blow to the shipyard . . .'

Howard didn't turn a hair, and Jenny thought that, though he was a bit self-satisfied, not to say pompous, he was really very nice. Paul Britton would have been contemplating her mother as if she were some deplorable laboratory specimen, but Howard was looking at her as he looked at everyone, with impassive courtesy and detachment.

What was going on under that bland exterior? Jenny wondered, mildly irritated by the knowledge that she hadn't got to the bottom of Howard yet, and didn't think she ever would.

But it didn't prevent her from having a most agreeable evening. Not once did Howard mention the shipyard, or even the kind of weighty topics which Jenny would have expected to interest him, like assassinations, and reparations, and the troubles in Ireland and the Near East. Instead, he proved fascinatingly well-informed about

310

the latest books and plays and art exhibitions, and Jenny sat and listened enviously and thought what an extraordinary man he was.

It was a pity that he always managed to sound as if his judgements were as unassailable as the laws handed down from Sinai, but that was Howard, after all, and he was perfectly good-humoured about it when Jenny had the temerity to disagree with him about Professor Coué and his campaign to persuade people to keep repeating to themselves, 'Every day in every way I am getting better and better.' Howard thought it was all nonsense, but Jenny wasn't so sure. They had a lovely, almost frivolous argument about it and Jenny suddenly thought how easy he was to get on with; large, urbane, competent and comforting.

He insisted on sending her home in a taxi, and she was able to tell him truthfully, as she left, that she hadn't enjoyed an evening so much for years.

4

IT WAS almost midnight on a Friday in October 1922 and everyone at Rashilea Terrace was in bed and asleep when the telephone rang in the hall.

Jenny, struggling to wakefulness, thought that the sound was a part of her dreams, and then, recognising that it wasn't, stumbled out of bed and hurried downstairs, pulling on her pink blanketcloth dressing gown as she went. How long had the thing been ringing, and who could be telephoning in the middle of the night? Something dreadful must have happened.

Her hands were shaking as she picked the instrument up, unhooked the earpiece, and said a little thickly into the daffodil-shaped mouthpiece, 'Hullo? This is Jenny Jardine speaking.'

All she heard was static. She wished she'd taken time to find her slippers. There was a draught straight from the Arctic coming under the front door.

'Hullo?' she said again, this time more loudly, more wakefully and much more irritably.

She had to jiggle the hook several times to attract the operator away from the old sweetie-wives' blether she was having with someone else at the exchange, and then there was nothing but more static for almost a minute. But eventually the call came through.

It was Natasha, of all people, and Natasha in a high state of nerves.

Since Jenny had left Provost Charters, she had had almost no contact with Natasha, except by way of Christmas gifts and formal little notes of thanks. Something must have happened to Paul or Sir Albert, she thought, although in either case she would have expected not a phone call but a telegram. If that. An unheralded invitation to the funeral would have been more likely, she reflected sourly.

'Natasha,' she shouted into the mouthpiece. 'Will you speak more clearly and more slowly. I've no idea what you're saying. Where are you? What's wrong? Do you know what time it is?'

'What does that matter! It is entirely necessary that I talk to *some*one. I am in London, and I have tried to reach Paul at Provost Charters but no one answers because one can never hear the telephone ringing in that stupid house.'

Oops! Jenny thought, beginning to relax a little. That's no way to speak of Ye Olde family home! It didn't sound as if anything terrible had happened after all. Resigned, she sat down on the hall chair and curled her feet up under her dressing-gown.

'Well, I'm here, Natasha, and you woke me up from my beauty sleep. What's the matter?'

'I have just read the newspapers. Have *you* read the newspapers?'

'Only the *Herald*, and I've only had time to skim through it.' Lloyd George had resigned as prime minister the day before and the *Glasgow Herald* was full of it, but there was a limit to Jenny's interest in the Welsh Wizard.

'I knew it, otherwise you must have telephoned me. The photograph! You did not see it. It would have been on the front page if it had not been for these silly politics.'

'*Which* photograph?'

The misery in Natasha's sudden wail carried even over four hundred miles of line. 'Of Matthew! Of my darling boy!'

Jenny's heart contracted. Please, no. Nothing could have happened to him. She would have known; surely she would have known?

'Yes?' It was difficult to get the word out in anything like her normal tone of voice.

'He was trying to fly under Niagara Falls, in some ridiculous aeroplane. Not over them, you understand, but *under* them! Through the space between the water and the cliff over which it falls.'

312

'And there was an accident, I suppose?' Jenny heard herself sounding perfectly flat. Twice before he had been reported dead, and had survived. A third time . . .

'Oh, no. He did not succeed, but there was no accident.'

Jenny couldn't stop herself from yelping, 'Then what on earth is all the fuss about?'

With a sniff that even Sir Albert would have been proud of, Natasha announced tragically, 'He was not alone. There was a young woman in the plane, too. And they were trying to fly under Niagara Falls because it seemed to them an appropriate way of celebrating – of celebrating – the fact that they had just been *married*!'

5

MATTHEW brought his bride home in the middle of April 1923, in time for the start of the flying season, and Natasha, to Jenny's horror, summoned the entire family to a party at the London flat to welcome them.

'Well, I shan't go!' Jenny said distractedly to Allie, who had also received an invitation. 'How she has the brass neck I can't imagine!'

Allie, who had known Jenny since she was a toddler, found both the remark and the tone in which it was uttered unexpectedly illuminating. Thoughtfully, she held out a frock and said, 'Here, try this on.'

She had always considered Natasha's attitude towards Matt to be about as pure as the driven slush, but had never known how Jenny felt about him. Her apparent lack of interest when his name cropped up might have meant anything or nothing. Allie had been tantalised. He was, after all, a very attractive young man.

The newspaper photograph suggested that Mims was a very attractive young woman.

But so was Jenny, now that she'd stopped looking so harassed. It had been as much of a relief to Allie as to Jenny herself when she had succeeded in re-establishing herself at the yard as John Jardine's wee lassie, whom everyone had known since she was so high and who could probably put a puffer together with her own hands and no need for a blueprint. It had been a close thing, though. Right up until last year, she'd kept on running to

313

Allie for advice and reassurance, and although Allie was patient enough, she wasn't patient to the extent of listening to an entire evening of Jenny's woes. Finally, she'd had to say, 'Jenny, I've *left* the yard, remember? I'll still listen to things that matter, but not to what Wullie Mackie said to Jamie Thomson about the third row of rivets above the plimsoll line on the starboard bow!'

She smiled to herself at the memory. Then, through the fitting room curtain, she said, 'Well, I shall certainly go. I'm bursting with curiosity, and if you're not then all I can say is that you're not human.'

Jenny – desire, conscience and commonsense warring furiously within her – emerged into the salon looking flustered and still smoothing down the skirt that fell in graceful folds from a low waist to six or seven inches above her ankle bone.

'Oh, yes!' Allie said with deep satisfaction. 'Made for you.'

Jenny surveyed herself in the glass. Allie was right. The long, straight line suited her very well, and the wide, shallow neck seemed to give poise and sophistication to her fair, bobbed head. The sleeves were fitted to just above the elbow, swelling out from there to the wrist in an elegant trumpet-shaped flounce. But it was the colour that was the ultimate persuasion, the new light red, halfway between coral and geranium. She always felt happy in red.

'It's lovely, Allie,' she said regretfully. 'But when would I wear it? It's Paisley we live in, not Paris.'

Allie's eyes met hers in the mirror, and Jenny had no difficulty in interpreting their message. She primmed up her lips and thought about it for a moment. Allie was right. In a frock like this she could take on the world. In fact, it would be her *duty* to take on the world.

Slowly, she said, 'I was thinking of taking Beth to London to see the royal wedding, as a kind of belated birthday treat. She thinks it's terribly romantic, a commoner like the Lady Elizabeth Bowes-Lyon marrying the king's son. Personally, I've never understood what's common about being a ladyship and I can't imagine why little girls find royalty so fascinating. But there you are. It's the twenty-third of April, I think.'

'Oh, dear, how very awkward for you,' Allie said sympathetically, 'when Natasha's party's on the twenty-fourth. It would offend the family irrevocably if you were in London and didn't go!'

'It would, wouldn't it?'

6

AFTER the start, it would have been like an evening spent wallowing in golden syrup if it hadn't been for Sir Albert, because everyone was being implacably charming to everyone else. Especially the former Countess Natasha Mikhailovna Efremov and the former Miss Mimosa Weber.

Jenny and Allie were first to arrive, accompanied by Bertha, who had insisted on putting them up at her flat in Westminster. 'I can always find you a bed,' she'd said, and Jenny hadn't realised she meant it literally until they'd had to clear away a mountain of books, pamphlets, labels and envelopes in order to discover where the beds actually were.

Bertha, one of those well-adjusted souls who never saw any need to make excuses for themselves, had merely remarked, 'Well, women over thirty may have the vote now, but it isn't good enough. So we're mounting a campaign to widen the franchise. Can I lift a subscription off you?'

Paul and Natasha's flat was in predictable contrast, high in a block overlooking Kensington Gardens. It had a fine view of the Albert Memorial, though not everyone regarded that as a point in its favour.

As they entered from Kensington Gore, Jenny said, 'Of course, these so-called mansion flats are really no more than a dressed-up version of the Glasgow tenement,' and Allie smiled, and went on smiling as the porter ushered them through a mirrored and carpeted entrance hall to a gilded lift, which wafted them comfortably up six floors and then decanted them onto a mirrored and carpeted landing with three beautifully polished front doors to choose from. There was a pleasant smell of beeswax and lavender.

Jenny said stubbornly, 'Well, the *principle's* the same.'

A neat little parlourmaid showed them into a bedroom where they left their coats and hats, and then led them along a mile or two of corridor to the drawingroom, where Natasha, Paul and Sir Albert were waiting for them.

To Jenny's annoyance, it was exactly the kind of room she dreamed of living in, huge and airy and fresh-looking. Everything that could be painted white had been painted white, with the mouldings picked out in gold, while the furniture was classic in style and delicately proportioned, mostly made from softly glowing fruitwoods and upholstered in green; not just a single green but, cleverly, three or four different ones, with a splash of subdued pattern here and there. On the walls were a few landscapes and seascapes in pale, rich colours, vibrant with light and shade. Jenny knew just enough to guess that they must be Impressionists.

She had no time to take in more, because Natasha was drifting towards them, her arms extended and on her face the bewitching smile she usually reserved for personable young men.

In obedience to their hostess's decree that since the party was to be just a family affair and *quite* informal, Jenny was wearing the dashing red frock and Allie a sober but stylish grey two-piece. Bertha's only concession to the occasion had been to remove the brown cotton overall she wore at home over her jumper and skirt. 'You needn't think I'm competing with That Woman,' she'd said.

Sensible Bertha. Because Natasha, predictably, had interpreted her own dictate with maximum latitude and was gowned in an ankle-length creation of champagne-coloured silk voile, sleeveless, very nearly topless, inset with gold lace and heavily embroidered with pearled sequins and gold glass bugles. There was a string of pale amber beads reaching almost to her knees, and her hair had been bobbed by a master. She looked sensational.

'Paris,' murmured Allie knowledgeably. 'Callot Soeurs.'

Jenny had time to reply with no more than a 'Hah!' before Natasha was upon them.

'Darlings! How wonderful to see you again after such a very long time. Allie, you simply do not change!' she announced fulsomely, and to Bertha, less fulsomely, 'Bertha, you do not change either.'

Then she stopped. 'But my poor Jenny! You are so thin. Are you quite sure that this important position of yours – company secretary, is it? – is not too much for you? You must take more care. You look almost haggard!'

But before Jenny could respond, Bertha surged to the rescue, exclaiming in tones of the most profound admiration, 'That's something no one could say about you, Natasha. You're wearing awfully well. Thirty-nine next birthday, isn't it?'

The elder Mrs Britton, preparing to slay her with a glance, was frustrated by the arrival of another guest. '*Thirty-four!*' she hissed as she turned away.

Allie looked at her sister sternly. 'A sadist, that's what you are,'

316

she said. 'And who d'you suppose this is? I don't recognise him as a member of the family.'

Jenny knew who it was, though she hadn't seen him since the days when Provost Charters had been a way-station for convalescent officers. 'Major Granby Fox,' she said. 'One of Natasha's most devoted admirers. She probably needed an extra man to make up the numbers. Oh, and here's Howard. How nice.'

Howard was looking very imposing, and beautifully and discreetly tailored, as usual. Though Jenny was no expert, she couldn't imagine him going anywhere but Savile Row for the dark business suits which were the only thing she had ever seen him wear, or in which she could even imagine him. But tonight her eyes dilated as she took in the informal splendour of his grey double-breasted lounge suit; he was even wearing a turned-down collar and a dark grey tie with small blue motifs on it.

He was really quite good-looking in his own way, a bit like a statue of an ancient Roman senator, one of the fleshier ones, with smooth brown hair, eyes that were difficult to see, being rather tightly cramped between their heavy upper and lower lids, a forehead, nose and chin of commendable solidity, and a mouth that resembled a new moon when he smiled. 'Handsome', with its connotations of glamour and personal magnetism, wasn't a word one would have used to describe him – Howard himself would have thought it very vulgar – but he had undeniable presence.

'Goodness,' Jenny thought, surveying the lounge suit again, and smiled brightly at him.

He came straight to her side, which was gratifying. It was even more gratifying when he said, 'My dear Jenny, you should always wear red.'

7

THEY were standing, fashionably sipping Manhattans and chatting, when the guests of honour arrived and everyone fell silent in mid-sentence. Everyone but Howard, who had more respect for his sentences than to cut them off in their prime. Dutifully, Jenny heard him out. Howard was full of surprises tonight. Egyptian antiquities, it seemed, were his hobby.

'. . . unfortunate that we will not know for some time whether the

Tutankhamen material includes any mathematical or astronomical papyri, since Carnarvon's death earlier this month will naturally impede the progress of the excavations. Ah, the happy couple.'

And then Jenny was able to transfer her look of faintly glazed politeness from Howard and his unexpected hobby to the two people standing in the doorway.

She felt her stomach turn right over, because Matt looked more relaxed than she had ever seen him, and years younger, and handsomer than she would have thought possible.

If it had ever occurred to her that she might have fallen out of love with him, she would have known in that moment how wrong she was.

It wasn't easy to look from him to the girl at his side – to Mrs Matthew Britton – and discover that she was a raving beauty, despite the very ordinary white blouse and navy skirt and the unfashionable length of her glowing hair. She showed no trace of nervousness, and the smile on her mouth was like the wings of a bird, hovering, while her eyes were luminous and green like young leaves with the sun behind them. She couldn't be more than twenty-one, but she looked as if she had the world at her feet. And why shouldn't she? After all, she had Matt.

Jenny abandoned her virtuous attempt to sympathise with the girl over being tossed, like some early Christian martyr, to the full family assembly of lions.

Then Natasha was gliding forward, her glass raised gaily in the air, and holding up her lips to be kissed, and gushing, 'Matthew, my darling boy! And this is – Mimosa?'

The girl's smile deepened, sharpening the lovely line of her cheekbones, and she said, 'Mims, *please*. And you must be Tasha. I have heard so *much* about you and all of it *wonderful!*' Her American accent wasn't strong and it sounded as if the emphases, with their curiously caressing note, came naturally to her, but Jenny thought she sounded suspiciously glib. Matt must have told her that Natasha loved being buttered up.

Matt put an arm round his wife's shoulders and smiled down at her.

'Don't say I didn't warn you, sweetheart. Tasha's idea of informal dress is not the same as other people's. Doesn't she look gorgeous? But we've come straight from the aerodrome at Croydon, Tash darling, and we hadn't time to change, so you'll just have to put up with Mims' blouse and skirt and my plus-fours.'

His eyes scanned the assembled company and Jenny found that she was sensitive to every gradation of the smile in them. Quizzical for Sir Albert; warm for Allie and Bertha; questioning over Granby Fox; reserved for Paul and the same for Howard.

She was so absorbed that she was scarcely even aware of it when he reached the end of the line and his glance came to rest on her own serious face; didn't at first, realise that the sudden quirk of his mouth was for her, or the faint, conspiratorial flicker of one eyelid, not quite a wink, that only she could see – as if he were saying ruefully, 'Family gatherings, my God!'

For a fraction of a second her eyes gazed blankly into his, and then she blinked, and felt a pulse begin to flutter at the base of her throat, and the only thing she could think of to do was raise her glass and say animatedly, 'To Mr and Mrs Matthew Britton! Welcome home.'

8

NATASHA, of course, had made sure that Matt was on her right at dinner and Granby Fox on her left, and Jenny listened and watched with a terrible fascination as she flirted spectacularly with both of them.

At the other end of the table, Paul was putting Mims through a deceptively casual *viva voce* on her past history and present ambitions. Jenny, separated from them by Howard, could hear enough to deduce that he was making very little headway in the matter of his new daughter-in-law's background, which interested him, and a great deal in the matter of her passion for flying, which didn't.

'. . . worked in a drugstore to pay for my lessons . . . *loved* planes since I was six years old . . . something mysterious and *magical* about flying . . .'

It turned out that Matt wasn't wholly engrossed in Natasha. Glancing along the table, he said, 'She's obsessed, you see? Says flying's more thrilling than love and far less dangerous!'

It wasn't the kind of remark calculated to appeal to his father, although Sir Albert guffawed and Natasha gave a trill of artificial amusement.

Mims pouted prettily. 'There's something else, too. It's more of a challenge. Men take women seriously in love, but not in flying. You have to *make* them admit that women are *just* as good as men in the air!'

319

'My goodness,' exclaimed Natasha girlishly. 'Another ambitious woman in the family! You all make me feel quite useless.'

With mild interest, Jenny waited to discover which of the men was going to be first to reassure her.

It was Granby, he of the smooth brown hair and liquid brown eyes. Laying down his fish knife and raising his hostess's hand to his lips, he said gently, 'But you are unique in everything, and we prize your charm higher than rubies.'

Paul ignored the byplay. 'And does my son encourage you in this desire to fly?'

'Oh, Matt is *quite* unique. He admits I'm as good as any man . . .'

There was an exaggerated gasp from where her husband was sitting, and Mims tossed her head and climbed down a peg. 'Oh, all right! I'm *pretty well* as good as *most* men. Anyway, it doesn't bother him in the least to have me at the controls. He's a darling!' Although it had been patently obvious that Natasha thought ambition in women was something to be deplored, Mims either hadn't recognised it or didn't care, because she concluded, 'One day, I'm going to fly *solo* round the world!'

'Heavens!' Natasha exclaimed again, her voice clashing with Matt's as he remarked, 'Possibly. But not in a "Jenny".'

Startled, Jenny said, 'What?'

'Mims' favourite plane, the one we've been stunting around the States in. The Curtiss JN-D4, known as the "Jenny" because of the JN. I've heard it described as a collection of spare parts flying along independently in formation. Which is about right. Anyway, no sane aviator would try taking *it* round the world, or any other of today's planes, come to that. I'm afraid Mims' great ambition is going to have to wait a while. In the meantime, we're setting up a short-haul line.'

Mims opened her mouth, but Matt didn't appear to notice. 'Anyway, why are we boring everyone stiff with all this flying talk? I want to know what's been happening over here. You're looking very well, Jenny. That's a smashing frock!'

'Thank you,' she said, her demure gaze half on Matt and half on Natasha's decolletage. 'Just a little something my dressmaker ran up for me.'

He grinned appreciatively. 'And how's that adorable daughter of yours? I brought her a small memento from the States, by the way; it's in my coat pocket.'

'Oh, Matthew!' She was surprised and touched.

Mims peered round Howard's stalwart shirtfront at her. 'Matt says she's the most *divine* child and quite his greatest admirer.'

'Well,' replied the divine child's doting mama, making a swift recovery, 'she certainly followed him around like a puppy when he was at Provost Charters the Christmas after the war. It's very kind of Matt to remember her. She'll be thrilled.' Jenny could hear herself sounding middle-aged and maternal.

Mims, losing interest, turned away again and Jenny, healthily annoyed by the sensation of having been written off, decided she wouldn't have liked the girl even if she hadn't been married to Matt. Uncharitably, she wondered if Mims had married him for himself, or because he had a plane she could fly.

Then Allie said, 'Do you have any fashionable dress shops in Iowa, Mims?' She didn't even glance at Mims' blouse, and the stress on 'fashionable' was almost imperceptible.

The evening came to an end at last, and Granby, courtesy incarnate, escorted Allie and Bertha down in the lift. Mims was still taking a cloying farewell of Natasha when it reappeared, and Matt held the gate open for Howard and Jenny to enter. The three of them were still waiting patiently in its mirrored and gilded interior when someone on a lower floor pressed the button and the lift began to descend.

As two pairs of silk-stockinged ankles disappeared from view – those belonging to the bride, Jenny was pleased to observe, very much inferior to the rest of her – Matt placed an arm lightly round Jenny's shoulders and gave vent to a protracted, 'Whew!'

She couldn't help laughing, because she knew exactly what he meant, and it seemed he had guessed she would. Feeling close to him for the very first time, she thought how strange it was that it should have taken four years' absence to bring it about.

She had almost forgotten that Howard was there until he said, 'Feeling the strain, dear boy?' and Matthew, removing his arm, replied with more than a touch of self-mockery, 'If you but knew!'

And then the lift stopped on the second floor, and some people got in, and all that remained were polite nods and smiles and murmured courtesies.

9

AS THE Austin Seven, repulsively known as the 'Chummy', bounced and rattled its way over Chelsea Bridge en route for the digs Matt and Mims had taken in Croydon, Mims said dreamily, 'I think Tasha is just *divine*. So elegant, so charming, so – exciting!'

Matt said, 'Yes, I'd noticed.' And been relieved. It hadn't occurred to him until he'd seen the two women together just how alike they were, in temperament if not in looks. For a nasty moment, he'd wondered if they were going to start competing with each other, because Mims was a highly competitive young woman and he'd forgotten to warn her that, against Tash, she couldn't hope to win.

He sighed internally. Tash had put on a fine performance tonight. If her hand hadn't twice brushed his thigh under the table, even he might have been deceived.

'I guess,' Mims went on, 'that it must be something to do with her being Russian. That brilliance, I mean? Don't think I don't just *adore* the rest of your folks, but they really are too awfully British.'

'You mean, dull?'

'I guess so. You *don't* mind me saying so, do you, honey? Allie and Bertha are so respectable they scared the living daylights out of me, and your brother's wife – widow – well, she did too! I mean, she's so correct and so *reserved*. Wouldn't Emily Post just love her?'

Matt held his tongue. He wouldn't, he knew, have much success in convincing his wife that appearances could be deceptive. She would merely nod, and smile in sweet surprise, and completely fail to understand if he told her that Allie, Bertha, and Jenny all had personal experience of what life and death were about, and had done things, on their own and on their own initiative, that had really been quite adventurous. Mims understood 'adventure' only as something involving physical danger.

He put aside for future consideration his sudden discovery tonight that Allie, Bertha, and Jenny were all grown-ups; that, beside them, Tasha and Mims were adolescents who hadn't yet learned to look beyond their own desires and perhaps never would.

He found himself wondering what had happened to change Jenny Jardine so much over these last four years. From being a bossy little girl, she had grown into the touchy young woman of

Provost Charters. But now, in her mid-twenties, she had acquired self-assurance and style; she wasn't just anonymously pretty now, but good-looking enough to hold her own in any company, or any company that didn't include Tasha and Mims.

He'd forgotten what expressive eyes she had; one glance had been enough to tell him that, mysteriously, she had abandoned her role as critic-in-residence and become quite human. No more tickings-off? No more ill-disguised disapproval? Life wouldn't be the same. The fact that she'd usually been right when she ticked him off hadn't made it any more acceptable. No one enjoyed being made to feel a fool.

It had also been interesting to discover that her attitude to the family matched his own – a rueful compromise between detachment and involvement – and that her sense of humour was in good working order. Hoping that there was nothing in her apparent friendship with Howard, he gave a mental shrug, because there was no reason why the girl should remain a widow for ever, and Howard, on the face of it, would be a very good match indeed. If Jenny was prepared to marry a man who reeked of self-satisfaction, that was her problem.

Over the rattle of the car on the cobbles, he heard Mims say, 'Matt?' and returned to the present.

'Sorry, darling. My mind was wandering.'

He smiled, and she smiled back, pretty, kittenish, captivating as always.

They were approaching Tooting Bec Common and it was late, and there was very little traffic about, and he didn't really need two hands on the wheel. So he put an arm round her shoulders and said, 'It's chilly. Come on, snuggle in. Not much further now.'

She stayed where she was, the kittenish smile still in place as she told him brightly, 'No, I'm just dandy. But it surely has been a tiring day. I just know I'm going to be asleep the minute my head touches the pillow.' It was a plea he had heard with increasing frequency during the six months of their marriage.

He restored both hands to the wheel and slammed his foot down on the accelerator and to hell with speed limits.

It was a pity the Chummy's absolute maximum was 38mph, because it didn't do anything at all to relieve his frustrations.

323

10

FOR JENNY, returning to Rashilea Terrace was like going back to prison, and the Head Warder didn't improve things by whining on, and on, for days.

'Left here all by myself while my daughter goes off gallivanting! I could have died, and no one would have known. You've no feeling for your poor old mother. Here's me with my fingers worn to the bone looking after you . . .'

Jenny said unkindly, 'It was your corns last time. You should have had Aunt Effie or Aunt Mattie to stay with you, like I suggested. Beth, run downstairs and put these things in the laundry bag behind the scullery door. Mum, would you move over so that I can hang this dress up?' She had been home for only half an hour and her head was aching already.

Ever since her father had died, she had been hoping that one of her mother's unmarried sisters might be persuaded to move in, permanently, so that she and Beth could move out, but Nellie wouldn't hear of it.

'*Effie?* I'll not have yon one in the house. Sister or no sister, she's common, that's what she is and always has been. And Mattie's got a right sharp tongue in her head. I'd have to be gey stuck to have her living with me. No, thank you. Things suit me fine as they are.'

She had no intention of letting her daughter get away as easily as that. Twice, Jenny had found a nice little flat that would have done very well for herself and Beth, and twice her mother had had one of her 'attacks' at the mention of it.

The trouble was that Nellie Jardine, deprived of her husband and cut off from her son, with Jenny out all day and Beth at school, had needed a new interest in life and had found it in worrying about her health. Having convinced herself that she was suffering from one or other dread disease, she refused to hear anything to the contrary, even from the succession of expensive specialists her exasperated daughter had taken her to see. When they assured her, with all the cheerfulness of bringers of good tidings, that she was perfectly hale and hearty, Nellie had been deeply insulted.

Jenny was fairly sure that the attacks were a fake, but not sure enough. Was it possible for someone as stubborn as Nellie to *will* herself to have a seizure? Jenny didn't know, and so she was still here. Still here – with no prospect of escape for as long as her mother lived, which might be for another twenty years.

Waking one night with thoughts like these in her mind, Jenny lay and stared at the ceiling and wondered drearily whether the day might come when Beth felt the same about her as she felt about Nellie. It was something that didn't bear thinking about, but even as she thrust the idea from her mind she knew, in fear and pity, that to be unwanted must be the greatest tragedy of all.

Four

1

EVERYTHING, in the months that followed, seemed to conspire against Jenny's attempt to lead the kind of routine-filled, ordered life that might have dulled her senses. She had known what it was to be unhappy before, but never with such cold finality.

There was no logic in it. For almost five years she had recognised that she loved and would always love a man whom the law said she could never marry; which meant that his arms might embrace her, but his body never. She wasn't a slut. She would rather that her love starved to death than be killed by shame and self-loathing.

She knew it, and thought she had come to terms with it. But seeing him with his wife, someone who received, as of right, what Jenny could never have, had destroyed her resignation. It was as if all life, now, was being drawn into the vortex of this one great hurt.

Wherever she looked, there was disruption and confusion. Even the yard was having its worst year ever, with only one ship launched, a dredger, and only one order on the books, for a factory ship to service the new whaling grounds in the Ross Sea. The books showed a deficit for 1923 of £8,000. Brittons' wasn't nearly as badly off as Beardmore's who'd lost £218,000, but as Jenny pointed out sharply to a self-satisfied James McMurtrie, Beardmore's owed their losses to the fact that they had tried to do *some*thing rather than nothing, which meant their men hadn't all found themselves on the dole.

The whole country was suffering. There were three different prime ministers in eight months; the boilermakers were locked out; the dockers and engine drivers, and London's bus and tram drivers went on strike, one after the other. It made no difference that the third of the prime ministers was leader of the first Labour government in British history.

'And why should it?' demanded Jack, currently indulging a flirtation with Communism. 'Everyone knows Ramsay MacDonald's just a sheep in wolf's clothing, a big bawheid who kowtows to the king in knee breeches hired from Moss Bros.'

Jenny, who in general subscribed to the philosophy of 'what can't be cured must be endured', began to find herself worrying about everything.

She worried about Beth, naggingly, in a low key. The child was less isolated now that she was at school, less shy with strangers, but at home she alternated between unnatural docility and deliberate naughtiness. Once, in the early days at Rashilea Terrace, she had taken her mother's hand and whispered tearfully, 'I don't like it here, mummy', and Jenny had tried to explain that they had to stay for a while because granny needed them. Since then, the child hadn't complained – or not in words. But Jenny knew that Nellie and the house were bad for her, just as having no father or brothers was bad for her.

Jenny's worries about Beth were interrupted by the need to worry about Iris, whose six-year-old son, Sydney Junior, had been knocked down by a bus and spent weeks in hospital in a coma. He recovered in the end, but during the whole dreadful time it wasn't her husband Iris clung to, but Jenny. Driving her sister to the hospital night after night in the Renault she'd bought secondhand from Howard, Jenny found herself returning home almost blind with fatigue.

And when she wasn't worrying about Beth or Iris, she was worrying – stupidly and uselessly – about Matt. Not on a personal level, but about his flying. She knew how much it meant to him; knew, too, how important it was for him to prove himself to Paul, who still thought of his refusal to take over the yard as a betrayal, an act of contemptible self-indulgence.

Jenny didn't see how Matt and Mr Bonny could possibly be making a profit. The cheapest air fares were reckoned at fourpence a mile – four times as much as rail travel – so the only reason for passengers to fly, other than for excitement, was in the hope of a shorter journey time. But day after day there were items in the newspapers showing that they didn't save enough time to save money. One Handley-Page pilot had to make seventeen forced landings on a single flight from London to Paris. Another, lumbering along in a pea-soup fog, found himself so close to the ground that he had to swerve to avoid a church steeple. During the winter, eighty per cent of scheduled services in the northern half of the country had to be cancelled altogether.

Other countries subsidised their aviation industries, but British airlines, said Winston Churchill, Secretary of State for Air, would have to fly by themselves, for the time being, anyway. Jenny didn't see how they could, especially very small passenger airlines like Matthew's which must make a loss every time a plane flew with only one passenger instead of two. That was the trouble with scheduled services.

327

2

WHEN the inevitable happened and the small airlines were forced out of business by the amalgamation of the largest ones into what was to become the government-subsidised Imperial Airways, Jenny was too concerned about Jack's wife Lizzie to shed more than a tear for Matt.

Jack's marriage had, of course, worked out exactly as everyone but Jack and Lizzie had foreseen. Rejected by her parents, shunned by her brothers and sisters, bullied by her church, left to her own devices day after day, night after night, by a husband to whom politics were more interesting than wives, poor stupid Lizzie had suffered three miscarriages and one stillbirth and pregnant, again, was in a state of nerves bordering on hysteria.

Jenny was the only person she could turn to, the only person she could even talk to, and Jenny began to dread finding her waiting outside the yard gates when she left in the evenings.

Forcefully, she told Jack, 'That girl is going to die if you're not careful!'

Jack said she was exaggerating, but all right, he'd see what he could do. Yes, yes, yes, he'd spend an occasional evening at home and see that Lizzie made something more sustaining to eat than bread and marge. 'Now, go away, will you? I'm needed in the turbine shed.'

'Why, what's the matter? Shall I come?'

'Don't you dare. The turbine shed's no place for non-union labour, and that includes company secretaries – even if they do happen to be sisters of the shop steward.'

Watching him disappear into the engine shop, a seething Jenny knew that, even if he did mend his ways, he wouldn't mend them enough. She sometimes thought that, if he hadn't been the yard's best engineer, she'd have taken great personal pleasure in sacking him.

328

3

IN THE end, Jenny summoned up her courage and, without telling anyone, took a trip to the Cowcaddens in Glasgow.

It was moral rather than physical courage she needed. She wasn't frightened of venturing into a slum; it was only strangers who felt that way, people who didn't know that the Glasgow keelie's style was war, not brigandage. He reserved his violence for enemies he knew, foemen worthy of his steel, and scorned to waste it on folk who were too feart to fight back. Women were quite beneath his notice except as targets for a lewd joke.

Even so, she had been careful. After some thought, she had parked the car under the lights of Sauchiehall Street and walked the rest of the way, one of her mother's old shawls round her head, and studded golfing shoes on her feet. The men hanging around the street outside the tenements didn't even turn their heads.

Finding the place, she stopped at the close mouth to fill her lungs with relatively untainted air before she ventured in. She'd never forgotten the stomach-turning smells of a slum tenement, even though her mother had stopped taking Jack and her to visit their grandparents when they were still very small.

The paint on the close walls was ancient and flaking and scrawled all over, and there was no light on the stairs because the gas mantles had been shattered. But she had expected that and brought a torch that showed her stone steps deep in the filth of years – grit and mud, greasy newspapers still smelling of chips and rancid fat and malt vinegar, dog droppings, a child's woollen mitten, two or three folded, red-stained rags that had been used as sanitary towels, broken beer bottles, an old shoe full of holes. There was a WC on the half-landing with the door hanging on a single hinge and a yellow pool swelling out from under it, afloat with creased and sodden squares of newspaper and other residues from which Jenny averted her eyes.

Reaching the first main landing, she shone her torch in turn on each of the four front doors, their paintwork kicked and scarred. Someone was having a screaming, bawling fight behind one of them. There were no names to be seen and she hesitated, and then decided to go further up. If she didn't find the name 'Henry' on any door, she could think again.

But on the third floor, by which time she was beginning to feel queasy, she found it, engraved on a cheap brass plate. Everything was fractionally cleaner up here and even the WC didn't seem to be blocked.

She raised the knocker and let it drop once, twice, three times. From inside, she heard a man's voice say, 'There's someone chappin'!' but when the door opened it was a woman standing there. It would be, Jenny thought; catch a man getting up to answer the door.

The woman was thin and lined and expressionless, her hair floating in grey wisps and her lips pale and anaemic. The hands twisting in the old towel that did duty as an apron were scarlet.

Two children, pink hands; four children, patchy hands; six children, scarlet hands; eight children, hands that were red raw – unless you gave up the struggle against the dirt. Jenny knew the Henrys still had six children at home, aged between four and sixteen.

'Mrs Henry,' she said. 'I'm Jenny Jardine. Lizzie's sister-in-law. Can I come in?'

The woman didn't answer. Her face stiffening, she turned away, leaving the door open and Jenny standing there, hesitating, staring into the kitchen. There was another door that probably led into a second room, but there wouldn't be more than that. Jenny had never seen a place so cluttered. Three pallid children lay on a mattress staring at her dully, and there was another standing naked in the sink, waiting for his mam to finish his Saturday-night bath. Through the festoons of damp washing hanging from the pulley on the ceiling Jenny could see that the walls were covered with cheap prints of the saints with, in a corner, a makeshift shrine to the Virgin Mary, decked with artificial flowers. A kettle was boiling on the hob and there was a throat-catching smell of dampness and washing soda and urine and heat.

Mrs Henry was whispering to a fat man in a tattered vest and trousers sitting in the chair by the side of the fire. Mr Henry, Jenny thought, and took a tentative step inside.

His voice stopped her. 'Away wi' you, wumman.'

'But I'd like to talk to you about Lizzie.'

'We ken naebody ca'd Lizzie.'

Jenny took a deep breath. 'Can I not come in? It's silly shouting at each other like this.'

The man rose, big and sweaty and threatening.

'Mr Henry, Lizzie isn't well and she misses you. Will you not . . .'

The door slammed in her face.

She dropped her torch. By the time she found it, scrabbling in the dirt, she was shaking with tears of rage and frustration. She thumped the knocker with all her might. And again. And after an interval, again. But the door remained shut.

And so she had no alternative in the end but to pick her way down the stairs again and march back to where she had left the car. Her shawl had fallen off and she was looking flushed and feminine and young, but when two of the men in the street leered at her and asked, 'Are ye wanting company, hen?' she fixed them with such a sizzling glare that they recoiled in mock alarm and went back to reorganising the Celtic forward line.

She sat in the car for a few moments, recovering herself, and then started up and drove, very sedately, down Renfield Street, over the bridge, past the Kingston Dock, and out to the Paisley Road. She was at Halfway House before she stopped shaking. She had always thought that no human being deserved to live in the squalor of a slum tenement, but now she wasn't so sure.

Was it the dwellings that made the people, or the people that made the dwellings? Was it the church that made the bigots, or the bigots that made the church? What did God have to do with any of it?

4

BY SOME miracle, Lizzie had her baby this time, and it was a little boy and he was fine. She called him Anthony Robert, and for a few brief days was happier than she had ever been in her life.

And then Jack said, 'He'll be christened in the kirk. The priests are no' getting their greasy hands on any son o' mine.'

'But, Jack! I swore. I swore an oath to Faither O'Connor!'

'Well, you can jist un-swear it. I'll no' have it, and that's final.'

Nothing would shift him.

Even Jenny, perceptive though she was, didn't recognise until years later that it was then that Lizzie began to die.

5

BY THE autumn of 1924, Jenny was so exhausted by the strains of the last eighteen months that when Howard asked her to marry him, she said, 'Yes.'

In which she surprised herself considerably more than she did him.

She had been in urgent need of a respite from work and worry, if only for a few days, and when Howard remarked casually at a board meeting that the British Empire Exhibition at Wembley was well worth a visit – 'a most interesting showcase for all the latest advances, in engineering as in everything else' – she had seen in it her salvation. Even her mother had acknowledged, however grudgingly, that if it had to do with the yard . . .

So she had deposited Beth, much to Beth's delight, with her Aunt Allie, and departed in a hurry, before anything could happen to stop her. It was already the end of October and the exhibition was due to close on the third of November.

Howard offered to escort her to watch the closing ceremony, which was to be performed by the Prince of Wales. She didn't know whether he was taking her because he wanted to take her, or merely to demonstrate that, in the face of nationwide competition, he was capable of acquiring tickets for the best seats in the best-situated of the covered stands. But it didn't matter. It was wonderful beyond words to have somebody else being competent and reassuring for a change, and pure heaven to be treated as a pretty woman rather than a cross between a crutch and a soundingboard.

London wasn't at its best. The traffic was terrible, so bad that it had become necessary to paint white lines in the middle of the road to try and impose some order on it, and the rain was pouring down with a grim tenacity that made Jenny feel as if she were still at home. But she wasn't, so she didn't mind.

She even found herself repressing a giggle at the sight of Howard's umbrella, which was of such heroic proportions that she wondered whether he'd borrowed it from a hotel doorman. But it certainly sheltered them both very effectively and so spaciously that it didn't detract in the least from Howard's dignity.

They spent the first part of the morning dutifully admiring the

Palace of Engineering – six-and-a-half times the size of Trafalgar Square and the largest concrete structure in the world – and then, Jenny's conscience clear, took themselves off to the Ceylon exhibit so that she could gape, in what Howard called a charmingly feminine way, at a million pounds' worth of pearl necklaces. After that they saw the Canadian pavilion and the life sized-statue of the Prince of Wales carved out of butter, which inspired Howard to suggest that Jenny might care for some lunch.

On their way to the stand in the afternoon, they paused to watch some workmen with forks and crowbars trying to drain the perimeter driveway so that the massed pipers of the 1st and 2nd Battalions of the Scots Guards wouldn't disappear, gurgling, from view as they marched into the arena.

Feeling well-fed and cheerful, Jenny said, 'We should have brought them a puffer. It would be about the right draught, wouldn't you think?'

Howard looked down at her and laughed his unpredictable laugh. Then he said, with no variation from his normal tone of voice, 'This may seem to you an odd time, but I have been thinking for several months that we are unusually well suited. Perhaps you would care to give some thought to the idea of marriage? We can talk about it this evening at dinner. Now, shall we go and find our seats for the ceremony?'

'Oh,' Jenny said weakly. 'Yes, by all means. Let's.'

As they paddled through the flood, she remembered that Tom had proposed to her on the golf course. Perhaps she just wasn't the champagne and roses type.

6

THEY dined at Claridge's, after a pre-dinner drink served by a footman in a powdered wig, and it was unexpectedly pleasant and private because the tables were so far apart that they were scarcely even within hailing distance of one other.

Jenny was deeply grateful that Allie had made her bring a dinner dress. She hadn't been able to afford a new one because there hadn't been any dividends from her shares in the yard and her salary only just met the necessities of everyday living, but Allie had said, 'Take this one, on loan. I won't say "on approval" because even at a discount you couldn't afford it! It's a shocking price. But it seems a waste for it not to be worn, just once, by someone with the figure for it. After that, I fear it will be heigh-ho for one of those ladies with shapes as solid as their bank balances. Look after it.'

It was the most beautiful thing Jenny had ever worn – a black Fortuny satin, pleated like a Greek chiton. Over it went a loose, thigh-length black velvet jacket printed with a metallic design in copper-bronze and lined with bright scarlet. It didn't need any jewellery, which was just as well, since Jenny didn't have any.

She could see everyone else in the dining room identifying the designer and placing her among the Rich Rich, but all Howard did was raise one eyebrow and look half appreciative and half perplexed. To her annoyance, she found herself rushing into an explanation.

He smiled. 'I see! Even to my masculine eye it looked – ah – unexpectedly costly. It is also extremely elegant. In fact, I would suggest that, since you will of course have a dress allowance when we are married, you might care to draw against it in advance. It is an outfit which I should be happy to see again. You have admirable taste, my dear Jenny.'

'Since I'll have . . .? Will I? I mean, would I? Oh.'

She couldn't think why she was twittering like an ingénue, so she took a restorative sip of Château Margaux 1870 and said firmly, 'Howard . . .'

Not until he had finished extracting the truffle from the interior of his roast partridge did he raise his head, showing her the curving smile that made his upper lip, always sparely drawn in comparison with the lower one, disappear almost to vanishing point. It hadn't occurred to Jenny before that he was one of those men who looked as if they ought to be wearing a moustache.

She had paused to be sure of having his full attention before she went on, but he forestalled her, assuming that he knew what she was about to say. It was a habit of his that Jenny found disconcerting, because he didn't always guess correctly and there was a limit to how often one could respond, 'Yes, but what I was going to say was . . .'

Now, nodding as if in agreement, he remarked, 'Naturally, I am not conversant with either the niceties or the costs of feminine apparel. I will therefore have to rely on your guidance as to what would be a suitable sum, bearing in mind that I should not like you to look any less elegant than you do now. You will not find me unreasonable on the matter or, indeed, on the other arrangements it will be necessary for us to discuss at some stage. I do not anticipate any problems.'

Then he went back to his truffle.

Jenny, momentarily speechless, surveyed what she could see of him – thick brown hair, impeccably barbered and brushed smoothly back from a high forehead; prominent nose; broad, expensively tailored shoulders; pearl shirt studs; monogrammed gold cufflinks. His hands, although beautifully manicured, were powerful and stubby-fingered, and in Jenny's view didn't quite live up to the rest of him. But then, she was prejudiced in favour of men with hands that were long-fingered and flexible.

Howard was in his mid-thirties and had never been married. Beyond that, and despite the fact that they had been acquainted for almost six years, Jenny knew nothing of his private life. What she did know was that he had an excellent reputation as an accountant, and was a partner in one of the most respected firms in the City. One of the most profitable, too, she deduced, because he was clearly well endowed with worldly goods and she remembered something being said at Provost Charters that had made her think he hadn't inherited much from his parents.

Collecting herself after a moment, she laughed. 'Howard! I haven't even said I'll marry you!'

7

BUT Howard knew that the issue was not in doubt. Any young woman in Jenny's situation would be a fool to refuse such an offer as he had made her, and Jenny was not a fool even if, at times, she was sadly ingenuous. Some day, no doubt, she would learn that it was wiser to mistrust people than to trust them. Some day she would lose that elusive quality that he hadn't been able to identify until he had seen it reflected, unobscured by experience or artifice, in her daughter Beth; a candid interest in people, and a prejudice in their favour. He found it rather charming, even while he deplored the impracticality of it.

Disposing his knife and fork at the side of his plate in perfect alignment, he dabbed his napkin lightly to his lips, and looked into her wide, clear hazel eyes.

Responsibility had been good for her. Over the last five or six years, she had developed from being a pretty but rather insecure girl into a handsome and assured young woman. Howard knew she was grateful to him for his kindness in the early days, and found it satisfactory that she continued to defer to his opinions, even when they ran counter to her own. Which was just as it should be. Indeed, he would not have contemplated marrying her if things had been otherwise. As it was, he found her looks and manners unexceptionable – for which, he supposed, he ought to give credit to Paul and Natasha – and believed her intelligence to be sufficiently lively to do him credit without being so acute as to incommode him.

It was tedious to have to go through the motions of persuading her, but modern convention decreed that women should not snatch too obviously at the first decent offer made to them and Howard was a great believer in the convention. Without it, or the appearance of it, both business and society would disintegrate into anarchy.

Smiling, he said, 'My dear Jenny, you are a sensible woman, and I am a sensible man. In other words, we are two rational people who enjoy each other's company and are sufficiently well matched to form a civilised partnership. Your own domestic situation at present, as I understand it, is less than congenial . . .'

Which was one way of describing his intended wife's repellent parent and scarcely less repellent little house. Howard had studied Jenny carefully over the last two years, finding it needful to reassure himself that she would not develop into a carbon copy of her mother. That would have been too high a price to pay.

'I myself,' he went on, 'am tiring of my bachelor existence, although it has much to recommend it. Indeed, I daresay I may never become entirely uxorious. I value my independence too much. However, matrimony has its undoubted attractions. I think we might have some cheese to finish off this excellent wine.'

When they were free of waiters again, she began tentatively, 'Howard . . .'

'The shipyard? Yes.' It would do no harm to keep her in suspense for a few moments longer. 'You must try the Roquefort. It is in beautiful condition, although I would have expected it to be a week or two on the young side, considering the time of year.'

'Very well. But Howard . . .'

Inwardly, he smiled. Then, aloud, he said reassuringly, 'You have no need to worry, my dear Jenny. I shall not require you to give up your work at the shipyard. It is my impression that it would not suit you at all to be without an occupation, especially as I am frequently away from home on business.

'And while we are on the subject of "home", I have been giving the matter some thought and I believe I should buy a house in one of the better parts of Paisley or Glasgow – am I right in remembering Pollokshields as a tolerable address? We will need somewhere substantial, because my collection of Egyptian antiquities is growing, and I also require study space for my mathematical and astrological papyri. We will, of course, retain the flat in Mount Street for use when we are in London. I anticipate no serious problems in dividing my time between the two.'

But there was something still troubling her, it seemed. When she said *'Howard!'* for a third time, it came out almost as a shriek.

He raised his eyebrows in faint reproval. 'Yes, my dear?'

'Why *me*?'

'Why. . .?' He hoped she didn't expect him to begin itemising her charms.

'Well, you're clearly not in love with me, and there must be dozens of girls you could choose from. So why *me*?'

He was disappointed to discover that even the practical Jenny should have fallen victim to the picture-palace obsession with 'love'.

'Oh-h-h, dear,' he said. 'What, I wonder, do you mean by "in love with"? Romantically infatuated? Hardly a stable foundation for a lifetime of living together. Coffee in the sitting room, I think.'

She had a pretty, rather sweet mouth, but her lips were tight as she rose and sailed ahead of him out of the dining room.

It seemed to Howard that a little gentle discipline was called for, so he allowed her to cool her heels for a few moments while he congratulated the head waiter on the excellence of the dinner. Then, as they crossed the marbled hall, the strains of *The Sheik of Araby* floated down from one of the ballrooms, and he left Jenny wondering where he had disappeared to while he strolled over to the porter's desk to confirm that he had ordered a taxi for eleven, and to ask casually, 'Desert oasis tonight?'

'As a matter of fact, no, sir. South Sea island lagoon, I believe.'

Returning to Jenny's side, he took her arm, saying, 'There is a fashion for exotic decorations at debutantes' balls these days. It must be months since anyone has seen any of the ballrooms here in their natural state.'

'Oh?' The tight look had vanished, and Howard thought that, really, it was almost farcically easy to put people in their place; a simple matter of demonstrating that their convenience was not the most important thing in the world.

337

Even so, he was faintly irritated to find that Jenny was disinclined to let the matter rest. Entering the sitting room, she pointedly ignored a flunkey's attempt to steer them towards a table near the small orchestra – sawing away at *Rose Marie* – and headed for the quietest and most private corner.

'Now,' she said purposefully, when they were settled. 'Go on, Howard, please. You haven't answered me. Why me rather than anyone else?'

8

SHE waited with interest while he surveyed her, smoothing down his upper lip with the side of his forefinger. It was the nearest thing to a nervous habit she had ever identified in him, and one that he seldom resorted to.

'What, still at that?' he asked after a moment, tilting his head and crinkling his eyes. He had narrow, judicious eyes, with incipient pouches beneath them. 'Well, then. We enjoy each other's company and have, I believe, reasonably similar tastes. You are intelligent, even-tempered, efficient. You are the right age. You are presentable. You lack the dedicated self-interest that characterises so many of the eligible young women of my own class. You know how to dress. And, of course, I find you attractive in the more intimate sense. If that were not so, I should not have asked you to marry me.'

He smiled at her as if condescension couldn't have been further from his thoughts. Jenny didn't know whether to laugh merrily or tip the scalding coffeepot into his lap.

In the end, she did neither. In a very stately way, she said, 'Thank you. Now I know where I am, and your flattering opinion of me leads me to believe that you will understand – and endorse – my feeling that I should not make a decision on such an important matter without giving it deep and considered thought.' She paused for breath, something Howard never seemed to find it necessary to do, however convoluted his periods.

'I am going home on the overnight train tomorrow. Perhaps I could give you my answer some time during the day?'

Not that she had much need to think about it. She was tired of being a widow and alone, and the last eighteen months had shown

338

her that she could not go on as she was, taking everyone's burdens on her own shoulders while she herself had no one to turn to.

Marriage would solve so many of her difficulties, and the kind of marriage Howard suggested would leave her a good deal of freedom. He didn't excite her and she was even a little nervous of him, although she thought that was probably because she didn't yet know him really well. He was a perfectionist, too, and a bit self-satisfied, and occasionally pompous. But in someone who'd been as consistently kind and helpful to her as he had, those were pretty minor faults. They really got on quite well, and he was clever and safe and comfortable, the only man she knew whom she could even contemplate taking as a second husband.

Except for the man she loved, but could never marry. She had recognised months ago that it would be foolish to spend the rest of her life yearning for him.

Even so, she wept silently in Bertha's cluttered spare bedroom, all through the long November night.

9

'NO, *no*, and NO!' said Matt.

'But why not?'

'There's a small matter of money. That's why not.'

Mims screamed, 'But think of the *prize* money!'

'Dammit, can't you see beyond prize money? Can't you see that if we *don't* win it, we'll be bloody bankrupt!'

Mims, decorative even in greasy overalls and practical turban, marched across the shed that did duty as the office of the Gannet Charter Line and said furiously, 'You are just the most terrible defeatist. You're enough to infuriate *anyone*. You're so British. You've lost all sense of excitement. *I want us to enter for the King's Cup Air Race!*'

'Well, you'll just have to go on wanting! Anyway, what's wrong with being British? You're British, too.'

'Only by birth. And if you haven't lost your sense of adventure, you sure have a fine way of behaving as if you had. "We blue-blooded English know it all!" Well, let me tell you, it sets every red-blooded American's teeth on edge.'

'Oh, yeah? Well, your red-blooded American desire to gamble more than you've got, in the hope of winning something you want, sets *this* blue-blooded *English*man's teeth on edge.'

Mims' English father had died, an alcoholic, when she was only two years old, and her mother had soon afterwards met and married a second-generation American, one Hans Weber, who owned a general store in smalltown Iowa. Mr Weber, as far as Matt had been able to discover – because Mims rarely talked about her family and had flatly refused to be married from home – was a man of moods, and his generosity had varied with his moods so that Mims had spent her years of growing up either very flush with money or very broke. She hadn't a notion how to handle the stuff, either on a personal level or in business.

But she was a good pilot, and when she wasn't in the air she was never happier than when stripping down aero engines or checking the maintenance of airframes. She had ideas, too, and when she wasn't throwing temperaments or wasting money, they made a good partnership. A good business partnership.

Matt took a deep breath. 'Look, sweetheart, the King's Cup is an endurance race. It's 804 miles – from Croydon up the east coast to Newcastle, on to Renfrew, and back by the west coast again. You do it once, and then you have to do it all over again the next day . . .'

'So what? It's a race. You know how to race. You can win!'

'Thank you for that vote of confidence, but we – do – not – have – the – right – plane. Nor would Bill have time to tune it up, even if we did. Nor can we afford the fuel. Nor can we afford to break down somewhere inaccessible in the Borders or the Lake District when we have commercial bookings to fulfill.'

'You're just scared to take on Alan Cobham.'

'Of course I'm scared to take on Alan Cobham. He's the best pilot in the business and he's got one of the best planes.'

'But he's got the heaviest handicap.'

'*Will you leave it!* It's not only Alan. It's Hemming, and Frank Barnard, and . . . What the hell am I arguing for? We cannot afford to enter, and that is that!'

Suddenly her green eyes filled with tears. 'It's always going to be like this. It's always going to be "no" to all the exciting things there still are to do. All the things no one's done yet. Crossing the Pacific. And the North Pole. Flying over Everest. And though you've flown the Atlantic before – well, most of it – you won't even enter us for the Orteig prize for New York to Paris . . .'

'Which is twice as far,' Matt interrupted in exasperation, 'as Newfoundland to Ireland.'

She didn't even hear him. 'And no one's ever flown the Atlantic solo . . .'

She was right in a way. The world of flying was still wide open. The trouble was that Matt himself wasn't sure where he was going. He had wasted more than three carefree years stunting around the States as if there was no tomorrow, but he knew now that his days of flying for the hell of it had to be over, if he was ever going to do anything with his life.

He was determined, still, to build a passenger airline, partly, he supposed, because he had an adolescent need to prove himself to his father, but also because he loved flying so much, because it gave him so much pleasure to introduce other people to the beauty of the skies, that he wanted to open the magical experience to everyone. It was a curiously sentimental dream for a man who, on a personal level, had learned to be cynical about human relationships, but there was also, deep inside him, the belief that, if people could travel more and further, if it was easier for them to meet and get to know the people of other countries, then it might – just might – help to prevent another Armageddon.

He had become convinced that his dream, in the present state of flying technology, was impossible of fulfilment. Regular passenger flying wasn't going to become a viable proposition until the designers had learned how to reduce fuel consumption and allow planes to stay in the air longer. They were going to have to introduce streamlining to step up speed; adopt something like Lachman's notion of slotted wings to improve reliability; invent instruments that would make it possible to fly in the dark or in the fog. They were going to have to produce planes that, like trains, would run on time. To begin with, he hadn't had enough sense to think it through; it was as if his judgement, like every other serious faculty, had been suspended during the years after the war. Relying blithely on luck, he had set up a scheduled air service, and it had deservedly collapsed.

Afterwards, he and Bill Bonny had agreed that until there were radical improvements in aircraft design, what they had to do was find some way for their new Gannet Charter to stay in business. Which meant – as they saw it – economy, intelligence, and avoidance of risk.

But, gradually, an idea had been forming in Matt's mind. At Tasha's dreadful welcome-home party, Jenny Jardine had said, 'Well, if all the available planes are as imperfect as you say, why not design your own? If you know what's wrong with something, you're halfway towards putting it right. It applies with ships, and I don't see why it shouldn't apply with planes.'

He'd laughed, and said, 'Oh, come on!' but the suggestion had taken root, and now he and Bill Bonny had designed and begun to build the six-seater Britton-Bonny 1, which was going to be quite exciting in its way – if it worked. Matt who, ironically, had been encouraged by Jenny's father to find pleasure in working with wood, made himself responsible for the airframe, while Bill, with a little help from Mims, was in charge of the mechanics of the thing. Unfortunately, it was taking very nearly every penny of the scanty profits from the charter line. Worse, from Mims' point of view, it wasn't a dazzling little beauty designed for spectacular long-distance flight, but something sensible, safe and dependable.

Poor Mims, who had thought she was marrying the man she had know in America – the man who was only a small part of this other Matthew Britton.

She wailed, 'All the things that haven't been done! And even the things that *have* been done haven't been done by a woman.'

She was the only girl he had ever known who could look woebegone and beautiful at the same time, but he didn't take her in his arms and soothe her, because they had been married for almost three years and he knew that it would do neither of them any good at all. She was vivid, and appealing, and teasing, and she looked and behaved as if all she wanted in the world was to have a man plunge himself laughingly and luxuriously inside her; as if she was made for love, and would revel in it. But she didn't. And because she was a nice girl, and respectable, neither of them had found out until they were married and it was too late.

During the war, he had learned how to be celibate for long periods. But it was a very different thing to be celibate when you were living in perpetual proximity to an extremely desirable wife who just wasn't interested.

'I know, sweetheart,' he said wearily, because he was fond of her and sorry for her, as well as for himself. 'Just give it time. When the situation improves, I promise you, you'll be the very first woman pilot to do *something* the world is waiting for.'

10

THE evening before the wedding, Jenny said weakly to Howard, 'You don't mind if I don't come, do you? It's going to be *awful!*'

'Nonsense, my dear. Mere irritation of the nerves. I agree that it may be embarrassing, but no one can harm you. Just remember that. And, of course, you will have your husband to protect you.'

He handed her out of the car at the front gate of No.2 Rashilea Terrace and she could tell by the quality of his smile that he was about to take her in his arms and kiss her. Which he accordingly did, despite a certain reluctance on the part of his affianced bride. Howard had never lived in the kind of place where, no matter what hour of the day or night you came home, you could always rely on there being one of the neighbours peering out from behind the aspidistra.

The first time Howard had kissed her, Jenny had been hesitant and confused. It was more than eight years since her brief experience of marriage, and no one, either before or since, had kissed her with anything like the thoroughness that Tom had brought to it, a thoroughness clumsy with urgency and desire. She hadn't known what to expect from Howard.

In the event, it had been rather like the annual audit, like being taken through a well-defined procedure, step by carefully considered step. First the encircling arms, cradling her into the right position. Then the eyes looking down into hers with a faintly amused expression that seemed to say, 'We are grown-ups and know better than to take this kind of thing too seriously.' After that, a smooth lowering of the head until their lips met and began gently, rhythmically, to press together while his arms settled more comfortably around her. It had been several minutes before his tongue began to stray between her lips, judiciously and enquiringly, rather as if he were trying to decide whether her flavour was such as might recommend itself to a connoisseur. And even afterwards, when it became more demanding, she had no sense of being guzzled up in any uncouth fashion.

It had been remarkably pleasant, and she had felt the faintest of frissons pass through her body.

It had also been a very long kiss, during which she had time to become aware of how expert – even by her untutored standards – Howard seemed to be. He must have had a good deal of practice, she thought, a little shocked. And then, unromantically, she had ended the kiss by almost choking on a breath of laughter, because it was silly to think of Howard being less than expert at anything he did.

This evening, he did not prolong his embrace. It was June, and not quite dark, and tomorrow was very near. Tomorrow *night* was very near.

She didn't know whether she was pleased or annoyed at not knowing where they were going to spend their honeymoon, or how they were going to get there. All Howard had told her, his urbane smile toppling over into smugness, was that country clothes would do very well.

11

THE wedding was every bit as gruesome as she had anticipated.

Wearing a long, shadow-patterned cream silk frock and matching hat, with a bouquet of cream and pink roses clutched in her trembling hand, Jenny walked up the aisle on Jack's arm, her rigid gaze fixed on Howard's back and her mind repeating over and over again that all she had to do was grit her teeth and get on with it – or, as Jack had phrased it, 'pit a stoot hert tae a stey brae' – because it would all be over soon.

Unfortunately, she had always had good peripheral vision.

It enabled her to see that her mother and Natasha were seated side by side in the front row. And as if that wasn't enough, behind them were Matt and Mims, sandwiched between Aunts Effie and Mattie.

She felt slightly faint. What demon of an usher had been at work there? Almost at once, she knew it must have been Iris's husband Sydney. Dyed-in-the-wool bacon merchant that he was, he'd probably allocated the seating on a nice, tasty basis of alternating fat and lean.

Jack, misinterpreting the quiver that ran through her, pressed her arm reassuringly against his side. He hoped this marriage was going to be better for her than the last.

Jenny would have preferred a very, very, *very* quiet wedding, but Howard had thought they should do it properly. He would foot the bill of course, since she had no father. In the end, she had given in, not for Howard's sake, but because, full of guilty relief at getting away from Rashilea Terrace, she had felt she couldn't, for a second time, defraud Nellie of being Mother of the Bride.

She would never forget the effort of will it had taken her to tell her mother, 'Howard says he would have no objection if you decided you'd like to come and live with us. The house is big enough. You could even have your own little sittingroom, so that we wouldn't be under each other's feet.' She herself thought it was amazingly generous of Howard.

It had been nerve-racking but not difficult to follow Nellie's mental processes. At least half the joy of going to live in a big, posh house would lie in telling the neighbours about it. 'My daughter and son-in-law want me to go and stay with them, of course. In Pollokshields.'

But after the enticing first thoughts of being waited on, and ordering the servants about, and having a whole new field of gossip open up before her, Nellie had begun thinking less palatable second thoughts. There was the unacknowledged fear that she wouldn't know how to behave; the realisation that she'd never be able to loosen her stays except when she was going to bed; the suspicion that there mightn't be any Joneses for her to be one up on; above all, the recognition that, since it wouldn't be her house, her word wouldn't be law.

When, at last, she had said, 'What? Leave my own wee house? Oh, I could never do that!' it had been as much as Jenny could do not to hug her.

'Are you sure? Are you absolutely sure? Because you can't stay at Rashilea Terrace on your own. You'll have to have Aunt Effie or Aunt Mattie to live with you.'

And now, of course, she felt awful about it. A queer thing, conscience.

O perfect love, all human thought transcending . . .

And then the marriage ceremony. The words were really quite extraordinary when you listened to them, Jenny thought. A triumph of scriptural optimism over human probability.

Howard said, 'I do,' at the right time, and so did Jenny, and then she found herself with her new wedding ring on her finger, about half an inch wide and 22-carat, what else?

Jardine, Britton, and now Fournier. She knew she was being

idiotic, but she found it peculiarly difficult to sign the register, as if she were signing away everything – everyone – she had ever loved or wanted.

12

THERE was a fleet of cars to ferry the guests from Paisley Abbey to the Central Hotel in Glasgow for the reception, a thirty-minute drive. Jenny, ducking the confetti outside the abbey, whispered fiercely to Jack, 'Don't you dare let mum get in the same car as Natasha!'

Jack's spurt of amusement made him look ten years younger. 'Feartie!'

'Yes, well,' she said. 'It's *my* wedding day, and I'll be a coward if I want to.'

At the hotel, her grip like a vice on her champagne glass, she joined Howard in circulating among the guests. It was as well that Howard was equal to anything, including unassisted small talk, because his wife was much too busy eavesdropping on snatches of conversation that ought, by rights, to have turned her hair grey.

Aunt Effie, elf-locked and uninhibited as one of Macbeth's three witches, had an uncomprehending Mims in thrall. 'Huv you got a big faimly? There's nine o' us and we're maistly tumshie-heided but my sister's aye had an awfy guid heid on her. She wis a school-teacher wunst, afore she was merrit. I'm gaun tae live wi' her noo Jenny's got a new man.'

And Sydney Cockerell, just like the Ancient Mariner, had fixed Paul Britton with his glittering eye, and was initiating him into the arcane mysteries of the grocery trade. 'Now, jist take they sugar bags, yon wee blue paper ones. Ye know the kind?'

'Not intimately.'

'Aye, weel, the lassies behind the coonter are aye tearing them. But, see, jist throw wan o' them away an' that's a' the profit on a pound o' sugar gone.'

Jenny let out a faint sob of hysteria.

Sir Albert was having the time of his life, as deep in the patter with Aunt Mattie as if he had never been away, but Nellie, holding her champagne glass with her little finger crooked teacup-wise from its stem, was not similarly at ease.

Jenny had warned her mother that Natasha was a terrible snob, so that, if she had to talk to her, she was to be very careful what she said and restrict herself to generalities. 'Just don't give her the chance to talk down to you, that's all.'

These admonitions had had their effect, because Nellie was saying with paralysing gentility, 'The servant problem's terrible these days, is it not? My late husband, Mr Jardine, used to say he wouldn't give a docken for most of the ones who applied for employment with us. Mind you, he had very high standards, being a man. Is it not awfully difficult for you, with a big house like Provost Charters to look after?'

Natasha's golden eyebrows rose under the fashionably deep-crowned hat, which, Jenny was pleased to see, didn't suit her at all because her cheek-bones were too wide. 'No,' she said, surprised.

'Reelly? I suppose that's because there are so many members of the aristo-crassy in your part of the country.'

'I have no idea,' said Natasha, with a shrug. Clearly, having satisfied herself that dear Jenny's mother was precisely as vulgar as she would have expected, she was finding Nellie a bore. 'I do not concern myself with such matters. Employing servants is a task for the butler and the housekeeper.'

Nellie's mouth dropped open.

Jenny was just about to rush to her mother's aid when she caught sight of Matt, standing alone nearby, his lips compressed into an invisible line. He appeared to be having trouble with his breathing.

She hadn't seen him for two long years.

He sensed her looking at him and, turning caught her harassed gaze. And that, it seemed, was the last straw. His mouth relaxed, his eyes began to blaze with laughter in the lean, handsome, tanned face, and her heart performed several amazing gyrations before she was able to stop it and remind herself, He's only a friend, someone I know. Nothing more.

And then she found that his amusement was so infectious that she was able to laugh back at him, and to recognise that it really *was* very funny, and what was she in such a fuss about.

Mims escaped from Aunt Effie with impressive rapidity and materialised at Matt's side, whereupon Jenny fluttered her eye-lashes winsomely at her, and Mims promptly linked her arm in her husband's and looked up at him with a smile that was more vixenish than kittenish.

Howard said, 'Something amusing, my dear?'

Jenny turned to him and tried to collect herself. 'I'm sorry.

You probably didn't hear. It was just the conversation between my mother and – and Natasha . . . Never mind. It wasn't as funny as all that. You must introduce me properly to Mr Durand. I don't think I've met an art dealer before. I don't even know what they do.'

She sat through the wedding breakfast in a state of mild euphoria. The food was excellent, and the wedding cake beautiful, and when she went off to change into the cream linen going-away outfit with the scarlet trim it was every bit as flattering as it had looked in Allie's shop.

Beth said, 'You look awfully pretty, mummy!' and she gave the child an enormous hug, and told her she wasn't to be any trouble to Aunt Allie for the next two weeks. Beth said, 'I'll be good. I promise.' Jenny felt a foolish tear spring to her eyes. She had been quite upset, at first, over the way the child had been transformed by the knowledge that she was going to have a daddy, just like everyone else.

When she returned to the reception, Howard murmured, 'I must not tantalise you any longer as to our honeymoon destination, because the journey is part of it. Allie has lent us her house in Morar.'

He meant Crannoch Lodge, which Allie had inherited from her father, and Jenny was slightly dashed for a moment, thinking of the six or seven-hour drive ahead, and then pleased, because she had never yet visited the Highlands although she had always wanted to.

But Howard hadn't finished. 'The journey, I am assured, will not take more than about two hours. I thought it would be an exciting new experience for you to go by something other than ordinary, everyday transport, so I have chartered Matthew's plane. We can land on the beach, he says, and he will have to stay overnight, but you won't mind that, will you?'

13

SHE lived through the next twenty-four hours minute by minute.

The plane looked very smart and very small. It was painted a gleaming white except for the nose, which was a pale, warm yellow, and the wings, which had wide black tips. In line with the registration number on the sides were written the words, 'Gannet Charter'.

'We couldn't very well call it the "Bonny Britton Line", now could we?' Matt said. 'The gannet's a bird, of course, and the inspiration for the name came during our Atlantic flight in 1919, when we emulated one by nose-diving into the sea from fifty feet up.'

'It doesn't sound very reassuring for your passengers,' Jenny said lightly.

'It wouldn't, if any of them were ornithologists, but we've been lucky so far. Ah, here's Bill.'

So they were introduced to the taciturn Mr Bonny, mechanical wizard, and waited while Matt made his external pre-flight check. Then they climbed into the neat little cabin behind the open cockpit and sat down, face to face, in wicker armchairs anchored to the floor by a hook and eye contraption. The walls were painted white, with framed pictures of early flying machines hung on them, and there was a carpet on the floor.

Condescendingly, Howard said, 'Very civilised. Very civilised.'

'Thank you,' Matt replied. 'We do our best. Now, we'll be hanging around for about five minutes while the oil warms up and I do my instrument checks. We'll take off straight into the wind, and after that it should be quite a pleasant flight. It's a lovely evening and you'll have a view of the Highlands that probably not more than a couple of hundred people have seen in the whole history of the world. How about that?'

Jenny said suddenly, 'You sound so happy and relaxed. Has something good happened? Is the charter business going to be – a success?' She had almost said, 'more of a success than the passenger line.'

'Time will tell. No, it's just that all my troubles leave me the moment I have an excuse to get up in the air. Plus, of course, the charter pilot's equivalent of the doctor's bedside manner!'

Jenny hadn't known what to expect, and for the first few minutes clutched the arms of her chair rather hard, while trying to look as if she wasn't. But then Howard pointed downwards, and there below them and to the left lay the Clyde.

She could almost have wept because it was so inexpressibly dear to her and it looked so strange and beautiful in the early evening light, the familiar bronze green waters, the brown smoke, the gaunt skeletons of cranes and derricks, the hazed silhouettes of the shipping; the whole scene overlaid with the mellow chiaroscuro of some old painting. From here you could almost forget that so many of the yards were idle and so many of the berths empty.

349

The wings of the plane waggled, as if Matt was trying to say something, and then they banked across the water and dipped low over the Britton yard, and away again, and up towards Loch Lomond and the Highlands.

It was a different beauty then, though Jenny couldn't see it at first for the tears in her eyes. The landscape was a wondrous panorama of amethyst and indigo and green; of mountainsides lucent and soft and so close that Jenny felt as if she could almost touch them if she leaned out; of lochs that lay wide and blue and shimmering, reflecting the hills around them like magical mirror paintings.

And then at last they were within sight of the sea and the sunset, and there was a path of rose gold leading onward and beyond, right to the edge of the world.

14

THEY landed on the beach and walked up to the house, and Allie's housekeeper gave them supper, all three of them. Then Matt said goodnight, and went off with the handyman to anchor the plane down, just in case a wind got up in the night.

Howard smiled at his wife. 'Shall we go upstairs? I hope you are not too tired to enjoy an appropriate end to this exciting day?'

It had been so long since Tom, and everything this time was so different.

Howard obviously enjoyed his prowess, and Jenny tried very hard to behave as if she were enjoying it, too, because she didn't want to disappoint him. She didn't know, then, though she was to learn in time, that he would always find her pretences acceptable because all he required of her was an acknowledgement of his expertise; and his practised handling did indeed stir in her, occasionally, an unexpected hint of pleasure.

But sex, for Howard, had relatively little to do with bodily comfort or gratification; more often, it was a private celebration, a statement of self-satisfaction over something that had happened in the great, wide world beyond the bedroom. Jenny was to discover that, scorning to reach a climax in less than twenty minutes, he was capable, when particularly pleased with himself, of holding out for as much as an hour-and-a-half. It was he, not she, who noted the timing.

It was to be many years before she discovered why he had been so pleased with himself on their wedding night. All she knew then

350

was that, with his heavy, muscular body braced on rigid arms, he was playing some private symphony within her, the phrases soft or loud, simple or complex, straightforward or undulating, but always smooth and rhythmical and relentless. Towards the end he was driving into her so deeply that she felt as if she were being impaled on him and lifted into the air by the length and strength of his thrust alone.

After a few weeks, she was to find that, if she could blank off her mind, her body wasn't entirely averse to the physical side of marriage. But on that first night there was no way of blanking off a mind filled with misery, and guilt, and the knowledge that the man she loved was sleeping only half a dozen yards away.

Five

1

AS HUSBANDS went, Howard was a model.

He was away a good deal, mainly in London, which allowed Jenny to be very comfortable in the new house in Pollokshields. This was large, square, and Victorian – rather like the house at Castlehead, but built of red sandstone instead of grey – and it ran like clockwork under the ministrations of Mrs Simons, the live-in cook-general, and May, the house-parlourmaid. Mrs Simons' daughter, who was training to be a schoolteacher, kept an eye on Beth when necessary, and Mr Simons was both gardener and general handyman. Jenny had never been so pampered in her life.

After a few weeks, she was even able to look at the decor without shuddering. Howard had insisted she leave it all to him. As with the honeymoon arrangements, she was to know nothing until he surprised and delighted her with the finished result. She had spent the first two months of her marriage living in an hotel and hoping that he was going to be right about the delight. It would have been nice to be consulted.

She wondered a little at the enjoyment he seemed to derive from springing surprises on people, and decided it was one of his ways of emphasising that it was he who was in control. She had learned very quickly that life ran on oiled wheels as long as nobody crossed him, even though he wasn't unpleasant when that happened; nothing so specific. But he had a very definite knack of creating an atmosphere.

Where the house was concerned, she had resigned herself to something that Howard would see as consonant with his dignity – heavy velvet, and dark panelling, and stately furniture. In the event, she could scarcely have been more wrong, and her reaction was less of surprise than sheer stupefaction. Everything was so avant-garde that she had no yardstick to judge it by.

'The style of the future,' Howard told her, observing her astonishment with a certain smugness, 'as unveiled in this year's *Exposition des arts décoratifs* in Paris. Those of us in the know call it Art Deco.'

Jenny said, 'Oh.'

There was a great deal of white paint, which pleased her, but the panelling was as utilitarian as if the carpenter had merely tacked some slats on the wall and left it at that; John Jardine would have sacked the man on the spot. The lampshades made her think of a Chinaman's hat, the chairs and sofas were upholstered in a style suggestive of squashy corrugated iron, and everything else seemed to consist of circles, zigzags, and mechanical forms. The colour was mainly peach sparked with violent primaries and an occasional touch of gold, and there wasn't a hint of what Jenny would have called craftsmanship anywhere.

'It's very unusual,' she ventured.

Howard smiled his special fat smile, and she knew that, tonight, there was going to be one of the longer intervals between going to bed and going to sleep.

'And wait until you see the gallery upstairs with my Egyptian antiquities. I think you will recognise that this new decorative trend owes at least some of its inspiration to the Tutankamen discoveries. It makes a most sympathetic background for my collection.'

Although she had heard a good deal about Howard's hobby, which had begun, he said, with an interest in ancient taxation and the chance purchase of a mathematical papyrus, the full extent of his commitment came as a surprise. Her head was spinning by the time she had been shown the abaci and the writing boards, the button seals, the inscribed beads, the astronomical and mathematical papyri, the fragments from the *Book of the Dead*, the wooden sceptres, and the most splendid and largest of his treasures, a sarcophagus.

She wasn't sure that she fancied sharing the house with a coffin.

It didn't surprise her, after that, to discover that Howard had already established a reputation as an expert. The French art dealer, Etienne Durand, who had been his best man, was a frequent visitor because, whenever he had a new acquisition that required authenticating, it was Howard he consulted.

'Faience,' Howard would say. 'Sebennyte period, without a doubt. If you do not have an attribution, I would say you could safely place it as from the Valley of the Kings. And what is this? Oh, yes, an *admirable* little scarab with – what? – astronomical inscriptions? We will have to look more closely . . .'

Mr Durand, a small dark man with a small dark moustache, was always exceedingly courteous to Jenny, but she couldn't rid herself of the feeling that all he ever wanted her to do was go away.

Not that she minded. She was delighted to leave them to it, because she could find little to admire in the art and artefacts of ancient Egypt – except, of course, that such destructible things should have managed to survive intact through more than three thousand troubled years of history.

2

HOWARD was not in the least perturbed by his wife's lack of enthusiasm for his collection. He had expected it, and indeed, if she had shown any real interest he would have felt compelled to discourage her. It would have been most inconvenient to have her querying this, that, and the other, offering help with the cataloguing, and making a general – if decorative – nuisance of herself. Now that she could afford it, she had begun to dress very well indeed.

Had she asked him, he would have explained – though not in so many words – that he had no time for amateurs, who never did things as he wished to have them done. Not that many professionals did either, because Howard's standards were exceedingly high, so high that, although he had been blessed from an early age with an intellect, manner, and presence that would in themselves have sufficed to carry him far in both public and private life, he had still made it an inflexible rule to inform himself so meticulously on any subject coming within his field of interest that he was virtually infallible on it. As it happened, he found this no great challenge, but it so much impressed most of the people with whom he had dealings that it was very rare indeed for them not to bow to his judgement. He had the highest reputation of any accountant in London.

Even Glasgow's business community knew of him, so it had come as an undeniable shock to him to discover that his new wife – while recognising that she was married to someone quite out of the ordinary – had no real idea of the weight his word carried in influential circles. Howard, feeling himself a prophet without honour in his own country, reflected that it must be much the same for His Majesty, whose sons in their childhood had no doubt valued him as 'father' and failed to recognise – if they even knew of it – his power as king. It seemed that he was going to have to demonstrate to Jenny just how much he mattered to the people who mattered.

Apart, however, from this myopia, which could be cured, she was a perfectly satisfactory wife, welcoming him home with genuine pleasure, running the household with competence, never pleading a headache in bed, taking his advice on matters concerning the shipyard and generally behaving as a dutiful wife should, even when it put her to some inconvenience.

He found – which surprised him a little – that he didn't even mind having a child in the house. Beth was an appealing little thing who prefaced every sentence with the word 'Daddy', as if she didn't quite believe it. It was a rôle he had no objection to playing now and again, and Jenny was sensible enough to make sure that the child never plagued him for more than ten or fifteen minutes at a time. He quite looked forward, in a detached way, to his wife providing him with a son or daughter of his own.

As the weeks passed, and the months, he congratulated himself on having made a wise choice. Not that he ever made any other kind.

3

YEARS before, Jenny had discovered a new world when she went to live at Provost Charters. Married to Howard, she discovered another one.

He felt it desirable, he said, that she should meet all the right people, and Jenny soon discovered that he seemed to know everybody who was anybody. In fact, she was surprised and embarrassed by the exaggerated respect accorded to her as 'Howard Fournier's wife'. It pleased Howard, whose reputation was of overriding importance to him, but she herself didn't much like being looked on as somebody's wife rather than as herself. Though she wouldn't have dreamed of saying so.

In no time at all, she was travelling up and down to London so often for parties, theatres and balls, that the attendants on the Friday and Sunday night trains were greeting her as a regular. Howard's participation in such frivolous affairs – unexpected, at first, in a man whose personal style was more suggestive of leather armchairs and *fine* Cognac and Gibbons' *Decline and Fall* – had more to do with business than pleasure, but he confessed to deriving a good deal of amusement from watching people make idiots of themselves.

Jenny could understand it, even if she couldn't share his propensity for looking down on humanity as if from the heights of Olympus. But it was all quite entertaining, and more so for occasional onlookers like themselves than for the regular participants. There were society balls five evenings a week and every one exactly like the last, so that, night after night, the same platoons of perfectly groomed girls in their Paris frocks danced with the same platoons of smooth-faced young men from Eton and the Guards, to the same tunes – *It had to be you, Manhattan, Fascinatin' Rhythm* – played by the same orchestras; watched all the time by the same haggard-eyed chaperons drinking the same warm champagne.

Country house weekends were no more distinguishable, and Jenny had difficulty once or twice in remembering which house she was in. The men always wore the same ties and the same plus-fours; ate the same breakfasts of kidneys and bacon; tapped the same barometers with the same frowns of concentration; stuffed the same pipes into the same pockets; massacred the same game birds with the same guns. The ladies indulged in the same tea and toast; admired the same gardens; gossiped about the same friends and played the same croquet.

If it hadn't been for the plus-fours and the length of the women's skirts, Jenny sometimes thought, the year might as easily have been 1905 as 1925. How was it possible that people could behave as if the Great War had never happened? And then she recognised that they were defending the last bastion of the privileged days that had gone, turning blind eyes to the knowledge that the world no longer owed them a living, acting out a reassuring charade, like children in a brightly lit nursery with the house nightmare-black around them.

It was when she found herself thinking along these lines that she had her own darker vision, and saw with painful clarity the world these people were trying to ignore, the world of unemployment and sickness and hunger. The empty berths at the shipyard.

What was and what wasn't going on at the yard had become an ever more depressing chronicle that came between Jenny and her sleep. What *was* going on was a withdrawal of government support for heavy industry, and what *wasn't* going on was any shipbuilding worthy of the name. Brittons' was getting ever more deeply into debt to the bank, and it worried Jenny stiff. She couldn't understand why Howard didn't seem concerned at all.

Not even when May 1926 came round, and the country was faced with a nationwide strike.

4

'JACK Jardine, can you not understand what I'm telling you? We've a tanker in the fitting-out basin that's due for delivery in two weeks, and there's a penalty clause if we're late with it. And No.598's due for launch, and if Asterisk don't have it in time for the new season they'll never order another ship from us again. If you bring all the men out on this idiotic General Strike, the yard is going to go out of business! There'll be no more jobs for *anybody*.'

Jack didn't believe her. He never believed anybody who didn't have dirty hands. 'Aye, aye,' he said dismissively. 'But it's no' the point. The point is, there's a principle at stake. The coal owners are wantin' to cut wages and increase hours for the miners, and the miners are our comrades and it's time the rest o' us stood shoulder to shoulder wi' them. We huv to show the government and the bosses that the workers huv had enough o' being trampled on.'

Jenny always got annoyed when Jack – or anybody else – talked about 'the workers' as if no one but a trade unionist ever did a hand's turn. 'Oh, dear,' she said sarcastically, 'maybe I should have changed out of my tackety boots!'

But she didn't want to be at cross purposes with him, so she went on, 'Jack, you know perfectly well that I sympathise with the miners. I even sympathise with you, too. Loyalty's a fine thing. I just don't want to see you cutting your own throats. In the state the country's in, surely it's better for folk to be underpaid rather than not paid at all?'

Jack snorted. 'That's what the bosses aye say! But ye can save your breath to cool your porridge, lassie. The General Strike's goin' to happen and it's goin' to teach the government a lesson it'll never forget. We're goin' to win. And then the miners won't *be* under-paid.'

'Oh, great for the miners!' Jenny said furiously. 'And what about you, when you deign to come back to work and find the yard's gone out of business?'

He made a rude noise. 'My head doesny button up the back! Whit ye mean is, your dividends'll huv dropped a bit . . .'

'*That is not what I mean*! What I mean is that the yard is on the very edge of going broke and if you join this stupid General Strike

357

it could tip us over the edge. Jack, I know what I'm talking about. I really mean it!'

He was sombre for a moment, and she wondered whether she dared hope. But then he said, 'No. We'll huv to chance it. I've tellt ye, it's a matter of principle. Folk like you dinny ken whit it's like to be grudged a living wage.'

Jenny, careless of her skirt, sat down with a thud on the red-scrubbed stone steps. Jack refused to be seen talking to her at the yard, and wouldn't come to Pollokshields, so she'd been forced to waylay him in the close of the tenement where he and Lizzie lived. At least it was a cleaner close than the one in Cowcaddens.

'Don't you dare talk about "folk like me" and living wages, Jack Jardine!' she exclaimed. 'You can call me one of the bosses till you're blue in the face, but I only get paid about half what you do. Women aren't supposed to *need* a living wage.'

There was a momentary gleam of humour in his eye. 'Och, weel. A good engineer's worth twice a company secretary any day. Forbye,' he looked her up and down, and the humour had gone, 'ye dinny look as if ye're on the bread line.'

Any reference, direct or implied, to Howard's money always put her on the defensive, because however you looked at it – assuming you'd been born on the Clyde and had the right sense of priorities – accountants and lawyers came very near the top of the list of social parasites.

She decided the only thing to do was ignore it. She *had* to convince Jack that it would be fatal for the men to come out on strike, because he was one of the most forceful shop stewards in the yard and everybody listened to him. She decided to take it very carefully indeed.

She had come prepared. 'I can prove to you that we're on the brink of disaster, and it's not because the directors have been lining their pockets. I've brought the accounts. I shouldn't have done, and there'll be a terrible row if anyone ever finds out, but the yard's a partnership, as I see it, and I think you're entitled to know. Just don't go around telling everybody. Look, I'll explain to you . . .'

At this highly inopportune moment, a shadow fell across the close mouth. It should have been some passing neighbour, but it wasn't.

'Howard!' Jenny said, by no means pleased. She had told him she was going to drop in and see Lizzie.

'Ah, there you are, my dear.' He could scarcely have been

more bland. 'I'm glad you haven't gone. I was passing this way and thought I could give you a lift home.'

Tactfully, Jenny had come on a bus, but Howard had parked the big yellow Citroën Tourer right outside.

Jack's eyes were like flints. By tomorrow, everyone at the yard would know that he had been consorting with the bosses. 'Trying to undermine my position, Howard?'

'Could I do that?' Howard smiled. 'Even if I wanted to, which of course I do not.' Thoughtfully he glanced from one to the other of them. 'Well, well. Ever the optimist, my dear Jenny. Have you finished your – ah – unofficial strike negotiations?'

Sherlock Holmes in person.

With some bitterness, she said, 'Probably.'

'And Jack has proved impervious to sisterly advice? Well, never mind. In my own view, the strike is inevitable and I believe it may even do some good. It will certainly clear the air.'

He turned to Jack, 'Bring – er, Lizzie, is it? – over for tea some day, Jack, dear boy, if you should happen to find yourself short of occupation or – er – sustenance.'

It was extraordinary how offensive he could be when he set his mind to it, though in such a stately way that you often found yourself wondering afterwards if you weren't just being over-sensitive. Jenny, aware that answering back was a waste of effort, merely sat and simmered – 'sisterly advice', indeed! – but Jack had no reason not to say what he thought.

'I wouldny touch your bloody "sustenance" wi' a ten-foot pole. And ye'll no' find Lizzie trespassing on your hospitality ever again, either. I'll make sure of that.'

Jenny exclaimed, 'Jack!' but he thrust past her and disappeared upstairs. After a moment, they heard a door slam.

Turning to Howard, Jenny said, 'Thank you very much.'

5

THE General Strike took place as planned, and all over the country undergraduates had the time of their lives driving trains and buses, while society debutantes manned canteens and the strike pickets played football with the police who were there to control them.

Or so it said on the wireless. At the yard it wasn't nearly such fun.

Howard, in the tone of voice that didn't take the possibility of disagreement or disobedience into account, said at breakfast on the first morning, 'You will not go in while the strike is on, of course.'

Jenny glanced up from checking Beth's homework. 'I must. James will be too busy fussing to do any thinking, and I want to have a look at some blueprints. It occurred to me last night that it might just be possible to rearrange the schedules and adjust our purchase dates so that, if the strike doesn't go on too long, we could still manage to meet our commitments and prevent the yard from going under. Beth, pet, are you sure you've parsed this sentence properly? Surely "shilling" is the subject, not the object?'

Beth was almost dancing with impatience. 'Mummy, I haven't time! I'll be late. It it's wrong, it'll have to *be* wrong!'

'Oh, all right. Off you go, then, and take care.'

Howard disliked having to repeat himself. When Beth had gone, he said, sounding this time rather like Jehovah cutting a recalcitrant Israelite down to size, 'You cannot salvage the situation single-handed. Please remain at home.'

Jenny had discovered an unsuspected streak of contrariness in herself during a year of living with Howard, because whenever he told her to do something – and although his commands might be phrased as suggestions or advice, they were still commands – she felt a powerful compulsion to do the opposite. Maybe she and Jack were more alike than she had thought.

Increasingly, she found herself beginning to disregard his advice in matters to do with the yard, advice he had taken to dispensing with what she considered unnecessary frequency. After all, it wasn't as if she was a complete ignoramus! For the sake of domestic harmony, she didn't make an issue of it, and it never seemed to occur to him that she would do other than what he said, so she usually got away with it.

There was no possibility of getting away with it this time. Even so, to the yard she went, driving part of the way and then using a borrowed rowing boat to reach the office without having to run the gauntlet of the gatehouse, with its pickets and police.

And it was worth it. She got an amazing amount of work done – profitable work, because she did find a way of shuffling the cards into a viable hand. It was some compensation for the knowledge that Howard was displeased with her, and Jack alienated, and Lizzie deprived of the only person whose support she could depend on.

When, after nine days, the union leaders capitulated and the strike ignominiously collapsed, Jenny could have wept for Jack, who had thought of it as a selfless battle on behalf of the downtrodden masses, almost as a prelude to revolution, and now saw all his ideals betrayed by leaders unworthy of the movement they claimed to represent.

She scarcely knew whose side she was on, the stark contrast between Cowcaddens tenements and country house weekends blurred, in her mind, by common sense and the suspicion that revolution wasn't either the fastest or best way to right the world's wrongs.

'Such a waste,' she said to Howard. 'Nothing achieved, and the miners deserted by the other unions, in spite of all their fine talk, and left to fight their battle on their own again!'

Howard folded his tie neatly and reached up to take out his collar stud. 'That is no more than foolish sentimentalism. I doubt if a day has passed since the war ended when there has not been a strike somewhere or other, but I believe this defeat for the unions will prove salutary, and that the era of strikes may have come to a close. Industry can do nothing but benefit from the harsh lesson the workers have learned.'

Then, removing the stiff, round-tipped, slightly old-fashioned collar he affected, he went on, 'I wish I thought that you, too, my dear Jenny, had learned a lesson, because it is time you disabused yourself of this idea that you are indispensable to the yard.'

Jenny, who was already in bed, raised her eyes from the *Glasgow Herald* and opened her mouth. Really! There were times when she felt as if she was the only person in the world who cared whether or not the Britton yard survived. Indispensable was just what she was.

But before she could speak, Howard, watching her in the mirror of his dressing chest, went on, 'I would not like to have to forbid you to go on working there, but unless you recognise that I, as your husband, take priority over the shipyard, I may have to.'

It was a threat she hadn't foreseen, and the breath left her lungs with a gasp as he turned to look directly at her. His eyes were cold, although the customary faint smile still hung on his lips. It had never struck her before how little his facial muscles moved, so that you always had to judge your response from the depth of the creases round his eyes and the millimetric variations in the curve of his mouth.

Did he take priority? By all the conventions of society, he should. But Jenny wished he hadn't put it in black-and-white like that, because it took no more than a moment's reflection for her to admit to herself that she cared for the shipyard much more than she cared for Howard.

When they had discussed marriage that evening at Claridge's, he had made it sound as if it would be an arrangement convenient to both of them, not just to him, and she had assumed that, as long as she took care to see that everything at home ran like clockwork, he would have no complaints to make. She had thought it very enlightened of him to take such an attitude. And yet here he was behaving like some bewhiskered Victorian patriarch.

Usually, when he talked down to her, she was torn between irritation and amusement; Howard was Howard, after all. She had married him in the knowledge of it, and having made her bed etc. etc. Resigning herself to his faults had scarcely seemed an exorbitant price to pay for all he had done for her, and she was fond of him in an un-extravagant kind of way.

Refilling her lungs, she said, 'I'm sorry you feel like that. The last thing I want to do is upset you.'

Consideration or hypocrisy – whatever one chose to call it – was a natural part of the give and take of marriage, and Jenny had no qualms about trying to sound contrite, even if she didn't quite manage it. She hadn't much choice, because Howard was not the kind of person you argued with. His opinions were inflexible – 'unassailable' was the word he used – and arguing with him was like arguing with a brick wall. The only choice was to fight or give in, and Jenny couldn't afford to fight unless it was a life-or-death issue. She had too much to lose.

Inwardly, she sighed. He was so sure of himself. That, she often thought, was why after eleven months of marriage he still made her nervous, and sometimes more than nervous. How could she possibly contend with someone like that, when she herself, deep down, was sure of nothing except her love for Beth, and the shipyard – and Matt.

'The last thing you want to do is upset me?' he repeated, opening the door to the adjoining bathroom; beyond collar and tie, he never undressed in her presence. 'My dear Jenny, if that had been true, you would have paid attention to my wishes. But you deliberately flouted them. You have displeased me very deeply – you have no conception *how* deeply. Perhaps it is fortunate that I shall be away for the next two or three weeks. By the time I return, I will expect to find you in a more amenable frame of mind.'

The door closed behind him, and Jenny discovered that her lips were trembling. He had no right to talk to her like that. She was his wife, and perhaps she had gone against his wishes, but that didn't entitle him to behave as if she were of no more account to him than – than some barber who had cut his hair badly. She didn't understand him at all.

When he came to bed at last, Jenny's light was out and she was pretending very hard to be asleep. He didn't disturb her.

6

A FEW days later, Nellie Jardine, who had been complaining for months that she was always tired, was diagnosed as suffering from anaemia and whisked off to hospital. A week after that, she died.

Howard was in Paris, and Jenny phoned to tell him.

'Yes?' he said, as if he were waiting for her to go on with whatever else she was phoning him about.

'Well, I wondered . . . Which day should we fix for the funeral?'

'That's up to you, surely.'

She couldn't believe it. 'But it'll take you a day or two to get here, won't it? And then there are all the arrangements to make.'

There was the briefest of pauses. 'My dear Jenny, you cannot possibly be expecting me to abandon my business here and rush home simply to arrange or attend your mother's funeral? You can manage that perfectly well on your own. Or leave it to Jack, if you think it's beyond you.'

'It's not that. And anyway, Jack refuses to be involved.'

There was a trace of weary exasperation in Howard's deep, well-modulated voice. 'Then you and Iris and Aunt – er, Effie, is it? – will just have to do what is necessary. I see no problem. Now, if you will forgive me, I have an appointment in a few minutes.'

And that was all. Not a word of sympathy or reassurance. It didn't matter that it would have been a false sympathy. There were decencies that ought to be observed.

Jenny, replacing the receiver, felt the first tears pricking her eyes. She hadn't loved Nellie, or Nellie her, but the bond between mother and daughter had been strong; it was in the nature of things.

Throughout the days that followed, when, trying to tire herself out, she did far too much in far too short a time, she was haunted by guilt over their lack of loving. How much had been her fault? How much of Nellie had been the real person, and how much a product of feckless parents and youth in a Govan slum? Had Nellie Jardine ever known what it was to be happy? How much better might both their lives have been if they had made more effort?

Her brain told her that nothing she could have done would have made any improvement in their relationship, but the dull weight in her chest remained all through the days of arranging the funeral, and attending it, and expecting Howard to phone and ask if everything was all right, and clearing out No.2 Rashilea Terrace.

Nellie hadn't made a Will, so the house itself was to go to Jack, who was going to sell it and pay the proceeds into union funds; he didn't approve of owning property. Aunt Effie was just waiting to grab the furniture she'd need when she found some place else to live, and Iris was off with the EPNS and the linen before Jenny had time to turn round. One of the neighbours fancied the hand-painted china in the show cabinet, and another wondered if she could have the stormy-sea painting 'just as a wee minding' of Mrs Jardine.

Jenny said, 'Yes, yes, yes. If you want,' and took all the better clothes down to the Craw Road, where there were folk who'd be grateful for them, and asked the minister if the crockery and cutlery would be any use for parish meetings, and sat and stared at the old photograph albums and letters and couldn't think what to do with them. All she herself intended to keep from among the sad, tawdry relics of her parents' lives was her father's football medal; she could hang it on a neck chain, she thought.

And still Howard didn't phone to ask how she was managing.

It was the second week in July before she heard from him, and even then it was only to ask whether a letter which should have been addressed to him in London had been sent to Pollokshields by mistake. As an afterthought, he enquired, 'Everything all right? You've settled the Rashilea Terrace business by now, I imagine?'

'Yes. Thank you. I'm surprised you didn't phone sooner.' Her voice was flat.

'My dear Jenny, I know you are perfectly competent when you choose to be, and I have been busy. However, I expect to be home for the last week of July and the first of August. We can take a few drives up round Loch Lomond or perhaps go down to the Kyles. A little fresh air will do us both good.'

'Yes, Howard. That will be nice.'

Later, she thought forlornly that perhaps what was wrong was that he didn't have any imagination. It couldn't be that he didn't care enough for her to put himself out. It probably hadn't even occurred to him that she had been upset, and had needed him.

HE was perfectly bland, perfectly himself, when he returned. The weather was good, and they had quite a pleasant time picnicking here and there, both of them behaving as if nothing at all had occurred to mar their relationship. Normal life was resumed, except for the hurt and resentment in Jenny's heart.

One evening towards the end of August, he telephoned from London to say, 'I will be travelling north on the day train on Saturday. Oh, and by the way, I will be bringing a guest, a young man. Perhaps you would ask Mrs Simons to prepare a room for him.'

'Yes, Howard.'

'All well at home? And at the yard?'

'Not too bad.'

'Good. Very well, my dear. Until Saturday, then.'

There was nothing unusual in Howard bringing guests home for a day or two. In general, they were collectors or archaeologists, men who shared his interest in Egyptology, but occasionally there might be some applicant for a position with Fournier, Le Jeune and Partners; Howard liked to assess his employees' social acceptibility as well as their talent for figures.

But this young man was a surprise. Though he blithely introduced himself as Simon Pierre, there was nothing at all French about him. Jenny found herself wondering whether he might be a relative of Etienne Durand, but Howard, typically, didn't enlighten her.

Whoever Simon Pierre was, he was about eighteen years of age, with a swagger that failed to make him appear older and looks that weren't going to give John Barrymore any sleepless nights. Of average height and build, he had lanky fair hair, indeterminate features, a slight cast in one eye, steel-rimmed spectacles, and the kind of limbs that might have been specially designed for tripping over Chareau chairs and reducing Jean Luce porcelain to smithereens.

Neatly fielding a Marinot vase, Jenny wondered whether he was deliberately cultivating the kind of personality that would compensate for the deficiencies Nature had showered upon him; because, of all the adjectives that might have been used to describe him, 'unassuming' was not one. He wore suede shoes, came down to dinner whistling the *Black Bottom*, and scarcely stopped talking all evening.

Howard, smiling fatly, left it to Jenny to get on with it.

The Trocadero ... Frascati's ... the Duke of York playing in the doubles at Wimbledon ... had they seen Ralph Lynn in *Rookery Nook?* ... the Charleston ... the new Decalion gramophone with the patent alloy cast Transmitter Triple-tone sounding boards ... the Astaires in *Lady, Be Good* ... crossword puzzles ... dance marathons ...

Simon, it appeared, was going to be a Bright Young Thing if it killed him.

Jenny's diversionary tactics had no effect at all. 'Where do you live, Simon?'

'London. In Marlborough Place. That's in St John's Wood, if you know your way around the Great Wen. I say, do you know why whisky kills more people than bullets?'

'No.'

'Bullets don't drink!'

Nine-year-old Beth, who was always allowed to stay up for dinner on Howard's first evening home, thought this hilariously funny, and Simon, who didn't need much encouragement, went on, 'And d'you know what the waiter said when someone complained there was a fly in his soup?'

'No, what?' Beth demanded.

'He said, "Maybe it's one of those vitamin bees they've just discovered!"'

Beth hadn't heard of vitamin B, which rather spoiled that one, but the one about the man who fed mothballs to an elephant to keep the moths out of its trunk was a great success.

Jenny said firmly, 'And what do you do, Simon, apart from gad about?'

'I'm going to' Varsity next month.'

'Oh, where? What will you study?'

'Don't I wish I could go to college in America! What a place! And how about the movies? I swoon every time I even think of Clara Bow. But, I say, wasn't it terrible about Valentino dying? I've seen every picture he ever made!'

Before Jenny's mildly startled eyes, Simon's expression dislimned into something that was halfway between a sneer and a pout, and the muscles of his weedy torso heaved seductively.

I bet you can tango, too, she thought.

She hoped he wouldn't be staying long. Not that he was the kind of youth one disliked. Rather, he was the kind to whom one was perpetually having to stop oneself from saying, 'Oh, for goodness' sake, shut up!'

8

HOWARD didn't usually say much in bed, except to tell Jenny to widen her legs, or arch her hips, or press her fingers hard into his groin to help him hold back, so that he might prolong what he referred to as their mutual pleasure. He had told her once that it was a method favoured by the ancient Chinese, and she had thought, a trifle hysterically, that Howard always knew *every*thing.

Granted the favours of silence and moderation, she had learned to find, if not connubial bliss, at least some enjoyment in Howard's experienced love-making. Not so when he had one of his occasional talkative spells, or when his self-satisfaction required a virtuoso performance. Then, Jenny felt as if there was so much of him inside her that her whole body was choking. The power of him as he plunged into her, again and again and eternally, exhausted her until it became the grimmest of struggles to prevent herself from crying out, 'Enough, Howard. Enough!' It was self-preservation that stopped her, because she knew too well that he would only smile breathlessly, and say, 'Nonsense, my dear,' and go on for longer than he would otherwise have done.

On the night of Simon Pierre's arrival, Jenny had the worst of both worlds, because Howard was not only exceedingly vigorous but exceptionally chatty.

'You are learning well,' he said, driving into her with the slow, steady, calculated power that always made her think how right Jack had been about sex being just like a cylinder and piston.

Howard said, 'It is my tuition, of course . . . I feared at first . . . I might be disappointed . . . since Tom really did not . . . teach you very much . . .'

Jenny gritted her teeth.

'A pity, I have always thought . . . that women have no opportunity . . . as men have . . . to gain experience.

'Tighten your muscles inside and grip me properly. That's right. And now a beautiful long, slow corkscrew. Yes, *yes*. Again again. Yes.

'Muscular control is . . . most important . . .'

It must have been at least an hour, she thought afterwards, before he said the one thing that mattered.

By then he was lying full on top of her, plunged deep inside her, his hands clamped like vices round her buttocks, and his eyes smiling the familiar smile of self-esteem.

He opened his mouth and she waited for it to descend on hers, but instead, he spoke.

He said, 'Simon is my son, of course.'

Then he brought his mouth hard down, and his tongue thrust itself between her lips and, simultaneously, she felt the hot, torrential flood of him bursting inside her.

9

PINNED beneath him in such a way that she could neither struggle nor speak, she lay and raged silently, knowing it was all deliberate, carefully plotted for his own maximum satisfaction. Which included winning a victory over his wife. And when he freed himself from her, he did it so smoothly and suddenly that she could have made no move to hurt him, even if she had wanted to.

What she could so, and did, was deprive him of the pleasure of her anger, astonishment, even curiosity.

'Indeed?' she said, and rose, and went into their en-suite bathroom and had a long, warm soak. She wasn't always so obvious about it, but tonight of all nights she didn't want Howard's seed left to germinate inside her.

They had never, either before or during their marriage, discussed the subject of children. Howard took no precautions, so Jenny assumed he must want them, but she herself wasn't sure. Or not so much that. It was more that she wanted to feel settled and comfortable with him before anything happened. So, before the wedding, she had paid a very private and embarrassed visit to Dr Marie Stopes' clinic in Islington – the only one she had heard of. Unfortunately, of all the birth control methods the clinic suggested, there didn't seem to be any likely to escape the observant Howard's notice, in bed or out of it. So Jenny had relied on bathing and douching and, so far, she had been lucky.

When she returned to the bedroom, she half expected him to be asleep. She had not expected him to volunteer an explanation, and she most certainly did not intend either to be tantalised into asking for one, or to show that she cared.

But in this particular encounter, the honours – if such they could be called – were to finish up even.

Howard was still awake, propped up in bed reading *Mrs Dalloway*, and greeted her return in his own inimitable fashion.

Glancing up, he remarked, 'You did not allow me to finish, my dear. Simon is coming to live with us.'

It was the one thought that hadn't occurred to her as she lay morosely soaking in the bath.

'*What*? With us? You mean *here*?'

'Precisely. Yes. And yes.'

'Oh, no, Howard. Precisely no. *Definitely* no.' That he should have an illegitimate son was shocking enough; that he should expect his wife to take the boy in was going altogether too far.

'But I insist.'

She was no more prepared for a confrontation than she had been three months before, and she didn't need the lift of his eyebrows to remind her that he held all the cards. She couldn't even rush home to mother, now; not that it would ever have occurred to her to do so. Once had been enough.

Helplessly, she said, 'Howard, you don't seem to have any sense of what's right and proper!'

'On the contrary, I am a connoisseur. In any case, since the boy was born such a very long time before we were married, I fail to see any impropriety.'

It was logical in its way, but Jenny had spent twenty-eight years as a daughter not only of Nellie Jardine but of the Church of Scotland, and she knew what was proper and what wasn't proper.

She stared at him, wondering whether it was possible to argue morality with someone who didn't seem to speak the same language.

Howard sighed. 'These tiresome Old Testament beliefs of yours, my dear – so very provincial. Come back to bed, and let us talk.'

He was as bad as Natasha. 'You mean *bourgeois*,' she said. 'I am going downstairs to make a cup of tea.'

'What an admirable idea. I will have one, too.'

10

SHE returned to find that he had decided to favour her with an explanation, and was taken aback when it turned out to be quite reasonable and understandable; the first part, at least.

As she had already deduced, Howard had been only seventeen when he fathered Simon Pierre – Simon Pierre Fournier, to give him his full name. He had been, he said, very lonely, having been left behind in London when his parents moved up to the Clyde, where his father was to manage the shipyard. He had been living in digs, and the landlady's daughter had been pretty and sympathetic and some years older than he. A piano teacher.

'The kind of commonplace situation,' said Howard, 'for which clichés were invented.'

When Margaret became pregnant, Howard had still been under age and had, in any case, no desire to marry her.

'She would not have been a suitable wife for me, and the whole affair would have come as a serious shock to my mother, who was as deeply devoted to me as I was to her.'

Jenny tried to imagine Howard being deeply devoted to anyone, but it was difficult.

'As it happened, Margaret had no father, or there might have been problems, but her mother would have made a fortune had she ever chosen to set up as a brothel madame and was perfectly satisfied with the arrangement we finally reached. I made them an allowance during the early years and, when my situation permitted, set Margaret and Simon up in a small house in St John's Wood.

'Margaret's mother, of course, moved in, but she died a few years ago. Margaret herself died this summer; a perforated appendix, I believe. The boy is therefore homeless, and in my view too immature to stand on his own feet. He needs a guiding hand.'

Meditatively, he concluded, 'So there you have it. And do you know, looking back, I find myself quite amazed at the generous and forbearing nature of my behaviour throughout.'

In Jenny's opinion, scandalous would have been a better word, except perhaps for the original lapse; even if it was the most scandalous part of all in terms of convention, she found she could almost sympathise. She knew what it was to feel alone and friendless.

And then she looked at Howard, taking his ease in his expensive bed in his expensive house, resembling nothing so much as a large, sleek and self-assured cat, and recognised that the idea of her husband as a lonely, unhappy boy was so wildly improbable that it verged on the ludicrous. The only thing to be said in his favour was that, if Margaret had been a respectable girl, none of it would have happened. For how many years, Jenny wondered, had Howard continued to treat Margaret as an unofficial wife?

It was Simon she was sorry for, though she wasn't sure how long she would go on feeling that way when she had him under her feet all the time.

Aware that her words were an admission of surrender, she said, 'And how do you propose to explain him? I don't imagine you want to advertise his illegitimacy to the world.'

'I have no need to explain him.'

'No,' she snapped. 'No one is likely to ask *you*. But I shall be very surprised if a good many people don't ask *me*.'

'An orphaned cousin, on my mother's side. That is all anyone needs to know. You must learn, my dear, to carry things with a high hand. It is really the only way. You might add, I suppose, that he will be studying medicine at Glasgow University, though I shall be surprised if he studies it for long.'

'He should be going to Edinburgh for that.'

'What a very unpatriotic sentiment! Besides, a moment's reflection would tell you that, if he went to study in Edinburgh, he would have to live in digs, and the landlady might have a willing daughter . . .'

Howard's ponderous idea of humour was altogether too exasperating. Jenny picked up the tea tray and, insofar as it was possible to flounce with her hands full, flounced out of the bedroom and down to the scullery, where it gave her considerable satisfaction to drop the whole lot with a resounding crash on the stone floor. She didn't even have a twinge of conscience over the thought of Mrs Simons having to clear it all up in the morning.

11

ABOUT ten days later, Paul telephoned her at home. Natasha, it seemed, was about to pay a visit to Paris to replenish her wardrobe.

'Normally,' Paul said, 'I would go with her, but I have not been very well recently, and do not feel up to it. So Natasha has made up her mind that Matthew must take her, on what she calls her first "serious" flight.'

Jenny's imagination reeled.

She had seen Matt only once in the last year, when Natasha had given a truly dreadful 'special weekend' at Provost Charters to celebrate Sir Albert's eightieth birthday. During it, Howard – who had been displeased with Jenny at the time – had flirted a little ponderously with Natasha, keeping one eye on Jenny, while Natasha, with one eye on Matthew, had flirted outrageously with Howard, and Granby Fox, and several chinless youths from the more distinguished families in the county.

Meanwhile, Mims had flirted with Sir Albert and fifteen-year-old Nick, and Matt, after trying politely and unsuccessfully to flirt with Jenny, had given up and spent most of the weekend engrossed in blueprints and calculations and much thoughtful staring at the plane parked on the south lawn.

Shuddering at the memory of it, Jenny said weakly, 'How nice.'

'Doubtless. I myself vetoed the idea, for obvious reasons.' Although Jenny waited, he did not dilate upon the 'obvious reasons', but went on, 'Unfortunately, Natasha was upset by my veto and the last few days have been – er – somewhat volatile . . .'

Jenny knew exactly what he meant; everyone in the household reduced to a quivering jelly and the housekeeper giving in her notice.

'So, to cut a long story short, I have agreed. The reason I am telephoning is that I suddenly remembered that, at the last board meeting, there was talk of you going to Paris to see some ship brokers, but there was a problem over fluid cash?'

Despite herself, Jenny chuckled. 'You could put it like that. Either I went to Paris in search of future business, or we paid an outstanding bill or two. Notably to the drawing office suppliers.'

'That was it, was it? I couldn't recall. Anyway, there will be a spare seat in the plane next week and you are welcome to it, if it would help at all. Leaving on Monday and returning on Friday. At no cost to you or the yard, of course.'

'A spare seat? Oh.' She was so busy thinking how useful the trip could be that it didn't at first occur to her that there was a price to be paid, after all. The price of chaperoning Natasha and Matt. Temporising, she said, 'There would be hotel costs, too, of course. Ummm . . .'

She hadn't heard Howard come in.

Behind her, he said, 'I sincerely trust that you are not contemplating a trip abroad.' He had a most unlikeable knack of putting two and two together. 'It would displease me very much, when Simon has just arrived and you should be helping him settle in. Really, my dear, Paris on business! Take care that you do not develop delusions of grandeur.'

It put an immediate end to her hesitation. She had swallowed his reprimands over her behaviour during the General Strike. She had done her best to forget how badly he had let her down when her mother died. She had even accepted his illegitimate son into her home. But there were limits.

'Yes, Paul,' she said. 'I should be very happy to avail myself of your offer, and I will pay for the hotel myself, if necessary. Though perhaps you would ask Matthew if he knows of one that is both cheap and respectable? And thank you very much for thinking of it. Give my love to Nick and Sir Albert, won't you?'

Then she turned to Howard and said, 'I will go to Paris if I want to go to Paris. May I remind you that you do not own me!'

He didn't answer, but only because she stalked out of the room without giving him the chance.

Six

1

'THE girls want to go slumming,' Matt said, 'starting at the Dôme and then downhill all the way. And since I'm damned if I'm venturing into dives like the *Kasbek* as the lone male in charge of three gorgeous females, you, my dear Charlie, are coming too. You might even,' he added spaciously, 'bring a friend.'

Charlie Thompson, twelve years old but in every other respect exactly the same as he had been in Sarajevo during the long, hot summer of 1914, stammered, 'Oh, I say, Matt! You know I can't stand those places. All darkness and smoke and queer music and even queerer people!'

'Quite. Which makes it incumbent on you as a member of the Embassy staff to lend me your assistance in protecting the ladies. Now, let's see. I have to look after Mims, and you can squire Tasha . . .'

'Oh, I say . . .'

'. . . which leaves us needing someone for Jenny. Someone nice, because she's a nice girl.'

'Oh, but I say, Matt . . .'

Matt's eyebrows rose. 'Come into a fortune, have we? Don't need any more free hops between London and Paris?'

'That's blackmail.'

'So it is!' said Matt cheerfully. 'Meet you at the Vavin crossroads at ten?'

2

TO Jenny's surprise, it had been Mims who piloted them across the Channel, so Paul's unstated worry about chaperonage had been needless. Perhaps Mims' mind had been running along the same lines.

Mims said, 'I don't get the chance of long flights very often, because our goofy passengers just don't *trust* women pilots. But the Big Cheese says if the family can't put up with me, who can? Natasha, honey, you *don't* mind, now do you?'

'And the Big Cheese,' said Matt, appearing from under the fuselage, 'is going to travel in comfort in the cabin with the passengers, and leave the lady to get on with it.'

With what appeared to be perfect competence and assurance, Mims found her way across the Channel to France and, following the glimmering track of the Seine, brought them, as dusk was falling, to the centre of Paris where, with the greatest aplomb, she circled the Eiffel Tower and then the Arc de Triomphe before heading off to the north-east and the pool of near-darkness that was Le Bourget.

Natasha and Jenny didn't hear Matt say to her sharply, after they had taxied to a halt, 'And *just* in time. When you have passengers aboard, a safe landing takes precedence over sightseeing. Please remember that in future.' Nor did they hear Mims' furious reply. 'Don't you talk to me as if I was some amateur on my first solo flight. I could see just *fine!*'

Tasha wasn't happy, either, and not only because she was having to share Matt's attentions with Jenny and Mims. Having scorned to wear the woollen stockings, flannel body belt, and knee-length knickers that all the experts recommended, she was so cold that her teeth were chattering and she had no sensation in her feet at all. She was also temporarily deaf, because nothing would have induced her to stuff her elegant ears with anything so vulgar as cottonwool and glycerine.

She received no sympathy at all from Jenny, who was perfectly warm and well wrapped up but in a militant mood. Part of it was Howard, and part of it Tasha, but mostly it was frustration over not having been able to pour all her troubles out to Allie, who was as good as a Trappist monk where secrets were concerned but had inconsiderately gone off on holiday just when she was most needed.

Matt, packing them all into a taxi with the promise that he'd follow as soon as he'd put the plane to bed, sighed ostentatiously and said, 'Come on, girls, cheer up. For God's sake, take a deep breath of garlic and *Gauloises* and try to remember you're in Gay Paree!'

3

IT was three o'clock in the morning when disaster struck.

They were sitting in *La Fétiche* listening to indifferent jazz and drinking the nasty champagne that was obligatory in all the subterranean *boîtes* of Montparnasse, and Charlie Thompson was saying for the umpteenth time that *La Fétiche* wasn't at all the sort of place to which Matthew should have brought the ladies.

'Try telling that to Tash,' Matt replied. 'She's bored with Fouquet's.'

The nightclub was no more than a bare-walled, many-arched cellar illuminated with blood-red candles and furnished with primitive wooden tables and chairs. There was a black jazz trio squeezed into a corner, a dance floor large enough for six tightly packed couples, and the fug – compounded, Matt suspected, of drugs as well as *Gauloises* and clay pipes – was so thick that, as Jenny remarked, one could have sliced it up and taken a bit home as a souvenir.

The place was packed, but everyone turned as they entered – a sea of heads cropped and frizzy, faces grey and unadorned or garish in red and ochre paint, figures fat, thin and middling, bundled up or half naked, clothes that spoke of impecunious academe, comfortable trade, unsuccessful art, and aspiring revolution. Tash, Mims and Jenny had all dressed down for the occasion, as instructed, but Tash's idea of dressing down was still a bit rich for the palate of Montparnasse.

What gave *La Fétiche* its special flavour was that the waitresses and waiters weren't what they seemed. The big, buxom waitresses in their red-sequinned bodices turned out to be men, and the no less buxom waiters in their red-sequinned dinner jackets, women. When they weren't serving, they were inviting customers to dance, and Charlie was thrown into total confusion by his inability to decide which, if either, he could respectably stand up with, or even say no to without causing a riot.

There was one fine, manly girl who couldn't take her eyes off Mims.

To Charlie, Matt said, 'We won't stay long.'

4

JENNY liked dancing, but only with people she knew, and Charlie Thompson and his friend Jim Goodhue were the kind of dancers who were so busy thinking 'slow-slow-quick-quick-slow' that they couldn't hear the music. So when the musicians abandoned the *Gut Bucket Blues* for Mr Berlin's *Always*, she gratefully and almost without thinking allowed Matt to lead her through the blue, swirling smoke onto the floor.

It was heaven and hell united. Because after a moment the crush and the music closed the space between them, and Matt's hand in the small of her back moved down until it was just below her waist, and their bodies touched, soft and resilient, matched together, natural together. And after a while he drew their arms inwards until their linked hands were locked between their bodies, and it seemed to bring them even closer together, unifying them, swaying and private, in an invisible capsule that shielded them from contact with everyone and everything extraneous to their perfect physical compatibility and new self-knowledge.

They said not a word, nor did they gaze into each other's eyes or even think. Until the music ended, all they did was feel.

Jenny was in a dream – a beautiful, illicit dream – when they returned to their table and she found Natasha's eyes on her, pale and baleful as ice.

The look lasted only a moment, and then Natasha, with a lavishness of gesture and absence of inhibition that argued too much bad champagne, went back to entertaining Jim Goodhue with tales of Imperial Russia. It was surprising, because one of her peculiarities was that she rarely spoke of Russia as if she knew it personally; she always sounded more like a well-informed outsider.

'. . . and when the French ambassador gave his coronation ball for the Czar and Czarina, the police were so afraid of anarchist bombs that they insisted on the most thorough search, during which they emptied all the vases and unpotted all the three thousand plants that had been brought in for decoration. My father told me there was so much mud everywhere by the time they had finished that no one was able to dance at all.'

'Did they find any bombs?' Mr Goodhue enquired dutifully.

'Oh, no. But . . .'

Anyone acquainted with Natasha was so accustomed to her pausing artificially for effect, that it was only when the pause became unnaturally prolonged that Matt and Jenny raised self-absorbed eyes to look at her.

And then they saw that her brows were drawn together and her mouth open in an expression of amazement and disbelief, a disbelief that very soon gave way to horror. She was staring at someone with ferocious intensity, but it was impossible to tell whom.

One hand went to her throat and another to her mouth, and she breathed a shuddering, 'No. My God, no!'

She looked as if she were about to faint and Matt began to rise to his feet, but just then one of the waitresses detached himself from the crowd and moved forward to stand directly before their table.

He was a man of about forty – insofar as it was possible to judge under the brassy wig and painted lips – and there was a look about him that spoke of a lifetime of deprivation.

His eyes staring straight into Natasha's and a wondering half smile on his lips, he said throatily, *'Dobry vecher,* Natasha Mikhailovna.'

5

'BORIS! *Chto vy delaete tut?'*

The man's smile curled slightly at the edges. It struck Matt that he looked like a politician sneering at a question he didn't intend to answer. *'Pogovorimte.'*

'S udovolstviem!'

Matt said, Tash . . .' but she paid him no attention at all, and he sat down again cursing under his breath, as the Russian volleyed back and forth, incomprehensible but obscurely threatening. The other waiters and waitresses stood grouped by the bar, watching interestedly, and the music first of all lost beat and then tailed away. Even the glasses stopped clinking and the voices gossiping as the customers, too, turned inquisitively to follow the furious exchange between the rich, fashionable, foreign lady and the Russian who stood before her. Everyone could see that it was the man – the transvestite, the parody – who was calling the tune.

Since this was France, home of the theatre of mime, the customers of *La Fétiche* were quite used to reading faces and gestures and not in the least fazed by their inability to understand what was being said. They were soon completely engrossed and thoroughly enjoying themselves.

Matt sat and wondered what the hell to do while the two voices became steadily more urgent, rising higher and higher as they gained in passion. Tash, now, was on her feet, and her face was flaming.

It seemed to have been going on for an eternity when Matt, glancing restlessly at the others, observed the expression on Charlie's face, and remembered Bosnia. Did Serbo-Croat and Russian have anything in common?

'What is it, Charlie?' he muttered. 'Can you follow it?'

'Yes, I . . . Just about. I say, Matt, we'd better put a stop to this, you know. It's . . . Oh dear, oh dear. I do think we ought to get Mrs Bwitton out of here.

Tasha and the man were positively shrieking at each other by now, and waving their arms, and Matt didn't think it was just good old-fashioned Russian melodrama.

Matt glanced round the nightclub and hoped the customers weren't going to cut up rough when he put a stop to things. There were a couple of gentlemen sitting at the back who looked as if they might be off-duty adagio dancers and handy with a knife. A pity Keith Whalley wasn't here; he always enjoyed a good shindy.

'Charlie, is he threatening her?'

'Well, yes, he is. Sort of.'

'What the hell do you mean, "sort of"?'

'Well, it's not as simple as that.'

Good old Charlie!

Rising, Matt began to move round to where Tash was standing, white as a sheet again and three-quarters hysterical, with her fists resting on the table.

He had intended to grasp her by the arm and say firmly, 'Control yourself. Come along, we're leaving.' But he had taken no more than two steps when he saw the man's hand rise and read in his face the clear intention to strike. Natasha hadn't even enough sense to move back.

There was only one thing to do, and Matt did it. Putting one hand on the table, he vaulted over it as if over a gate, knees slightly bent and feet well to the fore. There was a most satisfactory thud as they connected with the man's jaw. Douglas Fairbanks couldn't have done better, and Matt would have been proud of himself if he'd had time.

As it was, it was more important to grapple the dazed Russian to his bosom, yelling at a hesitant Charlie and Jim, 'Get the girls out of here!'

And then the fun began.

It could have been worse. Matt hadn't intended to do more than hold the man back while Charlie got the girls out, and his intention was clear enough to discourage not only the more respectable customers but the academics and anarchists who, however hot they might be on political theory, were notoriously cool when it came to the low, vulgar actuality of fisticuffs.

The waiters and waitresses, however, were quite a different kettle of fish.

Matt, having been brought up never to strike a lady, was at a serious disadvantage when it came to brawling with a bunch of transvestites. It slowed him up terribly having to look twice before he landed a punch. One against ten wasn't the best odds, either.

Even so, ducking and weaving, sliding over, under and between the tables, muttering a breathless 'Excusez moi!' every time he tripped over one of the academics or anarchists whose feet kept getting in the way, he managed to avoid mortal scathe until he found himself pinned against the bar, confronted by a very large gentleman whom he recognised as one of the jazz trio. Whose fight was this, anyway?

Grimly, he settled down to it, shooting out a sideways punch occasionally to discourage the interlopers who were trying to murder him from other angles, but it was all getting a trifle out of hand when help came from an unexpected quarter.

Suddenly, there was somebody at his side, lined up with him against the bar, somebody who was socking away with a will, and at all the right people, to boot. It was somebody in a blonde wig. It was Natasha's Russian friend.

It was ridiculous.

Matt sent the pianist flying at the precise moment when the lady on his left walloped another of the ladies with sufficient verve to send him staggering. In the brief breathing space this gave them, the Russian pressed something into Matt's hand, and Matt just had time to glance down before the next wave moved in.

He was still hiccuping with laughter as he squared up to a strapping wench in a red-sequinned dinner jacket, whose bosom was threatening to burst through her boiled shirt, but there wasn't

380

much opportunity for laughing after that, and when Boris finally went under it occurred to Matt that it was time to leave. With a flying plunge, he succeeded in breaking a path through the opposition, making not for the main exit but for the passage between the toilets that led, he hoped, to the back door.

He had just got as far as the door marked *Femmes* when a heavy hand clamped down on his shoulder, the shoulder that had been perforated eight years ago just before the Armistice and still gave him trouble sometimes. The grip sent a paralysing numbness through him for a moment, and he staggered, and knew that the next blow was going to be the knockout.

And it would have been if Jenny Jardine hadn't popped out of the door marked *Hommes* and floored his assailant with a saxophone.

6

CHARLIE Thompson and Jim Goodhue – a racing driver *manqué*, if the screeching tyres and smell of burning rubber that accompanied their departure from *La Fétiche* were anything to go by – dropped Matt and the three women off before the stately portals of the Plaza-Athenée just after four.

Any woman other than Natasha would have retired precipitately to the calm of her Second Empire bedchamber to indulge in a satisfying bout of hysterics, and even Natasha might have succumbed if Matt had not said firmly, 'Oh, no, you don't!'

Mims put a protective arm round Natasha's shoulders and said, 'But she is exhausted.'

'*She* is exhausted?'

After a word with the desk, he shepherded his charges out to the open courtyard round which the hotel was built. Fresh air and silence had never seemed more appealing.

'Now,' he said, when they were settled with their coffee and cognac, 'What was all that about? In what cause have I just collected enough grazes and bruises to turn me into a peripatetic Union Jack? Out with it, Tash.'

'I have no idea what you mean. If you choose to indulge in vulgar brawling, it is quite your own affair.' But her response was mechanical, and they all knew it. After a moment, tears rose to her eyes and into her throat, and she began rummaging blindly in her purse for a handkerchief.

'Here, have mine,' Matt said, shaking some red sequins out of it. 'Who is Boris?'

Her eyes were huge and her distress unmistakably genuine.

'He is my husband,' she said.

7

THE reason no one said, 'Oh, my God!' was that they were all struck dumb.

It meant bigamy. It meant blackmail. It meant a great many other things, too, none of them pleasant to think of.

'I was sixteen,' she said, 'and I knew nothing of the world. One didn't, in Mother Russia, if one was young and female and of the nobility. But one thing I knew, that I loved Boris. Bori, I called him. He was a student, and my family would not have countenanced a marriage, or not for years. But we needed each other so much. And so we were married in secret.'

For a moment she was far away from them, and Jenny tried to imagine her as sixteen, and innocent, and romantically in love. But it was like trying to imagine Howard as a lonely, unhappy boy.

Natasha said, 'He had ideals, like most students, and to have ideals in Petersburg in 1905 was a dangerous thing. He and his friends marched with Father Gapon and the workers to the Winter Palace on that Sunday in January, the twenty-second, Bloody Sunday, to ask that the Czar should accept a petition.

'I was there with my aunt, in the Palace, watching, when the machine-guns opened up on them from thirty yards away. There were five hundred people killed and many others wounded.' She stopped. 'It was clear to me that Bori must have been among the dead, because I never heard from him again.'

Jenny didn't mean to sound carping, but it had been a tiring day. 'Didn't you try to find out?'

'How could I? My secret would have come out, and then my aunt would have sent me away to the country, buried me for ever. And I have always disliked the country. Oh! You do not understand *any*thing, you English!'

'Scots,' Jenny said automatically. 'You mean you just went on with life as if none of it had happened?'

'What else could I do? And now it seems that my poor Bori was only wounded, and arrested, and sent to Siberia.'

Matt put a hand to his fevered brow, murmuring, '"My poor Bori"!' while Jenny exclaimed, '*Only* sent to Siberia!'

'Well, he is alive, is he not?' said Natasha a trifle irritably. 'He was freed by the revolution but could not sympathise with the revolutionaries. So he escaped to Paris, where there are many White Russians whom he thought might employ him. But they failed him, and that is why he is working in that terrible place.' She sniffed mournfully, and said again, 'My poor Bori!'

Mims said, 'Here, have a sip of brandy. It will make you feel better.'

'Thank you. You are the only one who is kind to me.'

Ignoring this slander, Matt asked, 'So what was all the screaming and shouting about? Just a run-of-the-mill lovers' reunion, was it?'

Natasha's insecure composure vanished, leaving behind a shock and fright that were starkly real. 'He says we are still married and I must come back to him! Oh, Matt, what shall I do?'

Before Matt could answer, Mims exclaimed, 'How *awful*! But how *wonderful* that he should still adore you after all these years,' whereupon her husband, exasperation boiling over, recommended her not to be stupid.

'It's a classic blackmail ploy. I imagine "poor Bori" would pass out flat with horror if Tasha consented to go back to him. If not before, then certainly afterwards.'

Jenny couldn't suppress a giggle, and Matt went on, 'Why not try it? Why not say you will?'

'Because I do not *wish* to go back to him!'

Helpfully, Jenny explained, 'Matt doesn't mean that you really should.'

'Then why does he say so?'

'Stop!' Matt had the feeling that life was beginning to imitate art. If this wasn't a Feydeau farce, he didn't know what it was.

Except that tragedy was waiting in the wings. Bigamy was a crime, but that seemed a minor consideration in comparison with the fact that, if the truth ever came out, young Nick would be branded a bastard, and Paul Britton would suffer a blow from which he would never recover. Tash was the only person in the world he had ever loved, and although the years must have taught him that his wife had many imperfections, he remained obsessed by her and would do, Matt thought, until he died.

'Let's establish a few facts,' he said. 'First of all, did you tell Bori your married name, or where you live?'

He wouldn't have put it past her to have given Bori her full name, address and telephone number, but she said loftily, 'Certainly not. I am not stupid.'

'You're sure?'

'Of course I am sure.'

'Well, at least that will make negotiations easier.'

'Negotiations? Which negotiations?'

'The blackmail negotiations, my dearest and most darling Tash. Bori must surely have mentioned that he was short of funds?'

She admitted reluctantly, 'Well, yes.'

'How much?'

'He did not say.'

'What exactly *did* he say?'

'He said I had deserted him, and he wished for compensation! So I told him he lied, because it was *he* who had deserted *me*!'

Matt said, 'Your processes of reasoning, as always, fill me with awe. But on the whole, I think it would be safer if I were the one to deal with Bori in future.'

Jenny frowned. 'You can't. It would be terribly risky to go back to that place.'

'Without you, certainly!' He grinned. 'What were you doing in the *Hommes*, anyway?'

She laughed back at him. 'Well, in a place like that, it was six of one and half a dozen of the other, wasn't it?'

'*Touché!* However, there's no need to worry. Friend Boris himself came to my aid during the scrum, which suggested to me that he was anxious not to close the door on negotiations. More than that . . .'

He produced something from his pocket. 'Even a transvestite waitress, it seems, is not necessarily lost to the finer things of life. He gave me his visiting card.'

Only Jenny saw anything funny in it. 'Embossed?'

'Of course! I'll see him tomorrow – I mean today – and take Charlie with me as interpreter. In the meantime, I'm for bed. Come along, you two. Let's return to that flea-ridden dump of a hotel of ours and leave Tash to wallow here in luxury.'

He gave Tash a kiss on the cheek as they left, and submitted with good grace to having her arms thrown round him and her tear-stained face buried in his shoulder. With a gentleness she hadn't heard in his voice for years, he said, 'Try not to worry. We'll manage things somehow.'

8

MANAGING things turned out to be extremely wearing.

Matt succeeded in snatching just over two hours' sleep before he had to be off to Le Bourget to ferry an English businessman – 'Don't trust these Frog pilots' – to Tours and back. Fortunately, there were no mishaps and he reached Paris again just before six, where he collected a reluctant Charlie Thompson from the Embassy and set off for the rue de Paradis, which turned out to be just as scruffy as all the other Paradise roads, streets, squares and lanes Matt had encountered in a far from sedentary life.

This one appeared to be the heartland of the Paris crockery trade, and they had to pick their precarious way through mountains of china, glass and pottery in order to reach the building where 'poor Bori' had his attic, a barren place, as Matt had surmised, smelling strongly of borsch and raw onions, and sounding loudly of the amateur violinist next door, the baby downstairs, and the crockery merchants in the street taking their goods indoors for the night.

Matt and Charlie stayed for an hour. Afterwards, having extracted a promise from Charlie that he would do some asking around, Matt took a taxi back to the hotel and changed hurriedly into white tie and tails. Natasha had taken a box at the Opéra and had told him austerely on the phone that, upon reflection, she had decided not to permit herself to be *boulversée* by what was, after all, no more than a minor *contretemps*.

In later years, he was quite unable to remember which opera they saw that evening, because Natasha clung to her resolution only for as long as it took them to ascend the white marble steps of the Grand Staircase and find their way to their box. They were scarcely seated when she demanded, 'Did you see him?'

'Yes. But the curtain is about to go up and this is neither the time nor place to discuss it.'

It didn't stop Tasha from trying, with the result that, by the time the first interval arrived, all four of them were exhausted and the people in the adjoining box looked ripe for murder.

385

Matt said, 'This is too much for my nerves! Let's go. We can get a taxi to Maxim's and talk while we eat.'

But Natasha couldn't wait. As the taxi rattled and hooted its way past the Madeleine to the rue Royale, she exclaimed, 'Now, tell me properly, what did he say?'

'He says he's tired of living in a garret. Needs a nice, cosy income.'

'So?'

'So he expects you to provide it.'

Tasha's outraged 'I?' caused the taxi driver to turn his head, thus jeopardising the lives of three innocent passersby and the gendarme on duty at the crossroads of the rue St Honoré. 'How much?'

'Wouldn't say.'

Tash said, 'But you must have *some* idea?'

'He's wondering how much the market will bear.'

And then the taxi drew up with a screeching of brakes and they had arrived. As Matt was paying the man off, Mims, standing on the pavement, raised her voice for the first time. She was looking sensationally sexy in a frock she'd bought that day in the Bon Marché – a long streak of something slippery in a splashy pattern of blue and green, with a back cut so low that it didn't leave more than the last two of her spinal vertebrae unaccounted for. Matt found he was able to admire the picture she presented without feeling even a twinge of desire.

'This is just the screwiest conversation!' she said. 'You don't mean to *pay* him?'

He shrugged. 'We might have to. Come on, let's go in.'

To Jenny, the brass and mahogany that made the restaurant look like the ticket hall of a luxurious Métro station were the most welcoming sight she had seen all day. She was hungry, she had a headache, she hated opera – especially when the handsome young hero was sung by a tenor who turned the scales at not an ounce under seventeen stone – and she was also feeling thoroughly belligerent after hours of talking stilted French to ship-brokers who seemed unable to adjust themselves to dealing with a woman, especially a woman who was young and moderately good-looking. Tomorrow, she thought, she would buy some spectacles, leave off her make-up and perfume, comb her hair dead straight, and see if that made any difference.

It wasn't until the soufflé Rothschild arrived that she began to pay attention to the conversation that had been flowing back and forward, pointlessly, throughout the four preceding courses.

'Baloney!' Mims was saying. 'Boris doesn't know who Tash is. If she just disappears, he'll never find her.'

'Don't you believe it,' Matt replied. 'He'll guess she must be staying at the Ritz or the Plaza, or perhaps the Bristol, and all he has to do is hang around. Once he spots her going in or out, he can discover her name easily enough.'

'Pooh. We're only here for another two days.'

'Now, yes. But she'd never feel safe coming back to Paris again.'

Jenny intervened. 'Anyway, Mims, it's not only Paris that's the danger. It must be perfectly obvious to Bori that Natasha lives in England now, and he would just need to come over for a few weeks and he'd probably see her picture in the society columns. Or Matt's picture in the news pages, come to that.'

She had touched a nerve, it seemed. Mims tossed her bright head. 'When does Matthew Britton ever do anything newsworthy these days? It's men like Floyd Bennett and Dickie Byrd who fly over the North Pole. It's Alan Cobham who's on his way back from the first round trip to Australia. It's . . .'

Matt interrupted, 'Leave it, Mims. We've had all this out before, and there's no need to bore Tash and Jenny with it. You know very well that Cobham has Imperial Airways behind him, and Byrd had to put himself in hock for something over $100,000 to finance the polar flight. The situation's entirely different.'

'But you promised . . .'

'I didn't promise to bankrupt Gannet Charter so that I, or you, could do something flashy to satisfy our vanity. Forget it.'

Jenny had never regarded jealousy as one of her vices, and was ashamed at the pleasure it gave her to hear Matt being sharp with his wife.

Matt turned back to Tash. 'What I need to know is, can you afford one or two small contributions to poor Bori's welfare, just to keep him sweet? I've a notion it may not be for long.'

Mims said pettishly, 'It's screwy. Paying blackmail's a mug's game.'

'Mims is right.' Natasha raised her chin combatively. 'I do not see why I should pay anything to that man, and I think it is very wrong of you to suggest it.'

'*Can you afford to pay him?* Forty or fifty pounds would do it.'

She shrugged. 'Perhaps. Though I have nothing but my dress allowance and most of that is gone. If I want anything more, I always ask Paul.'

Drily, Matt said, 'Not this time, if you please. You would have to lie, and there have been enough lies already.'

Before Natasha could react, Mims pushed her plate away. 'So Tasha pays the man fifty pounds and everything is hunkydory, is it? Until the next time. I cannot see why Tasha shouldn't just confess to Paul! Goodness knows, he worships her. He'd forgive her.'

Thoughtfully, Tash nibbled on a walnut. 'It is perfectly true,' she said. 'Especially since none of it is in the least my fault. I truly believed that Bori was dead.'

Very politely, Jenny asked, 'I wonder why it didn't occur to you to tell Paul about Boris before you were married?'

She had half expected an eruption, even though it seemed to her a fair question, but Tasha didn't speak at all for several moments. When she did her answer was devastating. Naively, she said, 'I forgot,' and the astonishing thing was that they all believed her.

9

THEY hammered away at the subject for another hour, Matt and Jenny of the opinion that Paul should be told only in the last resort, Natasha veering like a weathervane, and Mims convinced that it would solve everything if Tasha confessed right now.

'It would put a stop to the blackmail, and Tasha's conscience would be clear.'

'Yes,' Matt said. 'And at what a cost.'

'Paul? Oh, come on. He'd understand. He's a grown-up, not some starry-eyed kid.'

Jenny said, 'It's not as simple as that. He has a very – a very special feeling for Natasha.'

And then she realised that it was all a waste of breath, that she and Matt and Mims had all made up their minds, while Natasha, the one who really mattered, was just sitting there assuming that someone else would solve her problems for her. As someone always did.

Urgently, Jenny wanted to go back to the hotel. She couldn't bear to sit here any longer, with Tasha, whom she detested, and Mims, of whom she was jealous, and Matt, whom she loved. She had never seen him in white tie and tails before, but she knew the look on his face, the weary cynical look that gave him such a pronounced resemblance to his father. With Paul, the look meant rejection of something that displeased him. In Matt's case, she had learned, with the perception that had grown over seven long years, that it was a defence. What was he defending himself against now, this minute? Natasha's demands, Mims' aggression? It didn't occur to her that she herself might matter enough to be part of the equation.

'I think,' she said, 'if no one minds, I'll leave you all to it. I have an early appointment in the morning. I'll take a taxi.'

Matt rose to his feet. 'We'd all be wise to have an early night.'

But Mims said she was still far too wide awake, and this was Paris, after all, while Tasha hesitated and then decided, 'No, I will stay. My head is going round and round. It is better for me not to be alone for a while.'

So, in the end, Matt made sure that they had enough money for contingencies, then settled the restaurant bill and found a taxi for Jenny and himself.

10

SHE talked feverishly all the way back, because they were so close that she could feel the warmth of his body and smell the faint masculine smells of pipe tobacco and leather and cognac.

'I would have expected you to agree with Mims,' Matt said absently, as they were heading back up the rue Royale. 'You know, good Presbyterian principles. Honesty is the best policy, confession is good for the soul, all that sort of thing.'

'That's Catholics you're thinking of. They're the ones for confessing. Personally, I don't think you can get out of things so easily, or not when you can only ease your own soul by destroying other people's happiness or peace of mind.'

It wasn't far from there, if by an indirect route, to the saga of Howard and Simon Pierre. She knew she shouldn't be telling Matt, but she couldn't help herself and she found him a sympathetic listener. He didn't seem very surprised.

She didn't know that the only thing it would have surprised Matt to learn about Howard was that he was, in cold fact, the model of rectitude he appeared to be.

For the last three years, Matt had made it a practice to be well informed about the economic scene because, in one way or another, much of what was going on affected the aircraft industry, and from

389

his business passengers, many of them rendered garrulous by pre- or post-flight nerves, he regularly picked up information that should, strictly speaking, have been confidential.

Their main worry, always, was the new American determination to undermine the British Empire's monopoly of world trade. As someone had said to him sourly, 'The Americans aren't like us. They don't want to govern the world, just to own it.'

What the Americans had begun doing, in order to bypass imperial tariff barriers, was buy into or take over British companies, not openly but through nominees. It wasn't illegal, but it wasn't all that legal, either, and Matt knew that Howard was deeply involved. Howard was a shrewd operator, and his air of unimpeachable probity, Matt thought, must be worth thousands to him.

Jenny was saying, '. . . and of course all young Simon wants to do is keep up with the smart set, which makes me worry about his influence over Beth. Frankly, it's no joke being landed with an almost grown-up stepson, and I don't know how to handle him.'

'Perhaps you should ask Tash for advice. She's the expert.'

He said it idly, and didn't notice the expression on Jenny's face, because he was too busy thinking that her anger with Howard was the anger of a woman who loved her husband, and had been let down by him.

He found it painful. Slowly and almost imperceptibly, Matt had come to realise that he cared deeply for her. There were times when he thought she was the only sane, honest, unselfish person he had ever known. He had learned, not from Jenny herself but from Allie, how she had sacrificed her own comfort for her mother's, and rallied round when her stepsister was in trouble; after that it had been Jack's wife, and now it was Howard's son. And all the while she had been slaving away at the shipyard, holding it together – it sometimes seemed – by her own unaided efforts. She was hag-ridden by duty, he thought, and far too nice for her own good. Even when she was being bossy, it was always in a good cause.

He loved her for all that, and because she was perceptive, and clever, and humorous in her own quiet way, and vulnerable. He badly wanted to take her in his arms.

He was paying off the taxi when she said, 'Don't think I'm upset because Howard's let me down. What makes me furious is the way he's always so – so – damned superior, when he has a skeleton like that in his closet!'

Matt was still trying to adjust his thoughts when, having collected their keys, they reached the upstairs hall and Jenny concluded, 'Honestly! I'm beginning to wonder if I'm the only person in the family who doesn't have A Past!'

He laughed. 'You flatter yourself. I don't have one, either. Sometimes I wish I had.'

This time, he didn't miss the expression on her face. The fox collar of her evening coat made a perfect frame for the neat, poised, fair head and there was unusual colour in her cheeks. She would have looked very kissable if it hadn't been for the flash in her big hazel eyes.

'*No?*' she said, as if his words had been the last straw. 'What about you and Natasha?'

11

HIS only thought was, 'She can't know!'

'What do you mean?' he said.

'I mean – what about you and Natasha? Just after the war, to be exact. She threw herself at your head and you . . .' She stopped, too well-brought-up, despite her apparent sophistication, to say what she meant.

'I became her lover?'

'Yes.'

They stood there face to face in the draughty corridor of the hotel in the rue du Cherche-Midi, clean and cheap but a little seedy, with the six bedroom doors opening off it, and the bathroom at the end. It smelled, like all small Parisian hotels, of simmering *daubes* and *eau de javelle*.

Matt's eyes went blank, and the brown paint gave way to green plants and the *eau de javelle* to Guerlain 'Jicky', and he was back in the conservatory at Provost Charters on Christmas Eve 1918, a grown man helpless with desire for his father's wife. For four years he had led a life of almost total chastity, and she had been single-minded and unscrupulous, her sexuality so irresistible, so potent that all of his mind, heart, and soul, his entire being, became as nothing compared to the thunder of blood surging in his loins; fire and ice, passion and pain. A live match looking for a powder keg.

But somehow he had held out against her. Across the years, he heard his own voice saying, 'There has been a very special kind of feeling between us for so long, a kind of conspiracy of warmth, and fun, and affection. It may not sound very much, but it has meant a great deal to me. Don't kill it, Tash. I don't want to lose you.' But he had lost her, of course, because after that night he had never felt safe with her again.

'No, Jenny,' he said. 'You're wrong. Nothing happened between us.'

'But in the conservatory! And on the stairs – I saw you. I heard you.'

He shook his head. He didn't remember any episode on the stairs. 'You must have misinterpreted something. Tash is demonstrative, you know that, and sometimes she goes too far. But we have never been lovers.'

Her eyes were still full of doubt, so he said, 'I mean it. I swear to you.'

And then she believed him.

She smiled a little shakily and said, 'I'm glad. Goodnight, then, Matt. Sleep well.'

12

HE tossed his key down on the bed and began to empty his pockets onto the chest of drawers. Then he stripped off tailcoat and waistcoat, and untied the white bow tie and began to wrestle with his collar stud, recognising more clearly with every passing second that those few words in the corridor had changed the whole relationship between himself and the woman he had come to love. Something had already changed the previous night, when they had danced together; and something else when she had been the one to venture back into *La Fétiche* to find him and tell him where the car was; and had gone on to save him from a nasty situation.

But that she should have asked about Natasha, and that he should have answered her as if she were entitled to know, had meant something important to them. Strangely, he couldn't quite work out what, because he was tired and unsure about many things, and far more worried about the threat from 'poor Bori' than he had allowed to appear.

Slinging a towel over his shoulder, he went out, putting the door on the latch, and turned towards the bathroom.

There was a frown still in his eyes when he glanced up and saw that Jenny had been before him, and was just about to re-enter her room, looking clean and fresh in her pretty cotton dressing gown, as if she smelled of soap and toothpowder and other wholesome things.

She smiled at him, a shy and polite smile, and he could see that she was just about to disappear inside and close her door against him as if he were a stranger.

And suddenly, some instinct told him why, and he took a step forward, his eyes blazing and his hands held out to her. And he could hear her in-drawn breath and sense her inner struggle before she put her own hands in his, and smiled again at him, a different smile.

Then they were inside her room, with the door locked and toothbrushes and towels and washbags falling around them like leaves in Vallombrosa, and all they could find to say to each other was, 'Oh, Jenny!' and 'Oh, Matt!'

Then he was kissing her.

It was a miracle, because his lips fitted hers, and she was at home in his arms, and he neither hurried nor held back, and he did what he did when he wanted to, when she wanted to, and part of the miracle was the way their needs coincided so that the moment was always right.

Jenny had no idea that Howard's cold-blooded caresses had taught her to yearn for something more than he had ever given her, something she had been on the verge of knowing when she sat in her room in Provost Charters in 1919 and first realised that she was in love with Matt.

But now, as Matt's lips explored hers, before he had touched her anywhere save where his hands rested while they kissed, she felt a thrill of sensation begin somewhere at the back of her thighs, and run up to her waist and then spread out all through her body until every nerve and muscle and sinew was melting and the marrow was draining out of her bones, and there was no strength in her but only ecstasy and a dissolving wonder.

She had been resigned for so long to believing Matthew forbidden to her that, once in a while, she had allowed herself to dream dreams idyllic beyond reason; she had thought she could afford to, because there was no possibility, ever, of reality being measured against them and perhaps diminished by them.

She should have been afraid, now, because of that. She should have been afraid, too, of what would follow in the cold and sordid light of day; the shame, the embarrassment, the guilt over his wife, and her husband, the secret that would mean a guarding of tongues for all the rest of their lives. She should have been afraid, above all, of the future, and a hunger ten times, a hundred times more intense for having once been satisfied.

But she was afraid of none of it. She breathed, 'No,' when Matt slipped her dressing gown from her shoulders, and then her nightgown; when he bared her body, and then his, and carried her to the bed. But it was someone else speaking, the Jenny who ought to be and usually was. The other Jenny, the Jenny deep inside, was breathing, 'Yes, yes, yes.'

She felt safe, and secure, and in heaven. And what she had known of sensuality in the past – Tom's clumsy haste and Howard's obsession with self – vanished in the discovery of what love could be, in the fine, delicate tuning of two beings in perfect accord, the perfect matching of passion and tenderness and need.

No one, in the whole of her life, had ever treated her with tenderness.

Afterwards, he kissed her lingeringly on the mouth, and brushed her fair, fine hair away from before her eyes, and spoke the words she had dreamed of for almost eight years. The words he was not entitled to speak, or she to hear.

'I love you,' he said. 'So very much.'

Only her eyes answered him, but he smiled a little, and brushed her forehead with his lips, and left.

13

'MY DEAR Bori,' Matt said, hoping that Charlie's translation was up to all the nuances, 'you must understand that I will have no hesitation in going to the police if we fail to reach agreement.'

The older man, by straightening his shoulders, tilting his chin, and allowing his eyelids to droop, contrived to achieve – despite the black eye and split lip – an air of impressive hauteur. Matt saw that he must once have been a good-looking chap. In his early forties, he still had a haggard distinction despite ten years in Siberia and another ten years of going hungry in Paris. Though he hadn't gone quite as hungry as he claimed.

Boris drawled, 'It can be of no interest to the police that I wish my long-lost wife to return to me. In France, they take a proper view of marital duty.'

'I am sure you are right,' Matt said politely, 'but it is not your matrimonial affairs in which I would expect to interest them.'

If you had the right connections, it was amazing what you could find out about someone in a matter of forty-eight hours.

Bori's eyes opened again. 'Not?' He looked disappointed.

'Not,' Matt confirmed.

Absently, Bori lit a Russian cigarette and exhaled, adding a powerful top note to the intricate fragrance of the rue de Paradis, then, remembering himself, offered the box to Matt, who accepted, and Charlie, who inspected the contents with the greatest of care before taking one from the middle of the box. Charlie, a devotee of 'Sapper', was a great one for poisons unknown to science and never taking the first taxi in a rank.

'What, then?' Bori said at last.

'I'm not sure how to put this without causing offence . . .' Matt hesitated elaborately. 'But perhaps I might call it – intelligence work?'

'I do not understand.'

'I didn't think you would.' It was why Matt had brought Charlie along, despite his suspicion that Bori was perfectly fluent in French. Failing to understand in two languages was by no means as easy as in one. From narrowed eyes, he directed a piercing stare at the Russian and, giving his best impersonation of a hanging judge, said, 'You are an agent of the Comintern.'

It was pitching it a bit high. If Boris was anything, he was a very minor informant whose job it was to report on the doings of the more raffish members of Paris's White Russian community.

'I?'

'You.'

'This is a lie!'

'This is the truth.'

'It is *not* the truth!'

Scintillating dialogue, Matt reflected, but it wasn't getting them anywhere and he had a plane to catch. 'I have proof,' he said, stretching it a little, and before Bori could launch into further denials went on, 'and I will present it to the *commissaire* unless you do as I say.'

It took them a while to sort things out, because Bori, on reflection, rather fancied himself as an 'agent of the Comintern'

395

and abandoned the rôle only with reluctance, when he saw that conceding the lowliness of his position – *if* he held any position, which he did not by any means admit – was the easiest way to prove that the police would not have the slightest interest in his activities.

Matt, following his reasoning with some difficulty, began to see that Bori and Tash had more in common than might have been thought.

But not for nothing had Matt spent four years playing poker in dugouts and RAF messes. 'The White Russians,' he said meditatively, 'have their own organisation for dealing with those who spy on them, particularly those who spy in the name of the revolution. I have no doubt at all that they would be interested in anything I might choose to tell them.'

For what was no more than an educated guess, it produced the most satisfactory results. Bori's complexion changed from grey to white, and the discussion thereafter proceeded not only more rapidly but very much more usefully.

Even so, Bori fought a voluble rearguard action, so that it was a relief when he concluded grandly, 'However, now that the Politburo has been purified by the expulsion of that traitor to the revolution who calls himself Lev Trotsky, I might be able to find it in my conscience to return to Mother Russia, if . . .'

If?

If Natasha would pay his fare.

It seemed to Matt to be quite a good bargain, even though, when he broke the glad news to Tash, she demanded to know why Matt had not volunteered to fly Bori home to Russia himself. 'Then I would have had to pay him nothing. Why do you not think of these things?'

14

MATT and Jenny had not been granted a moment alone or any opportunity to talk by the time they landed again at Croydon on the Friday, and Jenny, in the grip of the inevitable crisis of conscience, had convinced herself that Matt could have made an opportunity if he'd tried; that he hadn't wanted to try.

She felt cheap. She remembered her mother's dictum that men never respected 'girls like that'. She couldn't believe he really loved her. Quiet, sensible, conscientious Jenny who, at her best, was quite good-looking and sometimes even quite witty, but couldn't hold a candle to Mims or Natasha. What was she supposed to do now? Did he expect her just to go home, and pretend none of it had happened?

Not for months was she to recognise that she had worked herself up to a pitch of resentment over an imagined fault because she couldn't bear to face the real issues.

They had almost reached the Gannet Charter office when Natasha exclaimed, 'Oh! I have lost an earring!' which meant, since Natasha's earrings were usually diamond and rarely weighed less than three carats, that they all had to go back and quarter the turf in search of it. They didn't find it, and it wasn't in the plane.

Matt said, 'Let's be a bit more systematic on the way back.' Taking Tash by the shoulders, he pointed her in the general direction of the office and said, 'Tash, you and Mims follow that line of attack, and Jenny and I will follow this.'

Very soon, they had fallen behind sufficiently for Matt to murmur, 'We must talk. We have to make arrangements.'

'Arrangements?' she repeated stupidly.

'Well, there *are* one or two minor matters to be attended to!'

She bent to pick something up and discovered it was only a chip of granite with some quartz in it. 'Are there?'

'Divorce, for a start.'

After a moment, she dropped the granite chip again. It seemed as if he did love her after all.

'Well?'

'But why?'

'Oh, for God's sake, Jenny. Bigamy's illegal. We've just been into that, remember?'

Her legs were refusing to hold her up, so she sank to her knees and stared intently at another patch of gravel. Matt bent to look, too.

She whispered, 'What do you mean?'

'I want to marry you, you idiot girl!' He couldn't understand why it should bring tears to her eyes.

Then she said, 'But we can't.'

'What do you mean, we can't?'

'I'm your brother's widow.'

He remembered, then, the Table of Kindred and Affinity at the end of the Prayer Book, 'wherein whosoever are related and forbidden in scripture and the laws to marry together'. He and Tom, when they had been boys whiling away the hours in church, had thought it highly comical that they'd never be allowed to marry their wife's grandmother or their daughter's son's wife. Now, as clearly as if the book was open before him, Matt could see number eighteen in the list, 'Brother's wife.'

Natasha was calling to them, 'Have you found it?' so they had to shake their heads and straighten up and move on.

It was a long time before he said, 'Does it matter? Not being able to marry.'

'Of course it matters! I'm not a – a tart!'

'Oh, Jenny! With all our happiness at stake?'

She bent again, and turned her head away, and something glittered in the rough turf; but it was a tear, not a diamond.

'We couldn't be happy, not that way. And what about Mims?'

'It wouldn't hurt her. She doesn't love me.' Stupidly, because his mind was in turmoil, he added with a humourless half laugh, 'She won't even let me sleep with her more than once in a blue moon.'

'I see. So you just want a woman, someone more amenable!' It wasn't Jenny speaking and they both knew it, but somehow they couldn't break free from an exchange that immediately went from bad to worse.

'No, I don't. I could have dozens of women. It's you I want!'

'Dozens of women? I didn't think you were that kind of man.'

'I'm not, damn it! Why are you so determined to misunderstand me!'

'Perhaps I'm not the right woman for you after all. Oh, where is this *bloody* earring?'

Silently, he opened his palm.

At any other time, she would have laughed. Instead, seething, she stared at it. 'Where did you find it?'

'It was caught in Tash's collar.'

And then, before he could stop her, she called, 'Natasha! Matt's found it. Now we can all go home.'

15

THE telephone rang the following evening just as Howard, standing before the cheval glass in the bedroom, was buttoning up his grey Chesterfield overcoat. He had already taken his Gladstone bag and attaché case downstairs to the hall. After two busy but productive weeks in Glasgow, it was his intention to fit in a few hours in London before sailing for New York on Monday morning.

When he picked up the extension, he found that Jenny was already answering and waited, in case the call was for him.

It seemed unlikely, because she was saying with bright surprise, 'Hello, Matt! What is it? Did I leave something on the plane?'

'No. It wasn't that. Are you – er – busy?'

Matthew's voice didn't sound as decisive as usual and it seemed to Howard that 'busy' was not the word he had intended to use. 'Alone' might have been more like it.

Frowning slightly, he replaced the receiver, which gave its familiar tinkle as he did so. Eavesdropping was hardly consonant with his dignity and, in any case, Jenny must have heard him pick it up and would be waiting for the sound of replacement.

He gave himself a final survey in the glass and then, taking up black Homburg and leather gloves, made his way downstairs.

Jenny smiled at him as he entered the drawing room, and said into the phone, 'Just a moment.' Then, 'It's Matt. Natasha's lost an earring and they wondered if I could remember whether she was wearing it on the plane.'

To her husband's eye, she was looking a trifle flustered. Dear Jenny, such an incompetent liar. It was fortunate that she had such a rigid moral code, or he might have been suspicious; as it was, he was scarcely even curious. 'I hope it turns up,' he said. 'I'm off now, my dear. Don't bother to come out with me. And you have my New York number if you should need me. Look after yourself.' Then he bent to place a kiss on her cheek, and was gone.

16

MATT, holding on as instructed, cursed his own stupidity in phoning. It had seemed worth taking the chance, but he clearly couldn't have chosen a worse moment. When Jenny spoke again, she sounded distracted, as if she were listening for the sound of Howard's car driving away, and even when she recovered herself he could sense her guilt and consternation over the risk he had taken.

'Beth's in bed, and Simon happens to be out somewhere,' she said, 'but . . .'

In the end, their conversation was horribly rational. Jenny talked about Matt's duty to Mims, and hers to Howard, and said she had Beth to think of, and Simon too, because she had accepted the responsibility of being a second mother to him. She made it clear, however unintentionally, that she was still upset that he should think she might ever have consented to living in sin.

He knew himself that it was too much to ask of a decent woman, and the sense of doom was already on him when he said at last, 'Then we must try to take our happiness together, when we can.'

As he had known she would, she said, 'No. It would be wrong. It would be unfair to everyone, and to us most of all.' Her voice was very low, and very sad, when she added, 'But I will never stop loving you, and wanting you. Goodbye, Matthew.'

Seven

1

WHEN Jenny returned to the yard on the Monday morning, she walked straight into a major crisis. Which was only to be expected. Years earlier, she had formulated Jardine's Law, which was that whenever you went away, leaving instructions to cover every eventuality that could conceivably arise during your absence, you always returned to find that the unforseeable had happened and everyone was in a panic.

This time the panic was justified, because the bank had come to the end of its patience. Between 1914 and 1918, the yard's gross profit had been three million pounds. Now, eight years after the war, it had an overdraft of £154,000. It was a derisory figure by comparison, but this was 1926, not 1918, and the bank insisted that something be done. Or else.

For the next week, it was talks, talks and more talks, and it was the 'or else' that came first. The bank demanded liquidation and it took Jenny much recourse to facts and figures and confidential telephone calls to persuade them that selling up was not the answer, because none of the other yards could afford to buy Brittons' capital equipment or land at anything like an economic price. Which would leave the bank as the loser.

The next demand was for takeover; the bank would put in its own management. Then it was for a committee to enquire into the running of the yard. And finally, an outside expert on cost-cutting to be appointed as joint managing director with James McMurtrie. Disguising their powerful sense of relief, James McMurtrie and Jenny agreed.

It had been the most exhausting week Jenny could ever remember, made no easier by the lack of support she and James had received from the rest of the board. Sir Albert didn't want to know, and would have been of little help anyway. Paul was still suffering from the infection that had been plaguing him for the last two months, and was lackadaisical and short of ideas. And Howard, just when he was most needed, was inaccessible, on a liner sailing to New York.

Jenny, in desperate need of a breathing space after her return from Paris, had been relieved to see him go, but 'Relieved!' she thought later, as she tried to word a radio message to him and gave up in despair because it wasn't the kind of crisis that could be resolved in radio messages.

She telephoned him in New York when he arrived there, although by then everything had been settled. He had had, he said, a most pleasant and relaxing voyage.

There was a protracted pause when she had finished talking, and she didn't know whether it was because he was thinking or merely part of the crackling and delays that always made long-distance conversations so awkward.

Finally, he said, 'Well, well. You seem to have acquitted yourself with credit. I am surprised that the bank was amenable. If anything further occurs, you must telephone me again, although I may not be easy to get hold of. I shall be in Wall Street most of the time. Perhaps Saturday evening would be best.'

'Yes,' she said, 'but I won't phone unless there's something urgent. It's terribly expensive.'

There was nothing urgent, which was fortunate, because by the next weekend she wouldn't have dared to talk to him. She suspected by then, and by the following weekend knew for certain, that she was pregnant.

2

IT was Matthew's child, of course. She couldn't doubt it, because she had suffered Howard's attentions only twice during the last month and they had been very early in her cycle and she had douched afterwards, as she always did. Then she had left for Paris and, afterwards, on the very evening of her arrival home, Howard had departed for London and New York.

Matt and she had taken no precautions. She had even stopped him when she had sensed that he was preparing to withdraw from her at the vital, magical moment. To be wholly together, then, had seemed far more important to her than either wisdom or common sense, and afterwards she hadn't even thought to rise from her bed and do what she should have done. Instead, she had lain all the night long, lost in happiness.

She had no idea what to do, though all she wanted to do was

rush off to Matt and throw herself in his arms.

Instead, she thought and thought until she felt as if her brain would fall apart. She knew, unequivocally, that she should confess to Howard, but the idea terrified her. She was ashamed of it, because he wasn't a harsh or violent man and it was unfair to him that she should feel that way, but she couldn't help it. It was a relief when she heard her own voice again – arguing vis-à-vis Natasha and Bori and Paul – that confession wasn't necessarily right, not if it hurt other people. And Howard would be hurt; in his self-esteem, if nothing else.

If she were to be honest, that didn't concern her very much. What did, was that if she told him, and he couldn't forgive, then her child would carry the stigma of being a bastard all its life. And it wouldn't only be the baby who would be hurt, because Beth would learn about it, too; Beth, who was just ten and innocent, but not so innocent that she wouldn't understand that her mother had done something dreadful, even if she didn't know what. Jenny couldn't bear the thought of losing her daughter's love and trust.

In the end, she couldn't see that she had any choice at all.

When Howard arrived home, she broke the news of his impending fatherhood to him with wifely modesty, and saw, for the first time in all the eight years she had known him, the blood rise to his cheeks.

After a moment, he smiled upon her and kissed her. 'What a clever wife I have! Repelling takeovers, saving shipyards, and now producing children. I confess that I had been beginning to feel concerned lest you were one of those women who become barren after their first child.'

Jenny held her tongue with difficulty.

'Upon reflection,' he went on, 'I think I shall enjoy being a father again. I was an absentee father in Simon's case. This time I can be a real one, can I not? And when is the happy event?'

'I'm not quite sure. The doctor says you can never be exact. The beginning of June, probably.'

She saw his eyes flicker, and knew he was working it out, and told herself, as she had been telling herself for days, that 'the beginning of June' could be any time from the first to the tenth or twelfth. *Oh, baby, baby! Please be early*, she prayed.

3

AT almost the same time, Matt was saying to Bill Bonny, 'Tell me if this rings a bell. "If we don't go now, we never will".'

Bill's square, expressionless face creased into what passed with him for a beam of happiness, and his boot-button eyes shone as if someone had taken a brush and polish to them. 'Strewth! D'you mean it?'

'Why not? We know the bloody things flies in dear old temperate England. We need to know what else she does, and how long she'll go on doing it, and under what conditions. *You* know she's ready to test, *I* know she's ready to test, and if we don't get away before winter sets in we'll be wasting the better part of six months.'

Getting away, right now, was the whole sum of his desires.

He said, 'How's Maggie going to manage without her husband?'

'She'll be 'anging out flags. Wot about Mrs Matt?'

Matt's eyes were on the spark plug he was tossing in his palm. 'Not happy,' he said, and left it at that.

Mims had made the most appalling scene when he'd told her she wasn't coming with them on the BB.1's proving flight.

He had been deceived, during the months after they first met, by her charm, the charm she used to get what she wanted; because of it, she usually *had* got what she wanted. But later, when Matt had, as she put it, 'gone stuffy on her', when he had begun at last to set his mind to serious business and couldn't afford to go on letting her have her own way just because she was so pretty, she had abandoned charm as a weapon. Nowadays, she seemed to think that making a scene was more likely to work. In which she was quite wrong.

In the case of the test flight, she hadn't believed him when he swore they weren't aiming for long-distance or speed records, that they wouldn't be doing anything dashing.

'We'll simply be pottering along testing the plane's endurance and fuel consumption and landing needs; finding out how she responds to extremes of temperature and turbulence. All boring, routine stuff, except when something goes wrong, and when it does, I'd rather you weren't around.'

'Oh, *dandy*! But if that's the kind of testing you're aiming at, don't try and kid me that you won't be over-flying the Himalayas and the South China Sea and the Australian outback and all kinds of other exciting places!'

He couldn't deny it, and he felt guilty, within limits, because he knew she was deeply disappointed. It hadn't been easy to explain that she would be nothing but a hindrance.

'Think,' he said, 'if we had to make a forced landing in some tribal area where a white woman's never been seen before.'

'I'm thinking. So what?'

'Think about having to sleep in the open or in cheap dosshouses in places like Shanghai. No, make it Bombay; China's not the place to be these days.'

'I'm thinking.'

'Remember that we'd have to reduce the fuel load because of the extra passenger weight.'

But all he got was another, 'So what?'

And so it had gone on. Even the fact that she was to be left to run Gannet Charter while he and Bill were away scarcely alleviated either her fury or her misery.

He wondered what she was going to say when he told her that if he were killed everything he owned would be hers, including his share of the business and the new DH.60 Moth.

Probably, 'Oh, great!'

4

NATASHA had no idea why she always read the newspapers last thing at night, except that, for several years now, there had been no reason to hurry to bed. She did not doubt that Paul, who had taught her so much and given her such pleasure, still loved her and was still obsessed by her, but he was approaching sixty now, and tired.

Whereas she was only thirty-seven. The difference in age that had seemed so unimportant when she was twenty and he was forty had widened into a yawning chasm.

She flicked the pages. Lindbergh, Lindbergh, nothing but Lindbergh. The young man who had made the first solo flight from New York to Paris, and had just arrived back in America to acclamation that verged on the hysterical. Four million New Yorkers, the newspaper reported, had showered him with eighteen hundred tons of ticker tape and confetti during his four-day welcome home. He had been paraded up Broadway like some Roman conqueror, and could hardly move for the specially struck medals that had been pinned to his chest. People from more than sixty countries had sent him gifts estimated at a total worth of two million dollars.

Tash resented it. It should have been Matthew.

But all she knew of Matthew was what she had gleaned over the months of his absence from scattered news items. There had been one a few weeks ago describing how the BB.1 had had to be towed out of a quagmire in eastern Siberia. And another reporting that he and Mr Bonny had been arrested in Japan for taking photographs from the air; the Japanese had thought they were spies and had kept them in prison for a week. But a few days ago, it seemed, they had landed safely in Singapore. The press was making a story, though not a headline one, of the wartime poet-hero who had built his own plane and now seemed bent on testing it to destruction.

Lighting one of her Turkish cigarettes, Tash supposed that, when she had finished it, she might as well go upstairs. Life was *unbearable*!

She tossed the newspaper on the floor, but even as she did so, something caught her eye and she had to pick it up again and turn back the pages in search of whatever it had been.

POSTCARD DIVORCES
Russia makes it easy
Archbishop of Canterbury shocked

In 1917 the Bolsheviks abolished church marriage and replaced it by civil registration. Divorce by consent of both parties was introduced at the same time.

Now, ten years later, new legislation means that a husband who chooses to live with a woman not his wife, or a wife who is parted from her husband, needs to do no more than notify the registrar (the ZAGS) that he, or she, considers the marriage at an end. There is no requirement for the other party's consent, and no pleading before the courts. Just a postcard to the ZAGS and all is over.

The Archbishop of Canterbury, asked by our reporter for his reaction, said: 'I am deeply shocked. The Church cannot but condemn an act which makes a mockery of the whole institution of Christian marriage. It is an outrage against civilised values.'

Natasha read it through twice, then a third time, just to be sure. Then she jumped to her feet and threw up her arms, laughing luxuriously to herself like an excited child. 'Silly old archbishop!' she exclaimed.'

Then she went off to look for a postcard and a pen.

5

AS THE weeks and the months of Jenny's pregnancy passed, she became superstitiously convinced that the baby would be late.

Howard arranged to be at home from the end of May, but the beginning of June came and went. And the real date came and went. And another week passed, and still Howard said nothing that wasn't solicitous. Jenny might have been convinced if she had been less keyed up, but although the change in his expression was impossible to define, she knew that change there was. She perceived it not through sight, or hearing, or any of the orthodox senses, but by the ice-cold prickling of tiny needles somewhere in the small of her back.

Her nerves were so strung up that when the telephone rang early one evening she jumped with such violence that Simon and Beth laughed as if it were a great joke and even Howard smiled as he moved to answer it.

'Natasha, this is a rare pleasure . . . Oh, dear . . . What should you do? You will forgive me for being obvious, but if Paul has had a stroke, what you should do is summon a doctor . . . I see . . . Well, yes, I am his financial adviser, but . . . Yes . . . Yes . . . I must go and look at my diary . . . Have a word with Jenny in the meantime.'

Jenny had already levered herself to her feet. 'Natasha, how terrible! Is it bad?'

'The doctor says he is paralysed all down his right side and he may never be able to walk or speak again. Oh, it is so dreadful! He looks so sad lying there, my poor Paul!'

'Did the doctor say what caused it?'

There was silence for a moment, then, her voice rising, Natasha said in a rush, 'I could not tell the doctor, or Howard, but I can tell you, because you know anyway. And I need to tell someone, and Matthew is away and Mims does not answer the phone. It was the divorce postcard!'

'The what?'

'Do you not read the papers? There is a new law in Russia. You can be divorced by just sending a postcard to the registrar. So I thought, if I send a postcard, then Bori and I will be divorced and he will no longer have anything with which to blackmail me, if he should wish to try again. So I wrote the postcard – in Russian, you understand – and left it on the hall table for Marriot to post . . .'

Jenny closed her eyes. 'Don't tell me! Paul saw it?'

'Yes.' Faintly injured, Natasha added, 'I do not think it right that he should have read my correspondence,' but then her voice broke. 'I had forgotten that he reads Russian.'

Jenny couldn't think of anything else to say but, 'Oh, Natasha.' Of all the stupid women!

'So now he is in hospital and, of course, he cannot sign things or do any of the things he always does. And I have no idea what to do, so I must have Howard. There is no one else.'

'Sir Albert? Nick?'

'*Really*, Jenny! For these last three years Sir Albert has been living in another world, and Nick is only sixteen. Also, he is away at school.'

Jenny said weakly, 'Here's Howard again. Give my love to Paul, if – well, you know.'

Howard, accepting the phone from her, said, 'I think I must go to the rescue,' and she nodded.

The baby was five days old when Howard returned, a beautiful little boy with Jenny's colouring.

Howard looked at him with interest, and then raised his head, his masked brown gaze meeting Jenny's hazel one. 'I would have expected him to have blue eyes,' he said.

6

IT WAS a moment before she was able to gather herself together and say lightly, 'Why? Do blue eyes run in your family? The Jardines have always been brown or hazel. Isn't he lovely?'

The bedroom was full of flowers, and Simon and Beth had been working very hard, so that she had a wireless to entertain her, and Simon's gramophone within reach. Every time one of them brought her a cup of tea, which they did with unrelenting frequency, they wound the dratted thing up so that she could have yet another four minutes of Whispering Jack Smith, or *I miss my Swiss*, or *Bye Bye Blackbird*.

'Very good,' Howard applauded, the irony in his voice belying the words. He didn't give even another glance at the baby as he sank down into an armchair and, bringing the tips of his fingers together, surveyed them with a spurious interest. 'Not good enough, however. I am unconvinced. I was not convinced even when I left for Provost Charters, so I thought it might be productive to take Natasha's mind off her present troubles by enquiring how she had enjoyed the Paris trip last September.'

His voice became pensive. 'I sensed that, at one or two points, she was being evasive – so unlike dear Natasha! – but she had a most excellent memory for where everyone was, and when, and with whom. It never fails to amaze me how often people *will* try to divert questions about something over which they feel guilty by being extremely voluble about some other subject entirely. In this instance, her equivocation was most instructive, and my deductions were inescapable. Do you wish me to particularise them?'

Jenny said, 'No. You have Simon, I have Johnny.' She couldn't bring herself either to explain or excuse.

Her husband's brows rose slightly. 'Is that his name? I cannot say I care for it. But really, my dear, the one can scarcely be held to justify the other.'

'Why not? One law for men, and another for women?'

'There is that, of course. But I was thinking more of marriage vows.'

'Those matter to you, do they?' She flung the covers back and put on her dressing-gown, then began to wander about the room, possessed by an obscure but compelling need to be on the move.

'Naturally.'

She was waiting for him to go on, but he didn't.

A heavy silence lay over everything, so that the sharp, insistent chirping of a baby blackbird in the garden began to grate on Jenny's consciousness like some Chinese water torture. She was determined not to say anything herself, because there seemed nothing she could say without making matters worse, but if Howard continued just to sit there, she didn't know if she would have the strength to hold her tongue. She felt like a child summoned before the headmaster for punishment, or a sinner standing before the Judgement Seat. The knowledge that she was in the wrong by the standards of both church and society oppressed her unbearably; in the wrong about everything, perhaps even about adoring her baby. She remembered the minister once giving a sermon about the 'children of sin', but couldn't recall very clearly what he'd said, except about the little ones being destined to suffer for their parents' misdeeds.

Going to lean over the cradle and look at her son, she felt the intensity of her love for him as something warm and glorious inside her even while she clamped her lips between her teeth and recognised that she was on the verge of becoming hysterical.

The atmosphere in the room was a product of her own nerves, she told herself. It must be, because Howard was sitting there quite calmly in his chair, showing no trace of anger, as much of an enigma to her as he had always been.

His eyes were impervious under their lazy lids when at last he looked directly at her and said, 'And what do you propose to do now – you and your incestuous child?'

He knew how to hurt.

She could feel the blood draining from her face. She knew, and he knew, that there was no conceivable taint of incest in the baby now lying peacefully asleep in his cot. It was something she had had time to think about, and she knew that the prohibition on a man marrying his brother's wife – or widow – must have been necessary long ago, when families all lived together and jealousy could be a force for destruction; in the modern world it was no more than a legal leftover.

But that was something else she wasn't prepared to argue about.

Before she could speak, Howard went on, 'I take it, from the fact that you are still here, that you have no thought of marrying the child's father?'

She turned away from him so that he shouldn't see her having to repress her tears. 'I can't. You know I can't. It's against the law.' Then she swung round again, and it was like a physical shock to meet his eyes. They were fully open, now, and there was a glint in their brown depths that she couldn't interpret. Or was afraid to.

She said, 'What am I going to do? That depends on you.'

'Does it?' There was a barely perceptible pause. 'You cannot marry Matthew, but can you give me an assurance that you will not go rushing back illicitly to his arms?'

'Howard! I have made one – mistake, but . . .'

'The idea of "living in sin" shocks you? Well, well, I cannot say I am surprised. I have always found it amusing how we, in the Western world, sneer at the Chinese for their preoccupation with saving face, when we ourselves have turned it into an institution.

'So, it depends on me, does it?'

Suddenly, unbelievingly, Jenny knew that something had pleased him. She didn't flatter herself that it had anything to do with not losing her, but there was an expression on his face that, in other circumstances, she would have identified as a smirk.

410

He said, 'I take it you are hoping I will accept the boy as my own? Yes, I thought you might be. And since I have no desire to appear in the eyes of the world as a betrayed husband – a demeaning rôle that does not, I think, suit my personality – I will agree.'

She felt no sense of relief at all. Sitting down at the dressing table, she began with shaking hands to brush her hair.

He went on. 'Under conditions, of course.'

'Yes?'

'Does Matthew know the child is his?'

Her voice sounded rusty as she managed to reply, evenly, 'No. He left the country before I was even sure I was pregnant.'

'Wise fellow. Then you will not tell him. I will not forbid you to see him when – if – he returns from this expedition of his, because I recognise that to avoid all contact might give rise to comment within the family. And we do not want that, do we? But you will see him as little as possible, and never alone.'

That was a decision she had already made for herself.

'You will also,' Howard continued, with the air of a man ticking off points on his mental fingers, 'behave to me as a more dutiful wife.'

An involuntary spasm crossed her face, and he saw it in the mirror, just as she saw his reaction to it – the tightening of his face muscles into a look that wasn't Howard at all, a look that to her fevered imagination summed up all she had ever understood by the word 'malevolent'.

The blood in her veins flowed cold and sluggish for a moment until she reminded herself that mirror images were always unreliable, often cruel. Of all things, she *must not* give way to these stupid, inchoate fears. This was Howard, her husband – a responsible, respected man who valued his reputation and had every right to be angry with the wife who had deceived him. He wasn't someone who was capable of the kind of honest outburst of jealousy that would have cleared the air; certainly not of violence. If he had been, Jenny would have been no less distressed but much less disturbed.

'I was not, as it happens, referring to the nuptial couch,' he said contemptuously, 'where I will expect everything to continue as before. What I had in mind was your obsession, for example, with going your own way at the shipyard. In future, you will pay more attention to my advice.'

She rose and, moving over to the gramophone, began to tidy up the records.

'And if I don't agree?' It was then that she braced herself to look him full in the eyes, and her heart turned over and she was sharply

411

and unequivocally afraid for the first time, because now there was no question of it being her imagination. His gaze was cold and unblinking as a lizard's.

He shrugged. 'Agree or not, it will be open to me to divorce you any time I choose. Your venture into adultery is one of those things that I am at liberty to "discover" whenever it suits me.'

It was a threat she had foreseen. Divorce now – or later. What difference did it make?

But she hadn't foreseen what followed.

'I would take care that the child was not an issue in the divorce proceedings.'

Her heart lifted a little, because Howard seemed to be saying that Johnny wouldn't suffer, wouldn't be branded illegitimate in open court.

But even as she opened her lips to whisper, 'Thank you', he went on with what he had been saying and it turned out that it wasn't going to be like that at all.

He was smiling his most self-satisfied smile at her, and his finger-tips were steepled judiciously under his chin as he said, 'Because if, in the meantime, I have acknowledged – er – Johnny as "our" son, you will understand that I would have no difficulty in persuading the courts to judge you an unfit mother. Which means that they would be bound to award custody of the child to me.'

He stopped for a moment, surveying her, almost amiably assessing the shock on her face and the darkness in her wide, long-lashed eyes. Then, rising in his usual smooth, unhurried way, he concluded, 'And there you have it, my dear. If you wish to keep your child, you really have no choice at all.'

PART FOUR

1929–1939

One

1

FEBRUARY 1929 was a good month for dying, so numbingly cold that it was as much as the million-and-a-half in the dole queues could do to pick up their fifteen shillings from the counter, or the rich their Dry Martinis from the bar.

Sir Albert went on the fourth, an old man who settled down for a nap after lunch and never woke again. Everyone said that he'd had a good innings.

His son enjoyed the title of Sir Paul for no more than two weeks before he suffered his second stroke, the one that killed him. Everyone said it was a blessed release.

2

NATASHA looked magnificent in black, now that full warpaint was *comme il faut* and her hair had paled a little from its original butter-yellow brightness. If there was a fault to find it was in her increasing amplitude, slight but noticeable, which might have led vulgar people to regard her as a cosy armful.

'Oh, ho! What a cosy armful!' said Matt with more than a trace of malice, placing an arm round her waist and planting a brisk kiss on her cheek. 'What has happened to the hourglass figure we knew and loved?'

The physical contact was a mistake, even now. Or perhaps especially now. She swayed against him and he had to step back and make a great piece of work about removing his overcoat.

Airily, she said, 'Boredom and woolly underwear are what has happened to it! Nineteen months of being a virtuous wife and daughter-in-law.

'My darling Matt, I cannot tell you how terrible it has been, cooped up here with an old man and an invalid who did not at all resemble your father. I wished so often, and I am sure he also wished, that the first stroke had put an end to everything. It was not *civilised* to

415

linger on so, and he was always such a very civilised man.'

Matt sighed, but the sigh was not, as she thought, one of sympathy. He wondered if it had ever occurred to her that her own criminal thoughtlessness had been responsible for it all. If it had, she had been quick to forget; forgetting what she didn't want to remember was one of Tash's strong suits.

Matt had no idea what testamentary dispositions his father had made. If it had not been for the extreme coolness that had existed between them since Christmas 1918, he would have expected Paul Britton to do as most men of his class did, and bequeath the bulk of the estate to his elder son – his shares in the shipyard, the house and the land, and sufficient capital for their upkeep. Well, he would soon find out.

Mr Taverner, the lawyer who was to read the Will to them, was a dry stick who still favoured the style of the Edwardian era, and had a voice as dim and dusty as the Inns of Court.

'Good afternoon, Sir Matthew,' he said.

Sir Matthew nodded urbanely, doing his best to look the part.

A few minutes later, they were all settled in the library and Mr Taverner cleared his throat significantly and began:

'This is the Last Will and Testament of me, Poliphilus John Britton, of Provost Charters in the County of Dorset. I hereby revoke all Wills heretofore made by me. I appoint my nephew Howard Britton Fournier of the firm of Fournier, Le Jeune and Partners in the City of London, to be the sole executor of this my Will . . .'

Mr Taverner sniffed. In his opinion, it was always bad policy to entrust things to a sole executor and he had advised strongly against it, but the late Sir Paul had said that one man could be trusted to get things done more expeditiously and just as efficiently as two, and he had every faith in his nephew.

'I give and bequeath unto my dear wife Natasha Mikhailovna Efremov Britton the house known as Provost Charters and all the land belonging thereto as shown in the schedule herewith attached . . .'

'Good heavens!' said Natasha.

After that there were outright sums of £2000 each for Matthew and Nicholas, £10,000 for 'my granddaughter Alexandra Elizabeth', and some minor bequests to servants. Then everything became very much more complicated.

Mr Taverner explained it all to them afterwards, in words which, in his own opinion, would scarcely have taxed the understanding of a ten-year-old, but Natasha was still confused when she, Howard, Matt and Nick sat down to dinner that evening.

3

'PLEASE do not treat me as if I were an idiot, Howard. Of course I understand the *words*. What I do not understand is what they *mean*.'

Howard studied his soup with interest. 'Mock turtle,' he said. 'How delightful.'

Nobody volunteered to run him up an omelette.

Natasha said, 'Do they mean I have to ask you every time I wish to buy a new frock?'

'Not quite.' Howard broke into the roll on his plate and buttered it lavishly. 'The Will was drawn up in 1921, and drawn up according to my advice in a form designed to circumvent Lloyd George's new death duties.

'Now, you will recall that, in 1921, Paul and Matthew were at odds, while Nicholas was only ten years old. When Paul made the Will, it was his intention to review it eight years later, when Nicholas was eighteen and approaching years of discretion. That intention was frustrated by his stroke, and so the 1921 Will still stands.'

He glanced at Natasha, stoically finishing her soup. 'Do you follow me so far?'

'Yes.'

'Since Matthew was *persona non grata* and Nicholas under age, it seemed sensible at the time – I stress, "at the time" – to bequeath the house, land, and the shares in the yard to Natasha. I remember Paul saying how happy he was that you had grown to love Provost Charters as much as he did.'

Natasha stared at him. 'Yes?' she said. 'You have no objection to salmon, Howard?'

'None in the world. Where the shares in the yard were concerned, Paul naturally assumed that he would inherit Sir Albert's some day, to add to his own. We now know, of course, that Sir Albert chose to bequeath the majority of his holding to Jenny instead. To that extent, Paul's legacy to Natasha is something less than he had expected it to be; twenty per cent instead of forty-one per cent.

'Let us now come to the trust, which appears to be confusing you all. In simple terms, the residue of Paul's estate goes into

417

a temporary trust, the whole income from which is at Natasha's disposal. Until, of course, the termination date, which is 1936.

'Paul selected this date because it would be the year of Matthew's fortieth birthday, by which time Paul hoped – if I may paraphrase him – that he would have outgrown the desire to throw money away on ill-considered ventures into flying. It will also be the year of Nicholas's twenty-fifth birthday, by which time Paul hoped – once more I paraphrase – that he would have outgrown the tendency to levity and volatility which his father detected in him.'

Impervious alike to Matt's raised brows and Nick's air of offended innocence, Howard concluded, 'When the trust is wound up, the capital realised is to be divided equally between Natasha, Matthew and Nicholas. And there you have it.'

Natasha said, 'How fortunate for us all that you are such an *excellent* accountant!'

Howard smiled benignly and, reaching out, took her hand and raised it, with ponderous courtesy, to his lips. Matt felt slightly queasy.

Nick said, 'Does all this mean that Provost Charters is mother's to do what she likes with?'

'Yes.'

'So she could bequeath it to the local cats' home or the – or the – St Valentine Day's Massacre Relief Fund if she wanted to?'

'Yes.'

Nick sat back, twirling his wineglass between his fingers, and said with a man-of-the-world air, 'Well, I do think, Howard, old chap, that you rather let the side down, there. If you were advising father, I would have expected you to suggest a proviso about the place being kept in the family. It ought to go to me.'

Matt had been thinking very much the same thing, except that he had a different legatee in mind.

Howard said suavely, 'I am sure you may trust your mother to know where her duty lies.'

Nick worshipped his mother, but knew her far too well to share Howard's confidence. With a rapid return to normality, he said, 'Huh! Want to bet?'

This did not go down at all well with Natasha, so that Matt felt it necessary to lay a hasty hand on her glass and say, 'Steady on! Don't let your trustee see you slinging the crystal around, or he'll dock your pocket money.'

Natasha glared at him and then transferred the glare back to her ungrateful son. 'If my darling Matt is very, very good and very,

418

very nice to me, I shall leave Provost Charters to *him*, which would be right. If he does not kill himself first in his silly aeroplane.'

'No!' Nick exclaimed hotly. 'Matt doesn't care about the house. He's never even here. But I do. I *love* it.'

Matt was vaguely surprised, and it struck him suddenly that he didn't know his brother very well. Nick had grown into a handsome young man, with a good deal of his mother's charm and more than a touch of her wilfulness. Aware from a child that he could get exactly what he wanted by smiling his mischievous smile or, if that failed, roaring off into melodrama, he was thoroughly spoilt. What he didn't seem to have was any sense of purpose, which would have been acceptable before the war but not now. Nowadays, you needed to know where you were going.

Natasha surveyed her son with renewed disapproval.

'You *love* it?' she repeated in tones of disbelief. 'You *love* it? How *can* you love it? Have you learned nothing from being my son?'

Even Howard was taken aback.

'How *dare* you,' she went on, her outrage mounting and her eyes flashing magnificently, 'love a house that is in every way ugly, vulgar and uncomfortable? That is in the most repulsive of Victorian taste? That offends against every sensibility?'

She waved an arm and it wasn't too difficult to see what she meant, if you looked at the place as a place, rather than as 'the family home'.

Blankly, Nick said, 'But you love it too. Don't you?'

'Your father wished me to love it,' Natasha observed, as they pushed back their chairs and moved into the music room for coffee and *petits fours*, 'and I did so because I wished to be kind to him. But now he has gone, I do not need to love it any more.'

Matt found himself chuckling.

So many times in these last ten years he had wondered at himself; at how, in his youth, he had adored Tash without reservation, and refused to recognise in her even the slightest fault.

He had tried to put his feelings into words on that disastrous Christmas Eve of 1918, when she had done everything she knew to force him into making love to her; when it had taken every ounce of willpower he possessed to reject her, and she had known it. She had been upset, then, but not at all discouraged, and she still hadn't stopped trying. He suspected he would always feel a compulsion to keep his back against a nice, safe wall whenever she came within reach.

But now, when she was being so gloriously, nonsensically, disarmingly herself, he felt a rush of the old affection. She was Tash, and she was wonderful, and he still adored her even if he didn't trust her an inch.

'Well, I don't give a damn if you think I've got rotten taste,' his brother told her heatedly. 'I love Provost Charters, and I *want* it.'

4

NICK did want it, because it meant to him what he knew it had never meant to Matt, a childhood of freedom and happiness and small pleasures beyond the possibility of counting.

Memories not of stern nannies and mutton broth and parents who were strangers, but of drowsy summer afternoons with pigeons cooing on the lawn and the smell of strawberry jam seeping out from the kitchens; of fountains sparkling in the sun against a dark green backcloth; of rose arches, and ancient yews, and peacocks; of raiding the kitchen garden for warm, luscious Brown Turkey figs and being chased away by young Comstock, sixty if he was a day, but forever 'young' because his father had been head gardener before him.

And in winter there had been the scent of applewood logs and the fun of toasting muffins before the nursery fire, and skating on the village pond, and playing rummy with his idolised mother, who entered into the spirit of things as blithely as if she were a child herself. He remembered her hugging him to her one day, and saying that playing rummy with her own lovely boy was *much* more fun than playing roulette at Monte Carlo.

He knew it was all over, that the years of unshadowed love and security had gone, that he would never be so happy again, or so near to being the master of his fate.

'*Quoth the Raven, "Nevermore",*' he murmured under his breath.

He didn't fear the future, but the thought of facing it without Provost Charters and all that it meant to him was intolerable.

5

'I WANT it,' Nick said again, 'and *I will have it.*'

Matt's amusement vanished. He had thought, insofar as he had thought at all, that if his father left Provost Charters to him, he and Natasha and Nick could work out some way of sharing it. He himself had very little feeling for the place, but it was where the family belonged, after all, and it had occurred to him that Nick, after he came down from Cambridge, might like to make a stab at being a gentleman farmer. The land had never been properly utilised.

With a sudden, powerful sense of regret, he recognised that the place would be almost bound to go to Nick in the end, because he himself, it seemed, would never have a son to inherit it.

But that wasn't the kind of thought one spoke aloud. He said curtly, 'You will forgive us, Nick, if we don't regard your wishes as on a par with divine command. Tash is right when she says that Provost Charters should pass to the eldest son.' Then, smiling, he tried to lighten the atmosphere a little. 'Though the whole question is probably academic. In my own view, Tash is indestructible and will outlive both of us.'

Tash lit up like a beacon and exclaimed, 'My *darling* boy!' but Nick just went on standing before the fire, brooding handsomely, like Byron having misgivings about Missolonghi.

Matt glanced at Howard and found him watching them all with his usual air of being the only grown-up among children. He was beginning, as Matt had long suspected he would, to resemble a basset hound.

Matt took a deep breath and said, 'By the way, Howard, I know it's a bit late in the day, but I haven't asked. How are you enjoying being a father?'

6

MATT hadn't known until a few hours earlier that Jenny had borne Howard a son. He and Bill Bonny had been away for almost eighteen months, because the BB.1 had responded so well to almost all they asked of it that they had begun to wonder if it was a real commercial proposition, a plane not just for Gannet Charter but for a market that was beginning to open up as the last of the Great War planes were pensioned off.

So they had taken their time over the proving flight, making contact with potential customers, customers like Keith Whalley, now with his own bush-plane outfit in Australia. Keith reckoned the BB.1 was a beaut, if only they could add an extra refinement or three.

'In the outback in the Dry – that's summer to you, you ignorant Poms – she c'n get to 130°. Touching metal's like planting your palm on the backyard barbie, so balsa would be better than aluminium for fairing the struts 'n things. The heat thins the air, too, so there's days when every other take-off goes crook, but I reckon those flaps you've got on the trailing edge oughta give enough lift to compensate. What we need is better fuel consumption and some way of getting the cow off the ground when there's six inches of dust on it. Oh, an' yair! We c'd do with some gadget to see through the Bedouries – that's dust storms – if you've got 'ny ideas!'

Matt had said thoughtfully, 'There's a chap called Doolittle in the States. He's working on instruments for blind flying . . .'

It had all been amazingly interesting, because what Keith needed for Australia wasn't unlike what Carey and Udny wanted in the Rajputana, and the cabin insulation needed for the Himalayas was presumably no different from what would be needed for the Andes.

They'd come home, in the end, with enough ideas to get them started on the BB.2, a deliberately commercial version adaptable to the widest possible range of flying conditions. It would be on the drawingboard for a while yet because, before they committed themselves, they wanted to know more about the *Inflexible*, the monoplane that had been built by Beardmore's, on the Clyde, specifically to demonstrate the advantages of all-metal, rigid construction.

Matt hadn't heard anything of Jenny all the time he'd been away. He hadn't written to her, because there hadn't seemed much point, nor she to him. It would have been difficult for her, anyway, because his only addresses had been care of a succession of embassies and consulates, but he suspected that, having chosen to stay with Howard, she wanted only to forget her lapse from virtue.

It had been a shock to hear that she'd had a child, and peculiarly difficult to find out – without seeming to be interested – exactly

422

when. The end of June 1927, or perhaps it was early July, Tash had said, but she really didn't remember. She knew it was ages after Paul had had his first stroke.

Matt had been too abstracted to notice that the expression in her eyes was by no means as offhand as her words. Nor would it have occurred to him that she might have her own views about the boy's paternity, and no wish to see an unbreakable bond established between his parents if she could prevent it. She had drawn her own conclusions from Howard's deceptively innocent questioning, because in some things she was no fool.

So Matt had worked it out, and it seemed that the child couldn't be his, and he knew, anyway, that if it had been Jenny wouldn't have kept the knowledge from him.

But it pained him, with a raw and illogical pain, to think that she must have gone to bed with Howard so soon after their own brief and perfect hour together. What was love? he wondered suddenly. He had always suspected that it was possible to think oneself into love. Was it also possible to think oneself out of it?

7

FOR the better part of eighteen months, Jenny hadn't been thinking at all. She remembered that, after Beth had been born, she had been fidgetty and restless and depressed, but only for a few days. This time it went on, and on, and on, until she couldn't remember what it was like to be her normal self; wasn't even sure what her normal self was.

To begin with, she was driven by a relentless energy that wore her out, mentally and physically, but wouldn't allow her to sleep. She would get up in the middle of the night to feed the baby, and find herself hours later sitting in the kitchen surrounded by blueprints and estimates and notebooks. She worked like a Trojan at the office, and at home couldn't bear to sit still for more than five minutes before she had to be up and doing something.

It might have been bearable, merely an exaggeration of her normal busyness, if it hadn't been for the spells when the world seemed to stop, when she would be standing looking out of a window in daylight and then it would be dark and she wouldn't know what had happened to the time in between. And sometimes she had hallucinations, when she saw a tramcar that wasn't there, or failed to see a bus that was. It terrified her. She didn't dare drive the car.

She was always worrying about the children, too, about whether Beth had fallen off her bicycle in front of a bus, and whether Nanny was feeding the baby properly when she wasn't there, or stuffing his little tummy with cold mutton pie and chips. She knew she was being stupid, but she couldn't help it.

At least such troubles as those weren't too obvious to other people, but no one could avoid noticing how her moods varied, how she dissolved into tears at the drop of a hat. James McMurtrie was forever saying, 'Really, Jenny!' and she could see Mr Selow, the bank's nominee, thinking, 'God save us from women in business!' But she couldn't stop herself.

Mr Selow had been ruthless with his economies. The Dalmuir works had been sold off to Lithgows, the South Yard put on a care-and-maintenance basis, and the shareholding in Eastern Empire disposed of; every estimate was cut to the bone and every petty cash slip scrutinised as closely as a million-dollar bill.

As a result, 1927 showed an operating profit of £10,000, even though the overdraft scarcely dropped because of the interest charges. And in 1928 the Inland Revenue came to the rescue with a repayment of wartime excess profits duty. After that, Mr Selow packed his briefcase and left them to it.

But it had all been about money, not ships, and it broke Jenny's heart. The walls of her office were covered with paintings and photographs of the ships Brittons' had built in the ninety-three years of its existence, and on her desk there was a beautiful little scale model of a puffer that her father had made for her when she was a child. And she would look at them, and then out of the window at the two ferry boats and the tanker that were all that were in the berths, and then she would burst into tears.

This was where she belonged, her true home, the place where she had been happiest for all the thirty years of her life. Seeing it like this was like watching a beloved child dying, slowly, of some incurable, wasting, lingering disease.

8

WHEN Howard, who had remained in Glasgow for only three days after presenting Jenny with his ultimatum – just long enough to satisfy himself that she was suitably cowed – returned from another of his extended business trips to New York and found his wife a bundle of nerves, he was displeased all over again.

Especially when, at three o'clock one morning, waking and finding her missing from bed, he went downstairs and discovered her at the kitchen table, poring over a balance sheet as if her life depended on it.

She jumped like a jack-in-the-box and looked as if she were about to faint when she heard his abrupt, 'So!' from a couple of feet behind her.

'I seem to remember,' he said, 'making it a condition of our agreement that you should curb your passion for the shipyard. You appear to be doing the opposite. Do I take it that you *wish* me to divorce you and take the child away from you?'

He never referred to Johnny by name.

She couldn't explain the kitchen and the balance sheet even to herself. How could she explain them to Howard?

The tears sprang to her eyes immediately. 'Howard, I'm sorry, I'm sorry, I'm sorry! I'm not well. I don't know what's wrong with me, and I can't help myself. I don't even know what I'm doing half the time.'

He raised one supercilious eyebrow. 'I find that hard to believe.'

'But it's *true*. I have terrible blank patches in my mind. I start to do one thing and finish up doing something else, with no consciousness of what's gone on in between. And every time it happens, it makes things worse.'

She stopped suddenly, realising that it must sound to him as if she was unhinged. He must be thinking that, now, there was real substance in his threat to have her declared an unfit mother. But it wasn't like that. It couldn't be like that. She was just tired and overwrought. If only he would sit down, instead of standing there looming over her!

'My dear Jenny, you appear to be trying to persuade me that you are weakminded, which does not accord with my knowledge of you. I am more inclined to think that you are making excuses for disobeying my wishes.'

'No, no, no! It isn't like that at all. I've been trying so hard to behave well, to do as you want me to do. You can't *possibly* believe that I want to have Johnny taken away from me.' She was weeping in full earnest by now. 'I'd kill myself first!'

Even as she spoke, she realised that she meant it. If she had been herself, she would have fought, but as things were, all she wanted to do was find rest.

There was a pause and then Howard said, a little less coldly, 'Have you seen a doctor?'

'Yes.'

'And? Pull yourself together, for goodness' sake, Jenny. This display of emotion is most unbecoming.'

She swallowed hard and, somehow, managed to string a rational sentence together. 'He said it's not unusual after having a child, if a woman is depressed or overwrought.' What he had really said was 'overworked', but that was a weapon she knew better than to offer her husband.

'And what is the cure?'

'Time. He says I'll get over it.' He had also said that this new-fangled notion that after-birth depression was a clinical illness was nonsense. It was no more than a woman's self-indulgent bid for sympathy for having suffered an experience that women had been suffering for a million years without complaining. The remedy was simple, the exercise of a little self-discipline, and he would be obliged if Mrs Fournier would waste no more of his time with her imagined ills.

He had phrased it much more politely, of course, because he didn't want to lose a paying customer, but that was what he'd meant. Jenny, returning home, had taken her pen and blotted his name out of her address book so violently that the ink had come through on the other side of the page.

Howard said, 'I see. Well, I trust that your recovery will not take long. Possibly it might be hastened if you were to set your mind to it? You must recognise that it would inconvenience me seriously to have a wife who cannot be trusted to behave rationally when I bring guests home.'

Was that all it meant to him? She gazed up at him through her tears, tall and stalwart and heavier than he had been a few years before. It didn't show when he was fully clothed, but his dressing-gown was taut around the middle. He was thirty-seven

426

years old and Jenny, with a strange detachment, reflected that he would be overweight by the time he was forty.

She clung to her detachment like a shipwrecked sailor to a floating baulk of wood. That Howard should see her misery only in terms of the inconvenience to himself was perfectly characteristic and not something she should allow herself to brood about.

The trouble was that he had always been the centre of his own universe. From odd remarks he had made, Jenny had deduced that even his parents had considered him a very superior young man. 'My mother,' he had said once, 'appreciated me, and taught me to value myself.' His father, by contrast, had been something of a cypher, so that his suicide had caused no hurt to Howard's heart; but it had been a serious inconvenience in that it had upset his mother and might well have interfered with his career. Howard had the strongest possible dislike of being inconvenienced by other people, and Jenny had always known it.

She swallowed and said, 'I'm sorry, Howard. I don't want to inconvenience you.' She didn't say, 'You terrify me, because you know how to tear my emotions to shreds and don't even realise you're being cruel. I feel as if I'm fated to go through all the rest of my life with my nerves on edge.'

'Good,' he said. 'And now, I suggest we forget the whole matter. Perhaps it might be of benefit if I telephone your secretary and instruct her to make sure that, in future, you do not bring work home from the office.'

She didn't dare say, 'No.'

9

IN THE months that followed, Howard did seem to his surprised wife to be making an effort to be sympathetic, as if he wanted to help, and because of it she began to feel almost grateful to him, almost to forget how deeply she feared his harshness. He had a very strong possessive instinct, and she suspected that the fact of her being 'his wife' was behind his solicitude, but he had taken the trouble to consult a specialist in London, someone of up-to-date opinions, who had told him that Mrs Fournier, in all probability, was genuinely ill and that it would aid her recovery if everyone were as understanding as possible.

There was no one else Jenny could turn to for sympathy. She wouldn't have expected any from Jack or Iris, but Allie, for once, didn't understand at all and neither, of course, did the children. Simon whistled *Shakin' the Blues Away* until Jenny was almost ready to scream – and on one occasion did – and Beth looked at her nervously, doubtfully, so that Jenny burst into yet another bout of worried tears and Beth became frightened to look at her at all, because it seemed to upset her so much.

But it was the children's incomprehension that saved her in the end. Beth always listened to what Simon said, dazzled by his familiarity with all the latest fads, and impressed by the knowledge he had acquired during his career as a medical student, brief though it had been. After his third term, his faculty adviser had suggested that perhaps young Mr Fournier wasn't cut out for the task of healing the sick. So now he was pretending to read Arts at Cambridge. Jenny had fretted about it all terribly, since nobody else seemed to be doing so.

But then, when he was home for the Christmas vac in 1928, she overheard him telling Beth portentously, 'I think your mum's really gone round the bend, you know. We'll have to be jolly careful with her. Mad people can be violent.'

Suddenly, blessedly, Jenny found herself laughing. When the most violent thing she had ever done was sock someone over the head with a saxophone!

She realised, much later, that she wouldn't have been able to laugh if she hadn't already begun to climb out of the slough, but at the time it seemed as if laughter was the miracle cure.

There were to be a good many ups and downs in the months that followed, but by the middle of 1929 she was almost herself again. It was just that sometimes, still, she suffered a relapse. It was usually brief, not much more than a sleepless night or a tendency to become over-emotional about something unimportant. But by that law of Nature which decrees that one never does anything silly except when somebody is watching, she suffered oue of her relapses, rather publicly, at the Living Advertisements Ball.

10

SHE didn't quite know how she had been talked into going, except that, with Simon, it was usually easier to give in than resist. While he tried to decide what to do with his life, Simon was making a career of playing the ugly sophisticate, and he had a natural talent for argument which could be exceedingly trying in everyday life, admirable though it might have been if he had directed it to some useful end. It wasn't the browbeating kind of argument, just perseverance allied to a logic whose flaws you didn't spot until it was too late.

He had become almost inseparable from Nick, his fellow-under-graduate at Cambridge, and since Nick's mother was making up a party to attend the ball, and Jenny was in London for an engineering exhibition, Simon said she really couldn't *not* go. She didn't give in until she had made sure that Matt wasn't going to be there.

Natasha had been making up a number of very expensive parties in the months following Paul's death, during which time Provost Charters languished under dust sheets and the striking Lady Britton, who photographed well, appeared regularly in the picture papers, clad in black gowns that were the very obverse of mourning and squired by a succession of willowy young men – mostly Honorables. But the faithful Granby Fox was never far away, contentedly observing. After the war, Granby had spent an unlikely few years in the City before becoming a gentleman farmer, with the accent more on the gentleman than the farmer. Where his relationship with Natasha was concerned, it seemed to be one of friends and lovers, with the accent more on the friends than on the lovers.

The Living Advertisements Ball was in aid of charity and, as so often in the postwar world, a fancy dress affair. All guests were required to turn up looking as if they had stepped out of some kind of advertisement or publicity material.

Jenny, her sense of humour almost back to normal, had flirted briefly with a tin of Heinz Baked Beans, rejected that in favour of Warner's Rust-Proof Corsets, then, reminding herself that she was thirty-one years old and a respectable married woman, resigned herself to a simple evening frock and an assortment of houri-ish veils, intending to say firmly, when asked, 'Abdulla Cigarettes'.

429

The whole evening very nearly ended before it began when Simon presented himself to her for inspection. He had rejected with contumely her suggestion of a Bisto Kid, saying he intended something a lot more striking than that, and as Jenny surveyed the cream-and-brown checked kimono and the vast bunch of red roses and blue tulips surmounting his bespectacled head, she felt bound to admit that he had succeeded.

'What on earth are you supposed to be?'

'Cadbury's Sheridan chocolates.'

'Well, if you think I'm going to be seen in public with a figure of fun like you . . .'

Nick laughed uproariously when they arrived. The two boys, it seemed, had had a bet on about what might be done in the chocolate-box line and Simon had undoubtedly won. Nick, as the Pierrot from Caley's Jazz-Time Toffees, was very much handsomer but sadly unoriginal.

His mother was pretty original, though, decked out in soap bubbles made of silver paper and cellophane. The costume wasn't transparent, but it looked as if it was meant to be. Fine for a nineteen-year-old, Jenny thought, but really! Natasha would be forty next birthday.

It was a very high-spirited ball. Raucous would have been a better word, with all the Bright Young Things stopping dead in the middle of the floor every few seconds, and screaming gleefully as they spotted their friends and tried to identify their costumes. There was a good deal of gleeful screaming from the balconies, too, but that had rather different overtones; 'come-hither' was the only polite expression for it that Jenny could think of.

The atmosphere was thick with smoke and women's perfume, and crawling with streamers, and the band was ear-splittingly loud and not very good. In fact, there was something frenetic about the whole thing, as if everyone had started the evening two or three drinks above par.

It wasn't only the younger generation. Natasha's friends were equally excitable and more than a little glazed about the eyes. Jenny slapped away her partner's wandering hand and wished she hadn't come. The only dance she'd enjoyed so far had been with the eternally sober and sedate Granby, who had cheated by turning up in ordinary white tie and tails and claiming to be the butler on the Kensitas packet.

On the whole, Jenny thought she would cut her losses and slip away. Simon could find a taxi for her.

As she made her way back towards the table, she could see that he was showing off for all he was worth, and in the mood to make an exuberant and boringly public issue of her leaving. But this time she wasn't going to listen to any of his nonsense. This time, he would do as he was told.

Unaware that she was looking rather stern-lipped, and that Natasha, watching her, had misinterpreted it, she reached the table to find her hostess with one arm round the neck of a conspicuously squiffy young man, who was trying to pour champagne into one of Natasha's silver shoes with the apparent intention of drinking from it.

Natasha, waving a glass airily in her free hand, was saying loudly to him with an interest as spurious as it was extravagant, 'But *you* are a stockbroker, so you can explain to me. I am acquainted with I do not know how many people – people with panache and experience, of course – who are making a wonderful success of their businesses. Why, then, should the shipyard belonging to my late husband's family be having so many, and so very boring troubles? Might it be due to what-do-you-call-it – managerial incompetence?'

Then, turning her head, she affected to see Jenny for the first time, and smiled, and stretched her body voluptuously, and exclaimed, 'Ah, my dear Jenny. Did you have a divine dance?'

Normally, Jenny would have ignored it, but at that moment, unfortunately, she suffered one of her increasingly rare relapses into emotionalism. To have this idle, detestable woman sneering at her beloved yard raised in her such a violent surge of passion that, almost without conscious volition, she found herself hitting back with the only words that she knew would hurt.

Scanning Natasha from the top of her bubble-crowned head to her shoeless foot, she hissed, 'What a slut you are, Natasha. I don't know how you can *bear* to make such an exhibition of yourself, and at your age, too! Thank God Paul never knew what a bitch he had for a wife!'

There was dead silence, and then Natasha was on her feet.

'Slut?' she shrieked. '*You* to talk of sluts? When *you* are the one who goes whoring as soon as you are out of your husband's sight!'

For the briefest of moments, Jenny was mystified, and then she felt the floor tilt under her feet as she realised what she had done. Knowing she must be as white as a sheet, she gasped, 'Natasha! Stop!'

Natasha didn't, of course. She didn't even lower her voice. Her beautiful face ugly with rage, she screeched, 'I wonder why Howard and my darling Matthew were *both* so interested in *exactly* when your son was conceived? I wonder how . . .'

The people at the adjoining tables had all turned and were watching with broad and bibulous grins. One of the girls giggled and whispered in her partner's ear.

Somehow, Jenny regained a grip on herself and, in a voice that had the cutting edge of twelve years of loathing, exclaimed, 'Natasha, I apologise. Now, control your tongue, for heaven's sake. This is not the place . . .'

'I wonder how you have the insolence to go on pretending to be so very moral, such a boring little prude! I wonder . . .'

Nick and Simon were staring at Jenny, wide-eyed, and she knew that it all had to be stopped here and now before the ultimate disaster happened and some gossip columnist drifted over looking for copy.

She said tightly, 'Be careful, Natasha. This is a game two can play, and I can assure you that I know a great deal more about you and . . .'

For several moments, she had been aware out of the corner of her eye of the figure in the blue-and-white striped Kodak Girl dress who had arrived at the table just after the beginning of Natasha's outburst. Now she saw who it was.

She left the rest of her words unspoken.

Into the vibrating silence, the figure said, 'Tash, darling, I'm so *ashamed* to be late. The bouncer *almost* wouldn't let me in because he thought I was gatecrashing.'

Natasha turned. '*Dearest Mims!*' she carolled. 'I had no idea you were there! Do join us.'

Natasha didn't care what she said or to whom when she was in a tantrum, but Jenny was to wonder later, as, time after time, she replayed the nasty little scene in her head, if Natasha had known all along that Mims was listening.

Jenny had believed Matt, when he said that he and Natasha had never been lovers, but she knew that Natasha still regarded him as unequivocally hers. It had mystified her, always, the readiness with which Natasha had accepted Mims, how she had almost seemed to be making an ally of the girl. Had she just been waiting, and watching, for an opportunity to break up their marriage?

Mims said, bright and brittle, 'What a day! I just can't wait to sit down. Say, can I have some giggle water? I surely need it.' Then she glanced at Jenny, still standing, rigid, facing Natasha and said, 'Well hello, Jenny. I didn't recognise you in your seven veils.'

Miraculously, Jenny contrived a smile. 'Hello, Mims. Don't think I'm leaving because you've arrived. It's just that I have an early appointment in the morning.'

But Natasha wouldn't let it go. Before Jenny had time to add, 'Goodnight, everybody,' Natasha pursed her lips in mock meditation and said, 'Now where did we hear you say that before? Do you remember, Mims? Oh, yes. One evening in Paris, wasn't it?'

Jenny smiled again, and said, 'Simon, will you find a taxi for me, please?'

11

IT WAS three o'clock in the morning when Matt quietly put his key in the door of the little house in Ponsonby Place. They'd got it cheap because the previous tenant had been flooded out when the Thames burst its banks the previous year and had decided Harrow-on-the-Hill was a safer place.

Matt wondered whether Mims was back from the ball; whether she'd even gone. He hadn't expected to be home from France until tomorrow, but it had seemed a pity to waste such a beautiful night. Nothing could touch flying alone in the sky in the moonlight.

He was hanging up his coat when the door of the living room at the back of the house was flung open, and was still blinking in the flood of light when the figure profiled in the doorway exclaimed, 'You're back, are you? You *rat!*'

She meant it, too.

'Yep! That's me,' Matt said. 'Have a nice party?'

'Is it *true* what I heard tonight? Was it *you* who fathered Jenny Jardine's baby? *Was it?*'

He'd had a wearing few days, so that, after the initial moment of gut-twisting shock, he couldn't stop his angry retort and didn't want to. 'Well, you don't give me much chance to father *yours*, do you!'

'You admit it? You just stand there and admit it?'

'I'd rather sit down and not admit it.'

He had to push past her into the living room or he'd have been standing out in the hall all night, and when he turned he was momentarily distracted. 'You didn't go to a ball in that old frock, did you?'

'Why not? It's near enough like the Kodak Girl's and I hung a camera round my neck. You're always telling me to save money. *Don't change the subject.* Is that baby yours?'

She was still the most beautiful girl he'd ever seen, with the long, gleaming, waving red-gold hair, the pure bone structure, the large green eyes with their slightly winged brows, the mouth with the Cupid's bow and the generous lower lip that made her look as if she were always pouting a little. Her figure was slim and trim, but she never made any effort with clothes. It was as if she only wanted to be one of the boys.

She was beautiful even when she looked as if she would like to kill him.

'Jenny's baby? No, he's not mine,' he said, speaking the truth as he knew it. 'And I would very much like to know which malicious chatterbox suggested to you that he might be?'

'Never mind that. Are *honestly* sure it's not yours? Are you *honestly* sure it wasn't born nine months after that evening in Paris when you and Dear Jenny left me and Tash at Maxim's?'

There was only one thought in his mind, and that was to protect Jenny. Coldly, he said, 'This is a farrago of nonsense. Jenny is a respectable married woman, and I am a married man . . .'

She was quick. 'Not a *respectable* married man, I notice!'

He ignored it. He wasn't prepared to start justifying himself for the times when, desperate, he'd found comfort in other arms than his wife's. There hadn't been many, because he hated the self-disgust of the morning after.

He took two steps across the room and grasped his wife's shoulders so tightly that she exclaimed. Then he said, shaking her, 'Who has been filling your head with these ideas. Who has been trying to make trouble? Tell me!'

'Tasha told me, and she *wasn't* trying to make trouble. She's real and honest, the only one who is. She tells me the truth, because we're close!'

'Hah!' He released her abruptly. 'I might have known.'

'What does that mean?' She stood rubbing her shoulder, staring at him, and he sacrificed Tash without a moment's hesitation. 'It means she's jealous. For years, she's claimed to be in love with me. I sometimes think it's only because she's my stepmother and can't have me. But she thinks I belong to her. That's all it is, no more than that.'

434

'I don't believe you. Tash isn't like that.'

'Isn't she?'

Matt went to the drinks tray on the corner table and poured himself a stiff whisky, then sank down on the elderly sofa. If everything went as he planned, and it looked as if it might, they'd be able to afford some decent furniture soon.

Mims stood, frowning in concentration, and then snapped, 'No. It isn't true. Even if it was, what you've said just makes things worse. If she's jealous, she must have some reason for picking on Jenny. So what is it?'

'God knows. Because Jenny and I knew each other when we were children, before Tash ever appeared on the scene. Or because Jenny said something to annoy her . . .'

He could see from Mims' face that he'd hit the nail on the head. 'And perhaps because it gave her the chance to upset *you*. You're my wife. You're the person she should be jealous of.' He didn't even try to keep the bitterness out of his voice.

Mims said slowly, 'She doesn't need to be jealous of me, really.'

'No.' He took a gulp of whisky and thought that, if he'd been a woman, he might have wept.

Mims moved over to her chair and picked up the book she'd been reading. 'I'm sorry I blew my top. It wasn't really about what we've been talking about. I wouldn't care if you slept with every woman you saw, except that marriage is more than just sleeping together, isn't it?'

'Yes.'

'But I've discovered. . .' She stopped, as if she was trying to say something very difficult. 'I've never liked – bed – and I thought maybe I'd just been born without the right kind of feelings. But a couple of days back, one of the girls at the aerodrome lent me this.'

She held it out to him. Radclyffe Hall's *The Well of Loneliness*, published the previous year and banned under the obscenity laws. A novel about women who loved women.

Matt felt a cold chill of enlightenment run through him.

Mims said, 'I understand now. I understand everything I didn't understand before. I've recognised every single thought, every single feeling in the book, all the things no one's ever told me. I didn't know there were women like that.

'But I know now. And I know I'm one of them, Matt.'

He didn't say anything. There didn't seem anything to say.

She went on, 'It means that everything that's wrong between us, between you and me, has been my fault because I – I . . . Oh, God, I'm sorry, Matt! But I can't help it!'

So he put his arms round her and patted her head, and soothed her, as if he was just a friend. Just one of the boys. He wondered if Tash had somehow known it.

Two

1

SIMON said, 'Hic!' and then turned and wagged a reproving finger at Nicholas. 'Shhh!'

The girls giggled, so Simon said, 'Shhh!' to them, too, and, fumbling a little, fixed the monocle in his eye, the better to stare them down. He'd got the idea from Dorothy Sayers, but it was suddenly borne in on him that Lord Peter Wimsey wouldn't have found himself shooing a couple of floozies out of his stepmother's house in a Glasgow suburb at five o'clock of a December evening.

He hiccuped again. Liquid lunches were a mistake. He'd had a brief flirtation with drugs a couple of years before, under the combined influences of Sax Rohmer and the Bright Young Things. But though he'd never found any difficulty getting the stuff – there was a woman who ran a pub on Shaftesbury Avenue, and a German sausage importer who smuggled it into the country packed in the middle of the *extrawurst* – Simon had found it all a bit of a letdown. He didn't like the hangover effect and he hadn't met a single girl who could tell him what it was like to be lured into an opium den by a sinister Chinaman.

He said again, 'Shhh!' and then opened the front door and peered out carefully at the short driveway leading down between the chilly looking laurels to the gaslit street. All clear.

'Goo'night, ladies!' He gave a smacking kiss to the dashing blonde who'd been his, rubbing himself sexily against her, while Nick enveloped his brunette in a passionate final embrace. Then they slipped the girls ten bob each and shooed them out.

Quietly, Simon closed the door, saying, 'If we walked them home we'd jusht get in the way of their bishness,' and Nick giggled and said, 'That'sh true.'

Beth, standing on the stairs watching them, thought, 'Really!' as Nick smoothed down his hair before the hall mirror and remarked, 'Hot shtuff!' while Simon crossed his hands over the place where paintings had fig leaves and laughed. 'There's talent even in the provinshes if you know where to look.'

Then they both jumped a guilty foot in the air as Beth said, 'Honestly, you're terrible. What have you been doing? Mummy

437

would be absolutely furious. She says you're not supposed to cuddle people unless you're going to marry them.'

It was very much a thirteen-year-old paraphrase of what Jenny had actually said when, a few months before, she'd taken the occasion of Beth's first period to try and explain the facts of life to her, something Jenny's own mother had never done. Jenny had begun to see why, as she found herself taking refuge in prudish words and coy phrases. How *did* you explain to an innocent child? She'd thought that she'd better let Beth absorb the general principles before she went into detail.

Simon, who had long recognised that his looks were never going to get him into pictures, had now decided on the Bar as an alternative outlet for his histrionic talents, and responded accordingly to his stepsister's rebuke.

'Ah, ha!' he exclaimed. 'Mummy says that, does she? Hearshay evidensh, of coursh, but a clear case of do what I say, not do what I do.'

He turned and headed for the sitting room. 'Bishness to 'tend to.'

'Goodness, what a mess!' Beth complained, as all three of them began picking up cushions and plumping up sofas.

'What elsh does Mummy say about men cuddling girls?'

'She says you've not to, because it just goes on from there, and before you know where you are the girl's having a baby. And then you've *got* to get married.'

Nick shook his head owlishly. 'Well, Mummy should know.'

Screwing the errant monocle back in, Simon said ponderously, 'You're not defining your terms, old boy. What should she know? The shtep from cuddling to having a baby, yesh. But getting married? No. Can't have it.'

Nick thought about it. 'Ashtrue.'

'What?'

'That'sh true. Married already. Got a husband. Not allowed to marry the chap who cuddled her. Not allowed to marry Daddy. Very shad. Daddy's nicer 'n Howard.'

'No, he's not.

'Yesh, he ish.'

With dignity, Simon announced, 'You're pre – prej – prez-shyoodissed.'

But even as he applauded this achievement, Nick said dispassionately, 'No, I'm not. If I were Johnny, wouldn' want Howard for a Daddy.'

Beth stamped her foot. 'What are you talking about?'

438

Simon subsided onto the now tidy sofa and absently buttoned up his flies, a process interrupted by Beth's appearance on the stairs. Surprised, he said, 'Talking about Johnny's daddy.'

'But Howard's Johnny's daddy.' Beth looked at Simon doubtfully. He always knew an awful lot that she didn't know.

Suddenly, Simon became aware that things were getting out of hand, but although he racked his muzzy brain he couldn't be sure whether or not he'd said anything irrevocable. He hoped he hadn't. Jenny would murder him, and he was really quite fond of her.

So he did his best to cater for all eventualities by curling a forefinger round his nose and looking wise. ''S a secret,' he said. 'I don't know the secret. Nick doesn't know the shecret. Shut up, Nick. Beth doesn't know the shecret. Maybe there ishn't a shecret. Anyway, not shposed to know.' He giggled. 'The three wise monkeys, that'sh us. OK?'

2

JENNY noticed that Beth was rather quiet for the next few days, and twice seemed to be about to ask her something. But Jenny was rushed, and a bit impatient, and both times Beth finished up by saying, 'It's all right, mummy. It's nothing.'

And then she came home one evening to find that Beth wasn't there. By seven o'clock she was worried.

The boys, who were playing Mah-jongg with *On the sunny side of the street* going full blast on the gramophone, said they hadn't seen the child and, no, she hadn't said anything to them earlier.

So Jenny went downstairs and telephoned the homes of a couple of Beth's school friends in case they'd gone to the pictures.

Then she phoned Lizzie, in case Beth had gone to help with the wee ones, now that Lizzie was expecting again, but Lizzie, in the faint apology for a voice that was all she could muster nowadays, said no, she wasn't there either. Jenny had to talk for a few minutes, pretending she was not worried, and to frown over the nasty, racking cough that punctuated all Lizzie's utterances.

Then it was Iris. Had Beth gone to play with her cousins?

'Whit? A' the way here without you bringing her? Don't be daft. Whit's the matter? Is she lost? My Goad, I mind whit I felt like when I couldny find my two wee ones last Hogmanay,

439

and the Glen Cinema on fire and me watching them bringin' out the bodies. I nearly murdered my two when they came sauntering home an' said they'd been playing fitba' in the park. Och, Jenny, are ye no' worried sick?'

'No, I'm not,' Jenny snapped. 'Will you stop being such a Moaning Minnie!'

She was sitting wondering, 'Who next?' when Simon wandered in, looking hangdog. 'Ummm, Jenny, I've been thinking . . .'

When he reached the end of his heavily edited confession, she was too upset to be angry. Even as she said, 'Simon, how could you?' she was thinking, 'Oh, Beth, my poor pet!' For a moment, she was sure the child couldn't have run away, not when the two of them were so close, but then she realised that that made it all the more likely, and when she went upstairs, she discovered that Beth's toothbrush and facecloth were missing, and a clean nightie and some underwear.

She sank onto the neat little bed and sat for a moment with her head in her hands and thought, 'Oh, God, what have I done? What have we all done?'

Even so, she sent Simon and Nick out to scour the streets, just in case. Then she picked up the phone again. Allie was her last resort and perhaps the most likely. If Beth wasn't with her, then it would have to be the police.

She prayed while the phone was ringing, but when Allie answered at last, said brightly, 'You don't have Beth there, do you? The little monkey's gone off somewhere without telling me, and I'm getting worried.'

'No, she's not here. What's wrong, Jenny? Oh. Well, she must have had a reason. Do you know what it is?'

'I think so.'

'Are you going to tell me?'

'Allie, I can't. It's too complicated and – and – I just can't. I'm sorry.'

'Is it you she's upset with?'

'Yes.'

'I'm not surprised. I'll tell you frankly, Jenny, I don't know what's been the matter with you lately. You dash around as if the world's going to come to an end if you so much as sit down for a few minutes like a civilised being. You're obsessed with the yard to the exclusion of all else . . .'

Jenny interrupted sharply, 'Well, someone has to be. It would have closed down by now, if it hadn't been for me.'

'Yes, I know that, and you know that. But you can't expect

your children to understand. Do you ever spend time with them? Do you ever talk to Beth, or take her to the pictures? Do you ever play with Johnny?'

'Allie, that's not fair!'

'Yes, it is. It's high time you got your priorities sorted out.'

Jenny was by now completely overwrought, and her breathing was distinctly ragged. 'Allie, this isn't the time. You can say what you like to me when I've found Beth.'

'Where have you tried?'

Jenny told her, and Allie looked at her watch. It was ten o'clock. She wished the child *had* come to her.

She said, 'There's one place you don't seem to have tried.'

3

SHE got the engaged signal first, and then no reply, which seemed odd. So in the end she slipped on her warm coat, climbed into the car, and in fifteen minutes was tugging at the brass bell of a top-floor flat in Shawlands.

The hall light went on, and she could see movement through the stained glass panels of the door. Then the door opened and she said, breathless with nerves as well as the seventy-two stairs up, 'Hello, Mims. Is Beth here?'

With reluctance, she'd helped Mims find the rented flat. Many of Matt's charter customers had faded away with the Wall Street crash, unable to afford his services, but he himself was much more interested nowadays in his new plane, and was determined to build it on the Clyde. Or so said the newspapers, whose waning interest in him had been powerfully revived by his succession to a title. In the ten years after the war, he had been reduced in their columns from 'Major Matthew Britton, Poet-Hero' to mere 'Matt Britton, air-taxi owner', but now, suddenly, he was 'the legendary Sir Matthew Britton, thirty-four-year-old white hope of the aeroplane industry'. His plane was going to be a low-wing monoplane of metal monocoque construction, and have a retractable undercarriage and all sorts of other goodies.

What snobs they all were, Jenny had thought in intervals of wishing desperately that he and Mims weren't coming to live in the same city, even though it was only for a few months.

'Is Beth here?' she said again, and could see Mims hesitating, which was answer enough.

'Why Jenny, what a surprise. I thought it was Matt who'd forgotten his key.'

By then Jenny was inside the big, square hall with its multiplicity of doors. Three of them, she knew, belonged to cupboards and a fourth to the bathroom, while the remaining three led to the kitchen-livingroom, the sittingroom and the bedroom. It was a spacious-feeling flat with spacious rooms, but there weren't many of them.

Mims gestured towards the kitchen. 'The prodigal daughter is in there.'

With extreme politeness, Jenny said, 'It would have been nice if you had phoned me,' and then walked through the door.

It was a room that might have been found in nine out of ten other genteel Glasgow dwellings, its walls and paintwork done in practical shades of toast and margarine, and the furniture constructed largely out of two-by-twos dressed up with light oak varnish and brown leathercloth upholstery. On the floor was a large square carpet patterned in the strong brown and orange that didn't show the dirt – mainly because you averted your eyes too fast to see it – with an eighteen-inch surround of shiny cinnamon-coloured linoleum and a battered fireside rug before the black-leaded cooking range. The windows, large and handsome, were curtained in washed-out brown chenille, and on the walls, hung too high, were a few watercolours of grazing sheep and views of the Kyles of Bute. Scattered around on every flat surface were the crocheted mats, brass candlesticks and sailing-galleon bookends so dear to every Scottish housewife's heart.

Jenny couldn't have borne to live in the place, but Mims had said carelessly, 'Matt will hate it, but so what. It's an apartment, and we'll be out most of the time.'

A woebegone Beth was sitting by the range nursing a cup of tea and staring towards the door as if she thought her mother was going to eat her, but Jenny was so relieved that all she did was sigh smilingly and remark, 'What a worrisome child you are! Come on, pet. Time to go home.'

And then Mims was perching on the arm of Beth's chair, and putting an arm round her and hugging her, and saying, 'Let her stay, if she wants to.'

Jenny, with hours of acute worry behind her on top of an exhausting day, hadn't realised just how near the edge of her control she was until, seeing her daughter nestle in against Matt's

442

wife, she felt her heart turn violently over inside her with jealousy and dislike, with obscure uneasiness and an unendurable sense of being left out. It was as much as she could do to bite back a cry of, 'Leave her alone!'

And then, clear and hurtful in her memory, she heard her own mother saying to her, 'Don't paw your father; he doesn't like it.' Was that why, even today, casual physical contact took her by surprise and she had to make an effort not to recoil from it? It didn't come automatically to hug and cuddle her children the way other mothers did, though she had persuaded herself that it was only because she didn't want to spoil them.

Did they miss it?

In a moment of bitter enlightenment, she knew that they must, because the same flash of vision showed her what she had never admitted even to herself, that *she* missed it and had always missed it. Only twice in her life had she had someone to turn to in the certainty that their touch would smooth away her misery, assure her that she was loved. Tom, for four days. Matt, for a single hour.

Heavy-hearted, she didn't dare hold out her arms to Beth in case the child rejected her. So she smiled at Mims in a meaningless way and said, 'I think she should come home.'

Mims had been watching her curiously, this woman whose self-containment had made her nervous when they first met, and later contemptuous. She had written Jenny off as frigid and uninteresting; pretty enough, and well-dressed, if you cared for that sort of thing – which Mims didn't – but with none of the verve or flair that made Tash such a glory to be with. Jenny might get a good deal done in her own quiet way, but Mims had never seen anything special in her, or credited her with any great success in life.

Until Matt. And yet even that little episode hadn't changed Mims' view of her, because Matt was devastatingly attractive – for a man – and could be very persuasive, and Mims was inclined to think that, that night in Paris, he'd simply wanted sex and grabbed the opportunity, despite the lady's virtuous protests. Mims wondered whether he'd enjoyed it; she couldn't imagine Jenny being very rewarding in bed.

God! What a bore it all was! But Beth was an appealing little thing, with her soft complexion and innocent eyes.

Mims looked at Jenny ironically. 'Don't worry. Beth hasn't told me why she ran away. Just that there was something she couldn't quite cotton on to. She wanted to be somewhere else for a while to try and work it out.'

443

'She could have asked me.'

'Seems not.' Mims raised an eyebrow. 'And *I'm* no use because she says I wouldn't know the answer. But I wonder if she's right?'

Jenny was grateful for one mercy at least, but she didn't like the smile on Mims' face, so she said in the businesslike tones that were her unfailing refuge, 'I, however, have the advantage of knowing the question, so there is no need for any of us to concern ourselves. Come on, Beth, you're dead tired and it's time you were in bed.'

But Beth, silent and huge-eyed, just sat there.

Jenny thought, she *can't* be going to disobey me!

It seemed sensible to postpone the problem for a few moments, give it time to sort itself out. 'Mims, I'll just phone Simon, if you don't mind, and tell him all's well and he and Nick needn't stay up.'

She was hanging up the phone when there was the sound of a key in the door, and Matt walked in, unwinding the muffler from round his neck and saying, 'By God, it's cold, and the fog's coming down.'

Then he saw her. His hesitation was only momentary, and the pleasure in his voice was impersonal, dutiful. 'Hello, strangers! Just going, are you? What a pity. Come on, then, Beth. I'll give you a piggyback downstairs, if I can stand the weight!'

Beth, dainty as an Arthur Rackham sprite, jumped to her feet exclaiming, 'Oh, yes. Please, Uncle Matt!'

And that was one problem settled.

Down in the street, Jenny said, 'Thank you,' and Matt said, 'Don't mention it. Drive carefully. Goodnight.'

4

THE fog was thick and dirty and unpleasant to breathe. All her life, Jenny had been unnaturally distressed by mist and fog. Coughing, she said, 'Put your scarf round your mouth, pet, and don't talk unless you have to. We'll go by Eglinton Toll so that I can follow the tramlines. Keep your eye on the lampposts and let me know if we're in danger of wandering too far off the straight and narrow. What a pity there's so little traffic about.'

It took an hour, and both of them were raw-throated and bleary-eyed when they reached home, so Jenny made them some Ovaltine and filled a hot water bottle for Beth and tucked her up in bed. 'Don't ever run away again, my darling,' she said, giving her a convulsive kiss. 'I've never been so frightened. Sleep well. We'll talk in the morning.'

And what, she wondered as she went downstairs again, her head splitting, her nerves still fluttering from the fog, were they going to talk about? Her daughter was too young and vulnerable to be told the truth, but Jenny couldn't bear the thought of lying to her.

She made sure she had turned off the gas in the kitchen, and was just about to switch off all the lights and collapse into bed when she caught sight of a note by the phone.

It was a message dashed off in Simon's characteristic style. 'One: Dad phoned, will be home on Monday for the festive season. Two: Your brother Jack phoned. He says do you know your *** friend Matt Britton has offered Tom MacKellar a *** job in his *** plane workshop? He sounded a mite peeved. Happy dreams, and give Beth a clip over the ear from me. Si.'

Jenny read the message once, and then again, and then a third time. Tom MacKellar, the best engineer in the yard after Jack! One of the handful of key workers whom Brittons' had somehow or other managed to keep on paying through the years, even when no one knew where the next penny was coming from.

And Matt, of all people! Just when one of the smaller shipping lines had cancelled a desperately needed order for a Channel steamer because too many passengers were beginning to abandon sea for air travel. Jenny couldn't believe it. Already worn out, queasy, full of inchoate fears, and indiscriminately angry with the world and with fate, she found all her feelings boiling up until she could have screamed with misery and rage.

There was subdued rat-tat-tat on the knocker.

It was well after midnight, and she wasn't going to answer at first. But then she thought perhaps it was someone lost in the fog and looking for directions, so she opened the door on the chain.

It was Matt.

Just the person she wanted to see. Unhooking the chain, she said in a voice of honey, 'Do come in.'

5

HE didn't notice the vibrations at first. Slipping in like a fog wraith and closing the door swiftly against the murk, he said, 'You got home all right, I see. I suddenly thought I shouldn't have let you go, so I followed just in case you might be in difficulties. I assume you came by Eglinton Toll?'

'Of course I did. I'm not entirely stupid. Anyway, I've driven in worse conditions than these.'

He still either didn't notice, or wilfully ignored, the tension in her. 'I also wanted to apologise for Mims. I heard what happened. She should have phoned you.'

'Yes.'

'Do we have to stand here in the hall?'

She ushered him into the sittingroom.

'My God,' he said.

'Art Deco.'

'Oh.' He turned. 'Look, Jenny, since I'm here, there's something else . . .'

'*Yes!* There's Tom MacKellar, isn't there?'

His face stiffened, and his eyes focussed on hers, the vivid, gentian-blue eyes that would have turned any woman who possessed them into a raving beauty. 'Ah. I see you know.'

'I know. How *dare* you, Matthew Britton! One of our best men. When I think what shifts I've been put to, finding the money to go in his wage packet these last six years, because we can't afford to lose him, because we'll need him badly when the situation gets back to normal. When I've scarcely been able to find enough work for him to convince him that it isn't charity. When I've had to apologise, time after time, because we couldn't afford to give him a rise, but we'd see what we could do.' Her voice rose sharply. 'And then you come sauntering in and offer him, I don't doubt, the kind of princely wages unheard of on the Clyde! You and your *bloody* plane!'

He was sensitive about it. 'My *bloody* plane is going to knock spots off every other bloody plane on the market, and unless I get it going now, when prices are at rock bottom and I can buy up engineering equipment at liquidation sales and find the men I need, I'll never get it built and the last three years' work will all have been for nothing.

'I'm within sight of what I want, what I've always wanted, and I am not going to be stopped by weak-minded scruples over other people's misfortunes that don't happen to be my fault! Will you get it into your head, Jenny, that shipping's a thing of the past. The future's in the air.'

'It is *not!*'

'Oh, come on! Can you seriously believe shipbuilding's ever going to be the same again – with the chairman of the Royal Mail Group sent to prison for fraud, with only a single ship under construction on the whole of the Clyde, with the underwriters at Lloyds refusing to insure the new Cunarder despite government guarantees . . .'

The largest passenger liner in the world; the ship listed as No.534 in John Brown's books. 'You're behind the times,' she said. 'They started work on her this month.'

'And they'll probably stop again next month or next year because no one will discount the bills. Look the truth in the eye, Jenny. The days of sea transport are numbered.'

'Really?' she said with heavy sarcasm. 'Whereas the crash of the R101 has filled everyone with enthusiasm for the joys of travelling by air?'

His reaction was unexpected. His face went bleak, and he turned away from her, and leaned an elbow on the thin, artistic mantelpiece and said without expression, 'Don't try and use that as a debating point. There were forty-four people killed, and I knew thirty-seven of them personally.'

She was silent.

It was the first time they had found themselves alone in four long years, and suddenly he didn't know what the hell they were doing standing here arguing about future trends in the transport industry. Raising his head, he gazed at her, standing before him with her hair ruffled, her lipstick worn off, a high colour in her cheeks, and an air of dishevelment that made her look endearingly human and desirable. He said softly, 'Oh, Jenny. My Jenny,' and reached out to take her in his arms.

But she stepped back as sharply as if he had offered her violence, and her anger was suddenly white-hot.

'How can you? How can you? When my daughter . . . When I . . . When she's asleep upstairs in this very house and in the morning I'm going to have to *lie* to her about you and me . . . Perhaps it doesn't matter to you, to "the legendary Sir Matthew" with his disdain for convention and morality and all the standards ordinary people live by! But I can't look at things that way.'

She shook her head with a vehemence that, turning into a shudder, ran through her whole body.

His eyes were frowning at her uncomprehendingly. He couldn't understand what Beth had to do with all this. To do with them. 'What in God's name are you talking about?'

Even when she was angry, Jenny was usually controlled. But now, inside her, there was a half-hysterical voice shrieking, 'To hell with discipline and control, to hell with always being understanding about *other* peoples' problems. What about *my* problems!'

And so she threw everything at him, the whole sordid, disagreeable story of cause and consequence, of words and looks, of Natasha at the ball, and Simon and Nick, and Beth running to Mims . . .

She was so upset that she wasn't altogether lucid. When Johnny was born, she had promised herself that, despite Howard, she would tell Matt about his son, calmly and reasonably, when the opportunity arose. It was his right to know. And now at last the opportunity had arisen, and – though not very calmly – she had told him, and he was just standing there with a heavy look of concentration on his face, saying nothing.

'Don't you care?' she gasped.

And then he was grasping her by the shoulders, and his voice grated, '"She said this" and "he said that"'! *What's the truth, Jenny?*'

'Don't be so stupid! I've told you! Johnny is your son!'

He released her so abruptly that she staggered. Then, as if he didn't have enough air in his lungs, drew in a deep breath and slowly expelled it.

'I want to see him.'

'*No!*'

'Where is he?'

'He's upstairs! He's asleep!'

He turned and strode out of the room and began to run lightly up the stairs, his open trenchcoat flying behind him, and Jenny running after him, pulling on his coat tails, trying to stop him, whispering furiously, 'You can't. He's asleep. Be quiet, oh, be quiet! Stop. Stop, Matt. Stop!'

In the upstairs hall, he hesitated briefly. 'Where? Which room?' He laid a hand on the knob of the room that was Beth's and she shook her head furiously. 'Shhh! You shan't see him.'

His voice was low but she couldn't doubt the sincerity in it. 'Oh, yes, I will. If I have to wake every single person in this godforsaken house, *I will see my son*!'

She had no choice but to give in.

She didn't know why she had been blessed with two such beautiful children. Johnny lay there in the glow of the nightlight, three-and-a-half years old and fast asleep, his fine skin delicately flushed from the warmth of the pillow, his light brown hair silky and

448

tumbled, his eyelashes, ridiculously long and thick, curling over his infant cheeks, and his mouth soft, curving, innocent. His beloved teddybear, Tuffy, was tucked in beside him.

Matt's face was unreadable, but his hands were clenched tight as if he were having to restrain himself from reaching out and snatching the child out of bed and into his arms. Then Johnny stirred slightly, and Jenny pushed an unresisting Matt out of the way and bent down and murmured, 'Go back to sleep, darling', and kissed her son lightly on the cheek.

They went downstairs again carefully and quietly, and when they reached the sittingroom, Matt's face was chalk white.

'How could you do this?'

She knew what he meant, even though the 'this' was encyclopaedic in its scope. 'Easily enough. Everything I've done, every single thing since I knew I was pregnant, has been for him. Would you want to see your son branded a bastard all his life? Well, I wouldn't.

'From the very beginning, I couldn't bear the thought of him coming into the world burdened with our guilt, going through life shamed by his heredity. Raised eyebrows and whispers, the suspicion that he's isn't trustworthy, the certainty that he must be immoral, as if it runs in the blood. I couldn't think of him being scorned by every dreary little clerk who, for one reason or another, has to see his birth certificate. I couldn't think of him falling in love, and being rejected as unacceptable – because of us.

'I can assure you, Matt, I thought of all that before I made up my mind what to do. And there were other reasons, too.'

She shook her head, and he could see that it cost her a good deal to add, 'It's no use, Matt. You don't have any say in the matter. Howard has accepted Johnny as his, and as far as I'm concerned, that is the end of it. Now, I think you'd better go.'

As far as Matt was concerned, it wasn't – couldn't be – the end of it. But because he had been presented with far too much to think about, and saw very clearly the danger of reacting without first taking time for reflection, he said nothing but looked searchingly into her shadowed hazel eyes and noted the telltale little creases around them. It occurred to him that what she had just said, what had come as a sudden, brutal shock to him, was something she had been living with for more than four years.

There was one question he had to ask. 'Does Howard know?'

Her eyelashes fluttered, and she nodded her head.

What a mess!

She said, 'He mustn't know that I've told you.'

After a moment, he sighed. 'Very well. It would be better if I went. But we must talk, soon.'

This time she shook her head, but he thought she didn't mean it and wouldn't have believed it if she had told him she didn't dare.

It seemed best not to force things, he thought, to leave on a calm, impersonal note, but he couldn't stop himself, as he went, from murmuring, 'My poor darling,' and touching a light forefinger to her lips.

Three

1

THE cheering carried over the water, and a band played the National Anthem, and the stern of the *Queen Mary,* which had formerly been ship no.534, slid out from between the twin file of cranes that stood, motionless and erect as some skeletal guard of honour, while the tugs fussed around in mid-stream ready to give her bows a nudge when they needed it.

It was the twenty-sixth of September 1934 and it was raining when, at John Brown's yard, Her Majesty Queen Mary launched the great liner and gave it her name, but every heart on the Clyde was filled with thankfulness because for so long it had seemed as if it would never happen.

'God bless this ship, and all who sail in her.'

Jenny, watching with half the population of Paisley from the Watter Neb on the other shore, began searching through her pockets for a handkerchief, and there were many people unashamedly weeping, not all of them women. For well over two years, Jenny and everyone else at the yard had studiously avoided glancing across the oily bronze waters at the huge shell that had loomed there, empty and abandoned, since work on her stopped at the end of 1931 and three thousand men were made redundant. That she was regularly given a coat of paint only seemed to make it worse, and until the government had at last granted a loan for her completion, she had stood as a grim warning, a symbol of despair, a monument to dreams unfulfilled.

Her launch didn't mean the depression on the Clyde was at an end; far from it. But it meant *some*thing.

2

MIRACULOUSLY, Brittons' was still in business, still independent, though Fairfield's had been absorbed into the Lithgow group in 1933 and Beardmore's, after the spectacular quarter-century during which it had come near to leading the world in ships and motorcars, aero engines and dirigibles, had shrivelled until it was now little more than the Parkhead Forge which had been the source of it all, sixty years before.

There had been threats, of course, and still were. The most serious – other than bankruptcy – had come in 1932, with a bid from National Shipbuilders' Security Ltd, whose avowed and government-subsidised aim was to buy up and close down obsolete and redundant shipyards.

Howard, after giving the matter some private thought, had declared himself against the offer; as he had phrased it to his fellow directors, he did not believe the yard should be allowed to go under in such a way. 'The market is heading for recovery,' he had added, 'and I would be failing in my duty as Paul's executor if I sanctioned the disposal of the family's assets for a mere pittance.'

He found it mildly gratifying that his word should be law these days, because although he himself had only the ten per cent holding he had inherited from his father, Jenny had twenty-six per cent – five from Tom and twenty-one from Sir Albert. And Jenny, of course, never went against his advice. Not now. It meant that, between them, they could outvote anyone else with ease, except in the event of some unholy alliance between Natasha and James McMurtrie or Allie.

He had smiled drily to observe the warm, if surprised, pleasure on the face of his wife, who had, naturally enough, expected him to advise acceptance; the yard was no longer a profitable concern.

Their marriage was going very satisfactorily these days, he had reflected. Indeed, Jenny had not put a foot wrong in more than three years, so that he had felt able to tell her, more than once, that he was really quite pleased with her. It had helped her regain some confidence, without encouraging her to become over-confident, and she was so determined to remain in his good graces that he had begun to feel that at last he could rely on her to defer to his wishes even when he forbore to express them.

It had amused Howard then, and continued to amuse him, the extreme lengths to which she went in order to ensure that the boy wasn't a source of friction. From the moment he had become aware of people, the child had been tiresome in the presence of his 'father', whose custom it was to ignore him.

Simon, on the basis of his brief and half-remembered medical training, had hold Howard severely that the child's nervous stutter was an undoubted result of his feeling rejected, but Howard had

452

merely smiled. The boy was of no interest to him, a perfectly commonplace, healthy, child who, like all children, was far too intent on attracting the attention of his elders.

Howard had no objection at all when Jenny, as soon as the boy was old enough, began sending him away on occasions when she knew that Howard was to be at home for any length of time. Sometimes, he went to his Aunt Allie, who apparently enjoyed having him; sometimes, in the care of Beth, to Provost Charters, where they spent the long school holidays and had occasional visits to London as a treat.

Natasha, Howard knew, didn't welcome the boy with much enthusiasm, but she and Beth were very attached to each other, which was understandable enough, since Beth had a remarkable talent for getting on with people, and considerable sweetness of disposition. Howard had overheard her say once, in response to some critical remark of Jenny's, 'But Mummy, Tasha's so bright and nonsensical! She makes me laugh, and she's awfully kind to me. I like her!' Howard had never troubled to find out why Jenny and Natasha had always disliked each other so, but it was a source of satisfaction to him that, in deference to his comfort, Jenny should continue to send the children to Dorset despite her jealousy over the affection that had developed between Natasha and Beth.

It gave Howard satisfaction, too, to know that Matthew, visiting Provost Charters, had met the boy and knew him as the son of his cousin and the wife Matthew had once had the temerity to bed.

3

IT WAS Howard's weakness that, secure in the knowledge of his own ability to dominate, he had never taken the trouble to learn much about people. If appearances were satisfactory, he was satisfied. In consequence, he was entirely wrong about his wife.

Jenny had taught herself to recognise that, in everything that mattered, she was on her own – as much on her own as she had felt that night in 1919, at Rashilea Terrace, when she had waited for the R34 to pass overhead with the man she loved, and could never have, aboard it.

But she was a very different person now. Now she was strong enough to grit her teeth and play the rôle that was expected of her. Now, it was Johnny who was important, and she was prepared to go to any lengths to keep him safe and herself sane. If it meant sending Johnny away so as to ensure that Howard remained in a good humour, if it meant literally forcing her marriage to run on oiled wheels, then she would do it.

Somewhere, she had even found the strength to stop being afraid of Howard himself; he was no longer able to tear her emotions to shreds. By 1934, as a result of her strategy, they had come to lead something that, on the surface, was an almost normal, comfortable family life.

It gave Jenny a whole new perspective. She still didn't know her husband, because he rarely revealed anything of himself to her, but in learning how to handle him, she had learned, too, something of his strengths and weaknesses, so that it didn't altogether surprise her when his financial acumen proved to be flawed over the upturn in the economy he had forecast in 1932. She had been suspicious even at the time, and within two years he had proved to be quite wrong – at least where shipbuilding was concerned.

Because what happened was that everything got worse and worse, until the yard wasn't even able to pay wages, far less bills, and the bank refused to increase the overdraft, and the Bank of England finally stepped in with a loan because unemployment was at three million and another thousand redundancies on the Clyde were quite unthinkable.

But despite that, by 1934 there was nothing but a single paddle steamer on the way, and the yard was existing from hand to mouth on repair work. Once or twice, at dead of night, Jenny found herself traitorously thinking that perhaps they should have accepted the NSS offer after all.

She couldn't understand how, without any visible source of income, Natasha and Nick were contriving to maintain their expensive way of life. Nick had even gone off on a tour of Europe when he'd come down from university, returning from Germany, where he'd witnessed a parade of the Steel Helmet Association, deeply fearful of German militarism. And now Hindenberg was dead and Herr Hitler had declared himself Führer. Every night, as Johnny kneeled beside his bed and began, 'Now I lay me down to sleep, I pray the Lord my soul to keep,' Jenny found herself praying, too. 'Please God, let there not be another war.'

She had said to Nick, casually, 'With dividends as they are, I can't but admire the way your mother manages. But it's time you helped, don't you think? Have you decided what you're going to do?'

454

'I'm not going to be a wage slave, if that's what you mean! Or not yet. Damn it, Jenny, I'm only twenty-three. And if we're facing another Armageddon, I want to get my fun in first.'

Even Howard, regaled with smoked salmon and caviar at one of Natasha's more elaborate parties, had felt compelled to raise a faintly reproving eyebrow. 'My dear Natasha, you must not think that the family trust has somehow contrived to remain on the Gold Standard even though the country has come off it. With shipbuilding at a virtual halt, and the stockmarket in its present state, well . . .'

He had left it at that, and Natasha had smiled blindingly, and said '*Dear* Howard!'

Jenny wondered why he hadn't been more emphatic about it.

4

'COME on, mother,' Nick exclaimed. 'We must have a party, we really must! 1835 and all that! It's not every day the shipyard reaches its centenary. The ghost of Good Old Jockie will probably come back and haunt us if we don't have a proper wingding to celebrate.'

Natasha looked at him doubtfully. He had turned into a very handsome and unusually charming young man; not that she would have expected anything else, since he took after her. She was really quite fond of him despite the fact that he was what the English called 'a bit of a lightweight', with none of his brother's strength of personality.

The only thing she had against him was that he was almost twenty-four and everyone knew it, which meant that – although since Paul's death she had exercised regularly and been careful about her diet, and though her lovers assured her that she didn't look a day over thirty – everyone also knew that she must be in her mid-forties. It was a very lowering thought, and most unfair when she had so many other problems to contend with. Perhaps if she had her bedroom redecorated, it might make her feel more cheerful.

Nick couldn't understand why she should be hesitating. In general, she was prepared to give a party at the drop of a hat.

But then her ice-blue eyes brightened and she looked at him with her lips very slightly parted and that air of innocence which he knew to be deceptive, and said, 'What a clever boy you are! Yes. Certainly we will give a party. We will make it a really memorable occasion!'

All his suspicions were awakened, but although he demanded, 'Mama, what are you up to?' she refused to tell him.

5

THE party turned out to be not at all what anyone had expected, because Tasha, having decided that a mere dozen or so close family would not make of it the Memorable Occasion she had in mind, had expanded her invitation list to include a great many second cousins twice or thrice removed – most of them descendants of John Bell Britton the First via his nine daughters. They were no more than names to her, or indeed to Matt and Nick, but most of them were so surprised at receiving the invitation that they accepted.

As a result, when Jenny arrived at five o'clock on the Saturday afternoon, having driven down from London with Simon but without Howard – who, as so often, was in New York – she was astonished to find forty complete strangers partaking of tea in the music room.

By the cocktail hour the number had doubled, and Jenny, scanning the throng for a familiar face, found herself cornered instead by a commanding elderly lady who said, 'Wonderful old place, ain't it? That's the thing about England, of course. Nothing changes. Just look at the Continent these days! Vienna derelict, Berlin dull, Moscow a morgue, and Paris positively provincial. But we still have the Court, and the Season, and Ascot and Lord's. It's all a matter of keeping up standards, you know. Setting an example to the Empire.'

Jenny, trying to visualise Mr Gandhi having an example set to him by the debutantes at Queen Charlotte's Ball, murmured a distracted 'Yes', and excused herself to go in search of Simon, whom she found at the buffet with an unknown young woman, ecstatically arguing the case for Mr Olivier's Romeo as against Mr Gielgud's.

Simon had recently abandoned his monocle and grown a small fair moustache, which he thought made him look like Fredric March in 'Anna Karenina'. He was twenty-seven now, and a struggling barrister, and Jenny wondered whether he would ever grow up. Another ten years and the love of a good woman, perhaps . . .

In the end, she had supper with Allie and Bertha and Nick, but she couldn't go on avoiding Matt and Mims for ever, especially when she saw Beth talking to them and obviously in need of rescue.

After that foggy December evening five years ago, she had promised Beth that she would explain about Johnny when Beth was eighteen and old enough to understand, and she had kept her promise. But this was the first time that Beth had seen Matt since, and she was clearly tongue-tied.

It was the first time Jenny had seen Matt for much longer than that. For Johnny's sake, she had taken every possible precaution to avoid a meeting, and since he had been away a good deal she had succeeded. Not that it had made any difference to her feelings. Her heart, this evening, turned over as sharply at the sight of him as it had ever done.

He was looking amazingly well, radiating a vitality and leashed power that Jenny had always known to be there but were now on full view to the world. He looked like a man who not only knew where he was going but was well on the way to getting there. For so long, he had been just another wartime hero – a man of the past – but now, as the newspapers kept saying, he was one of the aeroplane industry's men of the future, someone to watch. He looked as if he knew it himself.

Jenny wished she didn't love him so much.

Approaching the little group, she tried to concentrate on her maternal pride in her sweet, pretty daughter, who was looking very appealing in a pale peach-coloured evening frock, with a flared, bias-cut skirt and deep fichu collar. Allie was training her to manage a new shop she would be opening soon, and she was so excited about it that Jenny couldn't have avoided knowing all about current fashion, even if she'd wanted to.

The new, clinging line, Beth had said, was wonderful if you had the figure for it. Jenny herself still had – or near enough, she thought wryly, as long as she took care to choose a heavy fabric like tonight's matt silk crêpe, made up in a fluid column of water green, with a matching velvet ruffle round the armholes in place of sleeves. As always, she found it irritating that Mims managed to look a million dollars in something that couldn't have cost more than three or four guineas.

Mims was monopolising the conversation on the subject of the MacRobertson Air Race to Australia the previous year, when Matt had taken her with him. 'We didn't expect to win, of course, but we got there and a lot of others didn't. It was really a proving flight for the BB 3, which isn't designed for high-speed, long-range flying, but . . .'

On and on she went, relentlessly vivacious, and Jenny's attention began to wander, even though she kept her gaze on Mims' face. It was safer than taking the risk of catching Matt's eye.

'. . . and Matt's already had orders for four planes, because it was a great advertisement. Jim Mollison and Amy Johnson had to drop out, they had so much engine trouble, but we had nothing like that at all.'

Jenny said, a touch sourly, 'Well, you had a good engineer, didn't you?' Tom Mackellar's defection still rankled, just a little.

It was a relief when Nick wielded the gavel his father had once used in his rôle of Justice of the Peace and announced that his mother wished to make a speech, and would everyone please take their glasses and go out into the hall.

Dutifully, everyone trooped out, and after a moment Natasha appeared and mounted a few steps of the staircase, then turned and gave everyone a spectacular smile before glancing at the papers in her hand.

'My dear friends,' she began, 'it is a great joy to me to have you all here tonight . . .'

She said all the right things with the greatest aplomb, tracing the history of the yard from its beginnings right up to the busy and successful wartime years and then dwelling lightly but with a sadness that was really quite touching on the depression that had persisted ever since.

'But although many other shipyards have gone under, ours has not, and although much of this has been due to the conscientious guidance of our cousin James McMurtrie, I am sure James will not mind my saying how much we all owe to the widow of my elder stepson, our dearest Jenny, now Mrs Fournier.'

Every head turned, following the direction of Natasha's gaze, and Jenny found herself blushing.

'Goodness gracious,' she murmured, quite overcome, and made the mistake of glancing at Matt, to find him laughing at her as warmly as if there had never been anything wrong between them. The blue of his eyes was as deep as ever, and his smile so brilliant that she felt dizzy, and her knees turned to water. It was fortunate that the years had taught her, at last, how to disguise her feelings.

Natasha resumed. 'And now to another matter. The world is changing, and I believe that we must change with it, adapting ourselves to what *is*, rather than what *was*.'

Jenny was conscious of Nick materialising at her side, and of Matt murmuring, 'Where did she get all this homespun philosophy? What's come over her?'

Nick chuckled, 'Your guess is as good as mine. Though I wouldn't have you think this is all her own work. She and dear old Granby were closeted together all day yesterday deciding what she was going to say, and by the sound of it, he won!'

'Oh, dear,' said Jenny mournfully. 'Here was I flattering myself that she had at last seen the light about my services to the yard, and it turns out to be only Granby being polite.'

'. . . and so, while we are here to celebrate the shipyard that still remains in the family after a hundred years, we are here also to say farewell to the house which has been the home of the family for the last sixty-five of those years . . .'

Still smiling as if butter wouldn't melt in her mouth, Natasha went on, '. . . because, believing as I do that it is out of tune with the times to continue living in a house designed for the more spacious, and sadly lamented days of the Victorian and Edwardian eras, I have decided that Provost Charters should be sold.'

'*Bloody hell!*' Nick hissed.

6

IT WAS quite funny if you weren't involved. As soon as the applause had died down and everyone began to drift away, Matt and Nick formed up on either side of Natasha and, like tall military policemen taking a rather small malefactor into custody, marched her off towards the library. They were pursued by Mims, but not by Jenny, who felt it was none of her business. Even so, she looked after them wistfully. It went against the grain not to be there when someone was telling Natasha a few home truths.

Inside the library, Nick and Matt exploded simultaneously, but where Nick was incoherent, Matt was very much to the point.

'If there is one thing you are not doing, my dear Natasha, it is selling Provost Charters! You can wipe that idea from your mind right now. You know perfectly well that the place must come to me or Nick in the long run, and even if you want to be rid of it, you have no right to sell it. And you're not going to.'

'Do not talk to me in that way! I will sell it if I wish. Paul left it to me!'

459

Nick said, 'But he can never have dreamed you'd do anything as awful as sell it! Just because you're bored with it, because you're never here.'

Matt knew there must be more to it than that. Natasha's chin was in the air, her colour high, and her bosom heaving under the elegant black-and-white striped sequin jacket that disguised, but didn't quite conceal the increasing voluptuousness of the white-gowned form beneath. She was feeling guilty about something more than they knew, and hoping she wouldn't be found out.

'It's money, I presume?' She didn't answer, so he went on, 'But you don't have to go to extremes. For God's sake, just tell us, and we'll sort things out somehow. Selling the estate merely because you're short of cash is like cutting off your hand because you've broken a fingernail. Mind you, a little economy in future wouldn't be a bad idea.'

She sighed extravagantly. 'Do not talk to me about economy. It is a great waste of money! I have tried buying cheap frocks, but then I find I cannot possibly wear them, so I give them to the housekeeper and have to go and buy something else I *can* wear. In the end, it costs me more than it would have done if I had not been economical in the first place.'

'Yes, well. That wasn't quite the kind of economy I had in mind. How much do you need?'

'Oh, I don't need anything now. Not any more,' she assured him blithely. 'I think perhaps you do not perfectly understand. I have already sold the house, you see.'

Nick yelped, 'What?' and Matt said, 'Oh, God!' and then sat down and put his head in his hands. 'How far has it gone? Have you exchanged contracts?'

'How should I know? I do not understand these things. But it is all complete, so you have no need to worry about trying to raise money for me. Though it is very kind of you to think of it. Besides, I am glad to be rid of this horrid house. I have never liked it.'

With no real interest, Matt asked, 'Who have you sold it to? Some dreadful girls' school, I suppose, or someone who wants to turn it into a golf club?'

'Oh, no,' she said sunnily. 'I would never sell it to anyone like that. You should be proud of me, because I have really been quite clever . . .'

7

JENNY was saying irritably to James McMurtrie, 'Honestly, James, if you didn't drink so much tea you wouldn't have so much trouble with your digestion,' when Nick appeared at her side and took her arm in a grip that wasn't to be denied. His fair, handsome face was like thunder.

He didn't say a word as he propelled her, protesting vigorously under her breath, towards the library, releasing her only when they were inside and the door firmly closed.

'Well, really!' she said, considerably ruffled.

Matt was leaning on the lectern, looking at her as if she had let the side down rather badly, Nick was glowering, Mims looking accusing and Natasha brightly interested.

Jenny's conscience was perfectly clear, so she said in a tone of pained enquiry, 'What are you all looking at me like that for?'

Matt's brows were heavy over eyes that, in this light, had become as dark as sapphires. 'You must know. Perhaps you would like to explain?'

'Explain? Explain what?'

'Oh, come on, Jenny!' He was impatient now. 'I wouldn't have expected this of you.'

'What in the name of all that's wonderful are you talking about?'

'Didn't it occur to you to try and stop him? Or at least to warn us? You must know how much Provost Charters means to Nick and me.'

'I . . . What . . .'

He frowned. 'Are you trying to pretend you didn't know that Natasha has sold Provost Charters to Howard?'

Abruptly, Jenny sat down on the nearest chair.

The silence in the room was intensified by the drone of conversation from the drawingroom and the sound of the gramophone from next door, where some of the youngsters had rolled back the carpet for an impromptu dance. *Cheek to Cheek*. You couldn't get away from Irving Berlin these days. Jenny hoped Simon wasn't doing his famous impersonation of Fred Astaire.

She said, '*Howard?*' her voice rising half an octave on the second syllable.

'Did you really not know?' Matt asked, but Mims interrupted. 'Sure, she knew. Didn't you, Jenny? You resent Matt so much for stealing Tom MacKellar from your *darling* yard – that and other things! – that you're just *dying* to see him robbed of his birthright.'

Whereupon Nick interrupted to say that it wasn't Matt's birthright, it was his, and Natasha said it most certainly wasn't, and Jenny said she didn't believe a word of any of it, and Matt said surely she must have had some inkling, and Natasha said Howard would never have told Jenny anything because he was very clever, but that she, Natasha, was also very clever.

It took a while before anyone thought to ask Natasha how much Howard had paid her for Provost Charters, and even longer to extract an answer.

After a protracted silence, Nick repeated dazedly, '£400?'

After a further protracted silence, Matt said, 'Just about the going rate for a desirable little three-bedroomed, semi-detached, pseudo-Tudor residence in Wembley.'

Faintly, Jenny asked, 'Did that include the land?' Five hundred acres of the best farmland in Dorset.

'Of course.' Natasha was surprised. 'What would I want with the land if I do not have the house?'

'And the contents of the house?'

'Those, too, naturally. All the bad pictures, and the Victorian furniture, and the *dozens* of footstools covered in Jacobean tapestry done by Paul's mother! Did she spend all of her life with a needle in her hand, that woman?'

Matt lit a cigarette. 'No. Mims, nip out and grab some whisky and some glasses, will you? This is going to be a long night.'

8

SINCE 1927 and Paul's first stroke, Natasha had left all her affairs in Howard's hands. She had not curtailed her spending, nor had she given any thought to the effects of the Wall Street crash or the depression. Her income had continued to come in as usual, and she had assumed that Howard was being very clever. Paul had always said he was.

It took a good deal of cross-examination to elicit from her that Howard might perhaps have said something about the falling value of the family investments. But since he could not bear, he had also said, to think of Natasha being anything less than her exquisite and expensive self, he would personally make up the difference and Natasha could repay him when the trust was finally wound up. Things were bound to improve soon.

'Did you sign anything?' Matt asked.

She shrugged. 'I do not remember. I sign so many things that I do not read. Paper, paper, paper!'

By nature sanguine, she had chosen to think – when she thought about it at all – that the difference between the true return on the trust's investments and the income cheques paid quarterly to her bank must be matter of only a few hundred pounds, if that. So it had been a severe shock when, a few months before, Howard had revealed to her that the total to date was close on £80,000.

'How could I have known,' Natasha demanded, 'that the investments were bringing in nothing, and that *everything* I spent was on loan from Howard?'

Matt said, 'He must have warned you,' but Natasha denied it absolutely.

After a moment's hesitation, Jenny intervened. 'He did, once, though not very strongly. I was there.' She could hear him now, and still couldn't make up her mind whether he had been deliberately underplaying it, or whether it was just Howard being Howard. The latter, she thought.

Natasha glared at her. 'If he said anything, he said it in such a way that it did not seem to matter!'

When the moment of truth came, he hadn't demanded to be repaid, though he had said it was a trifle inconvenient to be short of such a sum. But he had remarked that, from Natasha's point of view, and Nick's, and Matt's, repaying him when the trust was wound up would make a rather large hole in the capital realised.

'I did not wish,' Natasha explained reasonably, 'to be left a pauper next year, with nothing but a large house which I have always disliked. So when he suggested that he might be prepared to accept Provost Charters from me in exchange for what I owed him, it seemed the solution to all our problems. When the figures were balanced out, I even made a profit.'

'Of £400.'

'Yes. Well, £400 is not to be sneered at! And when the trust is wound up, Matt and Nick will profit as well because we will not need to repay anything out of it. So I *have* been quite clever, you see.'

Everyone was too familiar with Natasha's idea of logic even to react. Matt remembered once, in his youth, going shopping with her, when she had decided not to buy five hundred guineas'-worth of fur cloak she most certainly didn't need and, having thus saved five hundred guineas, had felt perfectly justified in spending it on something else she needed even less.

Mims, whose grip on matters of finance was, in its way, no more orthodox than Natasha's, said warmly, 'I think you've done swell.'

'I see it hasn't occurred to you,' Matt said, 'that investments which aren't producing any income are unlikely to produce much in the way of capital when they're realised.' He waited for it to sink in, and then went on thoughtfully, 'I am beginning to suspect that we may all be in for a nasty shock when the trust is wound up. What a pity it didn't occur to you to question your income cheques a long time ago, Tash!'

9

BY three in the morning, everyone, even the youngest of the cousins, had either departed or retired to one of Provost Charters' guest bedrooms.

Only Matt and Nick remained up, sitting by the fire in the library wondering if it was possible to salvage anything from the wreck.

'We need a good lawyer,' Nick said, but Matt shook his head. 'Try, if you like, but I should be very surprised if Howard has done anything illegal.'

'Maybe he'd sell it back to us.'

'If you can raise £80,000,' his brother told him cordially, 'go ahead. I certainly can't. And frankly, I'm more concerned now about the trust than Provost Charters, because if most of the capital's gone down the drain, you and Tash will be in real trouble.'

'You, too.'

'Me? No. I've never let myself count on it. When I came back from the war, dad made it very clear that my future depended on me, and me alone, and I've gone on that assumption ever since. I don't need the money, even if it would be nice to have. With Gannet Charter still chugging along, I can manage, and the planes we've designed and built are beginning to look like a very commercial proposition. In that sense the future's bright. I, at least, know where I'm going.

But you? Really, Nick, didn't it ever occur to you to wonder where the money for your butterfly existence was coming from?'

'Why should it? Mother gave me a decent allowance and said dad had always wanted me to have a few years' fun. He said you'd been robbed of your youth by the war, and it hadn't done you any good . . .'

'Thank you very much.'

'Don't mention it. And I was to have time to find my feet in the world, without being rushed.'

'Lucky you. And now you've got no home, no income, no future as a gentleman farmer, and perhaps no capital next year, either.'

Nick stared at him. 'God, *what am I going to do?*'

'Might I suggest you throttle your mother, for a start?'

'Yes,' Nick said gloomily, and then, trying to look on the bright side, went on, 'Though I suppose it could be worse. Just. At least we've still got the London flat. Oh, God! We *have* still got the flat, haven't we? She hasn't sold that as well?'

Matt grinned. 'Relax. And you've still got her shareholding in the shipyard, for what it's worth.'

'You know, I don't think I'm ever going to feel safe about anything again.'

With absent curiosity, Matt asked, 'What had you been meaning to do with your life before all this happened? It's something I've never known.'

'Neither have I.' Nick shrugged. 'When dad died I felt as if I was left dangling. There'd been no future laid down for me, and it didn't help not knowing whether Provost Charters would come to me or you in the end. I suppose, in a way, I've been delaying facing up to my uncertain fate by refusing to confront it. Do you know what I mean?'

'I think so.'

'And, of course, once you make decisions you're forging chains that tie you down for the rest of your life.'

'But if Provost Charters had been left to you, you'd have settled down quite happily to farm it and never even thought of "chains"?'

'Yes. You may not believe this, but that exhibition of temperament, the night after dad's Will was read, wasn't just an adolescent demand for something I couldn't have. I've always been happy here, for as far back as I can remember. I've always felt I belonged. Me to it, and it to me.'

'Whereas I associate it with a gruesome childhood and have rarely been back since. Yes, I take your point. But we could have worked something out, you know.'

'Could have? Oh well, it's all past tense now. I suppose I'd better start trying to think up some way of earning a lot of money in a hurry.'

'You don't have to *earn* money,' Matt said, sleepily sardonic. 'If you were a really enterprising young man, you'd marry it.'

'*Don't!*'

Nick's distress was so real that Matt found himself wide awake again. 'Touched a nerve, have I?'

Nick slopped the last of the whisky from the decanter into his glass and took a long swallow. Then, in tones throbbing with heartbreak, he confessed, 'Matt, I'm in love!'

He was sufficiently like his mother to be offended when Matt didn't clap a hand to his forehead and cry, '*Catastrophe! Horreur!*'

'Oh, dear,' Matt said.

'Her name's Francesca and she's only eighteen, and so sweet and shy, and I worship her. But her father despises me. He's abominably strait-laced and abominably rich and he calls me a drone, a lounge lizard – you name it! I even get my ears pinned back every time mother's name appears in the gossip columns.

'I've never had much hope, but now I've none, because I've nothing to offer her at all. If I were to propose, he'd think all I want is her money. And she probably would, too.

'What the hell am I going to do?'

10

'AND I think it was most improper of you,' Jenny said.

She could say things like that to Howard now, and get away with them, as long as she spoke calmly. She could even show she was annoyed.

'And I don't see why you couldn't have told me. It made me feel pretty silly.'

He wasn't giving her his full attention, but there was nothing unusual about that. He had a knack of conveying that there were very few people worthy of his undivided attention.

On this occasion, he was jotting down some notes for a broadcast he had been asked to make. Even the BBC now recognised him as a world authority on Egyptian antiquities, despite the fact that he'd never dug up an artefact in his life. But he was so familiar with his subject, and had such a good memory and eye for comparative detail, that his judgement of quality and provenance seemed to be almost infallible. Etienne Durand said that, especially with American buyers, Howard's opinion on the authenticity and probable value of an object were very often the deciding factor in a sale.

Jenny sometimes thought it was *so* like Howard to be interested in nothing but accountancy and antiquities. Dead figures, and relics of the long dead past. What a chilly mortal he was, under that benign overlay!

'If I had told you,' he said, 'it wouldn't have been such a delightful surprise.'

'Delightful!'

'Come now, Jenny, my dear. I have never yet met a woman who does not yearn to preside over a large country house. And Provost Charters does have a certain sentimental attraction.'

'*For whom?*'

His only response was an absent smile.

Doggedly, she persisted, 'Couldn't you have prevented Natasha from running into such shocking debt?'

He smiled again. 'Am I my uncle's widow's keeper? I warned her, and she is an adult, and of sound mind. Or so one supposes, although I have never seen much sign of it. In fact, she has always seemed to me a remarkably silly woman.'

Jenny was so much in accord with this sentiment that she would have abandoned the whole subject if it hadn't been for Nick. 'Yes, but Nick is terribly upset. And Matt,' she added without thinking.

'You expect me to shed tears for Matthew? I have very little sympathy with either of them. If they had been upset rather earlier in the day, the situation need never have arisen.'

'Really, Howard! How could they possibly have guessed that you were setting up in business as a moneylender!'

'Are you impugning my integrity?'

'Don't be silly. Of course not.'

'*What* a relief. And now, my dear, if you don't mind . . .'

She gave up and went off to see how Johnny was getting on with his homework.

11

THE rumours of rearmament began early in 1936. It was all very nebulous. No one really knew anything, but everyone whispered. When Sir James Lithgow, now as towering a figure on the Clyde as William Beardmore had been a generation earlier, acquired a controlling interest in what was left of Beardmore's, it fuelled the gossip, because one of the things Parkhead Forge knew how to do was produce armourplate. There was talk of small gun manufacture, too.

No one liked the word 'rearmament', but everyone was desperate for the work the actuality would bring. After fifteen years of bad times, of layoffs and means tests and hunger marches, it was easy to rationalise the arguments in favour of restoring the navy to what it had been and ought to be. *Rule, Britannia! Britannia rule the waves!*

The whole of the Clyde hung, breathless, on what would happen when the restrictive naval treaties expired at the end of 1936; waited and prayed that rumour would be translated into reality. But with the end of the depression reputedly in sight, a spark of hope had been kindled that made the starveling present even harder to bear.

To survive until the time came was all that mattered, and the Britton yard hung on grimly with everyone else.

But then something happened that, for Brittons', threatened an end before the new beginning could come about. The Dominie Line failed to honour a bill for £100,000, and it wasn't just a matter of money; it left the yard wide open to takeover. The same thing had happened to Fairfield's little over two years earlier, and Lithgows had stepped in, paying the claim of the billholders and securing the whole Bank of Scotland overdraft; which was how Fairfield's had become part of the Lithgow group.

Cash, cash, cash. The word began to haunt Jenny's dreams. By July, there was only one hope she could see, and it was lucky that Howard was about to leave, yet again, for New York, otherwise he would certainly stop her.

Matt phoned her at the office one day, out of the blue. 'I know you've been having a hard time, and I just thought . . . Well, there are some pretty solid rumours going round the aircraft industry that rearmament's on the way, and I thought it might cheer you up a bit, if you hadn't already heard.'

She was very much touched, and exclaimed, 'Oh, Matt . . .' before she had time to stop herself. But then she went on briskly, 'Yes, I had heard, thank you. I wish it would hurry up. We've yet another crisis on our hands, and I'm going to have to go off to Barcelona to see if I can sort it out.'

'Barcelona?' he repeated sharply.

'Yes. We've had a substantial enquiry from some brokers there, and if I can arrange a repairs contract with a cash advance, we might just be able to save our skin.'

'*No*, Jenny. Find some other answer. The political situation in Spain's getting nastier by the hour, and you might get caught up in something.'

She sighed, 'I know. But I'll have to risk it. James couldn't be trusted to go, even if he were prepared to, so there doesn't seem to be any alternative. I'll only be there for three or four days.'

'When are you going?'

'Next week. I'm leaving on the seventeenth.'

Four

1

SEÑOR Brocar said, 'Your figures have been most helpful, señora, and we will talk again when I have had the opportunity to study them more closely.'

The telephone rang, and Jenny graciously indicated that he might answer it, then waited, grateful for the brief respite. It was early evening, but still appallingly hot in the shipping office down by the Barcelona docks; even the sunlight striking through the slatted blinds seemed dusty and metallic, making her feel thirstier and more headachy than she already was. She would have given a great deal for a nice cup of tea, rather than the sherry which the señor seemed to consider a viable substitute.

'*Si!*' he said into the telephone for the third time, and then '*Bueno!*' a couple of times, and finally, '*Adiós!*' Jenny wondered whether it was the same man at the other end as it had been earlier on, or whether the señor's conversations were always so laconic.

When he hung up this time, however, he directed a rapid fire of Spanish at his assistant, who listened with an air of the most intense interest, then smiled at Jenny's carefully incurious expression and said, 'A little political trouble in the south, a few coups in the name of *el fascismo*. Every hour, on the hour! Seville first. Then Cadiz at four, Malaga at five, and Cordova at six. But nothing to concern you, my dear señora.' He waved an arm towards the square outside, flanked by the Atarazanas Barracks and the Divisional Headquarters of the military. 'We will have no trouble here.'

Jenny didn't quite know how to take that. From what she had read in the newspapers, it was the army that was most likely to indulge in political coups against the Popular Front government. So, who did Señor Brocar mean by 'we'? She smiled non-committally.

'But to return to business,' he said. 'I have no doubt we will be able to reach some accommodation. Perhaps I may telephone you at the Bristol? In the meantime, please enjoy your stay in our beautiful city. It saddens me that my own engagements prevent me from offering you my escort, but that is life, is it not? I would recommend, by the way, that you avoid the Barrio Chino, but you will enjoy the Barrio Gótico. And this evening you must sit at a café

470

under the trees of Las Ramblas and admire the passing scene.' He brushed her hand, pricklishly, with his moustache.

'Thank you, I will,' she said, as if she meant it. The opening ceremony of the People's Olympiad was scheduled for the following afternoon and the city was chock-a-block with athletes and spectators who wished they were athletes. Jenny could think of few things more exhausting than sitting watching them all striding vigorously up and down the boulevard. Nor, as a lone woman, was there much peace to be had at a café table.

She said, 'And I have been told that tomorrow, I must visit the Sagrada Familia.'

2

As it turned out, she was never to see the bizarre, wind-tunnelled spires of Gaudi's unfinished masterpiece, because next morning she was roused in the hot bright dawn by what she thought, at first, was one of her recurring nightmares of the Somme.

It was several moments before she was sufficiently awake to recognise that the gunfire was real, and not very far away, and that, although she didn't know it yet, the Spanish Civil War had broken out.

Her hotel, as it happened, was in the Plaza Cataluña, which was in the very heart of the city, and strategically important. More than that, it also formed part of the building that housed the two vital objectives of all rebels, everywhere, in the modern world, the central telephone exchange and the radio station.

That was why, even as, no more than half awake, she pulled on her dressing-gown and threw back the shutters to look out of the window, the plaza was already filling with armed men, some of them in khaki green, others in working clothes, all of them emerging at a run from the side streets; and why, by the time she had tied her sash and pushed the tumbled hair out of her eyes, there was a full-scale battle in progress.

Neither at the time, nor afterwards, was she able to make head or tail of what happened that day, because although the people on the ground knew who was fighting whom, no one else did. Uniform was shooting down uniform and civilian, civilian, with no visible regard for logic. The army was involved, and the Guarda Civil and the

Shock Police; Communists, anarchists and the militia; Falangists, Carlists and Fascists; and anyone else who happened to be passing.

Jenny, accustomed to the idea that the army and police were always on the side of law and order and orthodoxy, found it difficult to rid herself of it even though she knew that, in Spain, the army was right-wing and the government left, so it must be an army rebellion.

After a time, she was able to work out that, while the officers knew they were in revolt against the elected government, most of their men didn't. It was the only explanation for the sudden lull, and the flag of truce, and the shouting back and forth and the subsequent conference; the only explanation of why a great body of soldiers then turned their backs on their officers and walked over to join the men they'd been trying to kill a few minutes before. But it wasn't an end to the battle. Almost at once, amid wild cheering, the new allies turned and launched a concerted attack on the officers and their civilian auxiliaries, yelling some kind of slogan at the pitch of their voices.

It was very nasty. Jenny had never seen a real battle before, although she had seen the aftermath of several, but she knew that most British and German soldiers in the Great War hadn't really hated each other, or not individually. This was quite different. Even from where she stood, high above what was happening, she could sense the bitter personal animosity and the blood lust.

It went on for fourteen interminable hours. At some point during those hours, Jenny thought she'd better dress and got into her cotton travelling suit, which seemed the most practical. At some later point she ventured out into the corridor, wondering what had happened to the other hotel guests, of whom there were a hundred at least. Some she found hiding in cupboards or under beds, but most were cowering in the rooms at the back. They were well supplied with bread and cheese, olives and wine, and she was grateful for something to eat, but she couldn't stay there, not knowing what was going on. So she went back to her room.

From the fourth floor it was like watching some old silent film, with shouts and screams instead of a jingling piano. A young army officer, making a lone stand by the fountain, was beaten to the ground, bleeding and trying to protect his head with his hands while he was kicked and struck at with rifle butts. Boys of no more than sixteen or seventeen, armed with ancient carbines, lurked in ambush behind trees, emerging only to shoot. In one corner of the square someone had set up a machine-gun. There were charges and counter-charges, with the telephone exchange as the main objective. Neither side was taking prisoners. Raised hands and white handkerchiefs were no specific against the pistol or the bayonet.

Sickened, Jenny sank down onto her bed and tried to stop her ears against the madness. It must come to an end some time, she thought, but when it did – what then?

At some time after six, the anti-army faction turned a cannon on the Hotel Colon across the Plaza and the last of its defenders surrendered. Suddenly everything was quiet, with nothing but an occasional burst of shooting, not very serious, in the streets leading off the square. Jenny thought it must mean that the government had won, in Barcelona at least. But for how long? And what was happening in other parts of the country?

She went to the window and looked out at the detritus of the battle, the bodies, the rubble, the discarded weapons, the slinking cats. What now? Did everything go back to normal? And what of Señor Brocar, whom she had come to Barcelona to see? Who was probably a Fascist and possibly dead. What should she – or could she – do?

3

IT WAS almost dark and she had just turned away from the window when something smacked into the glass within inches of her back.

By some miracle the first of the bullets missed her, although she felt the draught of its passing, and she was already diving down and sideways by the time the others followed.

It wasn't someone firing casually, at random, someone euphoric in the aftermath of battle. It was calculated and deliberate.

She lay on the floor in the corner of the room for a full fifteen minutes, while bullets spat through the glass one after the other, making a series of neat little holes with rays spreading out like amateur drawings of a diamond. The firing seemed to be coming from a roof across the square, and she didn't dare try inching towards the door, because she had no way of guessing how much of the room was within the sniper's line of vision. Only when it was fully dark might it be worth the risk.

She lay and listened to the bullets striking the walls, smashing ornaments and pictures, biting into the furniture. Once or twice

473

she was sprayed with plaster, and a sliver of mirror flew through the air and embedded itself in the back of her hand. Picking it out and sucking the wound and tying her handkerchief round it helped to distract her mind from the shooting.

When it stopped at last, she had no feeling of relief or safety. For ten minutes she stayed in her corner and then, bracing herself, jumped to her feet and made a run for the door.

But even as she opened it, half a dozen ruffians erupted out of the lift and came rushing towards her, waving pistols and bayonets and shouting their idiotic heads off.

It was really too much! Unless the god of coincidence was working overtime, these thugs were related to the bullets – and they frightened Jenny a whole lot less. Indeed, if they had but known it, they underwent a brisk transformation in her eyes from a squad of murderous Latins into a bunch of over-excited Celtic followers homing in on a lone Rangers supporter. And that was a situation that Jenny Jardine, daughter of the Clyde, was competent to handle any day.

With a sigh of purest exasperation, she planted her hands on her hips and said in English and with great clarity, 'And what, may I ask, is all this fuss about? Perhaps you would be good enough to tell me what you think you are doing, firing on someone who carries a British passport!'

Fortunately, Spaniards were great talkers and these ones were more than happy to argue the toss before getting down to serious business. Skidding to a halt, they treated her to a tirade of which she understood not one word.

She said so. 'But what *you* must understand is that there are American and British warships in Barcelona harbour which will give very short shrift indeed to anyone who harms their nationals.'

'*Ay!*' screeched the man at the head of the group. '*Americana? Si?*'

'Certainly not,' Jenny replied coldly, and was irritated to find that she didn't know the word for 'Scots'.

'*Inglésa,*' she said.

She was just wondering where to go from there when, with devout thankfulness, she spotted one of the reception clerks peering round the corner of the stairwell. Imperiously, she summoned him. 'Ask these men what they mean by firing into my room. I might easily have been killed.'

After much shouting and gesticulating, it transpired that some-one had fired out of a fourth-floor window of the hotel at some

474

passing members of the Guarda Civil, so that retribution had been called for.

Jenny, well into her stride by now, laughed scornfully and asked if they thought that she, *she*, a law-abiding British subject, was the kind of person who would stoop so low as to take potshots at the constabulary? Then, with a dramatic gesture, she invited them to search her room and tell her if they found any evidence of firearms, recommending them also to count the number of holes in the window, made by their bullets, any one of which might have pierced her to the heart!

There was no doubt about it, melodrama was catching.

They did search, quite thoroughly, and then, finding nothing, moved on without apology to the next room and the next, kicking open the doors with what Jenny regarded as quite unnecessary violence. Fortunately, all the other guests had made themselves scarce.

Once she was quite sure that they had lost interest in her, she retired into her battered refuge, closed the door, and sat down on her bed, feeling sick from reaction, hunger, and exhaustion. There was something digging into her, and it turned out to be a spent bullet, which didn't make her feel any better.

She heard the searchers pass on their way back to the lift. There had been no renewal of violence, so presumably they hadn't found anything.

What on earth was she going to do? Wait until tomorrow, and then try to get in touch with Señor Brocar and/or the British Consul? *Were* there any British warships in the harbour? She couldn't believe that everything was going to be back to normal in a few short hours.

There was a very gentle tap on the door.

It was so near, so intimate, and so unexpected that she jumped a foot in the air.

Her voice quavering, she said, 'Who's there?' but no one answered and it took a considerable effort of will to go over, and turn the handle and open the door a slit.

The lights hadn't come on, and all she could see was the outline of a tall figure, clad in the Spanish labourer's ordinary garb of dark trousers and light shirt, open at the neck and with the sleeves rolled up to the elbow.

4

THE figure chuckled and said, 'The US Cavalry to the rescue. Jenny, love, you were born to be a memsahib. Talk about putting the natives in their place! Can I come in?'

'Oh, Matt. Oh, *Matt!*'

'Just passing. Thought you might need me,' he said, and then kissed her very, very thoroughly.

After a while it became necessary to draw breath, though it seemed a pity. Jenny said, 'What are you doing here?'

'Can we sit down? Well, the BB 3a just happened to be due for a test flight, and I just happened to point her in the direction of the Med. And then I was tuned in to French wireless and I caught the news about yesterday's doings in the south, and I just happened to think you'd be well out of it. So here I am. I was lurking behind your reception clerk on the stairs just now, but I thought I'd better lie low until our friends had departed.'

'How did you know where I was staying?'

He opened his mouth and she guessed what he was going to say, so she added her voice to his and they said in unison, 'I just happened to ring your secretary at the yard.'

She loved him so much. 'You were worried about me?'

'You could put it like that. How are you on a bicycle?'

'What?'

'My dearest idiot, I haven't got the plane parked outside, you know. I landed a minute or two before dark in a field beyond the western suburbs. It's miles too far to walk, and my impression is that all cars are being shot at because only Fascists and the *bourgeoisie* can afford them . . .'

'Oh, well, we'd better not have a car then! I wouldn't want Natasha to say I was dragging you down to my level!'

He kissed her again. 'So I swiped a couple of lonely looking bicycles.'

'But I have to stay and see Señor Brocar . . .'

'No, you haven't. If you think it's going to be business as usual tomorrow morning, I can assure you it isn't. The trouble isn't over. In fact, I'd be prepared to bet it's only just started. No.

476

We are going, and we are going now, before some thieving bastard finds my plane.'

'All right,' she said obediently. 'Just let me comb my hair and pay a visit.' It always struck her as very silly, at the pictures, when the heroine went rushing off on some great adventure without having enough sense to go the 'Ladies' first.

She was about to put her hat on when he stopped her. 'A scarf, if you've got one; hats and ties are out of fashion. No, better still, take that shawl that's pretending it's an antimacassar, and shove anything you need in a pillowcase. I'll carry it over my shoulder.'

'Ready?' he asked a few minutes later. 'Good girl! Then let's go.'

5

IT was an eerie, gruesome, horrid ride to where Matt had left the plane, and Jenny knew that she could never have done it on her own.

Matt, who seemed to have an unerring sense of direction, took them through streets that were pitch dark and empty of life, avoiding any where there was a hint of sound or movement. There were still sporadic outbursts of firing, but at a distance.

Even so, on several occasions they heard parties approaching on foot, raucous and argumentative and staggering a bit, and Matt had to drag Jenny hurriedly into some side alley where they could plaster themselves and their bicycles against a wall out of sight. They had to take cover, too, from the armed patrols racing the city from end to end in requisitioned cars, careering round corners, the men crammed inside them leaning out of the windows shouting and loosing off their rifles indiscriminately into the air. 'Christ!' Matt murmured. 'Their driving's more dangerous than their guns.'

They had been on the road for what seemed a very long time, and Jenny's unused calf muscles were aching abominably, when he said, 'This is hopeless. We'll have to find somewhere to lie low for a couple of hours until they've run out of steam.' So they sat, silent and half-dozing, in a deserted courtyard until after midnight.

Then they mounted their ancient bicycles again and began pedalling through the blackness that was full of obstacles – makeshift barricades, rubble, dead mules and dead humans. In the doorway of a convent where a single candle guttered lay the bodies of two boys, with their throats cut from ear to ear. Everywhere there was the smell of cordite and blood and burning. hanging like a miasma over the city.

It was two o'clock when at last they reached the plane, to find it intact and peacefully waiting. Jenny could sense Matt's almost overpowering relief and thought it was partly because they had survived the journey, and partly because he had been worried about his valuable prototype.

There was, indeed, something of both in it, but his main feeling was gratitude that now he was in control of the situation again.

'Stay here,' he whispered, and vanished into the dark.

After he had landed the previous evening and while there was still a trace of light, he had paced everything out and noted the configuration of the ground. Now, placing one foot precisely in front of and dead in line with the other, he paced the full length of his runway again. He had to be sure that no one of evil intent had tossed up a barricade that hadn't been there before.

Jenny jumped like a startled hare when he reappeared and murmured, 'In you get. No sense in hanging around. Sorry she isn't a nice, luxurious Handley-Page but she'll get us where we're going a lot faster.'

It hadn't occurred to her that he intended to take off blind, in pitch darkness, from a field of rough pasture. 'You mean we're going *now?*'

'I do. It's a pity there isn't more wind, but this little lady has plenty of power for a short take-off. Also, I have good night vision and some of the new blind flying instruments. If we wait till dawn, we might find ourselves getting shot at before we're out of range.'

She trusted him completely, even though she only opened her eyes when she knew they had left the ground, which happened a great deal sooner than she had expected. It was the strangest sensation to soar smartly heavenward at something like forty-five degrees, when you were used to staying earthbound for so long that you thought the plane had changed its mind and decided to go by road. 'Heavens!' she exclaimed. 'Can we go back, please? You've left my stomach behind.'

He held out a hand for hers, and kissed it briefly. 'Know something? I love you.'

'Me, too,' she said, with a sublime disregard for grammar. 'Where are we going?'

He grinned. 'How do you fancy breakfast in Provence?'

6

THEY flew in over the lagoons of the Camargue soon after dawn, when the light was milky and the edges of the brown waters were fringed and scalloped with foam, like cooling *cappucino*. Scattered amid the summer-grey vegetation below, they could see the moving figures of black bulls and white horses, and there were flamingoes skimming the water, white and jet and rose-pink.

Matt said, 'Tired?'

'A bit. And ravenous.'

'Not long now.'

She had the map on her knees. 'Where are we going? Arles?'

'Nothing so commonplace. Wait and see.'

They landed in a field at the base of a sheer limestone cliff face, blindingly white against the blue. The air was heavy with lavender and herbs.

When the plane had come to rest Matt pointed upwards and said, 'Breakfast up there.'

'No, really, Matt! It must be a thousand feet up! You can't be serious.'

'Nine hundred. But don't worry. I know a man.' He waved, and she turned and saw a man on a motorbicycle coming towards them along a narrow, winding track.

It was Matt's wartime friend, Jacques Le Long, who had been expecting them and was quite *enchanté* to meet madame.

'Indeed?' Jenny said and, eyeing Matt severely, congratulated him on his foresight.

Then they squeezed onto the back of the motorbicycle and went roaring up the hill to the fortress village of Les Baux-de-Provence.

7

THEY had *oeufs en cocotte* for breakfast, and croissants, and apricot jam, and coffee in cups as big as bowls. And they had it in a garden full of the morning sun, fragrant with peach, fig and olive trees, and thyme, and roses; a garden perched over a vast sweep of landscape that stretched almost to the Mediterranean.

Afterwards, Matt kissed Jenny lightly and said, 'I ought to present myself at the *gendarmerie* and explain about the plane, but you need some rest. Madame *la patronne* will show you.'

It was a big, cool room overlooking the valley, and Jenny was so weary that, after she had nearly dozed off in the bath, she tumbled straight into the lovely big bed without even bothering to find her nightdress. She was asleep before she knew it.

It was dusk when, drowsily and with a delicious sense of well-being, she opened her eyes and saw the stars beginning to show through the open window and smelled the soft warm scents and thought, 'This is heaven.' And then a hand smoothed itself lightly down the length of her body, and she discovered that Matt was there beside her, and her whole being began to melt even before the stars were blotted out and his lips came down on hers, and there was nothing in the whole wide world that mattered, except the two of them.

The physical rapport between them was magical, something to which their brief hour together in Paris, almost ten years before, had been no more than a prelude. Now, it seemed that with every movement, every caress, every touch of hands and lips, they were able to sense and meet each other's needs, so that there was a wholeness, a perfection about their lovemaking that might have been the stuff of dreams.

She had no idea whether it was two hours or two days later when Matt moved teasingly inside her so that she moaned and moved her hips voluptuously and murmured, 'Yes, please'.

But he laughed, even though she felt him quiver in response, and said, 'It is more, much more than twelve hours since we had breakfast. Arise, love of my heart, and let us stay ourselves with flagons against the night that is to come. And stop trying to behave like a vamp in a B-movie, you wicked woman. Up!'

It took them a long time to dress, because every movement seemed to draw them back together again, but in the end they went downstairs for supper in the moonlit, magical garden, and drank a young, cool Rhône wine and ate something chickeny with so much garlic in it that Matt said they wouldn't dare go near anyone but each other for days, which was fine by him. And after that there was a salad, and then a wonderful flan of buttery pastry covered with thin slices of lemon that tasted like the pure, fresh essence of all the lemons that had ever been. And good coffee and cognac.

And then it was time to go back to bed.

8

IN THE morning, someone from the hotel was going to Marseilles and Matt arranged for a telegram to be sent home in Jenny's name, saying that she was fine, and there was no need to worry. It was the only acknowledgement either of them made of the problems that existed, and would continue to exist, and some day would have to be faced.

In the meantime, they dropped out of the world, not even straying from the village of Les Baux, but wandering round the extraordinary ruins of the mediaeval castle that had been built into the mountain itself, so that there were still alcoves imprinted into the rock face, and windows, and a long, wide balcony hanging over the edge of a nine-hundred-foot drop.

Jenny shuddered. 'Why am I dizzy when I look over there, and yet not when I'm in a plane?'

'Because there's something solid linking you to the ground. In the air, there isn't. Or that's the theory, anyway.'

He grinned as they moved away from the edge. 'And if you're wondering why I brought you here, it wasn't just because I fancied seeing you in Provençal costume!'

Since most of Jenny's clothes still reposed in Barcelona, she had been forced to replenish her wardrobe in Les Baux, which wasn't exactly a centre of couture. In her garish skirt and embroidered blouse she felt rather like a souvenir doll, slightly ridiculous but wonderfully light-hearted.

'Oh?' she said.

'Uh-uh. It's because this was where they held the Courts of Love in the thirteenth century, where the troubadours composed verses in honour of pure and high-born ladies. The prize was a kiss and a peacock's feather.'

'Thank you! But I'd be a terrible fraud as a pure and high-born lady, and you haven't written a single poem since 1918. Have you?'

'No.'

'I'm not even sure I could lay my hands on a peacock's feather, either. But as for a kiss . . .'

'I had a peacock's feather once,' he said reflectively. 'The night my grandfather told me that the high birth of the Brittons was pretty fraudulent, too. Quite shattered my faith in human nature.'

It was amazing how little they knew of each other, and how much, over the next three days, they learned, almost without being aware of it.

Madame *la patronne*, within whose whaleboned bosom beat a heart of *crème caramel*, observed them wistfully and wondered what they could possibly be finding to talk about. Most of her English guests simply sat silent, staring at the scenery or writing postcards, but these two? – it was as if they had a whole lifetime to catch up with.

The gentleman had stayed at Les Beaux before, on three occasions, alone and only for a day or two; to recharge his batteries, he had said with the smile that turned Madame's knees to water. She couldn't believe that the vitality beneath his armour of lazy nonchalance ever needed recharging, but preferred to think that here he found refreshment for his soul.

Such a very handsome man, with a style more European than English; and handsomer than ever now with the distinguished wings of grey beginning to show above his ears. She knew from his passport that he was forty years old; the perfect age for a man. The woman, two years younger, was good-looking rather than beautiful, but she too had distinction and her eyes were wide and humorous, her manner crisp and yet charming.

With a sentimental smile Madame watched as, wandering through the village, strolling through the gardens, talking intently over the supper table, the two of them tried to pretend that they were not new lovers. But they couldn't disguise the look in their eyes.

9

FOR three days, they existed only in and for each other, and by the end of them knew all that they would ever need to know. They belonged to each other completely, two halves of a whole.

Not until they were airborne again and following the Rhône north over the summer landscape did they return to the real world and ordinary things. And they talked conversationally, above the noise of the engine, as if the last days had never happened.

It was the only way, because they both knew that, in the world to which they were returning, nothing at all had changed.

Five

1

JENNY arrived home from London on the overnight train, braced – if Howard was back from New York – to make light of her escape from Barcelona and to avoid naming names. For once she was grateful that he was always too busy to listen to detail; indeed, she had sometimes thought that, if she came home one day with the Crown Jewels in her shopping bag, all he would have said was, 'How nice. They will go very well in the display cabinet in the drawingroom.'

But on this Saturday morning in late July, Howard was neither at home nor on the high seas. It seemed that Waring's had completed the refurbishment of Provost Charters ahead of schedule, and Howard was already moving in. Jenny was annoyed to discover that he had taken Johnny along.

Over breakfast, she glanced through the post and messages that had accumulated during her absence, and found that her secretary had telephoned three times the previous day. Would Mrs Fournier phone back urgently?

With a sigh, Jenny picked up her coffee cup and took it to the phone with her. 'Madge?'

'Oh, Mrs Fournier! Thank heavens you're back!' She sounded as if the end of the world had come.

'What's happened?'

'It's Mr McMurtrie! He's been *arrested*!'

The very idea was so impossible that it didn't make any impression on Jenny at all. She said, 'Oh, dear. Don't tell me he's contravened the Temperance Code?'

'I'm serious! He really has! Yesterday morning. And there's nobody at the office who has any idea what to do.'

Jenny sat down abruptly, and used her free hand to pour a liberal dose of caffeine down her throat. 'Start at the beginning, Madge, and take it gently. Remember, I'm an old lady and rather slow in the uptake.'

James hadn't just been haled off to the police station to explain away the fact that he'd walked out of a restaurant forgetting to pay the bill. He had been arrested good and properly. For fraud.

484

Jenny, with nightmare visions of the yard being involved in something like the Hatry or Kylsant scandals, asked faintly, 'what kind of fraud? Who else is involved?'

It was a relief, of sorts, when Madge said, 'You know that company he formed recently, the travel firm. Well, he's accused of issuing a false prospectus.'

At least it had nothing to do with the yard, or not directly. But fraud was a criminal offence and carried a prison sentence. Even if James was proved innocent in the end, Jenny knew that during the months to come the entire shipping world would think of Brittons' as having a managing director who was a crook. No smoke without fire. Jenny didn't think the yard could survive it.

Madge's voice said anxiously, 'Are you still there?'

'Yes. It's a nasty one, isn't it! But there's nothing we can do until we know more about it. Everything will just have to go on as usual, for the time being at least.'

'Do you think Mr Fournier might have some ideas?'

'Perhaps. I'll try and get in touch with him. In the meantime, don't lose sleep over it. Anything else urgent? All right. I'll see you on Monday.'

2

UNFORTUNATELY, the Provost Charters telephone had not been reconnected. Howard objected to having unsupervised workmen calling their brothers in Timbuktu at his expense.

Jenny sat, seething, thinking how extraordinary it was that Howard was always inaccessible when he was needed. You'd almost have thought it was deliberate! She hesitated about sending him a telegram asking him to phone her, but that would mean the village post office or the pub, and the matter was much too serious for that kind of conversation, even if she could rely on him giving her his full attention.

'Mrs Simons,' she called. 'I'm going to lie down for an hour or two, and then I have to go back to London.'

3

MATT and Nick finished piling Anthony Hope and Dornford Yates into the back of the van, in amongst the diabolos and yo-yos, the Meccano set and the Dinky toys, the model theatre and clockwork train, and all the other sentimental relics of their childhoods. Howard had sent most of the contents of Provost Charters to auction, but had held back a few things that he thought Matt and Nick might wish to keep. 'Decent of him,' Nick had said.

And then, a few days ago, Howard had announced that he'd be obliged if they could remove their belongings at their earliest convenience, because he needed the space.

Matt, surveying the contents of the van, said, 'I don't want any of this old junk, Nick. Do you?'

'No.'

'Then what the hell are we wasting time on it for? I've been away for more than a week and there are any number of other things I ought to be doing.'

'I wouldn't give Howard the satisfaction of throwing out what belongs to me!'

'So we're going to cart it all the way back to London and throw it out *there*?'

'Yes. Well, I don't know. I've always been fond of that train set.'

Matt said disgustedly, 'Come on. Let's go and see if he's got the decency to offer us a cup of coffee.'

Howard had had the wall between the morningroom and the library demolished to open up a large, L-shaped space with north and east lights. It was to be the gallery for his collection, and they found him there, surrounded by chests that looked as if they'd been constructed to protect their contents against anything short of a howitzer battery. He was engaged in unpacking one of them, and Nick waited hopefully for the Michelangelo 'David', but all that emerged was a succession of small, drab tomb figures representing bakers or brewers or something.

He said, 'Sure you wouldn't like us to leave you the toy theatre?'

Howard smiled. 'Simon, open that vitrine for me, and then see what you can do about some coffee. Johnny will help you.'

Matt caught his breath. He hadn't seen the boy – his son – in the corner of the room, sorting through a collection of cigarette cards. 'What have you got there? Cricketers? That's a good one of Larwood. D'you know, I saw the famous bodyline Test at Adelaide in '33?'

Johnny was nine years old and neither his dad nor Simon had the slightest interest in cricket. His eyes lit up. He'd only met his Uncle Matt a couple of times before, but he thought he was the most wonderful person on earth.

And then Howard's voice, well-modulated as always but with an unfamiliar edge to it, cut into the little scene. 'Johnny, go and help Simon.'

4

A CAR door slammed outside, but all they could see was that it was the station taxi.

And then Jenny marched in, stripping off her gloves and saying, 'Oh, there you are, Howard. Why in heaven's name haven't you had the phone connected? That's eighteen hours out of the last thirty-six I've spent on trains . . . Oh. Hello, Matt. Hello, Nick. What a surprise.'

Matt sensed rather than saw her eyes flicker as she took in the sight of himself and Johnny, side by side, and for the first time it occurred to him that, despite the difference in their colouring, there must be a resemblance between them. Instinctively, he moved away. Painful though it was, everyone believed Johnny to be Howard's son, and for Jenny's and the boy's sake they must not be disabused of that belief.

Jenny removed her smart little hat, which was Burgundy-coloured to match her frock and shaped like an upside-down wine goblet, and ran her fingers carefully through her hair. 'Perhaps it's just as well you're here,' she said. 'Nick, anyway. Because it concerns you, too.'

'What does?'

'Howard, James has been arrested.'

With care, Howard placed one of the little figures in the vitrine and said, 'Oh, good.'

5

JENNY, still pushing her hair back into shape, sighed with exasperation.

'Howard, you're not listening! I said, James has been arrested. James McMurtrie.'

'I heard you, my dear.' He moved the figurine to a more flattering angle and studied it critically. Then the door opened. 'Ah, here is Simon with the coffee. Fetch another cup, Simon.'

'Hiya, Jenny! Black or white?'

'Black if it's good, white if it isn't. Howard, did you *understand* what I said?' He was just being irritating, she knew. It had always been one of his favourite tricks, keeping people waiting for an explanation of his more gnomic utterances.

Johnny had come running to her side and she hugged him close to her as she said firmly, 'Howard, you cannot possibly mean, "Oh, good!" Even allowing for the fact that James isn't anyone's favourite person, you must see that it's a disaster for the yard!'

'Yes,' he said, and his smile suddenly curved so deeply that it reminded her of nothing so much as the peak of a schoolboy's cap.

A fleeting glance across the room showed Jenny that Matt and Nick were every bit as mystified as she was, and that she wasn't just being stupid.

Weakly, she asked, 'Don't you even want to know what he's been arrested *for*?'

'The fraudulent prospectus, I assume,' Howard replied, positioning a second little wooden baker beside the first.

Jenny was annoyed all over again. To have come dashing all the way down here at the cost of yet another night's sleep, only to find that Howard already knew about it!

'You mean you knew?'

He said, 'Of course. I helped him draft it.'

'You *what*?'

'Now it is you who are not listening, my dear.'

There was a single chair amid the sea of packing cases. Helplessly, Jenny sat down. 'I don't understand. The scandal will ruin us.

488

Howard, must you go on unwrapping those things? It's terribly distracting.'

And then Howard stopped playing with his toys, and straightened up to his full height, and, turning, rested his hands on the frame of the vitrine and said, 'Of course. That was the object of it.'

The world did a couple of reverse twirls and then stopped.

Jenny, utterly bewildered, said, 'You mean you *want* the yard to be ruined?'

Howard didn't reply but just stood there smiling his most maddening smile.

Glancing at Matt, Jenny saw that he was watching Howard with his gaze narrowed and the long, curling mouth she loved tightened into a thin, hard line. After a while, he said slowly, 'Of course, I am not in touch with what has been going on at the yard, but I know something of your business reputation, Howard. And I also remember what happened in – 1909, was it? I was surprised how forgiving you were about that. But to have carried on a private vendetta for almost thirty years? Surely not.'

Howard almost beamed at him. 'My dear cousin! It seems you do have some imagination, after all. Though I see you are not acquainted with the old Italian proverb that says, "Revenge is a dish which people of taste prefer to eat cold".'

Nick, his blue eyes snapping, demanded, 'What in hell's name are we all talking about?' Jenny had every sympathy with him.

'Yes,' she said politely, 'Nick and I are feeling left out.' Her heart was like a cold, heavy stone inside her.

Matt, his shoulders propped against the mantelpiece and his hands sunk deep in the pockets of his old flannel trousers, said, as if he were still working it all out, 'A quarter of a century ago, Howard's father committed suicide, and his mother, my Aunt Pearl, blamed *my* father for it. Then Aunt Pearl died a few years later, reputedly of a broken heart. Unless I miss my guess, Howard has spent all the intervening years revenging himself by trying to ruin our side of the family.'

'Not "trying to", dear boy,' Howard said. 'Succeeding. I valued my parents and your father took them from me. So I decided to take from your side of the family everything that *you* valued. Which is why I am here at Provost Charters now. Which is why that foolish man, James McMurtrie, is under arrest, ensuring that the yard cannot possibly survive. And which is why I am afraid you will find, when the trust is wound up later this year, that it realises very little.' He shook his head sadly. 'The stockmarket has not

489

been performing at all well; even the most conscientious trustees have come to grief.'

With sublime self-satisfaction, he glanced round his silent audience. 'As an intellectual exercise, I have found it all most enjoyable. I am really quite sorry it is over.'

6

NICK was sitting with his head in his hands, Simon wore a thoughtful frown, and Matt looked as if his mind was still racing.

Choosing her words with extreme care, Jenny said, 'Can we get this straight, Howard? You have spent all the years since you've been on the board trying to ruin the yard?' She didn't care about Provost Charters. She didn't care about the trust. But *her* yard!

'I have, despite your best efforts, my dear. You have really caused me quite a lot of unnecessary trouble.'

She couldn't wholly believe in this extraordinary madness. It seemed impossible that she should have lived with him for eleven years without knowing anything of it. 'You mean, when I was trying to stop the men coming out during the General Strike, and you put what I thought was an unintentional spoke in my wheel, that was deliberate?'

'Yes.'

'And when the bank wanted to foreclose in 1926, but James and I managed to persuade them against it? You can't have had anything to do with that. You were on a ship to New York at the time.'

'Wiser to be out of the way, in case I should be called on to save the situation. Which I would have been reluctant to do, since it was as a result of my private intervention that the bank felt it would be wiser to foreclose.'

'I see. It didn't worry you, of course, that it wasn't just the family who would suffer; that all the men would find themselves on the dole?'

He didn't even acknowledge the question, far less answer it, and her thoughts continued to fly on down the years. 'But why did you veto the NSS offer in 1932? Their whole object was to close the yard down.'

'True. But they would also have paid money for it, so that Paul's side of the family would have benefited, in however small a way. You must see that I couldn't have that. My objective was bankruptcy.'

Jenny found that many things were becoming clear. She took another deep, uneven breath. 'And all those times you forbade me to go off and see brokers, and look for business?'

He inclined his head. 'Even such small successes as you achieved helped to delay my plans.'

She knew then, with a sudden, cold, charity, that there was something else, something else that had always puzzled her a little, something that was not easy to accept as just another piece in this whole deceitful jigsaw.

She said, 'And of course you married me so as to be absolutely sure of knowing everything that was going on at the yard. I imagine you also assumed that I would follow any advice you chose to give, however bad.'

'In which I made an error,' he conceded. 'But you must not think that I failed to value your charming person.'

A small voice at Jenny's side said, 'Mummy, you're hurting me.'

She hadn't realised how tightly she had been clutching him. After a moment, she said quite naturally, 'I'm sorry, darling. Why don't you go and put some more cards in your album?'

7

MATT, aware of an almost overmastering desire to resort to physical violence, clenched his fists tightly in his pockets and asked coolly, 'Has Jenny covered everything?'

'Of course not.' Howard gestured to Simon to move the empty packing case away and bring another, as if, even in the moment of his triumph, he felt it needful to convey that ruining a great many lives, however satisfying, was only one of many other matters vying for his attention.

'Let me see, now. Yes. At the time of the Washington Conference in 1922, I had private information that there would be a moratorium on new capital ships, so I encouraged the board to raise a loan to finance investment that was, of course, wasted when the Admiralty orders failed to materialise.

'Push it over this way, Simon. Yes, that will do.' He glanced at the label. 'Good. The chisel, if you please.'

Then, with an artificial air of meditation, 'What else? Really, there was so much! I vetoed going to the stockmarket at a time when the yard would have had much to gain. I insisted on certain safeguards in estimating methods which ensured that Brittons' tenders were always high. I made the purchasing department observe stringent costing limits. I refused to purchase raw materials on several occasions when prices were unnaturally low and about to rise . . .'

It was small satisfaction to Jenny to remember that, believing her husband's ill-judged rulings on day-to-day matters to stem from his unfamiliarity with the functional details of shipbuilding, she herself had unobtrusively countermanded them.

He went on, 'There were a great many other such instances. I have always had an influence over McMurtrie, so that it was easy for me to curb any tendency on his part to take purposeful action.'

Then he bent over and began to pry open the new packing case.

Matt was bitterly angry with himself for having been too occupied with his own concerns – and particularly with the new aircraft factory – to follow up his faint, long-standing unease about Howard. Though even if he had, he suspected that he wouldn't have reached the right conclusion. He would have thought Howard constitutionally averse to unmaking, as distinct from making, money. Now, he said, 'But by destroying the yard, you are forfeiting a part of your own income, even if at the moment it happens to be an inconsiderable part.'

Howard laughed. 'Have you ever known an accountant go short?'

'No-o-o. Certainly not one who reaps rich rewards from helping American industrialists to buy up British companies so that they can get round tariff barriers. Not one who has so little feeling for his own country that, when it's still reeling from a war in which a million of its men died for the sake of a better world, he's ready to encourage outsiders to bring its whole trade and economy to ruin.' It was something Matt felt strongly about, because he couldn't help remembering the war years, and his friends dying in the trenches while the profiteers, safe at home, prospered and grew fat.

Howard didn't turn a hair. 'One must go where the profit is, dear boy. And I have other sources of income, of course.'

He gestured towards his display cases. 'You should realise that I have quite a reputation as an expert on this kind of thing. Indeed, you might say that what Berenson is to the art of the Italian Renaissance, I am to the art of dynastic Egypt.' His fat smile dawned. 'And what Berenson is to the art dealer Duveen, I am to Etienne Durand. I dare say you would be astounded at the monetary value

492

he and others place on my appraisal of such antiquities as happen to come on the market.'

Jenny was taken aback. It had never occurred to her that M. Durand, who had turned up at Pollokshields over the last ten years with the frequency of a recurring decimal, might actually be paying Howard for his authentications. She had always thought her husband gave M. Durand his opinion and advice out of pure vanity.

8

NICK'S chair scraped back.

He had been sitting silent throughout the conversation, his head swivelling back and forth as if he were a spectator at a Wimbledon final, his brain following everything that was being said, but his intellect refusing to grasp it.

Now, suddenly, the enormity of the whole thing reached him. Because of something that had happened before he was born, Howard had had the infernal cheek to pinch the family home, the family shipyard, and the family inheritance, leaving him, Nicholas Mikhail Britton, no better than a beggar.

His fair-skinned face scarlet and his blue eyes flashing, he burst out, 'What are we being so bloody civilised about? Why are we sitting around here talking – *talking* – as if all this was the most natural thing in the world? Howard's a thief and a fraud. He must have broken every law in the book! Why aren't we calling a lawyer or the police or someone?'

'No phone,' Simon pointed out helpfully.

Nick turned to Matt. 'He *must not* be allowed to get away with this!'

'No' Matt agreed. 'But I expect he has been very careful not to leave himself open to proceedings under the law.'

'How true,' murmured Howard as, with a loud crack, the lid of the packing case sprang open under his ministrations.

Wildly, Nick demanded, 'Why did none of us ever suspect him?'

'Because one does not,' Matt replied with deliberation, 'expect one's relatives to be crooks.'

Howard looked up, and for the first time in their acquaintance

493

Matt saw something in the brown, lizard-like eyes that might have been hatred.

After that, the situation deteriorated rapidly, because Nick took three long strides forward, reaching for Howard's throat and snarling something on the lines of, 'You may escape the law but you won't escape me!' while Simon leapt to the rescue, yelling, 'Take your hands off my father!' Whereupon Nick, diverted, paused to say, 'Father? I thought he was your second cousin or something!' and Simon shouted, 'Never mind that! Take your rotten hands off him!'

Howard, perfectly capable of defending himself against Nick who, though much the same height, was a good fifty pounds lighter, merely stood and looked superior, until Nick brushed Simon aside and Simon glanced round for some kind of weapon. It was singularly unfortunate that the only thing his eye lit on should have been an ancient Egyptian sceptre labelled 'From the tomb of Tutankhamen, Valley of the Kings', which didn't look much but had cost Howard a great deal of money.

As Simon snatched it out of the packing case with the very clear intention of breaking it over Nick's head, Howard let out a bellow that stopped them all dead in their tracks and then hurled Nick aside and, brandishing his foot-long chisel in an unpleasantly purposeful way, made a lunge at Simon who, turning pale, took to his heels and fled the room, still clutching the sceptre and with his father in the hottest of hot pursuit.

'Well, I never!' said Jenny in mild disapproval as, from the window, she watched the pair of them disappear down the drive at an Olympic sprint. 'You know, I don't think I've ever heard Howard so much as raise his voice before. Who would have thought he'd turn into a homicidal maniac? Perhaps I'd better go and make some more coffee.'

9

MATT and Nick were very ready to give Jenny a lift back to the station, and despite a protest from Howard, who had become quite himself again once he retrieved the sceptre from a quaking Simon, announced that she was taking Johnny back to Glasgow with her.

As soon as they were well out of range of Provost Charters, Matt began to look for a decent hotel where they could have lunch

494

and hold a council of war. The latter was Jenny's suggestion, and it turned out that, once Johnny had consented to be tucked up in one of the hotel bedrooms for an afternoon nap, she had a good deal to say.

The more she had thought about things the angrier she had become, until by the time they began to talk she was fizzing with rage.

'For goodness' sake, Nick,' she snapped, 'will you stop moaning, or at least stop moaning in clichés! "The loss of my inheritance" may sound all very fine, but what we need now is a bit less of such woolly thinking. We can't do anything about Provost Charters, and I imagine we can't do anything about the trust. But the yard is not dead yet, and I will *not* have Howard killing it.'

Matt had never before experienced his darling in her rôle as dynamic business woman. A trifle taken aback, he asked, 'Can we prevent it?'

'Whether we can or can't, *we are going to*! On the train down last night, I drafted a statement for the trade press making it quite clear that James's misdemeanours, if any, have nothing to do with the yard and that in any case, to the best of the board's belief, they relate to nothing more than a possible error in the notoriously difficult field of technical documentation. With luck, that should keep trouble at bay for long enough to allow us to tender for some of the rearmament contracts everyone's talking about. Fortunately, most people in the business know James well enough to realise that he hasn't enough gumption to be a proper criminal.'

Matt said, 'It's a start, certainly. But it doesn't let you off the hook about having your managing director in jail.'

'No, I know, and it would be bad tactics to sack him straight off. He can resign later on.' The unfortunate James thus disposed of, she went on, 'What we need is an Acting MD right now, and it can't be an outsider for obvious reasons. Nor, the world being what it is, can it be a woman.' She said it with some bitterness because, if she herself had had a free hand, she didn't think the yard would ever have got into its present state. 'So it has to be you, Nick. There's no one else.'

Nick turned white. 'For God's sake, Jenny! I couldn't.'

'What do you mean, "couldn't"? Do you want to save some of your much-vaunted inheritance, or don't you?'

'Well, yes, but . . .'

'You've been on the board as Natasha's representative for the last three years, so you must know *some*thing. And it's high time you started doing some work instead of frittering your life away. Don't worry. I'll tell you what needs to be done. I'll tell you what to say to the bank, and the unions. I'll give you all the support you need, provided you pay attention to what I say! We can run things together.

'What you have to understand is that the unions have always disliked James; he's been taking men on and laying them off until they don't know whether they're coming or going. You, on the other hand, might just possibly get Jack on your side, if you can convince him you're really committed. Whatever he says about the bosses, he always respected your Great-Uncle Hamish for an honest and knowledgeable man, and what you have to do is prove to him that those are traits that run in the family.'

Nick said, 'But . . .'

Jenny, who had sat through enough board meetings under Sir Albert's chairmanship to have learned to treat all sentences beginning with 'But . . .' as quite unworthy of notice, swept on, regardless. 'All you have to remember is that, whatever the papers say about the Red Clyde, the men's only desire is to work, so that they can feed their wives and families.'

For a moment, she couldn't think why Matt and Nick were staring at her. Then she said, 'It's not only you men who know how to lay down the law.'

Matt laughed, and reached out for her hand and kissed it. 'My darling, you're wonderful.'

Nick said, 'Oh ho!' but his heart wasn't in it.

'And "oh ho" to you, too,' Jenny told him. 'Matt's got me mixed up with some other woman. And if you're thinking of the outrageous slander your mother came out with at the Living Advertisements Ball, you can just forget it. Now, go away somewhere and think about whether you're going to come and do something useful at the shipyard. I want to have a proper, grown-up business discussion with your brother.'

10

IT WAS several moments before she could bear to break away from his arms, but she said, 'Matt, you must be careful!'

'I know. I'm afraid it slipped out.'

She sighed. 'If only . . . Oh, well. But I was serious about talking. Let's sit down. I can't think when you're holding me.'

So they sat sedately on either side of one of the tables in the hotel card room, and she said, 'I decided this morning that I'm going to leave Howard. No . . .' She couldn't bear the way his face lit up. 'No, not because of us.'

His mouth tightened. 'I see. I don't matter enough to you, but the yard does.'

'It's not like that! You know it isn't. What you don't know . . . Oh, how can I explain it all? When Johnny was born, Howard guessed what had happened. He said he would accept Johnny as his but would always hold the threat of divorce over my head. And if he ever did divorce me, he would have me declared an unfit mother, so that Johnny would be taken away from me.'

Matt said blankly. 'My God, why didn't you tell me? The bastard! What a threat to hold over you, my poor darling.'

'What good would telling you have done? Perhaps I was wrong. If I was – forgive me. But you see, there's only one thing that matters. If I were to leave Howard for you – a man I couldn't legally marry even if we were both free – I'd lose Johnny. Could you imagine any court in the land allowing him to stay with such an immoral mother? I must have been mad last week, to run the risk, but I just closed my mind to it.' Her mouth trembled a little. 'I wanted you so much.'

Her wide clear eyes, amber fringed with green, met his across the table, and there was so much love in them that he would have forgiven her anything. Gone, as completely as if they had never been, were all the tiny doubts and reservations that had troubled his heart since he had known about Johnny; they had existed only because he hadn't understood what she was going through.

Her voice becoming stronger again, she said eagerly, 'But after this morning, things aren't the same. You see, Howard's given *me* a weapon, for a change. I've always assumed – goodness knows why! – that he had some feeling for me, but now I know he doesn't.'

She was an astonishing woman, this love of his. He said. 'I don't know whether to commiserate with you or congratulate you.'

'Oh, congratulate me! Though I doubt if my vanity will ever recover from it. But listen, Matt. What matters is that, if he only married me because of the yard, he doesn't need me any more! What I'm trying to say is that, since he hates your side of the family so much, it would still be catastrophic if I left him for you. But I don't *think* he'd be prepared to stand up and look a fool in the divorce court for anything less than that. So – I've an idea, and I think it might work. But I'll have to go back and see him now.'

The expression on her face made him laugh. 'You look as if you're proposing to manipulate him shamelessly!'

'You bet!' she said inelegantly. 'Goodness knows, he deserves it! I can't tell you how disgusted I was to discover what a hypocrite he is. I felt quite sick this morning, remembering how he's always made me feel so inferior. Oh, no, my darling! I have no qualms at all. Deceit and deception seem to be a way of life to him. Fine! Because two can play at that game.'

11

HOWARD permitted himself a look of mild interrogation when the station taxi decanted Jenny under the porte-cochère of Provost Charters for the second time in one day. This time, he was gratified to see, she was looking thoroughly subdued and faintly pink around the eyes.

'He's with some friends in the village,' she said, when he asked about the boy. 'I dropped him off because I thought we ought to talk without being interrupted. Where's Simon?'

'He caught the four o'clock train.'

Removing her gloves, she deposited them with her handbag on top of one of the packing cases, then wandered over to the window and looked out. 'It's going to thunder. Howard, I'm sorry I rushed off like that, earlier. I was a bit – upset – about the yard.'

'Understandable,' he conceded. He was pleased that she should have returned. It had been something of an anti-climax, after the Great Revelation, to be left alone with no one but Simon, especially as Howard had the feeling that none of them had suitably appreciated the masterliness of his strategy. There was something else, too. More than anything, he enjoyed the knowledge of intellectual supremacy and secret power and, with the whole intricate affair now out in the open, he had been feeling rather deprived. Othello without Desdemona. Hamlet without the Prince of Denmark.

He remembered, with satisfaction, that there were still one or two points on which Jenny remained to be enlightened.

She said, 'Shall I make a cup of tea?'

'What an excellent idea.'

498

She seemed unable to sit still, wandering around the room with the cup and saucer in her hand, bending over to look at the labels on the packing cases, trying in the sudden gloom to read the titles of the books on the shelves. The rain was bouncing off the windows by now and there was a whistling draught from somewhere. There was no fire in the hearth, so that the room was suddenly chill and damp and cheerless.

Howard didn't notice. He was waiting, with interest, to hear what she had to say for herself.

As always, his imperturbable silence forced the words out of her, hasty words, as if she were nervous. 'When we reached the station, earlier, I found we'd just missed a train, so I took Johnny into the hotel for lunch, and then I began thinking. And I realised we'd been so busy talking about the yard this morning that we didn't really talk about *us*.' She took a gulp of tea and went on, 'And I don't know what you want to do?'

'Do? In what context?'

'Well, I mean . . . I know now why you married me. And though I've tried to be a good wife to you . . .'

It was remarkably obliging of her to present him with such an easy opening. He raised a hand. 'Accuracy above all things, my dear. In recent years, I grant, you have tried to be a good wife to me. But in the early days – well! You know as well as I do how many times I found it necessary to punish you.'

There was a sharp clink as she replaced her cup in the saucer. 'To what?'

'Come, now! You can scarcely have failed to notice.' He sat back and crossed his legs.

'You mean threatening – er – warning me that you'd take Johnny away from me?'

'That, of course. Though I should perhaps relieve you of any mis-apprehension about my attitude to the boy. I should not like you to flatter yourself that he has ever been an irritant to me in the sense of acting as a living reminder of your infidelity. The only interest I ever had in him was as a possible weapon against Matthew. Unfor-tunately, I have never quite been able to decide how best to use him.'

It was quite dark in the room now, and Howard was unable to see his wife's expression, but her voice sounded perfectly normal, if tremulous, when she said, 'Oh, I see.' Then she wandered over to the window again and rearranged a curtain that had billowed inwards and wrapped itself round the back of a chair.

'No,' he said. 'I was thinking of other things. If you had not, for

499

example, disobeyed me by going in to the office during the General Strike and working out a way to save the yard from collapse, I might have satisfied your maudlin desire for my presence at your mother's funeral. And I might not have brought Simon to live with us. If you had not gone to Paris against my wishes, you would not have returned to the threat of a bank takeover at the yard. If you had not tried to mislead me into believing that the child you were expecting was mine, I would have not sown the seeds of doubt in Natasha's mind which I understand bloomed so spectacularly at the Living Advertisements Ball.' He made a spacious gesture with his arm. 'Things like that.'

She stood motionless for a very long moment, and then walked swiftly across the room and sank to the floor by his side, looking up at him.

'Oh, Howard,' she said. 'I'm so sorry. I have treated you so badly! And somehow it makes it worse that you never loved me.'

He thought about that, briefly, conscious that there was something not quite right but unable to put a finger on what. Feminine logic! But her apologies disarmed him and he said, 'Well, well. I fear I must have caused some injury to your vanity.'

She sniffed. 'It was awful,' she said. 'I've never felt so let down, so useless. And the thing is – I don't know what happens next. You married me because you needed me, and I've been nothing but trouble to you, and now you don't need me any more. What am I to do?'

It wasn't a matter to which he had given any thought at all. Indeed, he had simply assumed that life at home would continue as before. Magnanimously, he said, 'You may stay on.'

'Would you let me? Oh, Howard!' And then she hesitated. 'It's just that, knowing you don't love me, I'm not sure that I could. Go on sharing your bed, I mean.'

He considered it. That she had, on one occasion in the past, shared a bed with a lover, had not prevented her from sharing his own, and with apparent enjoyment. Was that the same? No, perhaps not. He did, after all, have an expertise in such matters that transcended the emotion she insisted on referring to as 'love'. Remembering their discussion on the evening he had proposed to her, he said reprovingly, 'You must remember that, from the very beginning, I disclaimed any romantic infatuation.'

'Yes, I know. But I thought you might come to love me in the end, and now it seems that you haven't. And – and I can't adjust myself to it. Not yet.'

He repeated sardonically, 'Not yet? And how long, may I ask, do you think it will take?'

She sank her face in her hands, and her voice broke as she said, 'I don't know. I don't know. I'm not sure I ever can, if I'm to be near you, and always – aware of you. When I have come to depend so much on you and feel so deeply about you.'

Surprised, though not unduly so, he rose and went over to the cabinet containing the decanters. It was not his custom to drink anything other than wine before six in the evening, but he had had three glasses of brandy this afternoon in justified celebration. Another, he decided, would not come amiss.

It was natural, he thought, that his wife, emotionally dependent on him, should have been confused by his revelations.

Feeling almost benevolent, he said, 'Perhaps you should take a holiday, my dear.'

'Do you think so? I *would* like to be on my own for a while, to sort everything out in my mind.'

He wagged a finger at her. 'Not too long. I must make it a condition that either we resume our married life in two weeks from now, or we part for ever.'

She jumped to her feet. 'But Howard! You can't ask that of me.' Her voice became a wail. 'I don't think I *can* make the adjustment so soon!'

'A little self-discipline is all that is required. And you know me, my dear Jenny. When my mind is made up . . .'

She began to walk about the room, hastily and in clear distress of mind, and Howard waited, occasionally sipping his cognac and trying to decide whether he would, in fact, miss her if she disappeared from his life entirely. Only from habit, he thought.

In the end, the rain still lashing against the windows, the wind howling, and the curtains billowing, she came to stand before him. 'Won't you give me longer?' she asked, her voice breaking.

He shook his head.

He couldn't see her face, but he could sense her bracing herself when she replied, 'Then – no, I can't, Howard, even though I'll be lost without you! Not so soon. Though . . . Oh, I don't know! If I were to come to you again when I'm settled in my mind, and ask you to take me back . . .' She shrugged her shoulders forlornly. 'And if you won't, you won't. After all, you don't need me now.'

'Very true.' As if they were no more than distant acquaintances, he enquired, 'And where were you thinking of going for your – ah – retreat?'

'I've no idea.'

'You realise, of course, that since I now have Provost Charters – and, of course, no more interest in the shipyard – I shall be selling the house in Pollokshields?'

'Will you? Yes, I suppose so.'

'And you cannot expect me to continue subsidising you, if we part. There will be no more dress allowances, no more money for anything.'

The room was suddenly illuminated by the headlights of a car coming up the drive, and through the storm they heard the repeated sound of a horn.

Jenny said, 'I told the taxi to come back for me.'

'I see. Well, we have concluded our discussion, have we not? Goodbye, then, my dear. And remember – two weeks, or never.'

She sobbed suddenly, and then reached up to kiss his cheek. He thought he could see a glint of tears. 'Goodbye, Howard. Look after yourself.'

As he watched the taxi disappear through the sheeting rain, Howard reflected that she would soon be back, and with her tail between her legs. It wouldn't take long for her to discover what it was like to be without a home, without money – and without *him*.

12

IT was fortunate that he was not present to witness the scene that took place soon after, in a private room at the Horse and Buggy.

Jenny, pale with relief and slightly damp around the edges, gasped, 'I've done it. I've left him. My goodness, what talent the movies have lost in me! Merle Oberon, Elsa Lanchester, Garbo, Mata Hari – or do I mean Theda Bara . . .'

Nick, laughing, exclaimed, 'Oh, to have been a fly on the wall!' while Matt demanded, 'You mean it worked?'

'Yes, yes, yes. I took care not to overdo it – at least, I did overdo it once, but he was so full of brandy he didn't notice. I played on his vanity *quite* unscrupulously, and went all the way through the grand renunciation scene, and he thought I was just being a silly woman and didn't make a single threat. Mind you, I'm sure it's not really going to be as easy as that, but the first hurdle's over. He – has –

actually – accepted – the idea that we should live apart. To be free of Howard! I can't believe it!'

It was Johnny who silenced them all, Johnny, who had been standing, puzzled, listening to them and wondering what they were all so excited about. At last, he tugged at his mother's skirt and, in a tentative small voice, asked, 'Mummy, does that mean we're not going to have to live with Daddy any more?'

Jenny gulped and, dropping to her knees, put her arms round him. 'Yes, darling. Do you mind?'

'Oh, no. I'm *awfully* glad!'

Six

1

IT WAS a long time since Jenny had had to worry about money, but now all she had was the pittance she paid herself at the yard. So she took the children to Castlehead while she embarked on the dispiriting task of trying to find a home she could not only afford, but afford to furnish.

Craftily, Allie didn't say a thing for almost three weeks. And then, one night when Jenny was at the end of her tether, she burst out laughing and said, 'You're a stubborn one, aren't you! I could have told you the very first day that you weren't going to find anything, but I thought you'd better see for yourself before I suggested you stay here.'

'Allie, I couldn't! It's *your* home.'

'Yes, and I'm getting gey tired of rattling around in it all by myself. I've only kept it so that Bertha and Connie have someplace to come. Connie always says that, while she and Ted like managing their own hotel, it's great to get away. Anyway, I've got enough rooms to house a regiment, so why not?'

'No, really . . .'

'Don't worry, I wasn't thinking of turning the place into a foundling home! You can pay something into the kitty. And honestly, I'd be glad of the company.'

She got more than she bargained for. First Jenny and Beth and Johnny. And then Nick.

And then Bob, and Gill and Muriel. Because Jack's Lizzie, ailing ever since Bob had been born in 1924, had had two more children before she died, at the end of 1936 and the age of thirty-six, of what the doctor said was tuberculosis. And perhaps it was, although Jenny thought that the TB had been compounded by heartbreak. When Jack had refused to allow his children to be brought up in the Catholic faith, forcing her to break her oath to her church, it was as if she had lost what little spirit she possessed and sunk into a grey, guilt-ridden apathy that nothing could lighten. Jenny, watching her long, dismal decline, found that she herself was no longer capable of even passing a church, whether Catholic or Presbyterian, without a shudder of revulsion. She wondered what Jesus would have made

504

of the inhumanity of those who preached His gospel on earth.

Bob was twelve, Gill ten and Muriel six, and Allie said, 'Well, they can't be left to Jack's tender mercies, can they? They'd better come here. What's another child or three, after all?'

Whereupon Jenny hugged her so hard and shed such a torrent of grateful tears that Allie felt compelled to point out that this was a new frock and far from cheap, and if Jenny wasn't careful it would shrink.

2

JENNY found it very strange that now, at last, she and Matt could speak to each other freely on the telephone even if their conversations rarely touched on what mattered. Jenny never voiced the hurt and jealousy she felt that Matt was still living with Mims, sharing a bed, sharing a life. And Matt never spoke of his deep desire to have his son recognise him as his father.

Luckily, it was almost enough just to be able to talk, even about impersonal things like Franco's capture of Toledo and the Jarrow Crusade and the new Channel train ferry; the Crystal Palace burning down and the re-election of President Roosevelt. And the King abdicating because he could either be a King and unhappy, or an ex-king and happy, married to the woman he loved. Matt reported that Natasha was outraged at royalty letting the side down by putting personal before public considerations, while Mims was one hundred per cent on the king and Mrs Simpson's side; why should they give each other up just because of some fuddy-duddy old tradition? Jenny didn't admit that she herself had wept buckets over the abdication speech, even though she thought His Majesty was lucky to have such a clearcut choice to make.

They talked, too, and inevitably, about ships and aeroplanes.

3

AT the yard, Jenny felt as if she was carrying the weight of the world on her shoulders. James McMurtrie hadn't resigned, but at

505

least he didn't show his face at Brittons' while he waited for his case to come up. It meant that Jenny now wasted a good deal less time sitting listening, when she could have been doing something more useful, but although Nick learned quickly, they still seemed to be fighting against impossible odds.

She and Nick became obsessive, unable to talk about anything except what would happen when the naval treaties expired. The orders for new capital ships were almost bound to go to John Brown, Cammell Laird, and Harland and Wolff, but what about the cruisers, destroyers, submarines? Evening after evening, Jenny and Nick sat in Allie's house at Castlehead and planned how they would reorganise the yard's capacity. If they did this with the engine shop, that with the plate shop, if they abandoned riveting completely in favour of welding . . .

The only good laugh they had was when Howard had the almost inconceivable effrontery to turn up at a board meeting. Jenny, who could have outvoted him easily, decided the risk was too great and, by the exercise of considerable ingenuity, contrived to ensure that not a single issue of importance was put to the vote at all. She also made what Nick disgustedly described as 'cow's eyes' at her husband all the way through the meeting, as if to assure him she was missing him dreadfully and would, in another week or so, arrive on his doorstep begging to be taken back. As a result, he treated her with distant condescension, and left quickly, as soon as the meeting was over.

Even so, it looked as if Howard might be going to win after all, because the yard was on the very verge of going under.

Nick and Jenny had reached the awful, impossible stage of drafting the final dismissal notices for the two hundred men still on the payroll when Jack burst into Nick's office one afternoon with some news that had just come through on the union grapevine from Nuffields.

'The government's placed an order in Sweden for Bofors guns and there's more to be manufactured under licence in England within months. Anti-aircraft stuff.'

Nick was staring at him so blankly that Jack thought at first that he didn't understand, so he exclaimed, 'D'ye no' see, man? That's no' whit ye'd call routine military replacements! That fool Baldwin's got his finger out at last. It's going to happen.'

With a thud, he sat down in the chair by the side of Nick's desk, and said shakily, 'Oh, Christ! It's really going to happen. After all these years, there's going to be work on the Clyde again.'

506

'He just sat there,' Nick reported that evening, 'with the tears pouring down his cheeks, and I realised for the first time what the depression's meant to the men. I've never been so ashamed of myself, the money I've wasted in my time, the fuss I've made about "my inheritance" and all the rest of it. It was too much for me, I can tell you. You should have seen the pair of us, sitting there bawling like a couple of kids.'

Jenny felt her own eyes stinging, but Allie said sombrely, 'It's a terrible thing that it should take rearmament to save the Clyde. Pray God it'll prevent war, not provoke it.'

4

IN THE aircraft industry things moved faster than in the shipyards, because the Chiefs of Staff were convinced that, if war should come, the Germans would begin with a bombing offensive.

Matt, one of the few aircraft designers who were also pilots with twenty years of flying experience – including combat experience – was hesitant at first about being co-opted as adviser to such bodies as the Air Ministry and the Committee for Imperial Defence. He wasn't, after all, a designer of military planes, and even if the BB.3a could be adapted, it still wouldn't be a patch on Mitchell's Supermarine Spitfire or the Hawker Hurricane.

But then he paid a visit to Germany, because the Germans were pleased to welcome foreign inspection of their aircraft factories. Matt, shown round one that was turning out 300mph bombers at the rate of two a day, returned to London and began to talk very hard to a great number of people. There was no longer any doubt in his mind that the government was going to have to adopt a far more ambitious programme than the Air Staff's famous Scheme F.

He saw little of his wife, because he was rarely at home, and when he was it was like sharing the house with a sister rather than a wife. They had had separate rooms for years, and Mims had become much less argumentative, much less demanding; it was as if she had come to terms with herself. Matt, now totally committed to the factory, had found a reliable man to manage Gannet Charter, someone with a better sense of company finance than Mims had ever had, so that she herself spent most of her time either piloting charters or tinkering with engines. In

507

that sense, she was happy enough, and they rarely quarrelled nowadays.

Matt had thought, many times, that for Jenny's sake he and Mims ought to part. He knew that Jenny must wonder why they hadn't. Loyalty to Mims had prevented him from telling her the truth about his wife's sexual affinities, which meant he couldn't very well explain that he stayed with Mims because in the physical sense it didn't matter, whereas in other senses it did. He had begun to feel deeply sorry for her, because her lesbianism, anathema to the world at large, left her isolated, and he knew that, as a result, she needed him very much. She had told him – and he believed her – that she had been unable to bring herself to put her newly discovered instincts to the test, and he found it strange and sad that the Victorian propriety of her upbringing should still hold her in thrall. What a lot the Victorians had to answer for!

Leaving Mims, he concluded, would achieve nothing except to hurt her unnecessarily; it wouldn't bring him and Jenny any closer.

And then, one evening at the beginning of July 1937, she said, 'Did you hear the news on the wireless? Amelia Earhart's disappeared in the Pacific. She missed the refuelling base at Howland Island and she and the plane have simply vanished. Oh, Matt, if only . . .'

It was years since Mims had mentioned her great ambition, and Matt, dedicated to his own ambitions, had been selfishly grateful that she seemed to have abandoned it, even though he knew how avidly she followed the record-breaking exploits of Amelia Earhart, Amy Johnson, Jean Batten, Ruth Nichols, Beryl Markham, and all the other women flyers who made the headlines.

And now it appeared that Amelia Earhart, who had hoped to be the first woman to girdle the globe, had failed almost within sight of success, and there still remained one great 'first' open to a woman.

Matt knew that his wife had married him because he seemed to offer the answer to all her hopes, because with him she could fly. But he had kept her, metaphorically if not actually, grounded all through their life together. He had failed her in more ways than one, he thought, memories of their first unhappy years together blotted out by the knowledge of his own commitment to a new and more enduring love.

He owed it to Mims to make up for all that had gone wrong with her life, and in the way that meant most to her. There had been good financial reasons once why any attempt at pioneering or record-breaking had to be ruled out, but not any more. Now, he could let her have a plane easily enough. Now, he had sufficient pull with Imperial Airways and other outfits across the world to raise all the money and help she needed. If she didn't go soon, she never would, because war would put a stop to all that kind of thing.

They were sitting in the little parlour of the house near the river, scarcely less scruffy than it had been eight years before, on the night when Mims had been reading *The Well of Loneliness*.

He raised his eyes from the engine specification he was studying, and said, 'If you want to be ready for next April, you'd better start training now.'

She stared at him, the lovely green eyes wide and disbelieving. She was thirty-five years old and, now that the petulance, the trace of hardness, had gone from her expression, more beautiful than she had ever been. The smooth-crowned, neatly waved hairstyle suited her and although she was still careless of fashion, at least he no longer had to wonder, with a shudder, what she was going to turn up in at some stuffy official reception.

She breathed, 'You're kidding,' and he grinned a little lopsidedly, and said, 'No, I'm not.'

Her heart felt as if it was in suspension. She had given up hope so long ago, tried to close her eyes to her own private vision of the stars, and now she was being offered them on a silver platter, because when Matt did something, he always did it properly. If he was encouraging her to go, he'd do everything in his power to make sure that she went in style.

'Draft out a plan,' he said, 'and then we'll talk about it.'

5

THE next months were the happiest of Mims' life.

Once she and Matt had agreed the route, he left everything to her on the understanding that whenever she needed his advice or help she would ask for it. She was surprised, when she began applying for landing clearances and all the other documentation she needed for the journey, to find how often he was able to smooth her path, even in the most outlandish places.

After that, she began making arrangements for spare parts, fuel and oil supplies at key points along the route. With extra tanks, she estimated that she ought to be able to carry eleven hundred gallons of fuel, enough to give the twin-engined BB 3b a nominal range of four thousand miles. Matt insisted on refuelling stops every two-and-a-half to three thousand. 'And even that's cutting it fine, when you never know what freak weather conditions you might meet.' Every variation from normal cruising at normal height used up extra fuel.

In the meantime, with Bill Bonny's help, she modified the engines to give an increased compression ratio, fitted the latest two-pitch propellers, and made a number of other refinements including a more comfortable seat and special radio antennae to extend the range.

One of the bodywork specialists painted the words 'Mimosa Weber' in huge green letters along the sides of the fuselage. She looked at it and almost burst with pride.

She modified herself, too, and that was most difficult of all. It meant sitting in the same position for hours, day after day. It meant disrupting her normal sleeping pattern, so as to become used to staying awake for long, irregular stretches. It meant teaching herself to keep her mind free from intrusive thoughts, because she was going to need total concentration on one thing only, the act of flying.

Matt and she had one major row, when he announced that he proposed to track her in another plane, a few hours behind. 'To pick up the pieces if anything goes wrong,' he said cheerfully.

'No, no and *no*! I don't want a nanny! I won't have one. This is *my* adventure and I won't share it, I *won't*!' Her eyes were full of tears. 'I want to be Mimosa Weber, solo pilot, not Sir Matthew Britton's wife with her husband tagging along, keeping an eye on her!'

In the end, he gave in, though with certain private reservations.

At last the great day came, and Mims had such a wild send-off from Croydon that she forgot her disappointment that Matt wasn't there, because he'd had to leave the country a few days earlier on something official that he couldn't avoid. But he'd promised nothing would stop him from being there on the tarmac, cheering, when she returned home in triumph.

6

THE plane handled like a dream. Paris, Brindisi, Athens flowed by under its bright wings, and Mims was able to toss the mohair knee rug aside and put on her sunglasses.

She felt a headache beginning, so she fished out the menthol cone and rubbed it across the back of her neck, just at the base of her skull, and was grateful when, after a moment or two, she felt the cool, surface anaesthetic begin to take effect and the tension to relax. It was probably because she'd been too excited to swallow anything all day except some tomato juice out of a tin, so she conscientiously chewed a handful of nuts and raisins and felt better.

And then the radio told her that she was approaching her first refuelling and night stop, Baghdad, though she could see it already, a great brown city split by a wide river and dotted with palm groves. She and Matt had stopped here during the MacRobertson race to Australia in 1934, but it was quite different, and far more thrilling, to settle the plane for the night herself, and confer with the friendly gentleman from Imperial Airways who was going to have it refuelled from the 50-gallon drums with 'Mimosa Weber' painted on them in large green letters. She was taken aback to find that the little crowd waiting on the tarmac was a crowd of journalists waiting for *her*.

She'd decided, on Matt's advice, to make a relatively short hop on the second day in case the first day was overly tiring, so she had no more to do than fly peaceably down the Persian Gulf to Sharjah, a sinister-looking concrete fort with a control tower at one corner and a barbed-wire entanglement round it, all of it contrasting strangely with the calm creek in which she could see fish jumping and oceangoing dhows chugging peacefully about their business.

Landing in a great, swirling cloud of sand, she taxied as instructed through the gap in the barbed wire to join the Imperial Airways plane already parked there. And this time she was careful to powder her nose and comb her hair before she climbed out to meet the welcoming committee, only to find that there weren't any journalists but just some armed bedouin soldiers and an inquisitive group of Imperial Airways passengers from the fort, which was also the hotel and smelled strongly of mulligatawny soup.

511

She took off from the hard-sand runway next morning at dawn, and lurched into the air with the plane feeling overweight again and sluggish from the topped-up tanks. But now that she and the plane had come to terms with each other and she was worrying less about the mechanics of it all, she began to feel the real excitement of the journey, the thrill of venturing into the unknown.

The hours passed, and the landscape beneath her changed from rippling cinnamon-brown desert, to smoky blue hills, to soft green waters. And then she was in India, and there was Karachi with its great docks and the Imperial Airways planes parked near a signpost saying, 'London 4093 miles'. She topped up her tanks again, and assured a mob of reporters that the plane was flying like a dream, that she hadn't had a moment's trouble with it, and that no, she was not finding the flight a strain but, on the contrary, revelling in every moment.

'Next stop, Rangoon,' she said, and a man from the *Times of India* asked why not Calcutta?

'Because this plane's so economical on fuel,' she answered gaily, 'and life isn't long enough to stop off in Calcutta!'

Everyone laughed, because everyone knew that Calcutta was the slowest and most bureaucratic city in the world.

She had no idea how the flight was beginning to affect her, how the heat and the thin air were clouding her judgement as she flew on over sand and rock, sturdy brown hills like battlements, and dry river beds scratched in the soil with occasional patches of lurid green where there was some unseen water course. The heat blasted off the earth so that the plane juddered and the windows were like open furnace doors, but it didn't trouble her.

At some time during the afternoon, she passed over Calcutta, and continued on round the perimeter of the Sundarbans, a wilderness of mangrove swamps, peaceful and pretty.

'Mustn't land here,' she told herself solemnly. 'Tigers. Evil, dangerous things.'

And then she was heading down the eastern perimeter of the Bay of Bengal towards Rangoon, and there were offshore islands lying in the water like jewels discarded from the Burmese regalia, and small towns with walls toasted by the sun. Bright yellow beaches. Bright green water. Bright birds. Hotsy-totsy. Ritzy, in fact.

Hey! The plane suddenly went skidding across the sky like a stone over ice. No right to do that. A heavy blue haze had appeared from somewhere. Nose up. Nose down. This was goofy! And then the plane started doing a tango.

There was a tower of cu-nim ahead that looked about 60,000 feet high, with evil thunderheads and lightning like searchlights. Mims thought she'd better go round it.

She was almost clear when there was a bang and the plane bucked like a bronco. Then it just went on flying as if nothing had happened. It really was the most *darling* plane.

The only trouble was that the lightning-strike had put the radio out of action, although as far as Mims could judge the instruments seemed to be OK. She sat and thought about it when she was back in calm air again, looking down on a sea like shining purple lacquer in the late sun and catching a gleam of gold in the distance that she took to be Rangoon's Shwedagon Pagoda. In relation to it, the compass was pointing just where it ought to.

To land at Rangoon as she'd planned, or go on to Bangkok?

She'd always wanted to see Bangkok and she ought to have plenty of fuel for the extra distance. Euphorically, she thought that her darling plane wouldn't mind, even if it was beginning to get dark, because she had all the latest in blind-flying instruments. Besides, the Siamese royal family were well known to be flying mad, and she would probably find better facilities there for getting the radio fixed and checking the electricals than in the bustling capital of British Burma.

So when she saw the Rangoon river ahead, the chocolate-coloured water and the oil tanks, and the handsome avenues lined with Flower of the Forest trees, she banked away to the left and the interior, reset the directional gyro, and headed south-east for Bangkok.

7

SHE should have been able to see Bangkok long ago, but everything was pitch black and she had to switch off the lights on her instrument panel because they ruined her night vision. The instruments wouldn't have helped anyway, because she knew now that the lightning had thrown the compass out as well as wrecking the radio.

She was lost, way off course somewhere in the interior of Siam, or perhaps even French Indo-China, and she didn't have enough fuel just to go on flying round and round until daylight. She dropped lower and lower, and opened the cockpit window, and all she could smell was the hot night and the jungle, and no trace of the salt that would have meant she was near a coast. All she could see was a solid canopy of vegetation with no real break in it anywhere. Now and again, over the steady drone of the engine she heard the yelp of a wild animal.

She was too low. Suddenly, she sensed something towering out of the jungle, something too compact to be a mountain but still hard and dangerous, some kind of rock pinnacle. Sharply, she took the plane up again, and one of the engines hiccoughed. And then the other. She rocked the plane to tilt the last drops of fuel from the tanks into the carburettors, but it didn't help. She found she was sobbing, quietly and steadily, as she tried to put the powerless plane into a glide, hoping there might be somewhere to land at the end of it.

But the plane wouldn't glide and there was nowhere to land anyway.

As she crashed, the last thing Mims saw, a pale shadow against the dark of the night, was a huge, mysterious stone face, with shallow, slanting, closed eyes, and a smile that was at once cryptic, sorrowful and profound.

8

MATT was in Rangoon, waiting for her. He had wanted to be sure she really was all right before the difficult leg to Darwin, where Keith Whalley was to meet her and give her all the final, intricate directions she needed for the Pacific and help her check every millimetre of the plane before the crossing.

He didn't begin to worry seriously until midday the next day, and it was three harrowing days after that, days of quartering to the north, west, and east in borrowed planes, of spending the hours of darkness in a succession of increasingly desperate telephone calls, that a report came in from Phnom Penh in Cambodia that a small plane had been heard some nights earlier, flying very low over the jungles of Angkor, two hundred miles east of Bangkok.

But although Matt, with the generous assistance of many people, flew and overflew the jungle, and then searched on foot through the sixty square miles of ruined walls and towers and water basins;

of niches, staircases and canals; of sculptures and friezes and the vast enigmatic images, Buddhist and Hindu, of a long-dead civilisation buried in the wilderness, they found no trace at all of the plane with 'Mimosa Weber' so proudly blazoned along its sides, or of its pilot.

9

MORE than a year later, Matt was sitting with Jenny on the silver sands of Morar, with the silver-blue waters and silver-white clouds spread out before them like the backdrop of a stage that the gods had never intended to be peopled. 'This is the only kind of peace that's real,' he said suddenly. 'The kind that human beings don't have a hand in.'

'What makes you say that?'

'Need you ask? It's twenty-five years since the "war to end war" began, and now here we are on the brink of another one.

'But it wasn't just that. All this empty calm suddenly made me think of the Buddhist statues at Angkor. The locals said there were hundreds more scattered through the jungle; they were always finding new ones. And every one of them with the same closed eyes and calm, omniscient smile. You only had to look at them to know that, if you, too, followed the Noble Eightfold Path, you'd find release. None of this nonsense about heaven and hell. Nirvana means total oblivion of the soul, utter rejection of the world of sorrows. The ultimate peace. But the more I've thought about it, the more I've come to see what a very human and pessimistic concept it is, after all.'

He waved a hand. 'This, though. This doesn't have anything to do with humanity. It doesn't accept, it doesn't reject. It just is.'

'So?' Jenny gave a sardonic chuckle. 'You're going to take up residence on some inch-square islet and become a hermit?'

'Nope.'

With sudden passion, she exclaimed, 'I wish you would!'

Matt, despite being chairman of a furiously busy aircraft company making Spitfires as well as his own BB.3e, had been back in uniform for months now in some hush-hush advisory capacity, and although he was above field rank she doubted if that was going to stop him from getting into danger. He'd had a talent for it all his life. With the anger of love and fear, she thought that, at forty-three, he ought to know better.

Taking her hand, he looked down at it, absently checking off the fingers, one by one. 'Everyone's going to be involved this time,' he said. 'Civilians as well as the Forces.'

'Thanks to your bloody planes!'

There wasn't an answer to that, but he said, 'You can't stop progress just by resenting it. It's people who invent new technology and people who decide how to use it.'

'I know. But I feel sick every time I think of another war. And you involved. I'll never forget you falling into my arms, all mud-stained and bloody, that day on the Somme.'

'You'll never forget *what?*'

Dropping her hand abruptly, he stared at her with the most complete mystification on his face.

She didn't know whether to laugh or cry. 'I was the ambulance driver who took you back to the Casualty Clearing Station. You were completely delirious, burbling on about the bells of Hell going ting-a-ling-a-ling, and claiming to be drunk on the waters of the Pierian spring, and goodness knows what all!'

'Well, of all the . . . "Jerusalem, Jeroooosalem . . ." Was that *you?*'

'Was I singing that? I don't remember.'

'I'll be damned. And I *thought*, the day I crashed the Hispano into the ditch at Provost Charters, that we'd met more recently than the shipyard. But I dismissed it. Why did you never tell me?'

'I don't know.'

They were silent for a long time.

Jenny said, 'Hostages to fortune. That's the trouble with loving people. And this time it won't just be you in the front line. Beth could be in uniform within months. Women aren't going to be treated like china dolls this time. She's single and twenty-two years old, and managing one of Allie's dress shops hardly counts as work of national importance.'

'No, I'm afraid she'll be among the first to go. Dear Beth! What a sweet little mite she was all those years ago.'

'She's still sweet; I don't know what I've done to deserve such a daughter. I'll be worried to death about her. And if this war goes on for as long as the last one, Bob and Gill will be called up, too. And, oh, Matt! Just think! Johnny's twelve now. Even he might be in danger.'

All he could think of to say was, 'Don't fret, my darling. It can't possibly last for five years.'

516

But both of them knew that it could.

He said, 'What about Nick?'

'I've no idea. He's in a reserved occupation, of course, but he's been ridiculously self-critical ever since he realised what a sheltered life he led before he came to the yard. He just doesn't seem to be able to make up for it. To himself, I mean.'

'Yes, I know.'

She sighed. 'I suspect he's going to find some way of going off to the war, just to salve his conscience. He's got a very good man as his deputy and, well . . .'

Matt sketched an X in the sand. 'And what about Howard? Is he still pestering you?'

It had been a surprisingly long time before Howard became difficult, so long that, when he did, it had come as a very nasty shock. Jenny, thinking about it, realised that he must have gone on for weeks and then months, waiting for her to come crawling back to him. He was very good at waiting. And when she didn't, he had chosen to assume that she was just being a stupid female. The alternative explanation, that she was enjoying life very well without him, would have been far too great an insult to his vanity.

Finally, at the end of 1938, he had written ordering her to return to him. No nonsense about him missing her; just a straightforward command. She had replied with the soft answer that would turn away wrath – she hoped – because what she needed to buy was time; the older Johnny was, the weaker became Howard's case for taking him away from her. Even so, it would be years yet before they were out of the wood.

Howard's next letter had been, for him, conciliatory. He regretted her absence. After that the threats had begun.

She said, 'It's too lovely a day to talk about Howard, but yes. I had a letter from his solicitors last week. He proposes to evacuate himself to America when war comes, and he wishes to take "his son" with him for the child's own safety. Unless I agree, he will institute divorce proceedings. And that, as his solicitor points out, would come to the same thing in the end.'

Savagely, Matt skimmed a pebble over the surface of the flawless sea. 'A bluff?'

'I think so. I have the very odd and distinctly unpleasant feeling that he really does want me back. Don't ask me why. Because he's possessive; because he needs to reassure himself; because the household isn't running as smoothly as it did when I was there.

'But the war's too close now. He'll sail very soon, and my lawyer tells me that means nothing is likely to come of the divorce threat. Oh, Matt, just think what heaven it would be if he found Another Woman!'

He put an arm round her. 'He'd never find any other woman who's a patch on you.'

'Thank you, kind sir.' She raised her face to be kissed.

'I do love you very much,' he said.

After a while, she spoke again. 'The only thing is, what if he's employed some kind of Philip Marlowe to keep an eye on me? It would be just like him.'

It had been at the back of her mind for three long years. That was why they were in Morar now, the only place where they could be together and feel safe, a place where everyone knew of approaching strangers hours before they arrived.

Matt chuckled. 'Well, if the fellow's spry on his feet, he'll soon be called up. And if he isn't, then we'll just have to keep one jump ahead of him, won't we?'

And so they sat, watching the soft blue dusk spread over sky and sea, knowing that the second Armageddon of their lives was only weeks away, and tried not to wonder how many years it would be before they were free to come to Morar again.

PART FIVE

1939–1945

One

1

JENNY had been twelve when, as a special treat, Big Davie Laing had let her take the helm of his new puffer, the *Marie Lloyd,* and steer her a whole fifty yards down river at a speed of something like half a knot. Children on the Clyde were given every encouragement to be 'boat daft'.

That had been in 1910. And here she was, thirty years later, at the helm of another puffer, the *Gould,* steaming across the Channel in the company of hundreds of other little ships, quixotically bound for Dunkirk and the evacuation of four hundred thousand Allied troops trapped on the beaches of Flanders.

Fishing smacks, tugs, smart white yachts, brown-sailed Thames barges, pleasure cruisers, dredgers, car ferries, cockle boats, motor launches, trawlers, minesweepers . . .

2

IT WAS almost nine months since that Sunday morning, the third of September 1939, when at a quarter past eleven precisely the prime minister, Neville Chamberlain, had made his broadcast to the nation.

His voice composed and almost toneless, he had said, 'This morning, the British Ambassador in Berlin handed the German government a final note that, unless we heard from them by eleven o'clock that they were prepared, at once, to withdraw their troops from Poland, a state of war would exist between us. I have to tell you now that no such undertaking has been received and that, consequently, this country is at war with Germany . . .'

It had come as a surprise only to people who had been wilfully blind, but there had been such a cold finality about the words that Jenny found herself shaking her head against the angry tears, and murmuring, 'Not again. Not again! It's so *stupid.*'

The children, who didn't understand, had said cheerily, 'Come on, it can't be as bad as all that!' They'd learn, she thought.

Within weeks, *Time* magazine in America had begun referring to the war as World War II, and some of its readers wrote to object. It couldn't be a 'world' war, they said, if America wasn't in it, and they didn't like the implication that she soon would be. No one knew how long it was going to take for the actuality to catch up with the name.

In Britain, nothing happened for months, except that there were notices in shop windows saying, 'No blackout material, no drawing pins'. Road signs and direction posts were removed in case they might be of use to an invading enemy, which very successfully confused people going about their legitimate business. It was difficult to get stockings, so more and more women began wearing slacks. Everyone developed a permanently aching shoulder from carrying a gas mask. Cinemas, theatres and dance halls were closed until people got so bored that they had to be opened again. There wasn't a hint of the great German bombing offensive.

Many of the women and children who had been evacuated to the country returned home again because there didn't seem much sense in staying away, when the only fighting was on the Continent. Butter, bacon, sugar and meat went on ration, but it wasn't too bad; you could manage quite well on four ounces of butter and almost two shillingsworth of meat a week, as long as you didn't want fillet steak every day.

On the twenty-sixth of February, almost six months after the outbreak of war, the *Queen Elizabeth,* sister ship of the *Queen Mary* and the greatest liner ever built, crept out of John Brown's yard to be nursed by her tugs fifteen miles down the Clyde, at walking speed, to the Tail of the Bank, from which she was to sail on her maiden voyage to America and there become a troopship. Everyone at Brittons' stopped work to watch, and to sigh. No bands playing, no confetti, no bunting. Only a giant, slow-moving shadow decked out in battleship grey, a ship so huge that there were only two tides in the year high enough to float her down to the sea. And this day's was one of them.

On the tenth of May, Mr Churchill replaced Mr Chamberlain as prime minister, and three days later made a speech saying, 'I have nothing to offer but blood, toil, tears and sweat', which led a number of cynics to ask, 'Whose?'

The answer was not far to seek, because, two days afterwards, Mr Churchill's French opposite number telephoned him to say that the battle for France was lost. The Germans had broken through and the whole French and British armies were in danger of annihilation.

3

TOWARDS the end of the month, Jenny was in London sorting out some queries over a new Admiralty specification, and mentioned casually as she was leaving that she must now go and look in at a yard on the Thames estuary, where they were converting a puffer for wartime duties and hadn't quite got the hang of the engine.

The Admiralty man said, 'Yes, puffers are notoriously cranky, aren't they? If it weren't for the problem of crewing her, I know someone who could make very good use of that one. We've just crewed a Dutch skoot with a coxswain who can't steer and a chief who's never handled a marine diesel before, but I'm told that to send a puffer out without someone who knows the engine would be a sheer waste of effort.'

'Nonsense!' Jenny fired up automatically. 'They may be a little eccentric sometimes, but . . .'

In the end, since she had an inquisitive turn of mind and full security clearance, she discovered what it was all about. The army had to be evacuated, but the beaches round Dunkirk shelved so gradually that destroyers had to stand off a full mile from the shore, even at high tide. The whole of southern and eastern England was being scoured for craft tough enough to cross the Channel and of sufficiently shallow draft to be able to ferry the men out from the beaches.

As a result, she found herself, some hours later, telling a harassed officer of the Nore Command, 'I drove an ambulance on the Somme when I was eighteen years old, so please don't give me all that nonsense about "not a job for the ladies"!' And at ten o'clock the same evening she and the *Gould* went chugging out of Ramsgate harbour as part of an armada of little ships being chivvied towards France by an escort of naval motorboats.

'Like a bunch of hysterical sheepdogs,' calmly remarked Mr Kellam, the *Gould*'s temporary skipper who, in everyday life, was a solicitor and weekend sailor. Since it wasn't a weekend and he had been snatched from his desk at the shortest notice, he was still wearing the black jacket and dark striped trousers of his profession.

'What an interesting vessel this is. Is it likely to bite me, do you think, if I rub it up the wrong way?'

Jenny, standing at his elbow in the draughty wheelhouse, smiled cursorily. She was clad in one of Bertha's practical brown overalls – several sizes too large for her – and liberally streaked with engine oil.

Glancing round the convoy, she said, 'What do you suppose possessed us to get involved in all this?'

Mr Kellam pursed his lips. '*Noblesse oblige*, perhaps? Can't leave the poor chaps stranded, if there's something we might be doing.'

Which summed up Jenny's own feelings precisely. She warmed slightly to Mr Kellam, even if he did have an impregnable calm that reminded her of Howard. It cheered her enormously to think that Howard would have forbidden her to do what she was doing.

'There's a thermos of soup in the foc'sle,' she said. 'I'll relieve you at the wheel for ten minutes unless Willie needs me.' Willie was the third and last of the crew, a very young lifeboatman who, although he didn't yet know it, was going to spend most of his time stoking the boiler.

4

JENNY surprised herself by feeling very little surprise at sight of the beaches. From a distance, they would have seemed as harmlessly crowded as Brighton on a Bank Holiday Monday if it hadn't been for the sound of artillery and the huge columns of greasy black smoke and tongues of flame rolling up from the burning oil tanks behind the harbour.

It didn't look like the prelude to three days of nightmare.

The first day wasn't too bad, because the crews of the little ships were still fresh and the men on the beach reassured by their arrival. The sea was calm, too, and there was a heavy mist that preserved them from the attentions of the Luftwaffe.

The men waded out in orderly fashion and clambered aboard the *Gould* one by one, each man waiting, on Jenny's instructions, until his predecessor had found a place. It wasn't altogether easy, because they'd had to remove the hatch cover in case it wouldn't take the weight of scores of men, and that meant a good many had to pack themselves into the hold.

Jenny didn't know whether the men were being so amenable because she was a woman, or because they'd already seen a number of other craft heel over and become useless. A puffer was pretty hard to capsize, but Mr Kellam and Mrs Fournier, as they punctiliously addressed each other, had decided there was no sense in taking unnecessary risks.

The day wore on, and the puffer went back and forward, back and forward, delivering well over a hundred men to the destroyers each time.

It was almost dusk when Willie reported that fuel was getting low, by which time even Mr Kellam was beginning to look a little frayed around the edges and Jenny was ready to drop from exhaustion. So they took their next load of men straight back across the Channel to Dover, a nervy business unescorted since, although mines didn't pose much threat to a wooden ship, there were fast German motor torpedo boats prowling the sea, and the puffer's habit of shooting off flames from the funnel head didn't make for an unobtrusive passage.

At Dover, they managed four hours' sleep on camp beds before they were off again, this time carrying substantial supplies of sandwiches and water, not for themselves but for the Tommies. Rumour had it that over fifty thousand men had been taken off the beaches the previous day, more than twice what the commanders of Operation Dynamo, tucked away in their headquarters under the White Cliffs of Dover, had dared to hope.

But when they reached the beaches this time, part of another small armada, they could see at once that things had worsened. The weather had changed. The wind was blowing inshore and building up a surf so that more and more of the small boats were being swamped and others were sinking under the weight of too many men. There were rowing boats drifting around without oars, but no one had time to retrieve them or find timbers that might be used to paddle them.

The German guns had moved nearer and were firing more methodically and some of the houses along what had once been the promenade were burning, and there were piles of dead men on the beaches, and burnt-out trucks.

The mood was different, too, and it wasn't so easy to control the men as they came aboard, exhausted, hungry, unshaven, many of them blood-stained and bandaged. They were clinging to the queerest things, like children to favourite toys. Someone had a portable gramophone, another a huge china plate with 'A souvenir from Brussels' written on it. There was a lone French soldier with a live goose under his arm, and a good many men insisted on bringing stray dogs aboard with them. Argument was time-wasting, and the mood of the men precarious, so the livestock shared in the evacuation.

Even so, things were still going not too badly when the skies cleared.

It was then that the planes swept in, wave after wave of them, Heinkels, Stukas, Me 109s, all of them bombing and machine-gunning, turning both beaches and sea into an inferno.

'We, at least, are fortunate,' remarked Mr Kellam thoughtfully. 'We may, like those poor chaps on the prom, be sitting ducks, but at least we are sitting ducks with something to occupy our minds.' Jenny knew little more about Mr Kellam than she had done two days before, but he'd volunteered the information that he had been a naval officer in the last war, which explained a lot.

Only one German fighter took a personal interest in them, a Messerschmitt. Jenny watched, mesmerised, as it dived in to strafe the *Gould,* but the pilot's judgement wasn't very good, and he missed, and the bullets ripped across the empty water, and Jenny went back to work again.

When darkness came, the whole of Dunkirk seemed to be a wall of flames roaring and darting into the blackness of the sky. The still air was suffocating with the smell of burning buildings and smoke from the blazing oil tanks. And there were other smells familiar from the Somme, of incinerated flesh and blood and mutilation.

And still there were long queues of men stretching out into the shining black water.

The *Gould* had managed to replenish her fuel supplies from a coal yard near the harbour, so there was no need to go back to Dover, but Willie had fainted clean away and Jenny had fallen asleep on her feet, so in the end they decided to lie offshore for a few hours' rest on the bunks in the foc's'le.

After that everything became quite unreal. Soon after dawn, the sky filled with Hurricanes and Spitfires engaging with the German fighters and bombers, but after a while the British planes disappeared and in no time at all the Stukas were coming in again, in massed waves, so that throughout that interminable morning – in a pandemonium of noise and with bombs and shells browning the sea until it was like oxtail soup coming to the boil – the *Gould* spent as much time picking up survivors from wrecked ships as from the beaches.

First of all the minesweeper *Skipjack* turned turtle, and then the destroyer *Keith* went down. The tug *St Abbs* had scarcely finished picking up survivors from the *Keith* when she herself was struck. She sank in thirty seconds, and then it was the turn of the *Salamander*, and then the *Havant*, and then the *Basilisk*.

Jenny was in the midst of ushering some French soldiers aboard the *Gould*, shouting hoarsely, '*En avant, mes braves*' – the only vaguely appropriate phrase her weary brain could think of – when she heard a tearing, shrieking sound directly above, and glanced up, and then was aware of a shattering explosion, and smoke plumes bristling with splinters, and pain.

To her annoyance, she found she was lying on the deck, with no idea how she had got there. And then everything went black.

5

WHEN she woke up twelve hours later, in a wonderfully clean, quiet bed in a clean, quiet hospital in Dover, she learned that the bomb had landed on the beach where it had been partly muffled by the sand. The admirable Mr Kellam had prised off a couple of planks from the wheelhouse, instructed Willie, a strong swimmer, to retrieve an abandoned rowing boat, and had then rowed her out to one of the destroyers, which was just about to make for Dover with a full load.

They'd had to dig several nasty chunks of shrapnel out of her left side, and the surgeon told her it would be a while before she was entirely herself again. But he didn't know Jenny. Within three days, she was quite well enough to be sitting up getting annoyed about the newspaper report of Mr Churchill's speech in the House of Commons on the fourth of June.

'We shall fight on the beaches, we shall fight on the landing grounds, we shall fight in the fields and in the streets, we shall fight in the hills; we shall never surrender.'

The only word she could think of was impertinence. To turn what all those men had been through into the materials of cheap and vulgar oratory! It was outrageous.

Even when Matt arrived to visit her, she remained dewy-eyed only for a moment or two before she demanded, 'How dare That

Man call it a colossal military disaster? "Wars are not won by evacuations," forsooth!'

Matt hadn't known in what state he would find his beloved, and he couldn't help grinning.

'Here, have a chocolate,' he said.

'Matt Britton, where did you get those? I haven't seen a chocolate for months.'

'Well, it *was* a disaster, you know,' he said, his diction slurred by a coffee cream.

'Nothing of the sort! The retreat *to* Dunkirk may have been a disaster. But the evacuation *from* Dunkirk was a victory of the best kind. We saved almost 340,000 of those 400,000 men! Nobody thought, to begin with, that even a tenth of them could be taken off.'

He said suddenly, 'Are there any hospital rules that prevent me from kissing you properly?'

'I don't know.' She blushed. 'I've never been in hospital before.'

So he tried it, and no one raised any objections, though a passing nurse gaped enviously and wondered what Mrs Fournier had done to deserve such a divine man, and one with all that gold braid, too.

'And now we've settled that little matter,' Matt said after a while, 'perhaps you will tell me what the hell you were doing letting yourself get tangled up in the whole business? You and your bloody puffers. Couldn't bear to let the dratted boat go on its own, I suppose?'

'*Boat*? You mean ship. And anyway, where were you when we needed you?'

He didn't have to ask what she meant. 'Just because you didn't see us very often didn't mean we weren't there. The RAF went out on well over two thousand sorties trying to keep the Stukas away, and pretty savage ones they were. We lost about a hundred planes and seventy-six pilots.'

'Yes, but . . .'

'Which we could ill afford. My dear, sweet Jenny, the Germans are getting set to invade, and we have, this day, precisely 466 serviceable fighters to pit against three-thousand-plus German fighters and bombers. Now, I know we're all expected to be supermen, but just think about it.'

'Is it really as bad as that?'

'In a word, yes.' He moved a little stiffly in his chair and she looked at him suspiciously.

'What's the matter?'

'Nothing.'

'Yes there is.'

'It's all right. I got a bit wet, that's all.'

'How?'

'Fell in the water. Have another chocolate.'

'How did you fall in the water?'

'Oh, hell! You're as bad as a nagging wife. I got shot down and had to ditch in the Channel.'

She nearly choked. 'You *what*? Do you mean to tell me you've been up in the air fighting Germans when you're supposed to be sitting in an office giving people mature and sensible advice?'

'Fighter Command was short of pilots, and I happened to have a few hours to spare.'

'*Honestly*, Matt. Haven't you got any sense?' The tears sprang to her eyes. 'Didn't you have enough of fighting last time? You're forty-three years old, but you still insist on being out there, risking your neck. You go romping into trouble as if it's the most natural thing in the world to do. It's really *very* unfair to the people who worry about you. I've no patience with you!'

She couldn't think why, when she was so upset with him, he should be sitting there with his gentian eyes alight with love and amusement.

Until he said, 'Romping into trouble? Look who's talking.'

6

JENNY was back at work by the middle of July, and furiously busy. The Admiralty was screaming not only for aircraft carriers and battleships but smaller vessels in impossible numbers; seven hundred escort ships and fast minesweepers, five hundred magnetic minesweepers, almost two thousand trawlers, six hundred motor torpedo boats, motor launches and other small craft. A total figure, Jenny calculated bitterly one day, that spread out over the years of the depression would have kept every man on the Clyde comfortably employed.

But that was past history now. The Britton yard had its share of the new orders, as well as much urgent work on conversions and repairs, and Jenny kept having to pinch herself to persuade herself that it was really happening. This was what things should be like, what they had been like long ago. She felt a renewed excitement every day at seeing all the berths full again and everyone working just as they had done when she was a child. Except, as always, for the handful of men who only worked when someone in a bowler hat came round.

There was no rest at work, and none at home, although everything there was frustration rather than excitement.

She missed Beth terribly, because Beth had stayed at home, feeling increasingly unsettled, for the first few months of the war and then said, 'This is silly. I'm going to be called up some day soon, and I might as well go now, when at least I'll have some choice about which of the Services I can join.'

When Beth had been born, Jenny, with memories of her own childhood still fresh, had sworn to herself that she would never dictate to her children, and would always give them credit for having sense; that she would dispense advice only when she knew they hadn't enough experience to make a rational judgement of their own. It had worked quite well, she thought. But it meant that, desperately though she wanted Beth to stay at home until the last possible moment, all she could say was, 'It's your decision, my pet.'

And so Beth had gone straight into the Wrens, where she had become a cypher clerk. 'Not because I specially wanted to be,' she wrote, 'but the powers-that-be thought my experience in the fashion trade had probably given me a good eye for pattern! Marvellous, isn't it?'

Even without Beth, the house was bursting at the seams with people, not only family but a succession of billeted-out Polish and Free French officers. And there were rationing and shortages to be contended with, too. Since Allie's cook had decided to evacuate herself to the country and it was as much as Allie could do to heat up a tin of soup, Jenny, after a few weeks that were later to be immortalised in family legend as the Beans-on-Toast Era, had no choice but to take charge. The family then discovered, to its dismay, the true meaning of delegation of responsibility.

'There isn't an onion to be had in the shops,' Jenny said, 'and if I have to think up one more way of making turnips edible I will go on strike. So Bob will just have to dig up the lawn and plant it with vegetables.'

'But I dunno a thing aboot gardening,' protested the luckless Bob.

'Well, you can learn. That's what brains are for. Johnny and Muriel will help you with the planting and weeding. And Nick, do you remember when you were about six or seven, and I had you looking after the hens at Provost Charters?'

'Y-e-e-s.'

'Well, I've managed to get hold of some laying ones, so you can knock up a henhouse at the back, and take charge of them again. It'll give you an interest in life.'

'Getting a herd of cows, too, are we?' he asked.

She ignored the provocation. 'Allie can do the shopping, because it's not as if you need to know anything about cooking when there's no choice anyway.'

'Thank you very much,' Allie said.

Under Jenny's reign of terror, the food at Castlehead swiftly improved. The most trying thing about the whole business was that Gill's domestic science teacher at school insisted on teaching her pupils all the latest and most loathsome Ministry of Food recipes and made them take the results of their labours home with them. Waste not, want not.

One of the Free French officers turned green when he tasted his first spoonful of oatmeal and cheese soup, and Jenny didn't blame him.

7

JENNY was up and down to London almost as often as she had been during the first years of her marriage to Howard, only now it wasn't in luxurious first-class sleepers but in dreary, packed trains that were always late, trains whose windows were covered with a thick coat of paint and couldn't be opened after dark because of blackout regulations, and where the atmosphere after eight or ten hours was an intolerable fug of smoke and bottled beer and sweaty serge uniforms.

But, tiring and uncomfortable though the travelling was, most of her necessary journeys to consult with the Admiralty brought her a private reward, the reward of seeing Matt. Her own experience at Dunkirk had given her a new perspective on life and death and it seemed to her that, when there might well be no tomorrow, today was all that mattered.

Now, whenever opportunity offered, she went straight to his flat among the rooftops near Whitehall and let herself in with his spare key, and hoped he would be there. If he wasn't, she waited, and sometimes he didn't come, and sometimes he did.

One night during the darkest days of the Battle of Britain he came stumbling in, grimy, unshaven, and almost blind with fatigue.

It had been a day when wave after wave of German bombers had swept in over the coast, their purpose to destroy every RAF base in the south-east of England. Fighters had been wrecked before they could take off, hangars flattened, ground crew killed, power cables cut, landing fields turned into lunar landscapes.

Fighter Command was already two hundred pilots short, and those who were still able to fly were very near the limits of their endurance. And so Matt himself, quite improperly for someone whose expert judgement was officially considered more important than his ability to handle a Spitfire, had gone up himself.

To Jenny, he said, 'If this battle we are fighting now is lost, it will be the end of the war. And of everything else, too.' It was as much as he could do to get the words out.

Almost fifteen years had passed since they had first become lovers but, looking at him then, Jenny knew that the passion in her heart was stronger than it had ever been, that her love was something that would outlast her life, its intensity untarnished and undimmed, no matter what lay before them.

The tears of thankfulness pricking her eyes, she bathed him and put him to bed like a baby, and when he woke restless in the small hours and found her beside him, he tried to make love to her and fell asleep in the middle, so that when he woke again they were still locked together. By then he could manage to smile, and move tantalisingly inside her, and tease her into taking command; and for a while she was able to dull his pain over the half-trained boys he had watched plunge to flaming death the day before.

8

EXACTLY a week later, the Air Ministry issued a top priority alarm to all RAF commands – 'Invasion Alert 1'. It meant that, within the next twenty-four hours, the German army was expected to launch a seaborne invasion across the Channel.

But nothing had happened by the late afternoon, when Matt was at Bentley Priory, Fighter Command HQ just outside London, and the report came in that, according to radio crossbearings, huge formations of German bombers and fighters had set out from Calais.

With Air Chief Marshal Dowding, Air Vice Marshal Park and others, he went to the balcony of the Operations Room to look down on the huge map of the Channel and south-east England spread out on the table below. Girls in WAAF uniform, wearing headphones through which they received messages from the wireless operators, were using long, magnetic rods to push different-coloured blocks across the chart. Some blocks represented RAF, some enemy.

It was a familiar enough sight, because all Ops Rooms were laid out to the same pattern. What wasn't familiar was the speed at which the girls were raking the blocks across the table; and the other thing that wasn't familiar was the numbers. It didn't look like an invasion, but it was going to be the biggest raid yet.

Even so, everyone knew what was going to happen, because it always did. When the German formations reached the English coast, they would break up into sections, some of them heading for aircraft factories, some for the oil refineries along the Thames, and some for airfields or the industrial complexes of outer London. In more than a year of war, inner London – the London of history – had never been a target. Rumour had it that this was because Herr Hitler, when he had conquered Britain, wanted to ride along the Mall in state and take up residence in Buckingham Palace. He probably had visions, too, of kicking Winston Churchill all the way round the corridors of Westminster.

The RAF was used to the Germans' bombing routine, and its fighters were preparing to go up as usual. Once the attacking formations split up, the squadron leaders would yell 'Tally ho!' into their mouthpieces and the waiting Hurricanes, Spitfires and Defiants would pounce.

On the seventh of September, therefore, the senior command officers stood and watched the girls moving the blocks around, and waited for the three hundred Dornier and Heinkel bombers with their escort of six hundred Messerschmitts to divide into separate striking forces.

They seemed to he holding on for longer than usual.

They continued to hold on.

Matt, with a cold feeling in the pit of his stomach, was just thinking, 'What if, this time, they don't split up?' when Dowding's *aide* said, 'That's funny. They don't seem to be splitting up, do they, sir?'

By the time Park and Leigh-Mallory had succeeded in redirecting their heavily outnumbered fighters into the right patch of air, the

Luftwaffe had blown up Woolwich Arsenal and rased half of London's docks as well as most of the districts of Silvertown, Canning Town, Limehouse, Barking, Tower Bridge, Poplar and Millwall.

As the afternoon gave way to evening, people on the outer fringes of London thought, for a confused moment, that the sun was setting at the wrong point of the compass. Matt himself, overflying the raging fires of the East End in his own BB.3e to try and assess the damage, felt as if he were gazing into the very heart of hell.

The London Blitz had begun.

9

SIX months later, it was the turn of Clydebank.

Jenny had just arrived at the yard on fire-watching duty when she heard the stomach-curdling, rising-and-falling wail of the Air Raid siren. And then the drone of planes. Neither she, nor any of the half-dozen others also on duty that night, could believe it at first. Until now, the west of Scotland had escaped all but some fairly desultory attacks from the air, because it lay almost beyond the Luftwaffe's operating range.

Jenny had seen the London docks the autumn before. Great mushrooms of black and brown smoke, shot with crimson; bridges and catwalks reduced to tangled wrecks; cranes toppled in the water; ships sunk; the river itself aflame with the oil spilled on its surface; hundreds of people killed, thousands injured.

And all of that despite the anti-aircraft defences and the efforts of RAF Fighter Command.

It couldn't be going to happen here.

The Clyde didn't have any proper anti-aircraft batteries or fighter cover. Its sole defence was the decoy towns, the empty spaces of the Kilpatrick Hills on one side of the river and the Gleniffer Braes on the other, both of them ingeniously sown with chinks and cracks of light so that, from the air at night, they looked like badly blacked-out factory sites.

It was an idea that might have worked with one or two bombers, but not with waves of them, because the fires started by the first wave illuminated the landscape for those that came after.

Throughout the whole of that night, and the night that followed, Jenny stood on the office roof and waited – and waited – for the next wave to swing across the river and release the bombs that would reduce the Britton yard, after more than a hundred years of enterprise and endeavour, of struggle and heartbreak, to a pile of smoking rubble.

Waited and watched, with the yard's fire engine standing by and sandbags and stirrup pumps scattered around like tickets after a football match, as the burgh of Clydebank across the river, the place that had grown with the shipyards, was reduced again to the waste land it had been before John Brown's was ever heard of.

It had never been a pretty place, full of desirable residences and historic monuments; just a desert of barren streets and crowded sandstone tenements, a place where ordinary people worked and lived. Jenny tried not to imagine what it must be like to be in one of those tenements now, floor upon floor upon floor of people, with the high explosives raining down. Most folk, she thought, must be running out of them and away, to the inadequate shelters, or into the streets or the hills away from those tumbling mountains of stone that the bombs were transforming, minute by relentless minute, into cairns for the dead and dying.

Daylight revealed a Clydebank that was no longer recognisable, a chaos of buildings flattened or collapsing, of dead bodies, fires smouldering everywhere, the air choking with dust, craters in the roads, the injured buried in the rubble, paving slabs tossed around like confetti, dazed and homeless people, lost children, stray dogs.

And the same thing was to happen all over again that night.

By the time the second night of the blitz was over, there were only seven dwellings out of the twelve thousand that had once been Clydebank which still remained standing and whole.

Jack was one of those who were killed. Consistent in death as in life, he had gone across the river to address a strike meeting, of shipyard apprentices, and there had been a direct hit on the building.

No one was very sure how much of what they finally buried in the cemetery was actually Jack, because all that it had been possible for the Civil Defence people to do was sort bits of shattered bodies into piles, each with an approximately correct number of limbs, and tag each pile with the name of someone who, not so many hours before, had been alive and now was dead.

In a way, Jenny would have expected to feel more sorrow for Jack's children than for Jack himself, but the loss of their father didn't seem to worry them very much; it was almost as if they were having to work at it.

Bob said, 'Och, well, he was a hard man, and Gill and me'll never forgive him for how he neglected our mam. Anyway, he was never home. We didny know him.'

It was then that the tears came to Jenny's throat and she found herself leafing through her memories of a brother who'd been born to trouble as the sparks flew upward; stiff-necked, obsessive, stubborn as a mule. A thick-headed idealist who'd thought you could force people to see the light. She knew that, by ordinary human standards, he'd been criminally negligent towards poor stupid Lizzie, and yet he'd wept when he knew that the men on the Clyde were to be given back their work and their self-respect.

She didn't know, herself, whether she'd loved him, because in maturity he hadn't been a lovable person. And yet there'd been warmth and humour in him once, before he'd set himself up as an unsuccessful David against the Goliath of the world's ills. Whatever he'd become in the end, Jenny thought, she'd never forget how he'd protected her when they were small, or how kind and funny he'd been the night before she and Tom ran away to be married. She might not have loved the other Jack, but she'd been fond of that one, and always would be.

10

THE inexplicable thing about the Clydebank blitz was that, with the great wide river lying there below them, its bank lined for miles with shipyards and half-built vessels of war, the German bombers had missed the lot.

They'd killed hundreds of people and flattened a whole town. But to their real objective, they had done little more damage than shatter a few windows and send a scattering of grit over the blueprints.

Two

1

AS HIS official car swept round the last bend in the unkempt drive, Matt saw Provost Charters again for the first time in almost five years and could have wept. The house had been requisitioned at the beginning of the war as a training centre for special air units, and he had inspected enough such centres to know what to expect. The average country house hadn't been designed to be kicked around by hobnailed boots.

He had thought he was prepared, but what he hadn't allowed for was that he had never known the other houses in a normal, civilised state, whereas Provost Charters had been his home.

And now the windows were criss-crossed with sticky tape so that those which hadn't been shattered by cricket balls wouldn't be shattered by bomb blasts. One corner of the porte-cochère was shored up with timber, as if someone had driven a tank into it. The marbled floor of the hall was pockmarked with missing tesserae, and there were Boy Scout tracking marks scrawled on the pillars as well as other symbols, more adult and more explicit. The Venus in the stairwell didn't look any more like the Venus de Milo for having had her arms chopped off, and all the attendant nymphs had acquired painted moustaches.

The CO's office was in what had been the morning room, and Matt, standing waiting for the man to get off the phone, found himself remembering a scene long forgotten, the scene over his 'poetry' on the day his mother had walked out of his life for ever.

He hadn't thought about his mother for years, the woman who had borne him and, by rejecting him, had helped to make him what he had become. She had been neat and smooth and rather cat-like, he remembered, with large slanting violet eyes and pencil-thin eyebrows, and the lazy, touch-me-not air of a puss who didn't want to play and would be obliged if you would go away and leave it alone. She'd had long, shining dark hair parted in the middle and drawn loosely back into a knot at the nape of her neck, and even when she was unwell, as she frequently was, had always looked amazingly pretty in a bitchy kind of way. He hadn't discovered until a few years ago that she'd died in the 'flu epidemic of 1918.

The CO saluted him smartly. 'Coffee or something before the inspection, sir?'

'No. And I'd like to see round the building first before we go out to the grounds.' The man didn't look altogether happy about that, and bad luck to him, Matthew thought.

The musicroom was now the men's recreationroom, and they seemed to be using the carved overmantel as a dart board. There were pin-ups all over the place, and on top of the piano, now covered with beer-glass stains and cigarette burns, was the sheet music for *Kiss me good-night Sergeant-Major*.

Matt was reminded of Grandmother Lutetia and her monthly ballad evenings when he and Tom had been summoned down to the musicroom, and their mother had played for them while they all sang *England, my England*, *Linden Lea*, the *Kashmiri Song*, and *Land of Hope and Glory*. They would have enjoyed themselves enormously if their grandmother hadn't always told them, 'Now, remember. I expect you to sing with plenty of spirit – but don't shout'. What wouldn't they have given to be able to let off steam a bit!

The drawingroom, now full of aircraft-plotting charts, brought back memories of Sunday readings from improving books; of the Christmas influx of relatives, mainly maternal, when Matt and Tom had had to submit to being peered at over their great-aunts' spectacles, jollied along by Uncle Stephenson, giggled at by distant girl cousins, preached at by Aunt Pearl, and looked down on by Howard, fatly smiling.

The staircase was in a bad state, Matt noted as the CO rushed him round, and the bedrooms not much better. And then they were at the top of the house, where the nursery and schoolroom had been, and the CO was saying, 'Only dormitories here, sir', and the whole past world of childhood was flooding into Matt's mind as he listened to the man going on about bedding and blanco and boots.

'Yes,' Matt murmured, 'naturally . . . of course . . . I see.'

And all the while he was tasting the Gregory's Mixture Nanny had fed Tom and himself every March 'to clear out the system', and being reminded of the violent spring-cleaning every April, when the schoolroom carpets and curtains and tablecloths had disappeared for days on end and Nanny had thrown out all the boys' butterfly specimens, birds' eggs, conkers and pieces of string, and decided which of their toys were to be given to the poor; usually without telling them. That was how they had lost the splendid train set Great-Uncle Hamish had sent them. Nanny had said all it did was collect dust, but that was because she never gave them time to play with it.

In summer, there had been the village cricket match, and Harvest Home in the autumn, and in November they had been set to snipping coloured paper into chains and decorations, and making dreadful Christmas presents. And then Christmas itself, and the excited awakening in the dark, hearing the rustle of the stockings hung on the bottom bedpost and wondering whether this year there might be something different in them. There never had been. It was always a tangerine in the toe, sugared almonds in the foot, an apple in the heel, and a box of pencils in the leg. The more important presents were opened later, round the tree.

And after all the excitement, it had been back to what Grandfather Albert jocosely referred to as 'auld claes and parritch'. Old clothes and porridge. It had been one of those jokes that Grandmother Lutetia had never appreciated.

'Right!' Matt said. 'We'd better go and have a look at this obstacle course of yours.'

It was a pleasant day in early May, and there were still some daffodils that had escaped the clumping boots, and the cow parsley was sending up its deceptively delicate leaves. But there was no sign of the peacocks, and the goldfish had gone from the water garden, and the fountain was just something to be leapfrogged by high-spirited young subalterns when they were less than sober. God help the man, Matt thought drily, who misjudged it and caught himself a crack in the family jewels.

The Blackmoor Vale looked wonderfully peaceful under the blue, unshadowed sky, and there was no more than the faintest of breezes. Down to the right Matt could see the Norman turret of the village church, standing where it had stood for more than eight hundred years, and knew that, lying in its shadow, were four graves that bore the name of Britton. The road on the other side of the Vale had probably been a track in Roman times, and down on the floor of the valley was an age-old landscape of trees and hedges, pastures and fields, and small figures going about their changeless labours.

Matt stood and gazed, oblivious to the energetic noises of men running and jumping and rolling and climbing, and the interminable chatter of their CO, who was thinking privately that he'd been inspected by some pretty rum brass hats in his time, but this one beat the lot.

Until that moment, Matt had never been conscious of any warmth of feeling for either Provost Charters itself, or the English countryside. But now he found that everything had changed; perhaps, he thought later, because both house and landscape were in such peril. Or perhaps because he was weary, and the contrast with a bombed and battered London so acute.

Whatever the reason, while one part of his brain told him he was a sentimental fool, the other half recognised that this, before him, was what he had been fighting for; what everyone was fighting for. Something kindly, beautiful, peaceful and stable. Something that, even to those who dragged out the whole of their lives in the dirty, drab industrial cities, had a special and mystical meaning. Whatever the reality of the twentieth-century struggle, however irrelevant this ancient landscape might be, it still was, and always would be, what was evoked whenever the name of England was spoken. A tag from Kipling drifted into his mind. 'If England was what England seems, An' not the England of our dreams, But only putty, brass an' paint, 'Ow quick we'd drop 'er! But she ain't!'

This, before him, was 'the England of our dreams', the vision, the ideal, that lay at the heart of it all.

He turned away, and as he did so, caught the CO's expressionless eye. He was tempted to say, 'And up you, too!' but restrained himself and signalled his driver, who was standing waiting at a respectful distance, to bring the car round.

As he was driven back to London, he reflected that he'd better not reveal to Jenny that he'd had a vision of England. He'd never heard her advocating home rule for Scotland, but he wouldn't put it past her to demand home rule for the Clyde.

And then the smile in his eyes faded, because without having to think about it he had come to a decision. If he survived the war, he was going to get Provost Charters back from Howard, whatever it cost.

2

NATASHA had had a most unhappy time during the two years after she had sold Provost Charters to Howard. The family had been quite harsh to her and she would not have known how to manage if it hadn't been for the faithful Granby. Until the dividends from the shipyard began to come in again, she had found herself having to rely on his little gifts to make life tolerable. There had been nothing extravagant, of course, nothing that she couldn't accept with perfect propriety. A fur wrap or two, a diamond necklace she'd been able to sell – after having it copied in paste – a few hampers from Fortnum and Mason. He'd even asked her to marry him once or twice, but she sensed that he had no great desire to give up his hedonistic bachelor existence and was only asking in order to be kind. Since she disliked being condescended to, she had said no. Besides, marriage would have curtailed her social life, which continued to flourish even if her swains were no longer as young as they had been.

When she had, of necessity, divided the London flat in 1936 and sold half of it off, it had turned out to be a blessing in disguise, because when war came, it meant that she was able, as a woman living alone in a flat with two bedrooms, to avoid having strangers billeted on her, whereas no protestations of matronly modesty would have availed her if she had had six.

Everyone congratulated her on her bravery in remaining in London, servantless, with bombs dropping everywhere, and she felt no compulsion to confess that she had sometimes wondered whether she was doing the right thing. But she had always hated the country, so she had stayed, and in a way quite enjoyed it. With external events providing a sufficiency of drama, she wasn't bored and had no need to stir things up just for amusement.

Her spare bedroom was much in demand. There were friends, of course, and family. Allie stayed sometimes, because Bertha had been bombed out of her flat and had gone off to do good works in Portsmouth or some such place. Even Jenny stayed once or twice, since she and Natasha had not so much forgiven as decided, for the time being, to ignore the worst of their past differences. It made Natasha feel quite old to have fallen out of the habit of needling Jenny and thinking of ill turns she might do her, and cutting things she might say.

There was Beth, too, passing through London on her way home on leave. Natasha had a soft spot for Beth, because Beth was such a sweet girl without being at all wishy-washy, and made it clear that she thought Natasha was funny and nice, and that it was time old feuds were laid to rest. And there was Howard's son Simon, who had mysteriously detached himself from his father and become an honorary Britton. He was in the army, on the legal staff, and at thirty-four just as ugly and just as exuberant as he had ever been.

And finally there was Nick, who hugged his mother convulsively and remarked on how calm she was. 'Positively serene! Are you feeling all right?'

He had become a mystery to her during these last years, and she found herself scarcely able to recognise her charming, careless boy in the dedicated man he had become. And now, of course, he was doing something she would never have foreseen.

'It is quite ridiculous! Why should you go off and risk your life in the navy when you are doing work of national importance at the shipyard!'

'I'm not. Not really. I've been training a deputy these last three years, a good man who's worked his way up from the engine shop. He knows far more about technical matters than I do, and he and Jenny are getting along well. And there's another chap from the drawing office doing the administrative work. They don't need me.'

Natasha, with the aid of a fish slice, succeeded in detaching a dried-egg omelette from the pan and placed it on a lukewarm plate in front of her son, who eyed it dubiously.

'You mean,' she said, 'the shipyard does not need you, but the navy does?'

'I know it sounds silly, put that way. Christ, mother! This tastes like old shoe leather.'

'I imagine it does,' she conceded. 'I do not make good omelettes. Or anything else. I was neither born nor bred to hover over a saucepan. So, why are you going?'

'Call it conscience. My life has always been too easy.'

'Pfff! How silly.' She surveyed him, frowning. 'You do not look very happy about what lies ahead?' Indeed, she thought he looked grim, coldly fearful, almost resentful, and certainly not as if he had any expectations of glory. But then, this was a war that not even the young had welcomed.

Reminiscently, she said, 'I remember what a glow of excitement Matt was in when he went off to join up in 1914. As if it was all something noble and wonderful.'

'Well, he learned his mistake, didn't he?'

She sighed. 'I suppose so. War is so stupid.'

3

THE doorbell rang persistently one morning, just after six o'clock, and Natasha dragged herself awake and into the sapphire blue velvet dressing-gown with the satin revers, then brushed her hair and pinched some colour into her cheeks, and went to answer it.

'Dear God, at last!' Matt said. 'I was beginning to think you'd fled the country.'

He was in full uniform but so thick with dust that the crinkles round his eyes and the long, deep lines that ran from his nostrils to the corners of his mouth looked crusty and packed with sand, like river beds in a drought.

She stood in the doorway staring at him. 'Let me in!' he said, hammering feebly on the air. 'Let me in! I am innocent!'

And still she went on staring at him, because she had discovered something about him at last. It had always mystified her why, when he was so like his father in looks, he was at the same time so much handsomer, so much more attractive. And now she knew. It was the humour, and the vitality. Paul had affected his leisured, supercilious style for so long that it had become a part of him, and although he had been witty, he had not been humorous. It occurred to Natasha that wit was a cold thing, but humour was warm.

She said, 'Not too innocent, I hope,' and stood back to let him in.

He had been *very* like Paul during and after the Great War, when he too had cultivated a laziness, a nonchalance that held people at arm's length. But somewhere in the 1920s he had lost that. She thought suddenly that perhaps he had been having a difficult time, because the impression of intense vitality – the flame at which lesser mortals could warm themselves – had only come in the 30s when he had begun to be successful and sure that he could do what he had set out to do.

She had loved him since he was eighteen, and now he was – what? – forty-five, and she was fifty-two. It was acceptable.

Her smile curved. 'What have you been doing? Do you want breakfast?'

'Yes, please,' he said, adding hurriedly, 'I'll cook it. Nick warned me.'

'Ungrateful boy! But since it is you, you may have a special treat. A friend has given me a tin of American bacon, and we will open it.'

'Tash, you're an angel. And?'

'And toast. And I have learned to mix butter and margarine so that it does not taste as bad as margarine, though it does not taste as good as butter. I have also some home-made rhubarb-and-ginger jam which Jenny brought me last time she was here, which I do not like. You may eat all of it if you wish. In fact, I hope you will. And there is real coffee.'

'Did anyone ever tell you you're a wonderful woman?'

'Breakfast first, and you may tell me later. But why are you here?'

'A bomb, what else? I got home last night after a very tiring official day to discover that home was no more. So I have spent the night digging my neighbours out of the rubble, and generally amusing myself scrunching through broken glass and falling into craters, delivering stray children to the WVS, and tossing sand buckets at incendiaries and naughty words at the Luftwaffe.'

One thing people in London had learned over the last year or two was to appear to make light of tragedy.

Natasha saw now that his hands were raw and bleeding. 'You want to wash,' she said. 'With luck, there may still be a little warm water in the bathroom.'

Afterwards, he borrowed a frilly apron and cooked the bacon and made the toast and put the coffee on, and when they had breakfasted he looked better. So she went round behind him, and began to massage his shoulders, and then leaned over and kissed him. Although she perfectly understood that he had come to her this morning only because there was nowhere else to go, it was an opportunity not to be missed.

When he had left her, that night in the conservatory at Provost Charters more than twenty years before, she had murmured, 'I can wait, my darling. I can wait.' She hadn't even conceded the possibility of defeat. And in the intervening years, she still hadn't doubted. His marriage hadn't worried her at all once she had met his wife; she had known immediately that Mims, poor Mims, was more interested in women than men. Jenny had been different, and Natasha had done her best to drive a wedge between them, even though she didn't think of straitlaced Jenny as being serious competition.

She was moderately sure, now, that nothing had come of that little affair, not even young Johnny. It had been Howard, wishing

544

to stir up discord in the family, who had put that idea into her head. And if there was a look of the Brittons about the boy – well, Howard was half Britton himself. Not for years had she seen Matthew and Jenny exchange a word or a look that she could have categorised as suspicious.

It surprised her a little that, after all this time, she herself still wanted Matthew, even if, in the wanting, there was a streak of simple exasperation over how elusive he had always been. She had never accustomed herself to being denied what she desired.

But here he was, at last. Her Matthew! Still her dark Adonis, despite the distinguished wings of grey in his hair; still the one man who had always filled her with a sense of something that was half sentiment and half physical desire. She had learned after Paul's death that there were other men who were just as expert in bed as her husband had been, but although her body revelled in the simple sexuality of it all and such encounters satisfied her overriding need, it depressed her sometimes that love had always been missing.

And now? Now, of course, as a mature woman dealing with a mature man, she knew better than to throw herself at her darling boy, to try and break down his barriers by the violence of her own physical allure and his need, as she had done all those years ago, when she had only succeeded in frightening him off. She knew better, too, than to resort to the seductive little movements and surreptitious touches that had proved equally unavailing in the years between, so that he had become careful not to approach her too closely.

So she made her voice deliberately sultry, and faintly mocking, when she said, 'You must need a bed.'

Provocatively, she smoothed her hand over his hair and brought her body so close to his that her breasts, straining within the blue velvet house-coat, brushed temptingly against his shirt-clad chest. She knew he *must* be sexually aware of her. Men always were.

But he showed no trace of shock or embarrassment or desperation. It annoyed her quite considerably when, instead, his whole body went limp and he began to laugh helplessly. Then he rose and took her by the shoulders, and pressed a kiss to her lips that was not unlike the sardonic, punishing one he had given her the day he came back from the Great War. But this time the kiss had no underlying message at all.

Afterwards, his voice still shaking, he said, 'Tash, you're incorrigible! You sounded exactly like Dietrich trying to vamp Jimmy

Stewart or someone. Yes, I want a bed, but frankly, my dear, I don't want yours!'

He could see the reactions chasing each other through her mind. She wasn't accustomed to being rejected, and certainly not to being laughed at, so there was a rising anger until it dawned on her that to be angry would make her look ridiculous. And after a moment she became unsure of what to do or say next, and looked at him doubtfully and with a curious innocence; if she had but known it, he was nearer to giving her a good, honest hug then than he had ever been. In the end, his amusement began to infect her, and a reluctant gleam came to her eye, and expanded into a slightly shamefaced smile, and ultimately into a real, honest-to-goodness giggle.

'Give up?' he asked.

'Give up.'

'No more assaults on my virtue?'

She sighed. 'No more.' It was over now. 'You may have the spare bedroom for ever and ever, without fear.'

And then a thought occurred to her. 'But you must pay a price.'

He was immediately suspicious, and more so when she smiled upon him as lavishly as if she had been twenty-one again, and he a fourteen-year-old whom she had taught to tie his tie with style.

She said, 'Since I am not a good cook, and you *are* . . .'

'On the evidence of a few rashers of bacon?'

'There is no doubt in my mind. So, for as long as you are here, you must do the cooking.'

'A pleasure, ma'am!' He sat down and, planting his elbows on the table, said wistfully, 'Of all the gorgeous food we used to eat before the war, do you know what I most long for? Not oysters at the Savoy but breakfast in the station buffet at Perth. It used to be the best breakfast you could get anywhere, except for the coffee. Ayrshire bacon, and a perfectly-fried real fresh egg, and pork slicing sausage, and wonderful morning rolls, and lovely salty butter, and thick-cut marmalade . . .'

'Don't!' she said. 'Now, what *I* would like would be, first, caviar and vodka at the Ritz, and then . . .'

It was surprisingly pleasant, after all the sensitive years, to be just friends, and Natasha regretted it deeply when after only ten days, Matthew decided he must make an effort to find somewhere else to live.

More than that. She was exceedingly annoyed by the fact that, *because* they were just friends, she found herself having to pretend to amusement when he told her he was moving because 'a certain lady', hearing that he was sharing Tasha's flat, had – as he put it – 'hit the roof'.

<h1 style="text-align:center">4</h1>

THE war dragged on, and on, and on, so that it became hard to remember what things had been like before it began, and impossible to imagine it being over, even when, after more than two years, America at last came in.

The only difference that made, at first, was that the country suddenly became full of GIs – nice boys, most of them, Jenny thought, if rather prone to behave as if the British hadn't been doing anything since 1939 except hang around waiting for the Yanks to come and get things going.

1942 dragged to its end with the Russians taking the full weight of German might and even winning victories. Then the GIs landed in North Africa, and in 1943 the Russians drove the Germans back on the Eastern Front, and there were Allied landings in Sicily, and Italy surrendered.

Jenny, by that time, was worrying not only about Matt and Beth, but Bob, too. She knew where Matt was, most of the time, but censorship meant that every time there was a major battle on land or sea she found her nerves wound up for days, in case Beth or Bob had been involved. And then, when no telegram boy appeared, she was able to wind down again, just a little.

By the spring of 1944 Britain was like a huge armed camp in readiness for D-Day, and the Allied landings in France. It was then that eighteen-year-old Gill volunteered for the WAAF.

Jenny said despairingly, 'Oh, Gill, why? Why couldn't you have waited until you were called up?'

Gill shrugged. 'I'm sorry, Auntie Jenny, but it'll make a change, and I hate being a shorthand-typist.'

She had always been a difficult girl. It was she who, more than Bob or Muriel, had borne the brunt of her mother's long illness and dying, and Jenny had tried very hard to make it up to her, to coax her out of her shell, but she hadn't been very successful. Perhaps, she had thought sometimes, she had been too brisk, too bracing. Whatever the reason, she had never managed to get close to her.

And that made it much, much worse when, only a month later, the doorbell rang, and this time it *was* a boy with a telegram. And Jenny tore the dreadful thing open at last, and it wasn't about Matt, Beth, or Bob, but Gill, who had been killed in an air raid on the training camp. It was weeks before Jenny managed to overcome her guilt at the small voice that whispered to her, even as she grieved, 'If it had to be one of them . . .'

But then, for a change, something really good happened.

5

NICK, home on leave late in 1944, was strolling along Piccadilly, admiring the sandbags and wire netting and the boarded-up shop windows, when the siren sounded. He hesitated, because he detested the tube stations crammed with people taking shelter, and always wondered how much shelter they actually provided. If the truth were told, he hated London, too, these days; it was quite unlike itself. He felt more comfortable at sea.

He glanced towards the Circus which, without Eros, didn't look much like itself either, and as he did so, caught sight of a girl in the uniform of an ATS officer walking briskly towards the station. He could only see her back, but . . .

He broke into a sprint.

She turned as he drew level with her, and he grinned at her and said, 'Hello, Francesca. Going my way?'

In nine years, she had scarcely changed at all. Despite the crisp, efficient uniform, she still had that waiflike look, and the nervous trick of lowering her eyelashes when she spoke. Her smile was still just a little lopsided and questioning, as if she hoped you might smile, too, but wasn't convinced of it.

And his heart still turned over at the sight of her. He didn't know why; had never known why. Something to do with chemistry perhaps. He still adored her. He didn't care, now, what the hell her father thought of him, and he didn't care what she thought, either, as he snatched her left hand free from the strap of her shoulderbag and raised it so that he could see whether she wore a ring.

Laughing a little shyly, she exclaimed, 'Unhand me, sir!'

'Certainly not. Never again, in fact. Where are you stationed? I've got three more days' leave. I'm a reformed character and I can produce any number of witnesses to prove it. Will you marry me? Oh, Francesca, please say you'll marry me.'

She stared at him for a moment, because he was so very different from the boy she had been in love with when she was seventeen. He still had fair hair and eyes that were piercingly blue. He was still tall and lithe and goodlooking in an indefinably foreign way. But he looked as if he had been through a good deal since they last met.

So had she. She had been engaged at the beginning of the war to a nice, cheerful young man, a family friend, but he had been killed ten days before the wedding, and she had realised afterwards that it probably wouldn't have worked, anyway, because deep down she had been hankering after someone else. And still was. For the man who, standing by the battered side windows of Swan and Edgar's in the middle of an air raid, was asking her to marry him. At last.

'What took you so long?' she said.

6

BUT still the war wasn't over, even though, by early 1945, British and American troops were putting increasing pressure on Germany from the west, while the Russians did the same from the east. The trap was closing.

Though it wasn't closed yet, which was why, one bright spring day, young Johnny Fournier very nearly broke his mother's heart by appearing before her in RAF uniform, saying, 'I've volunteered. Well, I had to get in before it was over, didn't I!'

He was so young, so eager, so proud. So very much what his father must have been all those years ago, in August 1914.

Jenny said, 'My goodness, don't you look handsome! Why didn't you tell me?'

'I wanted to surprise you. And I know it sounds silly, but ever since you told me Matt was my real dad, I've wanted a chance to prove that – oh, I don't know – that I'm worthy of him, I suppose. I've always liked him and admired him so much, and, well . . .'

He didn't have to go on. Jenny knew what he meant. He was determined that Matt would have no cause to sneer at him as Howard had done.

With a little difficulty, she said, 'I don't think Matt would have been in the least disappointed if you'd decided to wait until you were called up. He's very understanding, you know, and he loves you a lot.'

'I know *that*! But it's for the sake of my own self-respect, really, if you get down to it. Don't be cross with me, mum, there's a love?'

'Am I ever cross with you?'

'No, but you needn't think I'm blind! You're not exactly bowled over with joy.'

It was a near thing, but she managed to sigh and smile, and say, 'We'd better have a glass of sherry to celebrate, hadn't we?'

7

AND then, at last, in May 1945, Herr Hitler was defeated, and everyone went wild with relief. Outside Buckingham Palace, fifty thousand people danced and sang, blew whistles and waved flags, kissed and hugged perfect strangers, and cheered and cheered and cheered.

And while the Royal Family was appearing on the balcony of the palace, Mr Churchill was appearing on another balcony, in Whitehall. He, too, was waving to the crowds, and had taken the trouble to change into his famous siren suit for the occasion. He conducted the throngs below in a rendering of *Land of Hope and Glory* which brought tears to the eyes of all the elderly ladies who were his most ardent admirers.

And, it soon seemed, almost his only admirers, because the general election that followed two months later ended in a Labour landslide. It was thought that the servicemen's vote had been the decisive factor, because servicemen had not been as impressed by Mr Churchill's conduct of the war as civilians had been.

It was therefore Mr Attlee who had the pleasure of informing the nation in mid-August that, consequent upon the vaporisation of two Japanese cities by atomic bombs, VJ Day – Victory over Japan Day – might now be celebrated.

'The last of our enemies is laid low,' he said.

8

JENNY, who distrusted all politicians impartially, whatever their hue, said, 'The last of our *foreign* enemies, he means. I sometimes wonder whose side the government thinks it's on.'

Tash was holding a party to celebrate VJ Day, and Jenny, looking round, couldn't help but count the cost of the six years that had passed. Nor did she know whether the full cost had yet been reckoned.

Two weeks before, she had received a telegram saying that Johnny was missing in Burma. She hadn't slept since. She hadn't thought about anything else.

Let him not be dead, she prayed.

She didn't realise how blankly intent her face was until she suddenly saw that Nick, across the room, had put boyishly waggling hands to his ears and was grinning at her as if to say, 'Wakey! Wakey!'

She smiled back, thankful that he was recovering so well. Not long after he and Francesca had been married, his ship had been torpedoed in the Baltic, and he had had to have a foot amputated because of gangrene and been invalided out of the navy. But he and Chesca were coping wonderfully. Chesca was one of the deep-down-nicest people Jenny had ever met, which was amazing when you considered the big, domineering and remarkably dislikeable man who was her father. But Chesca had somehow managed to retain her own quick intelligence and startlingly acute sense of the ridiculous, and Jenny thought she was exactly the right wife for Nick.

Matt materialised at her side. They had become very good, in public, at simulating a long-standing, casual friendship. 'What are you looking so pleased about?' he asked.

'Oh, just thinking I couldn't have found a better wife for Nick if I'd chosen her myself.'

'Busybody!'

But though he was smiling, she began worrying all over again because he looked so deathly tired. Ever since April, when almost by chance he had been present when the concentration camp at Belsen had been liberated, he had been suffering from appalling,

551

recurring nightmares. He hadn't told her anything about the experience, but she had seen newspaper photographs and she could guess. He always appeared so vital, so unruffled, so in control, that it was easy to forget how much imagination he had. But at least he was still alive, and whole.

There was a bustle at the door, and Jenny turned, wondering who it could be. Bob was still in Germany with the army, and so was Simon. Could it be? she wondered, her heart leaping . . .

And it was. It was Beth. 'Oh, darling, darling! I didn't think you would be able to get leave!'

'It's all right, mum, there's no need to smother me.' But the words were accompanied by Beth's lovely smile and a hug that spoke volumes. She said, 'We made a special effort to get here, because I wanted you to meet Joe. Mum, this is Joe de Roos. Joe, my mother.'

He was American, a captain in the army, and Jenny was doubtful at first because he looked very serious and rather hatchet-faced. But when he smiled she thought what nice eyes he had, and when he spoke it was with the most beautiful slight drawl.

'I am one hundred per cent delighted to make your acquaintance, ma'am. I have heard a great deal about you from your daughter. She thought these might help you to like me.'

Nylons, of course. Jenny wasn't used to being called 'ma'am' except by Matt when he was being sarcastic, and said rather distractedly, 'Oh, thank you. It's very kind . . . Have you been an American long, Captain de Roos?'

She had intended to say, 'Have you been over from America long?' but her slip of the tongue had the happy result of making everyone laugh and putting an end to all embarrassment.

Beth said, 'He's a Founding Father, sort of. His family went over to New Amsterdam in the 1600s.'

'And a pretty fair bunch of ruffians they were, too, I can assure you, Mrs Fournier.'

Beth turned to him in mock disapproval. 'Don't give the show away like that. She might take against you, and we can't have that when you're going to be her son-in-law.'

Her mother couldn't think of a thing to say, except, '*Oh, Beth!*

9

THE telephone rang, which surprised everyone because they wouldn't have expected the operators still to be on duty.

Natasha said, 'Jenny, it's for you. It's Allie.'

Allie had refused to make the journey to London, because she was in her mid-sixties now and, she said, too old for long, tiresome train journeys at short notice.

Why should she be phoning? Jenny's hand was shaking as she raised the handset to her ear.

Matt watched her, his own hand covering his mouth and his eyes empty, as if the light behind them had been extinguished and his heart left waiting in the dark.

Through the noise of the party he couldn't hear what she was saying, nor could he see any change in the carefully unemotional expression on her face.

It seemed an aeon before she replaced the receiver and turned and said, 'A telegram. It was delayed. It was from Johnny. He's all right.'

Matt thought she was going to faint. But she didn't. She managed a wavering smile, and said again, just in case he hadn't understood. 'It's all right. Johnny's all right.'

PART SIX

1946–1953

One

1

'SO we painted the pillar boxes green,' Johnny reported cheerfully.

'Why?'

'We thought it would be a change.'

Jenny gave up. When she had been in her teens, university was something you didn't even bother to dream about, and she couldn't help but feel that the children ought to recognise how lucky they were. But Johnny and Bob had ex-servicemen's grants, and Muriel had won a bursary, and not one of them showed a sign of gratitude, even if they were vociferously proud of their *alma mater* and its five hundred years of history.

The house rang to yells of 'Ygorra!' and Bob fell in love with some girl called Polly Conn – who turned out to be a course of lectures in Political Economy – while Muriel, reading first year zoology, brought a frog home to dissect on the kitchen draining board. It wasn't unusual for them to arrive home at breakfast time, still in full evening dress, after an all-night debate or one of the tribal events with names like Daft Friday which Jenny felt it wiser not to enquire into too closely. And when she was tempted to, she remembered how drab her own youth had been and let it all flow over her smiling head. The world had undoubtedly changed for the better.

Even so, on the phone to Matt, she said, 'It beats me! You'd think the ex-service students would have a sense of responsibility, but they're the ones who paint pillar boxes and throw bags of flour at the Rector.'

Matt laughed. 'I know the feeling. I did the equivalent myself when I went to the States in 1919. It's called forgetting. But I was wasting time, and they probably aren't. I've often thought that if I'd settled down to work straight away, instead of fooling around, it wouldn't have taken me nearly so long to get to where I am now. I shouldn't worry about them, Jenny. I imagine they're really working quite hard in the intervals of letting off steam. And if dashing around at dead of night repainting the pillar boxes on University Avenue cheers them up, why not? The world's a drab enough place.'

It was true. The end of the war had proved not to be an end, after all. An end to fear of death and destruction, certainly, but in every other way, the greyness and weariness of war remained.

Britain was broke. There was a housing shortage. Rationing had become even tighter when President Truman, three days after the surrender of Japan, abruptly terminated the Lend-Lease agreement that had helped to sustain Britain during the war; now everyone had to manage on a shillings-worth of fresh meat and twopenceworth of tinned meat a week. Even bread was rationed now, as it had never been during the war. There was talk of nothing but austerity, and wage restraint, of black marketeers and strikes, of 'export or die', and the queue of fifty thousand servicemen waiting to be divorced from their wives. Half the population seemed to be emigrating to Australia or New Zealand.

The only – and rather shameful – consolation was that it was worse abroad. The newspapers were full of the cold war in Europe, the civil war in China, Zionist terrorism in Palestine. The dismantling of the British Empire had begun, and India was partitioned into two independent states, Hindu India and Muslim Pakistan; in the riots and migrations that followed, four hundred thousand people were slaughtered. A few months later, Gandhi was assassinated. There were race riots in South Africa.

2

'HEY!' Matt said. 'Are you still there? What I phoned about was that I think I can snatch a few days off in April. Any chance of a nice secret week in Morar?'

'Yes, please. Definitely, yes please.'

Jenny had been exceedingly annoyed when Howard returned from America in 1946 and, as calmly as if he had never been away, resumed his campaign to make her return to him.

'I don't suppose,' she told Matt forcefully if inaccurately, 'that I have resorted to bad language more than half a dozen times in my life, but Howard really is the sheer bloody limit! I can't imagine what he thinks he's playing at, because I don't believe he really wants me back after all this time. He's just a rotten bully! He's only doing it to annoy me.

'I mean, it can't be some subtle preliminary to divorce, can it? After all, Johnny's grown up now, so that threat doesn't apply any more. And I shouldn't think he could cite something that happened twenty years ago as grounds – could he? Of course, there's desertion, but I've been leading such a pure and blameless life since I left him – everybody knows *that*! – that it would look in court as if I thought *anything* was preferable to going on living with him. Which is true, but I don't think he'd fancy that kind of affront to his vanity! What *is* he up to? Ooooh, I'm so cross!'

But although she was able to sound brisk and half-humorous about it, it worried her. There had been a widespread social reaction against the sexual laxity of the war years and the newspapers played it up for all they were worth. However restricted the number of their pages, they were always able to find space for a nice, titillating scandal. And the trouble was that Matt was now a distinguished public figure, the kind who was cited as a model for the young, and although he found it funny – ridiculous, in fact – Jenny could see no sense in going out of their way to invite gossip. She was convinced that if Howard petitioned for divorce it could do Matt a great deal of damage in unseen ways.

'Hell's teeth!' Matt expostulated. 'I can stand it. You don't think my whole business empire's going to come crashing down just because my morals aren't above reproach? You'd be the one who suffered.'

'And Johnny. What if Howard could still have him declared a bastard after all these years?'

'Most unlikely. I'll try and find out, if it'll make you feel happier.'

But he couldn't persuade her to recognise the benefits of divorce – beyond seeing the last of Howard – and it transpired that the whole thing was irrelevant in any case, because Howard eventually made it clear that he wasn't manoeuvring for divorce. In fact, he said, he would *never* divorce his wife.

Jenny, pointing out to Matt for the hundredth time that he and she could never be married anyway, was relieved.

And no, she still wasn't prepared to live in sin.

'No, no, no!' she said. 'I'm perfectly well aware that I used to keep going on about the morality of it, but I've grown out of that. No, it's the same problem as with divorce – worse, even. It's the scandal. Oh, *why* won't you see how harmful it could be!'

Nothing Matt could say would budge her, even though he said a good deal. It was a pity, if not surprising, that he left out the one thing that might, just possibly, have persuaded her. He didn't tell her because Jenny herself never confessed to him how often she was overcome by a private, miserable fury over the harshness of fate. She loved Matt so much, wanted so much to be with him always, but she didn't tell him because it was a cliché of life that it was only women who gave much thought to love and need, subjects of relatively little importance to men – who, as everyone knew, had weightier matters on their minds.

Matthew could have told her otherwise, that without her he was incomplete; but he didn't, or not in so many words. Somehow, he had always assumed that she knew.

So Allie's house in Morar continued to be their refuge, and they fled there whenever the opportunity arose. Apart from Johnny and Beth, Allie was the only person in the world to whom they had confessed to being lovers, although, as Allie said herself, she could hardly have failed to guess. But she knew little more, because Jenny didn't want her ever to be forced into the position of having to lie for them, either to Howard or to the press.

Now, Jenny said again, 'Morar? Oh, Matt, what heaven! I'll ask Allie, but I'm sure it'll be all right. It can be chilly in April, mind you.'

'So what? Sheepskin jackets and gum boots. See you soon, my darling.'

3

NICK was back in charge of the yard again, a yard that, miraculously, was still buzzing with activity, as it had been during the war. But he and Jenny seemed to spend all their spare time arguing about the future.

Nick was convinced that the Clyde's full order books and full employment were no more than a phase.

'Look! Japan and Germany may be paralysed now, but when they come back into competition they'll come with new machinery, new techniques, new everything. And with the traditional market for fast passenger ships declining – as you know very well it is – the competition for tankers and cargoes and ore carriers is going to be cutthroat. And I tell you frankly, Jenny, I can't face a repetition of the depression.'

'*You* can't? You only had about six months of it. I had fifteen years.'

'Then why the hell are you arguing? Matt says the shipbuilding *kind* of industry is doomed, and I think he's right. Give it another twenty years, and machines will be doing a good deal of what men do today. We have to look ahead.'

Jenny didn't want to look ahead. To her, it was always people who mattered, though she knew she could be pretty illogical about it. She was the first to weep over the depopulation of the Highlands – and the first to rush off to them in search of peace and quiet.

'But what about the men?'

'I don't know. New industries, maybe. A bigger variety of jobs even if they're done by fewer people. I've been talking to Matt . . .'

'So I gathered!'

'. . . and it's his notion we might expand the engineering shop and begin to make a transition from marine to aero engines. In partnership with him, of course.'

'What you might call a united Britton, in fact?'

He grinned. 'It's a thought, though, isn't it? Matt was right in 1918 when he told father the future was in the air. He was just too much ahead of his time. But now he's doing jolly well in the fortune-making line after all the years of blood, toil, tears and whatever, and if he can do it, why shouldn't we?'

Jenny said, with a trace of sarcasm, 'Especially since some of us prefer making money to inheriting it?'

'Chesca's been talking, has she?'

'She did just happen to mention that if you ran into your two small daughters on the street, she doubted whether you would recognise them. She tells me you're never at home because you feel that, having more or less inherited your rôle in the shipyard, you have to work twice as hard as anyone else to justify it.'

'Something like that,' he admitted.

'Well, good luck to you,' Jenny said cordially. 'How well I remember the days when I practically lived at the yard myself. Not any more. Age brings wisdom, and I am thinking of retiring.'

He couldn't help laughing at her. Her figure was as good as it had ever been, and her hair as fair. She still had gorgeous legs, even if Dior's 'New Look' deprived the viewer of much of what wartime Utility had revealed. There were a few wrinkles, of course, round eyes that could still brim with very youthful mischief. She was fifty, just, but if he hadn't known he'd have guessed at not a day over forty.

'Stop fishing for compliments,' he said.

561

4

BY the beginning of 1949, the idea of a 'united Britton' was on the verge of becoming a reality.

Between them, Nick, Jenny and Matt had hammered out most of the basic problems, and things had reached the stage where a formal meeting had been called, complete with lawyers, accountants and technical advisers.

Nick and Jenny were both on edge because, whatever happened, they were going to be out of their depth. It was all very well for Matt, whose business had so many tentacles by now that it would have been impossible for him to avoid delegating, but Nick and Jenny were accustomed to overseeing every detail themselves and being familiar with every legal and administrative intricacy touching on the yard's status as an exempt private company. That was all going to change now, and even though they had spent days puzzling over the new Companies Act, they still didn't feel they had a proper grasp of what they were in for. It wasn't that they didn't trust their lawyers, just that their habit of mind made them uneasy if they weren't *au fait* with everything.

Nick, in particular, was wary of the key decision that had to be taken, whether their association with the Britton-Bonny group was to amount to no more than a working agreement, or something much more closely integrated. Matt might be his brother, but Nick damned well wasn't going to let the yard lose its identity in a merger!

Matt, noting the belligerent gleam in his brother's eye, grinned to himself. Normally, he wouldn't have felt the need to be present at a meeting such as this; he didn't believe in employing extremely expensive dogs and then doing the barking himself. But it was a family affair, after all, and he wanted to be sure that Nick and Jenny weren't put at too much of a disadvantage. He had even suggested that the meeting be held at the yard, rather than at BB's head offices in London.

Anyway, it amused him to be here. Although his father had transferred a five per cent holding in Brittons' to him when he was born, it was the first time he had ever entered the famous boardroom, with its portraits of the frock-coated and bewhiskered Victorian worthies whom he found it impossible to think of as his ancestors. There was a very fetching one of Grandfather Albert, too, looking remarkably like H.M. Stanley – 'Dr Livingstone, I presume?' – and another of Paul Britton, inappropriately kitted out in riding dress and looking wonderfully arrogant.

It was only as he turned to take his seat that he realised, with a sense of shock, that it wasn't, in fact, the first time he had ever been in the boardroom. He had been here once before, had come running, sick and breathless, into a place imposing with dark panelling, acidulous with gaslight, hazy with cigar smoke that began swirling as he flung open the door and broke the news to the men sitting frozen round the great walnut table that Uncle Felix had hanged himself.

Brrr, he thought, and turned his attention firmly back to Nick, who was opening the meeting with the usual emollient chairman's remarks.

'. . . a Victorian shipyard that made the family's fortune, but Victorian times have gone, the Victorian fortune has gone, and it may not be long before the shipyard ceases to be a viable proposition in its present form. It seems that the time has come for Brittons' to make a new start in today's world.'

It was half an hour later, and one of Matt's legal eagles was saying in his pernickety voice, 'It is Sir Matthew's contention that . . .' when the door opened without warning to reveal a dramatically poised, blonde, petite, slightly plump, but exquisitely clad figure which beamed upon them all impartially and exclaimed, in an accent that still, after almost forty years, retained a trace of its native Russia, '*Darlings!* Am I late?'

5

NATASHA had been very much surprised to receive a visit from Howard at her flat near Kensington Gardens. First, a telephone call from his secretary, and then the man himself, as commanding a figure as ever; more so, in fact, since he had put on weight in the twelve years since she had last seen him. Instead of being stalwart, he was very nearly stout. He resembled, Natasha thought, one of those dogs with dewlaps, and bags under its eyes. Did she mean a bloodhound? She wasn't sure. But his tailoring was still perfect – even if he looked rather as if he had been corseted in Savile Row facecloth – and his air was as Olympian as ever.

She knew that Matt and Nick disliked him intensely as a result of his taking over Provost Charters, and there had been something about the shipyard, too, although she hadn't paid much attention at the time. She had thought that, if it was almost out of business, anyway, Howard's attempts to manipulate things could hardly be said to matter. And afterwards, when the yard had begun to be profitable again – under her darling Nick's management – she had merely shrugged and reflected that no harm had been done.

There was no reason at all, she thought, for her to be unpleasant to Howard, especially when she was still privately grateful to him for taking Provost Charters off her hands.

Even so, she had been just a fraction suspicious when the maid ushered him into her drawingroom.

'Champagne and flowers? How very charming!' she said. 'I do not remember such tributes from you in the past. Not a case of Greeks bearing gifts, I hope?'

'No, merely the influence of seven years in America. It is pleasantly ironic that "old-world courtesy" should have become the prerogative of the New World.'

When they were seated, he said, 'I thought you might like to know what is happening at Provost Charters.'

'Not in the least!'

'Ah, but it is no longer the house you dislike. There was a great deal of damage done during the war, when it was requisitioned for military purposes, and when I returned it seemed to me that demolition rather than rebuilding was what was needed. So I have had all the Victorian additions pulled down, and what now remains is the original house, just as it was in Georgian times. Simple, tasteful, elegant.'

'Are you trying,' she asked flirtatiously, 'to make me wish it was still mine?'

'Perhaps.' He looked down into his glass.

Natasha's heart began to flutter. She remembered how, in the 1930s, he had continued to send her substantial quarterly cheques, even when the stockmarket was doing badly, because he had said he could not bear to think of her being anything less than her exquisite and expensive self. They were about the same age, or perhaps Howard was a year younger; she couldn't remember. It was a pity he had a problem with his weight.

He raised his eyes again, smiling. 'It occurred to me that, since you have always had such admirable taste, you might care to advise me on a few decorative matters. The house is almost complete, but

564

I must confess that it needs a woman's touch.'

She was moved, just a little. Meltingly, she said, 'My poor Howard. It seems most unjust that you should have to come to me.' Then, less meltingly, 'Not, of course, that Jenny ever had any taste!'

'Jenny?' he sighed. 'Don't speak of her. I miss her, you know. But I suppose she will be happy, now. I fear that the proposed merger of the shipyard with Britton-Bonny will make it all too easy for her to live in Matthew's pocket.'

'*What?*'

'Don't you think so? Oh, how I regret it! All of it.' His tone was reflective. 'I have always been fond of Jenny, and as attached to young Johnny as if he were my own son.'

'*Wasn't he?* I mean, isn't he?' She found it exceedingly difficult to modulate her voice when what she really wanted to do was scream.

'Oh, no. He is Matthew's. Surely you knew?'

Her mind went flashing back through the years. So! Although she had finally decided that there was no real substance in her suspicions, she had been right all along! Paris. And the unease she had sometimes sensed under the surface when they were talking together. And Matt evading her own caresses.

It had been Jenny who had been on the catch for Matthew, of course. The Jezebel! The hussy! The deceitful little ... It was the last straw when, suddenly, she remembered Matt refusing to stay on in her flat during the war because a very special lady was jealous. Now she knew who that very special lady was, and she could have scratched her eyes out with fury. Just because she herself had resigned her claim on Matt, it didn't mean for a moment that she was prepared to let Jenny have him!

She knew very well that her cheeks must be scarlet, but Howard misinterpreted the signs. Leaning forward, he took her hand and said, 'Natasha, my dear, how very kind you are. I can see that you feel deeply for me in my uncomfortable situation.'

She fluttered her admirable eyelashes at him, but she couldn't flirt and think properly at the same time, so she stopped again, and it wasn't long before she said, with a fair assumption of sympathy, 'But we cannot allow Jenny to let you down even more than she has done already. It would be unthinkable to have her and Matthew working together, day after day. It quite makes me shudder! No, I know what you must do. You must stop the merger!'

'What a clever idea!' He gazed at her admiringly, but then shook his head. 'No, I can't. My holding is only twenty per cent

– the ten my father left me, and a further ten which I acquired from McMurtrie when he was in – er – pecuniary difficulties just before the war.'

'Did he go to jail? I can't remember.'

'No, but the whole affair did nothing to enhance his reputation and he decided to retire from business.'

'Oh.' She gave the matter another moment's thought. 'So, your twenty per cent is not enough?'

'Alas, no. Jenny has twenty-six, and Nick and Matthew have another five each. I would be outvoted.'

Arithmetic was not Natasha's strong point, but a few simple figures weren't beyond her. She said triumphantly, 'But I have twenty per cent also.'

'You mean you would add your vote to mine?'

'But of course! What are friends for?'

Howard beamed at her, and she basked in the pleasant glow of his gratitude while she reflected that it was going to give her the greatest possible pleasure to spike dear Jenny's guns.

6

'I HAVE come,' she said grandly, 'to cast my vote on this very important issue, and I have brought with me Mr Fournier, who also wishes to cast his vote. Who are all these people?'

Two more chairs were drawn up to the table and the mousy woman who was there to take notes provided Natasha and Howard with pads and pencils and sets of papers covered with figures and graphs and analyses in which Natasha had no interest at all.

'Technical advisers,' her son told her irritably. 'Mother, it's lovely to see you, of course, but there was no need for you to come. I always act as your proxy. You know that.'

'Only when I am not here myself, you silly boy. But today I *am* here, and I wish to vote for myself. This is a very handsome table, but I do not like the panelling.' She wished the portrait of Paul was not looking down on her in that disapproving way.

Nick, poor boy, seemed harassed. 'But we won't be taking a vote. It's not that kind of meeting.'

Natasha was surprised but not troubled. Glancing at Howard, she waited for him to strike the blow that would astound them all.

HOWARD said, 'I believe, Nicholas, that it would be of help both to your mother and myself if you explained precisely what is going on. We both have a strong financial interest in the yard, you know.'

'Yes, but I've told you. It's neither a board meeting nor a general meeting. You really have no right to be here.'

'Come, come!' Howard's voice was almost arch. 'You are scarcely going to throw us out? And you would not wish to give us the impression that you have something to hide.'

Matt wondered what the hell he was up to. Surely it wasn't possible that he was still trying to exact revenge for his father's death; that, having failed to wreck the yard in 1936, he was prepared to start all over again, even though, this time, his victims had been very thoroughly forewarned? For a moment, Matt almost admired him. Talk about perseverance!

It was clear that one of the things he was up to at this precise moment was trying to demoralise Nick, in which he was likely to succeed. Nick had enough of his mother's temperament to blow his top at quite the wrong moment if he were deliberately provoked. And Jenny, poor darling! It wouldn't take much to demoralise her, either. She hadn't seen her husband since before the war and had been living in hopes of never seeing him again. She always said that, in retrospect, he made her think of a very large and disagreeable slug.

Nick sighed with exasperation. 'Oh, very well,' he said, and launched into an explanation about the revival of foreign competition; and how postwar reconstruction would put former enemies at a huge advantage over the nominal winners of the war; and the shrinking market for passenger ships because of competition from aeroplanes, whose technology had advanced by leaps and bounds because of wartime demands.

Howard said, 'Yes, dear boy. We know all that. But whether a merger with Britton-Bonny is the best way of overcoming these putative future problems is what, at this moment, concerns us. It appears to me to be a sad waste of time and money to sit here hammering out details that will be quite simply irrelevant if your shareholders are opposed to the principle of the thing.'

Matt could feel his associates carefully concealing their impatience, and was irritated. If he had been in their shoes, he would have been thinking that this was not the way meetings should be run, and hoping it didn't indicate serious flaws in Brittons' management style.

Tactfully, he intervened. 'Nick, if you'd like to sort this out privately, we can leave you for ten minutes or so.'

But the look Nick cast him, as he said, 'No, no. That's all right,' was one of unabashed pleading.

Jenny, slightly pale, said, 'Perhaps it would be a good time to have tea, since we've been interrupted. Will you see to it, Madge?' Then, as her secretary put down her notebook, beckoned the woman over and murmured some further instructions to her.

When Madge had gone, Jenny glanced round the table and said, 'Since there is now no one taking Minutes, perhaps we can consider the official business temporarily suspended. Nick, why don't you tell Lady Britton and Mr Fournier what we have in mind? In general terms, I mean.'

Whereupon Howard had the brass neck to say benignly, 'My dear wife, how delightful to find that you are still as businesslike as ever.'

Jenny felt her skin crawl. Indeed, she was possessed by such a strong physical revulsion that, if Howard were even to brush against her in passing, she thought she would be sick. All she wanted to do was the one thing she couldn't do, rush to Matt's arms for protection. She wondered if he guessed. Probably not. He thought she was a grown-up and sensible woman, long past the age of irrational fears.

How could she – how *could* she! – have tolerated Howard's touch for all those years? She could only marvel at the strength she had drawn from knowing it was for Johnny's sake.

The tea lady entered, with Madge right behind, just as Nick finished his résumé, and there was an interval of clattering and murmuring while cups were distributed.

Madge murmured something in Jenny's ear and Matt, watching intently, thought he saw relief in Jenny's eyes. Then she said audibly, 'Go and have your own tea, Madge. We won't need you for a little while.'

But Natasha and Howard had been consulting, and Howard raised his voice. 'Not so fast, my dear. Perhaps your secretary should stay. Lady Britton and I wish to move that an Extraordinary Meeting should be constituted here and now. I believe the rules permit it when a quorum is present?'

Nick, floundering, looked at the yard's solicitor, and then at Jenny, who said thoughtfully, 'It's not a situation that has ever arisen before, or not to my knowledge. I would doubt it, though. Not only the quorum, but the lack of notice. Madge, would you go and find the Articles, please? I believe they're in the top drawer of the grey filing cabinet.'

The faintest flicker of surprise crossed Madge's face but only Matt, knowing his beloved, was suspicious.

They waited, and they waited. Matt's legal eagle began breathing heavily through his nose. Jenny poured everyone a second cup of tea.

It was a full ten minutes before Madge reappeared, looking flushed and explaining that the Articles hadn't been in the grey filing cabinet after all. 'They were in the green one.'

'Oh, dear,' said Jenny. 'I'm so sorry.'

Natasha, shifting a little in her chair, remarked to Howard in an audible undervoice, 'I do not understand why she should be finding it so difficult to answer a perfectly simple question.' Howard's reply was no less audible. 'You must forgive her. I believe she may find my presence somewhat distracting.'

Ignoring both of them – though with difficulty – Jenny began leafing through the pages. She knew the answer about the quorum as well as she had known where the Articles were filed and on what page she would find the relevant clauses, but she needed time.

Within minutes of Natasha's and Howard's arrival, she had identified the fast one Howard was hoping to pull. But she was just as mystified about the whys and wherefores of it as she knew Matt must be. Why on earth, after all these years, should Howard still want to see the yard heading for disaster? Surely he must recognise that, whatever he did, Matt and Nick were now far too strong for him?

And then he had addressed her as 'my wife', and she had seen the lizard look in his eyes and known the answer. It wasn't the Brittons who were the target. Not any more.

She it was who, with the assistance of Nick – and a bit of luck – had at the very last moment frustrated Howard's previous attempt to ruin the yard, when, thinking he had already won, he had gone so far as to boast about it. She had played further havoc with his vanity not only by leaving him, but by staying away. And in these last years, she had even stopped being conciliatory in her letters to him. He had thought her a puppet, and discovered she wasn't.

And so he was trying to punish her, as he had punished her

569

when they lived together. He couldn't use Johnny as a threat any more, but he knew how much she loved the yard, and that she had the largest single holding. If the yard failed, she would be the one to be hurt. It was almost as if he couldn't live without vengeance.

She raised her head at last, by which time everybody except Howard had been reduced to a state of profound, if concealed, irritation. 'Here it is,' she said. 'I must have gone past it the first time. It says not a quorum, but a full majority.' She handed the sheet to Nick, who read it carefully and handed it to Natasha, who glanced at it and handed it to Howard, who also read it carefully but didn't hand it on to anyone.

Matt wondered which of his associates was going to be the first to have a breakdown and run screaming from the room.

8

'GOOD,' said Howard. 'It is not of importance, since we have not only a quorum but a full majority present. Seventy-six per cent in all. And there are provisions for a meeting at short notice. So I will first apologise to Matthew on the company's behalf for dragging him here on a wild goose chase. Because we will not be proceeding with the proposed association between the Britton shipyard and Britton-Bonny Ltd.'

He looked round magisterially, showing no disappointment at the lack of expression on most of the faces round the table. Lawyers and accountants who had cut their teeth on poker dice didn't give anything away if they could help it.

But Nick hadn't had their training. 'Now, just a minute, Howard!' he exploded.

'My dear Nicholas, you may go through the motions of protesting if you wish, but I must point out that, of those present in this room, both Natasha and I are unalterably opposed to merger, and between us we have forty per cent of the vote – while you, my wife and Matthew can muster only thirty-six per cent between you. I insist that you constitute a meeting here and now, when I will put the motion that Brittons' should neither at this time *nor in the future* agree to combine any of its interests with those of any other company.'

'You can't do that!'

570

'Yes, I can.'

The yard's solicitor opened his mouth. 'Well, there may be grounds for . . .'

And then the door opened, and Jenny was able to say, 'Allie! I'm so glad Madge was able to get hold of you. We do rather need your fifteen per cent of the vote. Unless you've come to side with Howard and Natasha, of course?'

Howard's eyes were like slits as he stared at his wife, but Jenny was much too busy finding a chair for the smiling Allie even to look at him.

Natasha, turning, exhaled a suffocating blast of Abdulla No.7 into his face. 'Howard, does this mean we will be outvoted?'

Then, glancing round and reading the promise of retribution in the baleful eyes of her darling Nick and the uncomfortably tight expression round the mouth of her darling Matthew, she recognised for the first time that although she was here only to play games, they weren't.

In a rather plaintive small voice, she said, 'Oh, dear.'

9

AT LUNCHTIME a couple of weeks later, Matt emerged from a very different meeting with his mind full of turbo props, turbo jets, and the need to reduce fuel consumption per pound of thrust, and said to his secretary, 'Lay on some sandwiches and coffee, will you, Sylvia? Oh, and let me have *The Times*. I haven't had a chance to look at it today.'

But although his eyes scanned the columns, his thoughts were elsewhere. The morning's talk of engines had started him thinking about the shipyard again and he found himself reflecting, for the umpteenth time, that something was going to have to be done about Howard. For the next year or two – now that Matt and Nick had put the fear of God into Tash – the fellow would be pretty well hamstrung in any attempt to interfere with its management, but when Brittons' became a public company, with shares offered on the open market, it might be a different matter. There was something else, too. Howard's reappearance on the scene worried Jenny, even if she didn't show it, and as far as Matt was concerned, that was the clincher.

Wondering if the day would ever return when 'sandwiches' didn't mean, 'Spam or corned beef, sir?' Matt chewed away conscientiously and tried to refocus his eyes on *The Times*. They had come to rest, he discovered, on the parliamentary report page – a sure sign that he wasn't concentrating. He had employees whose sole task it was to keep him up to date on that kind of thing. But even as he moved his glance on, something caught his attention.

The Lords, it seemed, had been discussing a Private Member's bill introduced by Lord Mancroft.

Matt read the report of the Honourable Lord's opening speech not once but three times, after which he discovered that he had lost his appetite and was in need of something a damned sight stronger than coffee.

He pressed the intercom. 'Sylvia. In order of priority, whisky, then get my solicitor on the phone, and then see that I'm not disturbed for at least an hour.'

10

SOME little time later, the phone rang in Jenny's office at the yard.

'Hello, Matt,' she said in surprise, her heart leaping as it always did. 'Yes, I'm alone.'

His tone was politely enquiring, but there was an unusual vibrancy in his voice. 'Have you seen the papers today?'

'*Don't* ask me that! Every time someone asks me whether I've seen the papers, it always turns out to be something nasty. It used to be things like you having a crash, or getting married, or Natasha discovering about divorce postcards . . . At least we're past all that now.' She paused suspiciously. 'We are, aren't we? What is it? Don't keep me in suspense. Tell me!'

'I would, if you'd shut up for a minute. There's something in the parliamentary report . . .'

'Who ever reads the parliamentary report? Oh, my God, don't tell me they're going to nationalise shipbuilding?'

'Will you belt up, woman! Here am I trying to break something to you gently . . .'

She giggled. 'Oh, all right. It was just that you sounded like

Alger Hiss getting ready to pass on the closely guarded recipe for his mother's pecan pie. Bursting with Top Secret tidings!'

'Hah! Well, the news is, my dearest dear, that parliament has passed a law which permits a man to marry his brother's widow.'

There was dead silence on the other end of the line.

Then Jenny said faintly, 'What?'

'You heard.'

'Goodness me!'

'It's news to you, is it?'

'Of course it is!' Then, suspiciously, 'What do you mean "*has* passed"? I haven't seen anything about it in the papers.'

'Well, you wouldn't,' he said cordially. 'Or not lately. It was a while back.'

'Oh, *really*, Matt! What does "a while back" mean?'

He didn't answer, and she sat staring at the pictures on the walls, her emotions in turmoil, while he allowed a theatrical pause to develop. She could almost see the smile on his face. In the end, she was forced to exclaim, '*Matt!* Will you stop being so exasperating! What does "quite a while back" mean?'

And then he told her. 'It means twenty-eight years ago,' he said.

She felt very strange indeed, almost as if she were going to faint. After a moment, she stammered, '*Wh-a-a-a-t?*'

'Twenty-eight years ago,' he repeated helpfully. 'The Act was passed in 1921, but they mentioned it in the Lords yesterday in connection with a proposed new Marriage Enabling Bill.'

'But what . . .'

'You want the details, do you? Well, it was – is – known as the Deceased Brother's Widow's Marriage Act. It was an amendment to the Deceased Wife's Sister's Act of 1907. I've got it all written down here.'

She exhaled an audible breath. 'I don't believe it. I've never heard of it. It *can't* be true!'

'Oh, yes, it is, my love.' Then, in tones of extreme affability, he went on, 'I can't tell you how much I look forward to hearing your excuses. Because, you see, my own conscience is clear. I was in the States in 1921 when the Act was passed, and since it's not the kind of subject that crops up in everyday conversation, and one doesn't buy a new Prayer Book every year simply to keep up with the Table of Affinity, I am entirely guiltless. But you . . . I'm *ashamed* of you.'

She was relieved that he couldn't see her blushing as she heard her own voice echoing down the years saying, not once but many times, 'we can never marry'. And now it seemed it wasn't true. She had been in love with Matthew for thirty years and two months precisely and . . .

She said defensively, 'Well, it wasn't legal for a man to marry his brother's widow when I first thought about it! Because that was before 1921.'

'*Was* it?' She'd never told him precisely when – or why – she had discovered she was in love with him.

And then he went on, 'Well, in that case, I'd have expected you to be *more* likely to notice the law being passed.'

He was perfectly right, of course. Clutching at straws, she wailed, 'But it would be English law, not Scots law, and I only used to read the *Glasgow Herald* in those days. They probably didn't even report it. Oh, Matt, I can't bear it!'

'Talk about getting your just deserts! When I think how often you've told me we could never marry, even if we were free – and I believed you, God help me!'

And then something struck her, and she exclaimed, 'Howard! The rat! *He* knew what the law was. He must have known. I remember saying to him, when Johnny was born, that you and I could never marry, and he looked at me in the queerest way. But I didn't make the connection.'

Across four hundred miles, Matt could hear her fist pounding on the desk. 'Of course, of course, of course! He kept threatening to divorce me for as long as Johnny was young enough to make it a real threat. And then he changed his tune and began refusing to divorce me, because he knew I might find out we *could* marry if I was free. Ooooh! Couldn't you just murder him!'

Matt laughed. 'We'll certainly have to do *some*thing about him.' And then his voice changed and he said, 'But at least there's one thing we can settle now, this minute.'

'What?'

'My dear, darling, beautiful, ill-informed Jenny, will you marry me? Allowing for contingencies like getting divorced from Howard, of course.'

'I beg your pardon?'

'You heard.'

There were paeans of glory ringing in her heart, but she couldn't resist the temptation to get her own back, just a little. She said, 'I don't know if I'd want to get married again.'

'You *what*?'

'Well, what's the point in getting married?'

'Christ! If you don't know the answer to that . . .'

'Oooh!' she said, shocked. 'You randy old man!'

'I am fifty-two years old,' he reminded her wrathfully. 'A mere stripling. And if I hear so much as another cheep out of you, I will withdraw my offer.'

11

MATT himself had been free to remarry since 1945, seven years after Mims' disappearance, the term which, under the law, was required to elapse before a missing person could be presumed dead.

The final proof, strangely enough, had turned up a few months later. The remains of both plane and pilot had been discovered by the Japanese during their occupation of Cambodia, and someone who remembered the search had passed the news on as soon after the war as was practicable. Reliving those painful weeks in his memory, Matt had found some small comfort in the fact that Mims seemed to have crashed, quite literally, into the stone arms of one of the gigantic Buddhist statues hidden in the jungles of Angkor. She must have died instantly. Or, he thought wryly, gone to Nirvana.

At the end of March 1949, Jenny abandoned all her scruples about scandal and formally asked Howard for a divorce. It was no surprise when he replied, What? Divorce the mother of his beloved son, Johnny? Certainly not. And, of course, his wife had no grounds for divorcing him. Besides which, it would be unseemly for a man in his position to appear in the divorce courts.

Jenny would have been very surprised indeed to hear that Howard had been celibate for the last dozen years; on the other hand, nothing would have induced her to employ a pair of dirty raincoats to prove that he hadn't.

Matt and Jenny couldn't think what to do, but it occurred to them to call a family conference, in case anyone else might have an idea.

12

MATT began by breaking the news that he and Jenny had long been deeply attached to each other and that, if Jenny's divorce could be arranged, they hoped to marry.

It ranked, as he later remarked, as the flattest 'important announcement' he had ever made.

Nick, fishing in his pockets, said, 'Yes, well. We all know that. Chesca, have you pinched my cigarettes?'

Natasha murmured, 'Eh! *La belle affaire!*' and went back to studying a slimming article in *Vogue*.

Muriel said, 'Well, that's a relief! It was getting awfully boring, pretending we didn't know.'

And Allie said, 'What's brought this on? I don't understand why Jenny didn't divorce Howard years ago. I'm sure she could have found cause.'

It was with deep embarrassment that Jenny made her confession. 'Well, we didn't know it would be legal for us to marry. "His brother's wife", and all that stuff.'

'Goodness.' Allie peered over her spectacles. 'You should have asked me. I could have told you.'

Matt grinned lovingly at his pink-cheeked wife-to-be and then, settling back in his chair by the roaring log fire at Crannoch Lodge, said, 'It is necessary to settle Howard's hash once and for all. Jenny wants a divorce. I want my son. And we all want Provost Charters.'

'Oh, hear, hear!' Johnny said. He had grown up to be very like Matt in looks, in a rather indefinable way, but he hadn't lost the slight nervousness that had afflicted him since childhood; the nervousness for which Howard was entirely to blame. Howard, Johnny said, had always made him feel small and insignificant and unworthy.

The funny thing was that he had decided to make archaeology his career. Jenny wondered sometimes whether it was an indirect way of trying to get his own back by beating Howard at Howard's own game.

Now, he said, 'Incidentally, did I ever tell you I met a chap in India, an American, whose father's got one of the world's finest collections of Egyptian antiquities? Pays the Horrible Howard a packet for his advice. Holds him in very high esteem, he said.'

'Hah!' said his mother. 'No judgement!'

Nick had been looking slightly uneasy since the mention of Provost Charters, and Matt fixed him with an enquiring eye.

'Yes, well,' Nick said, casting a wary glance at Chesca, 'it's like this, Matt. I don't know if you were thinking of trying to buy Provost Charters back from Howard, but I – er . . .'

'Can't afford it?'

'No, it's not that. Chesca's got a bit of money of her own, and she's been trying to persuade me to use it to make Howard an offer he can't refuse. I wouldn't have done it anyway, as it happens, but the truth is that I, personally, don't want Provost Charters back.'

Natasha stopped dead in the midst of rearranging the Kashmir shawls that protected her from the Arctic gales coming in through all the windows and doors. 'Well, really!' she exclaimed. 'After the fuss you made when I sold it! All that talk about the home of your childhood and the emotional deprivation you were going to suffer through having it taken away from you!'

'That was then.' He had the grace to look a trifle shame-faced. 'But this is now. And I don't want to possess anything I haven't worked for. It's more than that, too. I'm completely committed to the yard and the aero engine works nowadays, and Provost Charters is simply too far away. Chesca and I thought we might buy a bolthole in the Highlands. I've heard of a place further north, near Kinveil. D'you know it? There's an old castle there.'

Matt nodded, trying to conceal his relief. After the day during the war that had exorcised all his childhood miseries, he passionately wanted Provost Charters back. For himself and Jenny. And for Johnny.

'However,' Nick said more strongly, 'don't think I'm not one hundred per cent behind you about getting the place back from that blighter Howard, if you want it yourself.'

'I do. I will even confess that I made Howard an offer in 1946 and was turned down flat. I thought that, since the place had been so knocked about during the war, he might be glad enough to get rid of it, but all he said was that he was looking forward with the greatest pleasure to the task of restoring it. Which, of course, he has now done.'

They had all seen the pictures in the glossy magazines of 'Provost Charters, country home of the distinguished Egyptologist, Mr Howard Fournier'. It looked charming.

Tash said with an irritable sigh, 'Muriel, pass me that pole screen! I can feel my face getting quite roasted from the fire. How I dislike these dreadful Highlands!' Jenny glared at her out of pure habit, but she went on imperviously, 'You know, I am still of the opinion that one could almost like Howard for what he has done. Provost Charters, as it was, was one of the ugliest houses I have ever seen.'

Matt and Nick were outraged.

'What?' Matt exclaimed. 'You can't have forgotten the Venus who looked as if she was carved out of Lux toilet soap!'

'Or,' said Nick, 'the dragon overmantel in the musicroom!'

'Or the stained-glass Lancelot and Guinevere!'

'Or the Botticelli seashells!'

'Or the battlements!'

Jenny called them to order. 'That's quite enough. What are we going to do about Howard?'

'Throttle him?' Nick suggested cheerfully, but Matt had a better idea. 'Bankrupt him. Now, that would be what I'd call poetic justice.'

Eighteen-year-old Muriel, who considered the whole thing shockingly frivolous and was anxious to get on with the argument she'd been having with Bob about the morality of the atomic bomb, said helpfully, 'Howard can't live much longer, can he? He must be quite old by now. When he dies, it should be easy to buy it back from whoever he leaves it to.'

Unfortunately, all she did was attract disapproving glances from everyone. The family, united as it had never been before, was determined to *do* something.

The only trouble was that, although they worried away at the question for days, they still couldn't think what.

Two

1

THE Geiger counter burst into a cheerful little song-and-dance routine, when what it should have been doing was sitting muttering and scratching its head and conveying a general air of, 'Well, now, what have we here?'

Johnny surveyed it with interest.

He knew he'd done everything according to the book. With the most meticulous care, he'd extracted six grams of elementary carbon from the samples and spread it evenly inside the brass cylinder. He'd sealed the cylinder ends into the Geiger counter, evacuated the air and replaced it with the standard filling mix of argon and ethylene. Then he'd twiddled a few knobs, given it a slap on the rump, and said encouragingly, 'Hi-yo, Silver! Let's go.'

Nothing wrong there.

Except that radiocarbon was a weak beta-particle emitter at best, and he shouldn't be getting the answer he was getting.

He gave the matter much thought before he rang his friend Brockhaus. 'Arnie,' he said, 'You know your dad gave me samples from two of the things in his collection, the sarcophagus and the writing board? But I've been thinking. He wanted me to do some more and, really, I might as well do them all at the same time. Another five or six, maybe?'

'Great!'

Arnie's dad was not only very rich and possessed of an enviously large collection of honest-to-God antiquities, but dead keen on modern technology. When he'd heard that the friend his son had met in India was working in Chicago, in a laboratory where they were experimenting with radiocarbon dating, you couldn't have stopped him with a steamroller. Frederick Arnold Brockhaus the Second was going to be The First Collector in The World to have his collection authenticated by atomic science.

Johnny hadn't had any objections. Suitable research material wasn't all that easy to come by.

He'd said, 'You do understand the principle, don't you, Mr Brockhaus? All living things have a proportion of C-14 in their make-up. That's the radioactive isotope of carbon. But when a tree's cut down or a person dies, the C-14 in the timber or the bones begins to decay. It's a slow process. After 5568 years – plus or minus a thirty-year margin for error – there's still half as much left as there was to begin with. D'you follow?'

'Well, sure. Simple mathematics.'

'Yes, the principle's straightforward enough, but the practice, I can assure you, isn't! To find out how long it is since the tree or person died, we have to measure the radioactive level of whatever carbon remains, and to do that we need what you might call neat carbon. It has to be separated out from a sample of whatever we want to test, and unfortunately we can't separate it out without destroying the sample.'

'How big a sample?'

'That's the problem. With something like bone or ivory, we need almost five ounces, so if you wanted us to test a – well, an ancient ivory plaque or medallion, there wouldn't be much of it left by the time we'd finished. Frankly, with something like that, I'd advise you to wait a few years until the technique is more refined. Wood, on the other hand, is easier by its very nature. We can work on much less.'

Mr Brockhaus's brow had lightened. He had plenty of Egyptian stuff that wouldn't miss a few splinters from the underside, he said. And he reckoned he could afford to sacrifice them in the interests of scientific progress.

Johnny had said it was jolly generous of him, and perhaps just one or two to start with.

2

AND now Johnny had a nasty little problem on his hands.

Arnie's dad, casting his bread upon the waters with the abandon of one who expected a whole chain of bakeries in return, sent him chunks of seven more ancient Egyptian treasures, so that Johnny finished up by testing samples from nine items in all. And even allowing for the fact that, with solid carbon, counting efficiency was far from infallible, he couldn't in the end doubt his results.

This time he didn't call Arnie. He called Matt in London.

When he had finished, Matt said, 'Aren't you glad you changed your name from Fournier to Britton when you came of age?'

'Not 'alf!'

'The question now is, can you manage a swift trip home?'

'I should think so.'

'Good.' Johnny could hear the smile in his father's voice. 'We've got him at last, my boy! We've *got* him!'

3

MATT said they didn't want women cluttering the place up, and Jenny told him loftily that she did not, in any case, have the slightest desire to sit and listen to them all making fools of themselves.

So they compromised, and Jenny sat down to a solitary dinner at an hotel in Salisbury while Matt, Nick and Johnny set off for Provost Charters in Matt's new A.C.

Since it was his habit to drive as if the roads were as little frequented as the skies, within half an hour they were sweeping up past perfectly tended lawns to the handsome new porch of a house no longer recognisable to the two men who had been brought up in it.

It annoyed Matt that the new Provost Charters was such an improvement on the old. All the grosser features of Sir Albert's venture into late-Victorian Gothic had vanished, leaving a simple, uncluttered square building with pleasantly proportioned bays, French windows opening straight onto the terrace, and an air of accomplished sophistication.

It was unmistakably a 'gentleman's residence'.

Matt couldn't think what Howard was doing, displaying such good taste, though Jenny could have told him that the one thing Howard had in common with his son, Simon, was an unerring instinct for what was about to come into fashion and a readiness to adjust his own taste accordingly.

They were admitted by a handsome housekeeper, a woman in her early forties, who ushered them into Howard's library, giving them time to note that, at least in some ways, the interior was still familiar.

Nick remarked on it and Howard said, 'Yes. Grandfather Albert simply tacked the drawing and dining rooms, the conservatory, and the music and morning rooms onto the outside of the existing house, so they were easy enough to demolish. And although the decorations were in a sad state when the house was derequisitioned, the walls themselves were perfectly sound. A good deal of the work that had to be done was paid for, of course, by government compensation.'

'You've managed to extract cash from the Treasury already?' Matt asked drily. 'Congratulations.'

'Strings, dear boy, strings. May I offer you a drink?'

Howard had put on a good deal of weight, although he wasn't fat. Not quite. And he had become very jowly so that he did, indeed, look like a basset hound, just as Matt had always thought he would.

It was a warm summer's evening and instead of sitting round the fire they gathered by the window, where they could admire a prospect of lawns and trees that would have warmed the heart of Humphry Repton himself, if only there had been a fallow deer or two to finish everything off.

'The grounds, of course, were a shambles,' Howard said, 'and since all those small, separate gardens needed so much upkeep, I decided it would be preferable to opt for a wider vista.'

It was exasperatingly clear that Howard had no intention of asking why he was being honoured by this deputation, so Matt said, 'Do you have a special gallery for your antiquities, or have you given all that up?'

'Good gracious, no. I have had the old servants' wing reconstructed. Are you interested? Would you care to see it?'

'Not in the least,' Matt said. It didn't worry him at all to have Howard write him off as a philistine. 'But Johnny would.'

For the first time, Howard looked directly at the young man he still claimed as his son, but whom he had not seen for sixteen years. His expression was one of smiling disbelief.

Johnny, remembering how coldly Howard had condescended to him as a child, found he still had to make an effort to speak to him without stammering. 'Yes, I've a considerable interest in archaeology and antiquities. A professional interest, I should add. I'm a physicist.'

It was satisfying to see Howard's eyes go blank, as he wondered what physics had to do with antiquities.

Matt intervened maliciously. 'Don't you keep up with modern technology? You should, you know. You would learn the salutary lesson that the war wasn't just an interregnum, but a watershed.

Those of us who were adult before 1939 – we're yesterday's men, now.'

Howard's long upper lip curled. 'Surely not. Not the great Sir Matthew Britton, distinguished spokesman of the aeroplane industry?'

'Oh, yes. Me, too. It happens to be necessary for me to keep up with all the latest developments, but they're not bred-in-the-bone; I wasn't shaped by them the way the next generation's going to be. Have you any idea how fundamentally the discoveries of the last few years are going to change people's lives? Atomic power, transistors, electronic computing machines, supersonic flight . . .'

Howard sipped his port and sighed. 'I am sure you are right.'

'Sorry,' Matt said, grinning to himself. 'Go on, Johnny.'

'Yes. Well, you see – er – Howard, splitting the atom didn't just mean atomic bombs. It's taught us a lot about radioactivity, and there's one application I'm specially interested in. Have you heard about radiocarbon dating?'

Howard shook his head and continued to sip his port, an expression of boredom on his face.

'Willard Libby, the nuclear scientist, has been working on it for some time. He's just about to publish. I'm sure you'll be interested, because the technique makes it possible to put a scientific date to archaeological remains.' He paused artificially. 'Including Egyptian antiquities.'

Nick, with honest regret, found it necessary to sit down, even though it spoiled the moment of truth. His artificial foot served him well, but he couldn't stand on it for any length of time.

Howard said, 'Indeed?'

'To cut a long story short, I have recently tested nine objects belonging to an American gentleman, a Mr Brockhaus. I found that three of them dated from somewhere around 1500 BC.

'The other six dated from somewhere around AD 1900.'

For the briefest of moments, Howard became entirely still.

Johnny, who was having a whale of a time, resumed, 'I didn't tell him about the six. I said the test hadn't worked. Because I already knew how he had built up his collection. He told me he always bought from Etienne Durand in Paris, and never without a guarantee of authenticity and assessment of value from one of the world's leading authorities – a certain Mr Howard Fournier.'

4

AFTER a while Howard moved over to the tantalus and refilled his glass. 'Not a guarantee of authenticity,' he said. 'Merely an educated opinion.'

Matt had no difficulty in suppressing any feeling of pity for the man who saw his world falling in ruins around his feet.

'It won't do, Howard,' he said. 'I can pull strings, too, you see. And someone fairly high-powered in Paris has had a serious talk with your friend Durand. It seems that for almost thirty years he has been acquiring, from some pretty diverse sources, modest fragments of the Egyptian past at modest prices, and then selling them dearly with a Fournier attribution.

'He hasn't committed himself any further than that, for fear of laying himself open to criminal proceedings, but my guess is that you received a percentage on every sale.'

Howard turned his head in supercilious surprise. 'And if I did? It is hardly a secret that Berenson used to receive one quarter of Duveen's profits in return for his advice. Why should I be content with less? It is perfectly legitimate business practice. I find myself unable to imagine what all this drama is about.'

'No doubt. But I haven't finished yet. Because I'd guess something else. When Carter opened Tutankhamen's tomb in 1924 or whenever it was, the market must have gone mad and, if I know anything about human nature, forgeries started pouring from the presses. Some of them would be cheap and obvious. But some would be made from waste wood that had been lying around for a couple of centuries, and some might even have been genuine but worthless stuff that was susceptible to being "improved". I wonder what you said about those in your "assessments"?'

Howard sighed ponderously. 'I have never endeavoured to persuade anyone, either Durand or his clients, that my opinion was anything more than an educated judgement based on style and condition. Never, during my entire career, have I claimed to "guarantee" anything. That being so, if other people have chosen to take my word as gospel, I can only say that they have brought their problems on themselves.'

Matt laughed. 'Very impressive, Howard! But though it sounds all

584

right here, it wouldn't sound so good in a court of law. On a subject where "expert opinion" has always been the yardstick, the expert has a very clear responsibility.'

And still Howard didn't move a muscle or give any sign of what he must be feeling. It was dark by now, and since their host wasn't showing any signs of getting up to put the lights on, Matt did.

Then Johnny chipped in. 'You can't hope to get away with it, you know. In this particular instance, I tested nine items and, frankly, if you can only get three right out of nine, you *have* to be either a fraud or else just plain incompetent.'

In Matt's experience, Howard had never had more than two expressions – Bland No.1 and Bland No.2. But now it seemed that he was capable of a third, and there was nothing at all bland in the way he stared at Johnny, his eyes no more than pouched slits and his lips so tightly clamped that they were invisible. It seemed that the boy's words had struck home at last, and Matt suspected that Howard had disliked the word 'incompetent' much more than the word 'fraud'.

Matt subsided into a chair, and said, smiling, 'Brockhaus was only the first, you know. The minute we start spreading rumours – which we'll be delighted to do – there'll be an absolute torrent of collectors and museums rushing to have their collections scientifically verified. And every time something you have authenticated is shown to be very far from authentic, it'll be another nail in your coffin. You're a crook, Howard, and you always have been. It's time your career was brought to an end.

'If you do what we say, we won't expose you. Otherwise, it will give me great personal pleasure to tell the world precisely what you are, and if that happens, you won't have a shred of reputation or dignity left. You'll be very lucky if you don't end up in jail.'

He had been hoping that Howard's control would disintegrate, that the façade of superiority would shatter to reveal the psychopath within. Because he didn't doubt that, in clinical terms, Howard was a psychopath, the kind of man who was oblivious to everything except what *he* wanted, who, if he had been violently inclined, wouldn't have hesitated to plant a bomb in a crowded place just to get rid of one person who annoyed him.

But his hopes were disappointed. The discipline of a lifetime held, and all that happened was that Howard's fleshy face tightened, and his eyes became lizard-like, and he snarled, 'Get out of my house, all of you! *Get out!*'

Matt smiled again. Then he settled back even more comfortably in his chair and purred, 'Oh, no. Not yet.'

5

NICK said, 'For God's sake slow down, Matt. My nerves won't take any more!'

So Matt dropped his speed to fifty, and they went cruising through the Dorset dusk, scarcely speaking. The sky was a soft, mysterious turquoise hanging like a gossamer veil over the stars and the shielded dark, while the hills were shapely and graceful, muted and shadowed and garlanded with trees that were themselves no more than moulded shadows, though still recognisably the trees of the English countryside, oak and elm and ash. It was very still, and the air smelled of summer and hawthorn.

Jenny was waiting for them, ruthlessly in control of herself. 'I've organised some sandwiches for you.'

But then she saw that Matt was gazing at her beatifically and it was altogether too much. Her hands hadn't stopped shaking for two hours. 'Oh, for heaven's sake! What happened?'

Matt said, 'He's agreed to let you divorce him. He will provide the grounds.'

Nick said, 'He's going to sell Provost Charters back to Matt at the 1935 price.'

Johnny said, 'He's going to let Matt adopt me legally as his son and heir.'

Matt said, 'And by routes we will arrange, he is going to refund their money to all the people he's defrauded over the years.'

Nick said, 'And finally, he's going to emigrate to New Zealand.'

Jenny said, 'Good heavens!' and sat down rather suddenly.

6

THEY decided they might as well spend the night in Salisbury.

Somewhere in the small hours, Matt woke up in the grip of a nightmare. It wasn't an uncommon occurrence; two world wars had provided him with the stuff of many nightmares. But this one was different. This time he was in a cold, draughty cathedral, and

586

although there were lights and activity in the distance, the cathedral was quite dark. And he looked up, and there was something hanging from the rafters above him, and it was a man, and he was dead, and it wasn't Uncle Felix. It was Howard.

'Don't be a fool,' he told himself as he sat up in bed and shook his head violently, trying to clear it. But he was in a cold sweat of fear. All those years ago, Felix had been rejected, condemned by the family, and he had killed himself. What if Howard . . .

Jenny said sleepily, 'Howard commit suicide? I never heard anything so silly in my life. You've had too much champagne.'

But it was no use and in the end they had to dress, and get in the car, and go back to Provost Charters. Jenny insisted on taking the wheel and complained all the way.

They stole up the drive on foot, feeling like a couple of burglars, and found the whole house quiet and dark except for one upstairs room.

Jenny hissed, 'Are you satisfied? Come on. Let's go back.'

'No. I have to be quite sure he's all right.'

'Well, I don't see how you're going to manage it, short of knocking on the door and asking. *Matt!* Really, Matt!'

He'd climbed up the ivy when he was a boy, and it was easier now because there was a kind of pergola affair over the terrace.

Jenny stood and fumed while, with great care, he inched his way up the side of the house and at last found his eyes on a level with the windowsill of the dimly lighted room, where he remained for what to Jenny seemed an eternity. Then, equally quietly, he made his way back down again.

When he reached the ground he was quivering all over and breathing erratically, but he didn't say a word, just took Jenny's hand and raced her back over the grass to where they'd left the car at the foot of the drive.

Then he subsided into a clump of night-scented stock and gave himself up to a fit of uncontrollable mirth.

She glared at him and demanded, 'What is it?' but he was laughing too much to answer. So she poked him in the ribs and said again, 'What is it? *Matt!*'

'It's all right,' he gasped at last. 'Your husband's safe in bed, and very much alive. Remarkably active for his age, in fact.' He showed signs of suffering a relapse and Jenny had to poke him in the ribs again, even more vigorously, before he was able to go on. 'The lady, certainly, seemed to be enjoying herself. A rather fetching piece. I think – I think it was the housekeeper!'

It was a moment before Jenny exclaimed, 'Oh, great! Well, you can just rig yourself out in a slouch hat and a dirty raincoat and swear to that in the divorce court. Now, can we get back?'

The housekeeper, really! She didn't know what the world was coming to.

7

THEY had a registry office wedding. In fact, they had two registry office weddings, and it confused the registrar very much when he found himself elevating Mrs Fournier to Lady Britton less than ten minutes after he had demoted the Dowager Lady Britton to Mrs Fox.

Natasha had decided, at long last, to reward the faithful Granby by making him the happiest man on earth. Everyone knew that it had come as a very nasty shock to Granby, who was nowadays less interested in winning the hand of his goddess than first prize for his giant marrows at the village flower show. But he bore it with fortitude, because he was after all a gentleman, and his bride – who was now sixty-four, though no one mentioned it – still a very lovely lady. Her eyes were still brilliant and her hair no less blonde, if perhaps less convincingly so, than it had ever been. If she was no longer the elegant sylph with whom he had fallen in love almost forty years before, the amply gathered skirt and intricately draped bodice of her Victor Stiebel dress disguised it very well. Gallantly, Granby offered her his arm, saying he had never thought he would live to see this day.

Jenny was laughing so much that she forgot she was wearing an extremely wide picture hat and found herself momentarily stuck in the doorway, which caused her to laugh even more and the vaguely disapproving expression on the registrar's face to deepen. He was a plump and well-polished gentleman, wearing a hearing aid, and he spoke very slowly and significantly as he took Matt and Jenny through the ceremony, staring intently into their eyes all the while.

Jenny was painfully aware that Matt was having as much trouble as she was in keeping a straight face.

'You know,' she said afterwards, 'I've just realised. All that beady-eyed till-death-do-you-part stuff and that unspeakably hideous vase of gladioli – he's got an inferiority complex. He's convinced everyone would really much rather be married in church and the registry office is a poor second best. Really! Why are my weddings always pure farce? I think I'll have to give up the habit.'

'You *think*?' demanded her husband.

And because it was, in truth, the happiest day of her life, she reflected for a moment and then, as one making a great concession, said, 'Oh, very well, then. I *will* give up the habit.'

EPILOGUE

2 June 1953

Epilogue

1

LONDON, still one of the liveliest, noisiest cities in the world, was jam-packed with people on the morning of the second of June 1953. It was raining – of course – but the British were used to that and it was, in fact, the only thing to carp about, because the Coronation of Queen Elizabeth II was pageantry at its functional best, a superlative display of antique splendours harnessed to twentieth-century needs.

It was what the country badly wanted, this feast of unrationed glamour after the eight drab years of postwar scarcity, and it was clear that the crowds jamming the Mall under the dripping trees were relishing every moment of it. Fat people and thin people, old folk and young, rich and poor, Britishers and foreigners, all of them shouting, singing and waving flags with cheerful and unquenchable enthusiasm.

Tall, distinguished, and damp, Sir Matthew Britton stood among them and reflected that it was a lot more fun here than it had been in the Abbey, from which he and Jenny had removed themselves with undignified speed the minute they had the chance. Fortunately, he had some sort of excuse, because one of the more reputable Sunday newspapers, hunting for a different angle on a story that was in acute danger of being overworked, had asked him if he'd do a critical assessment of the Coronation Day ceremonial.

'Popular bigwig tells all. Everything you never wanted to know about what Prince Philip said when the Archbishop of Canterbury trod on his toe. What Princess Margaret said when she tripped over her train. What the chaps in the Royal Mews said when the harnesses fell off the horses. That sort of thing,' the editor had said.

'You're joking.'

'God save us,' the man had gone on piously, 'from all the tripe the rest of Fleet Street's going to be churning out. What we need is a thousand words or so on the kind of impression the thing makes on a public figure like your goodself. You might toss in a few uplifting thoughts while you're at it.'

Amused by the idea, Matt had agreed and, after a bargaining session that would have stopped the traffic in the bazaars of

Casablanca, had got what he wanted; no editorial messing about with his copy, and an exorbitant fee payable to the Royal Air Force Benevolent Fund.

The descriptive material wasn't going to present any problems. It was a glittering, magnificent and yet curiously touching procession, impeccably organised, and Matt hadn't had any difficulty in getting hold of inside information about the planning that had gone into it; what the press called 'colour stuff'. He knew that the red morocco harnesses worn by the twenty-four state horses turned the scales at a hundredweight each and that the saddlers were going to have to be up in the morning very early indeed. He knew that every last footman had demanded time off to go to the chiropodist. He knew how much it had cost to have the Gold State Coach recushioned, retyred, and regilded, and all about the special light that had been fitted inside it, so that HM's new subjects could see her properly and, as one of the royal *aides* had put it, 'count every last jewel in her crown, from the Black Prince's cabochon ruby and the Stuart sapphire and the pearl drops that belonged to Elizabeth I right down to the three thousand diamonds in between.'

All that was fine. It was the 'uplifting thoughts' that were bothering him.

2

SUDDENLY, he laughed aloud.

Gold epaulettes, gleaming breastplates, waving plumes – and between the rear end of the bay carrying the Royal Standard-bearer and the front end of the animal with the Master of Horse on its back, a glimpse across the Mall of a small boy in a grey school-uniform jersey with a Union Jack in his hand and something much more intimate than bright and burnished cavalcades on his mind.

Jenny, beside him, said, 'What's the joke?'

'Memories! Memories! You know that chap who wants to write my biography? And the sort of thing they put on book jackets? Well, how about this? "The subject of this biography is Sir Matthew Britton – internationally respected airline chairman of today; formerly one of the country's most daring aviators; even more formerly a popular Great War poet; and more formerly still . . . the boy who disgraced himself at Queen Victoria's funeral."'

Her eyes brimming with companionable laughter, she said, 'Well, why not? You'd probably never have been what you are today if that hadn't happened.'

He hadn't thought of that. 'I wonder if you're right? If I hadn't disgraced myself, my mother mightn't have taken a dislike to me. My parents mightn't have separated, or my father fallen in love with Natasha. Uncle Felix mightn't have killed himself. My father and I might not have been alienated . . .'

3

'I MIGHT not even have had the wife of my heart and this ruddy great mob of a family.'

Never, until the last year or two, had 'the family' been much more than a conventional image to him, but now it was a substantial reality. And today, everyone was here except Nick and Chesca and their brood, because Nick found it painful to stand for any length of time.

He glanced round, smiling.

Jenny and Johnny, Bob and Muriel, Beth and Joe and their two little Anglo-American kids, Joe Junior and David Thomas, who was David after Joe's father, and Thomas after Beth's. Thirty-seven years since Tom had died. It was hard to believe.

Simon was here, too, though he wasn't strictly family. Jenny had been saying for years that the love of a good woman would make all the difference to him, and at last he'd married a nice girl, and become a proud father, and it hadn't made any difference at all. Simon would be Simon until he died.

And Tasha and Granby, of course; Granby was bearing up well, all things considered, and Tasha seemed to be enjoying having someone to order around and give in to her every whim.

Even Allie and Bertha, seventy-one and seventy respectively, had decided the Coronation warranted a trip to London. They were both pretty good for their age, although Allie had taken to leaning on a stick and Bertha was a bit hard of hearing.

He murmured to Allie, 'Remember the last royal procession we watched together?'

She peered at him over her spectacles, shaking her head, but she wasn't remembering a small boy proclaiming his urgent need. 'What changes,' she said. 'What changes.'

4

FURTHER along the Mall, an extra cheer went up. Matt said, 'That sounds like the Queen Mum's carriage on its way. Are you ready, darling? How about a ladylike Glasgow cheer?'

Jenny tossed him a far from ladylike grin and then, brushing aside a strand of honey-coloured hair that the wind had teased out from below her white straw hat, turned towards the approaching carriage with its royal burden of chiffon, satin and smiles, and opened her mouth wide.

She looked exactly as if she was about to let out a full-throated Ibrox Park yell. 'C'moan the auld yin! Get tore in! Kill um! Aw hey, melt um!'

Matt wouldn't have put it past her. For a craven moment, he found himself hoping that the Queen Mother wasn't familiar with the accents of darkest Glasgow, but he wouldn't have banked on it. And she was only too familiar with the nation's captains of industry – and their ladies. He drew a sharp breath.

But then, as the carriage rolled level, Jenny took pity on him and, precisely as she had intended, gave tongue to a perfectly respectable, five-decibel cheer that even Kelvinside couldn't have faulted.

He grinned at her. 'You're a wicked woman,' he said. 'And I love you very much.'

5

WHAT changes! Allie had said, and she was right. Not just, he thought, in the way that obvious things like cars and planes, atomic energy and computing science were influencing the whole tenor of life, nor even in the slow, social upheaval that, on the one hand, had eroded traditional wealth and power, and on the other offered someone like Bob, son of a shipyard worker, opportunities un-dreamed of fifty years before.

Matt sensed another kind of change, too, one reflected in

the almost superstitious note that marked the rejoicing along the processional route. He could remember the coronations of George V in 1911 and George VI in 1937, and although they'd been exciting enough they had been nothing like this. Today, it seemed as if all the cheering multitudes who lined the route were reading some mystical significance into the fact that the country once more had a queen entitled to reign in her own right; as if they were expecting the pretty, smiling figure in the golden coach to conjure out of the air some acceptable mid-twentieth-century substitute for all Britain's lost imperial grandeur and the international swagger that went with it.

It was almost four hundred years since the first Elizabeth had been crowned, and well over a hundred since Victoria had succeeded to the throne, an eighteen-year-old girl who had ended up ruling over six hundred million people and a third of the surface of the globe – the greatest empire the world had ever known.

But the empire had begun to disintegrate long before a postwar Labour government had decided to restore it to its rightful owners – a gesture that had been made to appear rather more selfless than it was. The real truth was that empires were profitable only when you were prepared to exploit them. If you didn't exploit them, you had to be very rich to be able to afford them, and the British couldn't afford their empire any more.

Nowadays, it was America, whose empire lay within her own frontiers, that was the richest country in the world, and the most powerful. Since the beginning of the century, all the omens had been right for her, and two world wars had helped; America's involvement in them had lasted little more than half as long as Britain's, and been much less damaging.

And there was more to it than that. America had the vitality Britain had lost, even if the time would come, sooner or later, when she too would lose her vitality. Nations were like people, and grew old.

Looking back, Matt could see that, for the last fifty years, the British had gone stumbling, shell-shocked, through the decades of imperial decline and America ascent, trying to pretend that the present wasn't really happening, that it was only an uneasy interlude, a temporary hiccup in history's grand design. Failing to recognise that, in reality, the glory was passing from their grasp.

And then it struck him, with a sense of irony and shock, that the history of the Britton family and the Britton shipyard throughout those years had been running in parallel with the history of the country. The riches, the pride, the slow loss of everything it valued, the descent into the abyss.

He himself had had to start again from scratch, to build a new empire from nothing, and Nick was doing the same, in a different way and on a different scale.

In which they were ahead of the land that had borne them. But now . . .

Like most people, Matt had heard a great many Coronation clichés about the 'new Elizabeth Age', and had thought drily, *If you wish long enough, Wish strong enough* . . . But suddenly, sensing the feeling amongst the crowds, he began to wonder whether perhaps all the rather cheap symbolism mightn't have something to be said for it after all.

Now that comparatively little remained of wartime austerity, now that British climbers had conquered Everest, now that there was a new young queen on the throne – if such fundamentally irrelevant things as these were enough to encourage people to look to the future, instead of to the past that had been so long in dying, well, at least they'd be looking in the right direction. Success and progress were, after all, a state of mind.

Reaching this happy conclusion to his meditations, he became aware of Jenny's voice speaking melodiously beside him.

'Matthew, dear heart!' she was saying. 'I don't wish to interrupt but, in case you hadn't noticed, the procession's over. What's the matter? Is it your article? Are you having uplifting thoughts?'

He grinned at her. 'And how!' he said.

Then, with an almost voluptuous satisfaction, he tucked her arm in his and dropped a kiss on the tip of her nose. 'Come on, then, love of my life. Let's go home.'